PRAISE FOR ROBIN PILCHER'S NOVELS

An Ocean Apart

"Warm and readable." —*The Washington Post*

"A warm, welcome tale of believable people and places, told by a born storyteller . . . *An Ocean Apart* is full of beautifully painted characters. . . . Though Robin Pilcher has his own literary voice, it is obvious that inheritance has brightened this first long, full tale."

—*The Anniston Star*

"Pilcher . . . writes of family and friends, love and death, grief and recovery with every bit as much insight and meticulous detail as his mother, celebrated novelist Rosamunde Pilcher. . . . Highly recommended." —*Library Journal*

"It is only a matter of time before the author becomes as famous as his mother."

—*The Midwest Book Review*

"*An Ocean Apart* is told by a born storyteller."

—*San Diego Union-Tribune*

"Pilcher's Scotland [is] peopled with faithful retainers, loyal workers, doughty veterans, cricketers, and dog lovers . . . it's a land Pilcher knows intimately."

—*Los Angeles Times*

"*An Ocean Apart* engages you from the s
from a nice touch of humor. A good, easy r
—G

"Rosamunde's fans will not be disappointed. . . . An enjoyable read."

—*Chattanooga Times Free Press*

"A fast, easy read with the happy ending the reader wants."

—*Knoxville News Sentinel*

Starting Over

"Pilcher's Scotland is a land of traditions . . . strong and rich."

—*Los Angeles Times*

"[*Starting Over*] offers light, entertaining reading and will appeal to those who like to escape but not be pandered to by overtly predictable situations. . . ."

—*Chattanooga Times Free Press*

"Every once in a while, a romance writer like Robin Pilcher comes along with a story that is just plain fun to read, that introduces characters that are worth getting to know, and that isn't necessarily predictable, even though it may tell a story we already know on some level . . . it is not surprising, then, that he clearly understands the expectations of the romance novel. What is also clear is that Pilcher, the son, understands much about families . . . and he encourages us with the thought that even in the worst of times there is the hope of starting over."

—*The Anniston Star*

"This is a warmly written, down-to-earth novel about human relationships."

—*Deseret News* (Salt Lake City, Utah)

"Pilcher has definitely inherited his mother's talent . . . and his second novel should prove that he isn't riding on her coattails.

[Pilcher's] characters are ordinary people enriched by [the] quiet rendering of their lives in a tale [with] lots of emotion . . . one of those smart, charming stories that leaves readers feeling content and very happy that they chose to read it."

—*Booklist*

A Risk Worth Taking

"Fans of acclaimed novelist Rosamunde Pilcher will queue up to read *A Risk Worth Taking*, a new novel by her talented son Robin. Robin Pilcher not only writes with his mother's style and fluency, but also writes about the same type of ordinary people . . . engrossing . . . more than one reader will relate to it with painful clarity. . . . Robin Pilcher, like his mother, obviously loves people and has a knack for conveying that . . . a poignant and thought-provoking book that makes one want to cheer for the Dan Porters in this world. This is a perfect novel for a wintry day."

—*Roanoke Times*

"This is an engaging character study of a person who once was riding the crest, but since has lost his self-esteem . . . the cast is a delightful ensemble . . . Robin Pilcher provides a deep look at what really counts as Dan reassesses his values and how he has lived."

—*The Midwest Book Review*

"A short novel that is one evening's reading delight . . . Robin Pilcher is good with the details of people's lives and his skill at dialogue makes for fast reading."

—*The Charlotte Observer*

"Pilcher offers a charming story about life in the new millennium and one man's pursuit of happiness, a tale that will appeal to both men and women."

—*Booklist*

"Pilcher crafts another engaging, happy-ending tale in the tradition of his mother, beloved British novelist Rosamunde Pilcher. . . . [Readers] will care about Dan . . . and his children and friends, and will approve [of] Dan's belief that risks are worth taking, and that life can be a great game."

—*Publishers Weekly*

An Ocean Apart

~

STARTING OVER

Also by Robin Pilcher

A Risk Worth Taking

An Ocean Apart

STARTING OVER

Robin Pilcher

THOMAS DUNNE BOOKS
ST. MARTIN'S GRIFFIN NEW YORK

THOMAS DUNNE BOOKS.
An imprint of St. Martin's Press.

www.stmartins.com

ISBN 0-312-35567-X
EAN 978-0-312-35567-8

An Ocean Apart originally published by
Thomas Dunne Books/St. Martin's Press in January 1999

Starting Over originally published by
Thomas Dunne Books/St. Martin's Press in January 2002

First St. Martin's Griffin Edition: October 2005

10 9 8 7 6 5 4 3 2 1

An
Ocean
Apart

For Kirsty,

of course

Acknowledgments

The writing of this book was always a possibility, never an inevitability. For it to have come to fruition, my deepest thanks go to my wife, Kirsty, who was always there to read a chapter, a page, a sentence, a word; to Ros, who constantly encouraged and dug her son out of a literary hole more times than can be admitted; to my sister Pippa and family, who guided a lost Scotsman around Long Island; to Matthew Gloag, Bill Lumsden and Tony Tucker for their infinite knowledge of the whisky industry; to Miranda Lindsay and Charlie Pank, two Oxford students split by a decade or two; to David Nichol, who helped me thrash out the constitutional issues; to Alexander Dundee for keeping me straight on the House of Lords; to Felicity Bryan, my agent, for being on hand always at the right time; and finally to Tom, my editor extraordinaire, who, having encouraged me to write over a period of ten years, gave his all when the time came.

CHAPTER 1

Jane Spiers drove with extreme caution through the pelting rain, her shoulders hunched over the steering wheel as she strained to make out the blurred outline of the road ahead. The windscreen wipers of the old Subaru struggled to cope with the deluge pouring down from the cold grey skies, and the feeble wheezing of the car's hot-air fan was of little help in clearing the steamy fog that had developed on the inside of the windows. That was Arthur's fault. He sat, enclosed in the boot by a large dog rack, soaking wet and panting heavily after his exertion on the moor. Jane opened the window a fraction to see if a little air circulation might help but shut it immediately when she felt the sliver of icy Scottish weather suck the warmth from the car. In all the forty years that she had lived in Scotland, she could not remember a May so cold and miserable.

Turning off the main road through a pair of lodge-gates, newly painted and bearing a sign marked PRIVATE DRIVE, she drove up the long tarmacked avenue, the tall oak trees on either side at last offering some protection against the elements. In this new-found shelter, the windscreen wipers' performance improved, and Jane crunched into a higher gear.

After half a mile, the drive opened out into a gravel sweep that rounded in front of the large Victorian house. Picking up one of her gloves from the passenger seat, Jane wiped the condensation off the windscreen, eager to complete the last few yards of her journey without running over either the trimmed edge of the grass border or one of the three black Labradors who customarily came bounding down the front-door steps.

On this occasion, there was no such welcoming committee, but even as she lurched the car to a halt in front of the house, Arthur sat up in the back and whined, his ears pricked forward and his nose pressed through the square mesh of the dog rack, anticipating a mad tear-around in the garden with his three black friends. Jane looked at his plaintive face in the rear-view mirror.

"Good boy, Arthur—you stay there," she said, pulling up the hood of her Barbour jacket and tightening the draw-string under her chin. "I won't be long."

Holding hard to the door in case the wind took it completely off its ageing hinges, Jane clambered out of the car, then, slamming the door shut, she scrunched her way in a half-run across the wet gravel and up the steps to the front door. With the informality of a frequent visitor, she opened up one of the heavy oak double doors and let herself in.

"Oooee!" she called out. "Anyone he-ere?"

No immediate reply. She took off her dripping Barbour and hung it on a hook amongst the collection of heavy tweed overcoats and waterproof jackets, then, clearing a space for herself on an old church pew, a dumping ground for fishing-tackle, hats and garden implements, she sat down to take off her sodden walking shoes.

"Hullo-o! Anyone here?" she called out again, and looked around to see if anyone had taken any heed of her call. The hallway of Inchelvie House stretched to the full height of the edifice, and was dominated by a huge central staircase which divided at right angles half-way up, leading to a balustraded landing above. Dark oak-panelled walls were lined with large family portraits intermingled with an eerie selection of crossbows, double-handed swords and shields, and above them, ranging to the highest point of the house, an array of about forty stags' heads, all rather old and moth-eaten. Jane smiled to herself, her own private thought always being that it was a toss-up as to which of these three adornments was the most hideous.

She left the pew and padded in her stockinged feet across the hallway. Approaching the bottom of the staircase, she became aware of a man's voice coming from the drawing-room. It was not a voice she recognized, more the deep, serious tone that might belong to a solicitor or chartered accountant, and instantly she wondered if she had chosen a bad time to call. She was caught in a moment of confusion, whether to try calling out again or just quietly leave, when a door opened in the far corner of the hall beyond the staircase and a small grey-haired lady appeared, precariously carrying a tray of tea and oblivious to her presence.

"Hullo, Effie," Jane said, as gently as possible, so as not to spread-eagle the little housekeeper and her load. Even at that, Effie stopped abruptly, making the contents of the tray shoot forward.

"Oh, Mrs. Spiers, whit a fright you gave me!" Effie said, steadying herself. "I didn't hear ye coming in."

Jane walked around the side of the staircase. "I'm sorry about that, Effie. I did call out twice, as loud as I thought decent." She smiled at the older woman, who was slowly recovering her composure. "I thought the dogs would probably have heard me. It's not like them to miss out on a good bark." She glanced towards the door of the drawing-room. "Tell me, is this a bad time to call? I have a feeling that Lady Inchelvie might have someone with her at this minute."

Effie shrugged up her little shoulders in a display of mousy mirth. "No, no, that's just the television you'll be hearing. Lady Inchelvie always has the volume up pretty high, and that's no doubt why the dogs never heard ye coming in." Effie always spoke quietly, as if everything she said were imparting some hugely private secret. "The snooker's on, ye see, and there's nothing she likes better than to watch the snooker." She moved forward, her eyes sparkling, ready to tell the best part of the tale. "Especially if yon Scottish laddie Stephen Hendry is playing. I think that she must be his greatest fan!"

Effie's face creased into another muted giggle, though it immediately gave way to a frown of concern when she noticed that Jane's jersey and tweed skirt were beginning to steam in the heat of the hall.

"Michty me!" Effie exclaimed. "You're surely awful wet! Dinnae tell me you've been walkin' oot on the moor wi' your dog on a day like this?"

Jane rubbed herself on the arm, Effie's observation suddenly bringing it home to her that she was indeed feeling rather damp. "If I didn't go out in weather like this, then Arthur wouldn't get a walk for about nine months of the year."

"Well, we canna have you standing around here catching your death," she said, bustling her way across the hall. "Let's get you in beside the fire, and then I'll away and fetch you an extra cup. Was Lady Inchelvie expecting you?"

"No, she wasn't. I just wanted to, well . . ." Jane stopped Effie by putting her hand on her shoulder. "Actually, the real reason why I'm here is that my husband asked me to pop in just to find out how everyone is. He's purposely not visited since Rachel . . . well, let's just say he felt that it would be better if I dropped in, sort of in passing, rather than him . . . as the family doctor, so to speak."

"Dinnae say any more," said Effie, flashing an understanding smile at her. "I'll no' tell Lady Inchelvie that you're here just yet. I'll just take in her tea-things and you go through to the kitchen, and we'll have a wee chat before you go in and see her. Does that suit you?"

"That would be just fine. Thanks, Effie."

Jane watched her scuttle off to the drawing-room, knock and enter, then turned and walked across to the door from which Effie had first appeared, and pushed it open.

The kitchen was large and utilitarian, unlike Jane's own, which she herself had lovingly converted into the hub of the house over the years. This was a complete throw-back to the green-baize-door era, all the walls being painted in a sickly yellow and cream easy-wipe gloss. There were no easy chairs, no wall decorations, just a plethora of pots and pans hanging from meat-hooks alongside three blinding strip lights above the enormous scrubbed pine table in the centre of the room, its austere cleanliness reminding her of a Victorian operating-theatre. She walked over to the old cream Aga at the far end of the kitchen and leaned on its spotless surface in order to induce some heat back into her bones.

The door opened behind her and Effie entered. "There we are now," she said, walking towards her. "Let's get the kettle on, and we can have a good natter over a nice cup of tea."

Jane moved to the side of the Aga, so that Effie could put the kettle on the hob. "Can I do anything to help?"

"No, no, you just away and sit down at the table. I know where everything is in this place. Now tell me, how is Dr. Spiers keeping?"

"Run off his feet at the minute," Jane replied, pulling out one of the kitchen chairs from the table and sitting down. "This wretched weather is really keeping the cold and flu bugs flying around. About half the children at Dalnachoil Primary School are off sick, and rather than get them brought into the surgery, he spends most of his day charging around from one house to another in the village."

Effie moved around her familiar kitchen like an automaton, taking cups and saucers from the pine Welsh dresser, then the milk from the fridge and putting everything on the table. "Aye, we're that lucky to have a man like Dr. Spiers around here." She took the steaming kettle off the Aga and poured water into the teapot, then, turning to face Jane, she took up her apron and rubbed her hands on it. "He really has been the saviour of this family over the past six months."

Jane noticed a weary expression had come over Effie's face.

"How *have* things been?" she asked.

Effie carried the teapot over to the table and sat down opposite. "Och, they come and go, up one minute, down the next." She poured out the tea into the two cups. "Lady Inchelvie has had to work like a Trojan this last month, getting all the grandchildren's things together to get them ready for returning to school. Mind, they didn't go back at the beginning of term, it being only a couple of weeks after their mother's funeral; and besides, I have an inkling that Mr. David was in two minds whether he should send them back there at all, thinking that they might be better off closer to him at the village school." She sighed and cocked her head to the side. "However, from what I can gather, it was the children's choice to go back and be with all their friends." She paused, seemingly unconvinced herself by the decision. "I don't know. Maybe a comfort for them to return to some sort of routine."

Jane took a drink from her cup. "I do think that's probably right, Effie. A different environment, yet a familiar one. Sophie has her GCSE exams this term, doesn't she?"

"Aye, she does. She's a grand wee girl—mind you, no' awful wee now, she's nearly sixteen years old, and that well-organized—just like her mother." As she said this, Effie suddenly faltered and swallowed hard, her composure suddenly under threat. "Oh, Mrs. Spiers, it's that hard getting used to not having Mrs. David around anymore."

Jane leaned across the table and patted the housekeeper's hand. "I know. My husband often wonders if cancer doesn't prepare a family better for the inevitable than, say, a heart attack or a road accident, but I don't think so. The loss when it happens is still devastating."

Effie was looking down in her lap, fiddling with her apron, her bottom lip quivering. Jane took a calculated gamble to continue the conversation.

"And what about the other children?"

Effie took a deep breath, and, almost for something to do, replenished both their cups even though Jane's was still three-quarters full. She delved into the pocket of her apron and brought out a handkerchief and wiped her eyes.

"Oh, they seemed to have coped better than any," Effie replied, managing to smile bravely, though her voice still faltered. "Even during the tea after the funeral, Charlie was badgering Mrs. David's brother to go out onto the lawn to kick a rugby ball with him. And wee Harriet, well, Sophie just seemed to take her under her wing. I don't really think the wee lass has taken it all in just yet. It's a blessing that all three are at the same school." She leaned across to Jane and said with a caring look, "Sophie will look after her, you can be sure of that."

Jane smiled and nodded. "Everyone plays a part in the healing process, Effie, not least you. You're as much a part of this family as any, and I know that everyone would have found it hard to cope without your being here."

The older woman went rather pink, not used to being praised quite so openly. She got up from her chair and cleared away the cups and saucers. "Och, we all do what we can under these kind of circumstances." She pulled open the dishwasher and started loading the racks.

Jane picked up the milk jug from the table and carried it over to the fridge, playing for time before asking the next question. "And what about David? How is he?"

Effie closed the door of the dishwasher and turned towards Jane. There was a moment's silence, an expression of concentrated bewilderment on her face as she tried to work out in her mind what to say. Then she just shook her head.

"I really canna tell, Mrs. Spiers. I mean, I have to say that he was wonderful as always wi' his children when they were home, playing tennis and fishing wi' them and all that, but even so, there always seemed to be something missing, as if he was only going through the motions. It was as if his mind was away somewhere else." She smiled at Jane and picked up a cloth from the sink and started to wipe absently at the draining-board. She stopped and nodded her head slowly. "Aye, now I think about it, it was the laughter that was missing." She looked across at Jane. "Maybe he's just finding it awful hard to concentrate properly on anyone but his wife. Dr. Spiers will no doubt have told you that he had nursed her entirely by himself since December." She turned away and looked out the window, and Jane heard her voice once again begin to falter. "I've a wee feeling that he was so devoted to her that some part of him died wi' her."

Jane went over to the little housekeeper and, putting her arm around her shoulder, gave it a comforting squeeze. "I can see that, Effie. I know that it must be really hard for you to talk about it, and I do appreciate you telling me." Jane felt that she had to break the melancholy of the conversation, and looked up at the clock above the Aga. "Heavens, it's half past four. I had no idea it was that late."

Effie turned from the sink, and on reaction looked up at the clock as well. "Och, Mrs. Spiers, what am I doin'? I shouldn't be going on so." She started to move towards the door, drying her hands on her apron. "Come on, I'll take you through to see Lady Inchelvie."

"Oh, please don't bother to do that," Jane said. "Look, I'll just show myself in. I'm sure that you've enough to do in here."

"Well, if you're sure. I'll have to be gettin' started on the potatoes for dinner. Lord Inchelvie has a meeting in the village tonight, so we'll be eating early."

"Absolutely. I've been enough hindrance to you." She walked over to the door of the kitchen, then turned to the housekeeper. "Keep your spirits up, Effie. You really are one of the mainstays of the household. Just keep being as cheerful as you always have been."

The volume of the television hit Jane as soon as she entered the drawing-room, the usually whispered tones of the snooker commentator sounding as though he were speaking through a megaphone.

". . . and if he can get a good angle on the pink ball, that should be the third consecutive frame to Hendry."

The three black Labrador dogs, however, heard Jane's entry above the noise, and, looking in her direction, each let out a short bark before realizing that it was a familiar figure. They left their place in front of the blazing fire and trotted over, their backquarters slewing from side to side with delight.

"Hullo, boys," Jane said, reaching down to pat their heads.

At the far end of the room, a figure moved in the high-backed armchair in front of the television. "Is that you, Effie?"

Unable to move any closer due to the keenness of the dogs' welcome, Jane called out, "No, Alicia, it's me—Jane."

Alicia Inchelvie peered round the corner of the chair, bowing slightly to look over the top of her reading spectacles. "Jane! How wonderful to see you! What a lovely surprise!"

She turned the television off with the remote control and rose to her feet, pushing a large ball of red wool onto the ends of two enormous knitting-needles. "Dogs, go and lie down and let poor Jane get into the room!"

Alicia walked rather stiffly towards Jane, her spectacles, now dangling by a cord around her neck, swinging from side to side as she walked. She was a tall and erect figure, dressed in her customary elegance of a tweed skirt and cashmere cardigan, with her grey hair pulled tight and gathered in a comb at the back of her head. It was the first time that Jane had seen her since the funeral five weeks previously, and although Alicia's whole comportment belied her seventy-eight years, it was obvious that even that short intervening period had taken its toll. There was now a drawn look on her face, a look of total fatigue, one that Jane surmised as being brought about by Alicia's own inner conflict to keep her thoughts of loss and anguish under control, so that outwardly she could appear strong and supportive to the rest of her family.

Two of the dogs took immediate heed of their mistress's request to return to the fireside. The other, an old greying boy with opaque eyes and obviously fading hearing, continued to wag his tail and gaze up lovingly at Jane, impeding any attempt she made to move farther across the room. Alicia's voice rose a full tone.

"HORACE!" she yelled in the direction of the dog. "GO AND LIE DOWN BY THE FIRE." She gesticulated like a policeman on point duty, waving on the old dog with one hand and pointing with the other, still clutching the knitting-needles, in the general direction of the fire. Horace looked sideways up at his mistress, her voice now having penetrated his senses, and, unclear as to why she held aloft those menacing objects in her hand, he slunk sheepishly away to join his younger companions.

"I'm sorry," Alicia said. "Horace is almost totally deaf now, rather like me. Can't hear anything unless it's at full volume. How are you, my dear?" She met Jane half-way across the room and gave her a kiss on both cheeks. "Come and sit down by the fire. What a revolting day! Would you like a cup of tea? I've just had one, but let me call Effie—"

"No, don't worry," Jane interjected. "I've actually just had one with Effie in the kitchen."

Alicia looked at her, surprised. "Have you? How extraordinary; I never heard you come in. How long have you been here?"

"Oh, about three quarters of an hour. No, actually I did want to speak to Effie about something." She smiled knowingly at her friend. "At any rate, I didn't want to interrupt the snooker!"

"Ah, so she's been telling you about my secret addiction, has she?" Alicia said, sitting back down in her chair. "I must say I get totally mesmerized by it, and it's such a treat to see so many young Scots being rather good at a sport! Really makes one feel quite patriotic, although I'm sure that being good at snooker reveals a somewhat misspent youth!"

"Absolutely," said Jane. "Who needs exam results when you can make money potting balls!"

They both dissolved into laughter, and Jane immediately felt at ease, any fears of how the overriding gloom of present circumstances might have affected her long-time friend expelled from her mind. They were still very much on the same wavelength, still able to laugh together.

Alicia put on her spectacles again, uncoupled the ball of wool from the end of the needles and resumed her knitting. For a second there was silence, as if her thoughts were taken up on a different plane. Then she looked up and smiled across at Jane.

"It's lovely to see you, my dear. I really have missed you. As you can imagine, life hasn't been filled with a great many happy thoughts lately."

"I quite understand. I should have popped in before now, but I didn't want to intrude." Jane watched Alicia as she concentrated on her knitting. "What are you making?"

"Oh, just something that Sophie started during the last holidays. It seems to be the rage at her school to have a chunky sweater with huge arms that come down at least six inches over the hands." She looked at Jane over her spectacles. "The waif look, I think. I took her into Inverness to see if we could find one, but they were all dreadfully acrylic, so we ended up buying a pattern and this rather garish wool." Alicia held the shapeless garment up at arm's length and wrinkled up the side of her nose in an expression of uncertainty as to what the end result might look like. "I have a feeling that it might look a little better on a large male gorilla than on Sophie."

"Well," said Jane, "I'm sure that if Sophie doesn't like it, there would be a welcome recipient at Edinburgh Zoo."

"You're not meant to agree with me Jane," Alicia retorted, feigning hurt. "You're supposed to say something like 'It's far too well-made for that!' " She laughed, then abruptly bundled knitting-needles, sweater, and ball of wool into one heap and threw it onto the sofa. "Anyway, I don't know why on earth I'm doing it when you're here. Come on," she said, getting up from her chair and manoeuvring her way through the prostrate dogs to put another log on the fire, "tell me what's going on in the outside world. I don't seem to have been in touch with anyone for so long."

It took Jane all of five minutes to fill Alicia in with the most important topics of local news: how the incessant rain had washed away part of the back road between Dalnachoil and Achnacudden, and how the local Territorial Army Brigade had come to the aid of the already overstretched roads division by erecting a temporary Baillie Bridge over the yawning gap; how Mrs. Mackenzie, the postmistress in Dalnachoil, had also been affected by the weather, bringing on a dreadful bout of arthritis which 'literally ballooned up my ankles, Mrs. Spiers, and I have to serve all my customers sitting on a chair behind the counter wi' my bedroom slippers on'; how everyone in the village had been asking kindly after all those at Inchelvie. And finally she told Alicia about how the influenza bug had hit the local school, and how Roger had taken it upon himself to visit all the children at home, rather than risk its spread by treating them in his surgery.

Alicia looked concerned. "You know, my dear, that husband of yours works far too hard. I mean, he really should have retired last year, shouldn't he? Maybe that's a silly thing to say knowing that the prime reason he kept going was to look after Rachel, but now can't he get one of his younger partners to do all these house calls? They really are going to have to start coping without him."

Jane sat back in her chair and sighed. "Oh, I know, and don't think I haven't put that argument forward on more than one occasion. What makes it more difficult is that I do have one of his partners phoning me up every so often to ask if I could gently persuade Roger to call it a day. I'm really caught between the devil and the deep blue sea. Anyway," Jane said, sitting up and looking at Alicia, "we're both in the same boat at the minute, aren't we? Having husbands who should have retired but are still working?"

Alicia smiled. "You're right, but mine are more exceptional circumstances."

"Of course they are. Tell me, how is George?"

"Like everyone else around here—totally exhausted, even though I think he's actually secretly enjoying his return to active duty. Nevertheless, if you've been retired for ten years, suddenly to have to start working again really comes as a jolt to the system. Not that he's hugely overtaxed. The new managing director at Glendurnich, Duncan Caple, is doing a wonderful job running both the business and David's marketing division, but George just feels that as he's the chairman and major shareholder *and* David's father, he should give support where he can, especially as the whisky market seems to be in such turmoil at the minute. I don't really pretend to know that much about it now, but there do seem to be an ever-increasing number of licensed trade dinners and marketing launches that George has to attend on behalf of the distillery."

Alicia paused for a moment, placing her elbow on the arm of the chair and resting the side of her face in her hand.

"But do you know, Jane, what we both find *so* energy-sapping is having to go back to a hectic daily routine we thought we'd left behind years ago! Having to get *up* in the morning, having to get children ready for going back to school, and then having them here all the time meant that one was always on call to entertain them. Heavens, just before he went back to school, Charlie had me out on the lawn operating the clay-pigeon trap! Can you imagine it? I'm absolutely hopeless with mechanical devices, and he kept shouting at me, 'Come on, Granny, you're useless!' as I launched off clays one after the other at about the level of his knees!" She laughed and sat forward in her chair. "Actually, come to think of it, this is about the first time that I've sat down and indulged myself for about a month!"

"Oh, I'm sorry, Alicia," said Jane, "and I come barging in and disrupt your peace."

Alicia waved her hand dismissively. "Don't be silly, my dear. This is exactly what the doctor ordered." She looked at Jane with a quizzical smile on her face. "Well, isn't it?"

Jane gave a surprised expression. "My word, that's intuitive of you." She smiled. "Of course, you're right; Roger did ask me to drop in to see you, just to find out how you all were. That's why I had a quiet word with Effie beforehand, just in case my timing wasn't very good." She paused for a moment. "She said that David is still keeping very much to himself."

"Yes, he is," Alicia said quietly. One of the Labradors had moved from his position by the fire and now lay at her feet, his head resting on her shoe. She bent forward and stroked his sleek black crown. "You know, the appalling thing about this whole affair is that he's going through something which neither you nor I have experienced. He has lost his life's partner. It's just so unfair." Alicia's tone had suddenly changed to one of anger and frustration. "Think of the many friends we have of our age who have lost their husbands or wives. That in a way is expected. But neither you nor I know what it's like, because it hasn't happened to us." She stopped talking and combed a loose strand of grey hair behind her ear with her fingers, her eyes looking at a point somewhere behind Jane's head. "I'm sorry, I didn't mean that. I think that that is the first time I've said it out loud. It's just that it makes me feel . . . well . . . so guilty."

"But that's natural," Jane said caringly. "The pain of losing someone close to you always seems to manifest itself in anger or guilt. But there is a positive side to it, and that is that David is extremely lucky, at forty-three years of age or whatever, to still have both his parents around to give their support. How could he have devoted so much time to looking after Rachel if you and George hadn't been there to pick up all the loose ends? Friends are great, but parents are better. And I'm sure that he's fully aware of that."

"I know, I know, but one just feels so useless. I wish that there was something, well, active that I could do to help him. If only he would let himself talk about it once in a while, but he just seems to bottle himself up. As far as I'm aware, he hasn't mentioned Rachel's name since the funeral. Outwardly, it's as if she never existed, but inwardly, I know he's in turmoil. It's a terrible thing to say, but sometimes I feel like grabbing the poor boy by the shoulders and giving him a jolly good shake." Alicia took a deep breath. "And then giving him a huge hug."

In the moment's silence that followed, Jane was aware for the first time of the wind and rain beating against the four large double-paned windows of the drawing-room. She looked over her shoulder and upwards at the black storm-clouds that spread themselves oppressively across the sky, and thought to herself how cruelly the elements accentuated the tragedy that had befallen this household. Her instincts told her that she shouldn't follow this line of conversation any further. Enough had been said for the moment, and it would serve no useful purpose to either Alicia or herself to continue it. She turned from the window and shook her head.

"Would you believe this weather for May?" She glanced up at the silver carriage clock on the mantelpiece above the fire. "It's only a quarter past five, and it's nearly dark." She did a double take. "Oh, my word, Alicia, a quarter past five! What am I thinking of?" She put her hands on the arms of the chair and pushed herself to her feet. "Poor Arthur has been sitting all this time in the back of my car, and I promised him that I would only be a moment. He'll probably have eaten his way through the dog rack by now."

Alicia rose stiffly from her chair. "My dear, you should have brought him in. The boys would have loved to have seen him."

"No, he would only have caused chaos. He's not as well-behaved as your dogs. Anyway, we had a lovely walk on the moor earlier on this afternoon, and he was soaking wet."

"Well, he's lucky to have such a devoted mistress to take him out on a day like this. I have to admit that I've been totally feeble. The boys' walk today consisted of my going to the front door, opening it and pushing them out for ten minutes. I am certainly not going out in weather like this!" Alicia went over to one of the windows and unhooked the cords that held back the huge room-high damask curtains. "And I really don't think that it is going to improve very much either. Better just to shut it out, don't you think?" she said, pulling the heavy curtains across the window.

Jane walked over to the middle window to do the same. As she unhooked the first cord, she looked out of the window at the darkness falling on the gardens of Inchelvie House. They were, even on this day, quite beautiful. Protected on either side by giant beech- and oak-trees, the long lawns swept majestically down to the dark frothy waters of the fishing-loch, their regularity split by meandering herbaceous borders with azaleas and rhododendrons in the early stages of bloom. Daffodils, still flowering due to the prolonged winter, bravely held their yellow heads high, a small splash of colour in defiance of the all-encompassing greyness of the day. To the right of the lawns, where two parallel paths ran between neat box hedges to the wall garden, Jane noticed that distinct changes had been made to the layout of the garden, the dark rich soil recently dug over to form two new flower-beds symmetrical to those on the west side of the lawn. She was about to turn and remark on this to Alicia, when a movement in the flower-bed farthest to the right caught her eye. She pressed her face closer to the window, cupping her hands around her eyes to cut out the light from the drawing-room behind her.

"Alicia, there seem to be . . ." Jane felt Alicia's arm brush hers as she came to stand beside her. She too cupped her hands over her face.

Alicia continued for her. ". . . two men standing out in the wind and rain digging holes in the garden and getting extremely wet."

"What *are* they doing?" She screwed up her eyes in an attempt to accustom her sight better to the fading light.

Alicia laughed. "My dear, don't you recognize them? It's David and Jock—you know, Effie's husband. They've been out there all day planting roses in that new flower-bed."

Jane turned and looked incredulously at Alicia. "In weather like this? What on earth for? They could end up catching double pneumonia if they're not careful."

"I tell you, it's more than my life's worth to try to stop them. For the past five months, that garden has been David's greatest therapy."

"Really? In what way?" Jane said, turning back to look out the window to where the two men were working.

Alicia drew one of the curtains across the window. "Do you remember when David gave up work at Glendurnich last December and moved Rachel and the family here from The Beeches after her first course of chemotherapy?"

"Yes, of course," Jane said, standing back from the window to allow the other curtain to be drawn across.

"Well, at that time George thought that it would be a good idea if David had something to occupy his mind, so he asked him to help look after the estate." Alicia moved away from the window and leaned against the back of one of the sofas, her arms stretched out at either side to support her. "Anyway, it became pretty clear to David that the farm manager was coping quite well without his input, and it just happened that while he was looking for some papers in the farm office one day, he unearthed these old plans of how the Inchelvie gardens looked when the house was first built. Apparently, some of the original flower-beds had vanished, I think probably sown out in grass about the time of the Great War, when manpower was scarce. So, on an impulse, David took it upon himself to reinstate the garden to its former glory, and that is where he has quite literally spent every free minute since. Whenever Rachel was receiving treatment in Inverness or just in the house asleep, David would head out to the garden, pore over his old drawings, and start digging away." Alicia laughed, raising herself from the back of the sofa. "Somewhere along the line, he roped in Jock to give him a hand. I don't think the old boy has ever worked so hard in his life."

They both walked over to the third window. It was now almost totally dark outside, but once again they cupped their hands around their faces to look out the window. The two figures had now moved closer to the house, and were dimly lit by the weak shaft of light that came from Jane and Alicia's window. David, bare-headed, with his hair plastered flat by the rain, stood talking to Jock, who, enveloped in a huge yellow fisherman's raincoat, peered from the shelter of an equally large sou'wester at the plastic-covered paper that David held in his right hand.

Alicia and Jane moved back from the window, both instinctively feeling that they didn't want to be caught looking out at the two men. Alicia turned and smiled at Jane. "The anger that that garden must have absorbed over the past five months has to be immeasurable."

She drew together the curtains of the remaining window and shut out the day.

CHAPTER

2

George Inchelvie closed the file on his desk, put the top on his fountain-pen and clipped it into the inside pocket of his tweed jacket. A squall of wind and rain hitting hard against the office window made him turn around in his chair to look out at the row of young silver birches, planted the previous year to give future shelter to the distillery's new car-park, as they waved their thin branches in submission to the battering that they were receiving.

He glanced at his wrist-watch. It was half past four. He pressed the intercom button on his telephone, and immediately the soft Highland tones of his young secretary lilted through the system.

"Yes, Lord Inchelvie?"

"Mhairi, I'm going to leave the office early today. I have a meeting in Dalnachoil this evening, and I want to get home before the weather gets any worse. Do you have any messages for me?"

"Let me just check, my lord." He heard the sound of turning pages crackle through the intercom. "No, I can't see anything."

"Right. You have confirmed with the Whisky Association that I'll be attending the conference in Glasgow next week?"

"Yes, and I've booked you into Devonshire Place for the Tuesday and Wednesday nights."

"Well done. If you could make sure that it's a twin-bedded room, just in case Lady Inchelvie wants to come down to Glasgow with me."

"Very good, my lord."

"Thank you very much, Mhairi. I'll see you tomorrow."

"Good night, my lord. Make sure you drive carefully, now."

"I will do, Mhairi," he said, smiling to himself at the young girl's motherly concern. He clicked off the intercom and leaned over to pick up the walking-stick that lay at the side of his desk. He rose from his chair, supporting himself both on the stick and on the edge of the desk, and stood for a minute, anticipating the sharp pain that would shoot down his left leg once he started walking.

He had never given much thought to the wound he had received in Holland during the war, even though at the time the bullet had only been two inches off shattering his spine, but now the incessant cold and wet weather, coupled with his advancing years, seemed to aggravate it more than ever before.

He swung through ninety degrees on his heels so that he was in line with the coat-stand, then, with the fingers of his free hand pressed deep into the base of his back, he took a step forward. It was like a hot knife jabbing into his left side, but he kept moving forward, knowing that it would ease off steadily after each step. He made it to the coat-stand, took down the old tweed overcoat and shrugged it onto his shoulders, and passing the stick from one hand to the other to maintain his balance, he placed the battered homburg on his head and opened the door of his office.

Making his way slowly through the open-plan trading hall of Glendurnich Distilleries Ltd., he headed towards the large glass double doors at the far end which led out into the reception area. He did not like the new layout of Glendurnich's offices but, even as chairman, he had felt that any criticism might be taken as being stuffy and nostalgic. During his more active days with the company, little had changed in the interior of the building since his great-great-grandfather Alasdair Corstorphine had produced the first bottle of Glendurnich Malt Whisky in 1852. Then it had been a rabbit-warren of small oak-panelled offices linked by narrow passages providing direct access to the distillery itself, and therefore constantly bustling with management, secretaries and distillery workers. George had always felt that, by design or default, it was this format that had created the autonomous structure on which the company had built its history of success, one which had been precipitated in 1882 through a chance sampling of Glendurnich's Finest Malt by the Prince of Wales in one of the many London clubs that he frequented. Within a week, the whisky's name had been brought to the attention of the discerning populace through the gossip columnists of every national newspaper. The future king, it was reported, had taken such a liking to Glendurnich's product that "now he feels that there is a worthwhile reason to visit his mother at Balmoral on a regular basis."

By the end of 1889, Glendurnich had doubled its production to 66,000 gallons a year, and in the following year the company was granted a Royal Warrant as purveyors of Scotch Whisky to the Royal Household. Then in 1906, Alasdair's son, Ralph Corstorphine, who found time to be both a Member of Parliament and chairman of Glendurnich, was granted an Hereditary Peerage for services both to government and to industry, choosing the name of Inchelvie after the vast rambling house that he had had built for himself on the moorland estate near Grantown-on-Spey.

Yet these accolades were seen as being achievements of the distillery as a whole rather than those of any individual, and the Corstorphine family never lost sight of that. The hierarchy in the company was built around the workers' knowledge of whisky distilling rather than on the basis of managerial status. One of George's abiding memories was that of his father, himself chairman of the company at the time, leaning against a radiator in one of the passages gleaning information on a point of whisky production from the two young McLachlan brothers, the distillery's stillman and mashman; they would be on the way to the workers' canteen, he on the way to a meeting.

But now the corridors, the individual offices, and the history had been torn out of the building on the recommendations of a London-based architect. George had been shown the drawings by David before the work was commissioned, and the architect, in his accompanying letter, had stated that his design would create *"a workplace in harmony with the requirements of modern technology, where staff could be flexible in utilizing the integrated computer system which in turn would provide an informational network that would optimize Total Quality Management and gear Glendurnich to attain new targets in the next millennium."*

George had thought at the time that the letter and the plans were balderdash. What was more, there had been no provision in the design to allow access by distillery workers to the new building, they having a canteen built nearer to their place of work, so that the turnaround time between shifts could be cut down.

George smiled to himself. Maybe it was a relief to the workers that they didn't have to run the risk of meeting the chairman and losing half their break-time in conversation with him. At any rate, having become involved once more with Glendurnich over the past six months, he had had to admit to himself that the new building, although impersonal, created a fresh and airy efficiency that had been lacking in the old corridors and stuffy offices. More importantly, it was able to accommodate those who held the twenty or so much-valued jobs that had been created by the continued expansion of Glendurnich.

But that didn't mean he had to like it. He walked at his own deliberate pace through the clusters of buzzing work-stations, past accounts, marketing, distribution, aware that his shambling figure must seem a total anachronism to those working on the hi-tech immediacy of the company's new business systems. Nevertheless, young faces looked up from their desks or turned from their computer screens, offering a polite "Good afternoon, Lord Inchelvie" as he ambled slowly past. He reciprocated the greeting to each with a smile and a nod, adding their first names when he could remember them.

George had made it three quarters of the way up the hall when a young man seated at the desk nearest the glass doors jumped up and held one open for him. He waited there for a full fifteen seconds, a smile beaming across his face, until George finally reached him. "There you are, my lord," he said.

"Thank you very much, ah"—George looked at him—"I'm sorry, I don't know your name."

"Archie McLachlan, my lord."

George raised his eyebrows in surprise. "My word, don't tell me you're a relation of the McLachlan brothers?"

"Aye, I am that. Gregor McLachlan was my grandfather."

"How extraordinary. I was just thinking about your grandfather and great-uncle when I came out of my office. They were both quite legendary in this distillery, you know."

The young man's eyes lit up with pride. "I was always led to believe that, my lord."

"Well, it's wonderful to know the family connection still continues." George glanced at the young man's desk. "You're in distribution, aren't you?"

"At the minute. I'm on a year's training scheme. I've done nine months in the distillery, and now I'm in the office for the remaining period."

"Jolly good, Archie." George put his hand out to the young man. "Let's keep more than one family tradition going here, shall we?"

Archie dived his own hand into the outstretched palm of the old man and shook it once as if sealing a deal. "I'd certainly like to think that, my lord."

George gave the young boy a smiling wink and walked through the door into the reception area. This was the one part of the building that the architect had not been allowed to alter. Four ancient brown leather sofas sat snugly against the panelled walls hung with old sepia photographs of the distillery from the turn of the century. An old, ornate grandfather clock ticked soothingly away between two glass-fronted mahogany cabinets, displaying bottles of Glendurnich specially packaged to mark historic occasions, amongst them the Victory Malts of 1918 and 1945 and the Coronation Malts dating back to 1903. Alongside the bottles stood photographs: a Royal visit; a presentation at a golf tournament; a huge racing yacht keeling at a gravity-defying angle, its ballooning spinnaker bearing the corporate livery of Glendurnich; and flanking the displays were two large silver trophies, spoils won by the distillery's own shinty team.

But probably the most important and invaluable asset of all was Margaret, the receptionist. There had never been any need for security at Glendurnich while she had been guarding the front door. A large and formidable lady, George had always felt that Margaret spoke to humankind as if it were, in its entirety, profoundly deaf.

She had acquired her first job in the typing pool forty years previously with a little help from her father, the distillery's head brewer. Then, five years later, she had been offered the position of receptionist, and thereafter it had been her domain, holding court behind her desk, one eye on the telephone exchange and the other on the front door. Her retirement had been mooted once at a board meeting, but it had been passed over as quickly as any resolution in the history of the company. Since then, it was widely considered that her departure would bear an ill omen for Glendurnich, similar to the ravens leaving the Tower of London. She also happened to be the prime reason why no changes had been allowed to be made to the reception area.

She looked up from her desk as George came through the glass door. "Och, is this you on your way home, then?"

"Yes, Margaret, I have a meeting in Dalnachoil tonight. I thought I'd leave a little earlier, what with the weather being so bad."

Margaret pushed her large frame from her chair and went around behind it to retrieve something from the floor, her enormous tartan posterior momentarily being the only part of her visible over the top of the desk. "Now if you'll just hold on a minute," her voice strained from behind the desk.

She re-emerged, blowing slightly from the exertion of her effort, carrying a large beige mackintosh and a multi-coloured golfing umbrella. "I'll just see you out to your car. We canna have you getting soaked to the skin."

"Now, Margaret, that's very kind of you, but really quite unnecessary—" George was unable to finish, his voice drowned by Margaret's swift rebuff.

"I'll not hear another word, my lord. Let me just get my coat on, and we'll brave the elements together, shall we?"

Margaret placed the umbrella on her desk and began clambering into her mackintosh. "And tell me," she asked in an almost normal pitch of voice, "how is Mr. David keeping?"

"He's all right, Margaret. He still has a few things to get straightened out, but I'm sure he'll be back at work quite soon."

"Well, I hope he will, my lord, because we all certainly miss having him around." She fastened the buttons of the coat and pulled the belt closed around her ample front. "If you could just say that I was asking after him."

"Of course I will. Thank you."

They were almost at the revolving door when the telephone rang on Margaret's desk. She hurried back, picked up the receiver and shouted into it. "Hullo, reception . . . yes, hullo, Mr. Caple . . . No, Lord Inchelvie is still here, but he's on his way home, he has a meeting tonight . . . very good, I'll ask him . . . very good, Mr. Caple." She put down the receiver and turned to George. "Mr. Caple wonders if you could just spare him a few moments. He says he'll be along right away."

George smiled. "That's what happens when one tries to sneak away early. Always found out. Thanks anyway, Margaret. I think you should just take your coat off again. I know how long Mr. Caple's 'few moments' are."

As Margaret went back behind the reception desk, the glass doors leading from the trading hall opened and Duncan Caple appeared. A tall, angular young man in his late thirties, he looked more like an accountant than the driven, dynamic business man he was. It was on these qualities that he had built his reputation, and the reason why David, a year before, had been instrumental in head-hunting him from a Jerez-based sherry company to take on the managing directorship of Glendurnich. However, even though George acknowledged him as being a man of immense capability in business, he also saw him lacking both in personality and social charm.

"George, old fellow, how kind of you to wait," Duncan said, walking towards him. George looked hard at the young man, already rankled by his informality and the way in which he always spoke to him in a slow and condescending manner, as if he himself were in the early stages of Alzheimer's.

Duncan reached him and held out his hand, a gesture that George felt was unnecessary as he had already seen him on three separate occasions that day. Nevertheless, he grasped the proffered hand and squeezed it as tight as he could to show Duncan that his befuddled brain was still capable of sending messages to the muscles in his arm.

"I don't want to be too long, Duncan. I've got to go to a meeting tonight."

"That's fine by me. I won't keep you. Maybe if we could just slip into the boardroom for a moment." He walked over to a door that led off the reception area, opened it and stood aside with his arm outstretched to usher George in before him. He turned to Margaret. "Hold all calls, please, until I'm finished with Lord Inchelvie."

Out of sheer devilment, George thought that he would assert his own constitutional rank over the proceedings from the outset. He walked straight over to the large ornate chair at the head of the boardroom table, hooked his stick on its back, and eased himself down between its two leathered arms, pulling the puckered flaps of his overcoat from beneath him and wrapping them around his body.

"Have a seat, Duncan," he said, pointing to the chair next to him.

Duncan sat down, then slid his back down the chair, stretching his legs out in front of him and crossing them at the ankles. He linked his hands behind his head and smiled, the informality of his actions a wordless snub to George's own small stand for conformity.

"How's David?" he asked abruptly.

George eyed him, wondering whether there was an ulterior motive for leading off with the question or whether it had come out of genuine concern.

He answered slowly. "Well enough. He still has a great deal to sort out at home, what with Rachel's estate and everything, but he's getting there."

Duncan puffed out his cheeks. "Good . . . good," he said, nodding his head slowly. "I'm glad to hear that."

He suddenly untwined his limbs and pulled his seat forward, leaning his elbows on the table and resting his chin on his hands. "Listen, George, we have a problem, and I can't really see a way of getting around it . . . well, the way things stand at the minute."

George was momentarily taken aback by Duncan's unexpected candour. "If I can be of some help . . ."

"Well, I think you can, George." He looked up. "You see, I think we should change our distributor in the States."

George shifted in his chair and looked hard at the young man. "What? You want to change from Lacey's? Why would you want to do that? They've been our agents for the past fifty years. I mean, Jim Lacey's a great friend of mine."

Duncan held up his hands, as if to stem the flow of words. "Maybe so, George, maybe so, but the fact is that over the past year, Lacey's have been slipping further and further behind their projected sales targets for Glendurnich. The latest Morgan-Graz MR report came in last week, and it showed quite blatantly that our market loss in the States corresponds directly with the rise in sales of Glenlivet and Glenfiddich. We simply can't afford to lose market share in this way."

George was silent for a moment, rubbing the side of his craggy face with his hand and staring towards the far end of the boardroom table. "You'll have to hold a board meeting. You can't make that kind of decision by yourself."

"I know, George; I'm calling one for the day after tomorrow. I have to take action on this straight away. I want a new distributor appointed by the end of this month."

"My God, that's the week after next!"

"I realize that, but it's urgent, and that . . . well . . . that is the reason I asked after David."

"What do you mean?" George asked.

"Well"—Duncan leaned back in his chair again—"I want David back at work as soon as possible."

George exploded. "Out of the question!" he said vehemently. "I mean, we can easily handle this ourselves, and David has more than enough on his plate at the minute. Anyway, you said yourself that he could take as long as he needed."

Duncan nodded. "Of course, but that was before all this came to light. Listen, we *can't* handle it ourselves. I'm going to be in London and Europe from the middle of next week, and you're going to be in Glasgow for the Whisky Association conference." Duncan paused, smoothing his hair back from his brow with both hands. "And David is still the marketing director of Glendurnich. I'm afraid it *has* to be his job to appoint the new distributor."

George rested his elbow on the arm of the chair and, closing his eyes, began rubbing his forehead in small circular movements with his fingers, his mind suddenly brought into involuntary conflict over his own instinctive paternal protection of his offspring and the continued well-being of his business. He had a mental vision of his son, who only a year before had himself been a vital and dynamic young man with his whole happy life mapped out before him, and who now spent every one of his waking hours endlessly and mindlessly digging in the garden at Inchelvie, never wishing to end his task lest his brain be taken over with thoughts of his dead wife.

Duncan watched him closely, noticing the colour drain from his face. He was about to say something when George spoke slowly.

"I do mean it. I don't think that David can take on anything like this just yet."

Duncan thought for a moment. "I was about to say, George, that it may be just what David needs—to get away from Scotland, to go somewhere completely different. I promise you it won't be too taxing. All David will really have to do is . . . well, just be there."

Lord Inchelvie sighed, realizing that for once the wretched man was actually showing some concern. "I know," he said, his voice sounding old and thin, "and I'm grateful for your understanding of the situation. But it's not just that. I'm pretty sure that David wouldn't want to be too far from the children just at the minute."

The smile slid from Duncan's face. He looked at George for a moment, then rose from his chair and started to pace up the boardroom.

"Listen, I quite see your point, but you have to look at it from where I stand. I was brought into this company a year ago to make sure that it grows. So far, I have achieved this. However, I cannot continue to do it without your full support. Right now, I am in desperate need of a marketing director. I cannot afford to lose further market share in our single most important overseas market." He turned and looked directly at George. "I really do need a marketing director right now. I'm sorry to have to say this, George, but if David is not able to fulfil his role, then I'll have to think about replacing him." Duncan had reached the other end of the table. He swung around briskly to face George before continuing. "Regardless of who David is, I'm afraid that I will have to ask the board to give this its full consideration at the meeting."

Duncan looked at his watch. "I hope I haven't kept you too long. Will you still be able to make your meeting?"

George nodded slowly and raised his hand in acknowledgement.

"Well, good night, then, and drive carefully. I think the roads may well be pretty dicey with all this rain."

He turned towards the door, opened it and left the room. George sat for a moment, then rose from his chair and shuffled over to the telephone on the table at the side of the boardroom. He lifted the receiver and dialled.

"Hullo, Hamish? . . . Yes, it's George Inchelvie . . . Listen, I'm afraid that I won't be able to make the meeting tonight . . . no, I'm sorry, but something has cropped up. Can you give my apologies? Thank you, Hamish. All well? . . . Good . . . my love to Christine . . . goodbye."

CHAPTER 3

Jock leaned his fork against his body and blew on his hands in a vain attempt to get some warmth back into his numbed fingers. As twilight set in, the rain seemed to come on harder, and the sound of David digging next to him was drowned out by the heavy splattering on his sou'wester and the arctic wind that whisked about his face. Jock winced as he picked up his fork, the dampness kneading at his arthritic shoulders. He looked over to David, who as always continued to dig without break, oblivious to the conditions in which he was working.

"Mr. David."

David straightened up, dug his fork into the ground and looked round.

"Mr. David, it's getting kind of dark."

David snorted a laugh at Jock's morose diplomacy, knowing full well that this understatement of fact was Jock's way of saying that they were both bloody mad to be out digging a garden in the pouring rain, with darkness falling so fast that they could hardly see what they were doing.

But that was Jock. As long as David had known him, and that must be, he thought on reflection, for the best part of his life, Jock had always been miserly with words. He would work away in the garden with such a dark look of solemnity on his face, it was as if he held the world in its entirety responsible for this inability to communicate. Yet under this hard exterior was a kind heart, and it had been Jock himself who had approached David at the outset of his task to restore the old flower-beds with a short, offhand statement to show his willingness to lend support. "Here, man, you've no idea how to handle a fork, do ye?"

After that they had worked together constantly, Jock greeting David each morning with a flick of his chin to the side and a sound emanating from his mouth that was as brief and as incomprehensible as a question mark. It was a perfect partnership. Neither wished to talk about himself or his thoughts; the physical act of digging and raking the new beds, planting the new roses, and watching their efforts take shape was sufficient to create a bond of understanding between the two men.

David looked up at the blackened sky and nodded. "Yes, Jock, I think you're probably right. Sorry about keeping you out so long. I was hoping that we might be able to finish this bed today." He pulled his fork out of the ground, stepped back off the flower-bed onto the grass, and for a moment surveyed their day's achievement. "Come on, we'll call it a day. We'll get the rest done tomorrow."

"Aye, if the Lord spares us," Jock said gruffly. "Gie me your fork, Mr. David, and I'll tak' the tools tae the shed."

David handed over his tool and fondly watched the old boy head off, his waterproof clothing creaking and rubbing as he walked. David delved deep into the inside pocket of his jacket and pulled out the grubby plastic folder that contained the garden plan. He started slowly towards the house, studying the drawings as he walked, then stopped and turned around to look back at the new flower-beds. The project was almost finished. Just that last bit around the variegated holly-tree to reclaim, and then the Inchelvie garden would be as it was before.

Yet he really didn't want the garden ever to be complete. It would break the spell of continuity which had existed since he started the job, his days of work linking the present with the past, linking this very moment as he stood there, rain dripping off his head and running down his face, with Rachel.

He placed both earthy hands on his face and pulled them down to his chin, clearing the water from his face and at the same time wiping away the unwelcome tears welling up in his eyes. "Shit!"

He slapped hard at his face with both hands to clear his head, then turned and began to jog across the lawn. As he rounded the side of the house he broke into an ungainly sprint, his arm movements restricted by his waterproof jacket and his loose-fitting Wellington boots burping out air as he ran.

He threw open the wrought-iron gate which led out onto the gravel sweep at the front of the house, slammed it shut, and heard it miss its catch and bounce open again behind him. He stopped and put his hands on his hips, and as he caught his breath, he heard above the wind the sound of a car going through its gears on the drive. He strained to see if he could make it out, managing only to catch the faint red glimmer of its rear-lights glinting through the trees before losing it to the darkness and the wind.

He shut and snibbed the gate, then, crossing the gravel, took the steps two at a time and threw open the front door, just as his mother was making her way across the hallway in the direction of the drawing-room. She swung round with a start. "David!" she exclaimed, clasping her hands to her heart. "What a fright you gave me!"

"Sorry about that," he said, smiling at her and holding up his hand in apology. He unzipped his jacket and threw it onto the church pew, then proceeded to toe one boot off with the other.

"How are you getting on, darling?" Alicia asked, coming across the hall towards him.

"What?" he said almost defensively, balancing on one foot as he pulled up his sock.

"With the garden, I mean."

"Oh, all right. We'll get that bed finished tomorrow."

"Well, I think that's marvellous, especially doing all that work in those dreadful conditions. You and Jock must be soaked to the skin. Has he gone home?"

"Yup, about ten minutes ago."

"Good, because Effie left half an hour ago to make him his tea. We were going to eat early, but your father has just telephoned to say that he's cancelled his meeting for some reason. So, half past seven all right for you, darling?"

"Yup, that's great." David placed his boots together and kicked them under the pew. Alicia pushed the dripping jacket to one side and sat down, trying to get below David's level so that she could make eye contact with her son. He caught her eye momentarily and gave her a faint smile before turning and walking towards the staircase. Alicia watched him go, and with a deep sigh, rose slowly to her feet and followed him across the hallway.

"I saw a car go down the road just then," David said, without turning.

Alicia stopped, surprised at being given this sudden and rare opportunity to enter into conversation with her son. "Yes, that was Jane Spiers," she said in a bright little voice, immediately being aware of the falseness of its tone. She cleared her throat to cover up for her overkeenness in grasping this slim and unexpected chance of communication, and continued in a more controlled voice. "She popped in for a cup of tea. I had just seen her off when you walked in. She was, well, just finding out how everything was, or is, so to speak."

David turned and looked at his mother out of the side of his eyes. She tilted her head and smiled at him.

"That was nice of her." He paused. "Well, I'll just, erm"—he pointed up the stairs—"go and have a bath."

Alicia nodded. "You do that, darling. Dad and I will see you down here at about quarter past seven."

As he walked slowly up the stairs, Alicia crossed her arms and leaned against the panelled wall, watching him until he was out of sight above her. She heard his bedroom door open and close behind him. She shut her eyes for a moment, shook her head and murmured to herself, "Oh, David." Then, walking back to the door of the drawing-room, she opened it and entered.

David turned off the gush of water that ran from the huge Victorian mixer tap into the bath, and bent over to stir up the peaty-brown water, still in its natural state from the holding tank, being fed by the spring high on the moor above Inchelvie. He threw off his dressing-gown onto the floor and stepped with one leg over into the bath, simultaneously taking his watch off his wrist. As he laid it on the chair beside him, he noticed that its face was misted with condensation. He rubbed it clear with his thumb. It was three minutes to six—just about news time.

He stepped back out of the bath and walked through the bathroom's steaming atmosphere to the mirrored cabinet above the basin. He opened it, took a small transistor radio from the top shelf, and closed the door, its mirror swinging round like a trap to catch the diffused outline of his face. He stood there staring back at his own unrecognizable features, a face that told nothing: not good looks or ugliness, humour or anger, happiness or sadness. It registered neither identity nor emotion, and he felt an obscure sense of comfort just looking at it.

He placed the transistor on the side of the basin and slowly brought his hand up to wipe the mirror clear. There it was, the face that he knew, its gauntness now accentuated by the muddy streaks left by his fingers when he wiped his face in the garden. Just one year ago, he thought to himself, that forty-three-year-old face had registered the thoughts and cares of a twenty-five-year-old, and now, one year on, it seemed to have doubled its age.

David reached up and threw the door of the cupboard open to break the spell of self-remorse, just catching it before it slammed against the bathroom wall. "Bugger it," he said out loud. "Will you stop thinking of yourself all the bloody time!"

He picked up the radio and turned it on, twiddling the dial to find the news, its speaker screeching a plethora of tones as if in defiance to its rough handling. Somewhere in the middle, he caught the merest sensation of the introductory bars of a song. He stopped and turned the dial backwards. There it was, then a voice-over, ". . . good you could join us this evening. This is Danny McKay on Moray Firth Radio going back in time with a beautiful track from Smokey Robinson and the Miracles—'Tracks of My Tears.' "

He held the radio in front of him as the bars unfolded into the song. "People say I'm the life of a party, 'cos I tell a joke or two." He cradled the radio in his hands as if he were carrying a small injured bird, frightened that if he moved it too much, it would suddenly stop breathing and die. "So take a good look at my face, can't you see the smile, it's out of place." Laying it down carefully on the chair next to his watch, he stepped into his bath and slowly lowered himself downwards, allowing the luxury of the water to flood over his body, and the memories to flood through his mind.

CHAPTER 4

That year, Oxford had uncustomarily shimmered in heat since the first week in May, bringing an early influx of tourists to streets already burgeoning with the youthful, buzzing throng of student life. The weekends were worst of all. On that particular Saturday, the volume of traffic going into town was horrendous, tailing back down St. Aldates as far as the police station. David sat in his stationary car silently cursing himself, realizing that he had been stuck in its baking interior far longer than it would have taken him to walk the distance from the Christchurch College tennis courts to the Kings Arms on Holywell Street.

He drummed his fingers impatiently on the steering wheel of the old Triumph Vitesse, craning his neck out the window to see if there was any sign of movement farther up the line, and then bringing his head back in to glance both at the clock and the temperature gauge on the walnut dashboard. It was ten to one. He was already five minutes late and he could detect light wisps of steam rising from the car's radiator. Dammit, he really *should* have just walked!

Leaning over to the glove compartment, he took out a handful of unsleeved tapes and proceeded to go through them, chucking the rejected ones onto the seat beside him. At that moment, the traffic ahead started to move. He let out the clutch without putting his hands on the steering wheel, and selecting a *Motown Greatest Hits* album, he pushed it into the slot of the new Phillips stereo tape deck, a recent and much valued twenty-first birthday present from his parents.

As the second track was finishing, David eased his car into a space between two rows of bicycles twenty yards from the Kings Arms. Jumping out, he locked the door and hurriedly dodged his way along the pavement to the large double doors of the pub. He pushed at them with both hands, only managing to get them a quarter of the way open, such was the resistance of bodies on the other side. Sliding through the gap into the hot, smoky atmosphere, he slowly threaded his way through the throng of lunch-time drinkers, stretching up to his full six-foot-two height to see if he could locate his friends. A shout rose above the clamour.

"Oi, David, we're over here!"

He looked round and spied Toby, standing on a chair and waving a beer-mat above his head, his square frame silhouetted by the dusty shaft of sunlight that angled through the window of the pub. He pushed his way towards him, eventually extricating himself at the crowded table where his friend now sat, resplendent in cricket whites.

"Look, I've got one in for you," Toby said, pointing to a pint on the table. He looked across to the person sitting opposite him. "Here, budge up, Henry, there's room enough for one more on that bench."

As David perched himself on the small space that Henry had vacated, a brown-haired girl sitting close to Toby's right-hand side on the window bench looked up briefly from the book that she was reading and combed her hair back off her face with her fingers. She picked up her glass and took a drink, her brown eyes catching David's gaze over the rim of the glass. For a split second, they lit up into a captivating smile, before she replaced the glass on the table and returned to her book, her hair once more falling back across her face.

Toby, who had been continuing a conversation with Henry, caught this interchange out of the side of his eye and looked quickly from one to the other. He leaned forward across the table. "Listen, David, if I could possibly drag your attention back here for a minute, I want to introduce you to Jane." He turned to the young blond girl on his left, who grinned inanely at him. David smiled and nodded a greeting at her. No doubt yet another of Toby's attempted first-year conquests, he thought to himself.

"Jane," Toby continued, "this is David Corstorphine—oops, sorry, the HONOURABLE David Corstorphine, second lieutenant-in-brackets-on-probation, I hasten to add, in Queen's Own Highlanders, and owner of one of the only private malt whisky distilleries in the WHOLE of Scotland, thus an extremely good guest to invite to a booze-up—"

"All right, Toby," David interjected, embarrassed by his friend's incorrigible attitude. "That'll do me fine."

"No, come on, let me finish. I'm building you up here." Jane let out a high-pitched giggle, giving Toby ample encouragement to continue with his monologue, and he proceeded to count out David's attributes on his fingers. "Oxford Blue at tennis, erstwhile lead guitarist with that well-known university band, The Tenement Blok, and owner of the most amazing car stereo in the whole of Oxford." He looked across at David. "There, that's it. I'm finished. That wasn't so bad, was it?"

David smiled sardonically back at him and took a drink from his glass, at the same time once more catching the eye of the brown-haired girl, who had again momentarily looked up from her book. She raised her eyebrows and almost imperceptibly shook her head before looking down again.

"So who won the tennis match?" Toby asked.

"We did—just," David replied. "That's why I'm so late. The final set went up to 13-11. What time does your cricket match start?"

"Two o'clock." Toby sucked in a shivering breath and executed a short drum roll on his knees with his hands. "And I'm nervous as hell. Somebody, in their infinite wisdom, has decided that I should open the batting."

"Hell's teeth!" David said, rubbing his hands together in evil glee. "I'm not going to miss that!" He got to his feet. "Come on, you'd better have another one. Build up your Dutch courage. What do you want?"

"Well, it'll have to be quick. Just a half of Flowers." He stretched his arms above his head, then placed one with awkward nonchalance around Jane's shoulder. "And you can get a half of lager for Jane while you're at it."

David pulled his wallet out of the back pocket of his tennis shorts and headed off towards the bar, leaving Toby to continue his somewhat clumsy seduction of Jane. He had only taken a few steps when he stopped and turned to look across the table at the brown-haired girl. "Would you like another drink?"

She continued to study her book, seeming not to have heard him above the general noise. He leaned over towards her. "I wondered if you would like another drink."

She glanced up, starting back with surprise when she realized that David was looming over her. "What? Oh! Well, that's very kind of you." She picked up her glass, drained it and handed it to him. "An orange juice would be lovely! Thank you!" She flashed her smiling eyes once more and immediately returned to her reading.

It took two trips back and forth to the bar to get the whole order complete on the table. Finally he placed the glass of juice in front of the brown-haired girl, and as he sat down she looked up and smiled a thank-you at him. Just then, Toby turned to witness this further exchange. He suddenly picked up his beer, drained it in one gulp and jumped to his feet.

"Right! The time of reckoning is nigh!" He clasped his hands theatrically across his heart and looked down at Jane. "But after the battle is won, I shall return to claim my prize!" Bending down, he delivered a long, loud kiss on the cheek of the giggling girl. Then he turned to David with a sly grin on his face.

"And I think I'll give one to your friend as well!"

Before David could utter a word to stop him, Toby had put his hand on the head of the brown-haired girl and bent down towards her. It had been his intention merely to give her a peck on the forehead, but the unexpected and unsolicited contact made the girl jerk her face upwards to look at him, her mouth open to issue some exclamation of surprise or rebuke. This movement and Toby's forward momentum were so perfectly yet unintentionally synchronized that he found himself administering a kiss not to the planned target, but directly onto her open mouth.

Her reaction to this unwelcome infringement could not have been more immediate. The book left her hands and flew up in the air, and David reached up and caught it with one hand as it sailed over the top of his head. Her arms flailed and her legs kicked out as she freed herself from Toby's embrace, throwing the table violently forward before it crashed back down again on its four legs. Glasses fell over and rolled across the surface of the table, liberally spilling their contents over the people who sat nearby. Warning shouts filled the air as everyone jumped up in the confined space, trying to avoid the cascading flow by opening their legs under the table or pulling their knees round hard against their seats.

In one movement, the girl rose to her feet and gave Toby a mighty open-handed clout on the side of the face. He reeled back from the force and sat down in a pool of beer.

"Sorry! sorry!" Toby exclaimed, holding his hands up in defence against a further attack. "I really didn't mean to do that!"

The girl looked at him angrily, her eyes narrowed. "What the *hell* do you think you're doing? How *dare* you?"

She started to move away, but as an afterthought she turned back and aimed a sharp and powerful kick at his shin under the table before stamping off towards the door of the pub, the packed and silent crowd parting for her as willingly as the Red Sea had parted for the Israelites.

As the door slammed shut, laughter first bubbled, then erupted everywhere in the pub but at their table. Toby sat with a shocked expression on his face, slowly rubbing his cheek with one hand and his shin with the other, while the others around the table, attempting ineffectively to wipe down their sodden clothing with their hands, glared disapprovingly at him.

"Sorry about that," he said defensively, holding up his hand in apology to the assembled company. He looked across at David. "Christ, she's a bit unpredictable, isn't she, your friend?"

Still clutching the girl's book in his hand, David sat shaking his head in disbelief at Toby's actions. "She's not *my* friend, you bloody fool! I've never seen her before in my life!"

"Come on! I saw you buy her a drink!"

"So? I bought her a drink. Doesn't mean you have the right to molest the poor girl."

"I didn't mean to do, well, *that*! It was a mistake!" he whinged, rubbing hard at his face and his leg. "Jesus, I hurt all over."

David got up from the bench. "Serves you bloody right, you twit." He took a deep breath. "Look, I've still got her book. I'll go and see if I can catch her and try to apologize for your . . . lunatic actions." As he turned and started to make his way through the crowds, Toby called after him in a disappointed voice.

"Does that mean you won't come to watch me bat?"

David stopped and looked back at him, shaking his head. "Listen, I'll try, but I think she's the priority right now, don't you?"

He pushed his way through the doors of the pub and stood blinking on the crowded pavement, trying to get his eyes accustomed to the bright sunlight. There was no sign of the girl. He moved ten paces to his left and caught a glimpse of her as she made her way purposefully along the Broad, dodging through the mass of pedestrians. He jogged along the pavement, clutching the book in his right hand, every so often jumping up to keep sight of her bobbing brown mass of hair amongst the mêlée of hatted heads and sunglassed faces. Then, finding it too hard to navigate through the crowd, he stepped out onto the street and started to sprint along the gutter.

He caught up with her just as she passed the gates of Balliol College, and slowed to a fast walk beside her, matching her pace. "Listen, I'm sorry about all that."

She looked sideways at him, then, without speaking, turned eyes front and kept walking.

"I just wanted to apologize . . ."

She stopped and turned to look directly at David. "Look! Let's just leave it, shall we?"

David held up his hands in an act of appeasement, the right still clutching the book. She took off again, taking David's lead in stepping off the pavement and making her way along the gutter. He sighed resignedly and watched her go, her long legs, clad in a pair of faded Levi's, stretching out and away from him, his eyes focusing on her neat denim-clad bottom as she walked down the street. It was only when he saw her veer across the Broad and disappear around the corner into Cornmarket that he was brought abruptly to his senses.

"Shit! Her book!" He took off at full tilt, dodging through the oncoming cars, taking the straightest line to the point where he had lost sight of her. Skidding his way round into Cornmarket, he saw her immediately, twenty yards in front, still striding up the gutter. At last he caught up with her.

"Look, I've got your book for you," he said, exasperated, holding it out towards her.

She stopped and turned to him. He smiled at her, trying to show that he was friend, not foe. "You left it in the pub," he said quietly.

The girl reached over and grabbed the book and was about to make off again when she turned to him, a thunderous expression on her face. "Do you know, there just happens to be one thing I cannot *stand* and that's the taste of beer, and what's even worse than drinking it is being forced to taste it via someone else's mouth!"

For a moment David looked at her incredulously, then felt the overpowering urge to start laughing. He stuck his hands in the pockets of his tennis shorts and glanced down at his feet so that she wouldn't see his reaction to her remark. When he eventually did look back up at her, his face still bore the merest hint of a smile.

"Well, I'm glad *you* think it's funny," she said sharply, and turned to walk off.

David quickly jumped in front of her, and held up his hands to halt her passage. "Please listen, just stop for a minute . . . erm . . ." He looked around, desperately trying to work out his next move. The shop immediately adjacent to them was an off-licence. "Look, would you stay here, *please,* just for a minute."

He moved sideways towards the off-licence, watching her warily in case she decided to bolt off again. He dived into the shop and reappeared thirty seconds later clutching a half-bottle of Veuve

Clicquot champagne. He blew out a sigh of relief when he saw she was still there.

"Look," he said, holding out the bottle towards her, "this is just a small peace offering to say I'm sorry for what happened in the pub. It was unforgivable, and I hope . . . well, I just hope that this'll help you get rid of the taste of beer!"

As they stood there, bumped and jostled by the passing crowds, David watched her closely. She started to bite at her bottom lip, and his heart sank as she half turned away from him. For a moment, he thought that this last chance to make amends had flown out the window when she looked back at him, her eyes creased into the same captivating smile that she had given him in the pub. Suddenly she broke into a laugh, and eyeing the bottle in his hands, slid her hands into the back pockets of her jeans.

"Well, that has to be the most expensive bottle of mouthwash I've ever been bought!" She paused for a moment, then, pushing her fingers through her hair, took a deep breath. "Look, what happened in the pub really doesn't justify you buying this." She paused and pulled an embarrassed face. "I think that I probably over-reacted a bit. Anyway, it's not really for you to apologize."

David smiled at her. "Well, I think someone has to." He offered her the bottle. "Okay, if not an apology, then let's just call it—an introductory offer."

After a moment's hesitation, she slowly took the bottle and clasped it in her arms next to the book. "Well, in that case, thank you, it's more than generous." She held out her right hand towards him. "And by way of introduction, I'm Rachel Devereux."

David took hold of her hand. "Hi, Rachel," he said, overwhelmed with relief that the whole incident was apparently finished with. "It's a pleasure to meet you. I'm David Corstor——"

"I know you are," Rachel interjected, a huge grin on her face. "Oxford Blue at tennis, titled, lieutenant in the army, what else was it? Oh yes, rock star . . ."

David felt himself blush. "Ah, of course, Toby's wretched introduction!" He looked up at her and smiled. "I think we'd both be better off if we forgot about that little interlude, don't you?"

Rachel smiled and nodded. "Maybe for the best."

"Good! So, which way are you heading now?"

"Back the way we came." Rachel flicked up her wrist and looked at her watch. "I was meant to be at the science buildings at two o'clock for a tutorial, but I don't think I'll make it."

David put his hand on her arm and turned her in the direction of Broad Street. "Come on, I've got a car back at the pub. Even in this infernal traffic, I think we've more chance of making it on wheels than on foot. At any rate, I'm going up that way." He glanced apprehensively at her as they walked. "Maybe I shouldn't really say this, but I'm meant to be watching Toby play cricket this afternoon."

Rachel looked sideways at him, a rueful smile on her face. "Yes, you're right. Better left unsaid."

They walked briskly up Cornmarket and around the corner into the Broad, sometimes divided and at other times pushed together by the crowds coming towards them. "So how does it work, you being here at Oxford and being in the army at the same time?"

"Well, I'm not really in the army yet. I'm what Toby quite rightly termed a 'second lieutenant-in-brackets-on-probation.' I joined up after leaving school, the army pay my way through university, and then, if all goes well with my finals, I do six months at Sandhurst and five years with the regiment."

"Right. So when *are* the finals?"

"God, I wish you wouldn't ask that question." He looked over to her, pretending to chew on the finger-nails of his right hand. "Next month!"

"Yeah, same as me."

"Really? I can't believe that. Which college are you in?"

"Hertford. Why do you say you can't believe it?"

"Well . . . because . . . well, I just thought that I might have met you before now. I mean, Oxford's not that big a place."

Rachel turned and smiled at him, but said nothing more until they had turned the corner of the Broad and were nearing the car. David took the keys from his pocket and Rachel walked out into the street to stand by the passenger door.

"Actually, I have seen *you* around," she said, looking at him over the roof of the car.

David stopped as he put the key in the door and glanced at her, a puzzled expression on his face. "Really? Whereabouts?"

"I don't know. Just around."

"Then why haven't I seen you?"

Rachel shrugged her shoulders. "I don't know. Maybe you just haven't been looking in the right direction."

The remark was laced with such possibly seductive innuendo that David felt an involuntary shiver of excitement course its way up his spine. He looked directly at her, catching the physical intent of the statement in her eyes.

"Obviously not," he said quietly to himself. Unlocking the car, he climbed in, and having bundled the pile of cassettes back into the glove compartment, he reached over to open the passenger door. Rachel threw her book onto the back seat and jumped in, wedging the bottle of champagne between her feet.

"The science building, then?"

She thought for a moment. "No, I don't think it's worth it. My tutorial will have started by now." She looked across at him. "Anyway, what the hell! I haven't had a break from my books in weeks. Maybe I'd be better doing something relaxing, like watching cricket."

David was taken aback by her suggestion. "Are you sure?"

"Why not? As long as I don't have to make physical contact with your friend Toby again!"

David let out a short laugh and, pushing the car into gear, he pulled away from the kerb and manoeuvred a tight U-turn on the junction of Broad and Holywell Streets, then headed back up Parks Road towards the university grounds.

He counted five cricket matches in progress as he drove the car as unobtrusively as possible around the periphery of the grounds, straining his eyes to see if he could make out any familiar figure on the pitches. He passed by the first game, and on to the second, and there caught sight of Toby standing in the crease at the bowler's end, one hand leaning on his bat, the other placed firmly on his hip, an air of confidence about his person.

"There he is!" he said, pointing Toby out to Rachel. "We'll park here, next to the sight-screen, and hope we don't get moved along."

"What's the sight-screen for?" Rachel asked, looking at the large white board that stood beside them.

"Well, it's positioned in direct line with the bowler and the batsman, so that the batsman can get a clear sight of the ball when it comes at him." David looked over at the score-board. "God, the jammy devil! He's only three runs off his half-century! No wonder he's looking so cocky!"

Rachel sighed. "If he's only got three more runs to make his half-century or whatever, why is he standing around doing nothing?"

"He's not facing the bowling at the minute."

"I've never understood the stupid game. When you're in, you're out there, and when you're out, you come back in here again."

Leaning forward, she picked up the half-bottle of champagne and pulled off the foil top. She rolled down the window and, twisting off the wire, exploded the cork towards the sight-screen, quickly putting the top of the bottle to her lips to catch the first frothing mouthful. She handed it over to David.

"It's over," he said, taking a swig and pointing towards the game.

"What, already?"

"No, not the game. 'Over' just means it's time for someone to bowl from this end. It's Toby's turn to face now."

Rachel shook her head. "It's a very stupid game." She reached over for the bottle and took another sip.

David watched the new bowler walk back towards where they were sitting in the car, turn twenty-five yards from the wicket and set off like an express train towards the crease. The first ball was a vicious outswinger at which Toby attempted to play a forward defensive shot, but missed it by a foot. He straightened and strutted up the wicket, tamping with his bat at various spots on the ground, obviously feeling that they were the major cause for his missing the last ball by such a wide margin. He returned to his crease, played a practice shot identical to the one that had just failed him, flexed his knees, and readied himself for the next ball.

"Wow, I'm not used to champagne!" Rachel said, leaning back in her seat. "I can feel it going straight to my head!" She rolled her head back and forth against the head-rest, then something on the dashboard of the car caught her eye. She leaned forward and pointed to the cassette player. "So, this is the famous stereo system that Toby was on about?"

David nodded. "Yeah, that's it."

"Can we put it on?"

"Don't see why not—as long as we play it quietly." Reaching forward, he pressed the on/off button and pushed the present cassette into the player. As the fade-out of Martha Reeves and the Vandellas hissed through the speakers, David watched Toby steer a ball off the edge of his bat for two runs.

"Come on, you fluky bastard," he said under his breath, "one more like that and you've got your fifty!"

As Rachel was tilting back another measure of champagne into her mouth, the muted, mellow guitar introduction filled every corner of the car. She suddenly sat upright, her body taut as she waited to hear the next bar. The instrumental gave way to the close harmony of the backing vocalists.

"Oh my God! It *is*! It's Smokey Robinson and the Miracles!" She reached forward and turned the volume button full on. "Oh, David, this just has to be the most beautiful, sexy song that has *ever* been written!"

The sound of the music was deafening within the small confines of the car, and instinctively David put his hand forward to turn it down, realizing that it could be no doubt heard by the players on all five of the cricket pitches.

"I think that that's just a bit lou——"

"Oh, please don't touch it!" Rachel said, reaching out and catching his hand to stop him. "Oh, *David,* this is just too fantastic for words!" She pushed open the door and jumped out, leaving it wide open.

"What *are* you doing?" he laughed.

But Rachel never answered him. Taking another drink from the bottle, she kicked out each foot to rid herself of her shoes and began dancing on the grass, moving slowly but steadily away from the car towards the sight-screen. David watched her for a moment, then dragged his attention back to Toby, who by this time was becoming increasingly agitated at the speed of the bowling. It was then that it suddenly dawned on him what was about to happen.

"Oooooh, hell's teeth!" he exclaimed out loud. He threw open his door and leaped out. "Rachel, you can't—"

He didn't go any further. Suddenly the visual impact of the cricket game became a stark and uninteresting antithesis to the spectacle that he was now witnessing. He swallowed hard as he watched Rachel gradually approach the sight-screen, her movements liquid as she danced, her rhythm perfect, her body picking up every sensuous particle of the song, and he found himself transfixed by the combination of the words, the music, her beauty and her motion. She turned, mouthing the words of the song directly at him, using the bottle as a makeshift microphone, "So take a good look at my face, can't you see the smi-ile, it's out of place," then again turned away from him, moving farther into the danger zone, gently swinging her hips and hands in complete symmetry and unison with the song.

A shout from the cricket pitch broke David's trance. He turned to look towards Toby's game. Everyone was gawking in their direction—all except Toby, who stood at the crease, waving his hand and yelling something at him.

"What?" David called back.

"I—said—get—her—away—from—the—bloody—sight-screen," Toby called out at the top of his voice. "She's—a—bloody—distraction!"

"You can say that again," David said to himself, and held up his hand in apology. He ran over to Rachel, who was now dancing directly in front of the huge white board.

"I think you'd better move," he said. "You're right behind the bowler's arm."

"No, I'm not. I'm miles away from him," she replied, continuing to dance, her voice now slightly fuzzy from the effects of the champagne.

David swept back his hair and scratched at the back of his neck. "Listen, I don't think we're going to be very popular with Toby."

Rachel said nothing but smiled wickedly at him.

"Come on, are you going to move, or am I going to have to carry you?"

Her reply was immediate. "All right."

David shook his head. "Oh, hell's teeth!" he said under his breath as he walked up to her. Putting one hand behind her back and the other under her knees, he picked her up off her feet, and as he half-walked, half-ran towards the car, Rachel linked her arms around his neck.

The whole episode had a dramatic effect on Toby. He was finding it hard enough to deal with the pace of this new bowler without the distraction of a sudden burst of music and the appearance of a girl in front of the sight-screen. As he held his hand up to signal his state of unreadiness to the bowler, he recognized David's car, and realized immediately that this was the girl who had given him such a hard time in the pub. It was, to Toby, an ill-fated omen. As David carried the girl away, he took up his stance once more, but when the umpire dropped his arm and allowed the bowler to start his run, his eyes were distracted from their normal line of concentration to watch David and the girl move towards the car. He never saw the ball. He only heard the thump and clink as it cart-wheeled his middle stump out of the ground and knocked the bails clean over the wicket-keeper's head. The fielding side erupted in delight and ran to the bowler, slapping his hands and patting him on the back in congratulations.

As soon as they reached the car, David dropped Rachel onto her feet and dived inside to switch off the stereo. When he reappeared, she was looking out towards the cricket game.

"Toby seems to be walking off the pitch. Does that mean he's out or in?"

David glanced over to the score-board in time to see the number 49 taken off the main display and relegated to the "Last Man" position, then turned back to view the dejected figure of Toby as he slumped his way back to the pavilion, slamming his bat into the ground as he went. David looked across at Rachel, who was biting at her lip, a cringe of embarrassment on her face.

"Oops, was that my fault?" she asked quietly.

David laughed. "I wouldn't worry too much about it. Anyway, I think he probably more than deserves it, don't you?" As Toby reached the steps of the pavilion, he turned to glare in their direction. David hastily opened the door of the car. "Nevertheless, I think the best thing we could do right now is get the hell out of here."

Rachel seemed to heed the suggestion immediately, but instead of climbing in, she reached over to the back seat and retrieved her book. She straightened up and stood directly in front of him, looking up at him. "I'll think I'll walk from here," she said.

"You don't have to."

"I know, but I need to clear my head. That champagne has just made me feel like going to sleep."

"Well, why don't you?"

"Because I have a mountain of work to get through this weekend, and because of today's . . . well . . . circumstances, I haven't even started." She clutched the book in her crossed arms and looked down at her feet. "But anyway, it was lovely to meet you—and thanks for the champagne. It was delicious."

She suddenly reached up and gave him a light kiss on the cheek, then turned away and walked off towards the gates of the cricket park.

"Do you want to meet for a drink sometime?" he called after her.

Rachel turned and smiled. "No, I don't think so."

"Why not?"

"Because I've only got a month before my finals, and I really don't want any distractions."

"I wouldn't be a distraction."

"I think you would."

"Well . . . er . . . what about after the finals?" David asked, desperate to prise even the faintest hope of commitment out of her. A thought came into his head. "I tell you what. Christchurch have a Commem Ball this year. Would you come with me?"

"When is it?"

"The twenty-third of June."

Rachel thought for a moment and nodded slowly. "All right, I'll come, but only on one condition."

"What's that?"

"You wear your kilt."

"Okay."

Rachel swung herself gently from side to side. "AND you bring your car and Smokey Robinson with you."

"That's two conditions."

Rachel smiled at him. "Well, that's the deal."

"Okay. Sounds good enough to me!"

CHAPTER 5

Effie pattered her way across the hall to the drawing-room door, knocked quietly, and popped her head around the corner. There was no conversation in progress, only the sound of the fire crackling in the hearth and the contented snoring of one of the dogs lying out in front of it. Lord and Lady Inchelvie sat opposite each other at the far end of the room, he snoozing gently in his large, threadbare armchair, a glass of whisky precariously balanced on one of its sunken arms beside him, while she, clicking away with her knitting-needles, watched the muted screen of the television.

"Excuse me, Lady Inchelvie," Effie said, almost in a whisper.

Alicia turned and dipped her head to look over the top of her spectacles at the little grey-haired head that peered round the door at about the same level as the handle. "Yes, Effie?"

"That's the dinner through in the dining-room now."

Alicia bundled up the knitting and placed it on the table beside her, then rose from her chair. "Thank you, Effie. I'm afraid that we're still waiting for David. I don't quite know what he's up to. I called up the stairs about a quarter of an hour ago, but he obviously didn't hear me. I think I'd better just nip up to his room to see if everything's all right."

"Och, don't you bother yourself about that," Effie said, appearing in full around the door. "I'm just away upstairs now to turn down the beds, so I'll give him a wee knock on his door." She looked across at Lord Inchelvie and smiled. "That'll give you time to wake up his Lordship."

"Oh, Effie, could you? That would be most kind." Alicia glanced over towards her husband. "I'm afraid the poor man's had a pretty tiring day at the office."

Effie paused for a moment. "Everything's all right, is it not, Lady Inchelvie?" she asked tentatively.

"Yes, of course. Why do you ask?"

"Oh, it was just that I was hoping that his Lordship was feeling quite well, what wi' him not going to the meeting tonight."

"No, nothing to worry about, Effie. Just something quite important has cropped up which he has to discuss with David over dinner."

"Well, I'm glad to hear it, then." She gave a quick smile in the direction of Lord Inchelvie and then waved her index finger in the air, as if conducting herself back into action. "Now I'll just away and see where Mr. David has got to."

Effie closed the door of the drawing-room and made her way to the staircase and, readying herself for the ascent by placing one hand on the banister and the other on her left knee for extra leverage, she began to climb the stairs, gently humming to herself as she went. Having made the half-way landing, she stopped long enough to catch her breath and to make a mental note to remove an over-conspicuous cobweb that floated high up on the large dark portrait that loomed above her before continuing on her way.

The door of the bathroom was open wide and the light off, but the steamy air that emanated from within still carried on it the smell of soap and after-shave. She hesitated, wondering whether she was a little premature in knocking on David's door. Her fist was about to come into contact with it when it flew open and David emerged, unaware of Effie's presence on the landing. They both started back in surprise.

"Oh, I'm sorry to disturb you, Mr. David," Effie said breathlessly.

"It was just that your mother and father have gone through to the dining-room, and they were wondering if everything was all right with you."

David, dressed in a clean pair of jeans, an open-necked shirt and bedroom slippers, smiled lightly down at her. "I'm sorry, Effie. I dozed off in the bath. I'm heading down now."

"That's fine, then." She stood there uneasily, her hands clasped together in front of her apron. "Well, I'll just away and turn down the beds."

David closed the door behind him as Effie scuttled off around the balconied landing. He walked to the top of the stairs and stopped, looking across the high divide of the hallway to the other side of the balcony where she was just about to enter his parents' bedroom.

"I'm afraid that I kept Jock out in pretty horrible conditions today. I hope he's not suffering any ill effects?"

Effie turned, her face briefly registering a look of surprise at David's concern over her husband before it broke into a smile. "Och, he's fine, Mr. David. He aye moans a bit when he's working out in the rain, but then again, he does the same when the sun shines. Jock has never been able to extract much pleasure from the weather, I'm afraid." She let out an affectionate sigh. "That said, you'd have a hard task keeping him away from the garden, whatever the weather!"

David did not reply, but simply nodded and smiled. He turned and took the stairs two at a time, his slippered feet creating loud flat echoes in the hallway as he descended. He crossed over to the dining-room and entered, and his parents, already seated at the top end of the large polished table, both looked up towards him.

"Sorry about that," he said, nodding a silent greeting to his father. "I fell asleep in the bath."

"Not surprising," Alicia said, getting up from her chair and walking over to the sideboard. She began to ladle a savoury-smelling stew onto a plate. "You must be exhausted after working out there in that dreadful weather."

George put his knife and fork down on his plate and sat back in his chair, chomping on his mouthful and pointing over to the far corner of the sideboard. "I brought the whisky through from the drawing-room for you, my boy, so help yourself to one."

"Thanks. I will."

He poured himself a sizeable whisky and added as much water to it again before sitting down at the table. While he settled in his place, his mother hovered at his side before placing the steaming plate of food in front of him. "There, that should be restorative."

"Thanks," David mumbled quietly, pulling his napkin from its ring and laying it on his lap.

Alicia returned to her seat and continued her meal. Over the past months, she had come to dread their dinners together, every night the mood of the whole proceedings being orchestrated by David's sombre and silent presence. Previously, it had been the time of day that both George and she had enjoyed the most, sitting quietly together uninterrupted, talking about their respective days and making plans for future ones. Now, if there was any conversation at all, it was still mostly between George and herself, but it was inevitably an exchange of words that sounded as thin and as falsely happy as a Linguaphone lesson. She knew that George understood this, and both came to prefer an uneasy silence to their chirrupy sentences, the three of them sitting together as if observing some monastic vow of quiescence, the high-vaulted ceiling of the dining-room amplifying the irritating sound of cutlery scraping against plate.

But she knew that tonight had to be different. In the drawing-room beforehand, George had told her of his meeting with Duncan Caple, and she knew that sometime during the meal the subject of the States would have to be broached. She therefore gave a small involuntary shudder of trepidation when she saw George put down his whisky glass and turn toward David.

"How are you getting on in the garden?"

The sudden break in the silence took David by surprise. He took a drink of whisky and wiped his mouth with his napkin. "Getting there," he said, his voice sounding croaky through lack of use. He cleared his throat. "I reckon that we'll have finished the whole thing by this time next week."

"Well, I think it looks pretty wonderful. You and Jock have really done a terrific job. I never thought that we would see the day when the garden would be restored to its former glory."

He took another mouthful of food, and silence once again fell over the proceedings, all three continuing their meal without looking at the others. David put down his knife and fork and turned to his father. "I thought that I might have a look at that bit of rough ground down by the loch next and see if I can't come up with a plan for that."

Lord Inchelvie stopped chewing and looked across at his wife. She was caught with her fork in her mouth, her eyes anxiously darting back and forth between her husband and her son. David picked up on the exchange.

"Is something wrong?"

His father sighed deeply and sat back in his chair, resting his elbows on its carved arms and linking the fingers of both hands together on his lap. His brow was furrowed deeper than usual, the loose skin on his thick neck creating a series of double chins as he looked down at his hands. He began to flick at one thumb-nail with the other.

"Well, in a word, my boy, yes."

A worried look came over David's face. "What is it?"

George Inchelvie looked back at his wife, who gave him the lightest of nods. "Well," he said, slowly, trying to pick his words carefully, "we have a slight problem in the marketing department at the distillery."

David paused for a moment, glancing back and forth between his parents. "Duncan should be able to sort it out, shouldn't he? That's what he's there for."

"Well, it's a little bit more complicated than that," his father continued. "There is only so much that Duncan can do, and he's finding himself a little short of human resources at the moment." He looked over at his son, realizing that he'd better just come out with it. "Listen, David, I know that you find it hard right now to give much thought to work." He paused for a moment. "But the fact is that we have this problem which I don't think we are going to be able to solve . . . well . . . without involving you." He watched as his son let out a deep sigh and began scratching at the back of his neck with both hands. "Duncan brought it to my attention today that our sales have slipped dramatically in the States. He was quite blunt about the fact that he wants to hold an extraordinary board meeting within the next few days so that we can appoint a new distributor over there as soon as possible."

George glanced over to his wife, who smiled reassuringly at him.

"I'm going down to Glasgow next week for the Whisky Association meeting, and, well, Duncan is heading off to Europe at the same time, so"—he began pulling at his ear-lobe with the thumb and forefinger of his right hand—"it's really just a question of who is going to be able to go over to the States." He quickly picked up his whisky glass and took a mouthful as a way of giving himself the excuse to be silent while his son came to terms with what was being said.

David leaned back in his chair and folded his arms. "What about Robert McLeod?" he said softly. "What's he doing at the minute?"

His father let out a short laugh. "Well, you know Robert better than any. He may be financial director, but he's hardly ever been out of this country, let alone to the States! He'd end up in Alabama or somewhere, and we'd have to send out a search party!" He smiled, but became serious once more when he realized David had not reacted to the light-hearted remark. "Anyway, like everyone else on the board of Glendurnich, Robert's getting a bit long in the tooth to be able to cope with something like this."

David shut his eyes and nodded slowly. "So, what you're actually saying is that Duncan wants me to go."

Alicia, who had been sitting quietly listening to her husband explain the situation, cut in. "Darling, the last thing we want in the world is for you to go out there, especially when we know that you don't feel up to it. We, of all people, understand this, David, but you also have to realize the predicament your father is in."

David rubbed at his forehead with the fingers of his right hand. "It's not only that I don't feel particularly up to it. It's just that I don't want to be too far away from the children at this precise time."

George paused for a moment, then reached out and placed his hand on his son's arm. "Listen, David, I do realize this, and I actually mentioned this very point to Duncan. However, he did say that he would make it fairly painless. Really, all you will have to do is to go over there for a couple of days to make the appointment. It will be a very simple operation and you'll be back almost immediately." He paused and looked once more at his wife for her silent support before continuing in a calm and reasoning voice. "Your mother and I also think that it might be a good opportunity for you to get away from here for a bit. I know that at the moment you might not think this is right, but I have a feeling that once you've made the break, it could be of benefit."

David picked up his napkin from his lap and threw it on the table and, pushing his chair away, he began to get to his feet. "Right—well, I'll give it some thought."

Alicia put up her hand, stopping him half-way out of his chair. "David, please . . . just sit down for a moment." She gathered her thoughts while he settled down once more. "David, your father and I are trying our best to do everything to help you at the minute . . . and it's very difficult . . . because we know how much you are bottling up inside yourself. We watch you every day becoming more and more introverted, and . . . well, it really is becoming too much of a strain on us old things." She looked at her husband, who sat silently in his chair, his face grey with fear of overstepping David's gossamer-thin tolerance level. "You see, life has to go on—not only for us, but for you—and, most important of all, for the children. We have to try to get back to some sort of normality, and everyone in the household is making the hugest effort to achieve this, even though the immediate past has been so damaging." She stopped and cleared her throat, her voice beginning to quiver with emotion. "I don't mean to be hard, David, but you have to come some way to helping us—and to start talking to us, otherwise I don't think that your father and I will really be able to cope with the situation much longer."

David glanced across at his parents, noticing the look of sheer sadness on his mother's face, while his father, issuing a gruff cough to cover for his emotions, took a handkerchief from his top pocket and loudly blew his nose. Somewhere deep in the turmoil of his brain, the sight of them showing their despair so openly pin-pricked at a sense in David which had been hitherto anaesthetized. He chewed slowly on his bottom lip before eventually speaking.

"For eighteen years of my life . . . I shared it . . ." He stopped, wrestling with his brain to get the word out, like someone who had suffered a massive stroke and was going through the agony of learning how to talk again. ". . . with Rachel."

He looked around the room and therefore didn't catch the slight movement that his mother made as she reached over to hold the hand of her husband under the table. David continued, his voice coming out in spasmodic phrases.

"We . . . were . . . one. We thought the same things . . . we laughed at the same things . . . we lived the same . . . we *were* the same . . . and . . ." He paused and took in a choking breath. ". . . now that she's no longer here . . . I feel lost . . . and empty . . . and I don't have any feelings any more. I find it difficult to show gratitude, because . . . my powers of being able to notice even the smallest kindness . . . seem to have been purged from my body." He wiped roughly at each eye with the back of his hand. "There is now . . . this huge void in my life . . . I have no senses . . . my emotions are gone . . . my self-confidence is gone . . . everything is gone." He glanced briefly at his parents. "But even if I can't feel anything, I do *know* . . . that you two have both been wonderful over the past six months . . . and I also *know* that I haven't shown my full appreciation for what you have done . . . but I do . . . appreciate it, that is."

"Darling, you don't need to—" his mother started.

"No, please," David interrupted, "let me finish." He got up from his chair, stuck his hands in the pockets of his jeans, and again gathered his thoughts before continuing slowly and methodically. "I guess

I've shut out everything in the world . . . because my own world no longer matches with it. For most of the time, I walk around existing as if nothing has happened to change my life . . . ever . . . then suddenly it's there, reality, right bloody there in front of me." His voice crescendoed as he angrily spat out the words through clenched teeth. "And just as I think, right, now you stupid bugger, this is where you can stand up and face it"—he paused and sat back down on his chair again before continuing almost inaudibly—"the shut-off valve cuts in again."

His mother looked across at him tenderly. "Darling, I know it might sound a bit of a cliché, but I really do think that this has to be nature's way. I would imagine it's a bit like losing an arm or a leg. To begin with, the mind numbs the senses, but eventually the reality, the pain, does catch up with you. It will catch up with you, David, and you will be able to face it . . . and you will come through it all right and begin to build your life again . . . I *know* so."

George and Alicia watched as their son stood up from his chair and walked up to the far end of the dining-room. He turned to face them. "You're probably right. Maybe I should go away, because I don't really want to be around here when it all does catch up with me." He stopped and began tracing a line down the pattern of one of the heavy damask curtains with his finger. "Because no matter how hard I try, I cannot . . . physically . . . move one step around here without thinking of Rachel. Everything and everybody reminds me of her . . . and I resent that . . . so I end up feeling . . . sad, depressed . . . even embittered towards those who are closest to me . . . like you two . . . and Effie . . . and, God forbid, even Jock sometimes!" He breathed out a shallow laugh and stuck his hands back in his pockets. "You know, I really thought that by staying out of our own house, it would make it easier. But it doesn't work. Rachel is everywhere."

He turned and walked back down the room towards his parents, giving them a forced smile of reassurance. He breathed out heavily. "Pretty hopeless, huh? Pretty bloody hopeless!"

Reaching across the table for David's empty whisky glass, George rose slowly to his feet, took his stick from the back of the chair, and picking up both his and David's glass with the fingers of his free hand, made his way to the sideboard. "I think that we could both do with another one, don't you, my boy?" he said with false cheerfulness in his voice. He poured two large whiskies, added a splash of water to each, placed one on the table, and slowly pushed it across to David with his stick. "One good thing, I suppose—there's plenty more where that came from!"

David looked at him and smiled and took the glass off the table. His father plumped himself heavily back down on the chair. "David," he said slowly. "There's never going to be a good time for you to make this trip, but I'm afraid that it really does look as if you will have to go. If you could bear to, I think that it would be a good idea if you came into work with me tomorrow, just to have a quick word with Duncan. Then, as soon as he's briefed you, you can bring the car back afterwards, and I'll get a ride back." He lifted the tone of his voice in an attempt to inject a tinge of light-heartedness into the overriding oppression of the conversation. "I was just telling your mother that I met a charming young boy in the distillery today by the name of Archie McLachlan. Turns out he's the grandson of Gregor McLachlan."

David smiled and nodded. "Yeah, I know Archie. I took him on for work experience just before I left."

"Well, he seems to be a very willing young man. I'm sure that he won't mind giving me a lift." He paused and looked across at his son. "Rest assured, David, that while you're away, your mother and I will give every support that you might need—with the children and everything. You'll only be away for a short period, and then, when you return, we can take it from there. If you feel you need a bit more time, then you can certainly have a look at that bit of the garden down by the loch." He looked across at David. "How does that suit?"

David didn't reply immediately, but bent forward and picked up the glass of whisky off the table. "Well, whatever plans Duncan comes up with, I don't want to leave without seeing the children."

"No, of course. I quite understand that."

David nodded slowly. "Right." He held up his glass to his parents. "Well, if you don't mind, I think I'll just take this up to my room."

He began making his way across the room, then, as an afterthought, turned back and walked over to his mother. He put his arm around her neck and gave her a kiss on either cheek. " 'Night."

"Good night, darling/my boy," his parents said in unison, and watched him walk to the end of the dining-room, open the door and leave. For a moment they sat there wordlessly, their eyes fixed on the door, both lost in their own private thoughts, before the movement of one broke the trance of the other.

"Well done, old girl," George said quietly, smiling across at his wife. "At least you started to get him talking."

Alicia did not reply immediately, but sat fiddling with an unused spoon on the table. "He's on a knife-edge at the minute, Geordie. He could go either way."

George leaned across and squeezed his wife's hand. "I know he is. I also know what he's talking about, this thing of being devoid of all feeling. I remember being like that during the war, seeing friends and comrades killed in battle, and just having to carry on." He took another drink of whisky. "I'd really forgotten until he started to speak about it."

"He will be all right, won't he?"

"Yes, I'm sure he will"—he slowly nodded—"but I'm afraid he's yet to suffer that cold hard shock to his system."

"You didn't say it all, did you?" Alicia said quietly.

"What? About Duncan's ultimatum?" He shook his head. "No, I couldn't. I think it's best to leave it as it is, and see how it works out." Pushing himself laboriously to his feet, he picked up his stick and walked round to his wife's side, placing his hand on her shoulder. "Come on, old girl, I think we're both pretty well emotionally drained. Let's turn in as well."

Alicia got up and linked her arm through her husband's. They walked together to the door, and as he opened it, she pressed the bell to signal to Effie that the dining-room was clear.

CHAPTER 6

For a moment, David stood motionless in his bedroom, his eyes closed, allowing its soothing quiet to envelop him slowly and gently ease the clamour in his mind. Putting his whisky glass on the dressing-table, he walked over to his bed and sat down heavily, leaning his elbows on his knees and rubbing at his face with both hands.

"Oh, *bugger*!" he said softly.

He fell back on the bed and lay looking up at the ceiling, wishing that there were an easy way to refuse his father's request. But there wasn't. Too much had been said over dinner, too many things had to be considered. He swung his legs over the side of the bed and sat up again. His parents were right. He did have to start getting some sort of perspective into his life, and even though the prospect of flying over to the States and having to conduct business once more with people that he had never met filled him with trepidation, he realized now that ending his closeted and protected existence at Inchelvie was inevitable—and that forcing himself into contact with others would, in the long-term, be healing.

Yet it really did terrify him. He got to his feet and walked over to the dressing-table and took a gulp from his whisky glass. In pouring it, his father had been over-generous with the whisky and less so with the water, and he coughed involuntarily as he felt it burn its way down deep into his stomach. He was about to turn back to the bed when he stopped, his eye caught by the photograph that stood propped up against the wall at the back of his dressing-table. He reached forward and picked it up. It was one that he had taken himself about two years previously—of Sophie, Charlie and Harriet in a boat on the loch, the soft evening light gently bouncing off the mirror-calm surface of the water and accentuating the glowing smiles on the children's faces. Sophie was pulling hard on the oars, her giggling face tipped up towards the sky as she tried her hardest to get the heavy craft on the move, while Harriet sat in the stern, looking open-mouthed over the side of the boat in the belief that she would soon pull out a fish with the help of her bamboo cane with string attached. Charlie meanwhile balanced precariously on one foot on the seat in the bows, his outstretched arms tipped to one side like the wings of a banking jet, as he half-heartedly fought his compulsive desire to fall overboard.

Smiling to himself, David opened up the top drawer of the chest and took out a pair of socks and gave the dusty glass of the photograph a wipe before placing it carefully back in its position. He took a pace back and stood looking at it for a moment, then his eyes dropped to another picture that had been concealed in the drawer. He hesitated, then took it out and, without viewing it, carried it to his bed. Falling back on the faded yellow eiderdown, he lay there looking up at the ceiling, the picture face-down on his chest. After a moment's meditation, he held it up.

It was a photograph of a wedding group—its colour almost faded out from having stood too long in direct sunlight—of himself and Rachel, flanked by an undisciplined gaggle of little bridesmaids and pages who strained at the leash, wanting to be anywhere else at that time but in the picture. To David's left, dressed in a black morning suit and looking somewhat out of place amidst the profusion of kilts, stood his best man, Toby, who leaned forward looking along the line at Rachel, a beam of sheer delight on his face. The photograph was one that had not been initially selected by the mimsey little wedding photographer, who had stated categorically that he didn't want to use the photograph as "it does not meet with my general high standards of portraiture." However, David had clandestinely saved it from the outtakes, as it was the only one that he really liked of the wedding, the reason being that as he looked towards Toby in admonishing seriousness, Rachel was looking directly at the camera, her face overflowing with laughter, having just secretly undone the buckle of his sporran, the shutter of the lens only managing to catch the image as a streaked blur as it fell to the ground.

David dropped the photograph back down to his chest and closed his eyes, suddenly cradled in the enveloping warmth of humorous nostalgia. He remembered now that he had chosen the photograph because at that time he had realized that it encapsulated every facet of Rachel's character. Direct, funny, incredibly beautiful. He felt his face break into a smile and he crossed his arms over the picture, hugging it to his chest, his pain gradually fading out of focus.

"Tell me again why Frank was called Frankie Push-Push?"

"What?"

"Frankie Push-Push. You remember—your friend at Oxford. Why was he called that?"

"God, what made you think of that?"

"I always think of things like that. They're all very precious memories—things like that."

David looked across at his wife on the bench beside him and reached over and tucked the tartan rug around her neck. Even though they were in the relative warmth of the old summer-house, he knew that she really shouldn't be out of her bedroom—not when it was this bloody cold.

"This is mad. You should be in bed."

"Come on, don't fuss. I'm all right. I just looked out of the window and saw you working, and I wanted to be with you."

Giving a shrug of resignation, David got up and walked over to the corner of the dark-pined room. He picked up an old paraffin stove and gave it a shake to check if there was any fuel in it.

"Should be enough," he said, removing the funnel and delving in his pocket for a box of matches. He lit the wick and watched as the thin yellow flame worked its way around each side to meet, then, replacing the funnel, he adjusted the flame until it glowed blue through the little window. Instantly, the summer-house was filled with its heady, comforting smell.

As he sat down again, Rachel unravelled her hands from the rug and pulled her woolly hat farther over her ears. "Well?"

David frowned at her for a moment before remembering her question. "Ah, yeah, Frankie Push-Push." He put his arm around his wife's shoulders and eased her gently towards him, ever conscious of her now constant pain. "Well, it was all a bit naughty really. He just happened to turn up at the flat one evening with a girl who turned out to be, well, somewhat loud when it came to love-making, and we all just happened to hear her yell out. 'Push! Frankie, Push!' probably at rather an important moment. Anyway, the next morning, I happened to call him Frankie Push-Push, really just as a passing remark, and he was so taken aback that he sort of blew out his mouthful of cereal across the table. After that, the name just stuck; actually, as it turned out, to his own egotistical pride and joy!"

Rachel's face broke into a wide smile. "I always loved that story."

"You knew it all along, didn't you?"

She turned towards him. "Yeah, but I still love hearing it." She moved awkwardly on the bench and let out a deep sigh. "It all seems so long ago."

"Twenty-one years, to be exact."

"I know. I'll never forget it."

For a moment, they sat together in silence, looking out onto the partly frozen loch, the opaque rays of the weak February sun glinting off the surface of the icy water. It was so quiet that even with the doors of the summer-house closed and the background hiss of the stove, somewhere, out on the lower reaches of the snow-capped hills, the distinctive and haunting sound of a single grouse could be heard, calling out its panicked chuckle. Rachel pulled the rug closer about her and let out a shiver, despite the heavy pine-tanged heat that filled the now fuggy interior of the summer-house.

"Do you remember how warm it was that morning after the Commem Ball?"

"That whole summer was boiling."

"That's right. It was, wasn't it? We had the roof of the car down—and then we tried to have breakfast with the Duke of Marlborough at Blenheim Palace."

David laughed. "Well, sort of. It was a pretty half-hearted attempt. I don't think he would have been too happy to be woken at five o'clock in the morning."

"No, maybe not. But then if we *had* seen him, we would never have ended up in that hayfield near Woodstock, would we?" She pushed herself in beside him to get the warmth from his body. "I can remember so vividly the smell of the hay—and the quiet. It was just like this. And then that fox appeared right beside the car—and he just stood looking at us." She let out a shuddering sigh. "My God, that was a magical morning."

David kissed her lightly on the side of her woollen hat. "Yeah, but there was something else, wasn't there?"

Rachel turned her head to look at him. "You mean Smokey Robinson?"

"Yup."

She grinned and nodded lightly. "Can you remember how many times you recorded that same track for me?"

"Not offhand, no."

"Twenty times. Ten each side. We must have played it about three times right through that morning—and we just danced—you in your kilt, me in my ball gown."

She swallowed hard, and David felt her body grow taut with effort.

"And still Smokey sang." She let out a short laugh. "You know, that was the one year of my life I kept a diary, and that was the sole entry for that whole week—'And still Smokey sang.' I wrote it diagonally across the page in big black letters. It said it all, really."

David could now feel the vibrations of her shivering against his body. "Come on, I think it's time that we got you inside." He put his arms around her to lever her gently to her feet.

She pushed his hands away. "No, not yet," she said, shaking her head. "I'm loving this—being outside again. It's just—*so* beautiful."

David held up his hands resignedly and sat down again, pulling her close in beside him once more. At that moment, they both became aware of a new sound, the faintest fluttering reverberation against the window-pane. A butterfly, having lain dormant in some dusty crevice of the summer-house, had been tricked by the heat of the stove into waking, and was now vainly attempting to make its way though the invisible screen into the open air. Rachel took a hand out of the rug and, leaning across, closed her fingers gently around it. For a moment, David heard the soft whirring of its wings against her palm before it stopped, content to rest itself in the moderate darkness of its shelter.

"Poor thing," she said, squinting through her fingers at the rich orange and brown of its colouring. "Doesn't stand much of a chance, does it? Either it stays in here and dies of starvation, or we let it out and it freezes."

David pulled her hand towards him and looked in on her little captive. "Yeah, the odds are pretty much stacked against it, aren't they?"

Rachel got to her feet and shuffled over to the door and opened it. She slowly uncurled her hand, but the butterfly seemed reluctant to move. She lifted it to her mouth and gently blew on its wings, encouraging it to fly. After a moment, it took off and was borne away on the frigid air. Rachel closed the door and stood watching until it disappeared.

"At least it will get the smell and taste of the world," she said, almost inaudibly, "even if it is only for a short time." She turned and shuffled back to the bench. "Better than being cooped up inside for the rest of its days."

David stared straight ahead, not wanting to catch her eye, understanding the simile that she was making and frightened by its direction. He felt her hand on his knee.

"We don't talk about it, do we?"

"What's that?" he said unconvincingly.

"Come on, my darling, you know—the inevitable."

David took in a faltering breath. "Darling, we don't . . ."

Rachel turned to him. "Yes, we do, David, we do. Because I really want to tell you that I'll be all right. I want to tell you that so that you can tell Sophie and Charlie and Harriet that I'll be all right—that I'll be safe—and that I'll be with you all wherever you go." She reached up and stroked the side of his face. "You know, you were without doubt the most handsome boy in Oxford." She let out a weak laugh. "I just could never quite believe that you would turn out as nice—and that it was me that caught you."

David leaned his face against her woolly hat, secretly using it to brush away the tears from his eyes.

"I'd really like to go back to Oxford, darling."

He cleared his throat before replying. "Would you?"

"Yeah. Very soon. Very, very soon." She pushed herself away from him. "But right now, I'm absolutely bloody freezing. Let's go back to the house."

Needing no further encouragement, David jumped to his feet and turned off the stove, then, helping her to her feet, he opened the door and put a supporting arm around her waist. As they walked close together across the frost-hardened lawn towards the house, David's leg bumped against a hard object in her coat pocket, making her wince with pain. He stopped.

"Are you all right?"

Rachel smiled bravely at him. "Yup."

"What have you got in there?" he said, feeling the side of her coat.

Rachel pushed her hand deep into her pocket and brought out a Walkman.

"It's my music."

"What is it?"

She stopped. "Here." She reached up and pushed one of the ear-plugs into his ear, then, standing close to him, she placed the other in her own, and pressed the "play" button. "It's the tape."

The song cut in immediately, filling his head with the words. "So take a good look at my face, you'll see the smi-ile, it's out of place."

He looked at her and smiled, shaking his head, incredulous. "You still have it?"

"Of course. All twenty recordings of it."

David linked his arm around her shoulder, and as they walked across the lawn, around the side of the house and up the steps to the front door, still Smokey sang.

Yet they never made it to Oxford.

The photograph fell onto the floor with a clatter, and even though he had been fast asleep, David sat bolt-upright, swung his feet over the side of the bed and stooped down to pick it up. He checked the glass. Nothing broken. He laid it on the bed beside him and bent forward, leaning his elbows on his knees, and rubbing his eyes with his knuckles. He glanced over at the clock. It was twenty to two in the morning.

He turned round, picked up the photograph and sat looking at it.

It had never been any different—from the moment they met to the moment they were married to the moment that she died. They had loved and laughed through life and through the procreation of life, and their children had loved and laughed with them. He was she, and she was he, their true bonding not having been made during the pageantry of the wedding, but three years before in that vast open Oxfordshire hayfield under the burning blue sky, witnessed only by the birds, the fox, the Triumph Vitesse—and Smokey Robinson and the Miracles.

He pushed himself off the bed, walked over to the dressing-table, and carefully stood the photograph up beside the one of his children. Then stripping off his shirt, he unbuckled his belt and kicked off his jeans, and fell into bed to sleep more soundly than at any time since the night that Rachel died.

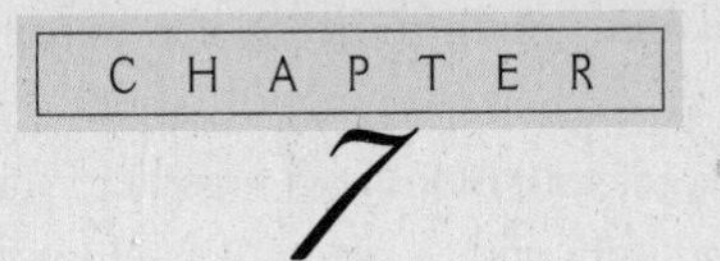

CHAPTER 7

The next morning David woke early and immediately became aware of an ache of anxiety gnawing deep in his stomach, a different and more frightening sensation than the cold realization of solitude which normally settled like a leaden weight around his heart. He pushed himself up quickly from the bed, as if fast action would help to shed this unwelcome feeling, and hurried out across the landing and into the bathroom. Turning the shower tap full on, he entered the cubicle before the water had a chance to heat up, and tilted back his head so that his face took the full force of the invigorating flow.

Yet the thought was still with him. Today he would not be going back out into the garden to work alongside Jock. Today, without option, he was having to return to a way of life for which he knew he was still both physically and mentally unprepared.

He bent down to retrieve the bar of soap which spun haphazardly above the outflow of the shower, and started to scrub hard at every part of his body, trying to scourge the cowardice from his being and revitalize the drive which he knew was locked away deep within him. In his mind, he went back over the conversation he had had with his parents the night before, remembering that for the first time he had suddenly understood their own feelings of anguish and vulnerability, feelings which lay just beneath an outward show of strength and support.

He shut off the water and stepped out of the shower, his skin tingling and his mind clearer. Still with the same sense of urgency, he shaved quickly and returned to his room. He put on a clean pair of boxer shorts and slipped into them, then, without thinking, pulled on his work jeans and started to do up the buttons. He stopped in mid-action.

"Oh, come on, get your bloody act together!" He pushed his jeans hard to the ground and, with a swing of his foot, kicked them back onto the chair, then, walking over to the wardrobe, he slipped his dark blue suit off its hanger and laid it on his bed. He stood back and stared at it blankly.

Somehow, he hadn't been able to bring himself to wear a kilt at the funeral. It was just too tangible a link with Rachel, and in some irrational way he had wanted to distance himself as far as possible from her on that day, hoping that it would make it easier for him to cope with the whole thing. So he had worn the suit—and he hadn't worn it since. He shook his head, his mind suddenly thrown into turmoil by an overpowering sense of rejection both to wearing it again and to his new routine. In one quick movement, he picked it up and threw it onto the chair next to his jeans. He pushed his fingers through his hair and glanced over to where it now lay, its pressed perfection standing out in powerful and self-assured contrast to the honest simplicity of his earth-streaked denims.

"Jesus, I'm not ready for this," he said quietly to himself.

He turned back to the wardrobe and took out a pair of fawn chinos and a navy-blue double-breasted blazer as a compromise both to conformity and to his feelings. He put on the trousers, along with a blue open-necked shirt and cashmere jersey, and pulled on a pair of socks before slipping his feet into a pair of dark brown boating shoes. Then, with one last huge intake of air, he strode over to the door, threw it open and walked out onto the landing.

They left the house at eight-thirty, David behind the wheel of the Audi Estate, with his father sitting hunched in his tweed overcoat next to him. Although it was David's own company car, his father had been making use of it while David himself had been working at home, and being more used to driving the garden tractor and on occasion his mother's small Renault, he found himself spinning the wheels on the gravel as he took off, being unused to the power of the big fuel-injected engine.

George looked across at him. "How are you feeling this morning?"

David nodded briefly. "Okay."

His father reached over and gave him a hard but reassuring smack on the leg. "You'll be fine, my boy. Don't worry."

The old man pressed the on/off switch of the radio, having become accustomed to listening to it on his way to work each morning, and thinking it better for David's sake that there be some form of diversion from conversation during their journey. The news programme *Good Morning, Scotland* blared from the speakers, and he quickly adjusted the volume and settled back to listen to the twangy tones of a sports correspondent discussing strategy with the manager of Glasgow Rangers Football Club.

As soon as David turned out through the gates of Inchelvie and onto the main road towards Dalnachoil, the clouds broke for the first time in about a month, allowing a fleeting splash of pale blue to push weakly through from above, followed almost immediately by a meagre ray of sunshine which glinted briefly on the windscreen of the car. By the time the Audi had reached the top of the main street of Dalnachoil, the streaks of blue had lengthened and the sun began to dart in and out through the clouds, bursting forth its unfettered light onto the houses of the village and casting swift-moving fluffy shadows onto the sides of the surrounding hills. As they drove along the main street, George raised his hand continuously to wave at acquaintances on the pavement, and David glanced in the rear-view mirror at the querying faces that followed the departure of the car, the villagers being unaccustomed of late to seeing both himself and his father driving off together.

Once out of Dalnachoil's speed limit, David felt a light unexpected surge of excitement slip its way through the barricades of dullness in his mind, almost as if he was at last managing to make a break from the confines of his small, sad world. He had never ventured farther than the village in the past month, and his visits there had been brief and only out of unavoidable necessity, always fearing that he might be caught up in understanding and comforting conversations with the locals. But now, driving out in his own car along the familiar road, he sensed almost a feeling of well-being as they wound their way southwards through the glen, flanked on either side by green sunlit fields which stretched away to clash against the brown blanket of heather moorland that rolled down from the hills above. He glanced over at his father, and for the first time in a long while was able to feel a sudden burst of intense love for the old man who sat with his eyes closed, his hand cupped around his ear to help him pick up the low tones of the radio. David reached forward to turn up the volume, and his father looked round and smiled.

"Thanks—that's a bit better," he said, dropping his hand to his lap. "Forgot to put in my bloody hearing-aid this morning."

At the bottom of the glen, David edged out at the T-junction, then pulled away in the direction of Aberlour, pushing the car hard so that he could feel the power of the engine press his back into the seat. The narrow road followed the contours of the Spey River, running swollen and brown after the spring rains. David took it fast but warily, being forced to slow from time to time to avoid hitting a variety of obstacles that he met on his way: first an ageing Massey-Ferguson tractor, which came hammering up the road towards him, black smoke belching from its punctured exhaust-pipe, while a large round bale of hay, bouncing wildly on its front loader, successfully impeded its driver's vision of the road ahead; next two blackface ewes that were lying in the middle of the road, soaking up the warmth from the tarmac, their heads thrown back as they cudded, like a couple of haughty old ladies complaining disdainfully to each other about this unscheduled disturbance to their peace; and finally a flashy new four-wheel-drive vehicle parked haphazardly at the side of the road, the empty fishing-rod holder on its roof indicating that its driver was somewhere down on the banks of the river, plying its pools and eddies for salmon.

Two miles before Aberlour, David turned right and crossed a high iron-latticed bridge that spanned the river, then immediately swung left past the large brown sign which bore the name GLENDURNICH DISTILLERIES LTD in gold lettering. The road had at one time twisted down the hill to the riverside in a series of hairpin bends, but had had to be re-routed to allow easier access for the long and unwieldly triple-axled lorries that delivered bulk malt from the maltings at Inverness and took off the casks of mature whisky to the bottling plant near Glasgow. Now it descended in one huge sweep, yet so designed to still leave the distillery completely hidden behind the screen of densely planted fir-trees, save for the two pagoda-style chimneys, the characteristic emblem of all Scotch malt distilleries, that sat over the old kiln-house and jutted their arrowhead-shaped tips above the cover.

Rounding the bend, he left the shelter of the trees and at once the distillery came into view below him. Set in a fifteen-acre site, it stretched out on a plateau twenty feet above the river, bounded by a series of tarmacked roads which, in turn, were bordered by a wide expanse of newly mown banks and lawns interspersed with bright well-kept flower-beds. The road dropped down the incline, so that David began at the same level as the dark grey metal roofs of the four identical maturation warehouses before descending to the plateau and driving alongside the original stone-built still-house and mash-house with their small white irregular windows, and then on past the malt silos to the new office block at the far end of the complex.

He pulled the Audi into the car-park and picked a space as close as possible to the main reception door. He turned off the ignition key, silencing both the engine and the radio simultaneously and, unclipping his seat-belt, he opened the door and got out. For a moment, he stood looking over towards the offices and found himself almost immediately stretching his arms high above his head to counteract an almost puerile sense of nervousness. He shook his head at this idiocy and walked around to the other side of the car where his father was already pushing himself to his feet with the aid of his stick. Putting a hand under his tweedy armpit, David gently heaved him upright, and the old man stood for a minute preparing himself for the first step.

He looked at David. "Ready?"

David smiled and nodded.

"Right. Well, let's make an entrance."

Margaret looked up from her reception desk as the revolving door swung round, and a huge grin spread across her face as she saw David follow in after his father. "Oh michty, michty me!" she said, pushing up her stout frame from the chair. "It's yourself, Mr. David!"

She bustled over towards them and grasped hold of David's hand even before he had time to offer it. "Och, it's wonderful, wonderful to see you." She looked him up and down, still clutching his hand. "My, I have to say that you're looking a wee bit on the thin side," she said, and then, after a short pause for reflection, "but I dare say it makes you look as handsome as ever!" She threw back her head and shrieked out a laugh that could no doubt be heard throughout the building.

"Jolly good, Margaret, jolly good," George cut in, "but David is only here for a short period today."

"Of course, of course," Margaret said quietly, suddenly embarrassed by her own over-ebullience. "I quite understand. But nevertheless, it's a pleasure to see you looking so fit and well, Mr. David."

David smiled at her and nodded. "Thanks, Margaret."

"Did Mr. Caple say at what time he would like to meet this morning?" George asked.

"Now he did that." She trotted over to her desk and picked up her spectacles and a piece of paper. She shook open the legs and placed the spectacles squint on her nose. "Right," she said slowly, holding the piece of paper out in front of her, "it says here could you all meet at ten o'clock in the boardroom."

"That's fine, Margaret. Many thanks. Just let him know that we'll be there." He took hold of David's arm and, turning him away from Margaret, glanced over at the grandfather clock.

"Look, it's twenty past nine now. I suggest you make yourself scarce until then, otherwise you'll only get press-ganged into doing some work. Go and have a walk around the distillery and we'll meet again in the boardroom at ten."

David smiled. "Right. Good idea."

Giving his son a gentle nudge in the back, George then stood watching as David hurried his way out through the revolving doors, almost as if he couldn't wait to be free of the building.

Arriving in his office, George was somewhat taken aback to find Robert McLeod there, standing with his hands clasped behind his back and looking out of the window. He swung round as George entered the room.

"Ah, George," he said in his extruded Edinburgh voice. "I hope you don't mind me waiting for you here. Mhairi told me that you had half an hour free just now, and I was really wanting to see you quite urgently."

George made his way over to the coat-stand. "Well, all right, Robert," he said, shrugging off his overcoat. "If you could just give me a second while I get myself organized."

As he hung his coat on the stand, he glanced out of the side of his eye at the neat, diminutive figure of Glendurnich's financial director and found himself smirking in mirth at David's desperate suggestion of the previous night that this man should undertake the United States trip. He walked over to his desk and sat down heavily in his chair.

"Ever been to the United States, Robert?" he asked, dropping his walking-stick to the floor beside him.

"No, I can't say I have."

"Didn't think so." Smiling broadly, George opened the top drawer of his desk, took out a pad of paper and unclipped his pen from the inside pocket of his jacket. Robert meanwhile had pulled across a chair from the far wall and placed it close to the other side of his chairman's desk, then, with a deft flick at each well-honed trouser crease, he sat himself down.

"Come to think of it, though," he said, a look of studied recollection on his face, "my wife and I nearly did take the two girls to Disneyland—I think when they were about fourteen and fifteen." He looked pensively over George's head and brushed minutely with his forefinger at the centre of his neatly clipped moustache, as if affectionately stroking a mouse. "That must have been about ten years ago. I think I cancelled the holiday because the exchange rate suddenly dropped." He came out of his remembrances and looked back at George. "Anyway, we much prefer the south-west of England for our holidays. There are so many wonderful golf courses down there."

"I'm sure there are," George said, glancing across at this pedantic little man who could be nothing but an accountant, so much so that he was quite happy to cancel plans to take his family on the holiday of a lifetime simply because the dealings of the international money markets meant that he would forfeit a few measly cents to his own precious pound.

Nevertheless, Robert was an excellent financial director. Having joined Glendurnich from a small firm of accountants in Edinburgh twenty years previously, he had handled the company's accounts with shrewdness and meticulous care ever since. Even so, he was a stickler for punctuality and time-keeping, never erring from his regular hours and always being the first away from the office exactly on the dot of five-thirty in the afternoon—which meant, in the summer at any rate, he would be heading straight for the golf course.

Yet for some time now, George had had a suspicion that Robert's interest in the company had been waning and he put it down to the fact that Robert may have had his nose put out of joint by Duncan Caple's own considerable financial expertise. Nevertheless, he felt it worthwhile to make a note on his jotter to remind himself to ask Robert at the end of their meeting about Duncan's concern over Glendurnich's United States sales figures.

"Well, Robert, what did you want to see me for?" he asked, putting his pen down and starting to glance through some of the morning's letters that Mhairi had marked for his attention.

Robert sat back in his chair and coughed once into his clenched hand to clear his throat. "Well, George, it's just that I think the time is right for me to take early retirement."

"What?" George looked straight up at him, a surprised look on his face. "For what reason?"

Robert crossed his legs and flicked away some specks of dust from his trousers with the back of his hand. "Because," he began slowly, "I think that I'm getting a little bit old for the job. I am very aware that the board of directors is now considerably younger than myself, and I am also beginning to find the whisky industry of today far too cutthroat."

George kept looking at him, waiting for him to continue. "Anything else?"

"Well, er, actually yes." He hesitated for a moment. "You see, I've been offered the job of club secretary at Drumshiel Golf Club, and I feel that it's such a wonderful opportunity that I just don't want to turn it down."

George sat back in his chair and swung it round to look out the window. For a moment he said nothing. "When are you thinking of leaving?" he eventually asked, his voice sounding thin.

"In a month's time," Robert replied jauntily, relieved that he had managed to break the news without receiving instant rebuke or mutterings about repercussions to the company. "That should give me enough time to get last year's accounts finalized. The new incumbent will then be able to start afresh without having to sort out any of my idiosyncrasies."

George continued to gaze distantly out the window, then, closing his eyes, he began to shake his head almost imperceptibly from side to side as a feeling of anger began to rumble away within his mind. Thanks, Robert, he thought to himself, this is exactly what I need right now! Not only do I have Duncan breathing down the back of my neck with regards to David's future with the company, but I also have David to deal with. He's not in any fit state to handle himself at present, let alone this American trip, and now you come traipsing into my office and tell me that we have to find a new financial director.

So you think it's time you bloody retired, do you? Well, *bully for you,* because I'm meant to have been retired for the past ten years, but here I am back again having to sort out everybody's damned problems.

Robert watched him closely as he turned back from the window, noticing that the usual ruddiness had drained from George's face, suddenly making him look extremely old. Concerned, he leaned forward in his chair and was about to ask the old man if he was feeling quite well when George took a deep breath and slapped the arms of his chair purposefully.

"Well, I suppose we'd better start looking for a replacement for you, Robert," he said in one expulsion of air. "You'll be a hard act to follow, you know."

"Thanks for saying so, George," Robert said, sitting back again, "but I really don't think it will be that difficult. I believe Duncan has already got his eye on the present financial director of the malting company in Elgin."

"Has he, by heck!" George barked out. "How long has he known of your plans?"

"I told him last week," Robert answered meekly, somewhat taken aback by the vehemence of George's retort. "He was very sad that I had decided to go, but felt that it was a good move for me."

Resting his elbows on the arms of the chair, George linked his hands together and chewed pensively at the side of his mouth. "What's his constitutional remit?" he asked abruptly.

"What do you mean, George?"

George glowered at Robert across the desk and repeated the question. "Is Duncan allowed to hire and fire employees of Glendurnich Distilleries Limited without consultation with the board?"

Robert nodded slowly. "Yes, I believe that that was one of the conditions to which we agreed when he joined the company."

George rested his elbows on the desk and began rubbing at his forehead with his fingers, suddenly realizing that not only could Duncan appoint whom he liked as financial director, but also that if this remit was taken to its extremes, it could have implications on his son's own future on the board of directors.

"God, why the hell did we agree to that?"

"I think," Robert replied timidly, aware that George was becoming quite irascible, "that we were all very keen to get Duncan as managing director."

George sat back in his chair. "Yes, I suppose so." He paused for a moment, looking back out of the window. "Robert, he didn't . . . erm . . . Duncan didn't ask you to leave, did he?"

Robert shook his head briskly. "Oh, no! Nothing like that. It really was all my idea. Heavens, no! I don't think even Duncan would have the nerve to do that!"

George smiled across at him. "I'm sure not, Robert. I'm sorry I had to ask you that, but I just wanted to make sure that things weren't going on behind my back."

Robert stood up, taking George's climbdown as an opportune point at which to end their meeting, and replaced his chair against the wall of the office. "No, not at all, George. Duncan can be a little, well, self-centred sometimes, but he's a good business man, and looking at the first draft of last year's accounts, I would say he's doing well for the company."

George looked across at him and nodded. "I'm sure, Robert . . . and thanks, I value your opinion."

"I'm happy, as always, to give it, George, and now if you'll excuse me, I must get on with those accounts." He grinned nervously at George. "Now that time is of the essence, so to speak."

"Of course, and Robert, thank you for all you have done for the company over the years. You've been a real stalwart."

With a fleeting smile, Robert turned briskly on his heel and left the room. For a moment, George stared at the closed door, then pressed the intercom button for his secretary.

Ten seconds later there were two small knocks on the door. Without waiting for a bidding, Mhairi entered the room, carrying a notepad and pen in her hand. The young secretary came over to

George's desk and stood in front of him. He looked up at her and smiled.

"Right, Mhairi. I wonder if you could confirm with Devonshire Place that both Lady Inchelvie and I will be staying on Tuesday night?"

Mhairi began to scribble on her notepad. "I take it that Lady Inchelvie won't be going to the conference?"

George shook his head. "No, no, she won't. She's really just taking the opportunity of the lift so that she can go on to Perth to visit the grandchildren at their school."

"Very good," Mhairi said, making a final full stop on her notepad. "Is that it, my lord?"

"Not quite. Could you telephone British Airways and book a return flight from Glasgow to New York for Tuesday morning?"

"This coming Tuesday morning, my lord?"

"That's right." He paused for a moment. "And I think you should make the ticket open-ended, Mhairi."

She waited, her pencil poised above the notepad. When George didn't continue, she asked, "And whose name should be on the ticket?"

George lifted his hand in apology. "Ah yes, sorry about that. It's for Mr. David."

Mhairi nodded and scribbled on the notepad.

"That's it, Mhairi. I'd be grateful if you could confirm all that."

"Certainly, my lord." She turned and walked briskly to the door. As she left the room, George swung his chair round to face the window and, picking up his pen, he began to turn it top to base, over and over, each time bringing it down harder on the surface of his desk. After a moment, he took the top off the pen and, with two heavy strokes, scored out his memorandum for Robert. He threw the pen on the desk and sat back in his chair, an exhausted expression on his face.

"I hope you're not up to anything, Duncan my boy," he murmured under his breath, "I just hope you're not up to anything."

Pushing open the door of the still-house, David was immediately met with the hot, heady smell of whisky distillation in progress. He climbed the four well-worn stone steps and walked out onto the steel-meshed floor that ran the full length of the high building, fifteen feet above the base of the still-pans. The still-house hissed like a pressure cooker, drowning out the clanging resonance of his footsteps on the grid flooring as he walked to the far end of the room past the four huge highly polished copper stills. He climbed the metal staircase and made his way along the narrow gantry that ran level with the highest point of the stills. Half-way along, he stopped outside a door newly painted in bright green and stencilled in white with the word CANTEEN. He hesitated a moment before pushing it open and entering.

Despite the overpowering smell of cigarette smoke, the workers' new canteen was bright and airy, having been converted from an old sky-lighted sack-loft when the old canteen was swallowed up in the refurbishment works. At one end, a loading door had been knocked out and replaced with a full-length window, so that from where he stood, David could see all the way down to the river below. At the other end, a modern Formica unit housed a stainless-steel sink, a refrigerator, and a microwave oven, while a brand-new Cona coffee-maker sat, still boxed, on the worktop, a marked indication that the work-force preferred their own vacuum flasks of hot sweet tea. The whole place might have resembled a smart well-appointed kitchen had it not been for the fact that the men, in illogical but pointed rebellion against their eviction from the old canteen, had voted to bring their furniture with them. The centre of the room, therefore, was strewn with an ill assortment of rickety, broken-backed chairs, gathered haphazardly around a long wooden table, its surface stained with mug rings and the dark brown, pitted lesions of cigarette burns. Above this was hung the wall's only adornment—a large calendar still turned to the month of March, which showed a blonde, well-developed young girl pretending to undo the wheel-nut of a lorry without the protection of a single stitch of clothing.

Around the table sat three men, all dressed in T-shirts and coveralls, drinking steaming mugs of tea and reading tabloid newspapers that were spread out in front of them. They looked across to where David stood and rose slowly to their feet, mumbling indiscernible greetings in his direction while casting embarrassed and uneasy glances both at each other and at the clock above the sink.

"Don't get up, please!" David said, also feeling embarrassed at their reaction to his entry. He looked across at one of the men. "How are you, Dougie?"

Pulling a fully laden ashtray towards him on the table, Dougie Masson stubbed out the butt of a self-rolled cigarette and walked over to David, wiping his hands on the back of his dungarees. He was as wide as he was tall, a little terrier of a man in his early fifties who had the sides of his head shaved down to a grey stubble to lessen the contrast with its polished dome. For twenty-five years, he had served in the army, at first with the Seaforths and then finishing off a proud and unblemished career as a colour sergeant in Queen's Own Highlanders in the same platoon as David. During that time, David, as a young and very green second lieutenant, had come to trust and rely on the experienced and much-respected little man, so much so that when they eventually demobbed together, he had felt strangely honoured when Dougie asked him if he might be able to pull a few strings with his father to get him a job in the distillery. Within a month, he was taken on as a trainee still-house operator, and since then their relationship had developed, not into a close friendship, but into an alliance built both on mutual respect and their ability to talk straight with each other.

Dougie grasped David's hand in a vice-like grip. "Good tae see ye back, Mr. David," he said in a voice that was as deep and as gruff as a gravel-pit. "Are you keeping yourself well?"

"Yup, I think so."

"Glad tae hear it." Dougie stood back and scratched at the taut thick muscle of his tattooed forearm. "The lads, well, we were all very sorry tae hear about your wife. That was a real bugger, sir."

David folded his arms and looked down at the ground, pushing a cigarette end under the table with his foot. "Yuh, I'm afraid it was."

Dougie glanced at him, then back to his workmates, who had

meantime gone back to reading their newspapers. He walked up close to David, gave him a brief wink, and nodded his head sideways in the direction of the door. "I'm just awa' back tae work, sir."

Understanding his message, David turned to follow him out, but not before raising his hand in silent farewell to the other two men. They looked up momentarily, reciprocating the gesture with a brief flick of their heads before returning to their reading.

"How're things with you, then?" David asked, leaning his elbows on the gantry barrier next to Dougie, as he looked down with a frown of concentration onto the still-house floor.

"Och, no' bad. Could be worse. We've been havin' a real bugger of a problem with that number three still over there." He pointed a stubby finger down to where an oxyacetylene welder stood amongst a cluster of tools. "Only just managed to get it sorted. That's why we're all a bit late in taking our tea-break."

"What was up with it?" David asked, looking down on the still.

"Och, it developed a leak in the steam kettle yesterday afternoon." He chuckled. "Bloody good thing that Jimmy has a big nose. It was him who picked it up in the condensate going to the boiler. Anyway, we had to empty the still overnight so we could isolate the steam valve, and we've just finished spot-welding the leak about an hour ago. We should be able to get the thing refilled this afternoon."

"Ah. Well done."

Dougie turned and grinned at David, knowing full well that a technical engineering fault in the distillery was not something of which he had great knowledge. However, when he noticed that David's eyes were focused blankly onto the still-house floor, the smile vanished from his face and he began slowly shaking his head.

"Och, Davie lad, ye're a wee bit distracted at the minute, aren't ye?"

David looked at him and nodded. "Yup, you could say that," he said with a long, heavy sigh. He turned round and leaned his back against the rail.

"So," Dougie asked quietly, "what have you been doing with yourself since, well, then?"

"Gardening, mostly."

Dougie rubbed abrasively at the side of his head. "Aye, well, it's good tae keep yourself occupied somehow." He turned to take up the same position as David. "So what brings you in here today?"

David reached out and took hold of the handle of a brush that stood against the wall opposite. He put his foot heavily on its head so that the bristles splayed out on the floor. "Well, I've got to go out to New York to do some business—and—as you can imagine, it's the last thing I bloody well feel like doing!"

Dougie crossed his arms and looked glumly down at his boots. "Aye, I can understand that." He let out a long sigh and began picking at a callus on his finger. "Will ye be seeing Lieutenant Eggar when you're out there?"

David stopped fiddling with the broom handle and looked quizzically at Dougie. "What do you mean?

"Lieutenant Eggar? Was he no' a friend of yours?"

"Of course he was. But why do you think that I would be seeing him?"

"Well, he's in New York—or somewhere's about. I've just read a wee bit about him in this month's regimental news. Hang on a minute"—Dougie pushed himself off the rail—"I've got it in my locker." He went back into the canteen, re-emerging a few seconds later with a copy of the magazine in his hand. "It came yesterday in the post. I just stuck it in my piece-bag last night to have a look at over the tea-break." He licked at a dirt-engrained thumb and began to leaf clumsily through the glossy pages. "Now where the hell—aye, here it is!"

He bent the magazine in half at the penultimate page and handed it to David. It was a small paragraph at the bottom under the column "Other News."

> Richard Eggar (2nd Lieut. QOH. 1973–1976) recently organized a reunion of Queen's Own Highlanders who, like himself, have put down roots in the United States of America. Now a vice-president of Dammell's Bank in New York, Lieu-

tenant Eggar said that he was well pleased with the attendance figure of fourteen, especially as three of the attendees had made the effort to fly over from the West Coast specifically for the occasion. Lieutenant Eggar, who is married and lives on Long Island, said that he would be delighted to meet with any QOH who might be visiting New York in the future. He can be contacted on 001 516 357 4298.

David raised his eyebrows and turned back to Dougie. "Do you mind if I borrow this?"

"That's nae bother. Just get it back tae me sometime."

"You'll have it by lunch-time," David said, placing the broom back against the wall and rolling the magazine into a scroll in his hand. "I just want to get that telephone number." He glanced at his watch. "Hell, it's five to ten. I'd better go. I have a meeting in five minutes."

As they began walking along the gantry together, Dougie turned to him with a kindly grin on his face. "Well, I hope I've brightened up your day a wee bitty."

"Yeah, you have, actually. Listen, sorry if I'm seeming a bit distant at the minute."

Dougie slapped him on the back. "Och, dinnae worry yourself about it. I think we know each other well enough. Just look after yourself, laddie, and dinnae do anything that I wouldn't do."

David let out a short laugh. "That's leaving me a wide margin." He descended the stairs, holding up the magazine. "I'll make sure this gets back to you."

"Aye, well, I'll be here or hereabouts."

The grandfather clock in the reception area had just whirred laboriously to a close after striking the hour of ten when David entered the building at speed and hurried across to the boardroom. Margaret, who was talking loudly on the telephone, swung round with a thunderous look on her face, but on seeing David the frown turned into a wide lipsticked grin and she simply waved heartily at him without interrupting her conversation.

His father was alone, sitting in his high-backed chair at the far end of the table and stooping down to suck the first mouthful from an overfull cup of coffee. He looked up when David walked in.

"I don't know how the hell she does it!" he said, his voice bordering on grumpiness.

David laughed. "Who's she and what does she do?" He walked up the room towards his father, pulled out the chair next to him and threw Dougie's magazine onto the table.

"Margaret! You ask her for a cup of coffee, and she comes in at the speed of light, dumps it down in front of you without one spilt drop, and look at it!" He gesticulated towards his steaming cup. "The wretched thing has a meniscus on it, it's so bloody full!"

He bent forward and slurped at his cup, then, pulling a large paisley-patterned handkerchief from his top pocket, he leaned back in his chair and wiped his mouth. "Did you go out to the distillery?"

"Yes, I ran into Dougie Masson."

"Ah, right. I haven't seen him for a bit. How is he?"

"Seems to be fine," David said, reaching forward to pick up the magazine. "He showed me this bit about an army friend of mine." He flicked through the pages to the article. "Seems he's working in New York and living out somewhere on Long Island." He pushed the magazine towards his father. "Thought I might give him a call to see if he has a spare bed for a couple of nights. Better than sitting in some hotel by myself."

George raised his eyebrows as he reached forward to pick up the magazine, not so much in interest at the article but more in pleasure at his son's seeming willingness to try to make the best of the New York trip. He gave the magazine a cursory glance before sliding it back up the table. "That's a terrific idea. Give him a call once we've finished . . ."

As he spoke, the door of the boardroom was thrown open and Duncan Caple appeared, bearing an armful of files and walking backwards as he continued to speak to someone outside the room.

"All right. Well, tell him I'll return his call in about half an hour."

He turned and back-heeled the door closed. "Sorry I'm a bit late. Got held up." He walked towards them, plunked down the files with a thud on the table and pulled out the chair opposite David. "Would it be all right if we kept this meeting quite brief? I'm expecting rather an important call from Japan at any minute." He looked across at David. "David, sorry, how *are* you?" he asked, a condescending tinge to his voice. "Apologies for having to call you in for this trip, but there really was no alternative. Anyway, as I said to your father, it'll probably do you the world of good to get away for a bit."

George began chewing quickly at the side of his mouth, furious at the crassness of Duncan's last remark. He caught the eye of the young managing director and fixed him with a steely glare.

"I think we'll just get the briefing over and done with as soon as possible, Duncan. David still has quite a bit to sort out at home."

The rebuke went straight over the top of Duncan's head. He glanced at David. "What? Are you going straight back after this? I thought you might be able to make a few telephone calls for me, seeing that you're back into the—"

"No, Duncan," George interjected pointedly, "David is going straight back after this!"

Duncan was silent for a moment. He was beginning to get fed up with having to carry the work-load of both David and himself, and fed up with the way that the Corstorphine family always seemed to close ranks on him whenever he was trying to achieve something for the company. He shook his head, taking on an air of truculent resignation.

"Oh, well, if that's what you've agreed between yourselves, then we'd better crack on with the briefing."

He picked up one of the files, flicked off the elastic holder, and opened it in front of him.

"I won't go into huge detail on this, David, as I'm sure your father has filled you in on the reason why I feel it necessary to appoint a new distributor in the States. Anyway, it suffices to say that it is essential that we improve or at least maintain our sales in the U.S. This simply has not been happening with Lacey's. Now, I managed to get hold of profiles on four different distribution companies, and from those have selected one which will go before the board on Tuesday."

George leaned forward in his chair. "I won't be here on Tuesday, Duncan. I'm traveling down to Glasgow for the Whisky Association conference."

The managing director sat back, resting his elbows on the arms of the chair with the palms of his hands held upwards at either side of him.

"It really is only a formality, George, as we discussed here yesterday. It has to be done." He turned towards David. "So, I've arranged your meeting with the new distributor for the Wednesday at ten A.M."

The lack of response from David made George glance along the table to his son, immediately noticing that, after his brief spark of excitement over the article in the magazine, he had returned to his own introverted normality, gazing as if mesmerized at the palm of his hand and rubbing it slowly back and forth with the opposite thumb.

This was too much for Duncan. Come on, man, he thought to himself, so okay, you're mourning your wife, but it doesn't mean that you have to show such a blatant disinterest in what's going on.

"Excuse me, David," he said sharply, "you may not think it, but actually what I'm saying is quite important."

David snapped his head up to look at him, fury suddenly flashing in his eyes. George saw it immediately and held up his hands.

"Okay, let's calm this all down, shall we? Duncan, you have the briefing document there. Just give it to David. That's all he really needs."

Duncan let out a resigned sigh. "Very well." He slid the document across to David. "The name of the company is Deakin Distribution. It's relatively new, but has had excellent results in promoting the sales of a couple of English gin companies over the past two years. They're based on Madison Avenue, I'm not sure where, but the address is in the file." He slapped his hands on the table and, pushing back his chair, got to his feet. "Well, I don't suppose there's much more to be said." He turned to George. "What about flights?"

"That's in hand. Mhairi's fixing it."

"Good." He picked up his remaining files and began to walk towards the door. As he passed behind David, he stopped. "Ah, just one more thing. I thought yesterday that it might have been an idea for you to pay a visit to Lacey's, just so that we finish with them in good grace. However, in retrospect I believe you should just leave it. I'll handle it from this end."

He went forward and put a reassuring hand on David's shoulder, but removed it immediately when he felt him flinch at the contact. For a moment, his hand remained hovering in mid-air, then, with a brief nod in George's direction, he turned on his heel and left the room.

A heavy silence enveloped the boardroom until George finally pushed back his chair, picked up his stick and began levering himself upwards. "He may be a good business man, but by God he can be an insufferable little devil sometimes."

David jumped up and helped his father to his feet. "Christ, I thought I was only a hair's breadth from thumping him."

George chuckled. "Yes, I realized that." He winced with pain as he took his first step forward, then began to shuffle his way towards the door. "Listen, old boy. I've booked you on a flight from Glasgow on Tuesday morning, and I've actually told Mhairi to make the trip open-ended. It's just that I thought that it might be, well, remedial or even beneficial for you if you stayed over there for a bit. Do some travelling or something. I mean, I shall leave it entirely up to you."

David shook his head. "No, I don't think so. I reckon I'll come straight back. The children will want to see me—and anyway, I'll have to be thinking about coming back to work quite soon. I can't have you filling in for me for ever." He smiled at his father. "About time you continued your retirement."

"Oh, goodness' sakes, don't worry about me! I'm perfectly all right! In fact, I'm actually rather enjoying myself!"

David laughed. "Yeah, I can see that." He paused. "Look, it's a really kind thought—and I might consider it just for a short while, but I'll need to speak to the children first. I'm going down to see them on Saturday at any rate, just to explain what's happening."

"Damned good idea." George stopped and walked back to the table and reached over for the telephone. "Now before you head off, just let me make sure I can get a lift home." He dialled a number and waited for a second. "Ah, Margaret, would you be kind enough to get that young man Archie McLachlan to come into the boardroom? No, he's in distribution at the minute . . . yes, that's him . . . thanks, Margaret."

He replaced the receiver and looked up at David. "Listen, I wouldn't worry too much about Duncan. He was making a meal of it, just because that's the way his mind works. You just handle this trip in your own way and at your own pace. I'll make sure you get all the backing you need from this end without your having to have any contact with him. All right?"

David nodded. "Yeah, probably the best idea under the circumstances."

There was a quiet knock on the door.

"Come in, Archie."

Archie McLachlan slowly opened the door and put his head round the corner, his eyes wide with uncertainty. "Did you want to see me, my lord?"

"Yes, Archie, come on in. You know Mr. David, don't you?"

Archie came forward and shook David by the hand. "Hullo, sir, nice to see you again."

"Archie," George continued, "Mr. David is heading back to Inchelvie right now, which leaves me without a car. Would it be going very much out of your way if you were to give me a lift back there this afternoon?"

"Not at all, my lord," Archie said, his voice lifting with the thought of this important assignment. He paused for a moment. "The only thing is I'm afraid that I've only got an old Ford Fiesta."

George let out a single loud laugh. "I don't mind what we go in, Archie, as long as it has four wheels and it moves."

Relief spread across the boy's face. "Oh, well, in that case, certainly, my lord." He began to edge his way back to the door. "If you would just like to let me know when you're thinking of going, and I'll get the car up to the reception door."

George held up his hand. "Now, don't go quite yet. I have something else I want you to do."

Archie stopped in his tracks and looked intently at Lord Inchelvie.

"Mr. David is going to the States next Tuesday, Archie, to appoint a new distributor, and I'm going to be in Glasgow on that day and the following one, while Mr. Caple will be in London and Europe from about Wednesday onwards."

"Right, my lord," Archie said, his brow creased in concentration at what his chairman was saying.

"I want you to be Mr. David's contact here for the time that he is away. If there is anything he wants, you deal with it yourself. You don't have to clear anything with anyone else in the company; is that understood?"

"Yes, my lord."

"Good. And Archie, check with Margaret each morning for any faxes that might come through from Mr. David. I shall tell her that they are for your eyes only. Everything must be carried out in the strictest confidence. All right?"

"Of course, my lord," he said.

"Very good. You head off now, and I'll get Margaret to give you a call when I'm ready to leave."

Archie nodded, and smiling briefly to David, he walked to the door and left the room.

David looked at his father. "You sounded like 'M' just then, giving James Bond his orders. What's up?"

George frowned. "I'm not sure. It's just that I have this sneaking suspicion that things aren't what they seem." He shook his head and smiled. "Maybe age is making me a trifle paranoid—I don't know."

He glanced at his watch. "Look, you head off now. That'll give you time to get back out in the garden with Jock this afternoon."

David shook his head and flicked through Duncan's brief in his hand. "No, I think that I'd better start reading up on this. I've got to start sometime."

"Yes," George replied, putting his hand on his son's shoulder. "I'm afraid that you do."

CHAPTER 8

As he turned the car in through the gates at Inchelvie, David saw Jock head towards him on the lawn tractor, carefully manoeuvring his way around the trees as he cut the grass verges of the drive. Feeling a sudden deep pang of envy for the old man and for the hard, yet undemanding simplicity of his job, his immediate impulse was to stop the car and tell him that they would continue immediately with the work on the flower-bed. But he checked himself and simply raised a hand in greeting as he drove past. No, he thought, you really do have to start sometime.

Parking the car at the front door, he ran up the stone steps and entered, then made his way across the hall to the drawing-room. Sitting down at his father's desk, he opened the document and found, stuck to the first page, the yellow Post-it on which he had written Richard Eggar's telephone number. He glanced at his watch. It was half past twelve. That would make it half past seven in the morning in New York. Maybe he could catch Richard before he left for work.

He picked up the receiver of the fax/telephone on the desk and dialled the number. The line cracked and whistled as it connected, followed within seconds by the single long ringing tone of the American telephone system. It rang four times before someone answered.

"Hu-llo?"

It was a man's voice, his vocal cords breaking as he spoke, so that the two syllables of the word ranged from base to falsetto, respectively, making David think immediately that whoever had answered the telephone was either suffering from a bad cold or had just woken up.

"Hullo, is that Richard?" As he spoke, he heard the man cough and clear his throat.

"Yeah, this is he." The voice was English, but tinged with an American slant.

"Richard, this is David Corstorphine. I was in Queen's Own—"

"David!" The voice, in its drowsiness, lifted a tone. "Hang on!" David heard a rustle of movement at the other end of the line. "Bloody hell, David Corstorphine! Where are you calling from?"

"Scotland."

"Scotland? Well, would you believe it? David! How the hell did you get my number?"

"It was in this month's regimental news. Something about you organizing some sort of get-together?"

"Oh, right." David heard a stifled yawn at the other end of the line.

"Sorry, Richard, have I woken you up?"

"No, not really . . . well, actually you have, but I should be up anyway. Just me being lazy. We were out at Montauk last night, and didn't get back till three o'clock this morning. Anyway, what am I talking about? This is crazy. I'm being phoned up at seven-thirty in the morning by a man I haven't seen in years. Could you give me a minute, David? I'm going to put you onto the cordless, so that I can get out of the bedroom."

The line went dead for a moment, and David sat twiddling the telephone cable around his finger.

"Hi, are you still there?" Richard asked, his voice sounding through the interference of the cordless phone.

"Yes, I'm still here."

"I'm in the kitchen now. Just bear with me while I put on the kettle. I'm dying for a cup of coffee." The interference swished as he moved around. "Right, that's it. So, David, how are you? It's great to hear you from you. What's the reason for the call?"

"Well, I was just wondering if—"

"No, hang on, let's get first things first. Tell me, how is the wonderful Rachel?"

David felt his mouth go dry. He tried to speak but nothing came out. For some reason, he had been totally unprepared for the question. All he had expected to do was to ask Richard if he could stay with him.

"Hullo, David, are you still there?"

"Erm . . . yes . . . sorry, Richard, sorry . . . I'm still here. Could you just hold the line a minute?"

Without waiting for a reply, he put his hand over the receiver and sat with his eyes tightly closed, a look of pained concentration on his face. Dammit, it had completely slipped his mind that Richard knew Rachel. Then of course he would have, because they'd been married for a year before he left the army. Now, thinking back on it, Richard had been with them on that mad skiing trip to Verbier. He could always press the "disconnect" button and call back later. No, what the hell good would that do?

"Hullo, Richard, sorry about that. Someone . . . er . . . just came into the room."

"Hey, that's all right. So, how is she?"

"Rachel . . ." David cleared his throat. ". . . died last month, Richard."

He heard nothing for a second except the continued crackle on the line, followed by the sound of a coffee-cup being knocked over on the sideboard or dropped to the ground. When Richard spoke again, his voice sounded distant and weak.

"Shit, David . . . shit . . . what . . . I mean, what happened?"

"Cancer."

"Oh my God . . . I'm so sorry. Did she . . . I mean . . . how long ago was this?"

"It was only diagnosed in October, and then by December, well . . ."

"Christ . . . what a *bastard* of a thing! Poor Rachel."

"Yeah."

"How are *you,* my friend?"

"Not . . . brilliant."

"Christ . . . I don't really know what to say . . . I mean, how are you . . . sort of . . . coping?"

"Not . . . particularly well. I'm staying with my parents at the minute."

"Right . . . and you've got children, haven't you?"

"Yup. Three. They've only just gone back to school."

"Jesus, I'm so sorry, David, for you all. I mean . . . shit! I'm so glad you telephoned to tell me."

David took a deep breath and cleared his throat again, realizing that Richard had given him the briefest opportunity to get away from the subject. "Look, Richard, that's not actually why I'm calling. It's just that, well, I have to come over to New York on business for a couple of days, and I was wondering if—"

Richard cut in. "Great! Can you come and stay?"

"Would that be all right?"

"Of course it would be. The only thing is that Angie is going back to Boston for a couple of weeks to visit her parents—but that's no problem, we'll just have to cope for ourselves. When are you coming over?"

"On Tuesday. I haven't got the tickets yet, but it'll be the morning flight from Glasgow, which gets into Kennedy at about twelve-thirty P.M., if my memory serves me correctly."

"And what are your plans for that day? Do you have a meeting?"

"No, it's not until the Wednesday at ten."

"Right, and have you any idea where the meeting is?"

"Somewhere on Madison Avenue."

"Okay, just hang on a minute while I get my diary. It's through in the sitting-room." David heard him move off through the house and then a frenetic rustle of papers before he spoke again. "Right, tell you what I'll do. I have an account with Star Limos here in Leesport, so I'll get a car over to Kennedy to pick you up. It's just over an hour's journey out here, so you can get the whole of Tuesday afternoon and the night to unwind, and then I'll take you in myself on Wednesday morning. My office is on Madison as well, and I'll bet you're only three or four blocks away from where I'm going to be anyway."

"Are you sure? I don't want to be a nuisance—"

"No way, José! Don't be stupid! I'm actually working summer-time hours at the minute, so I'm usually out here Friday through to Monday and then head off to the city for the remainder of the week. But while you're here, I'll just come back every night. That's no problem at all! Anyway, I've a mountain of paperwork to catch up on and the office can always E-mail me stuff if need be."

"Well, if you're sure, Richard, that really would be great. I can't tell you what a weight that is off my mind. It'll make my trip a great deal easier."

"It's a pleasure. Look, see you on Tuesday, okay? And, David . . . well, just *shit,* I'm so, so sorry about Rachel."

"I know. It's just one of those things."

"No, it's not. I know for you it's probably everything. Look, if you want to talk about it when you get out, I have really good ears. Anyway, enough said at the minute. Have a good flight, my friend, and look after yourself."

David dropped the receiver onto its base and sat rubbing his hands up and down his trouser legs, realizing they were trembling from the sheer effort of talking about Rachel. Taking a deep breath, he picked up the document, then immediately threw it back on the desk without opening it.

"Oh, bugger that!" He jumped to his feet and made his way out into the hall and upstairs to put on his work clothes.

CHAPTER 9

"This is meant to be the summer term!" Sophie said, pulling her blazer around her and tucking her hands under her armpits. "Summer terms are meant to be warm!"

The clonking contact of cricket ball against bat floated out on the chill breeze from the centre of the pitch, and a light ripple of applause sounded from the brave but sparse audience that encircled the game. The boys, who were fielding out on the ground, pulled their sweater sleeves down over their hands and jumped up and down to keep warm.

"Is it like this up at Inchelvie?"

Resting up on one elbow, David plucked absently at the daisies that carpeted the grass at the edge of the boundary. "No, it's been worse, actually. Last Thursday was about the first time that the sun broke through—but there wasn't much heat in it."

"I wish there was a switch we could turn on for summer," Harriet said, rocking herself back and forth as she perched on her father's hip-bone, "and then everything would become, well, summery just like that."

"Ow, Harry, don't do that! It's quite sore!"

Harriet let out a giggle and stopped momentarily, then, fixing him with a grin of wicked intent, began rocking again in short spasmodic bursts, testing out her father's resilience.

"Right, you little devil!" he exclaimed, swinging his arm round and pushing her down onto the grass. "War is declared!" He tickled her fiercely, making her shriek out in hysterical laughter.

"Dad, stop it!" Sophie said in an embarrassed whisper. "Mr. Hunter is watching us from the cricket pitch!"

David sat up, pulling a face at Sophie's reprimand, but continued to keep his younger daughter at bay by darting his hand back at her every time she tried to make a move.

"I don't think we need to watch the *whole* match, do we?" Sophie asked, pulling her knees up under her chin.

"Probably not." He looked over at the score-board. "That's the last batsman in for their team anyway, so they'll all be coming off quite soon. I think we should keep watching just in case Charlie *does* get the chance to bowl."

Sophie sighed. "It's just such a boring game, cricket."

She reached her hands behind her neck and pulled the elastic scrunchie on her mousy-brown pony-tail tight against the back of her head. David looked across at her and clandestinely studied her face. Tiny smile lines, creasing the olive skin at the sides of her mouth and eyes, were now the only indication that the hardened, unemotional glare which she had adopted since her mother's death was alien to her character. She wore it like a mask, as if in some way smiling or laughing might be construed as being disloyal to her mother's memory. On her upper lip there blossomed two small but angry spots, blemishes that in the past would have caused her as much anxiety as a smallpox outbreak, but which now were left untreated and uncared for. It was like looking at an incomprehensible abstract painting—textures of unhappiness, longing and dogged bravery all mixed together on a canvas of incipient beauty.

"That's exactly what Mummy thought," David said eventually. "She had absolutely no time for the game either."

Harriet sat up from her supine position at the mention of her mother and leaned across her father's body.

"What games *did* she like, then?"

David thought for a moment. "Well, you *know* she liked tennis—and—she was quite good at fishing. What else?"

"I know!" Harriet said, jumping across his legs and coming to sit between them both. "She liked cooking!"

Sophie sucked her teeth. "That's not a game, Harry!"

"It could be, though, couldn't it, Daddy?" She turned her face up to David, pressing her curly mop of jet-black hair against his arm, a pleading look in her eyes, willing his support in her argument.

"Well, I suppose you could fry eggs against the clock."

Sophie flicked up her head in disdain. "You would say that, Dad, just to agree with teeny-weeny."

Harriet kicked her foot against her sister's leg. "*Don't* call me teeny-weeny, Sophie!"

"All right, you two," David said, catching Harriet's foot as it flashed out for another strike.

Sophie turned, resting her cheek on her knee, and smiled lightly at her sister. "Teeny-weeny," she teased in a high-pitched voice.

"Sophie!" David laughed, "that's enough. Leave your extremely grown-up younger sister alone." He glanced across to the cricket game and saw with relief that at last Charlie was about to start bowling. "Come on, there's Charlie on now! Let's watch him."

Out on the distant pitch, Charlie sped into the wicket as fast as his spindly young legs would carry him, and with a somewhat over-complicated bowling action sent a looping ball towards the batsman. It was given a solid, yet sadly deserving blow, and as the young fieldsman chased off after it towards the boundary, Charlie stood watching him, hands on hips and disappointedly kicking the toe of his shoe into the ground. Taking this all as a sign for immediate congratulations, Harriet began clapping heartily and David grabbed her hands before her badly timed applause could be heard by her brother.

She tilted back her head and looked up at David. "Wasn't that any good?"

"No, not really."

Sophie let out a long sigh. "If he keeps bowling like that, we'll be here all day!"

Charlie's next ball was identical to the first, only this time the batsman, lulled into a false sense of security by the snail-like pace of Charlie's bowling, bounded down the wicket to take another fearsome blow at the ball—and missed. The diminutive wicket-keeper fumbled the ball into his oversized gloves and knocked off the bails, and an immediate unison cry of "Howzat" rang out from the pitch. The umpire raised his finger to signify the batsman's dismissal and the fielding side descended both upon Charlie and the wicket-keeper in a frenzy of excitement.

"Thank goodness for that," Sophie said, clambering to her feet. "Let's go into the school now."

"Hang on a minute!" David laughed, getting up and dusting off the damp grass clippings from the seat of his trousers. "Wait for Charlie. He's coming over."

They stood watching as Charlie ran towards them, his sweater thrown over his shoulder and his loose shirt-tail flying out behind him. He arrived in front of them, a grin spread across his freckled face, and blew upwards at the long string of auburn hair that fell in front of his eyes.

"Did you see that, Dad?" he asked excitedly.

"I certainly did."

"Not bad for second ball!"

David walked over to him and tousled his hair. "Not bad at all!"

"Can we go in now?" Sophie asked, running rapidly on the spot.

Charlie took no notice of his elder sister. "Dad, I'm not batting until number ten and they're going to have tea first, so Mr. Hunter said that we could go off for a bit."

"Where would you want to go?"

"McDonald's in Perth! Please, Dad! I'm famished."

The idea was greeted with an immediate shout of approval from Harriet. David looked across at Sophie.

"Is that all right by you?"

She shrugged noncommittally. "I don't really mind, as long as we go somewhere warm."

A quarter of an hour later, following a speedy drive around the Perth ring road, they sat in the car-park outside McDonald's with the tangy, sweet smell of fast food wafting about the fuggy interior of the Audi.

"Are you sure you don't want anything more than that?" David asked Sophie, who sat beside him picking at the smallest bag of fries that she had been able to order.

Sophie shook her head. "No, I'm not that hungry."

"Dad!" Charlie exclaimed from the back seat between slurps at his milk shake. "Harriet's just dropped a piece of gherkin on the floor."

"I don't like them," Harriet retorted quietly.

"Doesn't mean you have to throw—"

"All right!" David interjected. "It couldn't matter less." He turned in his seat and, picking up the offending object, jettisoned it out of the window. The children sat without speaking, munching loudly on their meals. David took in a deep breath.

"Listen . . . erm, I've got something to tell you. I'm going to have to go to America next week on business."

Sophie glanced round, a chip half-way to her mouth. "For how long?"

"Well, it should only be a couple of days. It depends really on how long it takes."

Charlie leaned forward between the front seats, licking ketchup off his fingers. "Does that mean you won't be coming down next weekend?"

"I don't know, Charlie. As I said, it all depends."

Charlie let out a moan of disappointment. "But we're playing Clevely Hall on Saturday."

"I know you are. But if I'm not back, I'm sure Granny will come down to watch you play."

"Granny doesn't understand cricket," Charlie whined. "She just spends her time talking to people and not watching."

"Oh, do stop moaning, Charlie!" Sophie said sharply. "It's really kind of Granny to come at all. Anyway, Dad will probably be back by next weekend." She looked round at her father, a flash of uncertainty in her eyes. "Won't you?"

David smiled reassuringly at her. "Well, it depends, but I'll certainly do my best." Stretching across, he took an over-cooked chip from Sophie's bag and, crunching on it, eyed the glum faces of Charlie and Harriet in the rear-view mirror.

"Listen," he said after a pause. "I know that we discussed this all before, but, well, now that you've been back at school for a bit, I wondered if you had any second thoughts about being away from home. It's just that I spoke with Mr. Hunter this morning and he says that he would quite understand if you did want to come back to Dalnachoil."

Sophie was shaking her head even before he had finished his last sentence. "No, I *really* don't think it would be a good idea."

"Can I ask why not?"

Sophie let out a long sigh. "Because we did discuss it, Dad, not just with you, but between ourselves as well. We all agreed that we didn't want to leave our friends, and well, since we've been back, Mr. and Mrs. Hunter have been really kind. We go up and see them every night and they, well, just talk to us."

"They don't play cricket *or* rugby at Dalnachoil," Charlie interjected quietly.

"We are really all right here, Dad," Sophie continued, "unless . . ." She stopped and looked across at her father.

"Unless what?"

"Unless you want us to come home."

David put his hand on her head and smoothed back her sleeked hair. "No, please, I really want what you want. It's just that, well, I thought it was worth asking the question again."

"*I* want to go home." The voice sounded so distant and so diminutive that everyone turned to look at Harriet. She was sitting contentedly munching on her hamburger and staring out of the window at a screaming child who had just covered the car-park with chocolate milk shake. Seeing everyone staring at her, she grinned broadly and readied herself for another bite. "Not now, though—in the holidays."

Everyone let out a groan of relief, then burst out laughing. David reached forward to turn the ignition key, but stopped when he felt the light touch of Sophie's hand on his arm.

"Dad?" A serious expression had suddenly come over her face.

"Yeah?"

"Are *you* all right?"

David paused for a moment, then smiled and slowly nodded. "Yeah, I'm all right."

"Good." She sat back in her seat. "Then we're all all right."

David looked round at the faces of each of his children in turn. "Yeah, we are, aren't we?" He fired up the engine. "Come on, let's get back to school before our master batsman misses out on his big moment!"

CHAPTER

10

Despite having left Inchelvie at six o'clock, the journey down to Glasgow Airport on Tuesday morning took one hour longer than planned, due to the endless stream of temporary traffic lights set up for roadworks between Perth and Stirling. Consequently, when David pulled the car to a halt outside the terminal, he had only time to bid a fleeting farewell to his parents before grabbing his cases from the trunk and hurrying into the building. At the check-in desk, the taut-faced girl glanced at his ticket, then told him, with acid delight spread across her over-made-up face, that the flight was due to leave in an hour and that she was only accepting late arrivals for Business Class passengers. Silently cursing the fact that he had the last seat on the plane, and that it happened to be in Economy Class, David had to use every ounce of his guile and charm to persuade the girl to allow him to proceed.

"Departure gate two then, sir," she said without a trace of a smile as she handed him back his documents, "and as fast as you can. The flight has just about finished boarding."

Returning her lack of animation with a flashing grin, David rushed through passport control and sprinted the full four hundred yards to gate 2 before thumping his way noisily down the telescopic bridge onto the plane. He was immediately the star attraction, The Man Who

Dared Arrive Late. Every seat was taken and every eye turned towards him as he walked up the aisle between the rows of disgruntled passengers.

His boarding pass did say that he was in seat number 21F, but when he arrived beside it, all three in the aisle row seemed to be already taken. A young woman in a garishly purple nylon shell suit sat in the seat nearest to him, clutching the pudgy fist of a baby girl who occupied the middle seat, while a hyperactive five-year-old boy, sporting a Celtic football strip with matching nylon track-suit bottoms, bounced energetically on the third seat, playing peekaboo with the elderly couple behind. David delved his fingers into the top pocket of his blazer for the stub of the boarding pass, finding it just as a stewardess approached him.

"Have you not found your seat yet, sir?"

"No, not yet." He handed her the stub, and she studied it for a moment before turning to the woman.

"How many seats did you reserve, madam?"

"Only twa," the woman replied in a broad Glasgow accent. "The wee yin is meant to be sittin' on my knee, but I wis hopin' this one wis free."

The stewardess smiled at her. "I'm afraid not. This seat is reserved for this gentleman."

David expected the woman to sigh heavily at this last-minute inconvenience, but instead she grinned up at him. "Och well, it wis worth a try." She unbuckled her seat-belt and, picking up her daughter, moved into the next seat. "C'mon, Tracy, you come onto my knee, darlin', and you, Darren, sit doon and dinnae be such a pest!"

Smiling a thank-you at the woman, David slumped down into his seat, buckled up, leaned back against the head-rest and let out a long sigh of relief.

That was cutting it far too fine. In fact, the past twelve hours had been cut too fine. He had really done very little to prepare himself for the trip over the previous two days, preferring to try to finish off the work in the garden with Jock and do most of his organization and packing on Monday evening. But then on Monday afternoon he had picked some daffodils from the garden at Inchelvie and had taken them to the small churchyard in Dalnachoil to put on Rachel's grave. Once there he hadn't wanted to leave, and consequently he had sat for hours, talking quietly to her until the sun eventually dipped away behind the hills.

The engines of the plane rose in volume and it edged slowly away from the terminal building. David turned his head to stare past the occupants of the window-seat as the plane taxied out onto the runway. He remained in that position until they had risen far above the river Clyde and had begun the ascent through the low cloud base. Once nothing was left in view below, he turned away, only to find himself being eyed with uncertainty by his three travelling companions. He gave them a smile, then suddenly realized that he was clutching tight to Darren's hand. "Oh, God, I'm sorry about that!" he said, letting go immediately and looking over at Darren's mother. "It's a natural reaction, I'm afraid. I always seem to grab hold of one of my children's hands during take-off."

The woman's face broke into a smile once more. "How many do *you* have?" she asked.

"Three."

"Jeez, twa's quite enough handlin' for me. You must be a glutton for punishment." She let out a throaty laugh which ended in two rasping coughs, and instantly David wondered how on earth she was going to survive the long non-smoking flight with the tantalizing sight of the pack of two hundred duty-free cigarettes protruding from the basket at her feet.

Darren, meanwhile, had not taken his eyes off David. "Mum's takin' us tae Disneyland," he said in an unanimated monotone.

"Is she?" David replied. "Well, you're a pretty lucky boy, aren't you!"

"Dae ye like Mickey Mouse?"

"Yeah, I think he's great! Is he your favorite?"

"No. I think he stinks."

"Darren!" the mother exclaimed, a look of embarrassed horror spread across her pasty features. "Dinnae be so cheeky tae the man."

"I'm no' being cheeky, Mam. You think he stinks too."

"Darren, that's ENOUGH, laddie!"

David smiled a fixed grin at the happy little trio, and as a form of diversion to return to his own company, he opened his brief-case and took out the Glendurnich document.

"Mam," Darren piped up again, "I'm needin' the bog."

His mother leaned across and whispered angrily at him. "How many times dae I have tae tell ye? It's no' called the bog, it's called the toilet."

"But, Mam, you call it the—"

"Darren!"

She undid her seat-belt and stood up, not noticing that the "Seat-Belt" sign was still on. A young stewardess came along the aisle towards her. "I'm afraid that you will have to sit down again, madam, until the captain has switched off the 'Seat-Belt' sign," she said, pointing up to the little illuminated light above the seat.

"My wee lad's desperate for the toilet. Can I no' tak' him?"

The stewardess, uncertain as to what to do, looked along the aisle for guidance from her superior, who was in the galley at the back of the plane. Hand gestures were exchanged, and she turned back to the woman.

"That's fine. I'll take you along with him, but the senior stewardess has indicated that it would be safer if you didn't carry the little one along."

The woman was beginning to get flustered, darting worried looks at the baby on her hip. "I canna leave her here by hersel'. Could you tak' Darren along for me?"

It looked as though a solution had been found until the stewardess put her hand out to Darren. He resolutely stuck both hands behind his back and began to wail loudly. "I want to go wi' you, Mam."

"Please, Darren," the woman pleaded in exasperation with her son. "Go wi' the nice lady."

David looked up at the scene, and wondered how it could possibly resolve itself. He didn't particularly want to become involved, but realized that if drastic action wasn't taken soon, young Darren would begin to flood the plane.

"Excuse me," he said, leaning across the seat towards them.

They all looked at him.

"I'm quite happy, if you want, to hold her until you come back."

The woman smiled at him. "Och, thanks, mister, but dinnae you worry yoursel'."

"I promise you, I don't mind. As I said, I've three of my own, so I'm quite an expert."

"Do ye really no' mind, mister? I'm afraid she's got an awful dose of the cauld."

"Come on, don't worry about it." He shoved his papers into the seat pocket in front of him and stretched out his hands to receive his charge.

The woman handed over the little girl. "There you go, Tracy. You stay with the nice man. Thanks, mister, you're a gem. I'll no' be a minute."

As the "toilet" party headed off up the aisle, Tracy sat on David's knee, staring at him in astonishment, her large brown eyes as round as the pacifier in her mouth, which thankfully was doing its job in preventing any outburst of protest. David gave the snuffling child a reassuring smile, then, thinking it better if she didn't have to suffer such a blatant reminder that she had been abandoned with a complete stranger, he turned her around so that the back of her head rested on his chest. He pulled in his chin to glance down at her, and thought that, for all the earthy coarseness of her mother, Tracy was beautifully turned out. Her tiny feet were tucked into a pair of cheap white plimsolls, and through the lace at the top of her short white socks were woven yellow strands of ribbon, matching exactly the colour of her little acrylic dress. Her soft, wispy hair was caught up in a white elastic band, making it sprout, like a tiny fountain, from the top of her head. David leaned forward to retrieve his document from the seat pocket, and with that, caught a whiff of the warm, sweet smell of baby, a cocktail so addictive, yet its ingredients so indescribable, save for the liberal sprinkling of Johnson's Baby Powder. It was a smell he had known so well in the past, a smell so powerful that, at one time, it had made him think that he could never live without a baby in the house.

Leaving the document where it was, he pulled Tracy close into his chest, the gentle movement of the little girl's body against his supporting hand seeming to calm his mind and dust away cobwebs from long-stored-away memories of his own children.

It was surprising that, during his first three months of working at Glendurnich, he hadn't been given the boot for sleeping on the job, as it seemed to be the only time that he could catch up on much-needed rest. This was all because of a small, vulnerable bundle of humanity called Sophie Rosemary Alicia Corstorphine, an angel during the day, who metamorphosed into a screaming scrap of unconsolable wretchedness in the early hours of the morning. Waking hours at night suddenly matched those of day, and even though it quite often resulted in a gritty-eyed tetchiness on the part of both himself and Rachel, she never lost patience with the baby. She would take it into bed in the middle of the night and, gathering up all the pillows behind her, would sit cross-legged gently rocking the baby, until its violent sobs receded to a gulping contentment as it sucked from her nipple. He, meanwhile, would be forced to lie pillowless, wedged into an eight-inch width of bedspace, with a hand and a foot stretched out to the floor to stop him from rolling out.

"Try singing to her," Dr. Spiers had helpfully suggested, and, not realizing that it all mostly took place at two in the morning, "or maybe take her for a walk in her pram to settle her."

So they tried one and then the other, only to find that Sophie would respond solely to a combination of the two. Consequently, the lights of The Beeches were often seen to burn brightly in the night, while David walked up and down in the hallway like some destitute busker, bleary-eyed and unshaven, singing soothing lullabies to his first-born child.

And then four years later, when Sophie had grown into a constantly happy, lovable child, thus making more than enough atonement for her ignominious start in life, Charlie appeared, live and kicking, with all the clichéd remarks about a future football star in the making. They battened down the hatches, prepared the pram in the hallway and the guitar at the ready, but it was as if he had been conceived by a different formula of genes (or, more likely, that he and Rachel had ironed out all their inexperience on Sophie), because the baby slept by night and grinned by day. By the time that Harriet appeared, there was enough baby-care know-how in the household for Rachel to afford to take a back seat while her eldest daughter, just turned seven years old, took control with an accomplishment and dedication that surpassed by far the efforts of any of the morose, disinterested au pair girls that had been employed in the past to look after herself and Charlie.

And as they grew, they became a unit within themselves, independent and content with each other's company in the games that they played: Sophie the organizer, Charlie the stuntman, and Harriet the cook, the chief bottle-washer, the alien from a different planet, but ultimately the baby. Yet their relationship with each other was not one of sugary-sweet perfection, their individual strength of character quite often being the cause of fervent disagreement, and games, on occasion, would culminate in vicious fights between the two elder siblings. While they ran to their mother to get first word in for comfort and mediation, Harriet would for a moment cast an uncomprehending look after them and then return happily to their now-abandoned game—to wash her teacups or to send her spaceship into warp five.

"Sorry we were so long, mister."

David looked round sharply from the window, his hand tightening instinctively on Tracy's stomach in the immediate thought that he might have unconsciously lessened his grasp on the baby. The woman was edging her way back into the seat, pushing a much-relieved Darren in front of her.

"Darren needed more than a pee. Och, would ye look at that! She's fast asleep."

David glanced down at Tracy. Her face was turned to the side, one flushed cheek squashed hard against the front of his shirt, her eyelids flickering, her pacifier hanging loosely in her mouth.

"My, she's lookin' awf'y hot. I hope she's no' comin' down wi' the flu or anything like that. Anyway, thanks again for your help, mister." She reached over and relieved David of his charge, and at once he felt the coolness of the plane's air-conditioning hit the warm little area which Tracy had occupied.

"Not at all. It was my pleasure," he said, smiling across at the woman. Then, pulling his blazer around him, he took the Glendurnich document from the seat pocket and at last settled down to read it.

Alicia stuck her spectacles on the end of her nose and looked up at the latest school photograph that hung on the wall outside the headmaster's study to see if she could pick out her three grandchildren amongst the other two hundred or so faces. Across the hall from her, the headmaster's nervous little secretary tapped ineffectively on the door for the second time.

"Come in!" a muffled voice bellowed out.

The secretary flashed a brave smile at Alicia before slowly opening the door and putting her head round the corner. "Mr. Hunter, I have Lady Inchelvie here to see you."

Without waiting for a reply she jumped back from the door, and within a second it flew open as if caught in a whirlwind, to reveal a tall, spindly young man in his mid-thirties with wild bushy hair and half-moon spectacles, the combination of which would have made his age indeterminable to Alicia if she hadn't come to know him so well over the past six months.

"Lady Inchelvie," he said, stretching out a long, bony hand. "I'm so sorry, I had no idea you had arrived. I've just been having to reschedule a boys' cricket match to another venue, because the girls are going to be using the athletics track around the one out there"—he waved airily with his hand in the direction of the front of the school—"and I do rather want to prevent them from coming under fire from one of the big hitters in our team." He smiled down at her from his lanky height. "Nevertheless, I do apologize for not springing up to meet you immediately."

"Not at all, Mr. Hunter," Alicia said, smiling at the dishevelled young man. "It's actually I who should be apologizing to you for being extremely disruptive and insisting that I should visit the children during the week. It's just that my husband was coming down to Glasgow for a meeting, and I thought that I would take the opportunity of a free ride!"

The young headmaster held up his hand. "Of course you should visit. Please, never think that you might not be welcome. It really is no imposition." He swung himself round to stand at the side of his study door, his gown billowing out as he did so. "Now let's go and have a seat in my office. Can I get you a cup of tea or coffee?"

"No, thank you very much," Alicia replied as she passed him. "I had an interesting cup of tea on the train over from Glasgow which tasted as if it might be a combination of coffee, tea and hot chocolate, so I think I've probably had my fair share."

Mr. Hunter let out a short, almost manic chuckle, then, having seen Alicia settled on the sofa, he slumped down with a *boing* of a loose spring into an armchair and almost disappeared from view. Alicia stifled a smile, realizing that he was built like a young giraffe—all legs and no upper body. He placed his elbows on the arms of his chair at about the same level as his chin. "I hear that Mr. Corstorphine is flying out to the States today."

"Ah, you're being kept abreast of the news, then."

Mr. Hunter smiled. "Yes, Sophie told us on Saturday night. She said that he wasn't too sure if he would be back by next weekend, but that he certainly would be for the leave-out. She was actually quite excited to talk about it."

Alicia paused for a moment, a worried expression coming over her face. "Mr. Hunter, how do you think they are? I mean, do they seem to be, well, bearing up all right?"

The headmaster pushed himself forward on the chair and, stretching out a long tentacle of an arm, momentarily touched Alicia's elbow.

"Firstly, Lady Inchelvie, I must tell you that they are never alone for a minute. Every member of my staff is looking out for them at all times and are under strict instructions to bring them straight to myself or my wife if there are problems. Then, as far as they are individually, all three are coping admirably. Of course, they all handle it differently. I think Charlie blots the whole thing from his mind, which might mean that there could possibly be a relapse at a later stage, but we'll cross that bridge when we come to it. He is as lively as ever, and a great asset to the Under-Thirteen cricket team. As for the girls, I really have to say that I am filled with admiration for Sophie in the way that she handles Harriet. For a girl of such tender years, her whole manner and decorum have been exemplary, and I have to say that she's one of the most resourceful, responsible and, without doubt, bravest girls I have ever had the honour of knowing . . . but . . ." He continued slowly, carefully picking his words. "I do know that the emotional upheaval within herself must be extreme, not only because of her mother, but also because she is at that chrysalis stage, Lady Inchelvie, and I have experience enough of being a headmaster of a mixed school to know that it is an extremely vulnerable time." He paused for a moment to change direction, noticing a slight quiver in Alicia's bottom lip, despite her upright and steadfast comportment. "Harriet is also fine. I know this because she is relying totally on her sister as a mother figure. Of course, one realizes that Sophie can never be a replacement, but there is still an order and sense in Harriet's life. However, I'm afraid that Sophie does realize this and that only increases the burden that she is carrying on her shoulders. Now, by telling you this, I don't want to appear alarmist, but only explain to you that I do understand everything that is going on, and that I do, I assure you, have it all under control."

Alicia smiled at the headmaster, feeling an urge to get up and hug the man for his kindness and the intuitive understanding he had of both the situation and her feelings. He rose from his chair, unravelling his legs like a couple of elasticised magic wands.

"Now let me see if I can locate them all for you. If you would just like to wait here, I'll quickly pop down to the classrooms. Will you be taking them out for lunch?"

"I don't think I'll get away without doing something fairly special with them."

"Well, you do whatever you want." He walked towards the door, then suddenly stopped and turned, hitting his head lightly with his hand. "Ah, dash, I almost forgot. I actually do need Charlie back here at two-thirty this afternoon. We have an inter-house cricket match on, and I'm afraid that his team would be quite bereft without him. Is that all right?"

"Of course. Sounds much more fun than lunch with stuffy old grandmother."

The headmaster raised his eyebrows. "As the boys would say, Lady Inchelvie, *don't you believe it*!" He turned and swept out of the room.

Alicia sat for a moment absently playing with a button on her cardigan, then, pushing herself to her feet, she walked over to the window to look out. Mr. Hunter was kind and understanding and in the nicest way persuasive. But she still worried. About the children, about David, and increasingly more about her husband. George was working too hard, taking too much on, yet she knew that he felt that there was no alternative at the minute. If she were to tell him that he had to stop going into the office every day or cut out the business meetings, he would just turn round and say that he was fine. But she had noticed him becoming more pale and tired as the weeks of his working progressed, and that really worried her more than anything. She shook her head slowly and looked out onto the cricket pitch that stretched across the vast lawn in front of the house. Near its centre, two boys were standing twenty yards apart, playing Gaining Ground with a cricket ball, straining every muscle in their skinny arms to see who could outthrow the other. A male voice sounded down below the window. "Come on, you ruffians, get to your class."

"Sorry, sir," they said in unison and ran off in the direction of the scolding voice, laughing and shouting as they went.

The door of the study opened behind her, and before she could turn around, a girl's voice shouted out. "Granny!"

Sophie rushed forward to greet her, circling the headmaster's desk and throwing her arms around Alicia's neck. She hugged her tightly, almost making her grandmother lose her balance.

"Hullo, darling, how are you?"

"I'm fine," Sophie said in a muffled voice, her face still buried in her grandmother's neck. She relinquished her hold and stood back looking at her grandmother. "I didn't know you were visiting today! Dad only said that you might come down at the weekend! How did you get here?"

Alicia studied her granddaughter's face, noticing that her smile did little to cover the look of sad exhaustion in her eyes.

"I've just taken the train over from Glasgow. Grandpa and I dropped off your father at the airport early this morning, and then he left me at the station. Grandpa has some meeting today and tomorrow in Glasgow. I thought that I might have stayed with him tonight, but seeing I'm quite literally on the road home, I thought it would be as well to catch the train from Perth to Carrbridge this evening." She paused. "So, tell me, how's everything been?"

Sophie levered herself up onto Mr. Hunter's desk and swung her bare legs over the edge. "Oh, all right, I suppose. Harry seems to be okay. I see as much of her as I can. Charlie's a pain most of the time, though. I go up to him every now and then at lunch-time to say hullo, and he gets all stupid and embarrassed in front of his friends." She let out a long sigh and turned to look out of the window. "Granny, do you think Dad's all right?"

Alicia walked over and took hold of her granddaughter's hand. "I think so, darling. Didn't he seem so to you on Saturday?"

"Yes. Well, in a way. It's just that he seems so . . . different—sort of distant. But I suppose it's understandable. I think he misses Mummy *so* much, Granny."

Alicia put her hands on Sophie's shoulders. "Of course he does, as you do, and all of us too. Grieving is the most terrible, painful thing for everyone, so one can only imagine what it must be like for people as close as your parents. But you mustn't start burdening yourself with his sorrow as well. You must think about *you,* Sophie. You've got your own life to lead, and, well, you've got exams and things very soon, so *please* don't worry. Your father will heal, I promise you—it might take a little time, but he will heal." She took Sophie's face in her hands and tilted it up to her. "Look, let's strike a bargain. Mr. Hunter has told me how wonderful you are being with Harriet, so you continue to look after her, and I'll make sure that Dad is all right. Okay?"

Alicia held out her hand, palm upwards. Sophie looked at it and, smiling, gave it a slap with her own. "Okay."

At that point, the door flew open and Harriet and Charlie burst in. Alicia turned, only having enough time to open her arms before the little girl jumped up from a distance of about three feet and circled her arms and feet around her grandmother.

"Watch out for Granny's back, Harry!" Sophie scolded.

"No, it's all right," Alicia said, kissing the top of her younger granddaughter's head. She looked across to Charlie, who had come to stand beside Sophie and was running a toy vehicle up and down the surface of Mr. Hunter's desk while at the same time surreptitiously trying to read one of the many letters that were strewn across the top.

"Charlie? How are you, my darling?"

"Fine," he replied, at first not breaking his concentration away from the letters. Then he swung round to face his grandmother. "Granny?" He had a look of such questioning seriousness on his face that Alicia thought that she was about to be asked her own personal views on "the meaning of life."

"Yes?"

"Have you got any sweets with you?"

"Charlie!" Sophie exclaimed, astounded at her brother's mercenary tactics. "You really are insufferable!"

Charlie's face creased into a wide grin, and they all broke into laughter. Putting Harriet down, Alicia walked over to the sofa where she had left her handbag, Charlie and Harriet following close on her heels. Alicia took three bars of Cadbury's chocolate from the depths of the bag and gave one to each of them, and they immediately started ripping away at the silver paper. Alicia held the third forward towards Sophie. "Darling, do you want one?"

"No, thanks, Granny. I don't feel like it."

Alicia moved forward and slipped it into the pocket of Sophie's dress. "Well, keep it for later. Share it with your friends or whatever. Now," she said, turning to them all, and at the same time looking at her watch, "Mr. Hunter says that I can take you out for lunch."

Charlie's eyes went wide with delight. "Can we go to McDonald's? We went with Dad on Saturday. It's really terrific, Granny!"

"Yes!" Harriet shouted in approval. "*Pleeeease,* Granny."

"Oh dear, I don't think that we can do that. For one thing, I don't have a car, and anyway, Charlie, Mr. Hunter has asked me expressly to get you back here by two-thirty this afternoon for your cricket match."

There was a groan of disappointment from the two younger children.

"We could go to the village pub," Sophie suggested. "I went there once with a friend of mine and her parents. It's only three hundred yards from the school and they do pretty good chips."

Alicia smiled across at Sophie and mouthed a relieved "thank you" in her direction. "Right," she said, "the pub it is!"

Charlie punched the air with his fist. "Yesss!" he said, darting towards the door. "Come on, let's go!"

"Just a minute," Alicia called after him, picking up her handbag from the sofa. "Let's get organized and all go out together, so that we don't disturb any of the classes." Taking hold of Harriet's hand, she moved towards the door. As Charlie opened it, Harriet looked up at her grandmother.

"Granny?" she said in a quiet voice.

"Yes, darling?"

"I think Daddy's gone away like Mummy."

The procession to the door stopped abruptly, and Alicia felt her face tingle with shock at the unexpectedness of the statement. She bent down and put her arm around Harriet's shoulders. "No, he hasn't, darling. He's just off to America for a short time to do some work. He'll be back soon. Didn't he say that he'd be back in time to take you home for leave-out?"

"Not that, Granny," Harriet continued, in a matter-of-fact way. "Daddy doesn't really seem to be in his body any more. He's somewhere else."

Alicia glanced up at the other two. Sophie stood looking at her sister, biting hard on her lip, while Charlie pushed the door shut with a sigh, his eyes focused on the door handle as he pulled it back and forth on its loose-fittings.

"Let's just go and sit down for a minute, shall we?" Alicia said, guiding Harriet back to the sofa. Sophie came over and sat on the arm, while Charlie stayed where he was, continuing to play noisily with the door handle.

"Now," Alicia said slowly, as she settled herself beside her granddaughter, "you tell me exactly what you mean."

"Well, it's sort of opposite to Mummy."

"I'm sorry, darling?"

"Mummy's spirit is all around us, but her body's not. That's what Sophie says. And Daddy's body is around us, but his spirit's not. So really it's opposite."

Alicia sat for a moment in silence, stroking the top of Harriet's head, trying to work out what to say. "Listen, darling," she said eventually, "I know that Daddy has been a little distracted over the past few months, and it must be really hard for you to understand why he *is* like that. But he is most definitely still with us, and I know that he thinks so much about you and loves you all very much. Now, I'm pretty sure that his trip to America will do him the world of good, and when he returns he'll be the way we have always known him." She peered round at Harriet's face. "All right?"

Harriet nodded, quite content with the explanation.

"Can we go now?" Charlie asked, opening the door.

"Good idea!" Alicia said as brightly as she could. "To the pub, then!" She gave Harriet a final squeeze and rose to her feet. "I didn't get any breakfast, so I'm looking forward to a great big plate of chips!"

Harriet ran to the door and followed Charlie out into the hall. Sophie, however, held back and stopped her grandmother by placing her hand on her elbow. "Granny?" Alicia turned to her. "I have a feeling he won't come back."

"Of course he will. He'll be his old self very soon."

"No, I mean, I think you're right about him needing to get away from Inchelvie and needing time to heal. I don't think he actually *should* come back for a bit."

Alicia patted the small slender hand that held her elbow. "We'll see, darling. But remember our deal. You look after Harriet, and I'll make sure Daddy comes back as the man we all know. All right?"

Sophie nodded, forcing a smile onto her face. Alicia took hold of her hand and kissed her on the cheek.

"I'll let you into a secret, Sophie. Mr. Hunter said that you were one of the most special girls he has ever met. Of course *he* didn't need to tell me that, but it's good for me and for you to know that you have a real ally here. And I'll tell you something else, my darling, and that is that I think you're turning into a very beautiful young lady, and I am so very proud of you." She pulled Sophie towards her and gave her a final hug before turning towards the door. "Now come on, let's catch up with those other two before they start disrupting the whole school."

CHAPTER 11

As the plane pulled up to the terminal building at Kennedy Airport, David watched with interest as his neighbour leaped to her feet even before the "Seat-Belt" sign had been switched off. She busily began to organize her children and to pull bags and jerseys from the overhead locker, eager to get off the plane and get on with her holiday. Others immediately followed her lead, but after ten minutes of muttered complaints about slowness in opening the doors and craning of necks to try to see why those in Business Class weren't attempting to make any obvious moves, most of them had sat down again, bags on knees, shaking their heads and raising their eyebrows at those who had shown similar impatience.

Two minutes later there were signs of movement farther up the aisle, and immediately the little Glaswegian family was on the move, Darren in the lead, pushing his way resolutely forward while his mother followed hard on his heels, with baggage and baby in arms.

David waited until the line from the rear of the plane was moving steadily towards the doorway before retrieving his brief-case and pushing himself out of his seat. He made his way down the aisle, stretching out his back and legs as he walked, stiff from having been crammed into such a small space for so long. He stepped out of the plane and relished for a fleeting moment the rush of warm air that squeezed its way through the gap between the fuselage and the air bridge before being met full-on by the chilling blast of air-conditioning that swept its way down the tunnel from the terminal building.

At the top of the air bridge he joined the herd of passengers emerging from other arrival gates and strolled leisurely down the long glassed-in corridor towards Immigration. As he went, he began to feel a quietening sense of relief come over him, realizing that amidst the massing throng of people on the move he was simply a statistical entity, anonymous, totally without history. He was of no interest to anyone, each person cocooned in his or her own thoughts and worries, as opposed to the one common, suffocating cloud of sadness that had come to hang over everything and everyone at Inchelvie.

He chose not to use the moving walkway and kept himself to the uncrowded side. Half-way along, his eye was caught by a flash of Celtic green on the walkway next to him and to his horror he saw Darren's head come bobbing along, a wide grin on his face as he delighted in his new-found game of running up the moving belt in the wrong direction, causing havoc with the flow of oncoming pedestrians. With that, the undecipherable pronunciation of his name rose high above the general noise of footsteps and chatter, and David caught sight of the boy's mother at the far end of the walkway, Tracy on her hip and her bags cast forlornly around her feet.

Once inside the Immigration hall, he took his place in the queue that snaked through the roped-off barriers to the line of fluorescent-lit booths. People fumbled nervously with passports and immigration forms, affording edgy smiles to one another as if they felt that they were about to be subjected to an intensive interrogation before being allowed into the country. Slowly, the queue shuffled forward until it was David's turn. He stepped into the booth and handed his papers to the young immigration officer.

"Are you here on business or pleasure, sir?"

"Business," David replied.

"And how long?"

"I'm not sure. Probably no longer than a week."

The young man nodded his head slowly. "Okay, and might I ask what your business is?"

"I'm in the whisky industry."

The young officer raised his eyebrows, a look of interest registering on his face, then stamped part of the immigration form and slipped it into the passport before handing it back. "Well, just keep it rolling in over here!" he said with a laugh.

"I will." He gave the young man a smile and was about to walk out into America when the officer spoke again.

"Just before you go, I wonder if you had a moment to explain something."

For a moment, David stood without replying, a frown of concern on his face as he tried to work out what the question might be.

"Surely," he said eventually, returning to the desk. "If I can."

The young man noticed his disquiet and smiled reassuringly at him. "There's nothing wrong. It's just that I'd like to know what 'The Hon.' means in front of your name? I'm new at this job and though I *have* seen it before, I've no idea what it means."

"Nothing much, to be quite honest. It stands for 'The Honourable.' It's just a courtesy title."

"Ah, and how'd you get it?"

"Well," he said, moving closer to the desk, embarrassed that someone might overhear their conversation, "it's just because my father is, well, a lord."

The young man's eyes opened wide. "Really? Does that mean you're related to royalty?"

"No, far from it!" David laughed. "As I said, it's just a courtesy title."

The young man cocked his head to the side. "Well, there you go. You live and learn. Thanks for the lesson, Mr. Corstorphine." He turned and called in the next person.

David recovered his suitcase from the carousel, cleared customs and strode out into the Arrivals hall. A sea of expectant people greeted him, some appearing immediately dejected on seeing that his wasn't the face for which they were looking, whilst others, with name cards held out in front, grinned hopefully at him. He picked out his driver, a small knuckle-headed man in a short-sleeved white shirt, black tie, and impenetrable Rayban sun-glasses, bearing a "Star Limos" sign with his name spelt phonetically underneath.

David approached him. "Hullo."

"You Mr. Costawfin?" the driver asked, chewing open-mouthed on his gum.

"Yup."

"Okay, I'm Dan, sir." In one swift movement, he grabbed David's suitcase and shook him firmly by the hand. "Car's just outside the building. If you don't mind, we'd better move fast before I get towed."

They made their way out into the glaring sunlight, and Dan aimed his remote at a black Lincoln Town Car. He threw the suitcase into the trunk and, having seen David into the back, leaped into the driver's seat and took off at speed, his tyres squealing on the hot asphalt.

Fifteen minutes later, they were heading east along the Southern State Parkway, the surrounding countryside changing with every mile that they drove away from New York City. Far from being the endless suburban sprawl that he had envisaged, the parkway was bounded by a screen of tall hardwood trees, which eventually gave way to dense, tangled expanses of spindly pines that stretched off into the distance on either side of the road. These, Dan informed him, were the pine barrens of Long Island, a haven for mosquitos and "a helluva fire risk."

Exactly fifty minutes after leaving Kennedy, Dan took an exit next to an enormous swivelling sign that said: LEESPORT OUTLET CENTER. At the top of the ramp he turned right and headed south along a wide stretch of road before clattering across a railway line and past a sign that welcomed visitors to Leesport. David gazed out the window at the houses, some with white picket fences enclosing gardens with neat, orderly beds of brightly coloured flowers while water sprinklers played on the lush green, mower-striped lawns. Beech-trees and native pines stood tall and leafy, wrapping their branches protectively around each house, granting it seclusion from its nearest neighbour. No two were the same, some gleaming white clapboard, others with brown cedar shingles, still others a mixture of the two. Wide-pitched roofs hung like stern eyebrows over shuttered windows while others, four-pitched and prim in their perfection, looked like wimpled nuns. Every hundred yards, bright yellow fire hydrants stood like sentries on the clipped, nurtured strip of grass that ran between the black asphalt sidewalk and the roadway, strategically placed to keep guard over the tinder-dry houses.

At the bottom of the road, Dan just made it through the traffic light and swung the car to the left. He glanced back at David. "Okay—so this is Leesport Village now, sir."

The thoroughfare was spotlessly clean, bordered by wide, white-lined parking spaces and fronted by a line of small shops, all in regulation-white clapboard, with paned display windows and flower-urns brimming with pansies, marigolds and petunias at their doors. The sidewalk was busy with pedestrians, old couples walking arm-in-arm, young mothers carrying babies on their hips, all dressed in summer clothes and all moving at an easy, unhurried pace. As Dan accelerated along the street, David looked out and caught some of the names on the small multi-coloured signs that hung above the shops: The Leesport Deli, Danby Real Estate, Helping Hands, Leesport Liquors, Jo-Ann's Fitness Center and, at the end of the street, the local sports shop, Lar Sport.

Two hundred yards farther on, Dan turned the Lincoln left up a narrow leafy street, past a green-and-white sign which read NORTH HARLENS, and pulled to a stop beside a letter box with "52" written on it in black lettering. The two-storied house stood back from the street, up a short concrete driveway bordered by wide strips of coarse zoysia grass, its frontage dominated by a high wooden sundeck, on which a table and chairs were neatly arranged. A couple of faded oars had been nailed to the wall like crossed swords. To the left of the deck, David could just make out, through a screen of shrubs, the shimmering blue of a swimming pool. There was nothing to set the house apart from any others that he had seen so far in Leesport, save for the network of scaffolding that jutted out from its farthest side and the heavy tarpaulin, flapping gently in the breeze, that covered a third of its roof.

Dan turned off the engine and pressed the switch for the trunk. "Here we are. The Eggars' house."

They both got out of the car, and as Dan took the suitcase from the trunk, a voice boomed out from the direction of the house.

"David, you old bugger!"

A tall, slim, blond-haired man came bounding down the drive towards him, his arms outstretched, and without seeming to slacken off his pace, he met David with a thump of chests and threw his arms around him, then gave him a bone-shaking slap on the back. "It's great to see you, my friend!"

"And you, Richard."

Richard stood back and eyed him up and down. "Christ, you haven't changed much." He stepped forward and roughly tousled David's hair. "Just a few grey hairs sneaking in there!"

He skirted round David and relieved the driver of his load. "So, you managed to track down the mad Scotsman, did you, Dan?"

"Yeah, no problem, Mr. Eggar." Dan turned towards David. "Have an enjoyable stay, sir, and if you want to get back to Kennedy at any time, just get Mr. Eggar to call the office."

David smiled and slipped him a twenty. "I will. Thanks, Dan."

They both stood in silence, watching as the car pulled away from the house, then David let out a long, relieved breath and looked up and down the street. "Well, you seem to have found a nice place to live. It's all so . . ." he paused, trying to think of an adequate word to describe what he had seen so far of Leesport, ". . . pristine!"

"Virginal, my boy," Richard replied in a mock Cockney accent as he walked back up the drive with David's bags in hand, "that's how I describe it—vibrant and virginal! Now come on, let's go crack open a few bottles of beer."

Richard led the way up a flight of steps onto the deck and crossed over to a wire-meshed screen door. He pushed it open with his shoulder and David followed him into a large, airy kitchen, its centre dominated by a long scrubbed pine table across which were spread Richard's work-papers. The whole room was aflame with dancing splinters of light that reflected off the open French doors as they gently swung in the breeze.

"Listen, I hope you don't mind roughing it a bit, old boy," Richard said. "You've slightly caught us at a bad time. We're in the throes of doing a major conversion job to the side of the house, so I'm afraid the roof is off the two guest-rooms." He opened the door and David followed him into the carpetless hall, their feet making imprints in the building dust that lay thick on the floor. Richard started up the stairs. "Just bloody typical of Angie, though. She starts something like this and then buggers off!" He walked along the narrow passage and pushed open a door with the suitcase. "So I hope you don't mind sleeping in here. It's my office. Not very salubrious, I'm afraid."

The room itself was only about eight-foot square, but was reduced in size still further by the wide shelf that extended round two walls, stacked neatly with filing trays and books. At one end, amidst a cat's-cradle of different-coloured wires, sat Richard's laptop computer, laser printer, fax machine and telephone. A single bed had been jammed in behind the door, the bottom half of which extended under the shelf. There was no wardrobe, but the jangle of clashing metal when the door was initially opened indicated that there must be a number of wire coat-hangers hanging behind it. Any daylight that might have entered through the two small windows was closed off by impenetrable roller blinds, which only added to the cell-like qualities of the room. Everything in the room was coloured light-brown with dust.

Richard put the cases down and looked around, his hands on his hips. "Hope it's all right."

"Yeah, fine," David said, trying to sound buoyant at the prospect of sleeping in what resembled an executive broom cupboard, "really fine. All I need is somewhere to lay my head."

"Good, well, the bathroom is right next door when you want it." He turned to leave. "Look, I've got a couple of calls to make, so get yourself organized and then come down and we'll have that drink."

He left the room and David stood for a minute surveying his filthy quarters. Jesus, maybe this hadn't been such a good idea and he'd be better off in a hotel somewhere. He felt an involuntary shiver run through his body and, putting his brief-case on the shelf, he began rubbing hard at his legs to try to relieve the aching that had suddenly developed. Putting his hand to his forehead, he wiped away a bead of sweat. Oh, no, don't say he'd gone and picked up a bug from that child in the plane! That was all he needed! He slumped back onto the sagging bed and stared up at the ceiling, a sudden sense of depression and uneasiness coming over him, and for the first time since leaving Scotland he felt the familiar dull ache of loneliness return to his body. Yet this time it was worse, the reality of his situation beginning to take a numbing grip on his ill-sorted and fevered mind—that now, in these characterless and unfamiliar surroundings, he was truly alone—an ocean apart from the children, and an ocean apart from Rachel.

CHAPTER 12

By dinner-time that evening, there was little doubt in David's mind that he had caught some fast-acting and virulent bug from the child in the plane. His whole body ached and his head thumped as he sat with Richard at the kichen table, eating rubbery, undercooked pasta and drinking too much wine, hoping that as soon as possible he would be able to excuse himself and go to bed. However, Richard hardly drew breath as he recounted endless stories and anecdotes of their time in the army together, and David, feeling duty-bound to play the polite guest, sat listening with a fixed smile on his sweating face.

At the end of the meal Richard stacked the plates in the dishwasher, then, without offering David an alternative, opened up a kitchen cupboard and took out two glasses and a bottle of whisky. Having poured two powerful measures into each glass, he sat down again and, after a moment's hesitation, broached the subject of Rachel, and David, not feeling in the mood to go into any great detail, proceeded to give him only the broadest outline on what had happened. However, as he talked, he noticed Richard's interest in the subject quickly wane, and almost imperceptibly the topic of conversation was guided away from Rachel and on to Angie. Soon David found himself in the role of sympathetic listener, as Richard, drinking two whiskies to his one, slurred on in an endless monologue about the problems they had encountered in their seven-year marriage—how she couldn't have children and how she made up for it by spending money as if it grew on trees, and now the final straw being this latest conversion, which she had started without his prior knowledge.

Until midnight David sat and listened, his face burning with fever and his eyes heavy with lack of sleep and jet lag. Then, unable to restrain himself any further, he let out an enormous yawn and pushed himself to his feet, an action which brought about an abrupt halt to Richard's outpourings. Mumbling abject apologies to David for burdening him with his problems and for keeping him from his bed, he too rose unsteadily to his feet and together they weaved their way upstairs.

With a sense of relief David shut his bedroom door and sat down heavily on the narrow bed, leaning his elbows on his knees and rubbing at his smarting eyes. He flicked his wrist over to look at the time. Half midnight. That meant he had been on the go for almost twenty-four hours. He let out a sigh of exhaustion and, heaving himself to his feet, made his way to the bathroom.

He gave his teeth a revitalizing brush and splashed cupped handfuls of cold water onto his face in an attempt to relieve the stinging in his eyes and the thickness clutching at his head, caused both by the flu and the overconsumption of wine and whisky. Then, returning to his bedroom, he undressed and jumped into bed, pulling the covers up around his chin to stop the uncontrollable shivering. He tried shutting his eyes, but his head seemed to be taking off in different directions, whirling in circles from Richard's endless chatter, and at the same time sinking in and out of the pillow with too much booze. He needed something to settle his mind, even just for a moment. He turned and scanned the small room for a magazine or a book to read, but there was only a shelf-full of company business plans propped up by a large legal encyclopaedia. He thought that he might have kept a newspaper from the plane journey, so he clambered out of bed and sprang open the catches of his brief-case. No luck. Only the Glendurnich distributor report. Better than nothing, he thought to himself. He took it out, closed the brief-case and got back into bed.

The next morning he was awakened abruptly by a clatter of coat-hangers as the door swung hard against his bed, and he looked up to see Richard's bleary-eyed and colourless face hovering above him.

"Richard? Whatsamatter?" he asked, bewildered.

Richard rubbed at his hair with his fingers. "Look, David, I'm sorry, but I'm afraid we've slept in. We'll have to get a move on. I'm going to telephone Star Limos right now for a car, 'cos I don't think I'm in a fit state to drive."

He hurried out of the room, and for a moment David lay in his bed while the throbbing in his head and the aching in his limbs began to register in his brain. He looked at his watch. It was half past eight. "Oh, *shit*!"

He threw off the bedclothes and jumped to his feet, the sudden movement exacerbating the overpowering feeling of nausea. He stood for a minute concentrating hard to bring it under control, goose-pimples pricking the surface of his shivering body.

"Oh, for crying out *bloody* loud! Why now?" He grabbed his sponge-bag and made his way through to the bathroom. There was no time for a shower, only a quick wash and a shave, before he was back in his room to riffle through his suitcase for clean underpants, shirt and socks.

"Dan'll be here in three minutes," Richard's voice sounded up the stairs.

A host of butterflies suddenly invaded David's stomach, and his fingers started to shake as he fumbled with his tie. Christ, he thought to himself, this is all I need. Bloody late for the meeting and a dose of flu to go with it.

He pulled on his trousers and, pushing his feet into shoes while still on the move, he grabbed his jacket and brief-case and ran downstairs.

Richard was already in the kitchen, flying around the room picking up bits of paper off different surfaces and stuffing them into his brief-case. "Sorry about this, David. Listen, grab a cup of coffee. It's in the percolator. I'm afraid it's left over from last night, but at least it'll be strong." A car horn sounded outside the house. "Christ, no time! That'll be Dan now! Come on!"

He ushered David out onto the deck and locked the door, then hurried down the steps, his guest hard on his heels. Dan was waiting for them on the street, holding open the back door of the Lincoln. They both bundled themselves in, and as the car powered off down the street, Richard slumped back against the head-rest. "Bloody hell, I feel rough! How're you doing?"

"Not too good. I think I've got the flu as well as a hangover."

"Christ, you poor bugger! You should have said something!" He paused. "Look, I'm going to come back tonight, but you'll probably be finished way before me, so I suggest you get yourself to Penn Station and just take a train to Patchogue. You can get a taxi from there." He delved in the pocket of his jacket, at the same time flicking open his brief-case. "There's the key of the house, and"—he took a mobile phone from the case—"I think you'd better call ahead and tell them that you're running about half an hour late." He shook his head and looked sheepishly at David. "I really am sorry about all of this."

The journey thereafter was completed in silence. Richard, green-faced in his sufferance of the mother of all hangovers, sat snoring loudly with his mouth open and his eyes closed, while David pulled his jacket tight around himself to try to curb his interminable shivering. Dan drove as fast as the speed limit and the traffic would allow, but by the time they reached the queue for the toll at the Midtown Tunnel, Richard's projected half-hour delay was already five minutes over schedule.

Dan looked round from the front seat. "Do you know where on Madison you're going, Mr. Costawfin?"

"Yes, somewhere between Forty-fifth and Forty-sixth East."

Dan nodded. "Right—that's easy enough. Just along Forty-second and up Madison. If it's all the same with you, Mr. Eggar, we'll drop off Mr. Costawfin first."

"Certainly, Dan," Richard agreed. "Without question."

The horn-blowing Manhattan traffic was heavier than Dan had

anticipated, with the result that it took a further ten minutes to reach the block of Forty-fifth and Madison. Bidding Richard a cursory farewell, David jumped out of the car, then proceeded to take another ten minutes of frantic searching to find the building in which the offices of Deakin Distribution were situated. By the time he came out of the creaking lift onto the fifteenth floor, the clock on the wall opposite read five past eleven. He looked up and down the corridor. At the far end, a polished brass plaque bearing the company's name hung on the wall beside a pair of large glass doors. He ran towards them and burst into the reception area so forcefully that the young blonde receptionist, her mouth open with fright, pushed her seat back from the desk, as if she felt that her office had suddenly come under siege from an Armed Response Unit.

David turned to catch the hinged glass door as it swung wildly back and forth following his forceful entry. "Sorry about that," he said almost inaudibly, trying to calm the situation by talking quietly.

The girl never took her eyes off him, but warily drew her chair back to the desk. "Can I help you?" she drawled, an annoyed slant to her voice.

"Yes," David said, trying to catch his breath following his exertions of the past quarter of an hour. "I'm afraid that I was meant to be here at ten o'clock, but I was held up. I'm from Glendurnich Distilleries Limited."

"And you are . . ." The girl ran her finger down the appointment book on her desk before looking back up at him with a sudden light and happy look on her face. ". . . Mr. Corstorphine?"

"That's right."

"If you would like to follow me, sir, the directors are waiting for you in the boardroom."

David followed her as she teetered along the narrow, newly carpeted corridor, her feet splayed out in stiletto-heeled shoes which made her tight-skirted bottom swing unnervingly from side to side in front of him. She stopped outside one of the doors, knocked and, without waiting for a reply, opened the door and stepped aside to allow David to enter.

A group of five or six men sat slouched in their chairs around a long boardroom table, some with their hands linked behind their heads. As he entered, they pulled themselves upright and swung round to look at him, then jumped to their feet in unison. A silver-haired man who had been sitting up at the far end made his way down the side of the table to meet him.

"David," he said, approaching him, his hand outstretched and a wide, beaming smile on his face. "Charles Deakin, managing director of Deakin Distribution."

David took his hand, and Deakin clenched it in his powerful grasp, giving it a shoulder-dislocating shake. He let go and clapped his hands together, as if wanting to start proceedings immediately.

"So you eventually found us," he said, pulling out a vacant chair for David and making his way back to his own at the head of the table. "I must apologize for not having sent you directions. I thought that you must have been to New York before and knew about our morning traffic!"

Charles Deakin had reached the top of the table as he finished his sentence and, turning to face David with a sardonic smile on his face, was joined in his moment of amusement by a rippling murmur from the rest of the assembled company. David smiled weakly. Apart from their managing director, all of those around the table were at least ten years younger than himself and dressed as though they were following a strict company code of attire—in razor-creased shirts, muted silk ties and brightly coloured gold-slided braces. He became acutely conscious of the fact that his own dark grey worsted suit looked old and dull, not only standing out in stark contrast against the vibrance of his companions' dress, but also perfectly reflecting the way that he felt within.

As Deakin sat, everyone around the table immediately followed his lead. David moved quickly to his own chair, realizing that he was in danger of getting completely out of step with the meeting. God, he thought to himself, what am I doing here? I should be in bed. Anyway, this was destined to be a mistake. I should never have agreed to come out here in the first place. His head pounded mercilessly, perspiration soaked the back of his shirt, and he became aware that his cheeks were shivering uncontrollably. He leaned forward in his chair, thinking that he should try to offer some explanation for his being late, but as he opened his mouth to speak, Deakin cut in.

"I'm afraid that we'll have to press on, David, as some of the guys have other meetings scheduled for mid-day. Alex here"—he held out his upturned palm in the direction of the young man beside him, who leaped to his feet and went to stand by the flip-chart in the corner of the room—"will be carrying out the presentation, and will introduce you to each of my colleagues in turn as he explains their individual involvement in the marketing and distribution strategy that we have laid out for Glendurnich." He opened the presentation document in front of him. "So, gentlemen, if you will all turn to page one, I'll hand over to Alex."

Deakin swung his chair round to face Alex, and there was a sound of acetate scraping against paper as the men opened their files. David, trying to keep up with proceedings, leaned over the side of his chair, picked up his brief-case and opened it up. The document was not on the top. It must be below the pad of paper. It wasn't there. He slid his hand to the bottom of the pile of papers and flicked his thumb through them. Nothing. He pulled open the flaps on the lid of the brief-case and stuck his hand down inside, but they were empty. A cold, terrifying sense of realization overcame him as his frowning concentration began to clear away hazy memories of the night before, and he remembered that he had taken it out to read in bed. Oh, no, he'd never put it back! It was still on his bed.

Alex, who had started the presentation, halted when he noticed David still scrambling inside his brief-case and stood looking in his direction, turning his black marker over and over and tapping its end impatiently on the palm of his hand. Charles Deakin, following the eye-line of his young colleague, swung round in his chair and looked down the table towards David. There was silence. David glanced up and saw that everyone was looking at him.

"Are you all right, David?" Charles Deakin asked.

David pushed his fingers through his hair and scratched at the back of his head. "Erm, I'm sorry—no—I don't seem to have the paperwork. I think I've left it behind."

"Not in Scotland, I hope!" Charles Deakin said with a chuckle, and his colleagues once more dutifully joined him in his amusement.

"No!" David said, a little too loud, thinking that he had to defend what little credibility he had left with the assembled company. "I mean, no, I've left it in my bedroom where I'm staying."

Charles Deakin nodded and smiled down the table at him. "No problem," he said slowly, as if he were about to explain a point to a classful of primary-school children. "If you would like to take Jack's copy and Jack, you share with Curtis."

Jack slid the document down the table, and David smiled an embarrassed thank-you at him. Deakin swung his chair back to face Alex. "Right! Let's get going."

Everything, from that moment on, came in a blur. Alex's voice sounded as if it were being played back through a slowed-down tape recorder, as the young man waarp-waarped his way through the presentation. He introduced each of the men in turn, and one by one they stood up, grinned in David's direction, and sat down again, their movements as slow and as fluid as the motions of weightless astronauts, without David's catching either their names or what roles they would be playing in the future marketing of Glendurnich in America. His mind drifted, a bizarre continuity in its train of thought. It started with his father, and how he had let him down so badly by making such a fool of himself at this meeting; then he thought of meeting his father in the boardroom at Glendurnich and how delighted he had been that he was to be staying with Richard; Richard, his friend, caught in a spiralling whirlpool of discontented unfulfilment with Angie, his wife; his own wife, Rachel, and the turmoil in his mind suddenly abated as he returned to Scotland with her, to long summer evenings down at the loch with their children, Rachel lying spread-eagled with laughter on the bank, while he, his jeans rolled up to his knees, waded into the loch to catch on camera the mad and uncoordinated antics of the children in the boat.

The last of the men around the table had sat down again, and the sudden break in activity penetrated his senses enough to make him realize that Charles Deakin was talking to him. He screwed up his eyes to clear his head.

"Sorry?"

Deakin repeated his question. "Are you married, David?"

"Yes."

"Great," the managing director continued immediately, "because we think that it would be opportune for your wife to accompany you on these PR trips. We Americans prize family tradit——"

"NO!" David yelled out.

Everyone sat back, startled at the sudden outburst. David clamped his hand over his mouth.

"I beg your pardon?" Deakin asked.

"No," David said, his voice choking. He had never said it before. No one had ever asked him that question. Everybody knew. "I'm sorry, I meant to say no—I'm not married."

There was a slight shifting of body weight in chairs, as the directors shot uncomprehending glances at one other.

"You're—not—married," Charles Deakin said slowly.

David looked along the table at him, feeling a tear suddenly trickle down his cheek and onto his hand. He shook his head once in the direction of them all, then, pushing out his chair, he jumped to his feet and, slamming his case shut, ran towards the door.

"You'll have to excuse me. I'm sorry, you'll have to excuse me."

He threw the door open and walked hurriedly along to the reception area. The girl smiled as he approached, then her face went expressionless as she saw the look on David's face. He strode past her without speaking, pushed open the glass doors, and left the offices of Deakin Distribution.

There was a stunned silence for thirty seconds following David's departure from the boardroom, broken only when Charles Deakin rose slowly from his chair. He cleared his throat.

"Well, gentlemen. I'm not quite sure what happened there." He turned and walked over to the window, the faces of his young executives following him as he went. He stuck his hands into the back of the waistband of his trousers and looked out at Manhattan. After a minute he returned to his place, gathered up his papers, and thumped their ends once on the desk.

"I think the best course of action would be for me to speak immediately with Duncan Caple at Glendurnich, and thereafter I'll circulate a memo to you all which will include the outcome of this meeting." He reached the door and turned round. "Thank you all for being in attendance." He pushed open the door and left the boardroom, leaving a crescendo of discussion behind him.

Tears welled up in David's eyes as he thumped at the elevator button with the palm of his hand. The panel showed lights on the fourth and twenty-third floors, but neither car seemed to be moving. He stood close to the door, his head bowed, willing one of them to reach the fifteenth floor before someone came out of the offices of Deakin Distribution to question him about his behaviour. A bell pinged once and the door farthest from him opened. He glanced in. It was empty, thank God. He dived into its haven of solitude, pressed the ground-floor button, and slumped back against the steel panelling. As the doors closed on him, he knew he was alone and, dropping his briefcase to the ground, he covered his face with his hands and broke into convulsive sobs, at the same time sliding down the panelling until he squatted on the floor.

Never before had he been so exposed to the reality of losing Rachel. Never before had he been so unable to control his emotions. But it seemed that, over the past twenty-four hours, fate had hit on a systematic plan to break down his defences, battering at his endurance, his emotions, his self-confidence, before delivering the final coup de grâce in the boardroom. It had worked. He felt no semblance of self-respect, no measure of ability, and now felt no inclination to suppress the one thing that he wanted to fill his thoughts with day and night—the memory of Rachel. He pulled his knees close to his chin and stared out in front of him, letting her name run through his mind over and over, like a jumping needle on a scratched record.

The doors clunked open on the third floor, and a black girl with a laden mail-cart held them back with one hand as she manoeuvred her vehicle in with the other. She looked down at David, leaned across to push the ground-floor button on the panel, and as the doors closed and the lift set off again, she squeezed herself back behind her trolley. She took a pack of chewing-gum out of her pocket, pulled a stick out with her teeth, undid its wrapper and pushed it into her mouth. She looked down at David again. "Hard day, huh?"

David continued to stare directly in front of him, his eyes vacant yet his mind focused on his thoughts. The girl shrugged her shoulders. "Never mind, friend," she said, looking up at the floor indicator just as the ground-floor light lit up. "By the looks of you, I don't think things could get much worse."

The doors opened and, with a hefty push, she rolled out her cart. David remained where he was, making no effort to move, not caring what happened to him and not really wishing to go anywhere else. He watched as the doors began to close on his solitude once more, but before they shut completely, a hand shot in and pushed them back. The girl leaned into the lift, her hand outstretched. "Come on, it'll do you no good goin' up and down the building all day. Just make you sick. Anyways, I might end up pushin' my cart in here again, and that'll only get me feelin' as depressed as you."

David looked up at her beaming face and slowly stretched up and took her hand. Effortlessly, she pulled him to his feet. "Let's go, friend," she said, guiding him out of the lift. "You'll feel better with some fresh air."

She walked him over to the doors of the building and took him outside onto the sidewalk. "You okay?" she asked, a concerned look on her face.

David looked at her and nodded, forcing a smile onto his face. He held up his hand in thanks and started to walk south down Madison, for no good reason other than that was the direction in which he was facing. The girl watched him for a moment, then, shaking her head, went back into the building.

He walked slowly, concentrating his sludged mind on moving one foot in front of the other, his legs feeling as if they were filled with a mixture of cement and jelly, the combined effect making him weave like a drunkard from side to side. He started to cross over Forty-fifth Street without noticing the signal and a cab screeched to a halt inches from his right hip. The driver slammed his hand on the horn and yelled something at him out of the window. He ran the remainder of the way to the sidewalk, finding that even that small amount of exertion had left him feeling exhausted, and leaned his back against the spindly trunk of a street-side tree, its thin branches waving in the blustering breeze that whirled through the shadowed streets. Despite the warmth in the air, he felt freezing cold, and with one hand pulled together his suit jacket and fastened the buttons. He tilted back his head to see at what point the skyscrapers ceased to cast their shadows onto the streets below, then continued his gaze on upwards until he was looking directly above into the unshielded warmth of the deep blue sky. Little things, he thought to himself, little things please little bloody minds.

He pushed himself off the tree and continued to walk aimlessly down Madison Avenue, on collision course with the side-stepping masses that approached him. Fifteen minutes later he had reached the block between Thirty-first and Thirty-second Street and stopped outside the open door of a pub, its glass window bearing the name FLANAGAN'S in gold crescent-shaped lettering. He looked in at the long bar, stretching thirty feet back into the depths of the building, every inch of it occupied by early lunch-time drinkers, and after a moment he entered and began to sidle his way through the crowd to the far end. A young barman in a white shirt and green bow-tie caught his eye and came down towards him, running a cloth over the bar as he walked. "What can I get you, sor?" he asked in a strong Irish brogue.

David looked around to see what others were drinking. The young suit next to him was drinking Budweiser from the neck. "Budweiser."

"Would that be bottle or tap?"

"Tap—and I'll have a Scotch malt as well."

The bartender held the beer glass under the gurgling tap. "Any particular brand?"

"I don't suppose you have Glendurnich?" he asked, almost sarcastically.

The barman looked over his shoulder at the mirrored display shelf half-way up the bar, then, leaving the beer-tap running, hurried his way up to check his stock, expertly judging his return just as the beer had begun to trickle over the top of the glass. He flicked off the tap. " 'Fraid not. Only Glenlivet and Glenmorangie."

David grunted derisively at himself. Stupid question. There it was, the proof of the pudding. That's why he was bloody well meant to be here, to get Glendurnich onto the shelves alongside its competitors.

"Would you be wantin' one then, sor?"

David let out a long sigh. "One of each."

As the bartender headed off to pour him the whisky, the young suit next to David vacated his bar-stool. Taking a huge mouthful of beer, he pulled the stool towards him with his foot and sat down, ready to numb his pain with alcohol.

Two hours later he lurched out of the pub and stood unsteadily in the middle of the sidewalk, his befuddled brain trying to decipher the barman's garbled instructions on how to get to Penn Station. More by good fortune than by better judgement, he had ended up only three blocks east of his destination, but nevertheless it took him thirty minutes of concentrated staggering before he found the station in his inebriated state.

The place was bustling with people even though it was only two-fifteen in the afternoon, and David, keeping close to the wall in fear of bumping into someone and losing his balance completely, skirted round the terminal until he saw the ticket office. He walked up to a vacant window and slumped forward, resting his arms on the shelf, his head only inches away from the glass partition. "One way to Patchogue."

The clerk pressed a button on his machine and shot out a ticket into the steel recess in front of David. "Eight-fifty."

Steadying himself against the window, David pulled his wallet out of his pocket, took out a ten-dollar bill and slid it into the recess. "Could you please tell me when the next train is?" he asked, trying not to slur his speech.

The ticket salesman looked at his timetable. "Two twenty-seven to Babylon, track seventeen. Change at Jamaica for Patchogue."

"Thank you," David said, this time hearing himself sound as if he had a severe speech impediment.

By the time he reached track 17, the train was already waiting. He clambered into the first car and sat down opposite a minute wizened albino man who wore a pair of blue-tinted spectacles and whose white hair poked through the plastic mesh of his red-and-blue baseball cap. He seemed to be working simultaneously on two crosswords, obviously photocopied from newspapers onto one piece of paper. David blinked at this near-surrealistic encounter, thinking that his imagination had become distorted with drink. But the little man was definitely there, checking the clues on each of his crosswords in turn and scribbling down the answers without once stopping to ponder the questions.

The train took off with a jolt and slid away from the platform, picking up speed as it entered into a pitch-black tunnel. David shut his eyes and tried to concentrate on synchronizing the natural swaying of his body with the movement of the train, but it made him feel sick, so he laid his head back against the seat and focused on an AIDS-Helpline poster that was stuck on one of the partition windows. With that, the train shot out of the tunnel and into Queens, the sun suddenly bursting so brightly through the window of the car that he had to put up his hand to shield his eyes. He tried shutting them again, but once again was overcome with nausea. He leaned forward, resting his elbows on his knees, and placed his hands over his face, finding it a bearable compromise—being able to cut out the glare, yet maintain his equilibrium by squinting through the gaps in his fingers at the chalk-faced dwarf opposite him. He remained in that position until the train conductor's voice crackled over the intercom.

"Jamaica. Change for Patchogue."

As the train drew into the station, about half the passengers rose from their seats. David grabbed his brief-case and followed, but once out on the platform he realized that he had no idea in which direction he was meant to go. He therefore tagged on to the larger of the groups as they made their way up and over the railway bridge.

It was the right decision, the Patchogue train pulling in just as he came down the staircase. Doors opened and a few passengers disembarked before the Penn crowd began to push their way in. David found a seat to himself in the corner, and for a moment wondered why others had chosen to squeeze themselves together so far from where he was sitting. His question was answered almost as soon as the train pulled out of the station by the sound of a flushing toilet from the door opposite him, followed by the sour, overpowering smell of urine. He put his hand across his mouth and nose to stop himself from gagging and turned to see the whole partition of the lavatory swing back and forth on its loose brackets as someone inside wrestled with the door handle. It eventually flew open and a gaunt middle-aged man appeared, dressed in a pair of coveralls and clutching a plastic bag in one hand and a can of beer in the other. He crossed over and sat down opposite David.

"Fuckin' lock's busted," he said, gesticulating with the side of his head towards the lavatory and taking an almost dainty sip of beer from his can.

David silently nodded and looked around, hoping that if he didn't make eye contact with his travelling companion he would be spared further revelations about his visit to the lavatory.

In comparison to this train, David realized that he hadn't quite appreciated just how clean the previous one had been. The imitation leather seats had at one time been two-toned, but now their fading colours were indistinguishable under years of grease-stains, and the windows were so smeared with engrained dirt that it was difficult to see out. He looked down at the floor and noticed a suspect trickle of liquid, originating at the rest-room door, which wound its way down the central passageway, its meandering course governed by the constant side-to-side swing of the train.

His travelling companion tilted back his head to catch the last drops of beer in the can and placed it neatly on the floor at his feet. Then, putting his hand in his plastic bag, he took out a second can, flicked open the ring-pull, and took another dainty sip. David thought about moving, but then simply shut his eyes and leaned his head against the hard metallic edge of the aluminium windowsill. He felt the feeling of nausea spread over him once more, this time made more acute by the smell coming from the lavatory. Why the hell should he move? This was exactly where he was meant to be, stuck in the corner of this filthy, seedy train with his chain-drinking companion, two losers together, the perfect theatrical scene for his own complete self-degradation.

He clenched his teeth and screwed up his eyes in an attempt to stop himself from sliding over the edge of the emotional abyss, but this time there was nothing to hold him, every saving foothold of pride and self-esteem at which he had grasped so many times in the past having been chipped away by the events of the day. He felt the first of the tears force their way through his tightly closed eyes and run in parallel lines down the side of each cheek before falling, their sly, discreditable work finished, onto the lapel of his suit jacket.

It was some time before he noticed that the beer-drinker had quietly moved away from him to the opposite end of the car.

CHAPTER 13

Having only gone through the motions of working that morning, owing to his unabating hangover, Richard decided that he could be of no further use to Dammell's Bank that day and slipped discreetly out of the office at two-thirty. He knew that it would take his last ounce of fortitude to suffer the tedious train journey back out to Long Island. Two hours later, he pushed open the unlocked door of the kitchen—an indication that David was home—and, chucking his brief-case onto the table, went over to the sink to fill up the kettle. As he plugged it in, a slight movement on the sofa in the corner of the room made him turn around abruptly.

"David? Jesus, what a fright you gave me!" He walked over to the sofa. "What the hell . . . ?"

He knew something was wrong immediately. David lay, his back turned towards him, making no move to acknowledge his arrival. He clutched a cushion tightly in his arms and his legs were drawn up into his stomach. Richard leaned across him and looked down on his ashen-white face. His eyes, swollen from crying, focused blankly into the fabric of the sofa.

"David," he said quietly, "what's up, old boy? Christ, you look all in."

David swung his legs round and sat up and rubbed hard at his eyes with his fingers. "Sorry, Richard. I'm so sorry."

"For what?"

David shook his head. "I don't know. Just being here. I shouldn't be."

Richard sat down next to him. "Christ, of course you should be here. What do you mean?" He bit hard on his lip, not understanding quite what had happened. "What is it, David? Is it . . . Rachel?"

David fixed his gaze out the window and slowly nodded.

Richard put a hand on his friend's shoulder. "Christ, David, I really am so sorry." He glanced around the room as if trying to search out an answer to David's problem. "Would you like a whisky or something?"

David shook his head. "No, I've already had a skinful." He pushed himself to his feet. "Listen, if you don't mind, I think I'll just get out of your way and go to bed. I'm not feeling too good."

Richard jumped up. "Yeah, of course. Do you want me to get a doctor or anything like that?"

David shook his head. "No, I just need to sleep." He walked to the door and turned round. "I'm sorry, Richard."

"Look, you really don't have to apologize, my friend. Just go to bed and sleep as long as you want. I'll be leaving pretty early tomorrow morning, but . . . er . . . listen, I'll tell you what. Angie's sister, Carrie, lives here in Leesport. She's always popping in, so I'll get her to organize something for you to eat, okay?"

David shook his head. "You don't need to bother—really."

"It's no bother, old fellow. Carrie won't mind at all. You just get to bed—and sleep." He paused for a moment. "Listen, Angie's got some pretty lethal sleeping pills. Do you want one?"

"No. I'll be fine."

"Okay." Richard walked over and patted him on the back. "But try to clear your mind, David."

David smiled and let out a shuddering sigh. "I doubt I'll ever be able to do that again, Richard."

"Yeah," Richard said quietly, "I know."

He waited until he heard David's door close before letting out a long, relieved breath. He walked over to the kettle and made himself a cup of coffee, then leaned his back against the sideboard as he tried to work out what he should do.

Carrie. He should call her first. No, maybe not. He went across to the table and opened his brief-case and took out his telephone book. He flicked through it to the correct page, then, picking up the telephone, he dialled the number and stood scratching at his cheek while waiting for an answer.

With a hot-water bottle tucked under her arm, Effie had made it to the half-way stage on the staircase when she heard the sound of the car scrunching to a halt on the gravel outside the house. She stopped, a puzzled expression on her face, then turned and descended the staircase and went over to the door of the drawing-room, knocked and entered. Alicia Inchelvie glanced up from her book at her, then swung round to look at the clock on the mantelpiece.

"Effie? Have you not gone home yet? It's half past nine!"

"Not quite. I was just going to put a hot-water bottle in your bed before I went—but—well, I was wondering if you were expecting someone. It's just that I'm sure that I heard a car stop at the front door."

"No," Alicia replied, putting her book down on the side-table and heaving herself up from the chair. "I can't think who would be coming at this time. Let's go and have a look."

As she walked across the drawing-room, the sound of the front door opening made the three dogs jump up from their place by the fire. Barking furiously, they skidded their way past her and out into the hall, their claws scraping on the polished wooden floor as they developed wheel-spin in their eagerness to find out who had entered their house. Alicia glanced inquiringly at Effie, then together they followed the dogs out into the hallway.

Surrounded by bouncing and panting animals, George Inchelvie slowly took off the scarf from around his neck and hung it on one of the coat-hooks.

"Good boys. That's enough now." He looked up as his wife and the little housekeeper came out of the drawing-room.

"George!" Alicia exclaimed, a concerned expression on her face. "What on earth are you doing home? I thought that you were spending another night in Glasgow."

George took off his coat and laid it on the pew. "I was meant to be." He steadied himself on his stick before starting to walk across the hall towards them. "Duncan Caple telephoned me at the hotel at about five-thirty. He said that he'd been on the point of leaving the office for his European trip when he'd had a call from this new distributor fellow in New York. Anyway, I had a fairly intensive conversation with him for about half an hour, after which I decided that I didn't particularly feel like staying away for another night—so I just drove home."

Alicia watched him closely as he spoke. If the economy of his slurred words was not enough to register his exhaustion, the colourless features of his face, its shadowed lines accentuated by the dim lighting in the hall, gave her the strongest indication that her husband had just about used up every reserve of energy.

"What's happened, George?"

He hesitated before replying, and Effie, realizing that her presence was no longer required, backed away towards the staircase. "Right, well, I'll just away and put the hot-water bottle in your bed, Lady Inchelvie." She bustled off, then stopped and turned back. "Would you be wanting a wee something to eat, my lord? There's a bit of the stew left over in the fridge, which I could heat up, or maybe a cheese sandwich?"

George shook his head. "That's kind, Effie, but no, I'm quite all right." A glimmer of a wry smile crossed his tired face. "I think I'll probably just make do with a whisky."

Alicia moved towards him and took his arm. "Come on, let's go and sit in the drawing-room." In silence they walked together across the hallway and into the drawing-room, where George sat down heavily in one of the chairs, grimacing in pain as he did so. "Bloody back is bad at the minute," he said, his voice croaking. "Too much driving."

"Too much of everything, Geordie," Alicia said, looking down at him and shaking her head. "Now, I'll get you a whisky and you tell me what's happened."

She went over to the corner cabinet and took out a glass and a half-full bottle of Glendurnich.

"Has David telephoned?" George asked.

"No," Alicia replied, pouring out a double measure and replacing the cork in the bottle. "Were you expecting him to?"

For a moment, George looked at his wife as he gathered his thoughts. "I'm afraid that David's meeting in New York didn't go too well."

Alicia handed him the whisky, then sat down on the edge of her chair, resting her elbows on her knees and eyeing her husband intently. "What happened?"

"I'm not sure. David apparently walked out half-way through, much to the surprise of everyone present. At any rate, that's what Duncan told me." He took a drink from his glass. "Anyway, that's only half the problem."

Alicia did not speak, but waited for her husband to continue. He chewed pensively at the side of his mouth before resuming. "Duncan feels that David's mysterious behaviour at the meeting is proof enough that he needs a complete break from his job. He says that he cannot operate Glendurnich without a marketing director, and he wants to appoint a new one as soon as possible."

Alicia sat back in her chair and closed her eyes. This was it. The worst had happened. She had never thought that it would come to this. "What did you say to him?"

"What *could* I say?" George retorted almost defensively. "I mean, even though the company belongs to the family, I can't exercise my own nepotistic muscle if David is not up to fulfilling his role. I know it's not his fault, but I have to understand Duncan's position as well." He drained his glass and took in a deep breath to compose himself. "Anyway, that's what I was negotiating with him on the telephone. What has been agreed is that Duncan *will* appoint a new marketing director, but I have managed to limit it to a one-year contract for the time being, and hopefully by then David will have managed to get himself together. If, at the end of one year, there is no change to the situation, then the contract will be extended at Duncan's discretion."

There was complete silence in the room, except for the rhythmic thumping of one of the dogs scratching at its neck with its back paw, and the ticking of the clock on the mantelpiece.

"What is happening with our lives, Geordie?" Alicia said eventually in a quiet voice. "Everything seems to have gone haywire. I mean, we have never had so many worries as we do now, and here you are, having to work harder than ever before." She paused and sat back in her chair and began brushing her hair over the top of one ear with her fingers. "I was so hoping that this trip might be the turning point for David." She looked across at her husband. "I really could not bear it if we found ourselves back to stage one with him, because I can't see how either of us will cope."

George nodded slowly, as if in submission to what his wife was saying. "I know. It's not good, and I just wonder where on earth he is at the minu——"

The telephone trilled noisily on his desk, and Alicia pushed herself to her feet and walked across the room to answer it.

"Hullo, Inchelvie . . . yes . . . yes, of course, Richard, how are you? . . . Why, what's happened? . . . Oh, no . . . oh dear, this was something I always dreaded taking place . . . Flu as well! . . . Oh, my word! . . . Oh, Richard, I'm so sorry . . . Yes . . . yes . . . but can you cope with all that? . . . I see, but does Carrie have time to do that? . . . Right . . . well, that is most kind, Richard. . . . Yes, I think you're right. The sooner he gets back here, the better . . . on the Monday-evening flight? . . . Yes, that would be fine. I'll arrange for someone to meet him at Glasgow on Tuesday morning . . . of course, and many thanks for letting me know, Richard . . . bye."

She replaced the receiver, keeping her hand on it for a moment before turning back to her husband to answer his unfinished question.

Knowing that the reception for his car telephone was better on the A9, Duncan Caple waited until he was south of Aviemore before punching in one of the three autodial numbers he had for John Davenport, chairman of Kirkpatrick Holdings Plc. The hands-free speaker crackled out three ringing tones before being answered.

"Hullo?" a female voice replied.

"Could I speak to John, please?"

"Yes, one minute, please."

Duncan heard the receiver being clunked down on the table, followed by the female voice calling out John's name. There was the sound of footsteps, the receiver being picked up again, and a man's voice spoke. "Hullo?"

"John, it's Duncan Caple."

"Where are you, Duncan?"

"In the car. Sorry to call you at home, John, but I thought it better if we were both out of our respective offices."

"Good idea. How did you get on? Manage to get hold of that information?"

"Yup, and it's exactly as you thought. Glendurnich *did* set up a stock-purchase plan specifically for distillery employees about twenty-five years ago, I think actually at the instigation of Inchelvie himself. Quite forward-thinking of the old boy, but he's always been a great one for boosting work-force loyalty. Anyway, the way it works is that if an employee wants to take up the company share option, he or she contributes fifty per cent of its value and the company forks out for the rest. However, to protect shares going out of the company, it was written into the original plan agreement that if any employee left and wanted to realize the capital value of his Glendurnich shares, he had to resubmit them to a pool system to allow existing company employees the chance of purchasing them. If they were not taken up by them, the family would then step in to purchase them. I also found out something else quite interesting: In the past twenty-five years, the Glendurnich work-force has expanded by thirty, mostly all within the office, but surprisingly only eight have left across the board."

"Which means?"

"Which means that, at this moment in time the family's shareholding in Glendurnich is quite seriously eroded."

"By how much, Duncan?"

"Well, I've found it bloody difficult to find out anything without causing suspicion. For some reason, Robert McLeod, the financial director, has never shown it in the accounts, but from what I can gather, I'm pretty sure that thirty-one per cent of the Glendurnich shares are now in the hands of the work-force."

"Excellent! I mean, it's not a majority shareholding, but it's a real arm-twister as far as we're concerned. And you reckon that the family are unaware of this?"

"They may very well be, but I don't think that they have an iota as to what the possible implications might be. Anyway, they don't seem to know if they're coming or going at the minute. My idea of sending David Corstorphine out to the States seems to have killed two birds with one stone. I spoke with Charles Deakin in New York earlier this afternoon, and not only have we managed to engineer his company's appointment as the new distributor, but also David seems to have suffered some sort of breakdown during the meeting and ended up by storming out of the building."

"Not the kind of behaviour one would expect from the marketing director of a bespoke malt whisky company."

"Exactly. So I immediately called old Inchelvie in Glasgow to break the news to him, and told him that we needed a new marketing director in place immediately. I actually felt quite sorry for the old duffer."

"And?"

"He agreed to it on a one-year contract. So you can tell Giles Barker to get up here straight away. He's got a new job!"

"Well done, Duncan. So what have we got? Deakin in the States, Giles taking on marketing. What about Robert What's'isname, the financial director?"

"That's fixed too. Robert McLeod is off to run some golf course at the end of the month, so I've appointed Keith Archibald of Northern Maltsters as financial director."

"Brilliant. So we're just about ready to start the campaign. When do you think that you'll be ready to begin dangling the carrot in front of the work-force?"

"Not just yet, John. I reckon I'll have to do some pretty heavy spadework on the old man first. He's so damned protective of his son, and judging from Charles Deakin's description of his behaviour at the meeting in New York, I'm pretty sure that once David's back in this country, Inchelvie will have to come to terms with the fact quite quickly that neither of them is capable of running Glendurnich. At that point I'm sure he'll be more than willing to negotiate with us, especially if the work-force are on our side. That's how I read the situation anyway."

"So, what's your plan of action?"

"Well, I'll get together a sale proposal with the help of Giles and Keith over here, and Charles Deakin in the States, and once I feel the time is right to approach Inchelvie, I'll coincide it with circulating the proposal to all the worker shareholders. It's a two-pronged attack, but it is imperative that Inchelvie and the work-force come to the same decision at exactly the same time. That about sums it up. Timing is of the essence."

"Well, if you say so. But don't leave it too long. You know how important it is for Kirkpatrick to get hold of Glendurnich as soon as possible. It's the missing link."

"Yes, I know."

"All right then, and by the way, I have had words with the Kirkpatrick board, and they have agreed on your fee note of half a million pounds, but that obviously depends on the successful outcome of the deal. Nevertheless, you could let me know sometime whether you will be wanting that as a straight fee payment or whether you want a proportion paid in Glendurnich shares."

"Right, I will do."

"Okay—well, keep pushing it as hard as you can. I'll contact you in a week to see how things are progressing."

"No, don't do that. Let me contact you. It's just that the old battleaxe on the reception desk at Glendurnich is as fiercely loyal to the Inchelvies as any, and I'm just not too sure how confidential telephone calls are when they pass through her switchboard."

"Maybe a replacement is in order, then, Duncan?"

"Maybe. In time. Trust me, I'll play it right. There's too much at stake here."

Duncan pressed the "end" button on the telephone and sat back in the BMW's plush leather driving seat, a smile of deep satisfaction on his face. Then, letting out a loud whoop of elation, he slammed both hands down on the steering wheel and pressed the accelerator to the floor, letting the powerful machine blast its way down the empty road, only easing back on the throttle when it had peaked at exactly twice the sixty-miles-per-hour speed limit.

CHAPTER 14

Although his influenza bug had virtually burned itself out within the first twenty-four hours, David felt no desire to leave the haven of his room during the next few days. Time became an unimportant entity in his existence, and the hours were only registered by the sound of Carrie who, at his own request, would simply leave a tray of food or a cup of tea outside his door, without venturing into his room. Through his window, light gave way to darkness, then back to light, but he never attempted to coincide any form of living pattern with it. He tried to sleep as much as possible, desperate to break away from the repetitive thought process that constantly gnawed at his mind, but much of the time he found himself lying awake on the bed or pacing the floor into the early hours of the morning.

Since Wednesday, he had left his room only to use the lavatory, returning immediately so that he might avoid coming into contact with either Carrie or Richard. All pride in his own personal appearance had become as unnecessary as any form of daily routine, and he now constantly scratched at his face, which itched with two days' worth of stubble. Yet obtusely, it satisfied his frame of mind, accentuating his self-induced penance and in harmony with his own deep lack of self-respect. Self, self. That was all it was now. Self-respect, self-disgust. In the past, to think constantly of Rachel had been acceptable to him, but somehow everything had become distorted, and his thoughts now were only of himself—no, probably *for* himself, his mind relentlessly churning over and over a catechism of words that helped to prove just how miserable and hopeless a human being he had become.

That evening, as he had done countless times before, he rose slowly from the unmade bed and walked over to the shelf and leaned his hands on its rough surface, his head, feeling like a leaden weight, drooping so that his chin rested on his chest.

Christ, what was it? What the hell was it? He had been all right when he came over from Scotland, and then somehow everything had gone wrong. Why? He had to try to reason it out. He pushed himself away from the shelf and continued to pace the floor, then stopped abruptly at the window, his actions frozen as he looked out at the darkening day, the merest splinter of enlightened thought breaking through the throbbing dullness in his brain.

That's it. You *were* all right when you came over from Scotland. You had felt quite happy being one of the crowd in the airport, because no one knew you, no one cared about you, no one had any idea of your past, present or future. You were a carefree nonentity. But that all changed the moment you walked into this house, because Richard *knew*. It's not just that you screwed everything up over here. You're frightened, aren't you? Frightened of your own identity, frightened to go back to Scotland, frightened to re-enter that tight claustrophobic environment where everyone knows you and everyone cares about you, and everyone looks at you with sad eyes, and talks about you in low whispers.

He walked over to the bed and fell back on it, gazing up to the ceiling. Keep thinking—that's it—keep thinking. What the hell *do* you want, David?

"I want to be—*alone*!" he said out loud, "just—*unknown*! I don't particularly want to be—David—fucking—Corstorphine—any bloody more!"

He turned over on his side and clutched his knees up to his chest. Free from responsibility, free from identity. It sounded like the song of a protest march. He snorted out a weak laugh and shook his head, the action amplifying in his ear the scraping sound of his stubble against the pillow. It was an impossibility, he knew that, but at least it was something on which he could concentrate his mind, something on which he was quite happy to expand his thoughts. He closed his eyes, and for the first time in two days the tightness in his head slowly abated.

He was awakened the next morning by a burst of sunlight shining through the window and onto his face. Blinking, he turned his head towards the door to avoid the brightness, and in his drowsy state suddenly became aware of an overpowering smell. He opened his eyes and found that he was lying with his hands linked above his head, his nose resting about six inches from his armpit.

"Bloody hell!"

He pushed himself up from the bed too quickly, and for a moment weaved unsteadily about in the centre of the room while his headspin subsided. He pulled off his T-shirt and forcefully discarded it onto the shelf, knocking over a small vanity mirror onto the floor in the process. He froze momentarily and stared down at it, wondering whether he had just condemned himself to a further seven years of bad luck. Slowly, he bent down and picked it up. It was unbroken. With a sigh of relief, he replaced it carefully on the shelf, and in doing so caught a fleeting glimpse of his new self. He held it up close to his face. His hair stuck up in punkish peaks from his head; his face, under its dirty cover of stubble, was pale and drawn, and the dark brown rings that surrounded his eyes seemed to sink them back into the depths of his skull. What did he look like? What single word could possibly describe this disgusting apparition?

A slug.

That was it. He was a slug—hiding away under its stupid, bloody stone.

The deep anger that suddenly built up within him seemed to trigger off a defence mechanism in his brain. That's it—no more. He glanced at his watch. It was seven-thirty. Right, you stupid prick, time to get your act together.

He grabbed a towel, picked up his sponge-bag and and walked out across the landing. He stopped. The door to Richard's room was still closed and he could hear him quietly snoring from within. He scratched at his head. God, what day was it? Richard must either be working from home that day or it was Saturday. In either case, he didn't want to be seen in his present state. He tiptoed into the bathroom and turned on the shower.

At first the water was cold, but it suited him, invigorating his mood as he scrubbed hard at his body with the sweet-smelling soap. Then, as the stream of water began to heat up, he poured out a dollop of shampoo and gave his hair the same purging treatment, repeating both operations before turning off the shower and stepping out of the bath, clean and renewed in body, if not in mind.

Five minutes and one and a half disposable razors later, he had rid himself of his stubble, finishing off by splashing stinging handfuls of after-shave onto the uncustomary softness of his face. Lastly, he gave his armpits an extra-long spray of deodorant before gathering up his belongings and heading back across the landing.

His room smelt so dank and airless when he returned to it that he immediately opened the window as wide as it would go, instantly feeling the warmth of the early-morning sun on his bare chest. He took a clean pair of jeans, shirt and boxer shorts from his suitcase and, having dressed, sat back on his bed and looked around. He didn't want to be there any longer. Its atmosphere had become too oppressive, too reminiscent of depression. He wanted to get away from it. In fact, right away from the house, away from where he was known.

He jumped up, galvanized into action by this thought. Picking up his wallet from the shelf, he put on a pair of boating shoes, then opened the door and quietly made his way downstairs and into the kitchen. He unsnibbed the French doors and let himself out onto the deck, carefully closing the door behind him.

He stood for a moment gulping in deep, reviving breaths of the fresh warm air before taking the wooden steps two at a time and walking down the driveway. He stopped at the bottom, looked up and down the street, then, with a decisive nod, turned right towards the main street.

The slug had made it.

It was too early for any of the shops to be open, so he strolled along the sidewalk looking in the windows at the goods on display. There were already a number of people about, walking dogs or carrying newspapers under their arms, and many of those who passed him smiled and said "Good morning." He reciprocated the greeting, each time feeling his spirits lift more.

Half-way along the main street, David came across the highest concentration of people outside the Leesport Deli. Men dressed in shorts and T-shirts leaned against large pick-up trucks parked at the side of the road, discussing their forthcoming day's work over bulging rolls and huge Styrofoam cupfuls of steaming coffee. The sight and the smell suddenly made David feel ravenously hungry, so he entered and joined on the back of the queue at the far end of the shop, filling in time until it was his turn by studying the menu on the long pegboard that hung above the counter. A continuous banter went on between those in the queue and the three young men in white aprons that served behind the counter.

"Who's next?" one of the young men called out, wiping his hands on his apron.

Already waiting for their order, those in front of David stood aside to allow him through to the counter. "How can I help you?" the young man asked, smiling at David.

David looked up at the list above his head. "Can I have an egg-and-bacon roll, please?"

"Okay, coming up."

The deli-man turned and bumped into one of his colleagues. "Lose some weight, Joe!" He let out a raucous laugh and ducked as Joe swung a mock punch at his head. He turned back to David. "How would you like your egg?"

"Er, fried please," David replied.

A ripple of laughter spread around the deli. The young man grinned at David.

"They all come fried, sir. That's about all we know how to treat an egg. Do you want it sunny side up or easy over?"

David smiled, embarrassed. "Er—sunny side up will do me fine."

The young man went off whistling and clattered some pans out of sight behind the freezer display before returning to the counter. "Anything else?"

"Yes, a large black coffee."

The young man worked like a trained cocktail barman, taking a Styrofoam cup from the dispenser and spinning it once in the air before pouring in coffee from a Cona pot. He snapped on a lid and, flicking open a brown paper bag, placed the cup carefully inside, just as a young, spotty-faced youth appeared from behind the freezer display, holding the roll wrapped in white greaseproof paper.

"Egg-and-bacon roll?"

"That's mine." The deli-man snatched it from the minion's hand and placed it in the paper bag alongside the coffee.

"Right, that's three-eighty."

David took his wallet from his back pocket and handed over a five-dollar bill. The young man rang it up on the till and gave him his change. "A dollar-twenty change. Enjoy, and have a nice day!"

"Thanks," David said, his face breaking into a smile at the all-American cliché. "I think I might just do that."

"Next?" the young man called out.

David turned away from the counter as the next customer moved forward to fill his place. He stopped and turned back to the young man. "I wonder if you could tell me how to get to the harbour?"

"Do you mean the marina?"

"Yeah, sorry, the marina."

"Turn right out of here, take the first on the right—that's Pearl Street—and just keep walking. If you walk about three hundred and fifty yards, you'll get your feet wet, so stop at about three hundred."

"Thanks," David said, grinning at the young comic.

"No problem," he said, and turned to the old man who had taken David's place. "Okay gramps, what's it to be today?"

David walked out of the deli into the sunlight with a smile on his face, his whole being lightened by the exchange. He decided not to indulge himself in the contents of his bag until he had reached the marina, so he took off at a brisk pace, following the young man's directions.

Pearl Street was like any other that he had seen in Leesport, a wide thoroughfare with secluded houses tucked away in their own grounds, separated from the sidewalk by fences. The road was crisscrossed with smaller streets leading off to rows of similar dwellings, yet, as he walked, he realized that the village was not in any way overbuilt, every so often coming across a grassed area on which there might be room for at least three more houses, this lending a healthy and clean openness to the surroundings.

The street eventually came to an end, opening out into a broad expanse of tarmac that led into the marina. David approached the small gatehouse at the entrance, and the old man who occupied it threw a cursory glance in his direction before looking away again. As there was no one else about, and heartened by the open friendliness shown towards him by the people in the deli, David decided to break the ice and engage the old man in conversation.

"Good morning." He stood purposefully beside the man's window, holding his paper bag in one hand and shielding his eyes from the glare of the sun with the other as he looked out over the marina. "Lovely day."

The man looked up and cocked his head to the side. "Sure is." With that, he leaned forward to turn up the volume of a television that was hidden below the wide ledge of the window.

David felt his face prickle with embarrassment at this blatant shun, but was immediately overcome with a devilish urge to persevere with the conversation, a reaction that was as much a surprise to himself as it was to be of a further nuisance to the old man.

"Is that the Atlantic over there?" he asked, a light-hearted innocence to his voice as he stared out across the marina. "Seems very calm."

The old man rose begrudgingly from his seat, realizing that he would have to respond before being left in peace again and, leaning out of his little window, jabbed a finger in the direction of the water. "That ain't the Atlantic—that's the Great South Bay." The action of his finger now changed to an up-and-over motion. "Atlantic's further over, beyond Fire Island."

David looked out to the long strip of land that lay about four miles across the bay. "Can you get over there?"

"Ferry goes from the marina every half-hour."

The old man, feeling that he had said enough, turned away from the window and sat back down in front of his television, effectively terminating the conversation. David pulled a face at the nape of his bristly little neck to acknowledge his gracelessness and moved away from the gatehouse. He headed off parallel to the marina, alongside a small public garden secluded from the road by a hedge of wild dogrose which fell untamed over a heavy two-rail fence, as simply fashioned and as rustic as a nursery rhyme. Twenty yards farther on, the hedge formed an archway over an iron gate on which hung a small brass plaque bearing the inscription THE LEESPORT RESIDENTS MEMORIAL GARDEN. He pushed open the gate and walked in.

The lawns and flower-beds of the little garden were beautifully kept, laid out in circular sweeps around the centre-piece of a large concrete plinth on which an old grey naval howitzer perched, pointing its flaking barrel out towards the bay. Beside it, the Stars and Stripes fluttered in the sea breeze atop a tall white flagpole. David walked around the side of the gun to the far end of the garden and stood for a moment gazing into the brackish waters of the bay as they lapped lazily against the vertical wooden pilings that protected the garden from erosion. He stepped back and looked around for somewhere to sit and spied an old wooden bench tucked under the barrel of the gun. Taking the cup of coffee and roll out of the paper bag, he sat down to enjoy both his breakfast and the view across the marina. All was tranquillity that morning, save only for the plaintive scream of gulls overhead, and the sound of the steel hawser-lines clinking like cowbells against the masts of the swaying yachts drawn up tight against each other along the wooden walkways that divided off the moorings.

This is perfect, he thought to himself, this is bloody perfect.

He didn't particularly want to move from the garden, but glancing at his watch, he was surprised to find that he had been sitting there for over an hour and a half, and realized that he should be heading back to the house to see Richard. He jumped to his feet, throwing his breakfast wrappings into the litter-bin beside the bench and, making his way across to the gate and out into the street, he waved heartily as he passed his grumpy friend in the gatehouse before starting back up Pearl Street.

The main street of Leesport was now filled with cars and bicycles, the sidewalks bustling with shoppers. As he weaved his way through them, David had the thought that he should buy Carrie a small token for her kindness in feeding "the invisible man" over the past few days. He caught sight of a flower shop on the opposite side of the street, and quickly crossing over the road, he entered in.

Half a minute later he reappeared, clutching a huge bunch of carnations in his arms while at the same time attempting to stuff the change from his purchase into his wallet. He took a couple of paces and half a dozen coins fell from his hand and clinked onto the sidewalk, rolling off in different directions. Swearing quietly to himself, he bent down to pick them up.

The last to be retrieved was a quarter which had rolled into the edge of the sidewalk, nestling under a flower-box attached to the wall of the next-door shop. Having recovered it, he straightened up to find himself facing a window display board covered with small white cards. He glanced up at the name. It was Helping Hands, the small employment agency that he had seen on arrival in Leesport.

As he turned to walk away, his eyes swept with casual interest across the job cards on the notice-board. He stopped in his tracks. Something had registered. He took a pace back and bent down to read the card in the bottom left-hand corner.

TEMPORARY HANDYMAN REQUIRED
for general garden work
experience preferred but not necessary
apply within

He stood up slowly, his eyes transfixed on the card, then stepped back from the window, his mind whirring with thoughts and ideas. Then suddenly, reason took over and he shook his head derisively at such an impractical thought. He walked away from the shop, but almost immediately came to a halt once more, and a young woman, who had been pushing a pram along the sidewalk behind him, bumped it heavily into the backs of his legs.

"Oh, I'm so sorry," she said, holding up a hand in apology.

David jumped aside to clear her path. "No, it's me who should apologize," he said, smiling at her. "Just having a moment of indecision."

The young mother laughed. "Yep, I just had one of those in the supermarket, but I put it down to post-natal syndrome."

David raised his eyebrows. "Yeah, well, I'm afraid I don't think that I could use that excuse."

The young woman pulled down the corners of her mouth and looked at him out of the side of her eyes in mock contemplation of this suggestion. "No—maybe not. But hey, I just thought, well, it's a beautiful day, why not go for it!—you should maybe do the same!"

Beaming a smile at him, she gave the pram a hefty push and continued on her way. For a moment David remained where he was, watching after her. She was right, he thought to himself, what the hell, and, turning briskly on his heel, he headed back to the shop and pushed open the door.

Although the office was only sparsely furnished with a sofa and coffee-table, two desks and a filing cabinet, David was immediately struck by the way in which it had been decorated, the soft pink of the walls picked out in the patterned loose covers of the sofa and in part of the zig-zag design of the fitted-carpet. One of the desks was occupied by a young girl, a pair of huge round spectacles balanced precariously on the end of her snub nose, whose fingers moved like lightning across the keyboard of her computer. At the other sat a large smooth-faced man of about sixty dressed in a brightly coloured loose-fitting shirt, its collar turned up to protect his neck from the two heavy gold-link chains from which were suspended a pen and a pair of horn-rimmed spectacles. His thick grey hair was combed back across his head, held immaculately in place by glistening quantities of styling-gel. As David entered, they both looked round in his direction, and the man jumped lightly to his feet and came around his desk to greet him.

"Hi, I'm Clive Hanley," he said, holding out his hand to David. "Can I be of assistance?"

David shook his hand. "Well, er, it was only an inquiry, really, about one of the cards in your window?"

Clive smiled at him. "Certainly, of course. Now what would you be particularly interested in?"

"The handyman."

"Okay—so—you want a handyman, is that right?"

"No—I was wondering about getting a job myself."

Clive paused, furrowing his brow, and looked David up and down. "I see . . ."

"Maybe I should explain a bit," David said, realizing that the man seemed a little non-plussed by his request. "It's just that I'm just over here from Scotland staying—"

"Scotland!" Clive interjected with a flourish. "I *love* Scotland! It's just so . . . *barren*!"

David waited for him to continue with his eulogy, but that seemingly was all he had to say on the subject of Scotland.

"Yes, well," David continued, "as I was saying, I'm over here staying with friends, and—well, I'm just hanging about the house at the minute, getting under everybody's feet, so I came out for a walk and just happened to see your sign in the window. I do have some experience, and well, it does say temporary."

"Right, okay," Clive said slowly, nodding his head. "Let's think about this for a minute. How long do you expect to be over here? You see, I would really need at least a month's commitment before I can put you on my books, otherwise it's just not fair to my clients."

David bit at his lip for a moment before replying. "Yeah, that should be all right," he said, taking instant decisions on his future as he went along.

Clive clapped his hands together conclusively. "Well, let's take some details, shall we? Come and sit down on the sofa, and I'll go get a form from my desk. Would you like a cup of coffee?"

"No, thanks," David said, holding up a hand, "I've just had one."

While Clive rummaged around in the drawers of his desk, David walked over to the sofa and sat down, casting a look around the office once more. Clive noticed this as he approached him, form in hand and, plumping himself down on the sofa next to him, he joined David in his appraisal of the décor.

"Not what one would expect of an employment agency, is it? I mean, I was quite happy with the yellow walls and green linoleum that were here already, but my friend insisted on doing the whole place up. He said that I couldn't possibly work in a place that didn't inspire me. Of course, I think he's done a wonderful job, but I sometimes wonder if it's not just a little bit like a beauty salon!"

With a laugh, he pushed himself forward to the front of the sofa and put the form on the coffee-table in front of him, then, placing his spectacles on the tip of his nose, he pulled his pen from its holder around his neck.

"Okay! Let's get started. Your name is?"

"David Corstorphine. C-o-r-s-t-o-r-p-h-i-n-e."

"And your address?"

David thought for a moment. "Uh, well, right at this very minute, it's Fifty-two North Harlens—but I think that I might be looking around for somewhere else to stay."

For a moment Clive held his pen above the paper while he contemplated this. "So, no problem." He started to write again. "How would it be if I just used this as your contact address, and if you do happen to move, you can always let me know."

"That's fine. Thanks."

"Okay—now, what's the next question? Ah, yes—are you married?"

David took in a deep breath. "No—no, I'm not. I'm not married." He exhaled with a sigh of relief. He had done it. The moment had passed.

"Now, what else?" Clive continued. "Ah yes—hobbies."

"I'm sorry?"

"Hobbies. Have you got any hobbies?"

Seeing that David was a little mystified by the question, Clive put down his pen on the table and leaned back in the sofa.

"I know that it might seem a little strange to ask a question like that, but it's just one of my eccentric little rules to try to learn as much as I can about a prospective employee. I just think that finding out about an individual's hobbies gives such a wonderful indication of his or her character." He pulled a face and placed both hands theatrically across his chest. "I mean, can you imagine how dreadful it would be if I ended up employing a serial killer!"

David smiled at the man, warming to his cosy antics. "Okay. Right. Hobbies. Well—I play tennis and a bit of golf—and I shoot."

Clive, who had resumed his writing, stopped, and looked slowly round to David, a startled expression on his face.

"No, sorry," David said, shaking his head, realizing that Clive had thought that his worst nightmare might have been fulfilled. "Forget that. It was rather a stupid thing to say. What else do I do?—Oh yes, right, I play the guitar rather badly."

"Classical, folk or pop?"

"What?"

"Sorry! My turn to be silly." Clive let out a short laugh and squeezed his hands self-consciously between his clenched knees. "It's just that I have been known to strum a little myself, though I'm far from contemporary. I'm really most partial to Peter, Paul and Mary, because they use such easy chord changes."

There was a moment of silence while he waited for David to make some sort of comment, but none was forthcoming.

"Anyway," he continued airily, bending forward once more over the questionnaire. "Let's get on with this. I think that's just about it." He gave it a final check-through, put his pen back in its holder, and jumped to his feet.

"There! So much for the formalities. Now let's go over and see what Dotti can come up with on her screen of wisdom."

David got up from the sofa and followed Clive over to the girl with the computer.

"Okay, Dotti," Clive said, leaning over the girl's shoulder. "As you are now no doubt aware, this is David."

The girl looked up at David, pushing her spectacles as far up onto her nose as possible with an index finger, and gave him a shy smile before returning to her screen. Clive put the completed questionnaire in front of her.

"These are his particulars, which you can enter later. Now we want to find David a job as a handyman, so let's bring up that file and see what we've got."

Dotti slid her mouse around the desk, clicking furiously. As the information came up, Clive scanned the screen while Dotti flicked down the list.

"We need to find something in this neck of the woods, don't we . . . okay. . . . Stop there, Dotti! That's it there! Newman." He turned to David. "They're new clients, David, I haven't yet supplied them with anyone." He turned back to the screen. "Where are they, Dotti?"

"Barker Lane," Dotti said.

"Yeah, that would be just perfect. Judging from the address, I reckon that their house would be somewhere down on the waterfront, along the marina? Do you want to give it a go?"

"Of course!" David said.

"Okay, Dotti, let's print out the address!"

Dotti set the printer whirring, and the Newman data sheet appeared on the print-out tray. Clive picked it up and handed it to David.

"Here you are, then. I'll phone Mrs. Newman and tell her that you'll be there first thing Monday morning, okay?"

David nodded.

"Now you'll need to know where the street is," Clive said, turning back towards his desk. "I have a map of Leesport somewhere . . ."

"No, honestly!" David said, stopping him in his tracks. "I haven't got much else to do over the next couple of days, so I'll just go and look for it myself."

"Well, if you're sure." He took hold of David's arm and guided him to the door, and as they passed the sofa, David bent down to pick up his bunch of flowers.

"Clive?" Dotti's sugary voice sounded out.

Clive turned to his assistant. "Yes, Dotti?"

"You haven't mentioned pay to David," she said quietly.

Clive brought both hands up to his cheeks and a look of horror lengthened his face. "Oh my God, what *must* you be thinking, David? I cannot imagine!" He began to walk back to his desk, but David put up his hand to stop him.

"Listen . . . erm . . . this may sound a bit strange . . . but I'm actually quite happy just to do the job . . . rather than get paid . . ."

Clive looked at him, not quite understanding what he was saying.

"You see," David elaborated further, "I only have a visitor's visa. I don't actually have a work permit. But I would really rather do the job and not get paid. I mean, I don't want to get you into any trouble."

Clive stroked at the side of his cheek with his hand and nodded slowly.

"Ah, so I get paid and you don't. Doesn't sound very fair to me." He turned to Dotti. "What do you think, Dotti? Any bright ideas?"

Dotti swung around in her chair, her nose wrinkled up to help secure her spectacles, her brow furrowed in thought. "Well," she said slowly. "I suppose what we could do is that if David does manage to find a place of his own, we could cover his expenses for food and rent. Then he would just be earning his board and lodgings."

Clive looked at David, a brighter look on his face. "How does that sound to you?"

"That sounds fine to me. I really don't need that much," David replied, relieved that the idea hadn't fallen foul at the last hurdle.

Clive looked over to his secretary, who was sitting with a huge grin on her face, seeing that her plan had been accepted. "You never cease to amaze me, Dotti," he said proudly. "You keep coming up with such wonderful ideas!" He ushered David to the door. "Now, give me a call on Monday evening and tell me how it went, and if you happen to have a new address by then, let me know."

David nodded and shook his hand. "I will—and thanks again."

As he headed off down the sidewalk, Clive remained standing at the window, watching him as he went.

"What a nice man," Dotti said, a smile in her voice.

"Yes, he is," Clive said slowly, "But quite a mystery, methinks."

Dotti got up from her desk and came over to stand beside him. Together they watched David's distancing figure. "What do you mean?"

"I don't really know." He turned from the window and walked back to his desk. "One could have quite easily taken him for a banker or some high-flying executive, but I don't know if you noticed his hands, Dotti. They're all calloused and as hard as leather. I mean, that man really has been a labourer." He sat down with a thump and let out a long sigh. "I hope we've made the right decision, Dotti. Do you think he's all right?"

"Yup, I think he's great," she said, making her way back to her own desk. "But I don't think he's Scottish, Clive. I mean, does he sound Scottish to you?"

CHAPTER

15

David took his time walking back to North Harlens, trying to work out in his mind whether his recent action was prompted by fateful inspiration or whether it was quite simply irrational stupidity. On a number of occasions, he stopped and thought about turning back there and then to cancel the job, as his mind churned through considerations of duties and responsibilities that he held for both his children and his parents. And then, on the other hand, if he did take the job, he would have to tell Richard of his plans fairly promptly, something made more difficult by the fact that his behaviour over the past few days could not have qualified him for The Perfect House Guest award. As he walked, he eventually came to the decision that it would be best not to say anything to anyone for the time being. He would go to the new job on Monday, and if it didn't work out, he would just pack up and return to Scotland mid-week, without anyone ever being the wiser.

But then, he really didn't want to go back just yet. No. Again that wasn't true at all. Of course he wanted to go back—he wanted to see the children more than anything, and he knew that he couldn't expect his father to fill in for him at Glendurnich for ever. Nevertheless, a return to Inchelvie at that very minute, with all its inherent connections with Rachel, would be a retrograde step, and even now, as he walked along the sidewalk, he felt his stomach knot tight with apprehension and foreboding at the thought of it. He was quite simply not ready for it, and he knew deep within himself that he *could* mend right here in Leesport, with its quiet, sunny surroundings, its gentle pace, and its friendly inhabitants who could take him at face value, without constantly having to make allowances in the way that they treated him.

That was, of course, everyone except Richard. Even though his friend could not have been more kind or understanding, he knew too much about him, and as such would always represent a link to his past and a threat to his anonymity in the future. If he were to stay, then he needed to get away entirely, to find a place or even just a room to rent to allow himself the space and time to get his mind straight again.

Having made a number of unnecessary detours in order to collect his thoughts, he arrived back at the house to find an old convertible Volkswagen Beetle parked haphazardly in the driveway. Its faded hood was folded down as far as the rusting support struts would allow, disclosing an interior that was littered with paint tubes and brushes, free-offer leaflets, chocolate-bar wrappers and empty Coca-Cola cans, while the steering wheel and gear-shift were freckled with tiny irregular twin grooves cut deep into the plastic, making it look as if both had been subjected to attack on numerous occasions by an inebriated rattlesnake.

As he skirted round the car, studying the assortments of dents and scratches that adorned its orange bodywork, a loud splash sounded out from Richard's swimming pool, followed by the manic barking of a small dog. He climbed the stairs to the deck and, walking over to the side rail, looked down onto the pool. A girl in a fluorescent yellow swimsuit was swimming lengths in a rapid overarm crawl, her long streaked-blonde hair flowing out across her back as her powerful strokes created a wake that washed against the side of the pool, soaking the orangy-brown miniature poodle who, barking incessantly, accompanied her length by length.

As she turned at the shallow end, the dog realized that it was caught up in a hopeless endeavour and sat down panting, continuing to watch her mistress through woolly eyes as she swam up to the deep end. David turned away to go into the house, but his movement was caught by the dog, and it came running round the edge of the pool and took up position at the bottom of the steps, squinting up at him and yapping furiously. Hearing the commotion, the girl, who by now had made it back to the shallow end, stopped swimming and stood up, wiping away the water from her face with the flat of her hands.

"Dodie! For goodness' sakes, be quiet!"

She blinked a couple of times to clear the sting of chlorine from her eyes, then, visoring them against the glare of the sun, she looked up at him. "Hi! You must be David. At last we meet! I'm Carrie."

"Oh, hi!" David replied, holding up his hand to acknowledge her greeting, a sign which the dog immediately took as a threatening gesture to its mistress, and resumed its high-pitched bark.

"DODIE!"

The dog turned and jumped up onto one of the sun-beds and sat there, scratching at its tight mat of untrimmed curls and yawning loudly.

"Sorry about the dog," Carrie said, sinking down into the pool and slowly breast-stroking the water away from her body. "She gets quite protective. Not that she could do much. She's only got two teeth!" She looked back up at him. "So, how're you feeling now?"

"Much better, thanks." He held up the bunch of flowers. "I bought these for you, just to, well, thank you for supplying me with all that food over the past couple of days—and to apologize for being so antisocial."

Carrie waved her hands in the air. "Oh, that is so *sweet* of you! God, you mustn't think anything of it! I just, well, feel so sorry—you know—for what happened to your wife. That was such a terrible thing."

David nodded and glanced down at his feet for a moment, before turning towards the house. "Listen, I'll go and put them in some water. Is Richard in?"

"I think so. I haven't been inside yet. I only just arrived before you and jumped straight in here, so I'm really not that sure. But hey, I'm only going to do another couple of lengths and then I'll be right in."

"Well, please don't hurry because of me."

"Okay!" Carrie said, and with a flourish of her hand she turned and duck-dived into the water and resumed her swim. Dodie, obviously feeling restored after her brief respite on the sun-bed, let out another of her high-pitched yelps and took up position once more at the side of the pool.

David had just finished putting the flowers into a jug of water on the draining-board when he heard the sound of Richard's footsteps on the upstairs landing.

"David?" he called out, as he came down the stairs.

"Yeah?"

He walked into the kitchen. "God, where the hell have you been? I was about to send out a search party."

"Sorry, I should have left a note. I decided on the spur to go out for a walk—see a bit of Leesport."

Richard smiled at him. "Good for you. So—how are you feeling?"

David nodded. "Better, thanks. Kicked off the flu, anyway."

"Right. And, er, how about, well, sort of in yourself?"

"Okay—I think."

"Good." They stood, an uneasy silence between them, the reservation of their male emotions making it difficult for either to know how to react to the other. The moment was broken by Carrie, who appeared through the French windows, rubbing her hair dry with a huge blue bathing-towel.

"Hi, Richard!" she said in a singsong voice. "What a nice friend you have! Look what he brought me!" She walked over to the jugful of carnations and took a deep inhalation of their sweet smell before turning back to David. "That really was the *nicest* thought!"

She was wearing a pink cheesecloth dress pulled over her wet swimsuit which made it cling to the contours of her slightly overweight body. Not a classically pretty girl, David thought, her nose was too pointed and her front teeth protruded a little. Nevertheless, she had an inexplicably attractive aura. Her skin was clear and unwrinkled, belying her age, which David reckoned as being not far off his own, her mouth seemed to be set in a permanent smile and her eyes sparkled with life.

However, all this ethereal beauty was more than offset by the appearance of her constant companion, Dodie. Seen close up, she looked as though someone, heavily under the influence of an hallucinatory substance, had set about her coat with a pair of curling tongs, so that she resembled more a discoloured old powder puff than a poodle. Only she didn't smell like one. Having jumped up onto the sofa, she now sat panting, looking directly at her mistress, and a doggie odour filled the room of which all except Carrie seemed to be aware.

"Jesus, Carrie," Richard said, wrinkling his nose up in disgust, "do we *have* to have Dodie inside? Can't you leave her in the car?"

"No, I can't," Carrie retorted, bending down to the dog. "Can I, Dodie-wodie? Last time I was cruel to you like that, you ate my steering wheel, didn't you, my little darling."

The dog responded by giving Carrie's face the once-over with its tongue.

"Jeez, Carrie, that is quite *revolting*! Her breath stinks!"

"Oh, well, you get used to it!" Carrie said light-heartedly as she straightened up. "Say, I'm kinda thirsty after that swim. Any chance of a beer?"

Richard glanced up at the wall clock. "Are you being serious? It's only eleven o'clock!"

"Well, it's Saturday, so there's nothing doing, and it's a beautiful day, and I want to get to know your friend."

Richard gave this a moment's contemplation before shrugging his shoulders and glancing at David. "She's right, of course. Always is." He made his way over to the refrigerator. "Three beers coming up then!"

They spent the rest of the day together by the pool, talking only when they felt like it and at odd intervals heading off into the house to bring out food and more beer. During the course of their intermittent conversation, David found out that Carrie was an artist whose itinerant lifestyle had, in her own words, resulted in her being "more successful at capturing scenes on canvas than men in matrimony." Yet there was not an ounce of bitterness or self-pity in the way that she said it. Both she and Dodie were free spirits, she said, living totally for themselves in their little house down by the marina.

That evening Carrie prepared a meal for them that was the complete antithesis to the inedible mess that David had had to endure on his first night in the house. They ate outside on the deck, the light of the setting sun bathing them in a warm red glow which seemed to match the spirit of the occasion. Carrie then succeeded in reducing both men to tears of laughter by recounting stories of her hippie days in San Francisco and her brief involvement with Hare Krishna.

"I was chucked out! I mean, I thought I was so *cool* at it! Then one day, I was out on the street and no one, I mean *no one* was interested in what I had to say about reaching the higher echelons of pure life enhancement, so, well, I had these big Doc Marten boots on, and I just sort of levelled a kick at this guy who was passing—and, er, I caught him between the legs. By mistake, I promise! I didn't mean to—sort of not, anyway!"

As night closed in around them, David sat back in his chair, a smile on his face, quite happy to allow the good-humoured, laid-back atmosphere flow over him, while Carrie continued to dominate the conversation, her scatty, disconnected monologues now directed towards giving a full account of her past painting trips abroad and the "true fulfilment" that each had brought her.

"Talking of which," she said, glancing at Richard, a sudden look of trepidation on her face, "do you have any idea when Angie's getting back?"

"Well, I spoke to her last night at your mother's and she thinks Wednesday. I hope to hell it is because I want to get this wretched conversion finished." He let out a deep sigh. "In her infinite wisdom, she decided to put off all further work until she returned."

"Uh-huh," Carrie replied absently.

"Why do you ask?"

"Well, it's just that, well, I'm heading off to Florence to paint for a couple of months, and she *did* say that she wouldn't mind looking after Dodie."

Richard groaned. "Oh, God, yes, she did mention that. I thought life was looking too good. When are you heading off?"

"Well, the flight's tomorrow evening."

"Oh, for heaven's sakes! What's going to happen to the dog between then and Wednesday?"

Carrie bit at her lip to stifle a laugh. "Well, I thought she could have just stayed—"

"Oh, not in the house, Carrie!"

"Why not?"

"Because she'll stink the place out! Anyway, I'm going to be at work all day, so there'll be no one to let her out. She'll just pee and shit everywhere!"

"She will not either! I've left her all day in the house. She just sleeps. I promise you, Richard, she has a constitution of a camel—or is it a hen? *Please,* Richard, all you'll have to do is let her out into the garden in the morning and when you come home in the evening." She paused and looked pleadingly at Richard. "It'll only be two and a half days."

Richard glanced a long-suffering look towards David, then took a long gulp from his wineglass. "Oh, what the hell! Okay, I'll agree to it on one condition."

"Which is?"

"That you give me full permission to attack her with a bottle of shampoo and some toothpaste every now and then!"

"Sssh!" Carrie held her index finger to her mouth and looked round through the fly-screen to where Dodie lay prostrate on the sofa in the kitchen. "Don't say it too loud or she'll hear." She turned back to Richard. "You can certainly try, but it never seems to make any difference!"

"Well, I'm going to give it a go, anyway." He tilted his head in the direction of the dog. "AREN'T I, DODIE?"

Dodie immediately lifted her head and pricked up her ears, then letting out one single bark, she flopped once more onto the sofa.

"Richard!" Carrie exclaimed in open-mouthed horror. "That is *so* cruel! You promise me you won't make her into a nervous wreck while I'm away."

"What is she now?" Richard laughed, then seeing his sister-in-law on the verge of rising to the bait, he leaned across the table and patted her arm in mock reassurance. "Don't worry, I'll look after her as if she was my own."

"Yeah, I bet!" Carrie gave him a distrustful look which she immediately managed to convert into one of sweet seduction. "Could you keep an eye on my house as well? Just when you're around, that is."

"Okay," Richard replied resignedly, leaning forward and pouring out more wine into their glasses.

"Thanks . . . and, Richard?"

Richard's face broke into a smile at the persistence of her requests. "Yes, Carrie?"

"There wouldn't be a chance," she said slowly, as if already expecting a negative answer to her question, "that you could get Star Limos to take me to the airport?"

"On my account, I suppose!" He laughed. "What time tomorrow?

"About four-fifteen?"

"Okay, I'll organize that," he said, leaning back in his chair. "Just a pity it's not Monday. You could have shared a car with David."

"Oh, are you going back to Scotland on Monday, David?" Carrie asked, and the sound of her voice resounded out loud and clear into the evening as a sudden profound silence descended upon the table. Her two dining partners eyed each other in turn, the smiles no longer on their faces.

Richard eventually cleared his throat and rubbed at his chin nervously. "I hope that's all right, David. I actually, er, spoke to your mother on Wednesday just to say that you weren't, well, quite up to scratch, one way and another, and I thought that you'd probably want to get back to Scotland as soon as possible. So I thought the Monday-evening flight would probably be the best one. Your mother said that there'd be someone to pick you up at Glasgow on Tues——"

He tailed off at the end of this explanation, realizing that David was not really listening to him. He leaned forward in his chair and rested his elbows on his knees, clasping his hands in front of him.

"Listen, my friend," Richard continued quietly, "I'd hate you to think that I'd gone behind your back. It's just that, well, I was actually quite worried about you, and I wasn't quite sure what I was meant to do."

David smiled and shook his head. "No, it's me that should be apologizing—not you. You've both been brilliant over the past few days, and I know that I haven't really shown you much appreciation for everything you've done." He shifted his weight on the chair, sticking his hands under his thighs. "It's just that . . ." He released one of his hands and scratched at the back of his head. ". . . Look, I have something to tell you which will no doubt come as a bit of surprise to you. I actually went into the little employment agency in Leesport this morning and lined up a job for myself as a gardener, and I'm, erm, starting Monday."

There was a complete silence, and David looked up to find both Richard and Carrie staring at him with looks of disbelief.

"But what about going home?" Richard asked eventually. "I mean back to Scotland?"

David let out a long breath. "To be quite honest, Richard, I . . . really . . . don't think . . . that I could face being back in Scotland just yet. I was walking around Leesport today, and I don't know quite what triggered it off, probably just the atmosphere of the place, but for the first time since Rachel died, I started to get everything into perspective, and I realized that heading back right now would just put me back to square one. I *know* that I have commitments, but well, I have a feeling that I've just reached rock bottom over the past couple of days, and I'm pretty sure that I'm on the way up again. So, in every way, I don't want to waste it—not only for myself but for my children and parents as well."

He took in a deep breath again before continuing.

"What you probably don't realize is that since Rachel became ill, I haven't been at work. I took time off to nurse her, and then, really as a form of, well, escapism, I suppose, I started to reinstate part of the gardens at my parents' house, and that's what I've been doing ever since . . . and I love it. I came over here on business because there was no one else in the company able to make the trip at that precise moment and . . . well, you know the rest of that story. Anyway, it was a complete fluke that I saw the job advertised today, and, as I said, I start on Monday."

David looked across to Richard and Carrie, who sat in silence, their sad eyes fixed on him. He let out a quiet laugh to try to break the gloomy atmosphere that he had created.

"I mean, I don't think that it'll be for very long," he said lightheartedly, "but it'll just give me time to get things in order, and I promise you, Richard, I won't burden either you or Angie with my presence. I'll get somewhere to stay as soon as I can."

"Hey!" Carrie suddenly exclaimed, making both Richard and David straighten in their chairs with surprise.

"Hey! Hey! Hey!" she said again, waving her hands in the air, looking as if she was trying to say something but couldn't work out how to put it.

"What's the matter, Carrie?" Richard asked, scowling at his sister-in-law for being so ebullient at a time when joyous reaction seemed totally inappropriate.

"It's obvious!" she said, jumping up from her chair and starting to dance around the deck in excitement. "David can stay in my house! That's it! He can stay in my house, and look after it. He can use my car, and well . . ." She stopped and grinned at the two men. ". . . Isn't that just a great idea?"

Richard raised his eyebrows and cocked his head to the side. "Well, it's an idea." He turned to David. "What do you think?"

David rocked forward in his chair, an excited look on his face. "Are you sure about that, Carrie?"

"Of *course* I'm sure!" Carrie said, resuming her dance around the deck. "Isn't it the greatest idea? You'd be doing us all a favour by looking after the place, because Richard wouldn't then have to be checking it out the whole time, and the battery wouldn't go dead on the car. Oh, it's great! I'm so pleased with myself!"

They broke out laughing at Carrie's flighty celebrations, and Richard reached for the bottle and began pouring out great splashes of wine into their glasses.

"Great thinking, Carrie!" he said, picking up his glass and raising it high in the air. "Well, I think we should all drink a toast to the newest resident of Leesport Village!"

Carrie sat down again and grabbed her glass, and all three clinked their glasses together at the centre of the table before taking huge mouthfuls of wine. Then, almost as if a huge black cloud had been lifted from their little gathering, they sat back in their chairs and breathed out huge sighs of relief.

"Well, it's all right for you, David," Richard said, turning to him. "You're all sorted out, but Angie and I are still going to be left to look after the dreaded Dodie!"

"Richard!" Carrie exclaimed, reaching over and hitting him on the arm, "you said you wouldn't be horrible to her. She's not the dreaded Dodie, anyway. She's the delightful Dodie!"

"All right, then, the delightful Dodie," Richard moaned, "but I still think we've got the rough deal!"

"Listen," David said, a pensive expression registering on his face, "if you want, *I* could quite easily look after the dog. In fact, the more I think about it, the more sense it makes. She'd probably be much happier at her own house, and anyway, she can quite easily come with me when I'm gardening. It really would be no problem, and I mean, I really like dogs. I've always had dogs."

He looked across at the others, expecting his offer to be accepted unconditionally, but was confronted by two very surprised faces, and for a moment he wondered if he had made completely the wrong suggestion.

"You don't mean that, do you, David?" Carrie asked quietly.

"Of course I mean it. I'd be quite happy to look after her—

anyway, for as long as I'm over here. She'd actually be doing *me* a favour by keeping me company!"

Carrie let out a yelp that wasn't unlike one of Dodie's and, jumping out of her chair, leaped towards him, engulfing his head in her arms.

"Oh, I think you're just the best!" she said, repeatedly kissing him on the top of the head. "Oh, how I cherish the day you walked into our lives!"

The ensuing commotion was loud enough to catch Dodie's attention. She let out one of her high-pitched barks and, jumping off the sofa, pushed her way through the screen door and locked her two teeth into one of the legs of David's jeans. Growling ferociously, she shook her head from side to side, as if determined to end the life of his Levi's.

"Come on, Carrie!" Richard laughed, suddenly feeling quite left out. "Give the guy a break! He's only said that he's going to look after Dodie!" He paused for a moment and looked down with little feeling of affection at the small, motley animal as it pulled hard on its quarry. Then he too slowly raised himself to his feet. "Actually, come to think of it, you're right! He's a bloody hero!"

With that, he threw himself forward to join Carrie in her adulation of "the saviour of the day," binding them both in tight with his arms, as if scrummaging down in a game of rugby. There was a loud crack as his extra weight was added to David's chair, and its legs slowly began to spread-eagle underneath him. With a crescendo of screams, the dissembled company pitched backwards and fell in a heap to the deck, allowing Dodie, amidst loud protestations and uncontrollable laughter, to have a field day in licking the faces of her incapacitated victims.

CHAPTER 16

Headaches were plentiful in the Eggar household the next day, the celebrations of the previous night having gone on well into the small hours of Sunday morning. Consequently, the plan to shift David and his belongings down to Carrie's house was delayed until the afternoon, a time when Richard felt he might be brave enough to venture out into the bright sunlight.

David, however, chose to clear his head by taking a walk midway through the morning, wanting at any rate to find out where he was meant to be working the following day. He made his way into Leesport, stopping to pick up a much-needed cup of black coffee at the deli, then, having asked directions to Barker Lane, he headed off in the opposite direction to the one he had taken the previous day.

Barker Lane was the last turning on the left before the Leesport Country Club, which lay just beyond the village boundary. He walked the full length of the road, eventually coming across the house in the bottom corner, opposite to where the road swung hard left through ninety degrees to run parallel to the bay, leading onto the marina half a mile away. The property was hidden completely from the road, the driveway descending in a bend through a screen of tall leafy birch-trees and high laurel bushes. For a moment, David stood at the head of the drive, spinning his empty Styrofoam cup around his finger while he considered taking a closer look. However, at that point a car came round the corner from the direction of the marina, and not wanting to give the appearance that he was loitering with intent, he decided to head back to North Harlens the way he had come, leaving his appraisal of the house until the next day.

Richard eventually managed to get his act together at four o'clock in the afternoon. Having bundled David's meagre belongings into the back of his car, they drove the four hundred yards down to Carrie's house, which happened to be situated right next to where he had eaten his breakfast the previous morning in the Leesport Memorial Garden. Both Carrie and Dodie were there to greet them at the gate, Carrie holding hard on to the end of a gushing hose, having been busy giving the plants one final watering before leaving. She opened the gate, then rushed away to the side of the house to turn off the tap. David took his two cases from the trunk of the car and followed Richard into the garden through the opening in the head-high, neatly clipped yew hedge.

If anyone wanted to look in on the property, the only unrestricted vantage point would have been from a boat positioned out on the Great South Bay. The easterly boundary was protected by a bank of high, waving pampas-grass that rustled and whispered in the warm afternoon breeze, while the dogrose hedge that ran around the periphery of the Memorial Garden encroached over onto the westerly side, spreading its weight across the collapsing picket fence that lay beneath it. Borders alive with flowering rhododendrons and azaleas, their heady scent brought out by the recent watering, skirted the lawn of springy zoysia grass which ran forward to the heavy wood pilings that jutted down into the waters of the bay. Still carrying his cases, David walked across the lawn to where it had been cut away into a steep gradient. Rough wooden steps had been sunk deep into the sandy soil to afford access to a small wooden jetty, where an old rowing-boat, its dark blue paint peeling away from its bows, nudged gently against its rubber-tyred mooring-post.

Richard and Carrie seemed to have disappeared inside by this time, so David made his way back across the lawn to seek them out. The house was nothing more than a tiny dark brown shingled shack tucked up into the farthest corner of the garden, next to the dogrose hedge. Yet it was far from shabby, its windows and shutters, downpipes and gutters all newly painted in brilliant white, its shingles giving off a strong aroma of newly applied creosote. The main entrance door was at the side of the house, while at its front, a screened veranda extended out from the French doors, its only furnishings two faded deck-chairs that were turned to face out over the waters of the Great South Bay.

There was a sudden scream from inside the house and Carrie appeared at the door lugging a huge suitcase and a folded-down painting easel, closely followed by Richard who, still suffering from his overindulgence of the night before, was making a half-hearted attempt to wrest some of the burden from his sister-in-law.

"Oh my God, David!" Carrie said, seeing him and dropping the suitcase heavily onto Richard's foot as he took it from her. "I've just realized what the time is! Star Limos will be at North Harlens right now, so I'm afraid I'm going to have to leave you to fend for yourself." She delved into the pocket of her dungarees and pulled out a set of keys. "Everything you need is on that. The saltbox, the car, and the little one is the key for the boat's outboard motor, which is in the sun-porch. By the way, there's a fax-cum-phone in the house which just use whenever you want."

Putting his cases on the ground, David took the bunch of keys from Carrie, giving her a puzzled look. "Right—and where might I find this saltbox, and what the hell do I use it for?"

Carrie flashed him a wide smile of enlightenment as she pointed towards the house. "You live in it, David! That's a saltbox, albeit a pretty small one. Don't ask me why they're called that. I don't know." She smiled and shrugged her shoulders. "I've never thought to ask." She turned and hurried towards the gate, against which Richard was now leaning, rubbing his sore foot.

"Oh my God!" she said, turning back to David, "I haven't said goodbye." She threw her arms around his neck and gave him a kiss on either cheek. "Look after yourself, David, and . . . well . . . start afresh—make this your new beginning."

David put his arms around her waist and gave her a long, tight hug. "Thanks, Carrie, I think I will."

Carrie pushed herself away and smiled up at him, her cheeks lightly flushed. "Wow! Go on squeezing me like that, and I may just decide to stick around," she said in a Mae West voice.

"Come on, Carrie," Richard called out.

"Coming!"

She turned and made her way out through the gate. Richard gingerly put weight on his foot and looked across to David. "Listen, you will telephone your mother, won't you? I feel slightly guilty about sticking my oar in on your business."

"You haven't at all—and I promise you I'll call her and explain what's happening."

Richard smiled at him. "You all right, old friend?"

"Couldn't be better."

"Well, if you need anything or want a swim in the pool, either give us a call or just come over."

"I will—and Richard—thanks for everything."

Richard waved his hand dismissively, then, holding both hands up in Al Jolson mode, he sang out, "That's what friends are for!"

There was yet another scream from outside the garden, and Carrie came rushing in once more.

"What the hell's wrong now?" Richard asked, exasperated.

"I haven't said goodbye to Dodie!" Carrie wailed. "You must have shut her in the house!"

Richard sighed impatiently. "Oh, come on, Carrie. Dan will get fed up waiting."

Carrie opened the door and Dodie appeared, jumping up and down in excitement. She scooped up the dog in her arms and planted a kiss on its head. "Bye, bye, my darling. You be good now, and look after David."

She bundled Dodie into David's arms and rushed out to where

Richard now waited for her in the car. David followed her through the gate and stood waving as the car turned with a squeal of tyres and headed up the road. As soon as it was out of sight, Dodie let out a wheak and tried to escape from David's clutches so that she could catch up with her mistress.

"Come on, dog," he said, getting a firmer hold on his charge, "you can show me round your house."

Dodie gave him a bewildered look and started to pant vigorously, an action which made David hurry back through the gate to release her from his grasp as quickly as possible into the safe confines of the garden.

The fact that Carrie treated her car as if it were a dustbin had no bearing on the way in which she organized her house. David stood in the doorway and looked around the small, lovingly furnished dwelling, warm with the sun that flooded in through the windows, each of them hung with red gingham curtains tied back with matching strips of ribbon. In the centre of the room, a round polished mahogany table, piled with magazines, sat between two armchairs with brightly coloured slipcovers, which faced a wood-burning stove whose blackened chimney stuck straight up through the roof.

To his left, on one side of the French doors, a high row of shelves, made out of bricks and planks, stretched up to the ceiling, each fully stocked with art books and paperback novels, while space had been made on its top shelf for an old turntable stereo system and Carrie's sizeable collection of records. On the other side of the doors, a roll-top desk lay open, its cubby-holes crammed with papers, while its leather writing surface was taken up completely with the telephone/fax machine.

To his right, lined against the back wall of the house, was the kitchen. Space for preparing a meal was minimal, but it still comprised all the necessities of a cooker, a fridge, and a sink. Above these, balanced precariously on nine-inch nails that had been driven into the wall, were four wooden storage shelves, their contents hidden behind curtains that matched those on the windows.

David dropped his cases to the floor and walked over to the heavy damask drapery that hung at the far end of the room. Behind this, he found a small double bed, which Carrie had sweetly made up for him with fresh linen, the corner having been turned down in a welcoming gesture over the top of the patchwork quilt. The only other furniture in the room was a pine chest of drawers, a bedside table with a lamp, and an up-ended packing case which served as a hanging closet. At the bottom of the bed, a door led off into a tiny bathroom into which was crammed a shower, a basin and a lavatory, the close proximity in the positioning of the latter two making David wonder whether the room hadn't been designed by, or even for, a minute contortionist.

He pulled open the drapery, hooking it back against the wall with the heavy sisal-rope loop, then, sitting down on the edge of the bed, he surveyed the whole scene in its entirety, noticing for the first time that every spare inch of hanging space on the walls was taken up with vibrant oil paintings: of beach scenes, of faces and figures, of streets, of exotic castles—all painted in the same distinctive style. He looked up at the one above his bed, and saw that it bore the signature "CL" in the bottom right-hand corner. They were all Carrie's work.

David grinned broadly to himself, then, falling back heavily on the bed, he gazed up at the ceiling, shaking his head in sheer contentment. This is perfect, he thought to himself, this is just perfect. He let out a chortle. Just a pity about the smell. The smile vanished from his face. Oh, Christ, the dog! Where the hell was she? He jumped to his feet and ran towards the door, hurdling over his suitcases on the way. He flung it open and was preparing to let out a loud whistle when Dodie scuttled in between his feet, bounced straight up onto one of the armchairs, and sat looking at him, her head cocked to one side.

"Good girl," he said, breathing out a sigh of relief. He shut the door and picked up his cases. "Right, come on. Let's get unpacked."

By the time the sun had shed its last dying rays on the day, he had everything in order, his belongings put away and his empty suitcases pushed out of sight underneath the bed. Not knowing if Dodie had been fed, he took out a half-used can of dogfood from the fridge, at the same time selecting a couple of eggs for himself. He spooned the meat into a plastic dish, which he had located under one of the armchairs, and gave it to Dodie who, judging by the speed with which she wolfed it down, seemed to suffer little from her lack of dental power. Then, while his eggs boiled furiously on the cooker ring, he pulled down Carrie's collection of records and, holding them in the crook of his arm, he began to flick through the covers.

They were magical, every one of them of his vintage: Jefferson Airplane, The Beatles, Bob Dylan, Joni Mitchell, The Velvet Underground, The Rolling Stones. He selected Dylan's *Nashville Skyline,* and placed it on the table, then, pushing the remaining sleeves back together again, he carried them back to the shelf. As he reached up, the bottom record slipped from his grasp and fell with an ominous clatter to the floor. Swearing to himself and grimacing at the thought that it might be broken, he picked it up and slid the record out of its sleeve. It was undamaged. Blowing out a puff of relief, he reached up to replace it on the pile when the title on the cover suddenly caught his eye. *Motown Greatest Hits*. He paused, holding the sleeve in his hands, then slowly, as if tempting providence, he turned it over. It was there. Smokey Robinson and the Miracles. He looked at it for no more than three seconds, then, quickly and decisively, he returned it to the shelf, sliding it in as far as it possibly would go at the bottom of the pile. "Start afresh," Carrie had said, "make this your new beginning."

To the strains of Bob Dylan he ate his boiled eggs, seated in one of the sagging deck-chairs on the veranda, while Dodie, perched on the other, willed him with plaintive looks to share his food with her. He peeled the shell off the top of one of the eggs and threw the contents to Dodie, who missed it with the first snap of her jaws, but then consumed it voraciously once she had worked out where it had landed. Later, having washed up his plates, he left them to drip-dry on the draining-board, then, wiping his hands on the seat of his jeans, he walked over to the desk and turned on the little light above it. He shifted the fax machine as far into the corner as it would go, then, opening up his brief-case, he took out a sheet of paper and a pen, and settled himself down to write a long, clarifying fax to his parents.

CHAPTER 17

"Oh, do get out of the way, boys!" Alicia shouted out, as she nearly tripped over the dogs on her way to the breakfast table, making the two brimming coffee-cups that she carried clatter unsteadily in their saucers. She was not in the best of humour that morning—she knew this, and it was so unusual for her to feel this way that it only seemed to aggravate her mood. Certainly the telephone ringing in the middle of the night hadn't helped, and although it had cut off almost immediately without even giving her the chance to lift the receiver, it had been enough to wake George. She had consequently spent the rest of the night with little chance of sleep, as he moved about restlessly in the bed, pulling the covers away from her, trying to find a position that would give him some relief from the nagging pain in his back. She was sure it was getting worse, and what's more, he now complained about—no, complained was the wrong word—remarked on other aches which seemed entirely unconnected with his war wound. She was worried—worried about this, and worried about the increasing demands put on him by the changes at Glendurnich. He had spent the whole weekend in the office with Duncan Caple, and now, on Monday morning, he couldn't even spare the time to come to have his breakfast.

She put down the cups on the table and walked over to the door and opened it. "Geordie!" she called out, her voice echoing around the hall.

"Yes?" George's distant voice sounded out from the drawing-room.

"What are you doing? Your breakfast is getting cold."

"Just coming," he replied.

Alicia returned to the dining-room and walked back to the far end of the table, sitting down heavily in her seat. She took a brittle piece of toast out of the rack and began to butter it, but only succeeded in making it break off into numerous shards on her plate. Sucking her teeth, she put on her glasses and picked up the newspaper and, giving it an annoyed shake, began scanning through the headlines just as George walked into the room.

"What have you been doing?" she said, looking at him over the top of her spectacles. Folding up the paper, she rose to her feet and walked over to the sideboard. "Your sausages are more like burnt offerings now."

"Sorry about that, old girl," he said, coming over to stand beside her. She gave him the plate, and he exchanged it with a long, handwritten fax. "This came in last night. I thought it must have been a fax when the phone cut off. It's from David."

"Ah, right!" Alicia said, a lighter tone in her voice, as she walked back to the table and sat down. "It'll probably be about his arrival time at Glasgow."

"Er, no, it's not," George said. "Just read it."

He took his plate over to the table and sat down next to his wife, and to avoid making eye contact with her while she read the fax, he picked up the paper and made a show of reading it, at the same time carving away at his over-cooked sausages. Alicia looked at him warily, understanding every one of his actions too well, and therefore realizing that the news was probably not going to be to her liking. She began to read.

George had laid his knife and fork together on the plate by the time Alicia folded up the fax and put it down on the table. She took off her spectacles and sat back in her chair without saying a word. George watched her, waiting to hear her reaction.

"Well?" he asked.

"Well," Alicia replied, shaking her head slowly. "I don't really know what to say. On one hand—yes—I can understand his point about getting away, and—well, if he comes back something like his normal self, then—yes, it's a good idea. But then he's talking about a month, I would say, at the least! So, for a start, he won't be back for the children's leave-out, which he said he would be, and then there are all these sweeping changes at Glendurnich." She paused. "I mean, I'm delighted that he seems to be better, but—well—my thoughts are now that if that's the case, then maybe he should come home, and start taking some of the pressure off you." She picked up the fax and unfolded it, starting to read it through again. "It really *does* seem that he's much better, wouldn't you say?"

George took a slice of toast and began buttering it, only to have as little success as his wife, a piece shooting off the side of his plate and onto the floor. He bent down laboriously to retrieve it.

"I don't think that he should come back just yet," he said, his voice strained from the exertion of his quest.

"What do you mean?" Alicia said. "Geordie, just leave the toast. Effie's going to be hoovering in here later."

"Dog's got it anyway," George said, straightening up.

"Listen, Geordie, I'm afraid that I have to disagree with you, because I simply cannot allow you to continue to work at this pace much longer. It was fine to begin with, when you were only just standing in for David, but now so much is happening, and I really don't think it's doing you any good at all. He has got to come back and help you."

George took a drink of his coffee and looked across at his wife.

"No, Alicia, I want him to stay out there. I was going to suggest it anyway before he left, that he should go to spend some time with the Richardsons in Massachusetts or the Penworths in Virginia, and that's why I bought him an open-ended ticket. So I'm quite happy that he's found this job." He paused momentarily. "I really do think that if he comes home right now, my dear, there is every chance his recovery would be short-lived. I grant you that he does appear to be better, but remember, it was only three days ago that his prognosis was entirely the opposite. I would think that the mending process has only just begun, and I want to make damned sure that when he does return, he's as near back to his old self as possible, so that he's quite ready to take over his position as marketing director once more. I mean, to put it bluntly, the future of the family involvement with Glendurnich depends on him."

Noticing the frown of concern registering on Alicia's face, George laid his hand reassuringly on top of hers. "Look, don't worry about me. I'm fine, I promise you. Anyway, today we have this new marketing director coming up from London, and even if it's not the ideal situation, at least he'll be taking some of the work-load off both Duncan and myself. To be quite honest, I've been feeling a bit guilty about some of the harsh words I've said about Duncan lately. He also expressed concern about my well-being over the weekend, and really he's as adamant as you that, once this new chap has settled in, I should take things a bit easier and not bother going into the office quite so frequently. And as far as the children are concerned, we'll just have them back here for the leave-out. These are all temporary measures, my darling." Draining his coffee-cup, he stood up and walked round behind Alicia, putting his hands on her shoulders. "Listen, David has given us his fax number. I suggest we write back a really positive message to him, saying that we stand full square behind him and that he should go ahead with his plans. Do you agree?"

Alicia looked over her shoulder and, placing her hand on his, she smiled bravely up at him and nodded. "All right, agreed. But as long as you really do start taking it a bit easier, Geordie. I don't want anything to happen to you."

George leaned over and planted a kiss on the top of his wife's head. "Nothing is going to happen to me." He let out a laugh, and started to walk towards the door. "I'm not ready to kick the bucket yet!"

He turned round and gave her a wink, at the same time leaning heavily on his stick and jauntily kicking one heel up behind him.

CHAPTER 18

The next morning, David was awoken both suddenly and prematurely by Dodie, who, having ventured onto his bed sometime during the night, felt that six o'clock was an apt time to give his face an unscheduled and somewhat unwelcome wash. With a start, he pushed her off the bed, then lay for a moment dazedly working out his new surroundings and listening to the birds noisily airing their dawn chorus outside in the garden.

From the other side of the room, the dog let out a wheak, and he turned his head on the pillow to see her standing hopefully by the door. He threw back the bedclothes and got to his feet and went over to open the door for her, and with two short barks, she slipped through the narrow gap and sped outside into the garden.

Having made himself a steaming cup of instant coffee, he was about to head to the bathroom when he stopped with a click of his fingers. He glanced at his watch and worked out what time it would be in Scotland. Exactly 11:05 A.M. He went over and sat down at the desk and, picking up the telephone, dialled a number.

He was midway through a gulp of coffee when a female voice answered. "Good morning, Hatching's School."

"Ah, hullo." He put the coffee-cup down on the floor beside him. "Would it be possible to speak to Sophie Corstorphine?"

"Who's calling?"

"It's her father—from America."

"Ah yes, Mr. Corstorphine. Now if I'm quick, I might just be able to catch her after break-time. Could you hold for a minute while I check her whereabouts?"

"Certainly."

A light scratching on the front door heralded the return of Dodie. He pressed the "monitor" button on the telephone and went over to let her in, just as Sophie's voice sounded through the speaker.

"Hullo, Dad? Hullo? Hullo?"

David dived for the receiver and turned off the monitor. "Hullo, Sophie?"

"Hi, Dad!"

"That was quick! I wasn't expecting you to be found so fast."

"No, well, I was just walking along the corridor on my way to a class when Miss Jenkins caught me. She says that you're still in America."

"Yeah, I am."

"What time is it over there?"

"Erm"—he looked at his watch—"precisely seven minutes past six in the morning."

Sophie laughed. "Isn't it ridiculous! We've had French, Biology and Maths already today, and you've only just got out of bed!"

"Yeah, it does seem a bit unfair, doesn't it? Hang on a minute." He paused long enough to hurl a cushion at the dog, who had just deemed his bed a suitable place to carry out her morning's ablutions. "So, how's everything going? Did Granny come down on Saturday?"

"Yes, she did *and* she was able to watch me playing tennis, seeing that Charlie's cricket match was cancelled. Clevely Hall had something like chicken-pox going round."

"Right. So did you win?"

"No. Mr. Hunter thinks it's because Rosie Braithwaite and I chatter too much on court."

"And do you?"

"Well, it's very difficult, Dad! If we suddenly think of something really important to say to each other, we have to say it straight away, otherwise we'll just forget!"

"So what was so important to say on Saturday?"

"Er," Sophie giggled, "actually, we were wondering what kind of shampoo we should recommend to one of our opponents, because she had terribly greasy hair!"

David laughed. "Well, that sounds *really* important, Sophie. Worth throwing the match for!"

"We *didn't* throw the match! We just, well, got rather hysterical and we couldn't hit a ball! Anyway, Dad, I'll have to get back to class."

"Okay, but don't go just yet. I, er, want to ask you something."

"What?"

"Well, it's just that . . . well, what would you honestly think if I said that I was going to stay over here for a short while?"

"What? In America?"

"Yes."

"Why?"

"Well, I suppose for a short holiday."

Sophie was silent for a moment. "How long's a short holiday?"

"I don't know. About a month, maybe."

He heard her tut down the line. "That isn't a *short* holiday, Dad!"

"Yes, I know. It's just that, well, I've sort of lined up a temporary job for myself, and a month is the least time that I can do. But I really don't need to do it, Sophie, if you would much rather I came home."

Sophie let out a long sigh. "No, I think it's a good idea, Dad. I said to Granny last week that you should stay out there for a bit, and anyway, I'm going to be revising for my exams all through leave-out."

"Did you really say that to Granny?"

"Yeah, I did! I think you need a change-of-scenery sort of thing."

David felt a sudden lump rise in his throat, hearing his young daughter say such reasoned words of understanding.

"But you will write, won't you?"

"Of *course* I will!"

"And you will be back before the holidays start?"

"I promise you."

"Well—no real objections, then. Do you want me to tell Charlie and Harriet?"

"I don't know. Maybe it would be better if I spoke to them myself."

"No, just write them a letter and I'll tell them. It'll probably go in one ear and out the other with Charlie anyway, and Harriet seems happy enough, so I won't go on about it too much to her. Listen, Dad, I'd better go. Write really *soon,* won't you, and whatever you do, don't forget my sixteenth birthday if you're not back for it, okay? Bye. Love you lots!"

David put down the receiver and sat for a moment staring at the wall, his mind torn between feeling relieved at her acceptance of the plan and sheer guilt at the impulsiveness of it all. He rose slowly from the chair. Well, it may be a complete disaster, anyway, in which case, as he had decided before, he would just go home. He took his towel from the tail-board of the bed and walked into the bathroom. Just play it by ear, that's the best thing.

He didn't really need to take the car to work that day. The Newmans' house was well within walking distance, and thanks to Dodie, he had more than enough time. However, he did want to go via the deli to get himself breakfast and something for lunch, and after work, he planned to stock up with provisions at Hunter's SuperSaver, before calling in at Helping Hands to tell Clive of his change of address.

He left the house at twenty past eight, stepping out into a day that promised to be as hot and as clear as the one before, the sky a glaring blue, with the morning sun sitting like a burning globe atop the waving bank of pampas-grass. He toyed with the idea of putting down the hood of the Beetle, but being unsure of how Dodie behaved in the car, he thought better of it. He opened the door and the dog jumped in, pushing herself between the two front seats into the back, where she sat panting with excitement. David climbed in after her and, putting the key into the ignition, went to fire up the engine. However, it was immediately apparent that Carrie's lack of automotive interest was all-encompassing, as it took at least a minute of fruitless cranking, accompanied by numerous backfires, before the engine eventually spluttered to life and he was able to start lurching his way up the road.

By a quarter to nine, he sat parked outside the Newmans' house, drinking coffee and eating the proverbial fried-egg sandwich, and smiling wryly to himself as he wondered what the workmen outside the deli must have thought of him with his little hippie vehicle and the poodle bouncing around inside. He drained the Styrofoam cup and, having stuffed his litter back into the brown paper carrier, he once more coaxed the engine to life and pulled into the driveway.

It was by far the largest and most opulent property that he had seen in Leesport. The gravelled drive, which led down to the rear of the house, was flanked by a wide expanse of well-kept lawn and overhung by the leafy branches of oak- and birch-trees that alternated on each side of its one-hundred-yard length. The house itself was a long Colonial-style building, the cedar shingles on its upper and lower stories being finished in different stains, giving it a two-tone effect. To the west of the house a large glass conservatory topped by a white balustraded veranda extended out to trap the evening light, while at the east end a passageway, subtly blended into the fascia, joined the old stable on to the main block of the house. A clematis montana bursting with pink flowers climbed over the entrance porch and meandered its way upwards to cover part of one of the dormer windows on the top floor, while flower-beds alive with azaleas and dwarf rhododendrons in bloom ran the full length of the house.

David drove slowly down the drive, trying to make his arrival as unobtrusive as possible, and pulled the Volkswagen to a halt next to a metallic-blue BMW 318 parked at the front door. Then, immediately thinking that this might be somewhat presumptuous of a mere gardener, he reversed and parked under the trees next to a long wooden shed, its sides and roof strewn with a tangle of trumpet-vine. He cut the engine, and Dodie, eager to get on with her new adventure, jumped forward onto the front passenger seat and sat blinking hopeful looks up at him.

"Stay here for now, Dodie," he said, putting up the window and leaving several inches open at the top for air. "I'll come and get you in a minute."

He stood looking at the house, trying to work out where best he should go. Two dustbins sat beside the banistered steps that led down from the door in the stable, and presuming this to be the kitchen, he made his way towards it. He climbed the steps and knocked on the door, and as he waited, a muffled yelp sounded out from the Volkswagen. He turned to see Dodie's face peering longingly at him through the side window.

"Sssh! That's enough!" he said in the loudest whisper he could muster.

This seemed only to act as further encouragement to the dog, and she now followed up her muted overture with the main performance, throwing back her head and letting out a long, plaintive howl. David took a quick glance at the back door, and seeing that no one had yet answered his knock, he ran down the steps and started back towards the car, waving his hand in a downwards movement at the dog.

"Dodie!" he called out, much louder, "get down and shut up!"

Dodie looked at him quite surprised, as if unused to being addressed in such harsh tones and, sliding her paws down the window, she slowly disappeared from sight. David turned back to the kitchen door, only to find that the whole episode had been witnessed.

"Oh, sorry!" he said, running back to the bottom of the steps. He looked up at the black woman who stood at the top, a grin stretched across her face.

"You havin' a bit of trouble?" she laughed.

David smiled and looked back at the car. "Sort of, yes. I've got a dog in the car who thinks she can order me around."

"Ah," the woman said, nodding her head slowly, "I'm glad it's a she. Obviously knows who should be the boss then!"

She was a large, happy-looking person, dressed in a strikingly bright pair of cotton trousers, a voluminous T-shirt and blue Reebok training shoes. David thought initially that she must have been in her early fifties, because of the faint wisps of grey that had begun touching at the edges of her tight black curls, but then, seeing her close up, he realized that it was almost impossible to guess her age, her face being as smooth and unlined as polished ochre.

"My name's David Corstorphine, and I—"

"Oh, of course," the woman cut in, her voice lifting in recognition of his name. "You've come from Helping Hands to do the garden."

"Yeah, that's right. Are you, erm, Mrs. Newman?"

She threw back her head and laughed heartily. "Heaven's sakes, no!" she said, putting forward her hand. "I'm Jasmine, Mrs. Newman's housekeeper."

David shook her hand. "Hullo, Jasmine, nice to meet you."

"Nice to meet you too, David. Come on in."

She stood aside and ushered David into the house, closing the door behind them. He had been right—it was the kitchen, a long, airy room with open rafter beams from which tracks of spotlights hung, its black-and-white tiled floor stretching the full length of the place. He was standing at the business end of the kitchen, from where he took in the custom-made units of reconditioned pine fitted with ultra-modern stainless-steel cooking hobs, deep freeze, refrigerator and eye-level oven. Dominating the centre of the room was a long refectory table with bentwood chairs pushed in around it. Its surface was scattered with open newspapers, cereal packets and plates, and in the middle stood a flourishing cactus, with a touch of surrealism added by a bicycle pedal, its chrome stalk pushed deep into the earth of the flower-pot.

Beyond the table, two sofas were grouped around a television, the space between them taken up with two enormous beanbags. The whole area was bathed in light from the three full-length French doors that extended the complete width of the far gable end, each being open to allow the warm breeze to blow into the room from the front garden.

"So," Jasmine said, walking over to the sideboard and flicking on the switch of the electric kettle. "Where you from? I love the accent."

"Scotland."

"Oh?" she said, leaning back against the unit and folding her arms. "You sure don't sound like any Scot I ever heard talk."

David smiled at her. "Well, it depends where you come from."

"Yeah, I guess it does." She pushed herself away from the unit and reached up for two mugs from one of the top cupboards. "Would you like some coffee?"

"Well, if you don't mind," David replied, putting his hands into the pockets of his jeans. "I don't want to hold you up."

"You're not," she said, picking up the coffee pot from the hob. "How you take it?"

"Black, please."

As Jasmine poured the coffee into the mugs, the urgent click-clicking of high-heeled shoes on stone flooring crescendoed towards them from the main part of the house.

"Jasmine!"

"In here!" she called out and walked out of the door in the direction of the voice.

David picked up his mug and, taking a cautious sip of the piping-hot coffee, started to move towards the French doors so that he could look out at the front garden.

"Listen, there's an old car out there with a dog in it that's going ballistic. Do you know who it belongs to?"

David stopped abruptly and swore quietly to himself.

"Yeah, it's all right. It's David, the new gardener from Helping Hands."

He turned and hurried over to the back door and craned his head against the window to see if he could catch a glimpse of the car.

"Oh, God, I forgot he was starting today. Look, I am so late, and I really need to get Benji to school, so maybe you could tell him what to do."

"Well, he's here in the kitchen."

There was a short pause before the click-clicking of the footsteps started again. David moved quickly away from the door and stood with his hands thrust into his back pockets, an inexplicable feeling of nervousness in the pit of his stomach at the prospect of meeting his new employer. Jasmine came back into the kitchen, followed by a tall, strikingly attractive woman in her mid-thirties. She was dressed in a fawn linen business suit worn casually over a cream silk blouse, its collar opened wide to reveal the full length of her slender neck. Her honey-blonde hair was pulled back from her lightly freckled face and gathered at the back of her head in a large gold clasp. She wore no make-up, save for the merest touch of pale lipstick on her mouth, and her only jewelled accessory was a pair of tiny diamond-studded earrings. In her hand she carried a brief-case, and across her shoulder, slung by a long strap, was a large crocodile-skin handbag.

"This is David," Jasmine said, grinning at him. "He's from Scotland."

"From Scotland, huh?" the woman said, coming no farther than where she had stopped next to Jasmine. "And do Scotsmen know more than Australians about gardening?"

David frowned, not understanding the context of her question. "I'm sorry?"

"Our last gardener was Australian. Actually he wasn't a gardener, he was a butcher. He could mow the lawns, but he treated everything in the flower-beds as if it were a weed. Do you know the difference?"

"Yes, I think so. I mean, yes, I know so." He inwardly kicked himself at the uncertainty of his reply.

"Good," she said, glancing briefly at Jasmine as if seeking approval that she had said enough to the new gardener. She looked back at him. "Well, I'm sure that Jasmine will show you where to find everything, and then you can, well, just get on with things." She caught sight of the clock on the wall. "Oh, God, Jasmine, look at the time! Where the hell is Benji? Could you find him and say I'll meet him in the car?"

"Okay." Jasmine disappeared off through the house.

"Oh, and Jasmine!" she called out after her.

"Yup!"

"Make sure that Germaine picks him up on time today. Benji said that he had to wait for at least half an hour outside the school last Wednesday."

"Okay, will do."

The woman turned and made her way towards the back door, and David, who still stood close by, quickly stepped forward and opened it for her. She glanced at him as she passed, a brief smile being the only acknowledgement of the gesture, and hurried her way down the wooden steps and along the path. David leaned forward out of the door to watch her go. As she approached the BMW, she began to talk urgently to a young boy who had emerged from the front door of the house and now walked unhurriedly towards the passenger door. He threw it open, slung in his school-bag, and got in. The woman revved up the engine and, with a spatter of gravel, reversed round in a tight arc and sped away up the drive.

David turned and walked back into the kitchen just as Jasmine entered through the other door.

"What a hassle!" She picked up her mug from the sideboard and took a sip. "Monday mornings are always like that." She made a face at the lukewarm contents of the mug, and throwing the remainder into the sink, she walked over to the table. "Give me a minute while I clear this up, then I'll show you where everything is."

"I suppose that that was Mrs. Newman?" David asked.

Jasmine turned from the table, her face aghast. "Oh, for heaven's sakes, I forgot to introduce you!" She picked up a stack of plates and carried them over to the dishwasher. "Yeah, that was Mrs. Newman. Jennifer, actually, she don't really like being called Mrs. Newman. She always moves like a whirlwind, so sometimes formalities just fly out the window."

"She obviously works, then."

"Yup, and how. She's what's called an account *ee*executive with an advertising company in Manhattan, so she's away mostly during the week, usually Mondays through Wednesday or Thursday. She and her husband have an apartment in the West Village."

"Ah, right."

He paused for a moment, wondering whether it was preferable to remain silent or continue asking questions that might be considered inquisitive. Silence sounded like the wrong option. "And Mr. Newman? What does he do?"

"Oh, he's some big shot with a computer company. He was here for the weekend but left earlier this morning. He's away most of the time." She pushed the cereal packets into one of the cupboards and put her hand on the top of the unit, letting out a sigh of concern. "Hard on them both, I think. Don't manage to see much of each other, only on weekends, sometimes not even that." She supplied the dishwasher with detergent, shut the door and switched it on. "But it's really hardest on Benji."

"So what happens to him?"

"Benji? He stays here with me." She picked up a cloth, and giving it a quick rinse under the tap, set about wiping the surface of the table. "Right now, it's just three or four nights a week, depending when Jennifer gets back, but during the winter, I'm here for the whole week."

"Right."

She finished the table with a flourish and hung up the towel on a hook beside the oven. "Okay, so that's done. Come on, I'll show you the garden."

She began making for the French windows at the front.

"Er, Jasmine, would you mind if we went out the back? It's just that I want to let the dog out of the car."

She looked at him warily. "I'm not usually very good with dogs. It's not some kinda guard dog, is it?"

David snorted. "No, it's a poodle."

"A poodle?" She raised her eyebrows in surprise. "What in heaven's name are you doin' with a poodle?"

"It's not mine. I'm only looking after it for someone."

Jasmine shrugged and walked towards the back door. "Okay, I think I can handle a poodle."

Dodie was delighted to see them, leaping up and down on the front seat of the car as she watched them approach. David let her out and instantly forgave her for having had yet another obvious gnaw at the steering wheel, in that she immediately gave Jasmine a rapturous welcome before endearing herself still further by picking up a piece of wood that was twice her own body weight and hauling it in circles around them.

Jasmine unlocked the door of the wooden shed next to his car and showed him where to find everything, then together they walked round to the front of the house. The garden was much larger than he had envisaged, the trees on either side of the lawn running down to the edge of the bay. Over to the right, sheltered from the wind on all sides by a high evergreen hedge, was the swimming pool, a section of its sparkling blue water just visible through the white picket gate, and beyond this still, David made out the high wire-netting of a tennis court above the hedge. The uniformity of the layout was cleverly offset by the almost random positioning of brightly coloured herbaceous borders, although the sparsity of vegetation in some was proof enough of the brutal treatment they had received at the hands of the last gardener.

"Pretty good, huh?" Jasmine said, surveying the garden with him.

"It's beautiful. It's so, well, peaceful."

"Yup," Jasmine said, nodding. "Sometimes too peaceful." She took a deep breath. "Okay, well, I'll let you get to work. You want anything, I'll be in the house."

She smiled and turned to make her way back towards the kitchen, then stopped and looked back at him. "Have you got anything for lunch?"

"Yeah, I stopped in at the deli on the way here."

"Okay, but come and eat it with me, and in future, don't bother with the deli. *I'll* give you lunch."

"That's very kind. Are you sure?"

Jasmine laughed and shook her head. "Of course I'm sure. Do I *look* unsure or somethin'?"

She turned and David watched her as she walked over to the French doors and back into the house. He looked down at Dodie, who was sitting at his feet staring up at him, her head cocked to the side, a twig now sticking out the corner of her mouth like a twisted cheroot.

"Right, Dodie, let's get started."

He reversed the sit-on mower out of the shed and started on the lawns that bordered the drive, and from the moment that he set the cutters in motion, he felt an instant and overwhelming sense of release. It was like a coming home, his return from the wilderness, and immediately the broken lines of communication and thought that he had had with Rachel in the garden at Inchelvie seemed reconnected. He smiled to himself, relishing the sweet smell of the newly cut grass, realizing now that this had been all that he needed since leaving Scotland, his whole spirit being further uplifted and revitalized by the heat of the sun on his body as he worked.

It took him the whole morning and the first part of the afternoon to cut all the lawns. Dodie ran alongside him for the first half-hour, but then, suffering from the heat and the sudden increase to her exercise regime, she chose to retire to the shade and lay watching him from beneath one of the blue awnings that were hung over the kitchen doors. David joined her and Jasmine for lunch at one o'clock, and the three of them sat together on the paved area outside the kitchen. They talked initially about Dodie, David explaining how his charge had come as a job lot, with a house and car attached. He only took the story back as far as Carrie, never mentioning Richard or Angie, and although to Jasmine his story seemed light and unconvincing, leaving many a question unanswered, she thought better than to ask them. She liked him; she liked his polite and unassuming manner, and his natural ability in displaying a genuine interest in herself. She talked easily about her employment with the Newmans, how she had started seven years ago as a domestic help, and how it had then evolved into her becoming their housekeeper, at the time that Jennifer decided to go back into full-time employment. Lunch went on much longer than it should have, and at two-thirty, accompanied by exclamations of horror at the time, they both jumped up from their chairs. David took off once more across the lawn on his mower, while Jasmine went into the house to continue with her work upstairs.

Having spent two hours giving Benji's room a much-needed clean, Jasmine was in the process of carrying the vacuum cleaner down the stairs when she heard the sound of a car pulling away on the front drive, followed by the sound of the back door slamming shut. She put the cleaner away in the cupboard under the stairs and walked through to the kitchen to find Benji helping himself to a carton of chocolate milk from the fridge.

"Hi, darlin', how's school today?"

"Gross," Benji replied.

"Did Germaine turn up on time?"

"She was five minutes late." Benji poured too much chocolate milk out into the glass, and it overflowed onto the sideboard. Jasmine picked up the cloth from beside the sink and was making her way over to clear up the mess, when Benji picked up the glass and deliberately flicked his hand across the spilt milk so that it sprayed over the floor.

"Benji!" Jasmine said, "Why'd'ya do that?" She bent down to wipe it up.

"Why'd'ya do that?" Benji said, imitating her voice, his mouth turned down at the corners. He carried his glass over to the television area, put it down on the floor and, flumping into one of the beanbags, he turned on the television with the remote control.

Jasmine finished wiping up the mess and rinsed the cloth under the tap, then, leaning her back against the sink, she folded her arms and watched him silently. He had really changed so much in the past year. He always had been such good fun, so full of crazy and wicked ideas, but now, ever since moving up to middle school, he had gotten all moody and uncommunicative, something she could understand of a kid in his mid-teens, but not for one of eleven years old.

Of course, it hadn't helped being kept back a year in elementary, because now all his friends were in the class above him, and he'd told her that none of them wanted to be seen around with him, because he was one year lower. And then, of course, the fact that he had put on quite a bit of weight over the past six months didn't help matters.

Not that he was hugely fat, and since he was tall for his age, he didn't look out of proportion. But he certainly was unfit-looking, and it had been enough for him to be excluded from any of the school teams. However, she couldn't really understand why this had happened in the first place. He didn't eat that much at home, and the only explanation that she could come up with was that he might well be heading off to the candy shop in Leesport at lunch-break, much against his mother's every wish.

But then again, she never felt like questioning him about it. She walked over to him and bent down and patted him on the shoulder. "Want a swim?"

"I'm all right," he said, not taking his eyes off the television.

"Suit yourself," she said, raising her eyebrows in defeat. She turned and was about to walk away when she heard above the noise of the television the sound of Dodie barking in the garden. Benji heard it too, and he raised his head and looked out of the French doors, craning his neck to see where the noise was coming from. "What was that?"

"That's Dodie. She's a poodle. She belongs to David, the new gardener. He's from Scotland."

Benji got to his feet and slumped over to the French doors and looked out to where David was working near the swimming pool. Jasmine followed, and standing quietly behind him, they both watched Dodie dancing around on the lawn with an old tennis ball, desperately trying to get David to throw for her. He turned from his work in the flower-bed and gave it a kick across the lawn. Dodie headed after it as fast as her legs would move and, having retrieved it, she made her way laboriously back to him, the ball slipping out of the side of her mouth every so often. Then, dropping it at his feet, she would let out another yelp, and David, in his own time, would start the process over again.

Benji leaned against the French door, his hands thrust into the pockets of his long baggy shorts, rocking himself back and forth against the doorpost as he watched this happen three or four times. "He's not wearing a skirt," he said glumly.

"What d'ya mean, a skirt?" Jasmine asked, perplexed by his statement.

"Scotsmen are *supposed* to wear skirts, Jasmine," he replied with a sigh of impatience at her ignorance.

"Now, for once you're wrong, Benji, 'cos I know they're called kilts."

"Skirts, kilts, what's the difference? All seems pretty girly to me. *And* he's got a girly dog."

Jasmine smiled and shook her head in despair at his mood. She turned away from the window.

"What do you want for supper?"

"Don't care much."

"Okay, I'll give you fried flies on toast, then."

"Jasmine?"

"Yuh?"

"Do you think what's-his-name knows anything about bikes?"

Jasmine turned back to look at him. He was still leaning against the doorpost, gazing out into the garden. "David? I dunno, Benji. Why?"

"Do you think he could put the pedal back on my bike?"

Jasmine smiled to herself. "I reckon he probably could. That is, if you ask him politely and start to remember his name properly."

Benji remained where he was, so Jasmine, thinking that a little active encouragement was in order, walked back towards him, pulling the pedal out of the flower-pot as she passed the table.

"Tell you what. If you put on your swimming trunks, then go get your bike and ask him to put the pedal back on, you can have a swim while he's doing it, okay? But you'd better hurry, 'cos I think he'll be headin' home pretty soon."

"Okay!" With a sudden air of excitement, he grabbed the pedal from her grasp and ran through the kitchen into the house. Jasmine watched him go, then, tilting her head to the side at this unexpected hint of hopefulness, she went to make a start on his meal.

It was Dodie who first alerted David to the boy's approach, suddenly rushing off across the lawn, yapping loudly. David turned from his work in the flower-bed to see what the commotion was about, and recognized the young boy he had seen earlier in the day getting into the BMW. He was dressed only in a pair of surf shorts, and was slowly pushing a bicycle across the lawn towards him. As Dodie reached him, he turned his bare legs in towards the bicycle in an attempt to protect them from her claws as she jumped up to greet him.

"Dodie!" David called out sharply. "Come here!"

For once, the little dog did as she was told, racing back to stand guard over her tennis ball, while the boy, eyeing her every inch of the way, continued warily towards him. David put down the hoe and stepped out of the flower-bed, wiping his hands on the back of his jeans. The boy stopped in front of him.

"Hi! How are you? I'm David." He walked forward and put his hand out to the boy, who tried desperately to free his own by juggling with the pedal that he was carrying, and in the process letting go of the bike. David lurched forward and grabbed hold of the handlebars before it hit the ground and laid it down carefully. The boy looked at him and smiled.

"So whom have I the pleasure of meeting?"

"Benji."

"Hi, Benji." He stuck out his hand again, and Benji stepped forward and shook it. "So what's been happening to your bike?"

"The pedal came off."

"Right—and you're about to fix it, are you?"

Benji looked at him and began scratching embarrassedly at his forehead. "Well, I was wondering—well, me and Jasmine were wondering if you could, well, maybe have a look at it, 'cos I've tried to fix it, but it just keeps coming off." He squatted down beside his bike and made a half-hearted attempt at putting the pedal back on.

"Right, well, if both you *and* Jasmine want me to do it, then I'd better get on with it, hadn't I? I'll need to go back to the shed for a spanner, though. Okay?"

Benji looked up at him, squinting into the sun. "A what?"

David bent down and took the pedal from Benji's grasp. "You'll see. I'll be back in a minute," he said, starting to walk back across the lawn. "Maybe you could keep Dodie occupied by throwing the ball for her."

When he had first entered the shed that morning, David had realized immediately that, even though the last gardener may have been lacking in horticultural skills, he certainly knew how to organize his workshop. Everything had its place, the garden implements hanging neatly from wooden dowelling-pegs stuck into the side beam of the shed, while the hand-tools were mounted in metal clips above the work-bench, the outline of each being traced on the mounting board, both for easy replacement and for recognition of what was missing. He chucked the pedal onto the bench and reached over and took down a 13-millimeter wrench, which, more by luck than better judgement, fitted the nut perfectly. He picked up the pedal and walked back out of the shed, and as he was sliding the bolt across on the door, he heard a distant splash coming from the swimming pool. He laughed to himself. Typical boy. Got bored with the game.

It took him just under a minute to get back to where the bicycle had been left. There was no sign of Dodie, either. He bent down to start fixing the pedal when he heard Dodie let out a yelp from beside the pool. He stood up and walked to where he could glance in through the gate to see why she was barking. Something was strange. There was not a ripple on the pool, and yet he was sure he had heard a splash. Dodie barked again. He turned and moved quickly through the gate to see what was happening. Dodie was sitting, a bemused expression on her face as she stared at its smooth, ripple-free surface. Benji was nowhere to be seen. He turned to walk away, and as he did so, his eyes happened to follow the line of Dodie's vision, and a sudden surge of adrenaline and alarm coursed through his body as he made out the dark outline of a figure, foreshortened by the refraction of the water, lying on the bottom of the pool at the deep end.

"OH, NO!" he yelled out, running around the edge of the pool, pulling off his deck shoes as he went. "OH, MY GOD, PLEASE NO! *JASMINE!*"

He dived in and swam down to the bottom, reaching out and grabbing the inert figure of the boy under the armpit. He pulled hard, expecting to have to drag the dead weight of the body upwards, when suddenly the boy seemed to come to life, kicking out with his feet, and they shot to the surface of the pool at the same time. Benji pushed the hair off his eyes and looked at him, spluttering out water.

"What's the matter?" he asked innocently.

David swam over to the side of the pool and grabbed hold of the edge as he caught his breath. He turned round to face the boy, who was now swimming sedately up the pool.

"What the *hell* do you think you were doing?" David shouted at him.

Benji climbed up the steps at the shallow end and received a rapturous welcome from Dodie. He turned to face David, a look of bewilderment on his face. "What d'ya mean?"

David swung himself out of the pool and turned round to sit on the edge, looking at Benji and shaking his head in disbelief. "What *do* you think you were doing? Christ, I mean, I thought you were drowned! I've never known anyone to do such a stupid, idiotic thing in my life!"

"I was holding my breath," Benji said, looking at him, his bottom lip beginning to quiver. "I can do it for a minute and a half."

"Well, it's a bloody stupid thing to do, and I don't give a damn what you do when other people are around, but you sure as hell don't do it with me. Okay?"

At that point, Jasmine came running in through the gate. "What on earth is going on?" she said breathlessly, looking at David and Benji in turn.

Benji stomped past her, a furious and mortified expression on his face. "He's stupid. He's just a—" He turned and looked at David, anger and tears burning at his eyes. "STUPID GARDENER!"

He ran out of the gate and headed for the house, and in the silence that followed, David could hear him sobbing his way loudly across the lawn. Jasmine threw her arms in the air and looked across at David. "Could you *please* tell me what's going on?"

David shook his head and kicked his feet in the water. "I'd just been getting a tool for his bike from the shed, and came back and found him lying in the deep end of the pool. I thought he was bloody drowned!"

Jasmine closed her eyes and slapped the top of her head with her hand. "Oh, David!" she said quietly, moving around the pool towards him, "I'm so sorry! That's Benji's ridiculous game. He's not supposed to do it. He's been warned so many times by his mother and me. Oh, good Lord above, I am so sorry."

David shook his head and waved his arm. "No, it's my fault. I've obviously over-reacted. It's just that, well, I was so bloody scared."

Jasmine crouched down beside him and put her hand on his shoulder. "Not surprisin'."

They remained in that position without speaking for more than a minute before David swung round and jumped to his feet. "I'm sorry, Jasmine. I didn't mean to shout at him like that."

"You've no need to be sorry, David. I just think it's pretty wunnerful that you reacted that way. I mean, you could have been so right, in which case you might have saved his life."

David glanced at her. "Maybe I should apologize to him?"

"No," Jasmine replied, shaking her head slowly, "I'll have a talk with him. Anyway, I think we should let the whole incident heat up in his brain. It'll be a real good lesson to him." She took hold of his arm. "Come on, I'll get you some dry clothes, and then I think you should be gettin' yourself home." She smiled up at him and gave a wink. "I reckon you've done enough for a day."

Clive and Dotti first stared unbelievingly at him when he walked into Helping Hands, before both burst out into fits of laughter. David raised his eyes heavenwards, not particularly wanting to share in their joke. However, he did realize that he must cut quite a comic figure, standing there with his little dog on its lead and dressed in a garish Hawaiian short-sleeved shirt and a pair of chinos whose cuffs ended three inches above his ankles.

"Yeah, well, I've already had some pretty strange looks in Hunter's SuperSaver."

Clive came round the side of his desk theatrically wiping non-existent tears of mirth from his eyes, and stood looking David up and down. "Oh, David, this is wonderful! So—Mrs. Newman insists that you wear livery, does she?" He burst out into fits of laughter again, and David smiled and shook his head at the ribbing.

"Oh, no, no, I must stop!" Clive continued. "It's just too cruel. Oh dear, oh dear!" He patted himself on the chest to regain self-control, then, bending forward and placing both hands on his knees, he looked down at Dodie. "And who may I ask is this?"

"Er, her name's Dodie," David replied guardedly, expecting Clive to make yet another of his humorous observations. "I'm afraid that I had to bring her in, otherwise she's quite likely to eat the interior of the car."

"Oh, aren't you just a bootiful creature?" Clive crooned as Dodie jumped towards him and started to lick at his hands. He straightened up fast as Dodie's powerful breath reached his nostrils. "Oh, my word! She does have a little problem, doesn't she?"

"That's putting it mildly." He reined in Dodie as Clive moved close up to him.

"Garlic pills," he whispered in his ear.

"What?"

"Garlic pills. Wonderful for canine halitosis!"

"Ah, right! Thanks for the tip. I'll get some for her."

"So, how'd it go today? And whose clothes *are* those?"

David recounted his day's experiences, getting more than a horrified reaction from Clive when he eventually explained how he had come to be wearing such bizarre clothes.

"Jasmine did point out that Mr. Newman was a little shorter than me, but it was either this or nothing. Anyway, that reminds me." He stood up, digging his hand into his pocket and bringing out the sodden piece of letter-head which he had picked up that morning from Carrie's desk. He opened it up carefully and handed it to Clive. "I managed to salvage this from my jeans. It's really why I dropped in. It's my new address."

"Oh, wonderful, so you found somewhere?"

"Yeah. It came with dog and car attached."

"Shore Road!" Clive said, reading the piece of paper. "That's pretty fancy, isn't it?"

"Not really. I'm in one of the little saltboxes."

"Oh, that's perfect for you! Now"—he started to pat at his pockets—"what did I do with that envelope?"

"It's here, Clive," Dotti said, turning from her computer screen, the envelope in her hand. "You gave it to me for safekeeping."

Clive tutted and raised his eyebrows in disgust at himself. "I'll be forgetting my own head next." He walked over to Dotti's desk and took the envelope, handing over David's address at the same time. "Be a gem, Dotti, and stick this on the machine."

He approached David and handed him the envelope. "I thought you should have some spending money, so I've made up a week's wages in advance for you."

David shook his head and made to hand the envelope back. "Clive, you don't—"

Clive stood back and held up both hands in refusal. "No, I insist. Really." He laughed. "If it makes it any easier for you to accept, I should maybe tell you that I do this for all my employees—just a little ruse I have for buying loyalty! And in future, all you need to do is drop in at the end of every week, and we'll settle up then. Is that okay?"

David slipped the envelope into his back pocket. "Yeah, perfect—and thanks again."

"Not at all," Clive replied, putting an arm on his shoulder and walking him to the door. "And for goodness' sakes, don't go saving kids from swimming pools every day. I don't want to have to start paying you danger money as well!"

Heavily laden down with the two carrier-bags filled with groceries, David fumbled the key into the lock of the saltbox and pushed open the door with his shoulder and, giving Dodie a whistle to get her inside, he kicked it shut behind him. Putting the bags down on the draining-board, he rooted around in one for a can of beer and made his way towards the veranda, taking a healthy swig as he went. He had just undone the bolts on the door when he noticed that a fax was sitting on the machine. He walked over to the desk, and instantly recognizing his mother's writing, he tore off the sheet and walked out into the veranda, plumping himself down in one of the deck-chairs.

My darling David,
Dad and I were delighted to get your fax and to hear that you are feeling so much better. I always had the notion that getting away completely from Inchelvie would do you the best good of all. Accordingly, we discussed your plan this morning over breakfast, and we are both of the opinion that it is an excellent idea for that period of time, and I am sure that it will enable you to eventually return to Scotland afresh and renewed.

What may come as a bit of a blow to you (yet in a way a mixed blessing to ourselves), is that Duncan Caple has felt it necessary to appoint a temporary marketing director in your place. Of course, it is not the ideal solution, but now that we know of your plans, it does allow you a breathing space, and also takes much of the pressure off your father. The new man starts today and Duncan has insisted that Dad should begin to take things much easier from now on, so let's hope!

I have no doubt that you will have already spoken to Sophie or even all the children about this, and of course, we are quite happy for them to come back here for their leave-out. By the way, when I visited them the day you left, Sophie said that she knew *that you wouldn't be back straight away. She's turning out to be a very intuitive young girl, that one! Knows her father better than his mother does!*

Do keep in touch. Faxes are wonderful—that is, as long as people on the other side of the world send them during our *daytime! (A little hint!)*

All my love,
Mama.

David folded up the fax and placed it beside him on the floor. He leaned back in his chair and closed his eyes, and instantly his mind was filled once more with weighty feelings of guilt and self-reproach for taking the job. Okay, so it had been a snap decision, but he would never have been able to afford the luxury of making it if he hadn't had his parents on hand to step into the breach.

Maybe he should just pack up and go home now. But there again, what was the point? This new marketing director had just started, so his job would be taken, albeit on a temporary basis, and the appointment would certainly take the onus off his father and allow him to return to his retirement. So what would *he* do? He certainly didn't want to go back to work in the garden. Well, not that one, at any rate. That would be a retrograde step, and he was past all that. But then again, he would have nothing to occupy his mind, and he would just open himself up to the danger of slipping back to where he had been before.

But what about the children? Were they now not only deprived of a mother, but a father as well? But in a way that was just a negative thought, because even though they probably had not given an enormous amount of reasoning to their decision, their instincts also had been to get away from Inchelvie and return to the different but happy environment of their school.

He pushed himself out of the chair and walked out into the garden, and stood looking out across the bay. No, they had *each* made the right decision, and their respective changes *would* help to start the long healing process. And at the end of term, that would be the time when they would get back together, refreshed and renewed.

He turned and made his way purposefully back towards the house, a plan beginning to form in his mind. Right, so he would return to Scotland at the end of June, a week before the children broke up for their summer holidays, and he would immediately take them off somewhere exciting and new, somewhere they could all make a fresh start at being a family once more.

He went into the living-room and, sitting down at the desk, he scribbled off half a dozen lines to his mother, laying it on top of the fax machine to send the following morning. Then, taking a piece of stationery from one of the cubby-holes on Carrie's desk, he set about writing a long letter to his dear, sweet, intuitive Sophie.

CHAPTER

19

Benji sat on the bench outside Leesport Middle School, listening to the shouts of his fellow pupils fade off into the distance as they made their way down the road towards main street. He got up and kicked at his school-bag that lay on the sidewalk, and looked at his watch. Come on, Germaine, it was twenty past four. He was the last one *again*.

He heard the main door of the school bang shut behind him and turned to see two boys come running down the path towards him. Recognizing one of them as Sean Dalaglio, his best friend in elementary school, he walked over to the end of the path to meet him.

"Hi, Sean! How're you doing?"

Sean walked past without looking at him, acknowledging his greeting with only a surly grunt. Benji watched them tittering secretly with each other before heading off down the road, now roaring with laughter and trying to push each other off the sidewalk.

He walked back to the bench, scraping his shoes along the ground, feeling the horrible and uncontrollable sensation of imminent tears build up inside him. He hated school. He hated everyone in the school, because he knew that they hated him. He sat down with a thump on the bench and opened up the side pocket of his school-bag and took out a candy bar. Why did his mother have to make him get a lift every day from that dumb Germaine? Everyone else walked to and from school, and they were all right. It was only 'cos *she* thought it wasn't safe. He even had to pay one of the boys to go down to the shops for him at lunch-time to get him his treats. It cost him twice as much as it should do for a candy bar, and because his pocket money didn't cover the cost, he had to sneak into his parents' bedroom at a time when Jasmine was busy downstairs to search the drawers of his father's desk for loose change. He felt guilty every time he did it, but then it was *their* fault. If they allowed him a bit more freedom, then he wouldn't have to do such a dishonest thing.

He glanced at his watch again. It was half past four. Come on, where *are* you, Germaine?

Adults were so . . . selfish. They only did what *they* wanted to do, what suited them best. Why did both his parents have to work? He *knew* his father must be pretty well off, because he always had big cars and quite often he had someone to drive them for him, and their house was one of the biggest in Leesport. He had lived there all *his* life, so it must have been bought when his mother wasn't working and was at home looking after him. It was so stupid. If she were home all the time now, then maybe she would see for herself that it was quite safe for him to walk to school.

Oh, come on, Germaine! Where *are* you?

What it all boiled down to was he only had one real friend and that was Jasmine. She could be pretty bossy sometimes, but she always played games with him if he wanted to. But it wasn't the same with her as it had been when Sean used to come round to his house. Anyway, she was probably going to get all pally with that idiotic Scottish gardener. Well, he *was* pretty dumb thinking that he was drowning, and then he had started yelling at him. How did he think he could get away with that? He'd only just started working for his parents. He was both stupid and rude—but then, that was probably why he was only a gardener. He didn't have brains like his own father, who was able to run a huge computer firm. Jasmine didn't have a boy-friend, though. Ugh, he couldn't *stand* it if they started dating each other!

He looked at his watch again and gave his school-bag another hefty kick. He stood up from the bench and started to walk up and down the sidewalk.

If only he could do something at school that would make everyone realize that he was all right. If only he could prove himself in some way. But how? He had tried his hardest at football, but he was much slower than the other guys on the team and could never keep up with the game, and as far as baseball was concerned, he was always striking out or dropping the ball. He had thought about entering this talent competition for poetry and music that the teachers were running, but they were putting each entry out over the school PA system every morning, and he *knew* that everyone would just laugh if he did something. It was all just so . . . hopeless!

He looked at his watch again. It was ten to five. He went back to the bench and picked up his bag. He was *not* going to wait any longer for stupid Germaine. If he walked home, then she would have to come looking for him, and that would serve her right, and hopefully Jasmine would chew her out. He slung his bag onto his shoulder and, glancing once more up the road to make sure that Germaine's car wasn't in view, he set off towards the village.

He enjoyed every minute of his illicit freedom, taking time to gaze into the shop windows in the main street as he passed by, eventually ending up buying himself a chocolate milk and a blueberry muffin in the deli. He munched his way to the top of Barker Lane and considered going on to the country club to watch some tennis, but thought better of it, knowing that Jasmine would be wondering where he was. Anyway, more than likely there would be some of his fellow pupils there being coached, and he certainly didn't want to see *them*. He turned down Barker Lane and headed for home at a slow, meandering pace.

He had walked far enough down the driveway of the house to see that the gardener's car was still parked by the shed when he heard the scrunch of gravel at the head of the drive as a car turned in. He turned and watched as Germaine's green Jeep came roaring in, coming to an abrupt halt beside him. Without turning off the engine, Germaine jumped out, a look of fury on her weaselly face.

"Where in God's name did *you* get to? I have been waiting for you outside that school for the past quarter of an hour, and I tell you, my boy, that I have one hundred and one better things to do than to hang around for *you*!"

"But you were very late, Germaine," Benji said quietly.

"It doesn't matter if I'm late. Your mother pays me to pick you up every day, so you just wait until I get there. Is that understood?"

"Okay," Benji said, looking down at his shoes. He heard the back door of the kitchen open and raised his eyes high enough to see Jasmine running along the path towards them.

"So don't you *ever* leave there again without me. Is that understood?"

"What's all the commotion about?" Jasmine asked as she reached them.

"This stupid boy walked home today," Germaine said, her teeth gritted in fury. "I have been sitting for *at least* fifteen minutes outside that wretched school waiting for him to come out, only to find that he's taken it upon himself to walk, *expressly* against the wishes of his mother, and I think you should give him a real good talking-to."

"Oh, do you?" Jasmine said, folding her arms and nodding slowly, "and what time, Germaine, did you arrive at the school to pick him up?"

Germaine started to bite at her lip. "*That* is irrelevant! He's *supposed* to stay there until such time as I decide to arrive."

"And what time did you *decide* to arrive today, Germaine?" Jasmine asked again quietly.

The frown on Germaine's brow deepened visibly as she became increasingly more angry. "I got there in plenty of time to pick him—"

"Okay, if I can't get a straight answer from you," Jasmine interjected, "I'll ask Benji." She put her hand on his shoulder. "Benji?"

"I left at ten to five, Jasmine, because I didn't think that—"

"Ten to five!" She glared at Germaine, her eyes like thunder. "Ten to five! That's thirty-five minutes late! Where *on earth* were you? You know he comes out at quarter past four."

"How *dare* you speak to me like that? Who do you think you are, you black—"

"I think you have said quite enough!" The voice came from such an angle that no one saw him approach. They all turned to see David walking across the lawn, a rake in his hand, with Dodie skipping along at his heels. Germaine looked at them both, a quizzical sneer on her face.

"And who the hell might you be?" she asked.

"It doesn't matter who I am," he said, his voice low and controlled. "I think you've said quite enough, so probably the best thing you can do right now is just get back in your car and leave, all right?"

Germaine looked from one to the other, then, turning on her heel with a yell of anger, she jumped back into her car, slamming the door behind her. She let down the window. "I'm going to make damned sure that Jennifer hears about this. I'll call her at the office."

"You do just that," Jasmine said slowly.

Germaine let out another cry of frustration, and having executed a noisy three-point turn, she threw up a middle finger as a parting gesture and roared back up the drive, spraying gravel onto the lawn as she went.

Having watched in silence as the car disappeared around the bend in the drive, Jasmine turned to Benji and put her hand on his shoulder. "Are you all right?"

"Uh-huh."

"Well, I think you acted real grown up, darlin', and I'm proud of you, so you've gone and done nothin' wrong as far as I'm concerned, okay?"

Benji looked up at her and smiled.

"Now, why don't you go and get yourself some chocolate milk out of the fridge, and I'll be in right after I've had a word with David."

Benji's face fell visibly, and giving a sullen glance in David's direction, he walked off towards the kitchen door. They stood silently watching him until he had entered the house.

"Oh, *goddammit*!" Jasmine exclaimed, slapping her hand hard against her thigh. "That really takes the cake!"

David shook his head. "Who *was* that, anyway?"

"*That* was Germaine. She takes—or should I say, *has* been taking Benji to and from school every day. She is always late for him, and today she was *so* late that Benji walked home. That was what all the shouting was about. What a *b* she is! Oh, hell, now what are we going to do?"

"Look, if you want, you can always borrow my car and take him," David suggested.

Jasmine raised her eyebrows. "That's very kind of you, David. It would be a great idea if I could drive!"

"Ah," David said, nodding in realization of the problem in hand. "Right. Well, in that case, the other alternative is that I could take him to school and pick him up—that is, if you agree with it. I mean, I'm here anyway, so it would seem to make sense—wouldn't it?"

Jasmine focused her eyes up the drive for a moment as she pondered the proposition, then turned to him, a smile on her face.

"Would you mind doing that?"

"Not at all. I'd be delighted."

"We'd have to clear it with Jennifer."

"Of course." He paused for a moment. "Actually, thinking about it, Jasmine, I wonder if we should consider clearing it first with Benji? I mean, I'm not exactly the flavour of the month right at this minute."

"Yup, I think that's a great idea." She grinned. "Just wish I'd thought of it. C'mon, let's go inside and ask him."

David stayed where he was. "Jasmine?"

"Yuh?"

"I wonder if you would mind if I did it. I really would like to clear up the misunderstanding that we had yesterday."

Jasmine nodded and moved off towards the house. "Okay. C'mon then."

They walked back along the path and up the steps to the kitchen door. As Jasmine opened it, she paused for a moment before turning back to David. "Listen, thanks for what you did back there."

David waved his hand dismissively. "Och, it was nothing. She was just a very stupid woman!"

"No, it meant a lot to me and I think probably to Benji as well. So thanks from both of us."

She started to go into the kitchen, but then stopped and turned to him once more. "Och!"

David looked at her. "What?"

"You said 'Och!' Now I know that that *is* Scottish!" She let out a laugh and entered the kitchen, leaving David to shut the door behind him.

Although there were tell-tale signs of Benji's having been there, like the open chocolate-milk carton being still on the table, he had obviously thought of something other to do than watch television. Jasmine walked over to the French doors and scanned the garden, but seeing no sign of him, she turned and motioned David to follow her through to the house. They went into the hall and stood at the bottom of the stairs, and Jasmine called out for him. Benji's muffled voice replied from somewhere above.

"He's in his bedroom," Jasmine said quietly. "If you go upstairs, turn left on the landing and it's the furthest room on the right, okay? Tell me how it went when you're through, so's I can give Jennifer a call. Good luck!"

David gave her the thumbs-up and headed up the stairs. He walked along to the end of the landing and hesitated for a moment outside Benji's door, working out how best he could eat humble pie before finally knocking.

"Yeah?" Benji's voice answered from inside.

"Benji, it's, erm, David. Would you mind if I came in for a moment?"

There was silence.

"Benji?"

"If you have to."

David pulled a face at this less than hopeful response and walked into the room. The boy was lying on his stomach on the bed, playing intently with a Game Boy, never raising his eyes for a second to acknowledge David's entry.

David stood in the centre of the floor and pushed his hands into the back pockets of his jeans while surveying the room, trying to find some talking point with which he could break the ice. It was wallpapered throughout with images of Superman carrying out gravity-defying stunts with an assortment of beautiful women held close under his Lycraed armpit. Light flooded into the room through the large dormer window, and he walked over to look out at the unimpeded view of the Great South Bay and over to Fire Island beyond. To the left of the window, a row of shelves was stacked high with a vast array of technological toys and plastic models of grotesque comic-book heroes, and underneath these, covering the whole surface of Benji's desk, was a computer system that looked complex and powerful enough to launch a rocket into space, its screen saver blipping out repetitive images that floated out to the surface of the screen before vanishing.

"That's pretty impressive," David said, nodding at the computer. He turned to see if Benji had reacted in any way, but he was still engrossed in his Game Boy, pushing hard at its controls as it sang out little tunes to register his rate of success and failure. David decided to persevere by trying out some inbred knowledge.

"I'm surprised you're still playing with a Game Boy. You've got CD-ROM over here."

He walked over to the desk and picked up some of the CD games that were lying beside the computer. Benji sighed deeply at David's unwelcome disturbance and pressed even harder at his controls.

Realizing that he was getting nowhere, David decided that the only option left open to him was the direct approach. He was just about to turn round to speak to Benji when his eye was caught by a small ukulele, tucked away forgotten on the top shelf, its small body emblazoned with the words "Hi from Hawaii!" He reached up and took it down and plucked at the strings. It was completely out of tune. He began fiddling with the wooden tuning-pegs, twanging the strings, and once he had it reasonably in tune, he strummed off a couple of chords before reaching up to replace it on the shelf.

"How d'you do that?"

He swung round to find Benji watching him, his mouth open, the now silent Game Boy held limply in his hands.

"What?"

"I thought that was only a toy. You made it play a tune."

David looked up at the ukulele. "Well, I don't suppose that one was specifically designed for playing." He took down the ukulele once more. "Probably just a souvenir, but it's got all its strings and it seems to work all right."

He played a number of quick chords, strumming hard and fast on the instrument, then, finishing with a flourish, he held his hands out at each side as if willing applause and gave Benji a quick bow.

"Where did you learn to do *that*?" Benji asked, his eyes wide. He slid off the bed and, discarding his Game Boy onto the bedside table, came across the room towards him.

"Well, I had this rather eccentric uncle who used to come to stay with us when I was a boy. He always brought his ukulele and made up silly songs for me. He taught me how to tune it first." David twanged the strings, singing out a word for each pitch. "My—Dog—Has—Fleas."

Benji laughed and, snatching the ukulele from David's grasp, plucked clumsily at the strings, singing out the tuning-ditty at the same time.

"There you are," David said. "You've just had your first lesson."

Benji's eyes shone with delight at his new-found skill.

"And then, once you've mastered that, you can start on the guitar."

Benji's eyes grew wider by the minute. "Wow, really! Can *you* play the guitar?"

"Well, I haven't for some time, but yeah, I reckon I could again. It's rather like riding a bicycle." David paused for a moment, realizing that this was a perfect entrée for his apology. "Speaking of which,

Benji, erm, the incident that happened yesterday when I was mending your bicycle . . . well, I'm sorry that I shouted at you over the swimming-pool thing. I didn't realize that you were an expert at holding your breath."

Benji smiled and shrugged. "Aw, that was nothing. Say, did you ever play in a group or anything?"

David laughed and shook his head at the boy's fickleness. "Yes, as a matter of fact, I did—at university."

"Wow! And did you write songs and stuff like that?"

"Sure. Not very good ones, but if the group played them loud enough, they didn't sound too bad."

"Wow! That's incredible! I thought you were just a gardener!"

David chuckled. "Well, I have just a few hidden talents."

Benji looked down again at the ukulele. "How old were you when you started playing this?"

"Oh, about eight."

"Eight! But I'm eleven," he said excitedly.

"Well, then, it's time you started to learn how to play, isn't it?"

"You mean you'd *teach* me?"

"If you want."

"Yay! And would you teach me how to write songs and things? I mean, I can write poetry. Would that be a help?"

"Well, you've got it made then. If you can do that, you can write songs."

Benji forgot to say "Yay!" this time, instead only letting out a high-pitched sigh that seemed to signify utter contentment. He looked up at David, a pleading look on his face. "Could you maybe start to teach me now?"

David shook his head and looked out the window. "No, not now. I think the evening's too good to sit inside teaching you how to play the ukulele."

Benji's face lengthened with disappointment.

"So I thought that we might go and play some tennis."

Benji looked up at him, his mouth open. "What?"

"I want to play some tennis. Is something wrong with that?"

"You can play tennis *too*?"

"Sure, why not?"

"*All right!*" Benji paused for a moment, his look of excitement suddenly dropping from his face, and he began fiddling with the pegs on the ukulele.

"What's the matter?" David asked. "Don't you want to have a game?"

"Yeah!" Benji replied. "It's only that . . ."

"Only what?"

"Only that I can't run very fast, 'cos I'm kinda . . . you know. . . . fat." He started turning the pegs of the ukulele round and round.

David slanted his head to one side and made a show of studying his physique. "I don't think you're fat. I would say you're more, well, powerfully built."

Benji looked up at him, an expression of sheer hopefulness on his face. "Do you really mean that?"

"Of course I mean that. I tell you what, in four years' time, I wouldn't like to meet you down a dark alley."

"What?"

"Well, you'd probably beat me up."

Benji's mouth broke into a wide grin. "No, I wouldn't! I'd beat up an enemy, but not a friend!" He laid the ukulele down carefully on his bed, then turned and raced towards the door. "Come on, let's go play some tennis."

"Benji," David said, staying where he was, his eyes fixed on the ukulele. Benji turned to see David beckoning him back with his finger.

"Yes?" he said quietly, looking at the instrument and trying to work out what he had done wrong with it.

"I watched you put that ukulele out of tune."

"Oh, sorry," he said humbly, going over to the bed and picking it up.

"No, it's all right. Only I want you to get it in tune for me by tomorrow, okay?"

Benji's face once more broke into a wide grin. "Okay!!" He put the ukulele down and ran back to the door. "Now can we go play some tennis?"

"Just one more thing."

Benji turned back again, this time letting out a groan of impatience. David smiled at him.

"Look, as you no doubt heard, Germaine is not going to be taking you to school any more, and—well—Jasmine and I were wondering if you would mind if I started to take you."

"What? In the Volkswagen?" Benji gasped.

"Well, if you don't mind."

"Wow! That's so cool! Can we have the top down?"

"Yeah, I'm sure we can. Why do you want the roof down?"

" 'Cos it's so cool, and . . ."

"And what?"

"Well, it's just that I was playing with Dodie yesterday and I bent down to get the ball, and she licked my face, and her breath is real lousy. That's why I stopped playing with her."

David laughed. "Okay, it's a deal." He walked over to Benji and held up his hand and they sealed the arrangement with a slap of palms. "Right, *now* let's go and play some tennis."

Benji threw open the door and ran off down the landing, and David reached the top of the stairs in time to witness him making it to the hall in four leaps, yelling out Jasmine's name as he did so. Jasmine came running through from the kitchen.

"Jasmine! David's going to teach me tennis, and then he's going to teach me how to play the uke——the uke——" He looked back up the stairs towards David.

"The ukulele."

"Yup, that's it. He's going to show me how to play the . . . *ukulelele*. He's taught me how to tune it already!"

As he ran off towards the kitchen, David descended the stairs to find Jasmine standing with an incredulous expression on her face. "For heaven's sakes, what did you *do*?"

"Oh, we just had a bit of private men's talk, and, well, he seems to be pretty *cool* about me taking him to school, so I think you're probably quite safe to make that telephone call now."

He blew on his finger-nails and waggled his hand to signify his own self-excellence, then, giving her a wink, he headed off after Benji.

CHAPTER 20

Sam Culpepper chucked the briefing document onto the boardroom table and sat back in his high-backed leather chair. He glanced down the table at the pensive looks on the faces of his two main account directors, who, in turn, stared at him in silence.

"Okay, so it's not that big, but I really want us to win this contract." He bent forward and picked up the cigar that was smouldering in the ashtray, and took a deep inhale of smoke. "Why? Because there are rumours that both Bates and Young and Rubicam have also gotten hold of this." He slapped his hand down on the document. ". . . And it would be one hell of a feather in our caps if we got it. I'd make damned sure that Media Week found out about it anyway!" He let out a loud laugh which immediately gave way to a crackling cough.

Russ Hogan was the first to comment. "To be quite honest, Sam, I don't think we stand a chance. We've never handled a liquor account before, let alone one based in the UK. I mean, the amount of research that we're going to have to put into this is enormous. I really wonder if it's worth it."

Sam slowly nodded. He could have bet a hundred bucks down flat that it would be Russ who'd come out with such a statement. Granted he was a good account director and excelled in smarming up his clients, but more often than not this was counteracted by his ability to sound off on a subject without giving much thought to what he was actually saying—and here was a perfect example.

Sam pushed himself out of his chair and walked over to the window, dragging on his cigar as he stared down at the clogged traffic far below on Fifth Avenue. He turned and looked at Russ.

"I think you're wrong, Russ. I think it *is* worth it." He returned to the table, flicked ash off into an ashtray, and leaned on the back of his chair, swinging it from side to side. "It took us over twenty years to build up Culpepper Rowan to the size that it's now, but I think we've hit a peak, and for the first time I'm concerned about the underlying strength—or should I say, lack of strength—of the company. Now, I may be wrong, but I think that we may have become just a little too complacent with the work that's ongoing. Our accounts may be numerous, but the majority are small. We don't have one big fish to fry."

"You're not trying to tell us that you think Tarvy's Gin is a big account?" Russ interjected, rankled by Sam's slanted accusation, and too thick-skinned to realize that it would be more diplomatic to allow his CEO to finish making his point. "I mean, you read out the UK sales figures just then, and I wouldn't say they're over-impressive. Okay, I grant you, these are probably indicative of the fact that it *is* a fairly new product in the UK, but there again, Sam, it's going to be totally new over here, and we'll be running up against the likes of Gordon's and Beefeater."

Sam held out his hands in exasperation. "But don't you see, Russ? Come on! What else did I read out?"

Russ leaned on the arm of his chair and bit at a finger-nail, not sure what his managing director meant. Sam looked at both his account execs. "Don't either of you see what I'm getting at?"

There was a moment's silence, broken eventually by the sound of Jennifer Newman's pen hitting her pad as she lobbed it onto the table.

"What you're saying—I think, Sam—is that it's not simply Tarvy's Gin that is important, more the fact that it is the new house gin for Gladwin Vintners, who also have Glentochry Blend Whisky and Valischka Vodka as house brands. You were saying that both of these command fairly sizeable market share in the UK, even though they are not prestige products. The gin is a relatively new product for them, so they give us the chance to push this one on a low promotional budget, and then, if it takes off, they might consider doing the same with their whisky and vodka products over here, hopefully through the same company. That means whoever wins the Tarvy's contract could eventually end up with the complete brand range of Gladwin Vintners."

Sam clicked his fingers and pointed at Jennifer. "Exactly. And that's what all the other top agencies in Manhattan would be thinking, and that's what they would be going for." Sam smiled at his female executive. "Thanks, Jennifer."

Russ chewed noisily on his gum and glanced across at Jennifer, giving her a look of light-hearted disdain at being upstaged. He turned back to Sam.

"Come on. There's nothing to back up that theory. It's pure supposition."

"Okay, so it is. But I really think we're going to *have* to start taking a few risks and spend a bit more time and resources on R and D, otherwise we could quite easily be brought down by our own complacency. I mean, we need something to put fire in our bellies, and I reckon that this account is as good a way as any of achieving that—and, as I said beforehand, the publicity would be terrific!"

Russ shrugged his shoulders in resignation. "Okay, so we do it. Who's going to handle it?"

Sam pointed his finger down the table. "I want you to do it, Jennifer."

She raised her eyebrows. "Why not? What's the timetable?"

"A month, to be precise." He watched tentatively her reaction to this, seeing her eyes widen as she began to understand the implications of his remark.

"Are you saying this proposal has to be completed in a *month,* Sam?"

"Yup, 'fraid so. This document has already been out for about three weeks, and I've only just got my hands on it." He opened up to the first page and began reading. "Proposals have to be submitted by Saturday, the fourth of July, at the latest, and Gladwin's will be announcing the successful agency on the seventh. So I'm afraid no Independence Day break for any of us this year."

Jennifer let out a long whistle as Sam looked up from the document at Russ.

"Okay, so it may be a long shot, but let's go all out to get this goddamned account!"

Half an hour later, Jennifer left the boardroom, cradling the papers and her notepad, laden with action points, in the crook of her arm. She walked along the corridor and was about to enter her office when her secretary appeared from the room opposite. "Jennifer, that's Jasmine for you on line two."

"Ah, right, thanks. Oh, Mandy, here," she said, handing her secretary the notepad, "could you type this up ASAP?"

"Sure thing."

"Thanks."

She walked into her office, and throwing the document onto the desk, she picked up the receiver and pressed the flashing button on the set. "Jasmine?"

"Hi, Jennifer."

"Nothing's wrong, is it?"

"No, not really."

"What does that mean?" Looping the telephone cord over her desk lamp, she walked around behind her desk and sat down. "Is there or is there not something wrong?"

"Well, there's nothin' wrong with Benji, which I guess is what you're meanin'. It's just that Germaine was real late in pickin' him up—I mean, all of thirty-five minutes late—and, well, Benji did the right thing and walked home."

"Oh, for Chrissakes, Jasmine!"

"Now don't start gettin' on your high horse, Jennifer! He did right. He couldn't go on waitin'. He didn't know if she was goin' to turn up or not!"

"Okay, so what happened?"

"Germaine came here just as Benji arrived home and started to tear strips off the poor boy, and er, I kinda got angry with her, I'm afraid, Jennifer, and she headed off, saying she was goin' to get in touch with you. She obviously hasn't yet."

Jennifer scanned her desk for a message. "No, I don't think so. I've been in a meeting for the past hour, so I wouldn't know. She probably won't at any rate. She knows she's in the wrong."

"Yeah, well, she sure as hell was out of line." Jasmine paused. "The trouble is, Jennifer, she's not goin' to do the run any more."

"Oh, God," Jennifer sighed, brushing her hand over head. "What on earth are we going to do now? I am *not,* repeat, *not* going to allow him to walk to school, Jasmine."

"Yup, that's what I thought you'd probably say. Okay, in that case I think that I may have come up with an alternative."

"What's that?"

"David has offered to take him."

"David? Who's David?"

"The gardener, Jennifer."

"Jasmine!" Jennifer leaned forward heavily on the desk. "You cannot be serious! We don't know him from Adam! I mean, he could be a—a child molester or something! I mean—"

"He is *not* a child molester, Jennifer. To be quite honest, I don't think I've ever met someone less like a child molester. He's a decent guy."

"Oh? And how can you tell that after he's only been there for two days?"

There was a pause at the other end of the line.

"Well," Jasmine said at last, "because Germaine called Benji stupid and then started in on a racial, and David came across the lawn and cut in and told her to go!"

"Ah—I see." Jennifer swore quietly at herself for being so one-track-minded. "I'm sorry, Jasmine. I didn't realize. What a bitch! How *dare* she?"

"It don't matter. Anyway, I can really vouch for David, Jennifer. I mean, he's here with Benji right now, out on the court teaching him how to play tennis."

"You're joking!"

"Nope, I am not! *And* he's going to teach him how to play the guitar."

"We don't have a guitar, Jasmine."

"Well, that other thing then. The uke . . . something."

"The ukulele?"

"Yeah, that's it. There's one in Benji's bedroom."

Jennifer sat back in her chair. "That's incredible! And is Benji quite happy with all this going on?"

"Jennifer, I haven't seen that boy look so plumb happy for the longest time!"

The door of her office opened and Jennifer turned in her chair to see Sam and Russ enter. "Hang on just a minute." She put her hand over the receiver, but Sam waved his hands at her to indicate that she should carry on with the conversation. Jennifer smiled and took her hand away from the receiver.

"Jasmine? Right, okay, if you think it's all right. I mean, it *sounds* all right, so yes, let David take Benji to school."

"That's great! I tell you truthful, Jennifer, I think that David could be the making of your boy."

"Well, let's not go overboard."

Jasmine laughed. "Okay, but you wait and see. I'll go tell them now."

"All right, and give Benji a big kiss from me." She put down the telephone and looked across at Sam and Russ who, by this time, had pulled up chairs opposite her desk.

"Everything all right at home?" Sam asked, a concerned look on his face.

"I guess so," Jennifer replied, nodding. "We've got a new gardener who seems to be something of a Superman. He's teaching Benji how to play tennis right now."

"That's great! Hey, speaking of which, we must get a game sometime! I haven't played this season yet."

"Well, come on out," Jennifer said, flicking open her desk diary. "Maybe not this weekend, because I want to get started on this." She pointed to the document. "But what about the one after?"

Sam put his hand in his inside pocket and pulled out his diary and began to leaf through it. "No, nothing on. Molly and I would love to do that."

"Okay, then that's a date!"

"Is Alex going to be around?" Russ asked, taking his own diary out of his pocket.

Jennifer smiled. "I could try to get hold of him and ask. Do you want to give him his yearly thrashing?"

"Well, he's about the only guy who can give me a decent game."

Jennifer and Sam gave each other a knowing look, and noticing this, Russ raised his hands in innocence. "It's true, I tell you!"

"Okay, I'll give him a ring." Jennifer jotted it down on her deskpad, then dropped her pen on the desk. "Now why I am being honoured with this visit from you both?"

Sam pushed himself out of his chair and stretched his hands above his head. "No reason, really. Only that we're going out for a quick drink and wondered if you would like to join us. Probably be the last opportunity that we'll all have for some time."

Jennifer smiled at both men, then shook her head. "That's sweet of you, but I'd better not." She picked up the document on the desk and started leafing through it. "I really want to get started on this."

Sam's face broke into a broad grin. "Great! I'm glad to hear it!" He took a pace over to Russ, who sat with a disgruntled pout on his face, and held out his hand. "That's what I call commitment, don't you, Russ?"

Russ looked round at him, and after a brief moment made a reluctant show of pulling a ten-dollar bill from the top pocket of his jacket and thrusting it into Sam's open hand. Jennifer's mouth fell open and she threw the papers back onto her desk, shaking her head in disbelief. "You two! You were betting on me coming with you, weren't you?"

"No, get it right!" Sam said, giving her a wink. "*Russ* was betting on you coming, while I, as always, had total confidence in you, and subsequently . . ." He folded the bill in two, placed it in his top pocket and gave it a little pat ". . . the outcome of our bet!"

"You men are such *babies*!" Jennifer jumped to her feet, and picking up her pen from the desk, made to throw it at them both.

"Uh-oh!" Russ exclaimed, ducking out of his chair and moving fast after Sam who, laughing loudly, had managed to beat a hasty retreat to the door. The two men pushed and jostled each other outside into the corridor, then Russ turned and stuck his head round the corner of the door. "Don't forget to call Alex!"

The pen hit the door a foot to the right of his nose. He glanced surprised at the point of impact, then, sticking out his tongue, closed the door quickly before further retribution could be administered.

"Goddamned schoolboys!" Jennifer said, smiling to herself. She walked over to retrieve her pen, then, returning to her chair, fell back into it and reached forward to pick up the telephone receiver. She pushed a button for one of the stored numbers and opened the document in front of her, closing it immediately when she heard an answer.

"Hello?"

"Hi, darling! It's me!"

"Oh, hi! Hang on, Jennifer, it's too noisy here. Just keep talking, though."

"Where are you?"

"San Francisco airport. I'm just about to catch a flight to Houston. Okay, is that better?"

"Yes, much."

"So, how're things?"

"Great! Sam's just given me a new contract to work on. Could be the big one for us."

"Glad to hear it. Listen, can you be quick 'cos I'm going to have to go."

"Oh—okay. In that case, could you just check your calendar and see if you're going to be back in Leesport the weekend after next? I've invited Sam and Molly out for tennis, and, well, Russ wants to come out to get his game of singles with you."

"Oh, hell, do I have to play him? It's just one big ego trip as far as he's concerned. I mean, he beats me every time."

"I know, darling. But can you make it anyway—for me?"

"Look, I don't have my calendar here, but I'll do my best to keep the weekend free. Okay?"

"Yeah, that's fine."

"All right. Well, I'd better be off."

"Okay. Have a good flight."

"Will do. See you."

"Yeah, see you."

Jennifer replaced the receiver and sat staring at the phone, suddenly feeling low at the lack of spontaneity in their conversation. "Love you," she said quietly to herself.

There was a knock on her door and Mandy entered the room and came across to her desk. "Here are your notes."

"That's great, Mandy. Going home now?"

"Yup, if that's okay?"

Jennifer lifted her head from her notes and smiled at her. "Yeah, fine. I'll see you in the morning."

As the door closed, she glanced back at the telephone, wondering if she should try calling Alex again. No, he'd said he was in a rush—it would probably just be a nuisance to him. She shook her head to support her decision, then pulled the file towards her and ran her hand down its centre to crease it open.

CHAPTER

21

There had been all-round improvement at the Newman household by the time the day of the tennis party came round. Firstly, Benji's tennis had now reached the stage that he could hold an extensive rally with David, even though David had to make sure that he kept hitting the ball to his forehand, otherwise it was quite likely to end up in the swimming pool. His ukulele playing likewise went from strength to strength, the only times that he was ever seen without the instrument being when he was playing tennis or at school, not yet having the confidence to show off his newly discovered prowess to his fellow pupils.

Despite this, he had decided that he would try entering a little song of his own for the school talent competition, his motivation for this being derived from the fact that David had himself written a little ditty about Dodie, specifically for Benji to play on the three chords that he had learned. However, throughout its first recital, Benji had criticized the song endlessly for its lack of accuracy and bad rhyming.

"So the chords are just straight G, C and D-Seventh—like that. Okay?"

"Yup. Can I do it now?"

"Hang on! You don't even know how it goes yet!"

"Okay. But I'll do it next time."

"All right. Now, are you listening?"

"Yup."

"Life is filled with such wonderful things
Like beer and hot apfelstrudel—"

"What's apfelstrudel?"

"It's a sort of a German apple-tart."

"Do you always eat it with beer?"

"No, I don't think so."

"Well then, why beer and hot apfelstrudel?"

"Because it rhymes, Benji."

"With what?"

"Just hold your horses! We haven't got there yet.

"But it's beaten by far
By a ride in the car
With Dodie the fun-loving poodle—"

"That's ridiculous! Can't you think of anything else to rhyme with poodle?"

"Hey, give me a break! It only took me an hour to write this!"

"An hour! But it's only five lines long!"

"Just wait, Sir Tim Rice, I haven't finished yet!"

"Who's Sir Tim Rice?"

"Listen, do you want me to go on or not?"

"Okay."

"We ride around the town
With the top folded down
And in Leesport I tell you that's freezin'—"

"No, it's not!"

"Not what?"

"It's never freezing in Leesport. Well, not in summer, anyway. In winter, it sometimes goes down to minus—"

"Benji!"

"Okay, I suppose you only used the word to rhyme with—"

"Look, do you want me to go on or not?"

"Sorry."

"Then the air becomes thick
You think Dodie's been sick
But it turns out that she's only breathin'."

"Hey! I like that!"

"Thank goodness! I've made an impression at last."

"Only *freezin'* doesn't rhyme with *breathin'*."

"Oh, forget it then!"

"No, please, David, do it again!"

"No. Couldn't be bothered. Anyway, I haven't finished it yet."

"*Please,* David, sing the whole thing! I promise I won't interrupt again."

"Promise?"

"Yeah, promise. Go on, how does it start?"

"Life is filled with such wonderful things
Like beer and hot apfelstrudel
But it's beaten by far
By a ride in the car
With Dodie the fun-loving poodle.

"We ride around town
With the top folded down
And in Leesport I tell you that's freezin'."

"Though it's not!"

"You said you weren't—"

"Sorry!"

"Then the air becomes thick
You think Dodie's been sick
But it turns out that she's only breathin'."

"Right, all together now!"

"Life is filled with such wonderful things
Like beer and hot apfelstrudel.
But it's beaten by far
By a ride in the car
With Dodie the fun-loving poodle.

"Well, she sits in her seat
Growls at all that she meets
'Cept the boy, and her boss who's a navvy."

"Is the boy me?"
"Yeah."
"Great! Er, David?"
"What?"
"Can I ask another question?"
"What?"
"What's a navvy?"
"A workman. That's me."
"Oh. Okay."
"Can I go on?"
"Okay."

"But although she goes wuff!
She's just a bundle of fluff
And you can use her to clean out the lavvy!"

"A lavvy?"
"A loo—a toilet. I don't know what you call it."
"Hey, that's really *rude*!"

"Well, those are the lyrics."

"I think it's great! But I bet I could do just as well!"

"Well, do it then!"

"Okay, I will. But can I do that one now?"

It soon became their constant anthem, both of them singing it out loud as they drove back and forth through Leesport on the school run, with Dodie, ever present in the back seat, lapping up every moment of reflected glory.

June had also brought out an abundance of new colour in the garden, which helped to create a fresh and exciting vibrancy to the already perfect setting of the house. Roses of every hue bloomed majestically, while flocks and Japanese irises, encouraged by the warm weather, stretched their spindly necks above the hydrangeas and spicy-smelling geraniums, splashing their pin-points of colour against the blue backdrop of the bay. The trumpet-vine that grew at the front of the house and climbed high onto the veranda above the conservatory broke open its flowers, spreading them outward so that they licked like tiny incandescent flames at the white wooden railings and the shingles around the upper windows.

This all helped give David even greater impetus in his work. He had found a small garden centre five miles out of Leesport on the Montauk Highway, where he had bought an abundance of herbaceous shrubs and bedding plants to fill in the gaps that had been left by the previous gardener. However, his eccentric appearance whilst shopping, pushing his laden trolley along the paths with a poodle attached by its lead to the handle, soon drew the attention of the young couple who owned the place, and subsequently, during his third visit, they introduced themselves and asked him into their office for coffee and muffins. Visits thereafter gradually lengthened in time, and even though they became firm friends, he eventually had to try stockpiling his lists in order to cut down both on the time he spent away from the garden and on his intake of caffeine.

Nevertheless, it was these friends, really genuine friends, that he had made during his short time in Leesport who helped him prove to himself that his own healing process was well under way. No longer did he wish to head home each night to sit alone in the house. He actively sought company, and when he was not having supper with Jasmine and Benji, he either dropped in at the Leesport Bar for a beer and a chat with the locals, or he was being invited out for dinner with new-found acquaintances. On one such occasion it had been at the house of Clive and his friend Peter. While David was made to sit at the kitchen table, the two men accompanied the preparation of the meal with a hilarious and obviously well-rehearsed two-man act, each singing and dancing around the other, saucepan and mixing bowl in hand, to the strains of an old recording of *My Fair Lady*.

But the closest relationship he had of all was brought about by his daily contact with Jasmine and Benji, the bond that he had now formed with the young boy helping to bring thoughts of his own children constantly to the surface of his mind. Every second night he would sit down to write each a letter, starting always by knocking off the number of days left to the end of term with the words "Then Holiday Time!!" written after the scored-out figure. He really missed them so much, and although he felt apprehensive about eventually having to return to Scotland, there was also a profound excitement at the thought of being with them again.

Yet at present it was the environment of the Newman household which gave him the strongest indication that he was returning to normality, both the simplicity of his own existence and the innocent, uncomplicated chemistry engendered by his two friends helping to reduce the tangled mess of barbed wire in his brain to a smooth, straight line of clear thought.

Consequently, life for him revolved around his work in the garden: the tennis matches with Benji, for which Jasmine, at Benji's insistence, had now been made to perch on a step-ladder at the side of the net, calling out what was invariably the wrong score, but all adding to the authenticity and importance of the occasion; the ferry trips to Fire Island with Benji, who, more often than not, was allowed to demonstrate his nautical skills by taking over at the helm; the evenings in the kitchen or on the terrace, drinking wine with Jasmine whilst Benji interrupted them constantly to sing Dodie's song or yet another line of his own "hit" single; and then Jasmine's driving lessons up the drive, which numbered only one and a bit, Jasmine having stormed off half-way through the second, leaving her passengers bent double with uncontrollable laughter at her total inability to master clutch control.

However, despite their ever-deepening friendship, David never mentioned anything about his past, unprepared to start revealing any of his innermost thoughts. This was not through any lack of trust or opportunity in confiding in Jasmine, but more that he was frightened of the reaction that he himself might have to his own revelation, knowing that it could so easily open up healing wounds and allow the infection of unwelcome sorrow to penetrate his mind again.

Friday had been such a beautiful day, with the sea breeze picking up enough to blow away the sticky humidity which had hung about since the previous weekend, that David had picked up Benji from school and, with Jasmine's permission, they had gone straight to the marina to catch the ferry to Fire Island. There they had spent the late afternoon and early evening, happily playing football on the beach and swimming in the sea, making it back across the boardwalk just in time to catch the last ferry home. Because it was too late to complete the work that he had scheduled for himself that day, David decided to return to finish off his tasks on the Saturday.

He arrived at the house at his usual time of eight-fifteen in the morning, to be met by Benji, who came running out of the kitchen still wearing his pyjamas. He proceeded to rattle off a garbled explanation about why he wouldn't be able to keep him company until later, seeing that his father was home and he wanted to play him his new song. David excused him, secretly relieved that he would now be allowed to complete the rest of the mowing without interruption.

By mid-day, the lawn tractor was back in the shed, and he had moved down to the flower-bed at the farthest end of the tennis court to plant the rest of the shrubs that he had purchased from the garden centre two days beforehand. He was in the process of digging in a new dwarf rhododendron when he heard voices coming from around the side of the hedge and turned to see five figures dressed in tennis whites slowly make their way towards the small summer-house at the other end of the court, chatting as they walked. Dodie let out a short bark to warn him of strangers in their garden.

"Dodie! That's enough!" he said quietly, watching them long enough to see Benji careering around the corner on his bicycle before turning back to his work.

"Benji! Watch out! You nearly ran over Sam!"

"Sorry, Sam! Sorry, Dad! HI, DAVID!"

David looked up and gave him a brief wave before returning to his work.

"Who's that, Jennifer?" David heard a female voice say.

"That's David, the new gardener. God, look, I'd better go and have a word with him. I haven't spoken to him since he first arrived. Listen, Alex, darling, why don't you play with Molly—no, that's not fair—Russ, you play with Molly, and Alex, you play with Sam."

"Christ, Jennifer, I *still* think it's too hot to play. I mean, it's the middle of the day!"

"Come on, moaner, you've been sitting on a plane all week. It'll do you good, and anyway, it might sweat off some of those extra pounds that total inactivity has put on your middle!"

There was an outburst of laughter.

"Thanks for nothing!"

"Can't I introduce Dad to David, Mom?" Benji asked.

"Yeah, why can't I meet Superman?"

"Sssh, Alex! For God's sakes, he might hear. Just go play some tennis."

There was the general mumbling of voices and the sound of tennis-racket covers being unzipped, and David had just heard the clink of the bolt being slid across on the court gate when a voice spoke at his side.

"Hi."

He turned in his bent position to look at a pair of long brown legs, his eyes following them upwards to the fringe of a short white tennis skirt. He stood up quickly, not wishing to make it look as if he was lingering on the sight, to find Jennifer standing beside him. He'd had only had a fleeting glimpse of her since their first meeting, that being on the previous Saturday, when he had come over especially to give Benji a tennis lesson. She had come out onto the veranda above the conservatory to watch them play for five minutes before going back into the house. Benji had said something about her being busy working on a new contract.

"Hullo. I hope you don't mind my coming over today. It's only that—"

"No! Not at all!" she cut in. She looked down at the rhododendron that he had just dug into the ground. "Are you putting in new plants?"

David followed her eye-line downwards. "Yeah, I'm afraid that the last gardener *did* leave a number of holes, so I thought I'd fill them in." He looked back up to her. "I hope that's all right."

"Of course it's all right. Where did you get them?"

"Oh, I found a small garden centre out on the Montauk Highway. They've really got good stuff out there."

"How much have you bought?"

"Oh, well, it's all right," he said, realizing that she might be thinking that a huge bill was imminent. "I just thought one or two here and there might help."

"But how are you paying?"

"No, I mean, that's all right. I just thought it would look better."

"But you must give me the bill. I can't expect you to pay for them."

"Well, I—"

They were interrupted by a ball coming high over the back netting of the court and landing on the lawn ten yards from David. He walked over and picked it up and lobbed it back over the netting.

"You must tell me how much I owe you, David."

He smiled, embarrassed, rubbing his hands together to rid them of the loose soil. It was the first time she had mentioned his name.

"Okay."

"And in future, if you go there, open an account, okay?"

"Right."

She turned and gazed around the garden. "It looks wonderful."

"Well, it's getting there."

"No, it's not. I think it looks wonderful now. I mean it. You really do know how to garden, don't you?"

David scratched at the back of his head. "Well, I have had a bit of experience."

They stood looking at each other for a moment, and David, unsettled by their lengthy eye contact, picked up his spade and made to start digging again.

"David?"

He straightened up again.

"I, er . . . well, I just want to say how much I appreciate what you're doing for Benji. He really loves his tennis with you, and his ukulele . . . and er, I'm quite happy to pay you extra for what you're doing, especially for taking him to school."

"For heaven's sakes, no!" David said, almost too forcefully. He smiled to mollify his tone. "I mean, no, I really don't want to be paid for that. It's a pleasure, believe me. He really is a great boy."

The remark had the most staggering effect on Jennifer, suddenly unleashing the full natural beauty of her face. Her mouth broke into a wide grin which wrinkled her cheeks into smile lines that had been imperceptible beforehand, her lips drawn back to reveal the perfection of her glistening white teeth. David was so taken aback by his own reaction to her that he looked down at the ground and started to kick nervously at the blade of his spade.

"Thank you for that." She let out a resigned sigh. "Well, at least promise me you'll open an account at the garden centre."

He looked up at her and smiled. "Okay, I'll do that."

"Jennifer!" Alex's voice called out from the court.

"What?"

"Are you all right?"

"Yes, fine."

"What're you doing? Gerry's arrived. Come and see him."

Both Jennifer and David looked to the other end of the court where a tall, thin young man was sitting down on the bench outside the summer-house. He was dressed in tennis whites, his hair sleeked tight to his scalp and gathered in a pony-tail at the back of his head.

"Okay, I'm coming!" She turned and gave David a smile. "See you."

"Right."

He watched her for a moment as she walked back up the side netting of the court, then turned back to his work in the flower-bed.

The players had just started on the second set when Jasmine came out from the house and called Alex to the telephone. David glanced out the side of his eye to see him leave the court immediately, asking the pony-tailed young man to take his place. As he ran towards the house, Jennifer, who had been knocking a ball back and forth with Benji on the lawn, watched him intently. After a brief discussion as to the score, the game continued, with the older man called Sam serving to the athletic and fiercely competitive Russ, who partnered Sam's dumpy little wife, Molly, at the end nearest to where David was working.

The first ball of the new game had hardly been hit across the net before Russ was jogging over to Molly to whisper urgent words of encouragement and new tactical ideas in her ear. The effect on her game was immediate, and of the next two balls that came to her, one was missed completely and the other dribbled harmlessly into the bottom of the net. Russ turned round and stood looking at her, hand on hip, his tennis racket over his shoulder and his head cocked to one side.

"Come on, Moll, what the hell's gotten into you? You were doing better than that before!"

"Sorry," Molly said meekly, returning to the backhand court and trying to give her partner the impression that she really was trying by crouching in concentrated readiness for the next ball to come to her. Sam wound himself up for the serve and it winged its way down to Molly's backhand. This time she made perfect contact, so much so that it sailed clean over the back netting of the court, landing at Benji's feet on the lawn.

"Oh dear!" she said, her voice faltering slightly. "I do apologize, Russ."

"That's game!" Sam called out from the other end, and proceeded to hit the balls down to Molly's end of the court. They finished in a clump against the back netting beside David.

"Right, your serve now, Moll," Russ said, his voice sulky at the thought of inevitable defeat. "Try and get them in."

Molly walked over to retrieve two balls from the back netting next to David, talking to herself as she did so.

"Oh dear! Oh dear! What *am* I doing wrong, I wonder?"

David tilted his head slightly towards her, never stopping his work in the flower-bed.

"Nothing," he said quietly.

Molly, being in the process of picking up a ball, glanced up at him. "Sorry?"

"You're doing nothing wrong. Just play to your husband's backhand. It's very weak."

"But I can't even get the ball over the net!"

"That's because they're playing to *your* backhand. Just run round the ball and play it on your forehand. You hit *them* well enough."

Russ turned round from his position at the net. "Molly! What's holding you up?"

"I'm coming." She looked at David and smiled.

David did not watch the next point, but listened to the ball being hit hard and often across the net. The rally ended with a shout of frustration from Sam, and a whoop of joy from Russ.

"Great shot, Molly! That's a helluva lot better!"

David smiled to himself in satisfaction as he dug his fingers into the ground to loosen the roots of a particularly stubborn dockleaf. He heard the squeak of tennis shoes approach him, and Molly bent down to pick up another ball.

"Thank you so much," she said quietly, and he turned to see her upside-down head grinning at him. He gave her a wink just as the weed came away in his hands.

———

Jasmine waited for Alex by the door that led into the hallway, and watched as he bounced his way up the steps at the side of the terrace.

"It's the phone in the study," she said, standing aside to allow him into the house first.

"Okay, thanks."

He walked down the hall and entered the drawing-room, closing the door carefully behind him, while Jasmine returned to the kitchen to finish putting the bottles of beer and iced tea into the cooler. She was just pushing the door of the refrigerator closed with her backside, a bowl of mixed salad in one hand and a plate piled high with tuna sandwiches in the other, when Benji ran into the kitchen.

"Have you seen Dad?"

"He's in the study, darlin'."

"Great! I want him to come and meet David," he said, running back the way he had come.

Jasmine called after him. "Just leave him be, darlin'. He's on the telephone right—"

"Dad, come and meet David!" Benji's voice carried through the house, as he yelled into the study.

She smiled and shook her head, and transferring the plate and bowl to one hand, she picked up the cooler in the other, and walked back through the hall.

The door of the study was slightly open, Benji obviously having failed to close it properly before running back out into the garden. Jasmine tutted and put down the cooler and walked over to the door. She was about to put her hand out to close it, when she heard Alex laugh quietly into the telephone.

"That's wicked!" he said in a hushed voice. "You shouldn't say those kind of things over the phone! Are you sure there's no one there that can hear you?"

Jasmine drew back her hand, wondering if she should close the door or just leave it as it was.

"Look, I really don't know if I can make it. I promised Jennifer that I'd be here this weekend." He laughed again. "I know you are. I'm horny too. But we'll just have to wait until next week."

Jasmine clasped her hand to her mouth and turned slowly away, feeling a sudden flush of panic burn at her cheeks.

"When are you off? . . . *Monday?* . . . Christ, you didn't tell me you were going away . . . yeah, and I want to see you too . . . goddamn it! . . . Okay, listen, I'll get out of this thing today . . . no, no, I'll just say I've been called away on business . . . no, just leave it with me. I really want to see you before you go . . . okay, meet you at your place in a few hours . . ."

Jasmine had heard all that she wanted. She tiptoed over to where she had left the cooler and, picking it up, hurried out of the door into the garden.

Alex put down the telephone and sat for a moment drumming his fingers on the surface of the desk. He turned to look out the window and caught sight of Jennifer and Benji hitting a tennis ball to each other on the lawn. Pushing back the chair, he rose and walked over to the window, where he stood watching them as they counted out the number of shots in their rally. It ended with Jennifer lobbing a ball high over Benji's head and he threw his racket up in the air in a desperate attempt to intercept it. He leaped to pick up the racket and the ball, then directed a yell towards the new gardener at the other end of the court. Jennifer looked round and laughed at the remark, as the man straightened up from his task and smiled in their direction, acknowledging whatever it was that Benji had said with a wave of his hand. As Alex watched this, he felt an unexpected pang of jealousy course through his body, as sudden and as powerful as an electric shock. He shook his head and turned from the window, giving the chair at his desk a kick as he walked towards the door.

"*Shit!* What a *fucking* mess you've made of this!" he said, slamming the door shut behind him.

Jasmine was on her way back to the house when he passed her on the terrace. Alex smiled at her, but she kept her eyes low and hurried past. He turned to watch her enter the house, then, pulling a face at her odd, unfriendly behaviour, he walked down the steps of the terrace and around the side of the hedge, arriving at the summerhouse just as the players were coming off court. Jennifer and Benji had brought their own game to an end and were moving across the lawn to meet them.

"Hey, Alex," Russ called over to him as he approached. "You really should have seen that! Molly played like a woman possessed! She won that match single-handed!" He turned to his blushing partner and gave her a kiss on the cheek.

Alex smiled and stuck his hands into the pockets of his shorts.

"Yeah, I wish I had," he said in a flat voice.

Jennifer looked at him, a worried expression on her face. "Are you all right, darling?"

"Yup." He glanced down at his feet and rubbed the toes of his tennis shoes together. "Listen, Jennifer, I'm afraid I've got some bad news. I've got to go."

Jennifer let her tennis racket fall limply to her side, and Benji ran over to his father and grabbed hold of his hand.

"You can't go, Dad. You haven't met David yet, and I want to show you how well I can play tennis now! Please, Dad!"

"I know, Benji, it's a real pain. I want to see you play tennis as well, and meet David, but this is sort of an emergency."

"How much of an emergency?" Jennifer asked.

"I'm not sure. That was Harry. Something's not good with the contract in Dallas. I have to meet him at the office in two hours. He says we can't afford to leave it until Monday."

Jennifer threw down the racket. "Oh, for heaven's sakes! Can't they manage without you for once?"

"Doesn't look like it. I may have to fly out there. I'm not sure."

Jennifer turned to the rest of the tennis party and held up her arms resignedly. "Sorry, folks."

Alex nodded. "Yeah, sorry about this, everyone. I'm afraid it's just the nature of the job!" He walked over to his wife and took her by the arm and led her around the hedge towards the terrace steps. "Look, I really *am* sorry about this."

Jennifer smiled and shrugged. "It's not your fault. It's only that sometimes I wish that we had the weekends to be a little more like a normal family—if not for our sake, for Benji's."

"I know." He paused. "Listen, I don't know if I will be going to Dallas, but I'm certainly heading back to San Francisco Wednesday night. So I was wondering if we might have an early dinner together?"

For a moment, Jennifer held off giving an answer, thinking about the work she still had to do on the Tarvy's proposal. Then she nodded. "Okay. Where?"

"We could try the new fish restaurant on Forty-eighth between Lex and Park. I think it's called the Ocean Floor. Supposed to be good."

"What time?"

"Have to be early, I'm afraid. Can you make it seven o'clock?"

"Yup, okay."

"Good. Well, look, I'd better be off. Apologize to Russ for not giving him a game."

"Oh, I think he'll survive," Jennifer sighed. "As will we all."

Alex smiled without looking at her directly. "I'll see you Wednesday then." He turned and began running up the steps.

"Alex?"

He stopped and looked back. "Yeah?"

"Could I have a kiss?"

Alex came down the steps towards her and gave her a peck on the cheek. "See you Wednesday."

He took the steps two at a time and, without a backwards glance, headed along the terrace and went into the house. Jennifer stood where she was, her arms folded, looking up towards the empty terrace. Then, with a shake of her head, she turned and walked slowly back to join the others at the tennis court.

"That's a goddamned shame," Russ said, taking a swig of beer from the bottle. "I'm not going to get my game now."

"Well, I sure as hell ain't going to take you on!" Sam laughed, sitting back in his deck-chair and taking a drag on his cigar. "I'm not going to risk spoiling an enjoyable afternoon by having a coronary."

"You don't need to play tennis to do that, Sammy," Molly said in a matronly voice. "You smoke too many of those things for your own good."

"Oh, don't start on that, Moll! Hey, Gerry"—he turned to the pony-tailed man—"why don't you give Russ a game?"

Gerry shook his head. "No, I'm really not into tennis as a competitive sport," he said in the mildest of Irish accents. "I just like to have myself a gentle run-around."

"Mom?" Benji had been sitting cross-legged on the ground, pulling up clumps of grass.

"Yes, darling?"

"Can I whisper something to you?"

Everyone turned to look at Jennifer, raising their eyebrows in intrigue.

"Okay."

Benji jumped up and walked over to his mother's chair, and putting his arms around her neck, he whispered in her ear.

"Oh, I don't think so, Benji."

"Why not? It's a great idea."

"I know, darling, but he's busy right now."

"Well, can't we ask him? Or at least ask Russ."

"Oh, this involves me, does it?" Russ said, moving towards Benji with his hands held out in strangle formation.

Benji screamed and sought refuge behind his mother. "Go on, quick, Mom, ask him before he gets me!"

Jennifer laughed. "Okay—Russ. Benji has suggested that you play David."

Russ stopped and looked at her inquiringly. "David? Who's he? I heard his name mentioned earlier."

Jennifer leaned sideways in her chair to look past Russ and pointed to where David was working.

"The gardener." She watched as he tamped at the ground around a newly planted shrub with his hands. "Look, Benji, I don't think he'll want to be disturbed. He's extremely busy."

Russ turned round and looked to the other end of the court. "Can he play?"

"You bet he can!" Benji said, moving quickly to stand by Russ so that he could convince him of the idea. "He's really good, Russ, 'cos he's teaching me how to play, and he can hit the ball real hard!"

"I think it's a good idea," Molly said quietly, and everyone turned to look at her.

"Now why would you say that, Moll?" Sam asked in a surprised voice.

Molly smiled. "Let's just say that he had a hand in turning my game around during that last match."

Russ looked at Jennifer. "Well?"

She shook her head. "Okay, Benji, you win! Go and ask him."

And with a whoop of joy, Benji ran off round the side of the court to fetch David.

Dodie, who had been sniffing around the pine-trees next to the shore of the bay, let out a short bark as she saw Benji approach, and ran past David at a gallop to greet him. David looked up from his work. "Hi! How are you getting on?"

"Great!—David?"

"Where's your father? I thought you were going to introduce me to him?"

"Yeah, I know," Benji said in a disheartened voice. "He had to go off to work."

"Oh, I'm sorry to hear that. Maybe I'll meet him next time."

"Yeah—but, David?"

"What?"

"Russ usually plays Dad at tennis, and Dad's gone now."

"That's a pity."

"Yeah—but Russ . . . well . . . David, would you play Russ?"

David pushed himself off his knees and stood up, and glanced to the other end of the court where everyone was looking in his direction. He turned back to Benji. "No, I don't think so."

"Why not?"

"Well—for a start, I'm not wearing any of the right clothes."

"You can play in those, can't you?"

"Well, then, I don't have any shoes."

"You're wearing shoes!"

"I know, but—well, I don't think I should, Benji. I've got work to do."

"Mom says it would be all right. Please, David, I think she wants you to, otherwise she'll have to listen to Russ grumbling all afternoon!"

David smiled at him and, after a moment's thought, nodded slowly. "Why not?"

Benji's face lit up. "You mean you'll play?"

"Yeah, if your mother doesn't mind."

Benji let out another whoop. "He's going to play you, Russ! He says he's going to play you!" He grabbed hold of David's hand and began pulling him as fast as he could around the side netting of the court.

Jennifer got to her feet and walked a few paces towards the corner of the court to meet them.

"I'm sorry about this, David. I hope you don't mind. It was Benji's idea."

"Yeah, I guessed that. Look, I'm afraid that I don't have proper shoes to wear."

"I told him that the shoes he's wearing would be okay, Mom," Benji cut in, still holding on to David's hand. "Dad's would be too small for him."

"I expect they would be." She looked down at David's battered pair of boating shoes. "They'll do fine, David." She turned and started to move back to the others. "Well, come on, you'd better meet your opponent."

Jennifer introduced David to Russ and the rest of the assembled company, Molly giving him the biggest smile as she shook his hand. Gerry jumped up from his chair and spun his racket round in his hand, offering it, handle first, to David.

"You'll be needing a weapon."

David bent down and cleaned his hands by rubbing them hard on the grass, then took the racket with a smile. "Thanks." He turned to look onto the court, where Russ was already hitting booming and faultless practice serves down to the far end. "Well, I'd better go and start doing battle."

After a brief knock-up, during which Russ had David running from one side of the court to the other in order to gauge the weaknesses of his new opponent, Russ felt confident enough in his appraisal of David's game to knock all the balls down to his end.

"Okay, we won't toss. You just serve." He walked over to the forehand court, giving Jennifer a smile and a wink before settling himself in readiness for the first ball of the match.

He made no contact with the serve at all. Not with the racket at any rate. The ball came over the net like a bullet, swinging straight in towards his body. The spin kicked it up viciously from the service line causing Russ to throw his head to the side to avoid being hit in the eye, and the ball struck him with a resounding *thwack* just above the left cheek-bone. There was a gasp from the spectators, followed by a muffled grunt of pleasure from Sam and a much less subtle yell of joy from Benji.

"Shit!" Russ exclaimed, standing stock-still and looking down the court at David.

He held up his hand in apology. "Sorry about that!"

Rubbing at his painful cheek, Russ made his way slowly across to the backhand court, and, giving his racket one quick spin in his hand, he readied himself for the next serve.

This time, the ball slammed down into the backhand corner of the service box, without a trace of the spin that had been put on the first serve. Having expected it to slew back in towards him once more, Russ found himself having to lunge sideways to try to reach it, doing so with such force that he continued on into the side netting. Dropping his racket, he spread-eagled his hands against it to prevent his face from being shredded through the wire.

As he turned to pick up his racket, there was a silence from the audience, save for a few throats being cleared. He walked back to the forehand court, glancing at Jennifer as he went.

"Where the hell's this guy from?" he whispered to her out the side of his mouth.

"Scotland," Jennifer said quietly.

"Hey! I didn't even know they *played* tennis there!"

He whacked at the soles of his shoes with his racket, more to vent his anger than for any constructive purpose, and once more settled himself down to face both the power of David's serve and the ignominy of his task.

By the time that four games had been played, Russ realized that he was no match for his opponent, never once being able to premeditate what he was going to do. If he powered a serve down towards him, David would take all the speed off the ball and plant it at such an angle across the net that Russ was invariably left stranded somewhere in the middle of the court. If he relied on his slower spin serve, then David would come in like an express train to hit the ball so early that it would be thumping hard against the back netting before he'd even had the chance to move off the baseline. Swearing in frustration to himself at being four games down and avoiding now the looks of the hushed spectators, he hit the balls hard down to David's end to prepare himself for the coup de grâce.

At that point, things started to go very wrong with David's game. Serves began to go inches wide or whack against the white tape of the net, and his returns either ballooned over the baseline or hit the side of the racket and skidded off to the edge of the court. Russ, encouraged by his sudden change in fortune, began to play once more to his audience, winking at them when he managed to win a point, or yelling out "Yes!" every time that David double-faulted. Within twenty minutes, Russ was poised at match point, victory and vindication for his earlier inabilities within his grasp. He swung a service down to the backhand court, and David, moving to the wrong side, missed the ball completely. Russ threw his racket in the air and ran to the net, and stood with his hand outstretched, happy to end the match at that point. David approached him and grasped his hand.

"Well played, Russ, that was good fun."

"Yup, good game. Damned lucky I began to read your game right. I thought you had me there for a minute."

They both walked off court to applause and many congratulatory comments on the standard and enthralment of the game. Benji, however, approached David with a profound look of disappointment on his face.

"We thought you were going to beat him, David, but you started to play like me!"

David laughed. "That's what happens in tennis, Benji. Things go right for a time, and then suddenly, *whoosh*! everything goes wrong."

Russ threw his racket on the ground and went over to the icebox and took out a beer. "Do you want one, David?"

"No, thanks. That's very kind, but if you don't mind, I think I'll just finish off what I was doing."

"You won't go brooding on defeat now, will you?" Russ said, flipping off the bottle-top and taking a mouthful of beer. "It was pretty evenly matched throughout."

"No, I won't do that."

Jennifer looked up at him from her chair. "You really don't have to go back to work, David."

"Well, actually, I do. I really need to get the rest of those shrubs in by this evening, otherwise there's every chance they won't last."

"Okay—but thanks again for giving Russ a game."

David nodded, then walked back around the court to continue his work in the flower-bed.

By five o'clock, the final shrub was in place. He gave each of the new plants a final watering, then, gathering up his tools, he made his way back around the side of the court, giving Dodie a whistle as he went. There was no one left at the summer-house, the tennis party having finished an hour before.

As he reached the corner of the hedge, Jennifer appeared around it, accompanied by Gerry. They stopped as he walked towards them.

"All done?" Jennifer asked.

"Yeah, they're all in."

Jennifer smiled. "David, I don't think you've been properly introduced to this mad Irishman, Gerry Reilly."

David stepped forward, and transferring his tools to one hand, stretched out the other. "Hullo, Gerry, pleased to meet you."

"David," Jennifer continued, "Gerry has a recording studio here in Leesport, and he's just had a . . . what is it again?"

"A new mixing console."

"Right—well, he's just had a new mixing console delivered, and he can't manage it into his studio by himself, so he was wondering if you might be able to give him a hand. That is, if you haven't got any other plans."

"No, I'd be delighted. I've got nothing at all on this evening."

"Oh, that would be great, David!" Gerry said, rubbing his hands together. "It's just that I've got to get it ready for this group coming in tomorrow, and I'd be struggling by myself. Look, I'll go and get my things from the house and meet you round at the back. Have you got a car?"

"Yeah."

"Okay, so you can just follow me. Are you sure this is no imposition?"

"Not at all. As I said, I'm doing nothing else."

"Great—well, see you at the cars, then!" He turned and ran back up the steps onto the terrace and disappeared into the house.

Jennifer made a move to follow him, then stopped and turned back to David. "You could have beaten him, couldn't you?"

"Sorry?"

"Come on, you know what I mean. You could have beaten Russ, couldn't you?"

David smiled and began to waggle his head from one side to the other. "Well . . . maybe."

"Why didn't you?"

"Well, I just thought that it might not be, erm . . ."

"Diplomatic?"

"Yeah, that sort of thing."

Jennifer flicked at a piece of grass with the toe of her tennis shoe. "Well, it's totally un-American, but nevertheless a very kind thing to do. My life would've been hell on Monday morning if Russ had lost."

David nodded. "Yes, well, I guessed he might not take it in the best spirit."

Jennifer laughed quietly. "You guessed right." She folded her arms and once again looked down at her feet as she smoothed over the grass with her shoe. "Well . . . I suppose I'll see you next week then."

"Yeah, okay."

She turned and made her way back to the steps, and David watched her as she stretched her long legs out to take them effortlessly two at a time. Then, giving Dodie a whistle, he set off across the lawn towards the garden shed.

CHAPTER

22

It was apparent from the outset that Jennifer's "mad Irishman" description of Gerry Reilly could not have been more apt. As David sat in convoy behind Gerry's ageing Maserati at the top of Barker Lane, Gerry suddenly pulled out into a non-existent gap in the traffic, causing a Chevrolet pick-up truck to slew dangerously to the side of the road and the driver to thump the heel of his hand on the horn. He then put his foot down so hard on the accelerator that smoke belched from its squealing tyres, and by the time David eventually managed to turn out himself, the car was a mere speck of red at the far end of the main street. Consequently, David found himself having to drive the Volkswagen harder and faster than it probably had ever been driven before in his vain attempt to catch up.

Two miles east of Leesport, David had practically given up all hope of ever seeing Gerry or the Maserati again, but racing round a tight right-hand corner, he came across the car parked at the side of the road, and he reckoned that it had probably been just good fortune that Gerry had actually looked in his rear-view mirror and realized that there was no sign of the Volkswagen. As he slowed, Gerry took off again, this time at a more gentle pace, and within one hundred yards he signalled to the right and pulled off the road. David followed him down an overgrown and rutted driveway, eventually coming to a halt outside a large weather-beaten barn. Gerry jumped out of his car and came round to open up David's door.

"This is very kind of you, David. I had a go at putting the console in myself last night, but just about did in my back and the bloody equipment at the same time!"

David got out and pulled up the top without securing it in order to prevent Dodie from jumping out, and followed Gerry towards the double doors at the front of the barn.

"Two of us should manage fine, though. It's just a question of slotting the new one in and connecting up."

He unlocked the small door that was set into one of the larger ones, and ushered David inside.

The front half of the barn had been converted into a huge open-plan room, the centre of which was adorned with a clutter of old sofas and chairs gathered round a large rough-hewn oak table. To one side, a kitchen stretched along the wall, separated from the sitting-room by a long breakfast bar, while the dining area was tucked away at the back of the room underneath a balustraded upper deck, upon which David could just make out the top of an enormous double bed. The whole place smelt strongly of old cigarette smoke and beer, as if it had been the scene of a wild party the night before.

Gerry went over to the refrigerator and took out two bottles of beer, and levering off the tops with the handle of a spoon, held one out to David.

"No use getting hot and bothered over the task, is there?"

He took a swig from his bottle and gestured with his hand for David to follow. He walked over to a door behind the dining-table and pulled it open, then pushed open a further door and flicked on a bank of switches, flooding light into the recording studio. It was only half the height and three quarters of the width of the living area, the front part being divided from the smaller back section by a sound-proof wall, in the centre of which was a large double-glazed viewing window. The room that they stood in was filled with musical equipment: two keyboards, a set of drums and a variety of guitars haphazardly strewn about on metal floor-stands, each of these being connected to a large input box below the viewing window by an entanglement of leads.

Through the window, two large Anglepoise lamps cast a speakeasy light over the gaping hole in the middle of the desk.

"Sorry about the mess everywhere," Gerry said, picking his way through the equipment. "The boys were in rehearsing last night, and didn't leave till about three this morning. They're not what you call very house-proud."

David followed Gerry's path through the instruments. "What kind of recording do you do?"

Gerry laughed. "Anything that makes a bit of money. Generally groups, but we do a few jingles for radio stations and the like, just to fill in the downtime." He held open the two doors that led into the control room. "That's how I met Jennifer, actually. I've done a couple of things for her company over the past year."

He walked over to the corner of the room and carefully pulled away a dust-sheet to reveal the new mixing console. "There she blows." He stood back to admire it. "Isn't she a beauty?"

David nodded, not really knowing if she was a beauty or not, but reckoning that if looks were dependent on the number of knobs and LCD screens that this machine had, then it certainly would be worth a wolf whistle or two.

"Right, David," Gerry said, squeezing his way in behind the console and edging it out from the wall. "If you could just get your hands in below, we'll get it up into its place."

David rid himself of his bottle of beer and bent down and levered up the console, and with a few manoeuvres around the room to get into the right position, they slotted it down on the desk.

"That's it! Perfect! Thanks a lot, David." He walked round to the back of the desk and picked up a handful of leads. "Now all I have to do is get all these bloody wires stuck into the right holes."

Retrieving his beer, David leaned against the ledge on the viewing window and watched as Gerry began pushing jack-plugs into their corresponding ports. "So, is it all different types of music that you produce?"

"Yeah, suppose so. I mean, I'm lucky enough to have been in the business for some time now, so I get groups seeking me out to produce for them. That's really why I moved out here to Leesport." He grinned at David. "Actually, to blow my own trumpet a bit, I've come to be known as the Pied Piper in the trade, seeing that I'm luring all the groups out here away from the studios in the city!"

"Seems a pretty good position to be in. Where were you beforehand?"

"I had a small place in the Village, but it just got too expensive, so I bought this place about a year ago. I thought at first it might be a bit of a white elephant, because I found out after I'd bought it that no insurance company would cover me for putting all this equipment into a wooden building." He gestured with his hand around the room. "So I had to brick up the bloody lot in the inside. That's why it's so much smaller than the other part of the barn, that and the soundproofing, of course. It cost me an arm and a leg, I can tell you."

"And obviously the bands are quite happy to make the trip all the way out here?"

"Well, it was a bit of a gamble, but yeah, they seem to love it! They book into a bed-and-breakfast in Leesport, and then, because most of the work is done in the evening or at night, they head off to the beach during the day, or the more sporty ones play tennis or golf at the country club." He looked across at David and raised his eyebrows. "It's quite funny, actually. The club has a strict dress code, and you can imagine the kind of clothes these guys turn up in to play their games."

David chuckled. "And they get away with it?"

"I've never actually witnessed what happens. I think it's better if they don't know who the culprit is who's bringing them here in the first place, but yeah, usually there's someone there who knows of the band, or their children know of the band, and they get to bend the rules a little. I think they try to get them out on the course or onto the courts before the old duffers come along and get the chance to complain." Gerry juggled with a handful of leads, shaking his head from side to side as he made a silent calculation as to where they should go. "Look, would you mind just holding on to these for a minute?"

David pushed himself off the ledge and took hold of the leads, while Gerry went round the other side of the desk and squatted down on his haunches to study the confusion of inputs on the patch-bays below.

"So most of the groups that you produce are quite well-known?"

"Yeah, you could say that. The lads here at the minute are popular on the sort of rock/folk circuit over here. Dublin Up, they're called. Ever heard of them?"

"No, can't say I have. I'm afraid that I gave up my musical career some time ago."

Gerry looked up at him. "You played, did you?"

David made a noncommittal gesture with his head. "Well, sort of. I had a group at university, but I've really done little since then."

"What instrument?"

"Lead guitar."

"Good for you!" Gerry said, swapping round two inputs on the lowest patch-bay and straightening up in front of the desk. He flicked a couple of switches on the console and feedback screeched through the two massive speakers behind David. Gerry quickly twisted two knobs and the noise subsided to a loud hum. He pointed through to the recording floor next door.

"That's the Gibson live. Do you want to have a go?"

David turned to look through the window at the bright blue guitar in the centre of the floor.

"Would you mind?"

"Not at all. Just give me a second, and I'll join you."

David laid down his handful of leads on the desk and pushed open the two doors. He picked up the guitar from its stand, slung the strap over his neck, and pulled out the plectrum that was stuck between the strings, creating a tuneless thwang that rang through the speakers as he did so. He played a couple of chords to make sure that it was in tune, then went through a couple of lead runs to get his fingers accustomed to the feel of the guitar. At that point, Gerry pushed open the doors and came through.

"Bert Jansch, yes?"

David smiled at him. "Oh, well, couldn't be that bad if you recognized it."

"Bad? I tell you, there's many a lead guitarist nowadays who couldn't do better!" He picked up a semi-acoustic Ovation from one of the stands and sat down on a leather-padded chrome stool. "Christ, you're some man for a gardener, aren't you? First tennis, then the guitar. What else do you do?"

David shook his head. "That's about it, I'm afraid. You happen to have witnessed the sum total of my talents in one day!"

"Thank God for that!" Gerry exclaimed, plucking at the strings of the guitar and adjusting the knobs on the machine head. "It's quite enough. Any more and you'd be making me feel humble." He played three quick chords. "Right then, David, that's it! The night is young, so let's get stuck in."

CHAPTER 23

Duncan Caple walked across the empty car-park at Glendurnich, turning his key-ring over in his hand to find the one that unlocked the front door of the office. It was seven o'clock on Monday morning, and even though the distillery throbbed with activity, having been in operation throughout the weekend, the office was completely deserted. He pushed the key into the lock and opened the door, and walked briskly to his office.

Placing his brief-case on the desk, he shrugged off his jacket and draped it over the back of his chair, at the same time pressing one of the autodial numbers on his telephone. While waiting for it to connect, he clicked open the locks of the case and took out a thick typed document. He sat down and began leafing through it as the distorted ringing sounded out from the telephone speaker.

After the tenth ring, he leaned forward with a silent curse, and was about to end the call when it was answered.

"Hullo?"

Duncan quickly picked up the receiver. "John? It's Duncan."

"Duncan! You just caught me. I was on the way out to the car. How are you getting on? I was going to call you today, but I never quite know when to ring."

"I know. Sorry that I haven't been in touch, but I just wanted to get this document ready before I made contact."

"So you've got it then?"

"Yup, and it looks good, though I say it myself. Giles has done a wonderful job in selling the idea, as has Keith with the figures. It all looks very convincing, even though it is fairly simplistic, but there again, it has to be put in such a way that all the distillery workers can understand what's going on. Having read it through in its entirety, I would have thought that we'd more than a fair chance of pushing this thing through to fruition."

"Bloody wonderful, Duncan! Well done! You'll let me have a copy?"

"Yes, I'll get one couriered down to you today."

"Great! So have you any idea as to when you're going to move on to the next stage?"

"Well, where are we today?" He pulled his desk calendar towards him and flicked over the page to look at the next month. "Right, it's the fifteenth of June, so . . . I think to be on the safe side, John, I would really like a month to get everything ready. I want to make damned sure that this whole thing succeeds, as I'm sure you do, and I just don't want to push it any harder than I need to. So . . . let's see now . . . how does Friday, the seventeenth of July, sound to you?"

"No earlier, huh?"

"No, I really think that if we left it until then, it would give me the best chance to make sure that it went through without a hitch."

"And you're pretty confident that there won't be one?"

"John, I've been up here for a year now, and I've seen how this place works. The Inchelvies pride themselves in having built Glendurnich on labour relations, almost to the point of extreme. Even though they hold only thirty-one per cent of the shareholding, if, to a man, the workers back our proposals, then the Inchelvies will go along with them. I can honestly vouch for that. And once you've had a chance to look at this document, you will see that the terms laid down will be more than attractive to the family itself."

"Right. And have you heard anything at all from Corstorphine?"

"Not a cheep. As far as I can gather, he's gone to ground somewhere in the States. Wallowing in his sorrow, no doubt. I don't think we'll have much bother on that account."

"Okay, well, you know what's going on. I'll put Friday the seventeenth of July in my diary, then. Now I want you to do just one thing for me, Duncan."

"Yes?"

"I really need to get in touch with you over the next month on a much more regular basis, so I want all lines of communication to be opened up between Kirkpatrick's and Glendurnich. That means telephone, fax and E-mail. I cannot be expected to keep tabs on what's going on through these hit-and-miss telephone calls."

"Fair enough."

"Well, as you know, it's impossible at the minute while your old battleaxe has control over the switchboard."

Duncan slowly nodded his head. "Ah."

"You'll have to get rid of her. It's important. As you said, you need time to set the wheels in motion, and we can't afford to have it being leaked out before the designated date. What's her name, anyway?"

"Margaret."

"Right. How difficult *would* it be to give her the push?"

"Well, I wouldn't like to give a firm answer on that one. She's well over retirement age, but she does wield a great deal of clout both here in the office and with old Inchelvie himself."

"Can't be helped, Duncan. Just keep Inchelvie at bay for a month by keeping him in touch on a more than regular basis from his house. Visit him if needs be, but just keep him so well informed on how the business is going that he finds no reason even to telephone the place. All right? And as far as Margaret is concerned, give her a substantial amount more than the redundancy due to her, and if you have to, let everyone know that she's been given a handsome ex gratia payment. Don't lose sleep over it. Just do it. Okay?"

"All right, John."

"Good! Well, I'll look forward to receiving the papers, and say well done to the boys."

Duncan put down the receiver and swung his chair round to look out of the window. He sat for a moment, rubbing at the side of his cheek as he worked out his memorandum to Margaret. Then, with a thin smile curling up the edges of his mouth, he turned back to his desk and, unclipping a pen from his inside pocket, he pulled forward a pad of paper and began to compose the receptionist's retirement order.

CHAPTER 24

Catching his breath as he rushed into the kitchen, Benji threw his tennis racket down on the table and turned triumphantly to David as he entered through the French doors.

"Beat you!"

"Okay, but you had a head start."

"But you're faster than me."

"Not much. I think it'd be fairer if you gave me a start."

"Oh yeah, right!" He walked over to the refrigerator, and pulling open the door, took out two cans of Coke.

"Here, catch!"

He threw the can erratically towards David, who lunged forward to catch it, but the condensation on its surface made it slip from his grasp, and it struck hard against the corner of the table and fell to the ground punctured, fizzing Coke in every direction. Jasmine, who had been in the process of taking a hot casserole dish out of the oven, turned to witness the sticky liquid spraying out across her polished floor.

"Oh, for Chrissakes, Benji, what the hell do you think you're playin' at?" She banged the casserole dish down on the sideboard, and shaking off the oven gloves, took a cloth from the kitchen sink and walked across to the table. "Just go and put your racket away where it belongs. Go on—do it now!"

Benji, taken aback by Jasmine's uncharacteristic reaction, glanced warily at David, who flicked his head to the side to indicate that he should do what he was told. David bent down and picked up the can, and covering the puncture with his finger, walked over to the sink and poured away the remainder of its contents.

"Sorry about that. It was more my fault than his."

"Well, you should have caught it, shouldn't you!" Jasmine sniped at him as she knelt down to wipe up the mess.

David pulled a face at Jasmine's mood, as surprised as Benji at her outburst. He walked over and squatted down beside her. "Look, let me do that."

She pulled her arm away from his outstretched hand. "No, I am perfectly capable of doin' it myself."

David straightened up and stood watching her as she wiped furiously at the mess.

"Jasmine?"

"What is it now?"

"Is something wrong?"

She stopped wiping for a second, then continued, rubbing harder on the floor. "Nothin's the matter with *me*."

She stopped again, and letting out a loud sniff wiped her eyes with the back of her hand. David went back down on his haunches and put his hand on her shoulder. "Look, there is something wrong. What's happened?"

She turned to look at him, tears in her eyes. "It's nothin' really. I just overheard something on Saturday during the tennis party, and . . . well, I could use some advice from you." Her eyes focused beyond David's left shoulder. "But not right now." She returned to her task.

David followed her line of vision to see that Benji had come back into the kitchen and was walking towards them. "I'm sorry," he said quietly, "I didn't mean to do it."

Jasmine laughed as she wiped at one of the legs of the table. "I know you didn't, and I didn't mean to yell at you. Just me being real bad-tempered. As David said, just as much his fault as yours."

The boy ran forward, and throwing himself on her back, kissed the top of her wiry hair over and over again. Jasmine spread-eagled her hands to stop herself from being flattened on the ground by the extra weight. "All right, Benji! You can get off now! I accept your apology."

"Great!" Benji said, slipping off the side of Jasmine's back. "Can we do it now, David?"

"In a minute. Just go and do a bit of practising. I want a quick word with Jasmine."

"Okay." He turned and raced upstairs.

Jasmine pushed herself to her feet and studied the floor just to make sure that she hadn't missed any of the Coke. "So what have you two got cooked up now?"

"Oh, it's his song. The school told him today that he has to have it ready for tomorrow morning. D-day has arrived! He has a slot on the public address system at a quarter to nine."

Jasmine smiled and walked over to the sink and began rinsing out the cloth.

"So . . . what do you want my advice about?"

Jasmine shook her head. "Nothin' that can't wait." She draped the cloth over the tap and turned to face him. "We'll get a chance to speak sometime when Benji isn't around. I don't want to risk havin' him hear what I gotta say." She picked up the casserole dish from the sideboard and placed it back in the oven, twiddling at a couple of the dials on the control panel. "Anyway, I think you've got a more important job on your hands than listening to me."

With a shrug, David turned and made his way through to the hall and up the stairs to Benji's bedroom. As he walked in, Benji looked up from where he sat playing the ukulele on his bed, the piece of paper bearing the words of the song spread out on his knees.

"This is soppy!" He threw aside the ukulele and scrumpled up the word-sheet, and letting it fall to the ground, he slumped back onto his bed.

David walked over to the bed and bent down to retrieve the ball of paper. "It is *not* soppy!" he said, carefully unravelling it and pressing it between his hands to iron out the creases. "Listen, I think this song is great. What don't you like about it?"

"It's all about *love,*" Benji said quietly.

"So? That's what all the good songs have been written about. What would you rather write about? Playing tennis?"

Benji looked at him, a sulky expression on his face. "Don't be silly. Who'd listen to a song about tennis?"

"Exactly. The words are great—and they're a bit different too. I mean, you've got a really good rhythm going in that first line—'I do love you, but you're breaking my heart, breaking my heart in two'—I think that's really great. It's very catchy."

"But everyone's going to laugh at me when it comes out on the PA system."

"Why? You know the tune, you can play it well enough and you sing it just fine. So why would the others laugh at you?"

" 'Cos they'll call me a sissy for singing about *love*."

David pushed himself farther onto Benji's bed and leaned back against the wall, his arms folded. "Okay, how much is it worth?"

"How much is what worth?"

"Well, let's say I'm your record producer and I say, 'Right, Benji Superstar, I'll give you ten dollars if they laugh at you, and twenty if they don't, would we have a deal?"

Benji looked hard at him, his brow creased with thought. "That's not much of a deal. You lose out both ways."

"Well, maybe I just know that they won't laugh at you. Okay, so I'll have to pay you out twenty dollars, but then I'm pretty sure I have a hit single on my hands, otherwise I wouldn't have made you the offer."

Benji was silent for a moment. "Do you really think it's that good?"

David nodded. "Yeah, I actually do."

"Gee!" Benji's eyes focused on open air as he contemplated his impending fame.

"So, do we have a deal?"

"You bet!" He leaped up from the bed, and picking up the ukulele, proceeded to play the first few chords of the song. "What do we do now?"

David pushed himself off the bed. "Well, we need to find a tape recorder."

Benji thought for a moment, then, placing the ukulele back on the bed, he leaped towards the cupboard at the far end of the room. He threw open the doors and rooted around inside, ejecting long-unused toys from its depth, eventually reappearing with an old plastic Fisher Price recorder. "How about this?"

David walked over and took it from him, and having given it a quick appraisal, chucked it dismissively onto the bed.

Benji's shoulders dropped visibly. "No good, huh?" he said, profound disappointment in his voice.

" 'Fraid not. The thing is, if we want to make a hit single, we're going to have to call in the professionals."

Benji swallowed hard. "What d'you mean?" he said quietly.

"C'mon. I'll show you."

Twenty minutes later, Benji stood half-hidden behind David in the centre of Gerry's recording studio, his ukulele held firmly behind his back and his mouth open in amazement as they listened to the ear-blasting music being played by the four musicians present. David felt the young boy tug at the back of his shirt, and he turned and bent down so that he could hear him above the noise.

"David, I think those guys are Dublin Up. They're *really* well-known!"

David nodded and gave him a wink, and Benji's mouth fell even farther open.

Inside the control room, Gerry looked up from his console and caught sight of them. He got to his feet and came through the double doors, then flicked a switch on the wall which immediately cut all sound from the instruments.

"What the f——"

Gerry held up his hand to the long-haired fiddler. "Watch it, boys. Kids present." He approached them and sidled a glance at Benji, who was trying to get in as close as possible to David's back. "So, Benji, I understand you've got a song you want to record."

Benji did not reply, but gave David an anguished look and shook his head.

Gerry winked surreptitiously at David. "A bit nervous, huh? No worries, everyone's like that." He turned to the group, who by now had rid themselves of their instruments and were lounging around on easy chairs and lighting up cigarettes. "Patrick, what were you like when you first went into a recording studio?"

"Shi——" Patrick grimaced. "I mean, pretty scared."

Gerry shrugged and looked back at Benji. "There you are, then. Even the lead singer of Dublin Up was scared. Would you believe that?" Putting his hand on Benji's shoulder, he guided him forward to the microphone in front of the viewing window and pulled forward a high stool. "Right, you get your backside up on there, and I'll adjust the microphone for you."

Benji did as he was told, but still tried to keep his modest instrument out of sight of the group. One of them, a lanky youth with a fierce Mohican haircut and a silver ring in his eyebrow, noticed this and suddenly let out a whoop of recognition.

"Hey, you've got a ukulele!" He walked over and took it from him. "Great machines! I learned to play on one of these." He stuck it under his arm and ran off some chords, and a smile slowly spread across Benji's face as he realized that the guy was only playing G, C, and D7.

"I know those chords, too," he said proudly.

"Well, in that case, you know as much about the ukulele as I do." He smiled and handed the instrument back to Benji. "So let's hear what you can do then."

Having placed an enormous pair of earphones on Benji's head, Gerry went into the control room, with David following hard on his heels. He flicked a couple of switches on the console. "Can you hear me, Benji?"

Benji nodded.

"Right, well, when you're ready, just sing a couple of the lines, so that I can get the balance right."

The boy gave David a look of sheer terror through the window. He leaned forward to Gerry's microphone. "Just take a deep breath and do it, Benji. Doesn't matter if you make a mistake. Gerry can do it as many times as it takes."

And with a brave smile, Benji began to strum.

On the initial take, he managed to get through the first verse without fault, but then, as he started the second, he played a wrong chord and doubled up with embarrassment. Gerry flicked the switch on his microphone. "Don't worry, Benji. That sounds great. We'll do it again, only this time, keep an eye on me, 'cos I'm just going to beat out the time with my hand. You seemed to speed up a bit at the end of the verse."

Benji's voice sounded through the speaker. "You'll throw me."

Gerry smiled at him. "No, I won't. Just watch my hand out of the corner of your eye. Are you ready?"

Benji nodded.

"Right, let's go again."

This time, Benji went through the whole song without fault. At the end, Gerry held his finger to his lips to indicate to everyone to keep quiet, then, after a few seconds, flicked off all the switches and gave the thumbs-up. Immediately, the muted sound of clapping came through the soundproof divide and Gerry and David watched as the group gathered around the grinning boy, giving him slaps of congratulations on the back.

They went back through into the recording studio. "Well done, Benji!" Gerry said, giving his head a light cuff. "All done in two takes! Not many professional singers can do that"—he turned to the group's lead singer—"can they, Patrick?"

The singer laughed. "I hope you're not implying anything by that remark!"

"Can I hear it now?" Benji asked excitedly.

"Sure you can." He went back into the control room and patched the song through to the massive speakers in the recording studio. Benji sat with an incredulous look on his face throughout, and at the end the assembled company once more broke into applause.

Gerry came back through from the control room. "Right then, Benji, you can either take it away as it is, or, if you want, I can add a few things to it."

Benji was silent for a moment. "What sort of things?"

"Well, we could put a drum beat to it and maybe a bit of bass."

Benji bit at his lip, a look of uncertainty on his face. Gerry smiled reassuringly at him. "Benji, it's your song. You wrote it and you played it. I'm just the mechanic, and I can, well, sort of fill it out a bit if you want."

"It won't sound stupid, will it?"

Gerry laughed. "Well, if it does, I'll have to pack up doing what I do and get another job."

Benji grinned and jumped off the stool. "Okay! Will you do it now?"

"Not quite now," he said, holding up his hands. He flicked his head towards the group. "I've got to get this lot sorted out first, but if David returns later on this evening, I'll give him the finished tape, so you'll have it first thing in the morning. Would that suit?"

Benji nodded.

"Okay, then!" Gerry said, giving him a slap on the shoulder. "You've done pretty well, my lad. You've a bright future in front of you!"

Outside the studio, Benji's excitement seemed immediately to diminish, and he ambled slowly towards the car, glancing thoughtfully at his feet. David eyed him as he spun his key-ring around a finger. "What's up?"

"David?" He paused. "You don't think I'll look stupid, do you?"

David shook his head. "Benji, I promise you that by this time tomorrow, you'll be a superstar at school"—he jumped into the car and started the engine—"and twenty dollars better off!"

He arrived at the house the next morning a quarter of an hour earlier than usual to ensure that Benji had plenty of time to hand in the tape at the school office. He sounded his horn twice, then repeated it a minute later when there was still no sign of the boy. The kitchen door opened, but it was Jasmine who appeared, giving him frantic gestures to come inside.

David got out of the car and ran over to the steps, taking them in two leaps. Jasmine was waiting for him in the kitchen, a look of humorous foreboding on her face, and pointed to where Benji lay face-down on one of the beanbags.

"What's up?" David whispered.

"Stage fright," Jasmine mouthed at him.

David raised his eyebrows and walked over to him. "Okay, Benji—you ready to go?"

Benji let out a groan and slowly pushed himself to his feet. "I feel as if I'm going to be executed."

David tried hard to suppress a laugh, but hearing Jasmine snigger behind him, he snorted it out through his nose.

"Sorry, Benji. I don't mean to laugh." He put his hand on the boy's shoulder and steered him towards the door. "Come on, let's go. It's going to be fine."

Benji shuffled towards the door, and as he passed Jasmine, she bent down and gave him a kiss on the top of his head.

"Go for it, maestro. Give 'em your best shot."

He thumped his feet down the steps and mouldered down the path towards the car. "More like they'll give me their best shot."

Jasmine picked up his school-satchel from the sideboard and handed it to David. "Is this going to work?"

"God, I sincerely hope so!" And with crossed fingers raised, he leaped down the steps in one and ran to join Benji in the Volkswagen.

Even though it was half an hour before school was due to begin, there was already a crowd of pupils milling around the main doors when they arrived. David pulled the car to a halt at the end of the path, and opening up the glove compartment, took out the tape and handed it to Benji.

"There you are, all ready for you. Now listen, there's a piece of paper in the cover. Make sure that you tell whoever takes the tape from you that they must read what's written before playing the song. Okay?"

Benji acknowledged him silently and climbed slowly out of the car. He walked round to the driver's door and David handed him his satchel.

"Will you wait?"

David nooded. "Okay, I'll wait right here until ten to nine."

Taking a deep breath, he turned and made his way up the path to the main doors. As he was about to enter the building, a boy, being hotly pursued by another, came storming out and careered into him, making the tape fly out of his hand. As if in slow motion, he watched it hover in the air then threw himself forward to try to catch it, but there were too many bodies around for him to get anywhere near it. He let out a strangled yell as he watched it fall towards the ground, but just as it was about to make contact with the concrete doorstep, a hand stretched down and caught it.

Sean Dalaglio straightened up, a grin spread across his face, and held out the tape to him.

Benji breathed out a sigh of relief. "Gee, thanks, Sean."

"Is that the song you wrote?"

Benji swallowed hard. "How d'you know about the song?"

"It's been announced out on the PA system already. Did you write it?"

Benji nodded.

"Is it good?"

Benji did not know how to respond. He turned to look down the path to the Volkswagen. The car was there but David was not. He looked around and saw that he was slowly walking Dodie up the sidewalk. He turned back to Sean.

"Well?" Sean asked.

"I don't . . . know." He pushed his way past Sean and ran along the corridor to the office and knocked on the door. Miss Trimble, the school secretary, opened it.

"Hello, Benji."

Benji held out the tape to her.

"Ah, this must be your song." She glanced round at the clock on the wall. "Well, your slot's in five minutes. We're just about to put on Chester Todd's poem, 'Seagull Over the Great South Bay,' and then it will be your turn, okay?"

Benji nodded and turned to go, then suddenly remembered what David had said.

"Miss Trimble?" he asked just as she closed the door. She opened it a fraction.

"Yes, Benji?"

"There's a piece of paper in the cover of the tape. It has to be read out before it's played."

Miss Trimble smiled at him. "All right. I'll be doing the announcement today, so I'll make sure to read it out beforehand. Is that all?"

He nodded and Miss Trimble closed the door behind her. He stood staring at the mottled glass for a moment, then, with a sigh of resignation, walked down the corridor to his locker. As he turned the key in the lock, the PA system crackled and Miss Trimble's voice sounded out.

"Good morning, boys and girls. The first of our entries for the talent competition today is from Chester Todd. It's a lovely poem called 'Seagull Over the Great South Bay.' "

There was a crackle as the tape recorder cut in and Chester's voice began reading.

"Over the bay the seagull flies
Then on a flagpole he does sit
The trouble is he cannot fly
When he wants to have a shit

"The seagull strains his—

The tape was suddenly cut off, as the whole corridor erupted into uncontrollable laughter. Boys leaned against their lockers and slid their backs down to the ground, clutching at their knees to suppress the aching in their stomachs, while girls clustered into tight groups, sniggering into cupped hands. Then they heard Miss Trimble's quivering voice again.

"I think that's enough of that. Chester Todd, please go immediately to the principal's office. Now, without further ado, I think we'll go on to the next entry. This is a song written by Benji Newman entitled 'I Do Love You.' "

Immediately there was a loud whooping noise from the boys in the corridor, and they all ran to crowd around him, letting out loud wolf whistles and wiggling their hips and blowing kisses at him.

That was it! He'd really screwed up this time. Why had he bothered listening to David? He should never have done this. He slammed his locker door shut and ran down the corridor to the lavatories and pushed open the door. Oh, no, there was a speaker in here as well! He darted round into an empty cubicle and pushed the door closed and locked it, and sinking down on the seat, he stuck his fingers in his ears and shut his eyes tight. Yet even in his silenced world, he could still hear the muffled tones of Miss Trimble's voice rambling on. What *was* she going on about? It had to be something to do with that note in the tape-box. He pulled a ream of lavatory paper off the roll and stuffed it into his ears, then, screwing up his face, he cut out all remaining sound with his fingers.

As he sat there, his elbows resting on his knees, he suddenly became aware of a powerful, rhythmic reverberation coming up through his feet. He looked up at the door of the cubicle and saw it rattling violently against the lock on the partition wall, as if someone were trying to get in.

"Go away!" he yelled out, momentarily unblocking his ears.

There was no one there. The reverberation was not man-made, but came from the speaker high up on the wall in the corner of the lavatory, blasting out the introduction of a funky, up-tempo song. He stood up and pulled the paper out of his ears, just as the vocals of the song began. "I do love you, but it's breaking my heart, breaking my heart in two." He pushed open the door of the cubicle and walked out, and stood for a minute listening to *his* song.

It was fantastic! It was like . . . real! There were drums and a deep thumping bass and something like a trumpet breaking in every now and then. But other than that, it was all *him*—with his ukulele! He had to go and tell David about it—he had to go see him outside, right now! He began to chew apprehensively on a finger-nail. But how? He would have to get past all those boys again. He walked over to the door of the lavatory and, after a moment's hesitation, pulled it wide open and stood back. The first thing he saw was a black boy from the class above him moon-walking past the door in time with the music. He moved forward and peered round the corner. The whole way along the corridor, kids were dancing around to the song. He edged out and walked towards the main door, trying to make himself as inconspicuous as possible by staying close to the wall.

Sean Dalaglio was the first to spot him.

"Hey, Benji!" he yelled out, running towards him. "That's a great song! How d'ya get Dublin Up to play session with you? They're my favourite group! Can you get their autographs for me?"

Benji looked at him wide-eyed. "You mean, Dublin Up are—" He gulped. "I gotta go, Sean."

He broke into a run and headed towards the main doors, and as he passed through the throng of dancing pupils, he was greeted with countless voices calling out "Great song, Benji!" and "You're sure to win with *that* one, man!"

He raced outside and saw David at the other end of the path, leaning against the side of the Volkswagen, a grin stretched across his face, and between the fingers of his right hand was held the twenty-dollar bill.

Benji started to run down the path towards him, but David suddenly held up his hand to halt him in his tracks and, at the same time, pushed the bill into the breast pocket of his shirt. Benji stopped and looked at him, a puzzled expression on his face. David flicked his hand at him, motioning for him to return back the way he had come.

For a moment, Benji stood where he was, then, with a look of utter disappointment, he turned round, only to be faced by a crowd of pupils who had silently gathered on the wide step outside the main doors. At the front stood Sean Dalaglio. Benji glanced round and gave David the broadest of smiles before heading back to school to run the gauntlet of congratulations from his friends.

CHAPTER

25

As the taxi edged forward in the solid Park Avenue traffic, Jennifer glanced at her watch. Five to seven already, and the restaurant was still another twelve blocks away. There was no way she was going to make it in the next five minutes. She leaned sideways, feeling the dampness of her shirt becoming unstuck from the dirty plastic of the seat due to the overpowering humidity outside and the lack of air-conditioning within, and looked past the driver to see the jam stretching up as far as Grand Central. She pushed herself forward in the seat and knocked on the partition glass. The driver reached back and slid it to one side.

"Ye, leddy?" he said in an accent that gave Jennifer little confidence in his ability to find the Empire State Building, let alone the Ocean Floor restaurant.

"Can't you cut across to Lexington or Third and try going up there? This is hopeless."

The driver smiled at her and nodded in agreement, at the same time holding up his hands and slapping them down hard against the orange acrylic steering-wheel cover.

"Yez, hopless!" he said, and remained where he was.

Jennifer stared at the back of his head, waiting for him to spin the steering wheel and make an attempt to cut off to the right, but he seemed happy to sit and wait for the traffic to start moving again, rocking his head from side to side in time to the strangled tones of the Middle Eastern singer that blared from his stereo.

She turned and looked around her in every direction to see if there was another taxi free anywhere nearby, but every one had its light off. Anyway, it would probably be out of the frying pan into the fire. She pushed her hair back off her forehead, feeling the dampness of it clammy on her hand, then, picking up her handbag, she took out her mobile phone and dialled Alex's number. It was engaged. She turned it off and threw it back into her handbag, and leaned forward once more to the open partition glass.

"Can't you at least turn on the air-conditioning?" she said angrily.

It was seven o'clock. Alex would be there by now. He was never late. She knew that, and that was why she had left the office in good time so that she could be there before him. But now it had been a full twenty-five minutes that she had been stuck in this taxi. She rolled down the window, only to be hit by a blast of air that was as hot as a hair-dryer and which only exacerbated her present discomfort. She rolled it up again and sat back to wait.

She hadn't seen him since the tennis party. He had left a message on the answerphone at the apartment, saying that he'd had to go to Dallas after all. "Unavoidable" was the word he had used. What was new? It was always unavoidable as far as Alex was concerned. Not that it mattered much. She had been working every hour that God had given her on the Tarvy's contract, so they probably wouldn't have seen much of each other at any rate. She shook her head. The bloody contract. Nothing she had produced so far gave her overwhelming confidence that they would secure it. Maybe Russ had been right. Maybe they were trying to bite off more than they could chew.

For no apparent reason, the traffic suddenly began to move again, and the driver turned and grinned, obviously thinking that theirs was now a well-bonded relationship following their brief but mutually misunderstood exchange of words.

"Ye, leddy, we move now!" He nodded contentedly and slowly the car began to roll forward up Park.

By the time they made it to the Ocean Floor, the time was edging towards twenty past seven. Having paid her budding linguist, Jennifer jumped out of the taxi and ran across the sidewalk into the restaurant.

The place was only half-full, with the consequence that she was greeted by three white-aproned waiters, obviously eager for any passing trade that they could muster. At that point, she spied Alex sitting over at a table in the corner of the room, laughing as he talked into his mobile phone. She cut a path through her welcoming committee, leaving them with frowns of resigned disappointment on their faces.

Seeing her approach, Alex quickly pressed the "end" button on the phone and tucked it away in the inside pocket of his jacket.

"Sorry I'm late, darling," she said, slinging her handbag over the back of the chair. "The traffic was lousy."

Alex got up and reached over the table and gave her a peck on the cheek.

"You looked happy just then on the phone," she said, pulling out the chair and sitting down. "Do I take it that all went well in Dallas, then?"

"Not really. That was just a social call to, er"—he faltered for a second—"to John. Now listen." He picked up the menu and made a show studying it. "I didn't know when you were going to arrive, so I've ordered you mussels and swordfish. I hope that's all right?"

"Fine." She reached forward to pick up her napkin, but was outmanouevred by a waiter who quickly plucked it away from her outstretched hand and, flicking it open, placed it on her lap.

"Good eat!" he said, smiling broadly at Jennifer.

Jennifer watched him turn and walk away. "Does no one speak English in this city any more?"

"What?" Alex asked.

"Oh, nothing," she sighed, shaking her head. She leaned on the table and cupped her chin on the back of her linked hands. "So Dallas wasn't a success, then?"

"No, not really." He reached over with the wine bottle and filled her glass. "I mean, I think it'll work out in the long run, but the company we're dealing with seems pretty edgy about the new system. It's just a question of earning their confidence."

Jennifer nodded slowly, understanding the implications. "Meaning that you're going to have to hold their hand for the time being."

Alex let out a long sigh. "Yeah, I'm afraid so. I'm heading straight back there after San Francisco." He glanced around the restaurant to see if there was any sign of their food, then pushed back the sleeve of his shirt and looked at his watch. "I hope they're quick. I can't be too long." He turned back to Jennifer. "So how's the new contract going?"

Jennifer leaned back in her chair. "We haven't got it yet, Alex. I'm just doing the proposal at the moment, but the problem is that it's completely new ground for me. I'm not really sure if I've hit it quite right so far, but . . ."

She tailed off, realizing that he wasn't listening. He was looking at his watch again and turning round to see if their food was arriving. At that point, a waiter came backwards through the kitchen doors and headed for their table with two plates held high in his hands.

"Mussels?"

Jennifer nodded and the waiter placed the steaming bowl in front of her.

"I get you finger-bowl, madam—and for you, sir, seafood salad."

"Thank you." Alex looked up at the waiter. "Could you see if we can get our second course as quickly as possible? I have a plane to catch."

With a smile and a bow, the waiter turned briskly on his heel and hurried off back to the kitchen.

"That looks good," Alex said, picking up his knife and fork. He looked across at Jennifer, who sat staring at him, making no move to start her meal. "What's the matter? Isn't that what you wanted?"

She shook her head slowly. "Alex, how long have we been married?"

Alex had taken a mouthful of salad as she asked the question, and stopped with his fork in his mouth. "Whop?"

Jennifer didn't reply, letting the question sink into Alex's brain. She picked up one of the mussel shells and tilted it back to her mouth.

"What was that supposed to mean?"

"We've been married thirteen years now," she said quietly, "just in case you've forgotten, but I could bet you that anyone here who just happened to witness how we're acting with each other would think that we've hardly ever met before. I mean, we're like total strangers! What have we talked about so far? Your business and mine." She leaned over the table towards him. "We have a life together, Alex. Thirteen years' worth of it, for Chrissakes!"

Alex let his knife and fork fall with a clatter to his plate and he raised his eyes to the ceiling. "Come on, Jennifer," he said in a whisper. "Don't start making a scene here. People will hear."

"I am not—making—a—scene!" she hissed at him between clenched teeth. She paused to compose herself. "It's just that every time we see each other, we seem to drift further and further apart. We don't seem to have anything in common any more—or do we? What's gone wrong? We did—no, that's not right—we *do* have a really good life together, Alex. You're my best friend. You're my lover, though one might not have thought it of late, and you also happen to be my husband and the father of my child. But nowadays, it seems to be all too much like a . . . a business arrangement."

Alex cocked his head to the side and continued to eat his meal. "Well, it was you who chose to go back to work. I didn't make you."

"Alex, I am not trying to fix blame. I just want for us to be . . ." Jennifer was interrupted by the waiter, who placed a finger-bowl down in front of her.

"Is our main course on the way?" Alex asked him.

"Yes, sir. On the way." He turned and left the table, and Jennifer continued. "I just want us to be together more, even if it's only on weekends."

"Well, you could always give up your job. You don't need to work. I'm successful enough."

"And how does one measure success, Alex?" Jennifer said, louder than she meant. Alex looked round the restaurant to see if anyone was looking in their direction. "Is it the number of zeroes that's on the paycheck at the end of each month? Or is it how much fun you have with your child, and how much you are involved with his upbringing? Does that count for anything? I mean, right now Jasmine and David seem to be the ones most involved with Benji, especially David, who—"

Alex picked up the napkin from his lap and threw it onto the table, and slapped down his hands hard onto its surface.

"Jennifer, are you comparing my contribution to Benji's upbringing with that of some . . . unmotivated good-for-nothing who just walked in off the street? Because if so, I resent that! Okay, Jasmine does a lot for Benji, but that's what's she's paid for, but don't start giving me all that crap about this guy David. Anyway, Jasmine works in order that *we* can work, so—come on, you tell me—how much time are *you* spending with Benji, O perfect mother? It cuts both ways. You do realize that, don't you?"

Jennifer finished off the last of the mussels and dipped her fingers into the bowl and wiped her hands on her napkin, then let out a long, resigned sigh.

"Okay . . . I know . . . you're right, it does cut both ways. The difference is that I have the whole thing going through my brain all the time. Do you?"

Alex didn't reply, knowing that whatever he said would be taken in the wrong light. The pause was long enough for Jennifer to realize that what she had intended to be a reasoned discussion was now turning into a heated argument. She reached over and put her hand on his.

"I'm sorry, darling, I didn't mean for this to happen. It's just that . . . well . . . I just want us to be together more—as a family. I know that might sound like a cliché, but the whole thing seems so hopeless right now!"

The waiter came over and placed their main courses in front of them. Alex glanced at his watch. "Christ, it's eight o'clock. I haven't got time to eat this. I'll have to go, or I'm going to miss the plane."

Jennifer nodded. "Okay," she said quietly.

"Are you happy to eat by yourself or do you want to leave it?"

"No, I think I've had my fill. Anyway, I don't know how good this place is. Those mussels tasted a bit strange."

Alex smiled at her and called back the waiter. "I'm afraid we're going to have to leave. We've run out of time."

"But you order food!"

"I know, but we have no time to eat it!"

"But you have to pay for food."

"Fine!" Alex snapped at him. "Just get the check!"

The waiter pulled a long face and stomped off, and Alex and Jennifer looked at each other for a moment before bursting out into fits of subdued laughter.

"You see what I mean?" Jennifer said. "It's catching!"

He bent down and picked up his brief-case, then paused before rising to his feet and looked across at Jennifer. "We'll work it out, darling. I promise you. But it just might take some time, okay?"

Jennifer nodded. "Okay."

He pushed back his chair. "Come on then. I'll get a couple of cabs."

The traffic was by this time much lighter, and Alex had no trouble in flagging down two empty taxis. He walked over to Jennifer and made to give her a kiss on the cheek, but she tilted her head round so that his lips came into contact with her mouth.

"I love you, Alex," she whispered.

He smiled at her. "Yeah, I know. Look, I'll give you a call when I'm back, okay?"

"Sure. Have a good trip."

He nodded, then turned and walked over to the cab and got in. It sped away from the kerb before he had time to close the door, and Jennifer stood watching until it had crossed over the lights on Park Avenue. Oh, Alex, you could have said it too. Not just "yeah." She put her hand to her forehead, feeling the first pangs of a headache coming on. It must be the humidity, or maybe just the after-effects of their stupid argument. That's exactly what it was—sheer stupidity, on both their parts. She screwed her eyes tightly shut to try to relieve the pressure building up in her head, and despite the heat she suddenly began to feel cold, with an involuntary shudder at the realization.

"You comin', lady?" the taxi driver called out to her.

Jennifer hugged her arms around her body and walked over to the car and jumped in the back.

"Where to?"

"Barrymore Street, please."

"West Village?"

"Yeah."

The cab sped off and took the lights on Park Avenue at yellow. By the time he had stopped at Fifth Avenue, Jennifer was shivering uncontrollably and her head felt as if it were undergoing a rhythmic pounding from a sledge-hammer. She tapped on the dividing glass, and the driver flicked it open.

"Yup?"

"Would it be possible to turn down the air-conditioning, please?"

"Hell, lady, it's roasting outside!"

"I know, but I don't think I feel too good."

The driver shrugged his shoulders and reached forward and turned a knob on his dashboard. The lights changed to green and he slewed the car round into Fifth Avenue, throwing Jennifer sideways in the seat. She put her hand to her mouth, feeling bile rise from her stomach and a choking sensation at the back of her throat. She reached forward and banged on the glass.

"Stop, please—now!"

The taxi pulled over to the side of the street and Jennifer pushed the door open before it had time to come to a complete standstill. She leaned out and threw up violently into the gutter, the whole scene witnessed by some passers-by, who instinctively withdrew to the far side of the sidewalk, uttering muted groans of revulsion. She closed the door again and fell back in the seat. The driver turned round slowly and eyed her.

"You been drinking, lady?"

Jennifer shook her head weakly.

" 'Cos if you been drinking, I won't have you in my cab."

"I haven't been drinking. I think I've eaten something."

"Well, for Chrissakes, don't throw up in my cab," he said, thumping his foot hard down on the accelerator, desperate to get her back home before she had a chance to do just that.

By the time they reached the traffic lights on Forty-third Street, Jennifer had had him pull over two more times, each session more violent than the one before. Her head now felt as if it was going to burst and she had to bend forward to try to relieve the unbearable ache in her stomach. Christ, she felt ill—it must have been the . . . she felt a sudden rush of pressure building up in her bowels—oh, no, please, God no, not that as well!

In her crouched position, she bent forward and knocked on the glass, and with a shake of his head, the driver immediately pulled over to the sidewalk again.

"No, no, don't stop. I just want to know where we are."

"Just coming up to Forty-second, lady."

"Well, could you turn left here, please."

"Left? But I thought you wanted to go down to the West Village."

"No, please, turn left. I want to go out to Leesport."

The driver spun round in his seat. "Leesport? You mean Leesport on Long Island? I can't go all the way out there. This is my busiest time!"

"Please. You have to. That's where my home is. I'm ill. Please. I'll pay you double the fare, I promise. Just take me there."

She slumped back in the seat, and for a moment the driver stayed where he was, staring at the ashen face of his passenger in the rear-view mirror. Then he pressed down his foot and sped away from the kerb, taking a left onto Forty-second Street towards the Midtown Tunnel.

Jasmine placed the cup of coffee on the table in front of David and sat down opposite him. He stared at the steaming cup, then slowly looked up at her.

"You see why I couldn't tell you when Benji was around," she said quietly.

David let out a long sigh. "Yeah, I certainly can. Just as well that he's staying with Sean tonight."

"Exactly. Mind you, I reckon it'll do him a lotta good staying with Sean again. You kinda pulled off something of a mini-miracle turnin' that one around, didn't you?" She took a sip of her coffee. "So what should I do about this goddamn mess?"

David shook his head. "I don't know, Jasmine. I really don't. I mean, I don't honestly think that we, or should I say you, can become embroiled in something that's not really your affair."

"Well, it *is* my affair, because I don't want to see Benji hurt."

"Yes, I understand that, but . . . well, Jennifer and Alex are adults. They have to sort it out for themselves. I mean, have you any idea whether Jennifer suspects anything?"

"No. As far as I know, she thinks everything's pretty much hunky-dory. Not that I ever talk about that kinda thing with her."

"Well, that's it, Jasmine. You've hit the nail on the head. You don't talk to her about that kind of thing, because it's really not your job. No, that doesn't sound right." He paused. "Look, you are probably the most loyal friend that she has, but this is her own very personal relationship." He pushed his chair away from the table. "I don't know. Maybe I'm barking up the wrong tree here. It's just that regardless of how well I knew a person, I wouldn't have ever wanted them to give me advice on something that concerned only myself and . . ." He tailed off, suddenly realizing what he was saying and, feeling his face instantly flush, he cast a quick glance at Jasmine.

"And what, David?" Jasmine asked quietly, her coffee-cup halfway to her mouth.

David looked at her stony-faced, struggling desperately to try to think of a way of diverting their dialogue away from the trap that she had inadvertently sprung on him. At that precise moment, the front doorbell rang three times in quick succession, and both turned simultaneously to look at the clock on the wall.

Jasmine frowned. "Who on earth would be callin' at a quarter to ten?" She got up from her chair and hurried off through the house. David stayed where he was, watching until she had left the room, then let out a long sigh of relief. Jesus, he'd nearly blown it that time. That was the past unconsciously weaving its way into present circumstances, and he had been caught completely unawares.

"DAVID! COME QUICKLY!"

The urgency in her tone made him jump up violently from the chair, making it fall with a clatter to the ground. He ran quickly to the hall to find Jasmine and a red-faced overweight man gently placing Jennifer down on the bottom stair and leaning her limp figure against the banister. She was ashen-faced, her pale shirt spattered with a yellow liquid that made it stick to her skin, and a nauseating smell permeated the whole area.

"What's happened?" David asked, glancing from one to the other.

The man turned and started walking back towards the door. "The lady's sick, sir, that's what's happened, and she's made one hell of a mess inside my taxi. Jeez, I didn't want to do the run, but she said she'd pay me double, and now I've gotta clean out the inside of—"

"All right," David cut in, holding up his hand. "Let's get one thing at a time. Just tell us what happened first." He looked over to where Jennifer sat slumped against the banister, clutching her arms around her stomach, a look of near-delirium set in her eyes. Jasmine had sat down beside her, a frightened look on her face, her arm around Jennifer's shoulders.

"Picked her up outside a restaurant opposite the Inter-Continental. New place, I think, so can't remember the name. Said first that she wanted to go to the West Village, then she was as sick as a dog about three times, and then made me bring her out here. She said she'd eaten something that didn't agree with her."

David looked at Jasmine. "Sounds like food poisoning. You'd better get the doctor fast, Jasmine."

"I can't leave her sittin' here, David. I gotta get her to bed."

"And I gotta get back to the city," the taxi driver interjected. "I gotta clean out the mess in the back of the car, and that's gonna take the best part of the night."

"How much is the fare?" David said, taking his wallet from the back pocket of his jeans.

"A hundred bucks, and that only covers the fare. As I said, I gonna have to—"

Jennifer let out a groan and keeled forward, throwing up a stream of liquid yellow vomit so forcefully that it covered her skirt and three feet of the floor in front of her, making Jasmine jump to the side to avoid being hit.

David had a shiver of recognition at Jennifer's plight, the whole scene sparking off a vision of instant déjà vu, as if a window, hitherto closed tight within his brain, had suddenly been opened.

"You must be prepared for the worst with chemotherapy, David," Dr. Spiers had said to him. "It can have some pretty unpleasant side effects. She'll be depressed, frightened and very sick, but you must just give her your support, David, all the support and all the love and all the gentleness that you can."

This was all too familiar to him, and God, he'd had enough experience of it to know exactly how to act. It was like a switch being turned on in his brain, and he moved forward to take control of the situation, his actions as if on autopilot.

He handed his wallet to Jasmine. "Pay him two hundred, then get hold of the doctor as fast as you can."

Jasmine rose to her feet. "But what about Jennifer, David? I gotta get her to bed."

"I'll do that."

She looked at him warily.

"Don't worry," he said, putting his hand reassuringly on her arm. "I know exactly what I'm doing." He turned to the taxi driver. "Thanks for bringing her out. We really do appreciate it."

The taxi driver dolefully grunted his acceptance of David's thanks and headed towards the front door followed by Jasmine, who still wore a look of worried uncertainty on her face. David skirted round the liquid on the floor and squatted down beside Jennifer.

"Listen," he said quietly to her. "I'm going to get you upstairs now. Do you think you can manage?"

Jennifer raised her head to look at him, her eyes barely focusing on his face. He placed his hand under her armpit and gently raised her to her feet, but her legs seemed too weak to carry her weight and she slumped forward against his chest. Wrinkling his nose at the smell of her clothes, he pushed her limp body away from him, and placing one hand round her back and the other behind her knees, he lifted her up in one swift movement and carried her up the stairs as fast as he was able.

Once on the landing, he suddenly realized that he had no idea in which direction her room was. He called down to Jasmine. "Which room is it?"

"Turn right and second on the left. Are you sure you can manage, David?"

"Yeah." He walked along the corridor and pushed open the door and, having pressed the light switch with his elbow, he carried Jennifer over to the bed and laid her upon it.

"Not down," Jennifer said weakly, trying to get herself back into a sitting position. "Feel sick like that."

David helped her back upright and felt an involuntary retch shudder through his body, caused by the putrid smell of vomit.

"Okay, try and stay like that for a moment. I'm just going to run you a bath, and then we'll get you out of those clothes." He looked over to a door that led off the bedroom. "Is that the bathroom?"

Jennifer nodded weakly, too ill to complain, and followed him with her eyes as he walked across the room to the bathroom.

Having turned on the taps, David grabbed a towel and returned to the bedroom to find Jennifer holding tight to the front of her blouse, a look of helplessness on her face. David leaned forward in front of her, resting his hands on his knees.

"Jennifer, you're going to have to trust me. I promise you, all I'm going to do is get you into the bath. Jasmine can take over after that, but I don't think she can manage to do the lifting work by herself."

The kindness in David's voice was too much for Jennifer. Her face suddenly creased up and she burst into tears, leaning slowly forward so her face rested on his arms.

"This is so . . . degrading," she said between sobs.

"No, it's not, Jennifer," David said, putting a hand under her chin and turning her face up so that she was looking straight at him. "There's nothing to worry about."

"It's not that," Jennifer said, pulling her face away from his hand and looking down into her lap. "I think that it may not be just the sick."

David squatted down on his haunches so that he could look up into her face. "Look, I promise you, I couldn't give a damn. I've seen a lot worse than anything you can show me." He paused. "I don't mind, Jennifer, if you don't mind."

Jennifer sniffed and nodded her head.

"Come on, then, let's get those clothes off."

Jennifer let go of the front of her skirt and put her hands to the side, and David calmly began to undo the buttons. He pulled the shirt off round her shoulders and let it fall to the ground, then, undoing the clasp and zip at the side of her skirt, he lifted her up enough to slide both that and her half-slip down over her legs.

At that point, he heard Jasmine's voice talking to him as she came up the stairs and along the corridor.

"I called the doctor, David. Thank God he lives just down the street. I reckon he should be here any min——" She walked into the room to find Jennifer sitting on the bed in her bra and pants, with David standing in front of her. "David! What are you doin'? You shouldn't be—"

David looked over to her and held up a hand. "Jasmine," he said in a quietly controlled voice, "could you just go and turn off the taps? The bath will nearly be overflowing by now. I'm going to get Jennifer into the bath and then you can take over."

Jasmine looked quickly at Jennifer, who turned enough to give her a brief nod. She went into the bathroom and turned off the water, swirling it around with her hand to check the temperature. Then, standing back from the bath, she found a position from where she could get a clear view of what was happening in the adjoining room.

"Right, now I'm just going to put the towel round you and get everything else off, okay?"

David flicked open the towel and wrapped it round Jennifer's shoulders, then, reaching round her back, he undid her bra strap and pulled the bra free, letting it drop to the ground beside the shirt. Having inched her forward enough to slip the towel underneath her bottom, he gently rid her of her pants, and wrapping everything up into the skirt, he threw the soiled bundle over towards the door. Then, pulling the towel tight around Jennifer's body, he hoisted her up from the bed and carried her towards the bathroom.

Jasmine stood aside as David entered, dumbfounded at what she had just witnessed. It had been a scene of such gentleness and caring that she felt instantly ashamed for ever considering that there might have been any other motivation behind David's actions. Every movement that she had seen him make was as if it had been rehearsed many times before—from the way he knew how to shift Jennifer's body weight with little or no effort to how he wrapped her in the towel and tucked it neatly into its own folds.

"You've done this before, haven't you, David, my boy," she said to herself as she watched him lower Jennifer's feet into the water. "Yessir, you sure done this before."

"Is the temperature all right?" David asked.

Jennifer nodded, and he turned to Jasmine, still with an arm around her waist. "Can you manage from here?"

"Yup, I reckon so," Jasmine said, coming forward and taking Jennifer's weight on her arm.

"Right, well, I'll just go downstairs and clean up that mess. Give me a call when you're finished and I'll come back up and get her into bed."

Jasmine nodded slowly and watched him as he left the room.

Then, turning to Jennifer, she removed the towel and gently lowered her into the bath.

The front doorbell rang fifteen minutes later, as David made his way down the stairs after having helped Jennifer back to her bed. He walked across the hall and opened the door, letting in a young man whose dishevelled appearance was indicative of the fact that he had obviously done more than his fair share of work that day.

"Sorry I couldn't be quicker. I was already out on a call when you phoned. So where's the patient?"

David pointed up the stairs. "Go right at the top and it's the second door on the left."

The young man took off up the stairs, then turned back to David. "Has she been sick since you called?"

"Yeah, once at least. Jasmine would know better. She's up there with Mrs. Newman."

The doctor nodded. "Good. Better to get it all out." He turned and continued his way up the stairs.

David stood in the hall until he heard the bedroom door shut behind the doctor, then, thrusting his hands into the back pockets of his jeans, he walked through to the kitchen and put on the kettle. He shook his head. He needed more than a cup of coffee. A large whisky would be better. He made his way over to the refrigerator and took out a can of beer, then, walking to the table, he picked up the chair that he had knocked over and sat down, pulling off the ring of the can and taking a long drink.

A flood of emotion suddenly coursed through his mind. Never had anything that he had done over the past few months brought back such vivid memories of Rachel. No, that wasn't right. She was constantly right there at the surface of his thoughts, but until this time it had been the happy, carefree memories of her that had occupied his mind, never the bad ones. Now he began to remember the countless occasions on which he had comforted his wife, gently stroking the soft patchy bristle on her head, being all that remained of her shining brown hair, while she, contorted in pain, bent over the basin at the side of her bed. Once she had finished, he would lay her down carefully, wiping her face clean with a wash-cloth. Then her hand would feel for his, and he would hold it, carefully so as not to hurt its thin covering of flesh, and she would open up her eyes and they would sparkle at him, exactly the same way as when they had first met, all those years ago in Oxford. And they never lost their sparkle. Never, until the day that she—

He heard the door of the kitchen open and, giving his eyes a rub and clearing his throat to rid it of the lump that had formed in his gullet, he turned to look at Jasmine. She smiled at him and walked over to the kettle.

"It's just boiled," he said, his voice still choked.

Jasmine looked at him and nodded and, taking a cup from the draining-board, she spooned instant coffee into it.

"How is she?" he asked.

"She'll be fine. The doctor gave her something to make her sleep. He reckons though that she'll have to get rid of it all herself. He doesn't know how long it will take. It can go on for some time, he says."

She poured water into her cup, and walking over to the table, she pulled out a chair and sat down beside him.

"You all right?"

David nodded.

"You look as if you've seen a ghost."

"No, I'm all right."

"Reckon now I can't say much to her about what we were talking about."

David sat back in his chair and shook his head. "No, I don't think so."

For a moment, Jasmine was silent, turning her coffee-cup round in circles on the table. "Can I ask you somethin'?"

"Yeah?" he said, picking up his can of beer.

"Are you a doctor or a nurse or somethin'?"

David stopped and looked at her, the lip of the can pressed against his mouth. "What?"

Jasmine leaned forward on the table towards him, an intent expression on her face. "David, you knew what you were doing up there. You said as much yourself. I saw it all. You've done that before—many times, I'd say. How come?"

David continued to look at her.

"Are you married, David?"

He said nothing.

"Because you were about to say something about you and someone else when we were talking earlier, just before Jennifer came back. Are the two things tied up, David? Is that why you're lookin' like you do right now?"

He turned and stared out of the window into the darkness.

"David? Do you want to talk about it?" Jasmine asked quietly.

He looked back at her, then began in a faltering voice. "Yeah, I was married. For eighteen years, actually. That was until April." He took a deep breath. "Rachel"—he paused and wiped at his eyes with the back of his hand—"had ovarian cancer. It was not detected till too late, and she underwent treatment for about six months. I nursed her the whole time—no one else—hence what you might call my expertise in the job. But she died in April." He turned and looked out the window once more. "And that's it, really. Now you know the whole story of David Corstorphine."

Jasmine sat with her hands clasped over her mouth. "Oh, Lordy, I didn't know, David. I'm so sorry. I didn't mean to . . ."

David shook his head. "No, you didn't do anything wrong. I was going to tell you sometime, but didn't really feel I was quite ready yet. Hadn't quite exorcized the ghosts of the past. That's really why I took this job—so that I could get away from it all. I didn't want to think, let alone talk, about it."

"And here's me puttin' my big foot in it. Oh, I feel awful. I didn't mean to get that out of you."

He smiled at her. "You know, Jasmine, you've been more help to me than anyone else. That's the truth. Both you and Benji. You've taken me at face value. You haven't once asked me about where I come from or what I've done. I really mean that, Jasmine, you couldn't have done more good for me. And as for Benji, well, just being with him has helped me realize just how much I've missed my own children."

Jasmine let her hands fall with a thump to the table. She sat with her mouth wide open. "Children? You have children?" she asked incredulously.

David nodded. "Three. Sophie, Charlie and Harriet."

"But where *are* they?"

"At school."

"Yeah, I guessed that, but who's looking after them at nights?"

"They're at a boarding-school."

"At a boarding-school? You mean they *live* in?"

David nodded.

"Do you mean to say that their mother died last April, and you have them at a boarding-school?" Jasmine exclaimed, shaking her head in disbelief and slowly rising from her chair.

"Yes, but—"

"That is . . ." She paused, trying to think of the right word. ". . . unforgivable, David! How could you do that? I mean, how old is the youngest?"

"Nine."

"*Nine?* But that's younger than Benji, David! *Nine?*"

"Listen, Jasmine, it may be difficult for you to understand this, but the children were all away at school before their mother was ill, and when the time came to choose whether to continue with their present school or find somewhere nearer home, it was the children themselves who chose to go back. You see, they have all their friends there; they're happy and secure; and for me, that is absolute. Even though *I* wanted them nearer home, I couldn't go against their wishes, because *that* would have been both cruel and self-indulgent."

Jasmine stood eyeing him, her arms folded and her head on a tilt.

"That's as may be, but what I can't understand is how you've felt able to . . . gallivant around having fun with Benji when your own children are . . . locked up in some boarding-school."

The remark hit a nerve, a painful one. He jumped up from his chair, banging his fist down on the table.

"That is neither fair nor true, Jasmine! I love my children, more than you can ever imagine! I have been in constant touch with them since I've been over here, and they with me. And if it's any of your business, I'm going back to Scotland at the beginning of next month, and we're all going off on holiday together. Anyway, I was only meant to be here for a couple of days, but then I realized that I couldn't go back, because . . ."

He slumped back down in his chair, his anger having worked its way deep into his mind to batter at the defences that had been hitherto holding so strong against his grief and sorrow.

". . . because I found that I just couldn't cope without my wife."

Fighting hard to control his emotions, he rubbed at his forehead with his fingertips, pressing them in hard to cause enough pain to act as a distraction. He took a deep breath. "I'm sorry, I didn't mean to shout at you."

He hadn't heard her walk round the table to stand beside him, but suddenly felt her hand resting on his shoulder.

"It's not you who should apologize. It's me. I'm too darned stupid to understand all that's gone on in your life. It's not for me to pass judgement on what you do and don't do. You know and understand your children much better than me, and I *know* that you love them better than I could ever imagine. I'm sorry. I should never have opened my big mouth."

David sat up and took a deep breath. "No, your reaction was quite justifiable. It does sound pretty harsh when you hear it cold like that. Just shows up all too clearly our difference in culture. What is it you Americans say about us Brits? Keeping the animals at home and sending the children off to kennels?" He let out a short laugh. "I can't make excuses for it, Jasmine, but I think you know me well enough when I say that it *was* the best thing for them under the circumstances."

She sighed and raised her eyebrows, then sat down heavily on her chair again. "Yeah, I guess so." She paused. "It's just a pity we won't get to meet them. How old are they?"

"Sophie's coming up to sixteen, Charlie's twelve, and Harriet—well, you know how old she is."

Jasmine nodded slowly. "Charlie's twelve. How about that? Pity we couldn't get him and Benji together."

"Yeah, they'd hit it off pretty well, too. Both born enthusiasts. Problem is Charlie courts disaster wherever he goes. That's why I over-reacted so, the time that I found Benji lying at the bottom of the pool. It was really Charlie I saw there, you know."

"For heaven's sakes, yes. God, you must have been scared some."

David gave a brief shake of his head. "You can say that again!"

She smiled. "So where are you taking them on their vacation?"

"Don't know yet. I'll fix it up when I get back."

She looked at him, her eyes bright. "I have an idea! Why don't you bring them out here?"

David gaped at her. "What?"

"Bring them out here to the States, to Leesport! I mean, why take them anywhere else? You know the place. You now have us and all your other friends over here. There's the sun and the sea, and the pool and the tennis here. Go on, David, it would be so much fun for them."

He smiled at her and shook his head. "No, Jasmine, I think not."

"Why not? Give me *one* good reason why not?"

"Because . . ."

"I know what you're going to say. Because no one knows about you and what's happened to you all, and you want to be able to guard your privacy. Is that it?"

"Well, in a word, yes."

"Well, in that case, bang goes your argument, because I know. So what other excuse do you have?"

David shrugged and scratched at his head. "I don't know, Jasmine. Maybe it would be better if I just finished off out here and went back to start again."

"No, it wouldn't," she said, her tone so sharp that it made David start back in his chair. She picked up a pencil that happened to be lying on the table and began to roll it over and over in her fingers. "Listen, David, I'm goin' to tell you something. This house has never been filled with so much happiness and laughter than since you been around. We really want to keep you here as long as we possibly can." She paused. "And I can tell you, that don't just go for me and Benji."

He looked at her quizzically. "Meaning?"

"Meanin' that I was with Jennifer just after the doctor left. I gave her the sleeping-pill, but she kept tryin' to sit up. She was pretty delirious, but she kept asking me, 'Where is he? Where is he?' over and over again. I said that I didn't rightly know, thinking that she meant Alex, but then she shook her head. 'Where's David?' she asked. I said that it was all right, you were downstairs, and with that, she kinda slid back against her pillow and went to sleep—just like that—with a big smile spread across her face." She let the pencil fall to the table. "The pill sure as hell couldn't have worked that fast!" "

David sat in silence, staring at her.

"David, you're right on two counts. First, we couldn't tell Jennifer about Alex. It's not our business. The other thing is, yeah, I *am* her best friend. I know her like a kid sister. Goddamn it, I *treat* her like a kid sister! And I sure as hell could not cope myself with this thing with Alex if it came out, and neither could she, especially not right now when she's sick. Whether you like it or not, you have gotten under all our skins. You've become our security, our—what was it Jennifer called you?—yeah, our Superman! You make things happen that ain't ever happened before in this household. And if you went right now, and Alex then decided to head off, I think the whole ship would sink."

David shook his head slowly. "I can't be around for ever, Jasmine."

"I'm not asking you to be around for ever. I realize that you have a life over in Scotland with the children an' everythin'. But if you bring the kids over here, it would at least keep you here too another week or two, and maybe by then, things might have gotten sorted out between her and Alex—or maybe not." She stretched out and put her hand on his. "Please, David, think about it, and think of all the fun the kids would have together."

He smiled at her. "My house isn't very big."

Jasmine grinned, realizing that the discussion was turning in her favour. "It doesn't matter! Kids love sleeping rough! Anyways, they could always come and stay here. Jennifer wouldn't—"

"No!" David cut in.

"Why on earth not?"

"Because I want no one else to know about my past, that's why."

"For what reason?"

"Because it would, well, just change everything. It would mean . . . that people knew about me . . . and that's what I couldn't deal with back in Scotland. I am quite happy with this identity of simply being David-the-gardener. I don't want to be known as David-whose-wife-has-just-died. Am I making any sense to you?"

Jasmine raised her eyebrows.

"I know it sounds quite underhanded, Jasmine, but what difference would it really make? I promise you I will tell Jennifer when the kids arrive, and then everyone else in my own time." He smiled at her. "As it happens, I was going to tell you first. Only you found out earlier than I had planned."

Jasmine slowly nodded. "So when d'you think the kids could come?"

"In about two weeks."

She looked at David, the excitement returning to her eyes. "Gee, that's wonderful! I could give you a hand to get some beds put up in your house. Hey, I can't wait to meet them! And to think of all the fun we'll have with Benji and with Dodie an' all." She suddenly sat bolt-upright. "Speakin' of which, where is she?"

Slapping his forehead in forgetfulness, David jumped up from his chair and looked around the kitchen, his sudden movement disturbing the dog, who had been lying, hidden from sight, deep within one of the beanbags next to the television. She stretched her woolly head up towards the ceiling and let out a loud yawn.

"Never far away," he laughed. He stuck his hands into the pockets of his jeans and arched his back, suddenly feeling very tired. "I think I'll go home now, Jasmine." He walked round behind her and put his hand on her shoulder. "Thanks for the talk, and for the great idea—and also for being a friend. I really appreciate it, you know."

Jasmine put her own hand up to her shoulder and patted the top of his. "Goes for both of us, David, I can tell you."

He gave Dodie a whistle, and Jasmine turned in her chair to watch him as he walked across the kitchen to the back door. "Be here usual time tomorrow?"

"Of course," David replied, and with a fleeting wave, he let himself and Dodie out into the warmth of the night.

Seeing that Benji was staying with Sean overnight, which let him fulfil his golden wish of walking to school, David did not need to leave the house quite so early the next morning, and consequently he decided to use the extra time to make some initial arrangements for the children's visit. Having called the airline in Glasgow and booked their flight, he realized that he might have been a little preemptive in doing this without first consulting the children, so he immediately put a call through to the school.

Mr. Hunter was delighted with the idea, saying that a trip to America would be a wonderful experience for the children and a fully deserved break for them all, especially Sophie, who had worked like a Trojan during the term, making him feel more than confident about the outcome of her GCSE exams. David heard him call through to his secretary to ask her to bring the children up to his study, and while she went off to search for them, the headmaster talked enthusiastically about how well each was faring, and how proud he had been not only of them, but also of their friends, who had given them all so much support. He had just begun to describe Charlie's latest endeavours on the cricket pitch when David heard the door of the study being opened in the background and the sound of voices approaching the telephone.

"Right, Mr. Corstorphine, that's them here now. I'll put on the speakerphone so that they can all hear you."

There was a click and David heard the sounds of their breathing coming down the line.

"Are you all there?"

"Hi, Dad!" David smiled to himself at the familiar enthusiasm in their voices.

"Hi, you lot! How're things going?"

"Great! Fine!" Charlie and Harriet replied in unison.

"Is everything all right, Dad?" Sophie asked, a worried edge to her voice.

"Yes, darling! Couldn't be better! In fact, the reason I'm calling is that I've just had this idea which I want to put to you all. You know that I said in my letters that we would all go off on holiday when I got home?"

"Yes," the three voices replied.

"Well, I just thought it would be quite fun if you all came out here."

"What, to America?" Charlie gasped.

"Yeah, to America."

"Wow! That's *amazing*! Do you get cowboys and things where you are?"

David laughed. "Not around here, I'm afraid, Charlie. I'm over on the East Coast, quite near New York. It's a place called Long Island. I'm sure if you asked your geography teacher, she'd show you where it is on a map." He paused. "Well, what do you think?"

"Would you be around, Dad?" Sophie asked uncertainly. "I mean, you wouldn't be working all the time, would you?"

"No, not at all. It would be *our* holiday, and, I tell you, there is so *much* to do out here. Swimming, tennis, windsurfing."

"I haven't got my swimming-costume here," Harriet's disappointed voice piped up.

"Don't worry about that, darling. I'm going to be telephoning Granny straight away, so I'll get her to send your stuff to the school, okay?"

"Yess!" he heard Charlie and Harriet yell out.

"Sophie? What do you think?"

"Yes," Sophie answered, a hint of excitement now in her voice. "I think it would be a great idea."

"Well, in that case, I can now tell you that I've already booked your flights, and I'm going to ask Mr. Hunter to arrange for a car to take you to the airport, and then I'll be in New York to pick you up. This is really exciting! I really can't wait to see you all again! Now listen, you'd better get back to whatever you were doing, okay?"

"Okay, Dad! We'll see you in America!"

There was a moment's pause as they left the room, then a click as Mr. Hunter picked up the telephone. "Well, you couldn't have wished for a better reaction than that!"

"No, you're right! Sophie, er, seemed a bit unsure to begin with."

"She's fine, Mr. Corstorphine, believe me. Maybe your reassurance was all that she required, because she certainly went off with a beaming grin on her face."

"Thank goodness for that. Now, Mr. Hunter, I'd be most grateful if you could arrange the car for them. I've booked them on a flight on the first of July . . . tell you what, I'll fax you all the details. That would be simpler."

"Very good, and I'll just go ahead and fix it up at this end. Well, I hope you all have a wonderful holiday. I think it's just what they all need."

"Yeah, I'm sure it's what we *all* need. Thank you again, Mr. Hunter."

David pressed the "disconnect" button and immediately dialled his mother's number. It was she who answered, and from the instant she spoke, he was aware of a happiness in her voice that had been so acutely lacking over the past months. Her reaction to the idea was as enthusiastic as the children's—"tickled pink" was the phrase she used—and she went on to say how everything now seemed to be turning out for the better. His father hadn't been required to go into work at all over the past two weeks, really due to Duncan, who had completely come up trumps by keeping him so well-informed with what was going on, quite often actually taking the time to come out to the house to see him. She asked David when he thought he might return, and he replied that he would leave it open-ended, but he reckoned that they would all be back sometime in the early part of August. Then, having asked her to collect the children's passports from The Beeches and to send them, along with some summer clothes, to the school, they ended the call with a final jocular comment from his mother about him beginning to sound quite American.

He drove to Barker Lane that morning with a sense of excitement and elation tingling in his mind, not simply with the thought of the children's coming out to see him, and how positive his mother had sounded during their call, but also with the relief of realizing that his secret was out, that Jasmine knew everything about him. It was like a weight lifted from his mind—no reason for pretence, no reason for keeping his guard up in front of her.

He entered the kitchen to find her laying out a breakfast tray for Jennifer.

"It's all fixed, then!" he said almost triumphantly, pouring himself some coffee. "They're flying out here on the first of July."

Jasmine took a sharp intake of breath and, with a yell of delight, hurried over and threw her arms around him in an all-enveloping bear-hug. "Oh, David, that's wonderful!" She clapped her hands together in readiness for imminent organization. "Listen, as soon as everything gets back to normal here, I'll help you find some foldable beds and sleepin'-bags. I'm sure we've got 'em stuffed away somewhere upstairs in the loft."

David smiled at her obvious excitement. "That really would be great, Jasmine." He leaned back against the sideboard and took a drink of his coffee. "So how's the patient this morning?"

"Much better. I slept in the next-door room last night just in case she needed me. Heard her get up once, but besides that, I'm pretty sure she slept through. Anyways, right now she's sittin' up in bed and sayin' that she might get up later on this morning. I told her just to stay where she was, and if I saw her down here, I'd chase her so fast up those stairs again that her feet would hardly touch the ground."

She laughed and, turning to pick up the tray, which was set with cup and saucer, a pot of tea and some toast and marmalade, she handed it to him. "I was just going to take this up to her, but seein' you're here *and* she's already asked to see you, I think we could kill two birds with one stone, don't you—nursey?"

She gave David a wink, and with a shake of his head at her gibe, he turned and walked upstairs.

Balancing the tray on one hand, he knocked on the bedroom door and, receiving a mumbled response, he entered in time to see Jennifer stuff something under her bedclothes and glance towards him with a flushed look of guilt on her face. She was dressed in a white, short-sleeved cotton night-dress, her hair hanging in loose strands against her washed-out cheeks, and the whole scene gave David the impression that he had just caught some impish child doing something that was very much against the rules.

She let out a sigh of relief on seeing him. "Oh, thank God it's you!" She retrieved a large acetate-covered document from under her bedclothes. "I thought it was Jasmine. She'd have given me hell if she'd caught me with this."

David laughed and carried the tray over to her bedside. "Where do you want this?"

"Hang on," Jennifer said, pushing back the bedclothes, "I'll just put this back in my brief-case." She scrambled on all fours across the double bed to the side nearest him, then tilted her head up, a grin on her face. "I went downstairs and got it early this morning before Jasmine was up, so I've had to hide it under the bed. Wicked, huh?"

David put the tray down across her knees. "So, how are you feeling this morning?"

"Okay. A little woozy, but the headache has gone and I haven't been sick again, thank God!" She took a piece of toast from the rack and crunched on it.

"Glad to hear it." He took a deep breath and turned to go. "Well, I suppose I'd better be getting to work."

"No, dom'p yep!" Jennifer exclaimed, her mouth filled with dry toast. She swallowed. "I mean, can you stay and talk for a minute?"

He stood for a moment, indecisively scratching at the back of his head. "Well, okay, if you want."

She reached forward as far as the tray would allow her and patted the bed, and out of habit, David found himself dusting off the seat of his jeans before he sat down. Jennifer poured herself a cup of tea and put down the pot, then for a moment just stared at the tray, lost in thought.

"David," she said eventually, still looking down at the tray. "I just, uh . . ." She let out a short embarrassed laugh. "I actually don't know what I want to say . . . no, I mean, yes . . . I do know. I just want to say . . . that what you did last night . . . was one of the kindest things I think that anyone has ever done for me in my life." She glanced up briefly and a smile flashed across her face before she looked back down to the tray. "So thank you." She looked up again and took in a deep faltering breath. "It sounds pretty inadequate, I know, but—"

"No, look, it was nothing," David interjected with a wave of his hand. "I tell you, we were all pretty worried about you. I think Jasmine's probably right. You should just take things easy for a day or two."

Jennifer nodded. "Yeah, I will." She took a long drink of her tea, then held her hand up mid-mouthful and gulped it down. "I know what I wanted to talk to you about. Benji's song. Jasmine says it's wonderful."

"How come you've heard about that so quickly?"

"Well, I sneaked along to Benji's bedroom on my way back from picking up the brief-case, and he wasn't there, so it was my first question to Jasmine this morning. She said that he was staying with Sean, and I said that I didn't think that they were friends any more, and then she told me the story of the song. How on earth did you pull it off?"

"God, I did nothing! Benji wrote and performed the whole thing himself, and Gerry added a bit of arrangement—with some help from this mad Irish bunch called Dublin Up. All I did was hang around in the studio looking spare!"

"Oh, come on, that's nonsense! It's just like the tennis. All this Scottish modesty infuriates me! I'll spell out exactly what you achieved, David, though I know I don't need to, because you know damned well yourself. Benji being accepted by his friends again, that's what. And you orchestrated the whole thing, didn't you?"

David rolled his eyes. "Now, listen, you've not been very well, and I don't think you should get quite so over-excited—"

"Oh to hell with you, you condescending brute!" With a cry of laughter, she whisked out a pillow from behind her and dealt him a blow on the side of the head. "Don't try to change the subject! Come on, SAY IT!" She whacked him again with the pillow.

"All right! All right!" David yelled out, covering his head with his hands in mock protection against the feeble blows that were now raining down on him in quick succession. "I give up! I admit it!"

"Good," Jennifer said quietly. She leaned back, panting from the exertion, the pillow still held poised for the next blow. "That wasn't so hard, was it?" She suddenly gritted her teeth, building herself up for another blow. "But I think you deserve one more for good measure."

As the pillow struck David on the side of the face, the bedroom door opened and Jasmine appeared.

"What's all the noise ab——? What on *earth* d'you two think you're doin'?"

Jennifer sprang back under the bedclothes as Jasmine approached the bed, giving David a reprimanding cuff on the side of the head as she passed.

"Honestly!" she scolded, fussing over Jennifer like a clucking hen, pulling the duvet cover up to Jennifer's neck and smoothing it down with her hand. "I can't leave you for a minute and you're revving yourself up. And as for you, David, you know how sick she's been. You should know better than to encourage her." She straightened up and looked at the two smirking faces.

"Sorry, miss," David said in a high-pitched voice.

It was enough to set Jennifer off. David looked up at Jasmine, trying desperately to offset the infection of Jennifer's reaction, and to his relief a huge grin spread across her face, and now they all burst out laughing.

"Okay, that's it! Enough's enough!" Jasmine said eventually, wiping a tear from her eye with the back of her hand. She walked to the end of the bed and put her hand on David's shoulder. "You—outta here!" She pushed him to his feet and guided him to the door and out into the corridor, then stopped just inside the room and looked back at Jennifer.

"Now, you get some rest, d'ya hear me? And no gettin' out of bed."

David stuck his head back round the corner of the door and winked at the trussed-up figure in the bed. "And no more scrabbling under the bed!"

Jennifer let out another snort, and Jasmine pushed him out of the door and closed it behind her. "What's that supposed to mean?" she said, a puzzled expression on her face.

"One day, Jasmine," he said, putting his arm around her shoulders and slowly walking with her along the landing, "all will be revealed."

Jasmine pushed herself away and gave him a hard punch on the arm. "Oh, git on with you! I don't know if I like you any more! You're behavin' way too happy!"

CHAPTER 27

It only took three days of cosseted convalescence before Jennifer was deemed fit enough by Jasmine to be allowed downstairs, despite having had a relapse during the afternoon of day one. Jasmine had at first blamed the shenanigans of the morning, but then later on that day, when Jennifer was having a bath, she had found the secreted brief-case whilst making the bed and, with many a moaning protest from Jennifer about being treated like a ten-year-old, she had removed it to the safekeeping of the kitchen.

David also came under fire from Jasmine's dictatorial leanings, something which he found quietly amusing. She had banned him from visiting Jennifer without her being in attendance, not so much that she felt that he would hinder her recovery, but rather because she had a sneaking suspicion that he had been in cahoots with Jennifer in smuggling the brief-case up to the bedroom in the first place.

Nevertheless, by Saturday the curfew had been lifted, and during a short handing-over ceremony in the kitchen, Jennifer was reunited with her brief-case, and given full permission by the "boss" to continue her work in the study. However, a combination of her illness, the break from work and the fact that Benji was at home made Jennifer feel lackadaisical about giving any immediate thought to

Tarvy's, and she decided to postpone any further work on it until Monday, when she would return to the office.

Consequently, she was able to devote the entire weekend to Benji. Taking him out in the rowing-boat, watching from the shoreline at his ever-improving attempts at windsurfing on the bay, and of course listening to "the song" over and over again, during each rendition of which Benji gave her a running commentary of every sound that had been introduced into the final mix.

But above all, she enjoyed the moments when David was around. At first she couldn't even explain it to herself, but then, on the Saturday afternoon, while sitting high on the umpire's ladder, giving out loud and biased judgements in favour of her son and killing herself laughing when David approached her and complained in true McEnroe style about unfavorable line-calls, she realized that this was all she strove for with Alex. This was family. This was happiness. For a moment, she wished that Alex could be there to be part of it. Then, almost guiltily, she understood that his being there would more than likely be a dampener, for David would no doubt see his own presence as an intrusion, and if she insisted on his joining in, it could quite easily lead to resentment from Alex.

That evening, having successfully exercised a bit of arm-twisting on Jasmine, she arranged a lunch-time barbecue for the following day, primarily as a thank-you to Gerry Reilly for his part in helping to produce Benji's song. As it turned out, Dublin Up were still in the process of recording their album, so the invitation was extended to include them, much to the delight of Benji, who saw a way to add to his already burgeoning reputation at school by inviting half of his class to the party.

It turned out to be an afternoon of riotous fun, precipitated by the fact that at last Jennifer had found something at which David was quite useless. His attempts at barbecuing were a complete disaster, and Benji and his friends spent most of their lunch-time running down the lawn with armfuls of charcoaled hamburgers and chucking them Frisbee-style into the bay. However, such was David's obstinance in giving up his post—"I'll get it right next time" he kept saying—that

Jennifer, armed to the teeth with skewer and spatula, finally had to drive him away from the barbecue. Thereafter the women of the household took over, Jasmine cooking everything to perfection, ably assisted by Jennifer, who used the water-squirter not only to keep the flames dampened down, but also to ward off David's sneaky efforts to return for another attempt.

The party stretched on through the afternoon into the early hours of the evening, with tense games of doubles on the tennis court, crazy antics in the swimming pool, and hotly disputed games of soccer, alternated with periods of indolent slouching both on the lawn and on the sun-beds around the pool. Age became immaterial as adult partnered child, and child conquered adult, with fierce rivalry developing between each team, for the most part engendered by the adult members.

There was only one occasion during the whole proceedings on which Jennifer had call to be momentarily concerned, this being brought about by a young female classmate of Benji's who had developed an obvious crush on the lead guitarist of Dublin Up. Having subsequently ensconced herself on his knee as he lay on the sun-bed next to Jennifer, the girl asked him quite pointedly why his cigarette was such a funny shape and why it smelt so strange. However, much to Jennifer's relief, and before there was need for her to exercise responsibility as the hostess, the young man snuffed out the suspect cigarette between thumb and forefinger and stuck it behind his ear. Then, in order to divert his young suitor from asking any more leading questions, he sprang to his feet, gathering her up in his arms, and lobbed her with calculated precision into the middle of the swimming pool.

As she heard Benji loudly bid farewell to the last of his friends at the front of the house and the sound of a car taking off up the drive, Jennifer walked slowly down to the bottom of the garden to retrieve an article of clothing left abandoned on the lawn. After picking it up she continued on down to the shore of the bay and stepped out onto the wooden jetty. She stood there hugging the shirt to her chest and listening to the cacophony of crickets that broke the quiet of the evening air, and watching the final rays of the setting sun as it shimmered pink across the gently undulating waters.

The perfect end to a perfect day, she thought to herself. No, it hadn't been just the day. The whole weekend had turned out to be the most relaxed, happy and—she consciously stopped her train of thought there, wondering if she dared admit it even to herself—yes, why the hell not—*intimate* time that she had experienced in years. She suddenly shuddered, despite the warmth of the evening air and, closing her eyes, she drew in the heady aroma of the pine-trees mingled with the tangy freshness of the salt water. Then, disregarding the mosquitos biting ferociously at her ankles, she walked slowly back up onto the lawn and meandered her way to the house, kicking out her bare feet in time with the chorus of a Lou Reed song that had begun to play over and over in her mind.

Oh it's a perfect day
I'm glad I spent it with you
Just a perfect day

By the time that David arrived at the house the next morning, Jennifer had already left for work, and Jasmine remarked with a delighted gleam in her eye that, for almost the first time in living memory, she had done so reluctantly. Nevertheless, whereas she had been morose about starting the new week, it was immediately heralded with a new buzz of excitement by the others in the Newman household, as David and Jasmine began to make plans for the children's arrival.

Benji was naturally irritated by their clandestine chats, so David decided to bring him in early on the plan, and sitting around the kitchen table after school that afternoon, he told him from the beginning about Rachel and the children, and about their imminent visit.

At first the young boy had mixed feelings about the whole affair. He couldn't believe that David had children of his own and hadn't told anyone, and at the same time there was a funny low feeling of resentment in his stomach when he thought about their coming out to the States and David spending all his time with them, and not with him any more. He also found it difficult to understand why David didn't want to tell his mother straight away, because he *knew* that she would be both amazed and excited that David had children.

David explained to him as concisely as possible that of course he would tell his mother, but that he wanted first to get the chance to explain things in full, as he had done with him. At first, Benji appeared despondent at not being allowed to break the news himself, but when Jasmine happened to mention Charlie's age, the boy's face suddenly lit up with intrigue.

"He's twelve?"

"Yup."

"About the same age as me?"

"Just a bit older, I'd guess."

"Do you think we might be friends, David?"

"I'm relying on it!"

"Wow! When's he coming?"

"Thursday of next week."

"Fan-tas-tic!!"

Thereafter, Benji was won over, and he joined in with as much enthusiasm as David and Jasmine in searching out the loft for the sleeping-bags and rummaging around in the rafters above the garage for the foldable beds and tent, the latter thrown in by Jasmine for good measure, just in case the walls of David's house couldn't cope with the sudden expansion in numbers of its inhabitants.

David realized quite early on in his organization of events that he was not going to be able to rely totally on Jasmine as a back-up, especially when Jennifer and Alex were around. Also he wanted his children to have a free run in Leesport, to come and go as they pleased, and if he were to take a few of his friends into his confidence, they would always act as a focal point for a visit from the children, or as a refuge if something went wrong. Consequently, he telephoned both

Gerry Reilly, even though he lived a bit out of Leesport, and Billy, the joke-cracking young man in the deli, and after work that afternoon, he went up to the main street to see Clive and Dotti. Although he had thought it only necessary to disclose the more general facts to Gerry and Billy, he felt comfortable in telling the whole story to Clive, who appeared suitably moved with emotion throughout, every so often dabbing at his eyes with a large paisley-patterned silk handkerchief.

The night before the children arrived, David felt as if it were he himself who was coming to the end of term. He woke constantly during the night to glance at his alarm clock and carry out mental calculations as to how many hours were left until it was time to get up, as well as working out what point the children might have reached on their journey. At six o'clock, he decided that he was not going to be able to go back to sleep and, jumping out of bed, he showered and dressed quickly and took Dodie out for a walk down to the marina. There he killed time by standing out on the farthest walkway, watching the sun rise over the horizon beyond the eastern reaches of Fire Island, making a deal with himself that he would only turn back when its lower tip had broken clear of the far-off sand dunes.

Having shared a breakfast of three shredded wheat with Dodie, he carried out a final check of the store cupboards to make sure that he hadn't forgotten any of their favourite foodstuffs, and gave the house one last look-over to see that all the beds were ready and made up—two in the screened sun-porch and the other in the corner of the sitting-room next to the desk. He then locked up the house and headed off to the garage to fill up the Volkswagen.

Benji and Jasmine were waiting outside the front door of the house when he arrived, both holding on to the ends of an old sheet that was stretched out between them. On it was written in big black blotched letters: WELCOME SOPHIE, CHARLIE AND HARRIT, with a blobby insertion caret adding the omitted E to Harriet's name.

"We're going to hang it outside your house, so that they see it when you get there," Benji said proudly, craning his neck over the side of the banner to admire his handiwork. "What d'ya think of it?"

"It's a work of art, Benji!" David exclaimed, standing with his head at a slant and giving it as much scrutiny as if he were admiring a van Gogh. "I reckon that that'll just make the start of their holidays."

"C'mon, Benji," Jasmine said. "Let's get this put away before it starts catchin' dirt." She turned to David as she pulled the sheet into tight folds. "You wantin' a cup of coffee before you leave?"

"No, I don't think so, thanks. I'll just take my time driving into Kennedy, and I can always grab a cup there if I arrive too early. You never know with these transatlantic flights. Sometimes they arrive an hour ahead of their time."

"When's it due? Just so's I know when to be down at the house."

"Twelve-ten. But then they'll have to get through Immigration and pick up their luggage, so I don't think that we'll be clear of the airport much before, say, quarter past one. There shouldn't be that much traffic on the parkway at that time of the day, so I reckon we'll be back by a quarter to three."

"Okay. We'll try gettin' there by two-thirty." She paused and smiled at him. "You excited?"

He nodded. "And how!"

"Well, in that case, I reckon you'd better jump to it! I'll see you later—and good luck with the kids. I got all kinds of butterflies workin' away in my stomach!"

"That makes two of us, then," he laughed, as he moved off towards the car.

As it turned out, it was just as well he had given himself so much time to get to the airport. There had been an accident on the Belt Parkway which caused a traffic jam that stretched all the way back onto the Southern State in Malverne. For an hour, he had remained in a stationary line of traffic, drumming his fingers impatiently on the steering wheel and glancing at his watch, while Dodie had amused herself by growling incessantly at the bearded truck driver whose vehicle edged forward alongside.

By the time that he found the most shaded place in the parking lot nearest the terminal, it was just after a quarter past eleven. Having opened the front windows an inch or two, he pulled up the canvas top of the Volkswagen and clipped it shut, leaving Dodie to feast herself on the knob of the gear-shift, and ran across the road to the terminal building. Pushing his way through the crowds as they stood in a series of zigzagging queues leading to their respective check-in desks, he glanced up at the information screen, only to find that he was on the Departures floor. He scanned around for a sign saying "Arrivals," eventually seeing it at the bottom of a flight of stairs twenty yards farther along the hall. Moving as fast as the thronging masses would allow, he made it to the steps and took them, two at a time, to the upper floor.

It was far less crowded than the Departures area, but nevertheless, there were already a cluster of expectant faces gathered around the chrome rail at the Customs door, watching and waiting for the first signs of their opening. The information screen indicated that the plane had just touched down, half an hour ahead of time, so he walked over to stand at one end of the barrier. Then, realizing that they still had to come through Immigration and Customs, he turned away and sought out a coffee bar. Ordering himself a black coffee and a muffin, he pulled out a bar-stool and sat down, and turned to watch for the doors to begin disgorging the passengers from Glasgow.

Twenty-five minutes and two coffees later, the doors eventually opened and the first shrieks of welcome resounded around the dome-like hall. A young child was pushed under the chrome rail by encouraging parents and walked apprehensively forward to greet an old couple who struggled bravely to co-ordinate the welcome that was expected of them while still trying to keep their overladen luggage trolley on its designated course.

Thereafter, the newly arrived passengers came thick and fast through the doors, some being welcomed by friends and families and whisked off to waiting cars, while others, casting lost looks around the terminal building, traipsed unsurely away in different directions, like sheep in desperate need of a sheep-dog to nudge some order and guidance into their lives.

Charlie and Harriet appeared first through the door, both coming out in reverse as it happened, Charlie shrugging up his haversack onto his back as he yelled to Sophie to hurry up. David slid off his bar-stool and made his way slowly towards the barrier, content to remain at a distance, quenching the deprivation that he had felt over the past month by savouring those few seconds in which they were unaware of his presence. They turned, suddenly shy as they stood scanning the smiling faces gathered round the barrier, then Charlie caught sight of him, and with a loud shout of "Dad!" ducked under the rail, getting his rucksack caught up in the process, and ran towards him. David stayed where he was, watching his son approach, strangely lean and lanky compared with Benji, his tight jeans and cotton gingham shirt making him appear unaccountably British.

Charlie hit him at speed and threw his arms around his waist. "Dad! We had a great time on the plane. I was allowed to go up with the pilot and watch him fly it! They wouldn't allow me to touch anything though!"

"I'm glad to hear it!" David laughed.

David pulled him in close to his body and leaned forward to give him a kiss on the top of his head, relishing the slightly musty smell of his hair. Charlie immediately pushed himself away and ran back to collect Harriet, who still stood where he had left her, having become entirely captivated by the sight of a young girl lying screaming on the floor of the terminal, kicking out her little legs in temper at her parents' luggage trolley as they tried their ineffectual best to calm her down.

"Harriet! Quick! Here's Dad!"

Harriet immediately broke out of her dream-world and an expression of yearning agitation came over her face as she looked around for her father. Then seeing him, she broke into a run, taking the long way round the barrier. As she came towards him, David bent down and gathered her up, feeling her arms and legs clamp around his body like some deliciously formed octopus.

"Hello, darling!" He nuzzled his face deep into the mop of thick black curls and kissed the nape of her smooth soft neck. "How are you?"

Harriet lifted her head off his shoulders and looked at him, her face a mere six inches away from his own. "Daddy?"

"Yeah?"

She glanced back towards the door. "That little girl is behaving *so* badly."

David laughed. "I know she is. I hope you behaved better than that on the plane."

Harriet turned back to look at him, a grin on her face. "Of *course* I did!" Her smile slid into a frown. "Except I was frightened quite a lot."

"Why?"

" 'Cos Charlie kept saying that the plane was *bound* to blow up!"

David raised his eyebrows and began walking with her towards the Arrivals door. "Oh, yeah, that sounds like him."

He stopped next to his son, who was leaning against the barrier, breathing on the chrome to make it fog up, then rubbing it hard with his hand to clear it.

"Where's Sophie got to, Charlie?"

"She's coming out with the stewardess. We had to have someone with us everywhere we went, 'cos they said we were too young to go by ourselves. It was really embarrassing, 'cos they put tags on us with our names. I pulled mine and Harriet's off when we landed."

"And I wanted to keep mine," Harriet whined.

"No, you didn't! You thought it was stupid, too. Here she is. Come on, Sophie, Dad's here!"

David moved to the side so that he could see her approach, and from the moment that she appeared around the corner, chatting animatedly to the stewardess as they helped each other with the luggage trolley, he felt a smile broaden across his face and a feeling of unbelievable pride rise up in his heart. She had changed so much, not only having grown upwards, but—well, sort of everywhere. Her long auburn hair was drawn back and gathered loosely behind her head with a clip, which seemed to accentuate the contours of her face. God, it had only been a month since he had seen her last, but it was enough for him to be aware of the metamorphosis that had taken place within her—no longer the gawky, self-conscious teenager, but a young fledgling fast breaking into womanhood. David let Harriet down onto the ground without taking his eyes off his eldest daughter, watching as she and the stewardess came round the barrier towards him, and noticing out of the side of his eye that a young boy, standing with his parents at the rail, also followed her progress with interest.

Leaving the stewardess to push the trolley the last few yards by herself, Sophie walked quickly towards her father, and just as she reached him, her face broke into a wide smile and her eyes sparkled, and in that brief, mind-shattering instance, David realized that it was as if Rachel had been re-incarnated.

"Hi, Dad," she said quietly.

For a moment, David stood entranced, shaking his head slowly at this incredible apparition, then moved towards her and pulled her in close to him.

"My God! You look wonderful!" he said, rocking her from side to side in his arms and kissing the side of her head. "Oh, it's so lovely to see you! I really cannot begin to tell you how lovely it is to see you!"

There was a loud tutting noise from beside him, and he looked down to see Charlie eyeing the stewardess and scuffing his feet across the floor.

"C'mon, Dad, this is embarrassing. Can't we go now?"

"Okay!" David exclaimed, giving Sophie a final kiss on the cheek. "Let's grab ourselves a horse and get the hell out of Dodge!"

Thanking the stewardess for her help, he took over at the helm of the luggage trolley and steered it towards the door of the terminal, his two daughters holding on to the handle at either side of him while Charlie ran ahead.

"Is this America now, Daddy?" Harriet asked as she jogged alongside David, trying to keep up with his brisk pace.

"Yup, this is it, darling, home of hot dogs, hamburgers and er . . . can't think of anything else that begins with *h*."

"And heat!" Sophie added with almost pleasurable relief, as they left the coolness of the air-conditioned building and walked out into the throat-searing swelter of the mid-day sun.

"Yeah," David laughed, "heat! And there's plenty of that, I can tell you!"

They walked across the road into the parking lot and made their way towards the Volkswagen. David had already given detailed descriptions of the car in his letters, and consequently both Charlie and Harriet spotted it at the same time and raced ahead, only to recoil sharply on reaching it, as Dodie suddenly jumped up at the half-open window and yapped fiercely at them.

"Is that Dodie?" Charlie asked, laughing uncertainly.

"Yup."

"She sort of suits the car."

"Why do you say that?"

" 'Cos they both look, well, battered."

"Well, for goodness' sakes, don't let her hear you say that! Dodie is very sensitive about her looks! I once suggested that she should consider having a fur-lift and she wouldn't speak to me for a week!"

"Really?" Harriet gasped, her mouth open as she stared at Dodie through the window.

"No, stupid!" Charlie retorted. "He's only joking!"

David unlocked the car, and pushing Dodie into the back seat, he reached over to release the catch for the front trunk.

"Can we have the top down, Dad?" Charlie asked, grabbing hold of a suitcase and dragging it round to the front of the car.

"Yeah, well, I guess we'll have to, otherwise I don't think there'll be room for all your stuff."

"Great!"

David squeezed Harriet's haversack into the last remaining space in the trunk and carefully shut the lid. Then, unclipping the roof, he folded it down, thus releasing Dodie's aromatic wonders to the world.

"Phew!" Sophie said, wrinkling up her nose. "What a niff! Bags I don't have her on my knee!"

David grinned at her. "Yeah, I'm afraid that she does have a bit of a problem. Someone suggested that I give her garlic pills, but I think she's built up some sort of immunity to them!"

"I'll take her!" Charlie said, reaching over the side of the car and ruffling Dodie's woolly fur. He turned and gave his elder sister a narrow look. "But only if I'm allowed to sit in the front."

The bargain was struck, and once the remainder of the luggage was jammed into the small compartment behind the rear seat, they set off on their journey back to Leesport.

Once they reached the Southern State Parkway, the traffic eased considerably, and as they bumbled along eastwards, David decided that this was the perfect opportunity to teach them the words of "Dodie the Fun-Loving Poodle." Three times through it, and Charlie and Harriet had picked it up completely, singing along with enthusiasm and rocking themselves side to side in time with the tune. Sophie, however, seemed reticent to participate, and as he accompanied his two youngest children through the verses, he eyed her in the rear-view mirror, as she sat leaning her elbow on the sill of the car and gazing absently at the passing scenery.

They eventually arrived at the traffic lights on Leesport's main street at exactly two-thirty, and thinking that Jasmine and Benji would have yet to complete their work on the welcoming banner, David pulled to a halt outside Helping Hands, giving the horn two quick beeps. He watched through the window of the shop as Clive and Dotti looked up from their desks and, on recognizing the car, both jumped to their feet.

"Why are we stopping here?" Charlie asked.

"I just want you to meet a couple of my friends." With that, the door of the shop flew open, and Clive came rushing across the sidewalk to the car, followed closely by Dotti.

"Well, for heaven's sakes!" he said, putting a hand to his cheek and surveying the incredulous looks on the children's faces. "Oh, David, they are simply wonderful! All so good-looking!" He grinned, giving his shoulders a cosy shrug, before offering his hand to each of the children in turn. "Hi, my name is Clive. You are? Sophie—hello,

Sophie, and—Charlie, and—Harriet. Well, I can't tell you how fantastic it is to meet you all! Oh, and by the way, this"—he turned and put an arm around his assistant, who smiled shyly, pushing up her spectacles onto her nose—"is Dotti." He sighed, surveying the children with a look of sheer delight on his face. "So where are you off to now? Straight to the beach, I'd guess."

David looked around at the children, who had not taken their eyes off Clive, riveted by his boisterous enthusiasm.

"Well, we'll go back to the house first and get the car unpacked, but then maybe a cool-down might be the order of the day."

"I think that sounds like a great idea!" He leaned his hands on the side of the car. "Now, any time you kids want to drop into the shop, you're more than welcome. Dotti has already got some Coke in the refrigerator, so come soon, won't you?"

The children smiled, mumbling a thank-you, and David turned the key and started the engine.

"We'd better be off, Clive. We're meeting Jasmine and Benji at the house, so we'd better not be late."

"Okay!" Clive said, jumping back from the car. "Remember now, any time you want, kids, just drop in!"

The white tip of the welcoming banner was clearly visible, fluttering high above the hedge, as David turned the car into Shore Street. He pulled to a halt outside the house, hearing immediately Benji's voice shout out excitedly from the garden.

"Jasmine, they're here!"

The gate flew open and he came running out onto the sidewalk. Then, stopping at a distance from the side of the car, he stood grinning and shifting his weight self-consciously from one foot to the other, as he was scrutinized by the new arrivals. David jumped out of the car and came round to the sidewalk.

"Right! Introductions!" He pointed to each of his children in turn. "Sophie—Charlie—Harriet. This is Benji."

There were a few uncertain murmurings as they acknowledged one another's existence, and David watched the whole scene with quiet amusement as he leaned over the side of the car and pulled the trunk lever.

"All out and we'll get the cases inside. Where's Jasmine, Benji?"

"I'm here!" a voice called out from behind the hedge. She appeared through the gate, a hammer under her arm as she wiped her glistening forehead with the back of her hand. "My goodness, you nearly caught us nappin' there!" She scanned the children, and her face broke into a huge smile. "Hi, everybody, I'm Jasmine. Now, Benji, I heard you bein' introduced, so you can go ahead and tell me who everyone is."

As the children clambered out of the car, Benji went through their names faultlessly, and Jasmine stepped forward to shake the hand of each in turn.

"Right!" David said, unloading the suitcases and putting them on the sidewalk. "Everyone grab something!"

Scooping up the two largest suitcases in an immediate test of individual strength, Charlie and Benji struggled with them through the gate into the garden.

"Hey, Sophie! Harriet! Come quickly!" Charlie's voice sounded out. "Come and have a look at *this*!"

The two girls picked up their haversacks and hurried through the gate to find Charlie standing in the middle of the garden, looking around in sheer wonderment.

"Isn't this great? Look, we're right by the beach! And look at the sign on the house! Benji says he made it himself!"

"You missed out the *E* in my name," Harriet said, disappointed.

"Harry, don't be so tactless!" Sophie scolded her.

"Yeah, sorry about that," Benji said quietly, pushing his hands deep into the pockets of his shorts. "I sorta got mixed up with the spelling—but I did put it in at the end."

Sophie smiled at him. "Well, I think it's great, Benji. It's really well done!"

Benji looked down at his feet, his face colouring with embarrassment.

"And I think so too!" Charlie said, grabbing Benji by the arm. "Come on, let's go and explore!" The two boys turned to run off together down to the jetty just as David came into the garden, carrying the last of the suitcases.

"Hang on, you two! Where are you heading off to?"

"We're going to explore, Dad!"

"Not just yet. We'll get the suitcases inside first, and I'll show you where you're sleeping."

"Yesss!" Charlie shouted out in excitement, and he and Benji ran back across the lawn towards the house.

It turned out that Jasmine had not only busied herself in putting up the banner, but had also gone through the house plumping up the cushions on the sofa and clearing away the cups and plates that David had left to dry on the draining-board. Harriet and Charlie were delighted with their bedroom out on the screened porch, both throwing themselves onto their beds and looking around to see what views were afforded them from their supine positions. However, Sophie showed little emotion at what the house had to offer, having placed her suitcase on her bed in the sitting-room and begun to unpack it with quiet and methodical efficiency.

"Okay!" David said, clapping his hands to assemble the company in the sitting-room. "Let's forget about unpacking for now. What do you think, Jasmine? The ferry to Fire Island?"

There was a whoop of joy from Benji, immediately echoed by Charlie and Harriet, who hadn't a clue what or where Fire Island was, but if Benji thought it was a good idea *and* it needed a ferry to get to, then it must be an idea worth agreeing with.

"Looks like you've hit on a good plan there!" Jasmine said with a laugh.

"Okay! Fire Island it is! Let's get your swimming things out of the suitcases, and we'll be off!"

Charlie and Benji ran through to the porch and began tearing at the contents of his haversack, while Jasmine gave Harriet a hand to sort through her belongings to find her swim-suit. David went into his bedroom alcove and took a pair of trunks from the top of his chest of drawers, and came back to find that Sophie had made no move to find her own.

"Can't you find yours, darling?"

Sophie looked up at him, her mouth lifting into a light smile. "If you don't mind, Dad, I don't think I'll come."

"Oh," David said, disappointed, "do come, darling. It really will be good fun. It's a beautiful beach, and—"

"Dad, I just don't want to!" She picked up a shirt from her suitcase and threw it down on the bed. "Do you really mind *that* much?"

For a moment, David stood staring at her, taken aback by the razor tone in her voice. He was about to answer her when he felt a hand on his arm, and turned to find Jasmine and the other children standing silently behind him. She walked towards the door of the house, gesturing with her head for him to follow.

"Come on, you lot," he said, waving his hand at the children. "Let's go out into the garden for a minute."

As soon as they were all outside, Benji, Charlie and Harriet ran off down to the jetty, yelling with enthusiasm as they went.

"Do you want to stay here for a while?" Jasmine asked quietly.

"Yes, I think I'd better. Would you mind taking them off for a bit?"

"Not at all! Tell you what, I'll bring them up to the house to swim in the pool, and then you two can join us later. How about that?"

"That would be great, Jasmine."

They walked down to the edge of the garden where Harriet stood watching Benji and Charlie competing with each other in a pebble-throwing contest off the jetty.

"Right, you lot! Slight change of plan! You're all going along to Benji's house to swim in the pool."

Letting out yet more whoops of excitement, the two boys ran back up the steps and headed straight past them to the gate. Harriet's return journey to the garden, however, was more laborious, pushing on her knees to give herself extra leverage as she climbed the steps.

She stopped beside her father. "Aren't you and Sophie coming, Daddy?"

"Not just yet, darling." He bent forward, his hands on his knees. "But if you go with Jasmine, Sophie and I will be with you very soon, okay?"

Harriet nodded and without a hint of shyness, slipped her hand into Jasmine's.

"Okay, Harriet!" Jasmine said, raising her eyebrows in delight and giving David a wink, "let's go catch up with the boys, then we'll have some fun!" They walked together across the garden and out through the gate, and as David headed towards the door of the house, he heard their voices on the other side of the hedge fading off down the street as they engaged each other in conversation.

David opened the door and walked back into the house. Sophie still stood beside the bed, unpacking her belongings. He picked up the kettle as he passed the sideboard and filled it up from the tap.

"Well, I'm going to have a cup of tea. How about you?"

Sophie shook her head without turning.

"No?"

She turned and flashed him a light smile. "No, thanks."

David leaned against the sink, folding his arms. "When I spoke to Mr. Hunter, he said that you'd done really well in your GSCEs. They went all right, then?"

"I suppose so."

Perplexed by the offhand reaction to his questions, David walked over to Sophie and put a hand on her shoulder. "Are you feeling all right, darling?"

She turned to him. "Not really," she said quietly. "I've just got this really bad tummy pain."

"Oh, darling, you should have said! Something you ate on the plane, d'you think?"

She raised her eyebrows at his misunderstanding of events. "No, Dad, not that kind! It's, well, you know—my time of the month."

David was silent for a moment as the realization of what she was saying dawned on him.

"Oh, for heaven's sakes, of course. I'm sorry, Sophie, I should have understood. No wonder you're feeling mouldy. Have you got, well, everything you need?"

She smiled at him as she continued to unpack. "Yup, I do, thanks." She stopped as she carefully laid a pair of trousers in the drawer. "It's just that, well . . . oh, never mind."

"No, go on, darling—please."

"Well, it's just that I'm still not very sure of myself, you know, dealing with all this, and sometimes I get panicky, and I find it difficult to cope—with swimming and things like that." She glanced at her father and bit hard on her bottom lip, then let out a faltering laugh. "I don't suppose it's the kind of thing that a girl discusses with her father. It's just that I haven't got Mummy any m——"

It was as far as she got. In that brief moment, the vulnerability brought on both by nature and by the long flight's disruption to her own body's time-clock broke through her steely resolve, allowing her emotions to burst through to the surface.

"Oh, Dad, I miss Mummy *so* much."

She ran towards him and circled her arms around his chest, her body heaving convulsively with shuddering sobs as she began to rid herself of the grief that she had been storing up deep within her for so long. For a moment, he held her in silence, kissing the top of her head over and over again, and feeling her tears slowly seep through the front of his shirt, wetting the skin beneath.

"I know you do, my darling, I know you do," he said eventually, tears welling up in his own eyes as he rocked her gently against him, "and I do too—so much so that it hurts, and I don't think that it ever will stop hurting. There is not one second of the day goes by when I'm not thinking about her." He pushed her gently away and, cupping his hand under her chin, he raised her face to look at him. "But listen, darling, I'm here for you now, I'm here for you all. Things were different for me back in Scotland, but they really have changed now, and they will keep changing—for the better, I promise you. I'm afraid we won't ever get Mummy back, no matter how much we wish and pray, but the most important thing is that we all have each other, as a family, and that's what Mummy would want—that we keep going and have more happy times, and laugh and joke just like we used to." He paused and looked around the room. "Do you know, she's here right now. I know she is. Right here in the room, and she's saying to us, 'That's it! Go ahead, you guys, do it for me! I'm cheering you on! Just keep laughing and joking and be happy, because if you're sad and down-hearted, you won't be like me any more, and I want to leave you my wit and humour and love of life and—beauty.' "

Sophie's face slowly broke into a sad smile and she pulled her face away from her father's hand and turned to look around the room.

"Do you really think she's saying that?" she asked quietly.

David smiled. "Well, something like that, only she's probably being a bit more forceful in the way that she says it."

Sophie snorted out a laugh, immediately following it by a hefty sniff, and David walked over to the draining-board and took a great wodge of paper tissue off the kitchen roll. He handed it to her. "Here, 'gie yersel' a tidy-up,' as Effie would say!"

Sophie laughed again, and taking a deep breath, she gave her nose a hearty blow and wiped away the tears from her face.

"All right?" David asked, putting his arm around her shoulder and giving it a quick squeeze.

Sophie nodded and handed the sodden mass of paper back to him. He turned and threw it into the wastepaper basket.

"Listen, I had a thought the other day that, well, seeing I missed your sixteenth birthday at home, we should have a party out here for you." He gave her a wink. "It's a pretty important birthday, you know, sweet sixteen and all that. We should celebrate it in style."

Sophie let out a long sigh. "Oh, I don't know, Dad."

"Why not? It would be great fun! We'll have it here and invite Jasmine and Benji—"

"Dad, it's a really kind thought, but, well, I feel a bit old to have a birthday party." She walked back to the bed to continue with her unpacking. "What would we do? Play games and things?"

David slowly nodded his head. "Yeah, I do know what you mean.

So, what kind of party would you like? Sort of . . . a discotheque or something like that?"

"I suppose," Sophie replied, shrugging her shoulders noncommitally.

"Okay, right, how about this for an idea? First, we'll have a small get-together out here—nothing too formal and certainly not childish—and we'll invite a few of my new friends who would love to meet you, and then, when we get back to Scotland, we'll have a real blowout of a party, either at The Beeches or Inchelvie, depending on how many friends you want to invite. And we'll make it the happening of the year—no, what the hell!—the century! What do you think of that?"

Sophie's eyes lit up with excitement. "Do you really think we could?"

"Yeah, too right we could!"

"And can I invite a whole load of friends from school?"

"Of course you can—and they can stay on as long as they like after it!"

Sophie ran forward and threw her arms around his neck. "Oh, Dad, that would just be so *cool*!" She reached up and kissed him on the cheek. "When can we have it?"

"Well, I think it would be best if we work all that out when we get home—but I promise you, we certainly will have one!" He pulled her to him and gave her a kiss on the neck. "But in the meantime, let's decide on a day for our Stateside hooley." He freed himself from her embrace. "No point doing it this weekend, because it'll be the Fourth of July and there'll be parties enough going on around here. So, how about next Tuesday? That should be enough time to get things organized!"

"Okay—so, what kind of party should we have?"

"How about a barbecue? I'm lousy at doing them, but you and Jasmine could help me with the cooking. Then afterwards, we'll head off to Fire Island on the ferry and veg out for the rest of the afternoon on the beach." He paused. "Actually, the best idea would be for you and Jasmine to organize all the shopping and everything, and I'll do the inviting. How does that sound?"

"Sounds good." She looked dubious for a moment. "But, Dad, I would rather it was a party for *all* of us. I mean, don't make a big thing about it being my sixteenth, because, well, there really won't be many others there of my age, will there?"

He nodded. "Okay, message understood. It's a deal, then?"

Sophie smiled at him. "Yeah, it's a deal!"

She spat on her hand and held it out, and for a moment David stood looking startled, suddenly remembering that this was the exact way in which he and Rachel used to strike their bargains. He slowly raised his hand to his mouth and, spitting on it, placed it in Sophie's hand.

"Right now, how about going to join the others? We'll finish the unpacking when we get back."

They turned towards the door, linking their arms around each other, and as David opened the door, Sophie stopped and glanced over her shoulder.

"Do you think Mummy's coming?" she asked quietly, looking up at him.

David smiled at her and turned round to look back into the empty room.

"Yup, she's with us all the way."

CHAPTER 28

Jennifer pushed the rear-view mirror of her BMW to one side to stop the glare of the setting sun from hitting her face, then switched on the radio to listen for the traffic report, wanting some guidance as to whether she should just stick to the Long Island Expressway or cut down the Grand Central Parkway, pick up the Van Wyck Expressway and take the southern route out to Leesport.

However, judging by the traffic build-up that she was presently experiencing in Queens, it was probably going to be a case of just sitting it out either way. It was a pretty dumb idea, at any rate, trying to get out of Manhattan on the eve of the Fourth of July weekend. All the world and his dog seemed to be on the road, but really she had no choice. Sam Culpepper had specifically asked her to be in the office on Saturday so that they could give the proposals for Tarvy's just one more look-over before it was overnighted to London. Her initial plan had been to head out to Leesport after that had been finished with, but then when Russ asked her to attend a meeting first thing Monday morning with some new clients, she felt that it would be better to spend the whole weekend in the apartment in the West Village, rather than having to face the start-of-the-week rush.

Nevertheless, she hated the idea of not being able to see Benji at all over the holiday weekend. So, on the spur of the moment, she had decided to head out to Leesport, so that she could at least spend a couple of hours with him before returning to the city early the following morning.

As she sat in the queue of cars, she glanced over at the thick typed proposal that lay on the passenger seat. She reached over and picked it up, letting the pages run across her thumb from beginning to end as if she were carrying out some form of superhuman copy-editing. She shook her head and chucked it back on the seat, lightly touching the accelerator to edge the BMW forward a couple of yards.

God, she hoped they'd get this contract. Sam had really set his heart on it, yet she still couldn't help but feel slightly apprehensive about its final content. Of course, the few days off last week hadn't helped. It had completely broken her flow, and consequently, over the past four days, she had found herself having to work well into the night in order to get back into the feel of it *and* to get it completed. Well, not quite completed. There were still a couple of statistics that she wanted to include in the report, but she had all the information with her, and she could just add them in on her laptop at home and take it into the office for printing the following day.

She let go of the steering wheel and linked her hands behind her head, stretching out her tired back.

But my goodness, those few missed days at work had been worth it, even though the reason for them had been thoroughly unpleasant, and the fact that she had had to work those long hours as a result. Having been with Benji for such an unbroken period of time, she had realized just how much he had changed, not only in the way he acted, but in himself, his whole body. Those mornings when he had come to sit on her bed before going to school and she had held him, she had felt no longer the soft flabbiness of his plump little body, but rather the beginnings of a fit young frame.

Yet she could take no credit for this change. It had been entirely David's doing, generating a renewed self-confidence and an almost tangible vibrance in the energy and enthusiasm of her son. David. She said his name again, feeling an unpremeditated buzz of excitement run through her, tingling her senses so much that a juddering shiver ran down her spine. She smiled and shook her head. No, it wasn't *that* kind of feeling. On the other hand, maybe it was. She couldn't work it out. It was just that being with him made her feel happy and relaxed and, well, almost tranquil without him having to do anything particularly special. Yet that was probably what made *him* special. There was no pretence with David. She knew exactly where she stood with him. He was kind, spontaneous, funny and totally trustworthy, and—come on, Jennifer admit it—attractive as hell, and, without doubt, one of the main reasons that you happen to be making this ludicrous trip out to Leesport.

The driver behind her blew hard on his horn, making her jump up in her seat and bringing her mind immediately back to concentrate on matters in hand. A gap of thirty yards had opened up in front of the BMW, which, at that moment, was being filled up fast by others who jumped lane in the vain hope that they could speed up their journeys in the process. Jennifer glanced to her right and saw the sign for the Grand Central Parkway. She flicked on her indicator and, turning round to beam a smile at the adjacent driver, she pointed to the exit, and within a minute she had used her charm to cut across three lanes of traffic, leave the LIE and begin heading southwards at a steady thirty miles per hour.

By the time that she descended the driveway to the house, it was just coming up to nine o'clock. She pulled the car to a halt, and picking up her papers and laptop from the back seat, she got out and hurried across to the front door.

"Hi, everyone!" she called out as she entered. She walked through to the study and dumped her stuff on the desk, then turned and made her way back into the hall, just as Jasmine appeared from the kitchen.

"Hi, Jasmine," she said brightly.

"Hi! Didn't think you was comin' home this weekend."

"You're right! I'm not supposed to be here, but I just couldn't bear not seeing Benji over this weekend. We've never spent a Fourth of July apart before. Is he around?"

"Not yet. He's still with David, but they should be home any minute now."

"So, how's everything been?"

"Really couldn't be better! And how are *you* feeling?"

Jennifer smiled at her. "Still a bit washed out, but I should be able to take things a little easier once this proposal's finished."

Jasmine nodded. "Do you want anything to eat?"

"Oh, Jasmine, that would be great. Just a sandwich or something would be fine. I've got some work to finish off, so if you could just bring it to the study . . ."

Jasmine turned to walk back to the kitchen. "Okay. One sandwich coming up."

Jennifer made her way to the study, and having laid out her work on the desk, she had just managed to bring the Tarvy's proposal up onto the screen of her laptop when Jasmine reappeared with a plate of ham sandwiches and a glass of beer. "Here you are," she said, putting it down on the table next to the desk.

At that instant, the front door opened and Benji's voice called out excitedly. "Mom!"

"In here, Benji!"

Bursting through the door, he ran over to his mother and threw his arms around her neck.

"Hi, darling! Where have you been until now?"

"We've been on the beach *all* afternoon. We only just caught the last ferry home, and then we went into Leesport to watch them get the firework display ready for tomorrow night. They set some off just to make sure everything was working. Didn't you hear them? Anyway, David said that we—"

He stopped when he heard the door of the study open. David entered the room, and Benji broke away from his mother and ran over to him. "David, can I tell Mom now?"

David ruffled the boy's hair. "Would you mind if I did it, Benji?"

Benji let out a disappointed moan, but before he could remonstrate still further, Jasmine walked over and put her arm around his shoulders. "Come on, Benji, I think we should leave Mom and David to talk, don't you?"

"Okay! As long as you tell her though." He ran from the room, with Jasmine following hot on his heels.

Jennifer watched them go, then turned to David, a smile on her face. "Hi!"

"Hi!" He put his hands into his pockets as he walked over to her desk. "Sorry about not getting Benji back here earlier. I didn't realize you were coming home this weekend."

She leaned back in her chair. "Well, I wasn't going to. We have to get this proposal off tomorrow, but I just wanted to see Benji, so I thought I'd come back for the night." She sighed. "Not that it'll be much of a night. I'll have to leave at about five-thirty tomorrow morning."

David nodded. "So, how are you feeling?"

"Great! Only I've probably undone all the good that I got out of the rest Jasmine made me take last week. I've had to work pretty long hours on this damn proposal, just to catch up."

"How's it going?"

Jennifer looked at the computer screen. "I don't know really. The trouble is I have nothing to judge it by. I *hope* it's all right, because Sam is really counting on me pulling this one off. It would really give the company *such* a boost if we managed to land it."

"Who's it for?"

"Oh, it's just a gin company in London. Tarvy's. You ever heard of it?"

"Yup, I know them well." He paused. "What I mean by that is, ah, I know the brand well enough."

"Oh, well, thank God for that!" Jennifer laughed. "At least *you've* heard of it." She reached over and picked up the market research report. "Tarvy's name doesn't even appear in this, but at least it gives me an idea as to what kind of sales figures we should be looking to achieve, and I tell you, it's pretty awesome!"

She tossed the report back onto the desk and let out a sigh. "Anyway, I can't really do much more. If we don't get it, well, that's that, but for Sam's sake, I sure hope that we're in with a glimmer of a chance." She smiled up at him. "Do you want a beer or something?"

"No, don't bother. I don't want to interrupt you."

"You're not," she said, getting up from her chair and walking towards the door. "I'll go get one for you from the kitchen." She turned back to him. "Anyway, I want to hear what the big secret is all about."

As her footsteps faded off down the corridor towards the kitchen, David turned and picked up the Morgan Graz market research report from the desk. Heavens, he hadn't looked at one of these for ages! In the past, he had read them as often as he had the daily newspapers. He shook his head and turned the pages, stopping abruptly as the familiar name of Glendurnich caught his eye. He glanced up at the top of the page. It was the top-ten world-wide sales listings for single-malt Scotch whisky brands. He scanned through the figures, a puzzled frown beginning to crease his forehead.

This wasn't right. Glendurnich was listed as being number four, exactly the same position they had occupied the year before. He looked down at the bottom of the page to check the date. It was the June issue. Okay, so they were world-wide listings, not specific to the United States, but the country was their single biggest customer, so they must reflect the sales over here. He scratched at his head, trying to work out if there was an alternative explanation. Maybe he was wrong. Maybe Glendurnich *had* reached a higher position while he'd been absent from the company, in which case, if sales had been on the slide, then Duncan was right in registering concern. But there again, he just didn't know.

He raised his eyebrows at the anomaly and quickly flicked through the remaining pages of the magazine. He was just about to close it when yet another name bounced out at him from the inside back page, making him shudder just in reading it to himself. Deakin Distribution. For a moment, he found his mind flashing back involuntarily to that appalling day in Manhattan, when every event that occurred and every action that he took seemed to be orchestrated to hasten his downfall. He blew out nervously at the very thought of it, then once more focused his eyes on the article. It was only a small piece in the bottom right-hand corner of the page, listed under the "Management and Appointments" column.

> UK's third-largest drinks company **Kirkpatrick Holdings Plc.** has announced the recent acquisition of New York–based distributors **Deakin Distribution Inc.**
>
> Kirpatrick's chairman John Davenport said that he welcomed the announcement, and that Deakin's had the proven ability to spearhead a new and aggressive sales drive in the USA, promoting their ever-expanding list of brand names.

David grunted derisively to himself, wondering if Deakin Distribution knew what they were letting themselves in for. "Aggressive" was a complete understatement as far as Kirkpatrick's were concerned, especially with that corporate shark, John Davenport, at the helm. He bit hard on his lip as it suddenly occurred to him that, as a result of his abortive meeting, Deakin's could now quite easily be Glendurnich's distributor. He closed his eyes in concentration, trying to work out in his mind what possible repercussions this might have on Glendurnich. No, it should be all right—for now, anyway. He knew for certain that Kirkpatrick's didn't have a malt whisky as part of its portfolio, so there shouldn't be any immediate conflict of interests. Nevertheless, he didn't like to think that Glendurnich was giving anything away to that company.

Just as he made a mental note to himself to check the whole scenario thoroughly when he returned to Scotland, he heard the sound of Jennifer's footsteps moving quickly back across the hall. He closed up the report and replaced it on the desk, turning round just as she came through the door.

"Sorry I was so long," she said, coming over and handing him the glass of beer. "Would you believe it, a woman selling cosmetics came to the door? I mean, not only at nine-thirty but also the night before a damned national holiday?"

David raised his eyebrows and took a long drink of his beer, while Jennifer sat back down at her desk. "So when do you expect to hear about the Tarvy's contract?"

"Tuesday. Ridiculous, isn't it? I don't know how they can expect to really study all the proposals in that short space of time. Nevertheless, that's what they want."

David looked at his watch, his mind still distracted by what he had read in the market research report and conscious that he had left the children alone in the saltbox. He drained his glass and put it down on her desk. "Listen, I'm going to have to go."

Jennifer looked up at him, a surprised expression on her face. "Hang on, what was it you were going to tell me?"

David scratched at his head. "Are you going to be back here on Thursday?"

"Yeah, I guess so. I was hoping that Alex would be here, but he telephoned last night to say that he has to be in Dallas for the next two weeks."

David nodded. "Would you mind if we left it until then? It's sort of quite important, so I'd rather take time to explain."

Jennifer shrugged her shoulders resignedly.

"Okay. In that case, I shall await the disclosure with bated breath."

David smiled at her and walked over to the door, turning back as he opened it. "Listen, best of luck with the account. Judging by the amount of work that you've put into it, I'm sure you'll be in with a shout."

"Thanks." She paused for a moment and squinted a rueful smile at him. "I don't suppose you'd be able to fix it, would you?"

David looked at her inquiringly. "Sorry?"

"No, don't worry. I was only joking. Just thought that you might have been able to cast a magical spell over this one as well!"

She gave him a wave with her hand, then turned back to her desk and resumed her work.

An unnatural quietness seemed to be radiating from the little saltbox when he got back to Shore Street, making David think immediately that something *had* to be wrong. He hurried from the gate to the door of the house and threw it open, breathing out a sigh of relief when he saw the children sitting cross-legged in the centre of the floor, gathered around a Monopoly board.

"Heavens, this is all very harmonious," he laughed.

Charlie looked up, a disgruntled look on his face. "Well, there's no telly and we were getting bored waiting for you. Where've you been? We thought you were only going to be five minutes."

"Yeah. Sorry about that. Benji's moth——"

"Hey, Harriet!" Charlie yelled out. "You can't do that! You're meant to be in prison!"

"All right, Charlie!" Sophie said sharply. "She didn't know!" She reached across the board and pushed Harriet's top hat back a square. "You'll have to wait until your next go, Harry!"

"Oh, pig's whistles!" Harriet exclaimed at being caught out. She rolled backwards onto the floor and bicycled her bare legs in the air, showering off the sand that had accumulated on them during the day on Fire Island. She turned her head and looked up at her father. "Daddy, do you want to play? You can be the ship."

"Not just at the minute, darling." He cast a caring eye over his children, noticing in the subdued light that each was beginning to show signs of a healthy tan following just two days on the beach. He walked over to Harriet and gently pressed his foot into her stomach, making her squeal loudly. "I've just got to make a quick telephone call, okay?"

He squeezed his way sideways past Sophie's bed to the desk and took his address book from his brief-case. Then, sitting down on the edge of the bed, he opened it at the correct page and scanned down the list of numbers until he found Gladwin Vintners. He was sure that he had William Lawrence's home number. Yup, there it was.

He picked up the telephone and dialled, turning to watch the game of high finance in progress while he waited for it to connect.

"Hu-llo?" a man's voice answered.

"Will, it's David Corstorphine."

"David, you old devil! What the hell are *you* doing phoning at two o'clock in the morning?"

David glanced at his watch, and then clapped his hand on the top of his head. "Oh, God, Will! I'm sorry! I'm in the States. I forgot totally about the time change. Jesus, I'm sorry! Look, I'll call you in the morning."

Will laughed. "Don't worry about it. We've just been out at a dinner party which turned into something of a marathon, so we're not long in anyway. So how are things? Are you out there on business?"

"Yeah, sort of. Listen, are you sure it's all right to talk now? I can always—"

"No, I promise you. I'm not even out of my clothes yet. So go on, what can I do for you at this ungodly hour?"

"Well, this may seem a ridiculous question to ask under the circumstances, but I was just wondering whether you were still handling the international sales of Glentochry?"

"Yup, I am."

"Right. You, er, don't happen to have anything to do with Tarvy's Gin as well, do you?"

"Yeah, funnily enough, I do. More by default than anything else. Gladwin's have recently set up a new marketing committee for the product, specifically to target the States, and I've been called onto it, ostensibly for my knowledge of the U.S. market. Why do you ask?"

"Well, it's only that I heard through the grape-vine that Tarvy's are looking to appoint a new advertising company over here."

"Christ, how the hell did you hear about that? I only just learned about that this week!"

"As I said, my ears were flapping the other day, and I just happened to hear word of it at a sales conference."

"Yeah, well, you're right. Gladwin's seem to be in an almighty hurry to get Tarvy's into the U.S. market, so they're looking to appoint a new agency ASAP. In fact, I'm going to have to spend the first two days of next week going through about five bloody proposals." He paused for a moment. "So what's your interest in Tarvy's?"

"None at all, I promise you. It's only that . . . well, listen, I know of one company that is putting in a proposal, and I can tell you that they're building up quite a reputation as being a pretty smart and up-and-coming lot."

"What are they called?"

"Culpepper Rowan."

"Yup, that name rings a bell. Have you got a vested interest in *them,* then?"

"Absolutely none! It's only that I know a couple of the directors quite well. From what I can gather about the company, it's extremely successful, but they're in need of a major international client to help them break into the big time, and I think that if they happened to be appointed, they would pull out all the stops for Gladwin's to get Tarvy's positioned as fast as possible."

There was a moment's silence at the other end of the telephone. "Well, I can't promise you anything, David."

"Oh, I quite understand that, Will. But if you could give their proposal just a little more than passing consideration."

Will laughed. "Yeah, okay, you pushy bugger, I'll do that!"

"Thanks, Will."

"Hey, listen, David, while you're on the phone, and talking of grape-vines and all that, is Glendurnich being attacked at the minute?"

David frowned. "What do you mean?"

"No, obviously it's not. Only I had lunch with Fraser Campbell of Dunmorran Malt the other day, and he said that one of the corporates had been snooping around his company."

"Christ, that's all we're needing in the industry! Which one was it?"

"Kirkpatrick's."

David felt his mouth immediately going dry. "Did you say Kirkpatrick's?" he asked quietly.

"Yeah. Word has it that they're trying to acquire a malt whisky for their portfolio, but if you've heard nothing about it, you should be safe enough."

David did not reply, but stood staring at Carrie's painting above the desk. He heard Will yawn at the other end of the telephone.

"Listen, mate, I'm knackered. Is there any more information I can give you, or can I go to bed?"

David shook his head to break his line of thought. "No—sorry, Will. That's all, and apologies for ringing you at such a ridiculous time."

"Don't mention it. And I'll keep Culpepper Rowan in mind."

Putting down the telephone, David sat back heavily on the bed and ran his fingers through his hair. Jesus, Kirkpatrick's couldn't be after Glendurnich, could they? Surely he would have heard. His father or Duncan would have been in touch with him.

"You all right, Dad?" Sophie's voice asked quietly.

He turned round to find the three children staring at him with concerned expressions on their faces.

"You've gone completely white," Sophie said.

David smiled and pushed himself up from the bed. "No, everything's fine." He clapped his hands together. "Right! Come on, Charlie and Harriet, time for you to get to bed!"

Ignoring their synchronized groans of protest, he reached down and scooped his youngest daughter up in his arms and, carrying her through to the porch, he dumped her down on her bed and tickled her stomach, and amidst screams of playful torture, she shot her legs up to her chin to protect herself.

"Daddy?"

"Yup?"

"Will you play Monopoly with me tomorrow?"

"Course I will."

"Can I be the top hat again?"

"Sure you can. Now get ready for bed!"

He bent over and planted a kiss on her forehead and walked back into the house, giving Charlie a pat on the top of his head as he passed.

He pushed Sophie's bed over into the middle of the room to make way for a seat in front of the desk, then, taking a piece of paper out of his brief-case, he sat down to try to make some order of the jigsaw of events that were swimming disconnectedly around in his mind.

There was really nothing to go on. Any pattern that he worked out was based purely on supposition and hypothesis. The only real concrete line of connection was Duncan's recommendation that Deakin's should take over the distribution of Glendurnich in the States, and that Deakin's had been acquired by Kirkpatrick's. Then again, Duncan's insistence in appointing them as the new distributor had come about because of a fall in U.S. sales, and he didn't have any solid information to hand proving whether they had or not.

He closed his eyes and scratched hard at the back of his head with both hands. You're probably reading too much into this, you bloody fool. Lack of brain usage over the past eight months has begun to make you paranoid. Anyway, Kirkpatrick's surely couldn't touch Glendurnich. It was a private company, shares held by his father and himself. And, hang on, yes, there would now be a few in the hands of the workers as part of the stock-purchase plan that his father had set up. But they wouldn't account for much. No, Glendurnich was undoubtedly safe from predatory attack.

But then again, how could he make sure that nothing had been mooted within the company? Whom the hell could he contact? Not Duncan anyway—if there *were* any firm pointers to connect Glendurnich with Kirkpatrick's, then they would most certainly be directed at him. Nor his father. There was no reason to worry him unnecessarily over something that was probably highly speculative.

Margaret was the obvious person, being without doubt someone on whom he could truly rely for her loyalty. But there again, he wasn't sure that her normal ebullient manner would be best suited for such detective work. Nevertheless, through her, he could get a fax safely into the right hands. But whose? He suddenly began clicking his fingers over and over. What about the young man his father had called into the boardroom just after the briefing? He thumped his head with his hand, trying to knock the boy's name back into his mind. What in God's name was it? Come on, his grandfather had worked in the distillery. Mc, Mc-something-or-other, Mc-McLachlan! That was it! Archie McLachlan!

"Dad?"

David turned to find Sophie standing beside him, dressed in her pyjamas.

"Yes, darling?"

"Are you going to be long? I'm feeling a bit zonked. I wouldn't mind turning in."

He glanced round at her bed, which stood hopelessly marooned in the middle of the room.

"Oh, hell, I'm sorry! Look, I promise you I'll only be five minutes. I just want to send a fax back to the office. Would you mind using my bed until I'm finished, and then I'll get yours sorted out. If Dodie's on the bed, just push her off, okay?"

With a shrug, Sophie turned and pushed through the curtain into his bedroom. There was an immediate growl from the dog, followed by a resounding thump as she was dispatched from the bed onto the floor. David picked up a pen from the desk and began to write.

Fax to: Archie McLachlan (VIA MARGARET)
Glendurnich Distilleries Ltd

From: David Corstorphine

Dear Archie,

I wonder if you could do a bit of investigative work for me. I have just heard through a friend of mine in London that a company called Kirkpatrick Holdings Plc. are looking to purchase a malt-whisky business. I know that there is probably nothing to worry about on Glendurnich's part, but could you just have a few discreet words with some of your associates to see if they have heard anything along these lines?

Also, I would be grateful if you could keep this between ourselves, and please do not *approach anyone on the board of directors. If you do manage to find out anything, please fax me back immediately at the number on the confirmation slip. If I don't hear from you, I'll take it that all is well!*

With best wishes,
David Corstorphine

David inserted the paper into the machine and dialled the Glendurnich fax number. Then, as it began to go through, he turned and picked up the chair, pushing back Sophie's bed into its customary position with his foot.

"Sophie?"

"Yes?" a sleepy voice replied from behind the curtain.

"Your bed awaits you."

CHAPTER 29

Since getting her job at Glendurnich Distilleries, Doreen McWhirter had arrived at the office every morning at eight-thirty sharp, even though she was not expected until nine, along with the other office workers. However, in order to assert the control that she felt befitting her newly appointed position as receptionist, she thought it necessary to be at her station to greet the directors of the company when they walked through the door, and also to show herself as a figure of dedication and responsibility to her fellow workers when they traipsed in at the scheduled arrival time.

Consequently, on that Monday morning she was both surprised and somewhat miffed to find that she was not the first to arrive, the main door having swung gently open when she had placed her key in its lock. She clipped her way across the reception area to her desk and studied the lights on her telephone.

Mr. Caple was in, the red light corresponding to his office telephone being the only one that shone out from the console. Doreen smiled coyly to herself and, picking up her handbag, walked around the desk and with a dainty jaunt to her step made her way over to the ladies' room. Placing the handbag on the shelf in front of the mirror, she took out her compact and lipstick, then, removing her winged spectacles, she began to give her face the gentlest of touch-overs.

She really liked Mr. Caple. She had known that from the moment she had met him at the interview. It was so pleasant to encounter a young man who was so organized, so particular in the way he liked things done, and she was sure that he had given her the job because he had recognized similar attributes in herself.

She snapped shut her compact and placed everything back in her bag. Then, having given the sides of her neatly cropped greying hair a quick flick with her fingers, she walked back out into the reception area and over to her desk. Pulling open one of the larger bottom drawers, she carefully laid her handbag on its side and slid the drawer slowly shut, making sure that no part of the soft leather would catch on its runners. Then, straightening up, she clapped her hands together once to signify that, for her, work was now under way.

She began her routine by walking across to the front door and picking up the newspapers that had been pushed through the letter-box. She placed them in order of size on the coffee-table that was positioned between two of the leather sofas, uncreasing each as she laid it out with two quick wipes of the side of her hand.

Having stepped back from the table to make sure that the newspapers appeared symmetrical also from the front angle, she made her way over to the fax machine to check if anything had been sent through over the weekend. There was only one message. She picked it up and walked back to her desk, reading it through as she went. At first, her face registered incomprehension, then, having read it through again, she looked up in thought, her eyes narrowed and her newly glossed lips pursed tight in disapproval.

Glancing down at the switchboard, she saw that Mr. Caple's light was now off. She strutted across the reception area and made her way quickly up the stairs and along the corridor to his office. She knocked and cocked an ear to await his reply.

"Yes?" his voice called out.

She opened the door and put her head around the side.

"Ah, Doreen! How are you this morning? Come on in!"

The receptionist smiled at his bright manner and entered. "You're up with the lark this morning, Mr. Caple," she said playfully, feeling a glow come to her cheeks as she said it.

"Work to do, Doreen! Nothing should stop for work!"

"Absolutely not!" she replied, letting out a merry little laugh. "I couldn't agree with you more!"

"So what can I do for you?"

She walked over to his desk, clutching the fax to her bosom. "I hope you'll agree with me that I'm doing the right thing. It's just that I found this fax on the machine this morning, and, well, in my opinion, I do not think that its contents seem to have the best interests of the company at heart."

The smile on Duncan's face was replaced with a quizzical frown, and he reached out his hand for the fax. "Then you'd better let me have a look at it, Doreen."

Doreen handed it over, quickly clasping her hands back to her bosom as she stood waiting in trepidation for his reaction. As Duncan read it through, he felt his stomach begin to tighten into a knot, and he had to make a conscious effort not to swear out loud. Looking up, he forced himself to smile at the receptionist before reading through the fax once more.

"Right!" he said eventually, tossing the page down onto his desk. "You did exactly the right thing in showing me this." He turned his chair to the side and stared thoughtfully out of the window.

"Well, I think that it's bordering on being a criminal act, Mr. Caple!" Doreen snipped tartly, pleased that he had agreed with her and thinking that this now granted her the right to speak her own mind on the subject. "I mean, fancy trying to go over the heads of the directors! And who, may I ask, does this man"—she leaned forward and spun round the fax on the desk so that she could read it—"this Mr. Corstorphine think he—"

"I'll tell you what we'll do," Duncan cut in, turning his chair round to face her again. "Until I've been able to make some inquiries into this, I think we should keep it entirely between ourselves. Tell nobody, especially this"—he glanced at the fax—"this Archie Mc-

Lachlan." He looked up at her inquiringly. "I don't think I know him, do I?"

"Well, he's presently working in distribution. As far as I can gather, he's on a year's training scheme, so he's not a full-time employee of the distillery."

"Ah," Duncan said, slowly nodding his head. "Well, as I said, Doreen, we'll keep this to ourselves; but in the meantime, could you do something for me?"

"Certainly."

"Could you find out how much longer young McLachlan has to serve before he completes his training scheme?"

"Of course." Doreen smiled knowingly at Duncan. "A very shrewd move, if you'll allow me to say so."

"Okay, well, let's leave it at that, and thank you for bringing this to my attention. I have a feeling that it might turn out to be an invaluable piece of information."

"I sincerely hope so," she replied smugly and, turning sharply around, she walked smartly over to the door and left the office.

Duncan waited until he heard her footsteps descending the stairs, then he jumped to his feet, making his chair shoot backwards. He turned and caught it before it banged against the back wall.

"Damn!" he said under his breath.

He picked up the fax and paced up and down the floor as he read it through again. He stopped and slapped the top of his head.

"Damn! Damn! Damn!"

He scrumpled up the paper into a ball in his fist and went to stand by the window, his eyes fixed blankly on the tall pines that stood beyond the car-park.

How the hell had David found out about Kirkpatrick's? Nobody else knew about it! And how long had he been keeping up clandestine contact with this guy Archie? Maybe more faxes had passed through the office without his knowing while old Margaret had still been here. Damn it, he had underestimated David. He thought that he was going to be away from the business for a hell of a lot longer than this! He turned and walked back to his desk, unscrumpling the fax as he went.

He pulled in his chair and sat down, reading through the fax once more.

He wasn't definite, though, was he? "Probably nothing to worry about on Glendurnich's part" he wrote. But, on the other hand, he must think *something* was up if he had expressly asked this guy McLachlan not to approach the board of directors.

He shook his head and pressed the automatic dialling code on his telephone, leaving it on speaker mode. He sat back in his chair, still trying to work out the connotations of the fax as the telephone rang.

The nasal tones of a female telephonist sang out from the speaker. "Good morn-ing, Kirkpatrick Hol-dings!"

"Mr. Davenport's office, please."

"May I say who's call-ing?"

"Duncan Caple, Glendurnich."

The telephone clicked, giving way to ten seconds of electronic Mozart before John Davenport spoke. "Hullo, Duncan. How are you this morning?"

"Not good, I'm afraid, John. We've got a problem. The receptionist here has just brought me up a fax which came in sometime over the weekend."

"And?"

"It's from David Corstorphine in the States."

"Go on."

Duncan leaned forward to the speaker and went through the fax slowly and concisely. At the end, he sat back in his chair and waited. There was silence on the line, save for John Davenport's heavy breathing.

"Christ, I thought you said that he was out of action!"

"Well, I thought he was! On the other hand, I wouldn't say there's any real evidence here to indicate that he's back *in* action."

"Hell, I would have thought that that fax was conclusive enough."

"Not really. For a start, he's based the whole thing on supposition. I honestly think that by coincidence he *has* heard a rumour of your plans to purchase a malt-whisky business, and he's just checking it out—nothing more than that. And besides that, I'm pretty sure the guy's not fit in the brain yet, because I make a point of asking his father about him, and he always replies that he's not ready to come home yet."

"Right." There was a short silence. "Then why do you think that he didn't want the directors to be approached? I mean, why did he not just fax you direct?"

"I don't know. I can't fathom that out either. At first, I thought that it might be that he'd been back in touch with Deakin's, but then we'd have heard from Charles Deakin if that had been the case. The way I read it is that the guy feels the whole thing is *so* improbable that he doesn't want to risk my witnessing him make a complete fool of himself again, like he did in New York."

John Davenport sighed. "Well, let's look on the bright side. Thank God he sent a fax, and thank God we intercepted it."

Duncan picked up his pen and began doodling on his desk-pad.

"So what do you want to do? Continue with the plan or, well, rethink it?"

John Davenport's voice exploded through the speaker. "*Christ* no! Listen, as you said, his whole fax is pure supposition! Kirkpatrick's has great *need* of Glendurnich, Duncan, and I'm not going to throw a whole year's positioning work out the window at this juncture! And remember, you've got half a million pounds coming to you if we succeed in purchasing the company. You don't want to kiss that goodbye, do you? Come on, we go ahead with it, but we'll just have to bring the whole schedule forward. We can't risk leaving it for another two weeks."

"Right. So you want to make it this week, then."

"I'm afraid so, Duncan. What do you think? Can you manage it?"

Duncan threw the pen down on the desk and fell back in his chair.

"Okay!" he said decisively. "We'll bring the schedule forward a week. I'll call a meeting of all personnel in the car-park at five P.M. on Friday, just before they head home, and go through the proposal with them then. That'll give them the weekend to mull it over. Then I'll pay Inchelvie a visit on Saturday afternoon and tell him about the offer."

"All right, but I really think you are going to have to start putting some fairly extreme pressure on him now, Duncan. You *have* to convince him that this really is the only way that Glendurnich will survive in the future, and make sure that he understands implicitly that we have the best interests of both the company and the family at heart. I would suggest you really push your trump card concerning the workers' thirty-one per-cent shareholding as soon as you've heard their decision on Monday, and maybe see if you can't get him to sign over some of his own shares as soon as possible after that. I'd feel happier if we had nearer the fifty per-cent mark before the whole world gets wind of this."

"Yeah, don't worry. I think we've worked out pretty well how to handle this whole thing."

"I hope so. I have to warn you that we *are* sailing pretty close to the wind with Glendurnich. While we're not doing anything strictly illegal, our actions could be classed as being 'over-manipulative.' "

"Yes, I understand that, John."

"Good! Now, what are you going to do about Corstorphine's fax?"

"Well, I thought at first that I might answer it by sending a fax straight from the computer—no identifiable signature or anything. But I think that's too dangerous, inasmuch as it *would* actually constitute an illegal action. No, I think we'll just leave it. I mean, at least he left open that option for us by saying that he didn't expect a reply."

"Okay, well, I agree with that. And what about this chap McLachlan?"

"Don't worry. I'll deal with him."

"Right. Just make sure you cover your back, Duncan, in every way. I've had to do it all my life, so I know what you're about to let yourself in for! And keep in touch on a daily basis from now on, or even more frequently if you want any advice."

"Will do."

"Well, best of luck, then. Just go for it, boy!"

The telephone clicked off before Duncan had time to reply. He switched off the speakerphone, then picked up the fax and slowly tore it into pieces and threw it away. He pressed the button on his intercom. "Doreen?"

"Yes, Mr. Caple?"

"What did you find out about McLachlan?"

"His apprenticeship terminates at the end of next month."

"Okay. Well, I'm afraid that I have no option but to bring it forward, Doreen, so could you ask him to come to see me right now, please?"

"Very good, Mr. Caple."

"And, Doreen?"

"Yes?"

"Thanks again for your assistance over this matter. I really think that that fax could have been very hurtful to the future of the company."

"That's exactly what I thought. I shall contact young McLachlan straight away."

CHAPTER 30

The atmosphere in the offices of Culpepper Rowan on Tuesday morning was one of tense expectancy, the whole place seeming to have taken on the air of a legal-appeals office that was awaiting word of a reprieve from execution. There was little laughter or chat, the executives choosing to stay in their own offices behind closed doors, and those employees who passed in the corridors did so in silence, exchanging only a fleeting nervous smile with each other instead of the customary light-hearted greeting or teasing remark.

The only contact that Sam Culpepper had made with the members of his staff that morning had been in the form of an internal E-mail, giving express instructions that if Tarvy's were to be in touch, then he should be the first informed. Consequently, every time the telephone rang, Jennifer stopped what she was doing and gazed mesmerically at the light on the panel, nervously biting at a finger-nail until it went out again. Then, with a sigh of resignation, she would set about trying to get her brain back to work on the proposal for Russ's new clients.

However, by mid-day, she had heard nothing from Sam, and realizing that it would now be five o'clock in the afternoon in London, she began to conclude that somewhere in an office, not very far away from theirs, a party was already under way to celebrate the winning of the Tarvy's account. She went back over in her mind every last detail of her proposal, knowing each heading and paragraph as if it might be the most personal record she had ever kept of herself. The more she thought about it, the more new ideas or angles which had been discarded seemed to spring to mind, ones which she now wished she had had the sense to include in the document. And the more consideration she gave it, the more despondent she became.

By one o'clock, the telephone seemed to have stopped ringing completely. That's it, she thought to herself, it's all over. We *definitely* didn't get it. She slumped forward on her desk and rubbed at her face with her hands. What a waste of effort! *Jesus,* why did Sam ever think that they might have a chance against all those big shots? It was like—David trying to take on Goliath! She suddenly snorted out an involuntary laugh, realizing the funny side to her pun, and a mental picture sprang instantly to mind of *her* David standing in front of an enormous Philistine giant armed with a garden hoe and a tennis racket. Knowing him, he'd probably win, too!

She pushed her seat back, and smoothing her hands over her hair and linking them at the back of her head, she swivelled round to focus on a couple of window-cleaners suspended in their cradle from the roof of the opposite office block, seemingly oblivious to their height above Fifth Avenue as they chatted.

The door of her office was suddenly flung open with such force that it crashed against the bookcase behind it, making her jolt round in her chair. No one entered, but she heard muffled voices outside in the corridor.

"Who's there?" Jennifer asked, leaning forward on her desk to see if she could make out what was going on.

"Come on, Russ, get it off!" a voice whispered.

"I can't! It's stuck!"

"Give it a shake!"

"What the hell's going on?" Jennifer got up from her chair and walked round the side of her desk. As she approached the door, there was a loud explosion and a champagne cork cannoned awkwardly off the ceiling, hitting her sharply on the toe and making her jump back with the fright.

"What the *hell* is . . . ?"

Sam's balding head came round the side of the door.

"Who happens to be a genius?" he said, his face set in such an asinine grin that it looked as if he were trying to get used to an oversized set of false teeth. "Who's just won us the Tarvy's contract?"

Jennifer felt her jaw quite literally drop open and she put her hand up to her mouth.

"*What!* But how? When? The phone hasn't rung for well over an hour."

Sam entered the room, shaking a fax above his head. "Maybe it hasn't. But who said anything about them using the phone?"

Jennifer clapped her hands to her head. "Oh my *God*! You mean we *got* it?" she said breathlessly, scarcely believing what Sam was saying.

"No!" Sam exclaimed, pumping the fist that held the fax in the air. "*You* got it, Jennifer! *You* got it for us!"

She staggered unsteadily backwards towards her desk and sat down when she felt its support behind her. "We got the contract?" she asked quietly.

Sam's face took on a look of impatience. "How many more times do I have to say it? Yeah, we got it, we—got—the—Tarvy's contract!"

Jennifer stared blankly over the top of Sam's head. "We got the Tarvy's contract," she stated as if in an hypnotic trance.

Sam put on his madcap grin again and stood nodding his head furiously in front of her. Russ came round between them and, handing her a glass of champagne, he gave her a kiss on the cheek. "What a wonderful woman you are, Jennifer Newman!" he said with a wink.

Jennifer's face suddenly broke into a smile as the news finally began to register, and putting her glass down on the desk beside her, she leaped forward towards Sam, threw her arms around his neck and began jumping up and down.

"We got it, Sam! We *got* it!"

"I *know!* I *know!*" he said, trying to get into step with her bouncing.

Jennifer pushed herself away from him. "Well, let me have a look at it!" She grabbed the fax from his hand, and began to read every word of it out loud.

7th July

FAX TO:	*Culpepper Rowan*
FOR THE ATTENTION OF:	*Sam Culpepper* *Managing Director*
FROM:	*Adrian Thompson* *Managing Director, Tarvy's Gin Ltd.*
RE:	*US Advertising Campaign for Tarvy's Gin*

Jennifer turned and smiled excitedly at her two colleagues before reading on.

Dear Mr. Culpepper,

Having given due and careful consideration to the proposals that were tendered for the above campaign, we have the pleasure of informing you that our marketing committee has unanimously agreed to offer you the above contract.

It should be known that the decision was reached, not only on the basis of your excellent proposals, but also on a recommendation made to a member of our committee by an associate within the drinks industry, namely that yours is a company that would be in the position to take immediate action in implementing soonest an advertising campaign for Tarvy's Gin. We see this as being an integral part of our projected plan to secure for ourselves a share of the U.S. market within this coming year.

I have already taken the liberty of booking a flight to New

York for both myself and our marketing director next Monday. We will be arriving at 2 P.M. U.S. time, so I would be grateful if you could confirm both acceptance of this contract, and also a meeting for 3:30 P.M. on Monday 13th July.

With best wishes, and again many congratulations on an extremely well-thought-out campaign!

Yours sincerely,
Adrian Thompson
Managing Director, Tarvy's Gin Ltd.

Jennifer's voice tailed off as she ended the fax, and she looked up with an incredulous look on her face.

"We got it, Sam! We goddamned well got it!"

Sam and Russ held their glasses up to her, and she in turn raised hers.

"To Tarvy's Gin!" Sam said with a laugh. "And long may it pour!"

They drank a long toast, and Russ came forward with the bottle to replenish Jennifer's glass. "So?" he asked, looking at her out of the side of his eye as he filled her glass.

Jennifer gave him a puzzled look.

"So," Russ continued, "who's this secret contact you have?"

Jennifer looked down at the fax again and quickly read it through once more. "I don't know. I—I was going to ask you the same question!"

Sam pulled on Russ's arm and guided the champagne bottle back to his glass. "Oh, who gives a damn!" He cast his eyes to the ceiling. "But whoever it is, may God look down on him or her at this precise minute, and lay a kiss on his or her brow!"

With a laugh, they raised their glasses up once more.

The combination of fast intake of champagne and a complete mood swing from one of deep depression to flying elation suddenly took its effect on Jennifer. She walked round behind her desk and fell back heavily in her chair.

"God, I feel completely and utterly emotionally *drained*! I have been sitting here all day thinking about it! I never imagined for a moment . . ."

Her voice tailed off and she glanced sideways out the window, picking out once more the two window-cleaners opposite. They were in exactly the same position, still continuing with their idle banter. God, in the last three minutes, right here in *this* office, future direction had been changed, not only for herself, but for Sam, for Russ—in fact, for the whole company! Yet out there, it was like a time warp—as if someone had pressed the "pause" button on a video machine.

She looked round at her colleagues, seeing immediately that their expressions had altered from ones of joy to querying concern. Sam stepped forward to the front of her desk.

"Listen, Jennifer," Sam said quietly, "they're not here until next week. I'm just going to reply to the fax right now and confirm everything. Know what I want you to do? I want you to get the hell out of this office, and I don't want to see you back here until Monday morning."

Jennifer looked at him. "But what about moving ahead with the contract?"

"There's nothing to do until they come! You've done it all already! We'll just be going over the proposals. So, as I said, get out of the office, go home to Leesport, and spend the rest of the week relaxing and spending time with Benji. Jeez, Jennifer, you sure deserve it!"

Jennifer closed her eyes and let her head fall back against her chair, the idea of being away from the office for nearly a week suddenly filling her with a euphoric sense of relief. She opened her eyes and looked at the two men who now both leaned forward on her desk, like a couple of praying mantises eyeing their next meal.

"Do you think I could, Sam?"

"Of course!" He smiled at her. "Just relax and get ready for the meeting on Monday!"

From that moment on, every action that Jennifer took seemed to be in total contrast to the frenetic way in which she normally ran her life. Having taken a taxi back to Barrymore Street, she spent an hour packing a suitcase that would normally have taken her ten minutes, and then, driving back to Leesport, she even found herself taking the unprecedented step of pulling over at a roadside restaurant for a cup of coffee. There was simply no hurry now. She had the best part of a week to herself, and she was going to savour every moment of it.

By the time that she arrived back at the house, it was half past four in the afternoon. Taking her suitcase from the trunk, she walked over to the front door and pushed at it. It was locked. Her immediate reaction to this was one of puzzlement, but then, smiling to herself, she sorted out her keys and unlocked the door. They had probably all gone to Fire Island. Anyway, wherever they were, there was no need either for explanation or for worry. David would no doubt be with them.

She let herself in and for a moment stood in the hall, listening to absolutely nothing, simply relishing the peace and quiet of the empty house. Then, carrying her suitcase upstairs to her room, she put it down on the bed, and crossing over to the bathroom, began running a deep and relaxing bath. As the water cascaded from the taps, she watched it transfixed, allowing her mind to indulge itself happily in the elation over her own success again and again.

The sound of the water beginning to gurgle through the overflow waste-pipe shook her out of the day-dream. She turned off the taps and made her way back into the bedroom, and picking up the telephone, dialled Alex's mobile number. While waiting for it to connect, she kicked off her shoes and began to undo the buttons of her shirt, listening to the hissing on the line before the staccato tones of a female voice machine cut in.

"The number you have dialled has not responded. Please try late——"

Jennifer replaced the telephone, and quickly slipping out of her clothes as she walked back to the bathroom, she slowly lowered herself into the steaming water.

An hour and a half later, having indulged herself for longer than she had planned, she stood in the still deserted kitchen dressed in a simple cotton frock, her wet hair pulled back into a stringy pony-tail.

She glanced at the clock on the wall. Just before half past six. Well, there was no point in sitting around the house waiting for them to return. If they had gone to Fire Island, they would be taking the ferry back pretty soon. Okay! So why not go to meet them and give them a surprise!

She considered at first walking the half-mile to the marina, but uncertain as to what their normal arrangements might be, she realized that they could have gone their separate ways by the time that she got there—and she really *did* want to tell David about her triumph.

She ran back through to the hall, picked up the keys of the car from the table and let herself out the front door, locking it behind her. Then, jumping into the BMW, she reversed hard round and took off up the drive in a flurry of dust and gravel.

By the time she arrived at the entrance of the marina, she knew for certain that she had made it before them, there being no sign of them either there or anywhere on Shore Street. Pulling the car over to the side of the road, she got out, and leaning on the door, she shielded her eyes with her hand and looked out across the bay to see if she could make out where the ferry might be. Once she had become accustomed to the glare, she caught sight of the little craft about half a mile out from the shore, plying its way towards the marina, the Stars and Stripes fluttering from its mast in the gentle breeze.

As she turned to make her way down to the marina, she glanced to her left and noticed David's orange VW parked farther along Shore Street beyond the Memorial Garden. She smiled and shook her head, never having realized before where he lived. She took a step towards the marina, then stopped. Maybe she could just go and sneak a look at his house. She glanced out towards the boat, and judging that it would take at least another ten minutes to reach the marina, she turned and made her way along the street.

She first became aware of the sound of music and laughter as she walked past the Memorial Garden. Her immediate thought was that it came from the garden, but as she passed the gate she could only see an old man walking slowly around the path with an equally aged dog on a lead. No, the noise was definitely coming from the house farther along the road.

She slowed her pace as she approached the gate adjacent to the Volkswagen, and standing to one side of the hedge, she peered round the corner and looked over the top of the gate. She could see nothing, the action seeming all to be taking place farther over to the right. She stepped across to the centre of the gate, and was just about to lean over to see if she could make out what was going on when a ball came shooting over to land beside her at the gap in the hedge. She took a step back and pushed herself against the hedge as someone ran over to retrieve it.

"All right, Benji," she heard Gerry Reilly's voice call out, a weariness dulling its usual bright Irish tones. "That's it! You boys have won. I think we should call it a day." There was a short pause. "Oh, for crying out loud!" he continued softly, as if talking to himself. "Who the hell's idea was it to start a conga?"

Jennifer slowly stepped forward from the hedge. What was going on? What was Gerry doing here? She moved towards the gate and, unsnibbing it quietly, she walked through into the garden.

The music came from the small house that was set in the corner of the property, the doors of its porch open wide to allow the music to filter out into the garden. A conga line was threading its way down towards a flight of steps at the front of the garden, led by a large, middle-aged man with an abundance of sleeked-back grey hair who wore the gaudiest shirt that Jennifer had ever seen. A man of similar age clung on around his middle, while behind him, Jasmine kicked out her legs to the side and threw back her head in laughter. As the line began to descend the steps, the tail of the conga flicked round, and Benji, who was taking up the rear, was catapulted off and rolled across the lawn with a shout of gleeful annoyance. He jumped up, and was just about to head off to join on the end again, when he suddenly did a double take, seeing his mother standing ten feet away from him. He ran towards her, rubbing his hands up and down the seat of his pants.

"Hi, Mom!" He turned towards the rest of the party. "Hey, David, it's Mom!"

Jennifer looked around. "What's going on, Benji?"

"It's a birthday party for Sophie, Mom! She's sixteen!"

As the line broke up, Jasmine made her way across the lawn towards Jennifer with a grin stretched across her face, but then slowed to a standstill when she noticed the look of utter bewilderment on Jennifer's face. David appeared from the centre of the now-silent melée and walked towards Jennifer, scratching nervously at the back of his head. Jasmine caught this action as he passed and grabbed at his arm.

"You never told her, did you?" she exclaimed, her voice aghast at the realization that Jennifer knew nothing about the children or the party.

David shook his head. "Not yet. I was going to on Thursday."

Jasmine hit her head with the palm of her hand and put her fists on her hips. "Oh, *David!*"

Jennifer stood shaking her head, her brows furrowed. "What *is* going on? Who *is* this Sophie whose birthday it is, anyway?"

David approached her. "Listen, I was going to expl——"

"She's David's daughter!" Benji cut in excitedly. "David's oldest daughter!" He looked around to see if he could find Sophie, but she was nowhere to be seen at that precise moment. He grabbed hold of his mother's hand and dragged her past David and Jasmine to where the others stood. "And this is Charlie!" He pulled his new friend forward out of the crowd, and then did the same with Harriet. "And this is Harriet! They're *all* David's children, Mom. Isn't it great?"

"Is this your mummy, Benji?" Harriet's sweet little voice cut through the commotion like a razor blade.

"Yup," Benji said proudly.

Jennifer could do nothing but stand and stare at everyone, her head suddenly feeling as if it were about to explode beneath the pressure of the countless emotions converging all at the same time. David was married? Her friend David was *married*? And he had children? And he hadn't *told* her? Everyone else in Leesport seemed to know about them, but he hadn't told *her*?

"Listen, this is really all my fault . . ." David started, but Jennifer stepped back, holding up her hand to stop him from speaking further. She cupped her elbow in her hand and covered her mouth, knowing that her bottom lip had begun to quiver involuntarily.

At that point, the door of the house opened, and she turned to watch a tall young girl appear, carrying a jug that clinked with iced lemonade. She stopped when she saw that everyone was looking at her.

"What's going on?" she asked in a subdued voice. "Why's everything gone so quiet?"

Jennifer looked down at her feet. So, this must be Sophie. She shook her head, suddenly realizing that she didn't care who the hell any of these people were anyway. Oh, she had been feeling so good, so . . . *happy*—and now? She looked up at David, feeling the tears begin to well up and burn at her eyes.

"Yeah, why stop the party?" She began to back off towards the gate. "I'll just . . ." She turned and hurried away.

"Jennifer!" David called after her, but she had gone.

"Oh, for heaven's *sakes,* David!" Jasmine cried out.

"I'm sorry, Jasmine, I didn't think—"

"No, you obviously didn't, did you? Don't you realize that it now looks as if Benji and I were part of some sneaky plan to hide it from her?"

"I know. I'm sorry, but I promise you, I'll explain everything."

Jasmine shook her head slowly and turned away from him. "Ain't it a little late for that?"

David swore to himself, then moved off towards the gate. He turned. "Listen, everyone, I'm sorry about this, but could we just put everything on hold for a minute?" He looked at Clive. "I think it would be a good idea if you and Peter took Jasmine and the children back to Barker Lane for now."

Clive nodded. "Of course."

"What on *earth* is happening, Dad?" Sophie asked.

"It's really nothing, darling," he said, walking towards her. "Just a stupid misunderstanding that's come about through bad timing on my part." He gave her a kiss on the forehead. "But the party will continue later, I promise you."

He turned back towards the gate and as he reached it, he felt a hand clutch at his elbow. He turned and looked down at Benji. "David," he said, a worried expression on his face, "I think Mom's crying."

David ruffled the boy's hair. "Yeah, I know, Benji, but I'll get it sorted out, okay?"

Benji turned without looking at him and went back to take hold of Jasmine's hand. David threw open the gate and began sprinting as fast as he could along Shore Street. He was moving so fast that he had run twenty yards past the BMW before recognizing it as Jennifer's car. He stopped and loped back slowly towards it, glancing in as he approached. Jennifer sat in the driver's seat staring straight ahead and clutching the top of the steering wheel. He opened the door. "Listen, Jennifer, I just—"

"No," she cut in, holding up her hand. She glanced up at him, a look of deep hurt in her eyes. "I don't want to listen." She fired up the engine and moved off, pulling the car round into the entrance of the marina. David ran after it and opened the door, squatting down on his haunches behind it so that she couldn't reverse away.

"Please, Jennifer. Just give me a chance to explain."

"No! Now would you get out of the way, please?" she said, fighting hard to control her voice.

David did not move from his position. "Not until you've given me a chance to explain."

Realizing that he was not going to move, she took in a deep breath, and pulling the keys from the ignition, she jumped out of the car.

"Please! Just leave me alone!" she said, as she strode off towards the marina.

David stood up and shut the door, then, catching up with her, took hold of her arm. She turned and raised her hand at this unwelcome contact, and he backed off hurriedly.

"Don't you *ever* touch me again, do you hear?" She shook her head in anger as she fought to find her next words. "I thought I could trust you! I thought you were—my *friend*!" She began walking away, then turned back. "I mean, *everyone* seemed to have known about all this except me! Even my own child! How do you think that makes me *feel?*" She spluttered out a gasping sob of anger.

"I was going to tell you on Thursday! I didn't think you were coming back until then."

She crossed her arms and nodded. "Oh, Thursday. That would have been just fine, wouldn't it? Let's keep it all a secret until after the party, then we won't have to invite boring old Jennifer."

"Oh, come on, that's stupid!" David snapped at her, losing his patience. "It wasn't like that at all!" He immediately held up his hands in apology at his tone. "Listen, I'm sorry about the party. It was just that Sophie's birthday was last month, so I thought we'd just celebrate it as soon as possible. There was no subterfuge or malice ever intended by that!"

Jennifer shook her head at the pathos of his explanation and turned and walked past the entrance gate. The same surly-faced little man who had been in the box when David had come down there on that first morning stood up from watching his television and leaned out of the window.

"Hey, you! Is that your car parked up there? 'Cos if so, you can't park it there. It's blocking the entrance!"

David glared at him. "Look, why don't you just—bugger off!"

The man was at first mystified by the retort, but then a thunderous expression came over his face. "Hey, who d'ya think you're talkin' to, you goddamned Brit? Stuck-up bastard. Don't you—?"

"You heard him!" Jennifer interjected with force. "Just *bugger off*!"

She turned and strode off, and David watched as the man, obviously stunned by the fact that an American *woman* could talk to him in such tones, slumped slowly into his seat and turned back to watching his television.

As Jennifer walked out onto the narrow gangway that led to the boats, David pushed past and turned to face her, successfully impeding her from going any farther. She stopped and looked at him, anger blazing in her eyes.

"Why didn't you *tell* me! I can't believe you didn't *tell* me! I wouldn't have minded, David! I just feel so—left out! I don't mind that you have a . . . wife and children, but why did you think you couldn't *tell* me?"

"I don't have a wife!"

"Oh, *right!*" she exclaimed, trying to push past him. "So how do you explain those three kids back there, or are you going to spin me some yarn about you gallivanting around Scotland fathering illegitimate children everywhere?"

"Oh, don't be stupid! Of course not."

"*So where the hell* is *your wife?*"

"*SHE'S DEAD!*"

The two words came out with such passion and anguish that they seemed to hang in the air, breaking immediately through Jennifer's anger to dig themselves deep into her innermost self. It happened so fast, and was so discordant with the preconceived course of her argument, that she found herself swallowing back the angry retort she had intended.

At that point, two yachtsmen, who were walking along the narrow gangway, excused themselves in passing, and both she and David stood aside in silence to allow them through. Jennifer turned and followed them with her eyes, thankful for the interruption to retrain her thoughts. She turned back to David and flickered a half-smile at him, but then, seeing the look of desolation on his face, she lowered her head and closed her eyes, devastated by her own self-centredness in not having allowed him to explain earlier.

"When?" she eventually asked in a quiet, faltering voice.

David remained silent for a moment before answering. "April."

"This April?"

David glanced out the side of his eye at her and nodded.

Jennifer let out a deep shuddering breath. "Oh, David! Why did you—"

"Listen!" David cut in, holding up his hand. "I wanted to explain to you properly. Believe me, I never wanted you to find out like this. It just happened that Jasmine found out, well, really by default, and I asked her not to say anything, because . . ." He stopped and turned to look out across the bay to Fire Island. ". . . because I wasn't ready to tell anyone. That's the reason I'm out here. So I could lose myself, and get away from constantly thinking and having people talk about it."

As he stood, still gazing out across the bay, he suddenly felt a hand slip into his, and he turned to look into Jennifer's upturned face.

"And do you think you could talk about it—with me—now?" she asked softly.

David paused for a moment, then slowly nodded.

"Well, come on then," she said, pulling him by the hand back towards dry land. "Let's find somewhere a little more private than this."

Two hours later, it had all been told and, with nothing left to say, they sat together in silence on the little jetty in front of the saltbox, gently skimming their bare feet across the surface of the water and looking out across the bay as the warming darkness fell about them. Throughout his explanation, Jennifer had continually asked questions with such intuition and understanding that he realized at the end of it that her knowledge of Rachel and the children probably now outmatched that of anyone else but his own closest family. It was at that precise moment that he felt more at peace with himself than at any time since Rachel's death.

The quiet was so enveloping that David caught the change in Jennifer's breathing as she let out a silent laugh to herself. He turned and looked at her. "What?"

She shook her head and, leaning back on her hands, she straightened out her legs and watched the water drip from her feet. "Nothing. I was just remembering *my* sixteenth birthday."

"God, I can't remember mine! Yours must have been a pretty special occasion."

"Oh, it was!" Jennifer put her head back and gazed up at the stars. "I was at a boarding-school in Richmond, Virginia, and my mother picked me up on the morning of my birthday and said she had a surprise for me. We flew up to New York, and we shopped . . ." She let out a short laugh. ". . . . and we shopped some more. And then, in the evening, we went to my first Broadway show." She paused, pulling her knees up under her chin. "It was *Jesus Christ Superstar*. I have never forgotten it."

David smiled and looked down into the dark waters. "Yeah. I can imagine." He let out a long sigh. "I think that's what I really fear most for my children. They'll miss days like that. They'll never have them."

Jennifer reached across and laid her hand on top of his. "David?"

"Yeah?"

"Would you let me ask Sophie to come to New York with me?"

"What?"

"Can I take Sophie into New York this weekend? I'd love to take her shopping, and then maybe go to a Broadway show."

"Would you really do that?"

Jennifer leaned over towards him, her face lightening up into that same smile she had given him when he had first complimented Benji on the day of the tennis party.

"I don't have a daughter, and I've never regretted it for an instant—except for one thing. And that was that I could never give her a day like the one my mother gave me for my sixteenth birthday. You've been so wonderful with Benji, David, and I would love more than anything to take Sophie."

"Well, I think it's a wonderful idea. We'll ask her. I'm sure she'll be bowled over."

"Good. We'll go into the city on Saturday morning, and we'll shop till we drop; then we can go back to the apartment in West Village, because we'll have it to ourselves, seeing Alex will still be away. Then we'll go to—now what would she enjoy?—I know! *Crazy for You*. That's on at the Shubert!" Her face beamed once more with excitement.

David laughed. "Now *that* will be right up Sophie's street!" He jumped up and, taking hold of Jennifer's hand, pulled her to her feet and then both walked slowly back along the jetty and up the narrow steps into the garden. When she got to the top, she turned as he took the last two steps behind her.

"Oh, by the way, I was going to tell you. We got the contract."

"You did! Well done! You deserved it in every way!" He put his hand out to give hers a congratulatory shake, but she crossed her arms and eyed him closely, as if trying to make out some follow-on to his initial reaction to the news.

He met her gaze. "What's the matter?"

"David, can I ask you something, and would you give me an honest answer to my question?"

"Well, I don't know what it is yet."

"Okay! So here's the question! You said that you gave up work to look after Rachel?"

"Yeah."

"Right! So what I want to know is—what do you do? I mean, what is your normal job?"

"Why do you ask?"

Jennifer turned and began walking nonchalantly towards the house. "Oh, it's just that one reason we got the contract with Tarvy's was because some unbelievably kind person and obviously well-connected with the company put in a good word for us." She turned and looked directly at him. "But neither Sam, Russ nor I have any idea who it could be."

"Ah, right," he said quietly, looking down at his feet to cover for the smile on his face.

"You don't happen, by any chance, to be in the liquor business, do you?"

He looked up and nodded noncommittally. "Well, sort of."

"What do you mean, 'sort of'? You either are or you aren't."

"Yeah, okay, I'm in the whisky industry."

Jennifer walked slowly back towards him. "And have you, by any chance, contacted anyone over the past week who might just happen to work for Gladwin Vintners?"

David stuck his hands in the back pockets of his trousers and looked everywhere except at Jennifer. "Well, sort of, yeah—but it was a social call as well."

Jennifer stopped directly in front of him. "You've done it again, haven't you? I only said it as a joke, but you managed to fix that too!" She gave out an incredulous laugh. "Your name *is* David Corstorphine, isn't it?"

"Yeah, why?"

"It's not anything like, well, Clark Kent or . . . something similar?"

"God no, you're looking at a mere mortal here."

Jennifer shrugged her shoulders. "Well, maybe." She reached up and gave him a slow and gentle kiss on either cheek. "But a particularly special one."

She turned and hurried over to the porch. "Come on, I haven't celebrated yet! Let's have a drink! God, I'm in need of one after this afternoon!"

David thumped his hand against his forehead as he followed her towards the house. "I'm afraid that could be a problem! I know for a fact that I don't have anything. I didn't have much at home, and I think Gerry ended up nicking the last beer. But look, I'll go straight up to the liquor store and get a bottle of wine."

"No, don't worry," she said, disappointed, as she entered the living-room.

"Honestly, it's no problem!" he said, picking up the keys of the Volkswagen off the table. "Give me five minutes, and I'll be back. Just make yourself at home. The place is so small that you'll probably find everything from where you're standing at the minute!"

As it happened, it was a good fifteen minutes before he returned. Having taken a bottle of champagne out of the cooler in the liquor store, he became embroiled in a lengthy conversation with Victor, the old man who ran the place, about the differing qualities of champagne that were now coming out of France. Eventually, he managed to get away, leaving Victor to continue his droning appraisal with some guy who had only come in for a six-pack of beer.

The moment he arrived back at the house, David moved quickly, fearing that Jennifer might have decided to go home. He ran across the garden, and entering through the porch, he found her sitting in one of the armchairs with Dodie on her knees.

"Sorry about that!" he said, beginning immediately to take the foil off the top of the bottle. "I was held up!"

"Don't worry!" Jennifer replied. "Dodie appeared from somewhere and has been keeping me company. Listen, David, I didn't know how long you were going to be, and I was a little worried about the children, so I rang Jasmine. Just as well, as it happens, because she was in somewhat of a state about this afternoon. Anyway, I put her mind at rest, and then got her to ask the children if they minded sleeping at the house tonight. They seem to be okay about it. Do you have any objections?"

"No, that's great—as long as it's all right by you."

"Yeah, sure it is! And anyway, I'd love to have them to stay whenever or for as long as they want! Please treat it as an open—"

She stopped talking, realizing that David was suddenly frozen in mid-action as he prised the cork off the bottle. He seemed to have become aware of the music that Jennifer had put on the record player, and was standing staring at the pile of records that she had taken from the top shelf and had left sitting on the table. She looked across at them.

"Oh, I'm sorry! I hope you don't mind. I just thought that I'd put on a record, but they all seemed, well, either doleful, or . . ." She laughed. ". . . a little too seductive, and I didn't think that I should give you the wrong idea! So I thought that there was no harm in a bit of Martha Reeves and the Vandell——"

Her voice petered out, as she noticed that David's face had drained of all colour.

"David, what's wrong?"

"Could you change the record, please?" he said quietly.

"Why?"

"Could you just please change the—"

It was too late. The song faded out, and the needle crackled unerringly on the spacer towards the next track. Jennifer watched as David shut his eyes, his whole face tightening as if he expected someone to deal him a final, mortal blow.

The quiet guitar introduction of "The Tracks of My Tears" sounded out around the room. David turned away and lowered his head, the bottle held limply at his side as he leaned his free hand on the back of the armchair. Jennifer looked up at the speakers, realizing now that it was the song. She walked over to him and took the bottle from his grasp and placed her hand on his shoulder.

"Is it the song?"

David slowly nodded.

"Was it yours? Yours and Rachel's?"

He nodded again.

Taking a grip on his arm, she slowly turned him towards her and looked into his lowered face, seeing the tears in his eyes.

"Oh, David!" she said quietly, "I didn't know! Come here!"

She pulled him against her, and as he rested his head on her shoulder, she suddenly felt a shudder run through his body and into her own as he broke down, the tears beginning to flow uncontrollably as she held him close to her.

"So take a good look at my face, can't you see the smi-ile, it's out of place."

She pushed him away, and, placing her hand gently on the side of his cheek, she tilted his face up so that he looked at her directly.

"You know, you must be the bravest man I know. You've come out here and you've managed to exorcize all these ghosts by yourself. And on top of that, you've fixed it for Benji, Jasmine *and* myself over and over again. It's my turn now. It's my turn to fix it for you. This is the last ghost, David, and I'm going to be with you every step of the way."

As the track came to an end, Jennifer left him and reached up and placed the needle haphazardly somewhere near the beginning. She turned round and took him again in her arms, and gradually, as the song continued, she felt him begin to move against her in rhythm with the music.

"Since you left me, you see me with another girl, seemin' like I'm havin' fun."

David held himself tight against her, feeling the warmth of her body, pulled close against him, loving the smell emanating from the softness of her neck. He closed his eyes as he felt her lips reach up and caress him below the ear. They moved in sequence across his cheek, eventually kissing at the side of his mouth. Then he felt it, the gentle pressure against his own lips, and he let them part, allowing himself to taste for the first time in what seemed an eternity the essence of all that he had longed for, and all that he had missed since losing Rachel.

Her name. Rachel. It was Rachel he missed.

He pushed himself away from Jennifer and stood, his gaze lowered to the ground.

"I—I'm sorry, Jennifer, I can't! I can't do this so soon after . . ."

Jennifer moved quickly over to the record player, using the opportunity to replace the needle on the record, this time hitting the introduction perfectly. She turned back to him, and gently took hold of both his hands.

"People say I'm the life of a party, 'cos I have a drink or two."

"David, nothing is going to happen, I promise you. I won't let it. We do nothing more than dance. That's all—but there is this one very beautiful and special ghost that we have to exorcize."

She pulled him back towards her, and this time her lips had no need to work their way to his mouth. He was there, waiting for her, ready for her, and together they began moving gently, as one, around the tiny confines of the living-room.

And still Smokey sang . . .

CHAPTER

31

Jasmine really didn't know what had hit her over the next couple of days. The house had suddenly lost its usual airy tranquillity and been turned into a place of vociferous mayhem. The route leading from the hall through the passageway and into the kitchen had come to resemble more the Indianapolis Speedway, and she would often find herself having to jump clear of a gaggle of screaming children as they burst through the kitchen like a litter of unruly puppies. And even though they spent most of their time outside in the swimming pool or on the tennis court, there always seemed to be a child at her side, either asking advice as to where something had been left, or where somebody was, or what time the next meal was going to be.

But she didn't mind. In fact, she revelled in it. Not only because she loved having so many children about her, but also because of the sheer relief she felt in not having to be party to any further clandestine fibs or secrecies. Jennifer was now part of it, wholly integrated into this new uproarious way of life that Jasmine herself had been enjoying, though somewhat guiltily, over the past week.

Furthermore, Jennifer seemed to be a changed person, having almost an aura of serenity about her that Jasmine had never before witnessed. Gone was the rushed and, at times, offhand formality of the business woman, replaced by a more gentle, relaxed character who appeared totally content in giving her complete and undivided attention to the new household. Yet despite being happy about this inexplicable change, Jasmine found herself becoming increasingly concerned about what effect Alex's wrongdoings might have on this new, more vulnerable, Jennifer if she were ever to find out about them.

A further change was that, without any hint of favour or encouragement, she had acquired a constant shadow in the form of Harriet. The child was always there at her side, either asking if she could help her cook or bake a cake, usually at a time when she was attempting to prepare yet another gargantuan meal for the troops. Jasmine eventually concluded that one of her main assets in attracting so much attention from the little girl was the colour of her skin, in that whatever they did together, Harriet would just stare up at her, her eyes wide with fascination, as she moved her head from side to side, quite unashamedly studying every pore on Jasmine's face.

David, meanwhile, had found it impossible to do any further work in the garden, not because he didn't want to, but because, on making his first appearance with a hoe and fork in hand, he was met with such a derisive cry of *"Boooriiiing!"*—for the most part orchestrated by Jennifer herself—that he was left with no option but to return his tools unused to the garden shed. Feeling almost heavy-hearted about it, he shut the doors and locked them up, knowing that he was probably doing so for the last time.

Nevertheless, there was now no excuse or covert reason for not devoting himself entirely both to his children and to Jennifer, Benji, and Jasmine. Moreover, as the week unfolded, it became apparent to him that, right here and now, he was in the company of those with whom he most wanted to spend his time. There were trips to Fire Island, excursions into Leesport in the Volkswagen, disruptive visits to the huge multiplex cinema in Sayville, always returning at the end of the day to Barker Lane, where tennis matches and swimming competitions continued well on into the evening.

After their first night in Jennifer's house, the children quickly came to the conclusion that it had far more to offer in terms of comfort and amenities than the saltbox in Shore Street, and it was therefore agreed, to a man, that they would prefer to stay there. Sophie at first felt a little guilty in letting her father return to the saltbox by himself, and subsequently cajoled Jennifer into asking him if he too wanted to stay. However, Jennifer secretly understood David's wish to return to the haven of his own house every night, knowing that he was still in need of a private space. She therefore immediately accepted his somewhat lame excuses that it would be less disruptive for Dodie, and that he was also half-expecting a fax to come in from his office in Scotland.

This distancing allowed David the perspective of standing back and observing his children as they blended, as smoothly as synchromesh, into the way of life of this household—a way of life that had been so much a part of his own over the past six weeks. Charlie and Benji had become an inseparable and independent unit, spending most of their time on the tennis court or out on the bay with the Windsurfer, taking it in turns to man the rowing-boat and yell encouragement to the other as he wobbled his way across the shallows. Harriet, meanwhile, appeared content to be anywhere in the vicinity of Jasmine, always being the first to run back into the house to seek her out if she had been away with the others for any length of time.

But what gave David the most satisfaction was the bond that was forming between Sophie and Jennifer. At first, he'd had fears that there would be a cool reserve on Sophie's part, especially as she might see Jennifer only as the person who had disrupted her birthday party. But he had not counted on Jennifer's intuition in understanding this for herself, and on that very same night when she had returned from David's house, she had gone up to Sophie's bedroom and had sat on her bed until well after midnight, simply talking to her and making plans for their forthcoming weekend in the city.

What was more, in seeing for the first time this woman, who happened to be no part of his family, so closely involved with one of his own children, he became almost imperceptibly aware of his mind creating a direct link between her and Rachel, and instead of banishing it as an invasive and unwelcome thought, he found himself quite at ease not only in accepting it, but also in being able to admit to himself just how important a role Jennifer had begun to play in his life.

Seeing that the promised continuation of Sophie's birthday party had not taken place on the Tuesday, David decided that, on the eve of Jennifer's and Sophie's departure to the city, he would take everyone, including the original guests, out to dinner in the Leesport Restaurant. As they were to number thirteen at the table, and not wishing to tempt providence, he also invited In-Deli-ble Billy (as the children had now christened him), having noticed that, during their countless visits to the deli, Billy had come to direct his wicked and teasing remarks to Sophie, and she in turn had reacted to them with a sparkle in her eyes and a flush to her cheeks.

As it turned out, the party was a wild affair, with all protocol regarding age and status being summarily discarded from the moment it began. Gerry had brought along with him two guitars, one of which he handed over to David at the end of the meal, much to the embarrassment of the children, and thereafter those who were willing stood up to do a party piece.

Of course, Benji was first to take up the challenge. He launched into his own song, then interjected it throughout with excuses about how it sounded much better when Dublin Up were playing with him. Then, amidst shrill protests from Sophie, Billy dragged her up from the table to perform a duet with "You're the One That I Want," and although it appeared at the outset to be a strong contender for The Best Entertainment Award, Billy became somewhat over-suggestive in his Travolta dance routine, and the act came to an abrupt end with Sophie running from the room with an embarrassed scream of "That's absolutely *revooolting*!"

David and Gerry were next to perform, singing a merry little tune which turned out to be slightly bawdy in content, earning them some stern looks of disapproval from Jasmine.

The finale, of course, was the best, coming as the direct result of a request from David. With loud yelps of encouragement from the assembled throng, Clive and Peter were pushed self-consciously to their feet, and after a few furtive whispers to each other in deciding which way they should initially face, they set about performing, in perfect sychronization of both voice and foot, their well-polished rendition of "Wouldn't It Be Lovely."

The next morning, David was up at Barker Lane at half past eight, eager to make sure that Sophie had everything she needed for her trip. However, he found himself more of a hindrance than a help, the two city-bounders already seeming to have everything in hand, so much so that Jennifer had told Sophie only to pack her night-things, seeing that the main reason they were going to the city was to shop! Feeling slightly embarrassed by this, David managed to catch Jennifer for a fleeting moment by herself, and stuttered his way around the subject of money. Jennifer, however, stopped him mid-sentence by simply reaching up and placing the tip of her forefinger on his mouth. Then, walking away from him, she began to reel off a string of expenditures, relating to the garden and to Benji, which he himself had incurred without reimbursement. Thereafter, David felt it best not to make another approach, but eased his conscience instead by slipping one hundred dollars into Sophie's purse.

At nine on the dot, the two girls (as Jasmine had begun to call them) were sitting champing at the bit in the BMW. Sophie gave an excited wave first to David and Jasmine and then to the three very tired-looking faces who peered out of an upstairs window, before turning round and pointing her finger à la "Wagons Roll!" up the drive. With a flick of her hand in a final gesture of farewell, Jennifer powered the car away from the house.

Exactly two hours later, they arrived in the West Village, and having parked the car in a space in Barrymore Street and deposited overnight bags in the apartment, they walked the short distance to Spring Street. There, Sophie spent the rest of her morning in a bemused trance, as Jennifer led her up from one shop to another. All the names that she had heard of, and had talked about with her friends at school, were there. Agnes B, Replay, Guess, and they went into every one and bought something for her, and for her alone.

They then took a taxi uptown and ate a late lunch in a restaurant on Madison Avenue. At the end of the meal, Jennifer ordered coffee for two, and being for the first time in the relaxed privacy of their own company, she broached the subject of Rachel. With almost a frightened reticence to begin with, Sophie suddenly found herself being able to open up to this woman whom she had come both to like and trust over the past week.

Having been allowed to leave their shopping bags at the restaurant, they took a taxi to Central Park. There the conversation continued as they walked side by side along the path by the lake, Sophie's arm linked through Jennifer's, only stepping away from each other to allow for the occasional erratic Rollerblader or single-minded jogger to pass unhindered. The more they talked, the more admiration and love Jennifer felt for this young girl at her side, realizing that she herself had never experienced such devastating loss and emotional upheaval in her own life.

When they eventually left the park, Jennifer decided that there was not enough time to go back to the apartment before the show. Consequently, they took a taxi straight to Broadway, stopping off to collect their bags on the way. Then, having ensconced themselves in a welcoming pub called the White Lion, they sat drinking Coke and eating chips, while studying the faces of the people who entered and, giggling uncontrollably, comparing their looks with well-known people.

They walked the remaining distance to the Shubert Theatre, arriving ten minutes before the curtain of *Crazy for You* went up. Having entrusted their shopping bags to the little lady who ran the cloakroom, and having stocked up with programmes, they entered the auditorium and sat down in their plush velvet seats just as the overture began.

To Sophie, it was the most magical thing that she had ever seen. She sat transfixed throughout the performance, listening intently to every song and humming the melody over to herself after each was finished, desperate to remember everything that took place during the performance. The man in front of her seemed to be the tallest person in the audience, but she didn't mind, because it meant that she could lean over to the side in order to look around him and, without excuse or self-consciousness, feel the warming comfort of physical contact with Jennifer as she did so.

After the show had finished, they stood on the sidewalk outside the theatre, feeling the sultry heat of the evening blow about their faces and, deciding not to take a taxi, they turned and walked off in the direction of the West Village, swinging their shopping bags to and fro as they jumbled through the words of the songs together.

By the time that they reached Twenty-first Street, their hands ached so much from carrying their bags that they succumbed to the lure of the taxi, and within a few minutes were deposited back outside the apartment in Barrymore Street. Jennifer unlocked the door and flicked on a light switch, then, dumping everything on the hall floor, she walked through to the sitting-room and sat down with a sigh of exhaustion in an armchair.

"So," she said, looking at Sophie, "what shall we do now?"

Sophie shrugged. "I don't know. Isn't it a bit late to start doing something now?"

Jennifer glanced at her watch. "Heavens, it's ten to twelve! I'd no idea it was so late! Maybe you're right. Do you just want to go to bed?"

Sophie wrinkled up her nose in disapproval of the motion. "Not particularly. I'm pretty hungry, though!"

Jennifer slapped her hands on the arms of the chair and jumped to her feet. "Yup, so am I! So what do you want? Do you like pizza?"

"Do I not!"

"Great! Me too! So tell you what we'll do, I'll phone for the best pepperoni pizza that money can buy, and while we're waiting for it to be delivered, we'll get into our night-clothes and you can pick out a video for us to watch. Then we'll just curl up on the sofa and pig out on pizza! How's that for an idea?"

Sophie nodded slowly, a contented grin on her face. "I would say that it couldn't be better!"

Five minutes later, having changed into her night-dress, Jennifer padded into the sitting-room in her bare feet and vaulted over the back of the sofa to sit beside Sophie. The video had already started, the opening credits being accompanied by some seriously eerie music.

Jennifer turned slowly to her young companion, a look of complete shock on her face. "Sophie, what on earth are we watching?"

Sophie smiled at her. "*The Amityville Horror*."

Jennifer's mouth dropped open. "Oh, Sophie, do we really want to watch this? Is there nothing a bit tamer?"

Sophie laughed. "Come on, Jennifer, it's only a *film*! Anyway, I thought we'd had enough sugary sweetness for one night. Time for a bit of nerve-tingling spice!"

Jennifer shook her head slowly. "Ooh, you evil girl!" She grabbed hold of Sophie's hand and squeezed it. "Okay, but if you're going to make me suffer this, I'm holding on to you good and tight. I just *loathe* horror films!"

Sophie let out a wicked chuckle and, pulling Jennifer's arm across her shoulder, tucked herself in against her.

Although they both heard it simultaneously, the noise at the front door was more like a soft scratching than a knock.

"Pizza time!" Jennifer exclaimed, jumping to her feet. "Last one there has to eat the box!"

They both ran for the door, and Sophie, having had more recent practice in the art of outwitting her siblings, sneaked under Jennifer's arm and made it there first. She threw it open, making the bunch of keys that hung in the lock jangle against the metal of the door handle. A couple stood in the corridor, locked together in a deep embrace, being so enwrapped in each other that it took all of two seconds before either of them realized that the door had been opened.

Sophie looked quizzically at them, thinking that neither looked very much like pizza-delivery people, then turned round to Jennifer. She stood behind her, stock-still, a look of sheer horror on her now ashened face, her mouth twitching as if she was trying to say something. Then, in the quietest voice she spoke, her tone registering both total disbelief and unbearable hurt.

"Oh, Alex, no!"

CHAPTER

32

Throughout the day on Saturday, there had been more than a few disgruntled moans from Benji and Charlie about not being included in the trip to the city, so, in order to take their minds off the unfairness of it all and to add some variety to their escapades, it was arranged for them to spend the Sunday with Sean Dalaglio. Jasmine, meanwhile, said that she wanted to take Harriet to visit her mother in North Leesport, so, David found himself to be a free agent for the first time in over two weeks.

Having allowed himself a lie-in until nine o'clock, he took Dodie for a short walk down to the marina, before setting about tidying up the house and ridding it of the clutter of camp-beds and sleeping-bags. He had taken everything outside to put into the Volkswagen, when he found himself consumed with guilt over the state of the car's interior, a week and a half's worth of ferrying children around having left it in a worse condition than when he had taken it over from Carrie. Therefore, having stretched the cable of the vacuum cleaner to its full length from house to car, he proceeded in sucking out a dust-bag's worth of sand and old candy wrappers, all which seemed to have worked their way into the most inaccessible crevices of the plastic upholstery.

As the electronic bells of the little Roman Catholic church on Champner Street began to summon the congregation to eleven-o'clock mass, he made his way to the bottom of the garden, a can of Pepsi in hand, and descended the steps to the jetty. He flicked off his deck shoes and sat dangling his feet over the edge as he watched a windsurfer skim his way across the bay about three hundred yards offshore.

God, this place really *was* perfect. He smiled to himself, realizing just how many times and on how many different occasions he'd said that over the past six weeks. But it was true. Never, for one minute, had it lost the special magic that he had felt that first morning when he had walked down to the marina and looked out across the bay. And now, on top of that, it had succeeded in casting its healing spell, not only over him, but over his whole family. But it wasn't just the place—it was the people as well. Everyone had played a part in his revitalization and in his own children's readjustment to family life, something which was going to make it so much easier for them all when they returned to Scotland.

Scotland. His mind turned to the distillery, and he wondered for the hundredth time if he shouldn't have asked Archie to fax him back regardless, the lack of response having left a niggling doubt in his mind that something untoward might be taking place. But then again, Archie would surely have contacted him.

As he finished off the last remaining drops of the can he started, turning his head quickly towards the house, positive that he had just heard the sound of a door banging.

"Hullo?"

He waited for five seconds, listening for a reply, then jumped to his feet and ran back up the steps. The side door stood ajar.

"Hullo?" he called out again as he walked across the lawn to the porch. He heard a scuttling noise from inside the house, and Dodie came bouncing out of the screen door, followed immediately by Sophie.

For a moment, David just stood looking at her, her presence there being so unexpected.

"Sophie?" he said, a confused tone to his voice. "What are *you* doing here? I thought you weren't due back until tonight."

Sophie said nothing, but ran over to him and put her arms around his chest, holding herself tight against him.

"Has something happened, darling?"

Sophie looked up at him, a worried expression on her face, and nodded her head.

"What? Tell me."

Sophie took a couple of deep breaths, as if steeling herself to speak, before she finally blurted out her explanation.

"It was so awful, Dad! We'd been to the theatre and then we went back to Jennifer's place and we were watching a video and waiting for the pizza to arrive, and then I opened the front door and there was this man and woman there, and they were snogging each other in the corridor." She pulled herself even tighter against her father. "It was Jennifer's *husband*, Dad!"

David stood with his eyes tightly shut, not wishing to hear the final sentence, knowing already what she was going to say. For a moment, he held his daughter in silence.

"When did you get back to Leesport?" he asked quietly.

"Last night—no, this morning, I suppose, at about three o'clock. We just packed our things and came back. Poor Jennifer, Dad. She was *so* upset all the way home."

David bent forward and kissed the top of her head. "Did you see Jasmine when you got home?"

"No, we were pretty quiet. I don't think Jennifer wanted to see anyone. Then, when I got up about an hour ago and went downstairs, there was no one in the house, but I found a note on the kitchen table from Jasmine saying that she had seen the car and explaining where everyone had gone today. That's why I knew you were here. Then I went into the conservatory and found Jennifer. She's just sitting there by herself on the sofa." She looked up at her father again. "I asked her if she wanted me to get you, and she just nodded without speaking. I was going to ring, but I thought it would be better if I came and saw you, so I borrowed Benji's bike."

David put his arm around his daughter's shoulders and began walking towards the house. "Listen, we'll just leave the bike here for now and go straight up there in the Volkswagen, okay?"

Sophie stopped and looked up at him. "Actually, Dad, I think it would be better if you went alone. To be quite honest, I don't want to go up there now."

"Right. In that case, will you stay here and look after Dodie?"

Sophie nodded.

David gave her a kiss on the forehead. "Look, I'll be back as soon as I can. And don't worry. I'll speak to Jennifer and see if I can help her to get something sorted out."

"She's such a lovely person, Dad, and it's just so horrible seeing her look so sad."

"I know. Well, let's see what I can do, okay?"

As soon as he arrived at the house, David caught sight of Jennifer through the conservatory window, sitting motionless on the sofa. He got out of the car and walked round the side to the French doors, watching her at all times through the glass. Yet her eyes never followed him, even though, at one point, he moved directly through her line of sight. He entered the room and quietly sat on the low coffee-table in front of her. Her legs were tucked up under her chin, her vacant eyes puffy with too little sleep and too much crying, her cheeks streaked with tear-stains. David reached forward and stroked the back of his hand up and down her bare arm.

"Jennifer? Are you all right?"

She didn't look at him, but took in a deep sniff. "That's a pretty stupid question for Superman. Does it look as if I'm all right?"

David glanced down at his hands and began flicking at one thumb-nail with the other. She was right. It was pretty stupid.

"Alex has been having an affair with his bloody business associate for three months, David," she said, her voice choking.

"Yeah."

Jennifer turned to him. "What do you mean, 'Yeah'? Did you know about it?"

David rubbed at his forehead with his fingers. "Well, in a way.

Jasmine had an idea that something was going on. She overheard Alex talking on the telephone the day of the tennis party. But she didn't know for certain, Jennifer, and once she'd told me, I didn't really think it was for us to say anything."

Jennifer nodded and looked away. "No, I don't suppose it was. I should have realized it myself."

As she said this, she leaned her face forward on her knees and burst into tears once more. David got up from the table, and squeezing himself down between the arm of the sofa and her back, he pulled her against him and began rocking her gently, as if comforting a distraught child.

"What did I do wrong, David? Was it my fault? What did I do *wrong*?"

"Nothing. You did nothing wrong. You mustn't blame yourself for this. It's totally Alex's fault that this happened."

"But why did he do it? Why did he think he *needed* to do it?"

"I don't know. I have no idea. It's just that maybe, well, sometimes people lose sight of what they've got, and as far as Alex is concerned, I think he's probably gone fucking blind."

"I thought we were good together, David. Maybe not perfect, what with the jobs and everything, but I thought we were good! And Benji as well. I really did think that we had everything going for us . . ." Her voice grew higher as she fought back the tears once more. ". . . and now I'm talking about it all in the past tense!"

David pushed himself off the sofa and sat down again on the coffee-table, taking both her hands in his and looking straight into her face.

"That's just it, Jennifer! You mustn't speak about it in the past tense! You *do* have it all—still! Listen . . . oh, hell! . . . I can't really explain this properly, but . . . you see, I don't . . . I *don't* have it all any more, Jennifer. I can't *help* but speak in the past tense, and I can tell you, I would give anything for it to be different. You know, when Rachel died, I became, well, self-absorbed and bitter, and I suppose completely selfish, but I realize now that, even though the hurt is still profound, I not only have the obligation of the children, but also the sheer joy of them as well. You still have both Benji *and* Alex. And what's more, Benji has Alex—and he really needs him, Jennifer. He loves him. He's his *father*! You can never lose sight of that. Please don't ever lose sight of that. Okay, I realize that Alex has behaved like a complete moron, but it's worth everything, your happiness and Benji's happiness, to try and get it all back together. You've got to work it out, Jennifer. Please try—even for me, try, because I tell you, I couldn't bear it if I went home knowing that this family, *your* family, which has become so—so important to me, should have suffered the same fate as mine—without it needing to happen."

She turned away from him, sadness expressed in every inch of her face, and slowly shook her head. "But how? Where would I begin, David? I didn't know anything was *wrong!* So how would I have any idea where to begin?"

"I don't know. I just don't know. God, we men can be such complete idiots in this way. But we've got to think about doing something." He paused for a moment to gather his thoughts. "I mean, did you say anything to him last night?"

Jennifer continued to shake her head. "No, nothing. I was too angry." She sniffed out a brief laugh. "I actually slammed the door in his face, which was really idiotic, since he had his own keys. Anyway, by the time that he let himself back in again, he'd got a taxi for his . . . his woman, and Sophie and I were about ready to leave."

"Why did he come back then?"

Jennifer let out a deep sigh. "Because he *said* he wanted to talk."

"And you didn't?"

"No, of course not! He'd just cheated on me, and I . . . I . . ."

Her bottom lip started to quiver.

"Keep going! And what?"

She blurted out her response. "And I was frightened he was going to ask me for a divorce."

David squeezed her hands to try to keep her attention. "And—did he?"

"No, he just kept saying that he was sorry and that he wanted to talk."

"So—then what happened?"

"Sophie and I left."

"And that was it?"

"No." She paused. "As I was getting into the car, he ran up to me and said that he was going to come out here this afternoon so that we could talk."

"And will you do it, Jennifer? Will you please speak to him? You've got to try! Just talk about what's important—in both your lives—and make him understand it as well."

"But why the hell do you think that I should ever want to?"

"Because in everything that I've asked so far, you've never said no!"

In the silence that followed, Jennifer just stared at him, biting her lip. Then she smiled faintly at him and nodded. "Yes, you're right. I haven't, have I?"

He reached up to give the side of her face a brush with his hand. As he did so, she caught it and held it against her cheek, and he watched as a tear fell from her eye and ran off down the side of his finger.

"Why are you such a special man, David?"

"God, I'm not. I can tell you that straight."

"Oh yes, you are." She paused and looked deep into his eyes. "I wonder why it couldn't have been me that you met all those years ago in Oxford." She smiled and took his hand round to her mouth and kissed it before returning it to her cheek. "Just the wrong time, the wrong place, an ocean apart."

She reached over and kissed him gently on the cheek, then, putting her arms around his shoulders, she pulled her face close into his neck.

"But we found a bridge, didn't we, my greatest friend?" she whispered quietly into his ear. "All these years later, we found a bridge."

David pushed her away from him and held her face in his hands, smoothing away the tears from her eyes with his thumbs. "Yeah, we did. And I'll never, ever forget you for it."

They sat together in silence, their total concentration in each other only being broken by the shrill sound of the telephone ringing. Jennifer slowly let go of David's neck and, with a smile, got up and walked through to the study and picked up the telephone. David listened to her as she answered it.

"Hello? . . . yes, hello, darling . . . yes, I'm fine . . . where are you? . . . right . . . yes, he's here, do you want to speak to him? . . . Okay, just hang on a minute." She cupped her hand over the receiver. "David, that's Sophie on the telephone. I think there may be something wrong. Her voice sounds a little shaky."

David hurried to the study and took the receiver from Jennifer. "Sophie?"

"Dad, I heard the telephone ring when I was outside in the garden with Dodie, and it just cut off, so I didn't bother coming in, but it was a fax coming through."

David could hear the anxious tone in her voice. "That's all right, darling, don't worry about it. It's probably only from Archie at work."

"No, Dad, it's not!" She paused. "Dad, is a stroke serious?"

"A stroke? Yes, it can be. Why do you ask?"

Sophie's voice faltered at the other end of the line. " 'Cos Grandpa's just had one."

CHAPTER

33

David sat by himself on the jetty below the saltbox, staring out across the bay, the crumpled page held tight in his hand. He took a deep breath and, unfolding it, began reading for the third time the scrawly handwriting of his mother.

Darling David,
I find this terribly difficult to write, but I'm afraid that there is no easy way to break this devastating news to you. Just before lunch-time today, your father suffered a stroke, and I am at this very moment sitting beside his bed in Raigmore Hospital in Inverness. The doctor has just left the room, and he said that he was in reasonably stable condition, but I can see for myself that there is very little colour in his dear old face and he has tubes sticking out of him in all directions. Nevertheless, he is sleeping quite peacefully at the minute, so I am taking the opportunity of this quiet time to write you what I am sure will turn out to be a long epistle, because I think it most important that you understand every detail of what led up to this.

There had been no warning of it happening. He really seemed to have been so well. However, late in the afternoon yesterday, Duncan Caple came to see him. I thought that he was only just keeping your father up-to-date on what was happening at the distillery, but after he had left, I went into the drawing-room to find your father in a complete state of agitation.

It appears that Duncan has not been as straight as we thought, David. Your father explained it to me, but I'm afraid that I was so concerned about him that I didn't manage to take it all in.

Nevertheless, it seems that a company called Kirkpatrick has put in an offer for Glendurnich. I don't know how long Duncan has been planning this, but it must have been for some time. He had already spoken to the workers at the distillery on Friday about it, because it seems that they hold 31 per cent of the shares, and then he tried to put extreme pressure on your father to begin the transfer of his own shares as soon as possible, saying that it was for the best for both the company and the family.

I did say to your father that he should get in touch with you straight away, but he wanted to leave it until today, so that he could go into the distillery to learn the full story—not from Duncan, but from one of the workers—and thereafter, he was going to fax you.

Anyway, as far as the events of today are concerned, I can tell you word for word what happened, because he telephoned me mid-morning from his office in the most frightful tizzy. He had left at nine o'clock (he was actually meant to be reading the lesson in church, but managed to get Roger Spiers to stand in for him), and went into the distillery and spoke to your ex-sergeant, Dougie Masson. Dougie didn't know very much about the ins and outs of Kirkpatrick's plan, but he thought that it must have been brewing up for some time. He also said that, having spoken to the other workers on Friday evening, after Duncan had announced the proposal, they seemed quite excited about the idea, as they realized that they would be making some money out of the deal. However, as you can imagine, Dougie was fiercely loyal, and said that he wanted no part of it.

What really hurt your father the most (and I also think what made him realize that Duncan had been totally dishonest) was that Dougie told him that two people had left the company under what he termed suspicious circumstances. One of them was Margaret, and the other was Archie McLachlan, the young man whom your father said he'd asked to act as a contact for you in the distillery. At that point in our conversation, he said that he was going to come straight home and fax you—and that was the last time I spoke to him.

The rest of the story I was given by the police sergeant who came to the door to tell me the news. Apparently, your father had stopped somewhere on the Grantown Road to allow a young shepherd to get his flock across the road. As the boy closed the gate behind his sheep, he waved to thank him for stopping, but the car never moved forward. He went over to the car and found your father slumped over the steering wheel. Thankfully, the boy then used his wits, and seeing that there was a car phone, called both the police and an ambulance. The sergeant did say that it was very lucky that the phone actually worked in such a remote area.

So here I am at his bedside. Jane Spiers kindly gave me a lift up here, and here I shall stay. But I'm afraid the doctors have told me that the prognosis is not good, David, so you must really try to get back here as soon as possible—not only to see your father, but also to stop this appalling thing that's going on at the distillery. I pray you'll be able to rally the troops behind you and get rid of that dreadful man Duncan Caple and *all his henchmen.*

I have just read this through again, and realize that you could be feeling guilty about all this taking place. You must not. Your father was right in allowing you the time to heal. If you had been here, you would still be mouldering around in the garden, none the wiser for what was going on in the distillery, and none the wiser in yourself. This was going to happen regardless. It has been planned for ages. But now I know *that you are better, and I know that you will come back fighting—for your father.*

I must go down to the front desk now, and ask them to fax this for me.

All my love, darling, to you and to the children,

Ma.

David scrumpled the piece of paper back up into his fist and hit it three times hard against his forehead.

Yeah, but what you didn't know, Ma, was that I *did* have a bloody clue that something like this might be going on. Dammit, it was over a week ago that I sent the fax to Archie!

Jesus, the fax! That was it! Both Margaret and Archie had gone, so it would have no doubt landed right on Duncan's desk. He knew exactly what he was doing! The *bastard* knew *exactly!*

"Is it bad, David?"

He glanced round to find Sophie and Jennifer, who had returned with him to give him moral support, sitting on the steps watching him.

"Yeah, I'm afraid so. We have to go back now."

Sophie let out an anguished cry and Jennifer put her arm around her shoulders and pulled her to her. As David ran back up the steps, he bent down in passing and gave his daughter a comforting kiss on the head, then hurried off across the lawn into the house. He picked up his brief-case and, placing it on the desk, he took out his address book and dialled the number of the airline in Glasgow. There were four seats available in business class for the evening flight. He booked them, and as he put down the telephone, Jennifer and Sophie walked into the room.

"Jennifer, could you do something for me?"

"Of course."

"Would you take Sophie back to the house and get everything packed up, and then get the others there as soon as you can?"

"Sure I will. Anything else?"

David thought for a moment, trying to get his mind clear. "Yeah. If you could maybe give this friend of mine in Leesport a call. His name's Richard Eggar. I'll give you his number. Explain to him that I have to go home, and ask him if he could pick up Dodie and the car from your house this evening. Also, could you ring up Star Limos in Leesport and get them to send a car around to your house in, erm . . ." In his mind, he quickly worked back from the time of the flight departure. "God, it'll have to be in an hour's time."

"Okay."

Jennifer came across and touched his arm. "Are you all right?"

He smiled. "Silly question."

"Yeah, sorry."

She reached up and gave him a kiss on the cheek, then, putting her arm through Sophie's, they walked together back out into the garden.

David picked up the telephone again and dialled the number for Inchelvie. It rang six times before finally being answered by a very faint, quavering little voice. "Hullo, Inchelvie?"

"Effie, it's David."

"Oh, Mr. David, have you heard the awful news?"

"Yes, Effie, I have, and I'm coming straight home tonight with the children."

"Oh, thank goodness! It's so awful, Mr. David. Your poor father!"

"I'm just so sorry I wasn't there."

"Aye, but you'll be coming home now, Mr. David. That's the main thing."

"Listen, Effie, I need your help. Do you think you can do something for me?"

"Certainly. Will I be needing a piece of paper and a pen?"

"Yes, I think you might."

"If you could just hold the line a wee minute then."

He waited until he heard her voice again.

"I'm ready, Mr. David."

"Okay. I'll go slowly, but if you want to stop me at any time, just say so. First, I want you to go to the top drawer of my father's desk. In there, you will find a black book with the words 'Glendurnich Telephone Numbers' written on it. Now, it has all the home telephone numbers of those who work in the distillery in it. Have you got that so far?"

"Yes, Mr. David."

"Right, I want you to find the numbers for Dougie Masson and Archie McLachlan."

"Dougie . . . Masson and Archie . . . McLachlan. Yes, I have that."

"Well done. Now, our plane gets into Glasgow at seven-ten tomorrow morning. Ring Dougie Masson first and tell him the time of the plane, and then I want you to ask him to hire two cars from Gillespie's Garage in Grantown and to put it on my account. Have you got that?"

"Heavens, what a lot to write!"

David suddenly had a vision of the little housekeeper writing feverishly in her loopy writing.

"I know. I'm sorry, Effie, but you're the only one who can do this."

"That's all right. I have it so far."

"Next, get Dougie to ring Archie. They can arrange with each other for the cars to be picked up and I want them to meet us at Glasgow tomorrow."

"Is that it, Mr. David?"

"That's it. Do you think you have that all?"

Effie went back through the list without fault.

"Well done. Just one final thing. I'm going to get Archie to bring the children straight back to Inchelvie, so they should be with you about mid-day. You will be there?"

"Yes, of course."

"Thank you so much, Effie. I'll see you sometime tomorrow, then."

"Very good, Mr. David."

He put down the telephone and let out a deep sigh, then turned to start packing up his belongings in the little house that had come to mean so much to him.

The limousine had already arrived at Barker Lane by the time he got there, and he felt quite thankful to see that it was Dan himself who was going to be driving them. The children were milling around, all looking a little bewildered by what was happening. As he opened the door of the car, Dodie jumped out to welcome Benji and Charlie, who came rushing forward to meet David.

"Do you really have to go, David?" Benji asked in a soulful voice.

"Yes, I'm afraid so, Benji. Now, come on, you two can give Dan a hand to get my things into the car."

As the two boys began to pull his suitcases out of the back seat, David walked over to the front door just as Jasmine and Jennifer came out.

"You got hold of Richard all right, then?"

"Yup," Jennifer said, handing a child's haversack to Dan. "Everything's arranged."

David nodded sadly. "Right. Well, I really think that we should just get straight off."

"Benji and I are coming too," Jennifer said quietly.

He looked at her, startled. "Are you sure?"

"Yes."

David nodded. He bent down and scooped up Dodie, then walked over and handed her to Jasmine. "Jasmine, could you look after Dodie until this evening?"

"Of course." She sighed deeply. "I was so sorry to hear about your father, David. I'll pray mighty strong for him. But I have to say I'm also real sad 'bout you all goin'."

David moved towards her and wrapped his arms around her ample shoulders, giving her a tight hug.

"Goodbye, my dear friend, and thank you for all you've done—for me and for my children."

"I've done nothin' special."

"Oh yes, you have. More than you can ever imagine. In a way, I feel I owe you my life." He felt himself begin to choke up, and cleared his throat. "And look after Jennifer, won't you? You realize that she now knows all about Alex."

Jasmine nodded. "Mm-mm. She told me."

"Things will work out. I know they will."

Jasmine grinned at him. "Yeah, sure they will—if you've had a part to play in it."

David turned towards the limousine. "All right, everybody in the car!"

The children clambered in, Benji and Charlie letting out a loud exclamation of glee as they simultaneously discovered the television and the drinks icebox. David stood aside to allow Jennifer to get in before him. At that moment there was a sound of crunching gravel at the top of the drive, and a dark blue Mercedes came speeding down towards the house. Jennifer groaned audibly, one foot in the car, and watched it come to a halt beside them.

Alex opened the door and got out, flicking off his sun-glasses and sliding them into the top pocket of his shirt. Benji, on seeing who it was, let out a yell of joy, and pushing his way past Jennifer, ran over and threw his arms around his father's waist.

"Hi, Dad! We didn't know you were coming today, did we, Mom?"

Jennifer smiled at him and shook her head. Alex gave his son a kiss on the top of the head, then looked up at his wife.

"Where are you going?" He directed his question to her alone.

"To the airport. David is returning to Scotland."

"And you're going too?" There was a hint of uncertainty in his voice.

"To see them off, yes." She looked at David and smiled. "David, I don't think that you have had the pleasure yet of meeting my husband, Alex, have you?"

David walked over to Alex and held out his hand. "How do you do, Alex."

Alex slowly took hold of the offered hand and shook it once. "Hi."

"I really can't tell you how much I've enjoyed working here. It's the most wonderful place. You must be very proud of it."

Alex looked at him and then at Jennifer.

"In fact, you must be very proud of everything you've got. I can say quite categorically that I have never before worked for such a wonderful family. So thank you."

Alex smiled bemusedly in acknowledgement of the remark, then looked at Jennifer. "When will you be back?"

"This evening."

Alex nodded. "Great. I'll see you then."

She climbed into the car, and Benji dived his way in after her, shouting out a loud farewell to his father. David glanced over at Alex, and then at Jasmine, blowing her a final kiss before getting into the car himself.

There was little said on the way to the airport, primarily because Charlie and Benji spent most of the journey trying to get the television to work, the reception being so intermittent that they had to press their ears to the speaker in order to be able to hear anything at all. Consequently, whenever anybody tried to talk, they were met by a barrage of hushing noises. Jennifer did ask for further details about what had happened in Scotland, but rather than explain, David simply handed her his mother's now-battered fax and let her read it for herself.

They arrived at the airport exactly two hours before the flight was due to depart. Dan parked directly outside the terminal and found a luggage trolley before taking his leave of them, explaining in his deep Bronx growl to "Mr. Costawfin" that it would be better if he stayed with the car in case he was moved on.

They were lucky in finding a queue for the check-in desk that wasn't too long, and having rid themselves of their suitcases, made their way across the enormous hall to the Departures gate, Benji and

Charlie finding enough time on the way to have their photograph taken together in a booth.

Sophie was the first to say goodbye to Jennifer, holding on to her as if her life depended on it, and thanking her over and over again for her time in Manhattan. Then Harriet gave her a kiss, and pulled out from the depths of her haversack a scrumpled-up drawing that she had discovered on the way there, and asked Jennifer if she would give it to Jasmine. Charlie's farewell was more formal, a solid handshake which nearly took Jennifer's arm out of her socket, before he returned to giggle hopelessly with Benji over one particular photograph in which they both had their tongues sticking out.

"It's just me, then," David said, standing in front of Jennifer.

"Yeah, it's just you." She folded her arms and glanced around the huge hall, not really looking at very much in particular. "I'm so sorry that you have to go back like this, David. I really hope your father will be all right."

David smiled at her and nodded.

"Will you write or call?" she asked. "I mean, just to keep in touch?"

He looked down at his feet. "I don't know. Maybe it wouldn't be a very good idea for a while, you know, at least until things are settled down with Alex. Maybe next summer you both could bring Benji over for a visit . . ."

He hesitated, noticing that Jennifer had looked round at him, a pleading look in her eyes.

"Well, just one call," she said, "so that I know that you all got back safely. That would be all right, wouldn't it?"

David nodded. "Of course."

Jennifer took in a deep breath and shook her head. "I really feel shell-shocked! What the hell is *happening*? Everything in my life seems to have gone completely upside down in the past twenty-four hours." Her eyes suddenly brimmed with tears, and she walked towards him and put her arms around his neck and pulled herself close in against him.

"David, I can't accept that I'll never see you again," she whispered into his ear. "I can't believe that you won't be just there—in my garden—in my life, ever again."

"What? Like a gnome?"

Jennifer laughed against his shoulder and he felt her tears wet on his neck.

"Yeah, Supergnome." Her voice choked. "Super, Supergnome! Oh, David, I just don't know how we're all going to cope without you!"

David pushed her gently away from him. "You will." He kissed her on both cheeks. "I know you will."

He smiled and stood away from her, then turned to his children. "Right, you lot, time to make a move."

Benji heard the words, and for the first time the realization of what was happening hit him. He ran up to David and held tight to his arm without speaking. David tilted back the boy's head to look at him.

"Listen, Benji, I want to see you in ten years' time either as lead guitarist for the most famous band in the world, or playing tennis on the Centre Court at Wimbledon; otherwise I'll think all my expert tuition has gone to waste. Okay?"

Benji nodded.

"Good boy. And you never know—we might get you and Charlie together sometime during the holidays."

Benji's expression turned to one of excitement, and turning to look at Charlie, he gave him a conniving grin. David reached down and gave him a pat on his backside that guided him towards Jennifer. "Now, you look after your mother, and tell her not to work so hard!"

He glanced up at Jennifer and gave her a wink, then taking hold of Harriet's hand, he walked with his family through the automatic doors, turning just as they were shutting behind him, to catch his final, fleeting glimpse of the two people who had helped, more than any, to give him back his life.

CHAPTER 34

"Oh, it's raining, Dad," Charlie said in a depressed voice, his face pressed to the glass of the window, as the plane broke through the clouds to begin its final approach into Glasgow.

David stopped writing and leaned forward in his seat to look out the window past his son. "Yeah, well, it might not be at Inchelvie. It looks quite clear over there to the north."

"But it never rained in Leesport."

David smiled and reached out and ruffled his son's hair, then, flipping over the cover of his writing-pad, he slapped his hand down on it in a gesture of completion. That was it. It had taken him the whole flight to work it out, but that was it. He had every piece of the jigsaw now in place, every one of those seemingly unconnected events linked perfectly together, running in sequence from the time that he had been asked to go out to America by Duncan right up to the present day.

There was no doubt now that it had all been a set-up, all meticulously planned to take full advantage of both his father's age and his own inability to cope with the situation. In retrospect, maybe they had left themselves wide open for such a thing to happen, either through complacency or inefficiency, but nevertheless, the way Duncan and Kirkpatrick's had acted was, quite simply, heinous. But he did know only too well that that was how big business was conducted, slithering its way just above the threshold of legality, and giving scant consideration either to personal damage or to the consequences resulting. And this was now all too bloody apparent, with his father lying so critically ill in hospital.

The plane thumped down onto the tarmac, and the engines screamed violently as the pilot engaged reverse thrust. Harriet, who was sitting in the aisle seat next to him, instinctively reached out and grabbed hold of his hand. He held on to hers tight, smiling to himself as he remembered the last time he had done just that with the little Glaswegian tyke on his way across to America. God, so long ago. But now he was back. He gritted his teeth as he thought about his prepared show-down with Duncan. Yeah, now he was truly *back*, in every bloody sense of the word!

Dougie and Archie were there waiting for them at the Arrivals hall barrier, Dougie dressed somewhat uncharacteristically in a dark suit that accentuated every muscle in his squat frame, and this, coupled with the expression of hooded seriousness on his face, made him look like a highly experienced Russian bodyguard. David smiled to himself, realizing that it was probably exactly what he was going to need that day.

"Hi, Dougie," he said, stretching out his hand.

"Hullo, Mr. David." He took a firm grip on David's hand. "Did you have a good flight?"

"Yes, thanks. No problem at all." He turned to Archie. "Hello, Archie."

The young man gave him a self-conscious smile and a brief nod of his head. "Dougie and I were just saying how sorry we were to hear about your father, sir."

"I know, Archie. It's very sad."

"Aye, it's more than that," Dougie cut in, flicking his head to the side in a knowing gesture. "I ken fine well what brought it on. It's just bloody criminal." He touched his finger to his mouth, realizing that he had just sworn in front of the children. "Sorry, sir."

David smiled and shook his head. "No, you're right." He took over control of the luggage trolley from Charlie. "So, come on. Let's go and sort it out."

They walked out of the terminal building and splashed their way across the rain-soaked road to the car-park. As they approached the cars, David turned to the younger man.

"Now, Archie, I want you to take the children straight back to Inchelvie, and make sure that you see Effie, the housekeeper, before you leave, okay?"

"Right, sir."

"Then, after that, go straight to the distillery. I want you there when we meet with Mr. Caple, but you must *not* park in the office car-park, understood? I don't want to risk you being seen, otherwise it might spoil the element of surprise. Go round to the loading bay at the back of the maturation warehouses and park over in the corner next to where the empty barrels are stored."

The young man nodded.

"Right. Now we'll go in convoy as far as Aviemore, and there we'll split, because Dougie and I are going to head straight up to Inverness to see my father. Okay . . ." David looked at his watch. ". . . so it's a quarter to eight now. We should be in Inverness by about half past eleven, if those bloody unmarked police cars aren't on the A-Nine. I reckon we'll be back at the distillery by half past one, so make sure that you are there by then, and keep an eye out for us coming down the road. Is that all clear?"

"Yes, sir."

"Okay, then, let's make a move."

He turned to Sophie, Charlie and Harriet, who had been standing silently beside him, and bent down and gave each a kiss.

"Now, you lot, go with Archie, and I'll see you this evening at Inchelvie."

"Will you tell Grandpa to get better soon, Dad?" Charlie said in a solemn voice. "Because he *did* say that he would teach me how to cast a salmon rod these holidays."

"Yeah, I will," David replied as lightly as he could.

Archie opened the back door of the car and Charlie and Harriet clambered in. Sophie held back for a moment, then took hold of her father's arm and led him away to a safe distance from the car.

"Dad, do you think we could go back to The Beeches tomorrow? I think we all need to go home."

David smiled at her, and putting his arms around her, he gave her a long hug.

"You're absolutely right, darling. We all *do* need to go home—back to where Mummy is."

He gave her a kiss on the forehead, then walked back to the car and opened the front passenger door for her. "Drive carefully, Archie," he said, looking into the car. "You've got a particularly valuable cargo on board."

The journey to Inverness took a little longer than anticipated, even though the weather, as he had predicted, improved as they headed north. The single-carriageway sections of the road were heavy with lorries, each having accumulated a tailback of cars that were boxed so tightly together that it made overtaking almost impossible. Although Dougie was quite adept at driving a half-mile stretch on the wrong side of the road to get clear of the hold-ups, Archie seemed to have taken David's last remark to heart, driving with such care and attention that Dougie had to pull over into a lay-by on two separate occasions to allow his car to catch up, then watch in seething frustration as a recently overtaken lorry and its parasitical line of cars trundled slowly past.

However, once they passed Aviemore, the traffic thinned out, and having seen Archie and the children safely on their way to Inchelvie, Dougie put his foot down, eventually pulling the car to a squealing halt at the main doors of Raigmore Hospital just before mid-day.

David asked Dougie to wait in the car-park, then walked in through the main doors of the hospital and approached the main desk. An elderly lady, whose gentle smile made it look as if she'd been specifically bred for voluntary services, looked up from where she had been writing on a shorthand pad.

"*Good* morning, can I help you?"

"Yes. I wonder if you could guide me in the right direction. I want to find Lord Inchelvie's room."

David watched as she wrote down his father's name on her pad. "And may I ask who you might be, sir?"

"Yeah, I'm Mr. Corstorphine, his son."

"Oh, I see. Right," she said, getting up immediately from her chair. "If you could just give me a moment while I get someone else to look after the desk, and then I'll take you to his room myself."

She turned and went into the office behind her. David watched through the window as she spoke to a colleague who was sitting having a cup of tea. The woman cast a glance at him through the window, then got up from her chair.

"Mr. Corstorphine," the lady said, as they both came out of the office. "If you would like to follow me, I'll take you up there now."

They walked over to the lift and took it to the sixth floor. David followed her along the spotless corridor, both standing aside to allow an old lady in a pink winceyette nightie to push her drip-stand slowly past them, muttering incoherently to herself as she went. At the end of the corridor, they entered a long ward, and David's guide stopped outside a door next to the nurses' desk.

"You'll find Lord Inchelvie in here, sir. I think Lady Inchelvie should be there as well."

David thanked her and turned to watch her leave the ward. As he put his hand out to push down the handle of the door, it opened and Roger Spiers appeared. On seeing David, he held his finger to his mouth and closed the door quietly behind him.

"David!" the old doctor said, holding out his hand. "How nice to see you! Well done, you getting back so quickly."

David shook his hand. "How is he, Roger?"

Dr. Spiers flicked his head to the side. "Not that good, I'm afraid. Nevertheless, he's pretty comfortable and I know for a fact that he's not in any pain, but, well . . ." He smiled warmly at him. ". . . like all of us of that generation, the old engine begins to get a little weary, and it becomes increasingly difficult to keep it from stalling." He looked round at the door. "Your mother's in there. She's been absolutely marvellous. Hasn't left his bedside since she got here"—he turned back to David—"so I know she'll be delighted to see you home, my boy." He gave his arm a reassuring squeeze, then shambled his way off down the ward. Taking a deep breath, David gently pushed down the handle and put his head round the door.

The small room was mottled with light that bled its way through the gaps in the closed blinds and a thin ray caught the side of his father's cheek as he lay motionless on the bed, accentuating the pallor of his once ruddy complexion. A network of tubes ran upwards from his body to the plastic drip-bottles that hung above the bed. His eyes were closed and his mouth open, but what little sound he was emitting was drowned out by the constant bleeping of the heart-monitoring equipment which flickered out its glowing light into the semi-darkness of the room.

As David watched, his mother stood up from where she sat knitting beside his father, and gently pressed his chin upwards, closing his mouth. Then, stroking her hand over his forehead, she pushed away a strand of hair that had by some miracle displaced itself, and giving her husband a smile that would never be acknowledged, she turned to sit down again, executing a double take when she saw David at the door.

"Oh, my darling, well done!" she said in a whisper, dropping her knitting onto the chair and coming over towards him. As David walked into the room, he noticed immediately the look of sheer fatigue and sorrow in his mother's eyes as she approached. He took her in his arms and held her tight.

"Let me have a look at you!" she continued to whisper, pushing herself away from him, yet holding firmly on to his arms. "You look so well! You're brown!"

David smiled at her and looked over to his father. "I'm so very sorry that I wasn't here, Ma. I really am so sorry."

His mother turned to follow his gaze. "My darling, it is *not* your fault that this has happened, and you must not even begin to think of reproaching yourself for it. I mean it. That was exactly why I made a point of explaining that in my fax. The doctor did say that it could have happened at any time." She turned back to him and reached up and kissed him on the cheek. "The main thing is that you're here."

David made no comment, thinking it neither the time nor the place to tell her that he had worked out what had been going on at the distillery. Instead, he walked past her and went over to stand by his father, reaching down and gently taking hold of his hand, taking care not to knock out the tubes that were protruding from his wrist.

"I've just had a word with Roger Spiers outside in the corridor. He says things aren't looking too good."

His mother walked around to the other side of the bed and stood looking down at her husband. "No, I'm afraid not. There was a marked deterioration overnight. They very kindly allowed me to stay in the next-door room, and they called me at about two o'clock this morning, because they were so worried about him." She let out a long sigh. "But he seemed to rally again."

David glanced over at his mother, and caught on her face an expression of unequivocal love as she looked down at her husband. "He's always been a fighter, David. He's very weak, but I have a suspicion that he's been holding out until . . . you got home."

David nodded and leaned over and stroked his father's face, feeling a lump tighten in his throat and his eyes begin to smart with tears. "Well, I'm back now. I hope you can hear, Pa, because I'm back now, and everything, I promise you, is going to be just fine."

He bent forward and gave the wrinkled forehead a kiss, wincing at the coldness of his father's skin against his lips. He stood up and looked over to his mother. "Listen, I'm going to go to the distillery right now. I want to get this whole thing cleared up and finished with today. But I'll be back later, once I've been to Inchelvie to see the children. Do you want anything from the house?"

His mother smiled at him. "No, I've got everything I need here."

They both moved to the bottom of the bed, and David gave his mother a hug and a kiss before walking over to the door. He turned to give his father a last look, then, on impulse, returned to the bed and gave the dear, brave old man another kiss.

"We'll get this sorted out. We really will," he said, addressing no one in particular, but hoping that both occupants of the room could take comfort from his words. He opened the door and walked out, closing it gently behind him.

They drove in silence back down the A9, Dougie intent on getting back to the distillery as fast as possible, while David was quite happy to use the time to look through his notes, trying to get all his facts as clear as possible in his mind. As Dougie drove across the bridge over the Spey and turned hard left down the Glendurnich Distillery road, David glanced at his watch. It was half past one. He took in a deep breath. This was it. The show-down.

They descended the hill and turned the corner above the maturation warehouses. Archie was there, his car tucked away between two rows of barrels at the most northerly point of the concrete apron. Dougie flashed his lights, Archie responded, and his car immediately shot out and came round the side of the sheds, pulling in behind their car as they levelled out at the bottom of the hill and following them onto the car-park.

As soon as Dougie had stopped, David jumped out and looked around to make sure that Duncan's BMW was there. It was. He turned round to Dougie and Archie, who had come to stand behind him.

"Right. Archie, has Dougie explained what's been happening here?"

"Yes, he has, sir," Archie replied seriously.

"Good. Well, as soon as things are back to normal here, I just want you to know that you are to be reinstated at Glendurnich. I take it that you don't have another job yet?"

"No, I don't!" Archie exclaimed, his eyes wide with delight.

"Right. That's settled then. Now, I want you two to be present in the boardroom, just in case things get a little out of hand, okay?"

They nodded briefly, and David suddenly realized that both were dressed very much smarter than he was, he still being in the clothes that he had worn when he left Leesport. He felt a wry smile come over his face. What the hell! Better wearing old clothes for this kind of job. Blood would no doubt wash out much better from denim.

"Right. Let's go."

As they walked across the car-park, David turned to see that Dougie and Archie were making up a V-formation behind him. He smiled to himself. Perfect. Just like the Westerns. Everyone had his gun hand clear for the show-down.

They each took a separate door, bursting into the reception area at the same time, making the woman at the desk start back in surprise. David walked over and leaned both hands on the desk, and the woman, her mouth pursed in displeasure at their unmannerly entrance, pushed back her chair to distance herself from the menacing figure that stood in front of her.

"Excuse me, but who on *earth* do you think—?"

"Just be quiet and listen," David said, holding up his hand. "I want you to get hold of Duncan Caple and both the marketing and financial directors, and tell them to meet me in the boardroom *right* now."

The woman looked at him, her right eye twitching with both fear and indignation.

"Don't be absurd! I—"

"I also want you to get in contact with Margaret, and tell her to get herself back here right now. Then, as soon as you have done that, I want you to vacate this desk. Is that understood?" He flashed her a brittle smile and turned and walked towards the boardroom, followed by Dougie and Archie.

"Excuse me!" Doreen called out after David, her voice shaking with anger. "But I have no idea who you are!"

David turned and gave Archie a wink, and as he and Dougie continued on to the boardroom, Archie broke formation and walked back to the desk. He leaned across, his face two feet away from the receptionist, relishing this moment of glory in his young life as he emulated every movement of his boss.

"You have just addressed Mr. David Corstorphine, son of Lord Inchelvie and the principal shareholder of Glendurnich Distilleries Limited. Now, if I were you, I'd get hold of Mr. Caple, Mr. Barker and Mr. Archibald right now, and tell them that they're wanted in the boardroom immediately. And then call Margaret. You'll find her number in the Glendurnich telephone book—probably at the top of the list."

Doreen looked at Archie, her former expression of self-importance now replaced with one of utter fear.

"What shall I say to her?" she asked in a thin, trembling voice.

Archie pushed himself away from the desk and turned to walk over to the boardroom. "Just tell her that Mr. David's back—for good!"

The young man took his time getting to the boardroom door, eager to hear Doreen talk with Mr. Caple on the telephone. In a faltering voice, she made her announcement, then, almost immediately, repeated it, and Archie imagined with almost sadistic glee the horror on Duncan Caple's face as he learned of David's presence in the building. Then, clenching his fist, he punched at the air, expelling through gritted teeth a silent Yesss before opening the door and walking into the boardroom.

When Duncan Caple entered two minutes later, accompanied by Giles Barker and Keith Archibald, David was standing looking out the window, his hands clasped behind him.

"David!" Duncan exclaimed, as he walked across the room towards David. "How nice to see you back. I was so sorry to hear about your fath——"

David turned and pointed to the table. "Sit down, all of you."

Duncan stopped in his tracks and held up his hands, a sardonic smile on his face. "Of course. So how did things go in Ameri——?"

"Just sit *down,* Duncan!" David hissed through gritted teeth, as he turned to face the window once more.

The managing director shrugged, then pulled out a chair and sat, the other two directors having already taken heed of David's request the first time round. Duncan crossed his arms nonchalantly, then suddenly became aware of both Dougie and Archie, who were leaning against the back wall of the boardroom.

"So what have we got here?" Duncan asked, casting a glance at them over his shoulder. "The heavy brigade? Are you going to get them to beat me up, David?"

David turned. "No, Duncan. They're actually here to stop me from beating you up."

Duncan reached forward and brought his hands hard down on the table. "Oh, *come on*! We can be a bit more mature about this, can't we? You know, it's quite easily explained—"

David held up his hand to stop him. "No . . . no, let me see if *I* can explain what's happened. You just sit there and listen for a change, and if I do happen to go wrong at all, *then* you can put me right."

He walked slowly around the table, glaring at the three as he went. They followed him with their eyes, the two directors visibly blanching as they waited for him to begin. David breathed deeply, trying to steady his emotions, and looking at Duncan's thin aquiline nose, he found himself wondering what it would look like pushed flat against his face. He stopped and leaned forward on the table.

"So how much were you going to get paid, Duncan?"

For the first time, Duncan's smile slid from his face. "I don't think that really—"

"Because it must have been a hell of a lot to make it worthwhile for you to do what you've just done."

He stared with such hatred at Duncan that the man began to rub his hands nervously together between his knees. David pushed himself off the table and walked over to the window.

"I don't know the time-scale on this, but I'm not really bothered. What I do know is that you have . . . *used* my father and myself to your own advantage, with the result that he is now lying near death in hospital." He turned and looked at Duncan. "And I want you to get something clear from the outset—and I'm really addressing all of you now—and that is whatever has happened or *will* happen to my father will be on your consciences for the rest of your lives. Maybe, at this very minute, it will mean very little to you, because I think that you're too pig-ignorant to understand that . . . but Christ, I tell you, it'll eventually catch up with you!"

David surveyed them all in silence. They sat in a row, Keith Archibald now biting at a finger-nail, as they waited for him to continue. David caught Dougie's eye, and his ex-sergeant gave him a wink and a nod of his head in encouragement.

"Right!" David said, turning back to the window. "So let's see how close I can get to your little plan." He paused. "In May, against both my will and my father's, you pulled me back to work, under the pretext that sales figures had slumped in the States. Number-one point. They had not, but you knew pretty well that the only person who might check up would be Robert McLeod, and you managed to slide him away from the company and replace him by—?"

He looked at the two directors, pointing his finger at each one. Keith Archibald slowly raised his hand.

"Right . . . you. Good. So Duncan, you decide to appoint a new distributor in the States. Deakin Distribution, a company run by a Mr. Charles Deakin, who just happens to have recently sold his company to a UK corporation called Kirkpatrick Holdings Public Limited Company." For effect, he spelled out the full name in short, pronounced bursts. "So . . . I am sent over there, and because you have already given Deakin a full briefing on my own . . . personal loss and state of mind, he is able to play heavily on that, to such an extent that he suddenly, quite out of the blue, is able to stress the importance of my having a wife."

He shook his head as he began to take in fully the ruthlessness of Duncan's actions.

"And bang! It works! I fly out of the office, in a worse state than ever before." He took in a deep breath before continuing.

"So that's me out of the way. Deakin calls you and confirms all has gone according to plan. You then contact my father and tell him that you now need a marketing director, because I'm not in a fit state to fulfil my job." He pointed to Giles Barker. "And you were brought in—from Kirkpatrick's, I presume?"

The three directors were by now looking extremely uneasy.

"I take it from your lack of interjections that I'm not doing badly so far."

Duncan shook his head, and blowing out an impatient breath, linked his hands behind his head.

"That only left you with my father to deal with. However, you managed to get him out of the way pretty easily by saying that there was no need for him to come into the distillery any more, and that you would keep him in touch by visiting him at home." He turned and stared directly at the managing director. "How very thoughtful of you, Duncan." He began pacing up and down the boardroom.

"Now, you have the full run of the distillery to yourself." He held up a finger and waggled it in the air. "Ah, but what about Margaret? She commands the switchboard. How can you begin to receive endless telephone calls from Kirkpatrick's without raising her suspicions? Easy! Get rid of her! So out she goes."

He paused for a moment, as he tried to get the next point into his mind.

"Okay, so what about this take-over? What made you think that you could buy out a company that was in the hands of private shareholding? Ah, the workers' stock-purchase plan. You found out that they now owned thirty-one per cent of the shares. Not enough to swing an outright purchase, but nevertheless, a good-enough thumbscrew when the time was right . . ." David turned and thumped his hands down onto the table. ". . . to approach my father!"

David took a deep breath.

"So what were you going to say to him? 'Listen, old boy, you're getting on a bit, and your son has lost all interest in the company and won't want anything to do with it, seeing that he's just had a nervous breakdown in the States. Much better that you realize your capital from the company now—anyway, thirty-one per cent of the shares are already owned by the workers, and they're all for making a bit of money out of the deal, which I'm sure you will agree is owed to them after *so* many years of faithful service. So why not *do* the right thing, *old boy*'!"

David spat out the last words in sheer fury at the three men who sat in front of him. He turned away and stood rubbing at his forehead with the tips of his fingers, his eyes tightly shut.

"But then, I found out about Kirkpatrick's, didn't I? And I began putting two and two together, even though my evidence was somewhat sketchy. So I faxed Archie through Margaret, but of course, Margaret wasn't there, so your . . . tame woman out there"—he pointed with a thumb over his shoulder towards the door—"brought the fax directly to you. And that not only spelt the end of Archie's involvement with the company, but also made you realize that I had an inkling of what you were planning."

He turned back and looked directly at Duncan. "But what gets me is that you continued. I can't believe that—unless you were being pushed like hell by John Davenport in London."

Duncan made no move to comment, and David shook his head. "Christ, I *am* doing well, aren't I? So you went on. You told the workforce on Friday, and then, on Saturday afternoon, you began to put the pressure on my father . . . and the consequences of *that* we all know too well."

Giles Barker broke the silence that followed by clearing his throat.

"So what do we do now?" David asked. "You tell me, Duncan: What do you think we're going to do now?"

Duncan pushed himself forward in his chair and linked his hands together, placing them in front of his chin. "Well, we could still go ahead with it. It would still be hugely profitable for your family. If you would just, for one moment, consider—"

David turned, a look of sheer horror on his face.

"*What?* I don't believe you said that! God, you are so *fucking* thick-skinned! Oh, no, Duncan, this is as far as it goes. Not only do I hold thirty-four point five percent of the Glendurnich shareholding, but under the circumstances that surround my father at present, I stand here in proxy of his thirty-four point five per cent shareholding as well! That is sixty-nine per cent, Duncan, just in case your mental arithmetic is not as sharp as your underhandedness. There is no way that you can swing this deal *now!* No, I think you have totally misunderstood my question. What I'm really saying is: What are *you* lot going to do now?"

Duncan was silent. He rubbed at his chin and glanced across to his fellow directors, who in turn looked back at him.

"I don't know," he said eventually. "What do *you* want us to do?"

David pulled out a chair and sat down opposite them, fixing each with a penetrating stare.

"Well, as far as I'm concerned, you have only one option, and that is to leave today, and never, ever set foot in Glendurnich again. But if you feel that you want to go against that option, then I'll tell you exactly what I'll do. Tomorrow morning, first thing, I shall call the Scottish correspondent of the *Financial Times* and the industrial editors of both *The Scotsman* and *The Herald,* and I shall issue them with a news release explaining exactly what has happened at Glendurnich. You'll agree with me when I say that I know the story well enough. And when it is printed, I doubt that you three will ever get a job again in this country." He leaned back in his chair. "I certainly don't think John Davenport will want to know you. He would no doubt put his damage-limitation exercise into overdrive and distance Kirkpatrick's as far as possible from your escapades up here. You'd take the brunt, I'm afraid."

He glanced over to Dougie, who was looking down at his feet, slowly nodding his head. There was a soft scraping on the carpet as Giles Barker and Keith Archibald pushed back their chairs and made their way over to the door. David turned and watched as they silently left the room, then stared over at Duncan, who eyed him with disdain, as if determined to make his final stand of dominance in the company. At that point, there was a knock at the boardroom door.

"Come in!" David called out.

Margaret put her head around the door, and he saw immediately that there were tears in her eyes.

"Yes, Margaret?" he asked in a concerned voice.

"Mr. David. I'm so sorry. Your mother has just been on the telephone." Her voice choked. "I'm afraid that your father died a quarter of an hour ago."

David looked at her and then over at Duncan.

"You fucking bastard!"

The fuse blew in his head and, fuelled by the resultant overload of anger and hatred, he moved so fast around the table that Duncan had no time to get out of his chair. David pulled back his fist as he approached him, and the man cowered away, clamping his hands to his head to protect himself from the blow. He swung with all his force at the side of Duncan's head, but just as he was expecting to feel the satisfying crunch of hard knuckle against soft cheek-bone, his hand was caught inches short of its target in Dougie's rock-hard palm.

"No, Davie!"

David turned to look through his blurred vision into Dougie's face.

"It would'na help, laddie. It just would'na help."

David turned away, and pulling his hands across his head, he walked to the far end of the boardroom and let out an anguished cry.

"Oh, no, Pa! Oh, no, no, no!"

He looked up at the painting that hung above the fireplace and stood, for a time indeterminable, staring into the kind, gentle face of his father. His eyes watched him, his smile enveloped him, and it slowly began to dawn on him that his mother had been right. The old man had picked his time. He had done all that he could, and he had clung on long enough to make sure that his son was there to carry on.

He turned. There was no one in the boardroom. The chairs were left pushed away from the table. It was all over. Glendurnich was unequivocally back in the hands of the Inchelvie family.

CHAPTER

35

As the haunting strains of "The Dark Island," played by a piper from the First Battalion, The Highlanders, skirled distantly from the hill above Dalnachoil, George, Fourth Lord of Inchelvie, was silently laid to rest in the grave next to his daughter-in-law. Not a sound was heard from the village, not a car driven through, as every one of the inhabitants of Dalnachoil, along with all the employees of Glendurnich Distilleries Ltd., were present at the funeral, packed into every available space in the tiny churchyard.

As the minister finished reading out the final dedication, David dropped the cord into the grave and looked up from where he stood at its foot to give the signal to the other bearers to stand down. With a long bow of his head, he turned and walked back to his mother's side, taking her gloved hand in his and giving it a reassuring squeeze. Sophie, who had been standing behind, holding hard to Charlie and Harriet, stepped forward, so that the Inchelvie household stood in line in front of the grave. Then, each giving a final bow of his head, they turned and made their way through the gravestones towards the path that led down to the gate.

When he reached the path, David stopped and looked over at his mother. "It's better to do it now," he said quietly. "Much better here than back at Inchelvie."

His mother looked round at the gathering and nodded. "Yes, you're probably right. What about the locals? Do you mind them hearing?"

David shook his head. "They've as much a right to hear what I'm going to say as any." He smiled at his mother. "It'll give them something to talk about at any rate."

He stepped away from her and walked back towards the grave. Everyone was looking at him. "If you could all just bear with me for a minute!" he called out at the top of his voice.

The grave-diggers, who were readying themselves to finish off their task, pushed their spades back into the soil and returned to lean their backs against the churchyard wall. David waited until the querying whispers had died down before he started.

"I had planned to say this to you all back at Inchelvie after the service, and I hope therefore you don't think it improper of me speaking to you here, especially in the context of what has just taken place. Nevertheless, both my mother and I think it apt that this should be said before the final curtain has been brought down on my father's life, because we both are certain that he would have wanted to hear what I am about to say."

He cleared his throat.

"I know that many of you here are not employees of Glendurnich, and even though I am specifically addressing them, I think it only right that everyone knows and understands the implications of what I am going to say and how important it is for the future of our community."

He paused as a gust of wind blew through the churchyard, rustling the leaves on the trees.

"You know, I consider myself incredibly fortunate to live up here in Scotland. We have a way of life, or what they now term 'a quality of life,' which is the envy of many in other parts of this country. But things are not always what they seem, as we all well know. We are a remote nation, especially up here in the north, but that remoteness only helps to strengthen the bond of belonging within our communities. We all look after each other—and we all respect each other, and this could be no more apparent than it is right now, with you all being present here—and I thank you for that from the bottom of my heart, not only for the support you have given my family today, but also for the care and understanding that you have shown towards myself over the past months.

"However, the consequences of remoteness can be fickle. Whereas it can bring us together, it can as easily split us apart, and this is nowadays all too dependent on what employment is available. We do what we can up here, we do with what's available, otherwise there is no option but to pack up and move into the cities where there are more jobs. And that is what erodes our communities. So, it is therefore essential that we protect for ourselves every available source of established employment—and Glendurnich is no exception."

David stopped for a moment and thrust his hands into the pockets of his kilt jacket.

"Last Friday, the employees of Glendurnich were called to a meeting to be briefed on the proposed buy-out of the company by a London-based corporate called Kirkpatrick Holdings Public Limited Company. The reason for this was that the employees, in total, own thirty-one per cent of the shares of Glendurnich, as the result of a stock-purchase plan set up by my father twenty-five years ago. Now I know that, to many of you, the idea of being able to cash in on this might seem extremely attractive, but what I want to put to you is that it could be a very short-lived bonus.

"What you must understand is that Glendurnich is almost unique up here. It is entirely independent, and at present it holds a significant share of the malt-whisky market world-wide. For over one hundred years now, we have never stopped producing whisky. Yet this industry is cyclical, which means that we do have periods of feast and famine, and I can tell you that I have seen what happens to small corporate-owned whisky companies in times of famine. They become a statistic. They become a minus figure on the wrong side of the balance sheet, and because they are only of minor importance to the actual company that owns them, they get closed down. Maybe not for ever—maybe just for a year or two, until demand rises again—but nevertheless they get closed down. And everyone loses his job.

"No one has ever lost his job at Glendurnich through redundancy, and, by rejecting the offer from Kirkpatrick's, I am going to make damned sure that it never will happen. Now, I'm not doing this for any selfish reason, or just for the good of my family, but for you, all of you being the extended family at Glendurnich. Your welfare is as important to me"—he turned and gestured with his hand towards his mother and his three children standing on the path—"as that of my own family, and that is why I could never live with myself if, say in five or ten years' time, I witnessed the closing down of the distillery and the subsequent loss of your jobs."

He paused and looked around the faces, trying to judge from their expression whether he had said enough to convince them.

"Now, I'm not going to say anything further at the moment, and I am certainly not going to ask you for your opinion on the matter right now, because it is neither the time nor place. Nevertheless, for those of you who would like to discuss this further, I am setting up a committee at Glendurnich, and I think it appropriate that that committee should be a true representation of the distillery as a whole. It will therefore consist of myself, Dougie Masson and Archie McLachlan, representing the board, the distillery workers and office workers respectively."

David cast his eyes to the ground for a moment before looking up again.

"That's it. Now, please, I do want you all to come back to Inchelvie where we can have a good few drams of Glendurnich malt and celebrate in style the life of a great man. And talking of which, I think by now you will understand the reason why I chose to speak to you here. Because in everything that I have just said, you would have heard exactly the same from my father."

David watched as sombre heads began to nod in agreement. As they turned their eyes back to the corner of the graveyard where his father had been laid to rest, David nodded briefly to the grave-diggers, and they stepped forward and began to shovel earth into the grave.

He turned and walked back to his mother and put his arms around her. "I'm sorry. That was a bit long-winded. Maybe I shouldn't have done it here after all."

His mother pushed herself away from him and smiled up into his face. "Darling, you were wonderful, and your timing was perfect. You said it all. Only your father could have said it with so much feeling."

She looked back towards the grave where the pile of earth was fast diminishing. "There are two people over there, David, lying side by side, who would be so proud of what you have just done."

David smiled at her, then took hold of her hand and together they walked down to the gate where the children stood waiting for them.

Just before six o'clock that evening, David helped the last of the workers climb unsteadily into the hired coach, and stood watching as the laden vehicle lumbered off down the drive. He turned to make his way back to the front door, but then hesitated, and instead walked across the gravel to the gate that led into the front garden. He pushed it open and rounded the high hedge to view, for the first time since he had returned, the new rose garden. It was in full bloom, every one of the bushes having taken root, despite the appalling conditions under which they were planted. David smiled to himself. Appalling conditions. God, how true *that* was, not only in terms of weather, but of circumstances as well. He walked along the grass path that ran between the borders, every so often reaching over to pluck off a deadhead. It had worked out just as he had planned. Every ounce of effort that he had put into it had come to fruition. And it was all for Rachel. The perfect memorial, representing, in every way, her pure, unadulterated beauty.

He bent down and dug his fingers deep into the earth around the roots of a lone dandelion, feeling the cool stickiness of it against the skin on his hand, so different from the warmth of the light, sandy soil to which he had become so accustomed in Leesport. He threw it onto the grass beside him, then rolled up a lump of earth into a tiny ball between his fingers. Two gardens so different, yet linking two women so alike, and even though one had touched his life for only a fragment of the time of the other, he knew that he would never be able to forget either.

CHAPTER 36

The wind and rain drove hard against the windows of the offices of Culpepper Rowan, causing the water to run in diagonal streaks across the tinted glass before settling in the sheltered crevices at the side. Jennifer stood with her arms crossed and her head resting against the cold pane as she gazed vacantly down onto the traffic far below on Fifth Avenue. It was only three in the afternoon, but the sky was so heavy with dark, scudding clouds that the cars were already driving with their headlights on. It all looked so depressing. Thank God it was only two weeks to the beginning of May, and then everything would hopefully transform to sunshine and warmth. Summer would be here.

But there again, it would be only the weather that would change. Not her life. As far as that was concerned, it might just as well be winter all the time—cold, colourless and dismal. It had been that way since November, when Alex had eventually left, and even before that, the effort of trying to work things out with him had been more stressful to deal with than his subsequent departure.

She turned from the window and went over to her desk and, slumping down in her chair, she reached forward and scrolled through the page on her laptop. She laughed scathingly to herself. THE page! That was all she had written. She was supposed to have finished the damned proposal by that evening, but every ounce of creative adrenaline had deserted her. It was as if her brain were swimming in syrup.

She guided the arrow up to the "save" option, then shut down her computer, gently closing the lid and sitting back in her chair. She just couldn't concentrate any more. And it seemed to be getting worse.

She pushed her chair away from the desk and stood up, and as she made her way back to the window, there was a brief knock on her door and Sam entered. "Hi!" he said, clapping his hands together. "Just wanted to find out how you were doing on the proposal."

Jennifer glanced at him, then turned away to look out of the window.

"Not good, huh?" he said morosely.

Jennifer shook her head.

"Well, tell you what, I'll get Russ to have a look at it. I think we should try to get something faxed to them by this evening." He walked over to her desk and picked up her telephone. "Yeah, Russ, it's Sam. Could you come to Jennifer's office? Thanks."

He replaced the receiver and came over to stand beside Jennifer, leaning his back against the window and pushing his hands into his pockets.

"You're not feeling too good, are you?"

"I'm sorry, Sam. I haven't been much use to you over the past six months, have I?"

Sam reached out and took hold of her arm. "Come on, you've said that before. You've done just fine. Things have been pretty difficult for you, and I can live with that. You'll get back into the swing of things soon enough."

Jennifer was silent for a moment, as she continued to stare out of the window. "No, I don't think so. I'm burned out. I have nothing really to offer you any more. I am beginning to think that it would be better if I just quietly packed up my things and left the company. You can't afford to subsidize my existence here. Anyway, I think that the time has come for me to get my priorities right."

"Meaning?"

"Meaning that I really want to spend more time with Benji and Jasmine at home. I think that's where I am needed the most right now."

Sam let out a long hiss. "Yeah, I suppose I can understand that, but I really don't want you to go." He paused, rubbing at the toe of his shoe with the heel of the other. "I don't, er, suppose you ever heard from Alex again?"

"No. Not directly, anyway. I had a letter from a lawyer in Dallas two days ago, saying that he was going to be representing him in the divorce proceedings."

Sam blew out disparagingly and shook his head. "Christ! What a bastard *he* turned out to be!"

Jennifer smiled sadly. "Well, he wasn't at one time, Sam," she said quietly.

"I know. I'm sorry. I shouldn't have said that."

At that moment, the door flew open and Russ walked in, laughing at a remark that someone had said to him in passing outside the office. "Yeah, Sam, what can I do for—?"

Sam held a finger to his lips to stop him from continuing. He turned to Jennifer. "Listen, I understand your reasons for wanting to leave the company, but I wonder if you might consider just holding fire for a time."

Jennifer looked at him. "For what reason?"

The expression on Sam's face suddenly transformed into a huge grin. "Because—I have just had a phone call from Gladwin Vintners. It seems that they have been *so* impressed with the way we've handled the Tarvy's account that they want us to take on the marketing of Glentochry Blend Whisky and Valischka Vodka over here."

There was a loud whoop from Russ and, stepping forward, he held his hand up in the air and slapped it down on Sam's outstretched palm.

"Goddamn it, Sam, you old son of a gun! You were right! You were absolutely right!"

"Well, I told you we could do it! I knew it was only a matter of time!" He turned to Jennifer. "And that's why I don't want you to go just yet. They have specifically asked for you to handle it."

Jennifer smiled at him, and shook her head. "You know, that's very sweet of you, Sam, and I really am delighted that you've got it, but I'm simply not fired up any more, and I don't want you to risk losing it because of that. Anyway, I don't think that I want to change my mind. You boys can handle it well enough."

Sam let out a groan of frustrated disappointment, then paused for a moment.

"Okay. How about this for an option? Gladwin's want us to fly over to London to meet with them and discuss the schedule. We don't have to produce a document. We don't have to produce anything, just show up for the meeting. Now, I really want you to come over with me, Jennifer, and I also would like you to bring Benji." He threw his hands up in a devil-may-care gesture. "Hell, I want you to bring Jasmine as well! Let's *all* go over! We'll stay at the Ritz, because I think that we damned well deserve it, and once we've had the meeting, *then* you can decide if you want to leave the company. Now, would you consider doing that?"

Jennifer looked at Sam for a moment, then suddenly seemed amused. "Sorry, Sam, I just had this wonderful image of Jasmine being waited on at the Ritz."

"Well, why the hell not?" Sam said, holding out his hands. "She's been through the mill as much as any of you. Come on, Jennifer, *please,* you'd do it for me, wouldn't you?"

Jennifer contemplated the suggestion. "I'd have to get Benji off school."

"Do it!" Sam exclaimed, rubbing his hands together as he realized that he was making some headway with his persuasion. "Come on! It would be great for all of us. And as I said, you can make up your mind one way or the other after the meeting."

"Okay."

Sam slapped his fist into the palm of his hand in triumph.

"But," Jennifer continued, "I couldn't go right away. I mean, I'd have to clear it with Benji and Jasmine first, *and* with Benji's principal at school."

"Yeah, that's no bother. We wouldn't need to go until the beginning of next week. That leaves you three days clear before the weekend." He paused and looked intently into her face. "So we have a definite yes?"

Jennifer smiled at him. "Yes."

"Great!" Sam cried out, pushing himself away from the window. "I'll go fix that up with Gladwin's, and book the flights *and* the rooms at the Ritz." He took hold of Russ's arm as he walked past him. "Russ, would you be good enough to get a copy of that proposal Jennifer's working on, and get something off to the client tonight? Doesn't have to be anything too great. We can stall them for a couple of days."

Russ nodded. "Okay."

"Good." He turned round to Jennifer and gave her a wink. "So, London, here we come!" And giving a little skip, he walked over to the door and left the office.

As the door shut, Jennifer made her way over to her desk and, pushing open the lid of her computer, she turned on the switch. "I'm sorry to load this onto you, Russ. I just couldn't get it going at all."

He shook his head. "Don't worry about it. I'll put something together for them for tonight. Don't forget, I'm a bit of a genius too!"

Jennifer pushed a floppy disc into the computer and transferred the document across. Then, ejecting the disc, she handed it over to Russ. He stood holding it in his hand, and knocking it nonchalantly against the tips of his fingers.

"How's, er, Benji doing—you know—without Alex around?"

Jennifer let out a long sigh. "Not good. He's really taken it all so hard. In fact, he hasn't really been the same since . . . well . . ."

"Since David left?"

Jennifer looked startled, then smiled. "My, that's pretty intuitive of you, Russ! Yeah. Since David left. He hero-worshipped him, really."

"Have you ever heard from him?"

Jennifer closed down her computer and shut the lid.

"No. Not since the week after he left. He called to say that they had arrived back in Scotland. His father died the day he got back. I haven't heard anything since then. Benji got a bunch of cards and a couple of letters, though, from Charlie, his son."

Russ continued to tap the disc against his fingers. "Listen—maybe I shouldn't say this, but—well—Benji wasn't the only one who kinda liked him, was he?"

Jennifer felt a flush come to her cheeks and she shook her head slowly.

"God, Russ, you've softened some! A year ago, I'd have quite happily laid down a hundred dollars against you noticing anything like that!" She paused as she walked over to the window. "But you're right. I think I can honestly say that he was the most special man I've ever met in my life."

There was a moment's silence.

"Yeah. He was some guy, wasn't he?"

Jennifer turned and looked at him. "How come you say that? You only met him once."

"Once was enough." He paused. "You remember that tennis match?"

Jennifer nodded.

"Well, it just happened that the following week, I went to watch a demonstration match at Flushing Meadows. It was really all put on for the crowds—a mixture of good tennis and good humour. Anyway, in the second set, the better of the two players obviously wanted to make it one set all, so that they could take the match to the third set—and he did it by making his serves and ground strokes go inches over the lines. Okay, so it was planned—but it was so imperceptible that I am sure that most of the spectators didn't realize that it was happening. But *I* knew, because David had done exactly the same thing to me the previous weekend."

He walked over to stand beside Jennifer and began fiddling with the cord of the window blind. "God, I can tell you that it fairly dented my pride. And then I thought to myself, well, hell, what about David? It never made any difference to him whether he won or lost. And then I realized that he hadn't minded humbling himself, because it was all above him, and in that way, he was above me. What was more, he made me understand that without actually having to show me up."

He let go of the cord and looked across at Jennifer, who was standing smiling at him. She walked towards him, and reaching up, gave him a kiss on the cheek.

"He touched everyone, Russ, one way or the other. I know that it sounds like a cliché out of a *Superhero Comic,* but sometimes I just wonder why, of all the millions of front doors stretched across the States, he came to knock on mine." She reached down and unplugged her laptop from the wall socket, then, curling up the cord, she walked back to her desk. "I mean, think of it, if it hadn't been for him, we wouldn't be planning this trip to London!"

Russ watched her as she opened up her brief-case and slid in the laptop.

"Why don't you go to Scotland?"

Jennifer glanced up at him. "What?"

"Why don't you go up and see him?" He walked across to her desk and leaned forward on it, looking directly into her face. "Go on, do it! If you want an excuse, say that Benji wants to see him. Just don't let him go!"

She paused for a moment, then smiled and shook her head. "No, Russ. I can't. I don't know what his life is like. I mean, everything would be completely different. It was just a moment in time, a very happy and unforgettable moment in time."

Russ looked down at the disc that he still held in his hand. "Yeah, maybe. Suppose it's just me being too impulsive. But listen, I'm coming over to London with you, so if you do happen to change your mind, you go and I'll cover for you. Is that a deal?"

Jennifer zipped up her case and nodded. "Yeah, that's a deal, Russ—but I won't be changing my mind."

He pushed himself off the desk and walked towards the door.

"Oh, I don't know. There's a good few front doors in the UK as well. Maybe fate will take you to his." He turned and smiled at her, and held up the disc. "Anyway, I'd better get going on this."

"Russ?"

He stopped with his hand on the door handle.

"Thanks."

Russ flicked his hand dismissively at her and walked out of the office.

Jennifer dialled the number of the house in Leesport.

"Jasmine? Hi, it's Jennifer . . . listen, this might come as a bit of a shock to you, but we've got to get you a passport by next week."

CHAPTER

37

Narrowing his eyes against the glare of the morning sun, the tall blue-coated doorman at the Ritz moved as agilely as a ballroom dancer around the portly female frame that tried to back out of the newly arrived taxi, finding himself in a quandary as to how best he could be of assistance to the woman without causing obvious affront. He skipped lightly around to her other side and held hard to the hand that was scrabbling blindly for support, and once she had extricated herself, Jasmine turned to him with a beaming smile on her face and blew out a sigh of relief.

"Thank you kindly, sir. Those taxis sure seem to be a lot easier to get in than out."

"Yes, they can be a little awkward, madam," the doorman replied with a diplomatic smile, and briefly touching the brim of his top hat, he glided around to hold the cab door open for the other four occupants.

As they climbed the steps and entered through the revolving doors of the hotel, Jennifer heard Jasmine gasp audibly as she stared in open-mouthed wonderment at the sumptuous interior of the reception area. "Now, this is what I call high-livin'!"

Jennifer laughed. "Well, don't start getting any big ideas about what we could do with the house in Leesport." She opened her handbag and took out their passports. "Could you just keep an eye on Benji, Jasmine, just in case he heads off on one of his exploration jaunts." She walked over to the reception desk, where Sam and Russ were already booking in.

"So if you could please just fill this in, Mr. Culpepper," the pretty young receptionist was saying brightly, as she handed Sam a registration form. "And this is for Mr. Hogan . . . and this for Mrs. and Master Newman . . . and you have a Miss Washington with you?"

"I'll do that," Jennifer cut in, smiling at the receptionist. "She's looking after my son."

"Very good, madam. But you will need to know Miss Washington's passport number."

Jennifer held up the passports in her hand. "Don't worry. I have them all here."

Having filled in their forms, the receptionist escorted them across the hall and left them in the capable hands of the head porter.

"Right then," he said, taking a number of keys out of the cubbyholes behind him. "You are all on the fourth floor. Mr. Culpepper room 410, Mr. Hogan 416, Mrs. and Master Newman 422 and Miss Washington 427. Now, I'll get someone to take you up, and your bags will be brought to you directly."

He called over a bellboy and handed him the keys, and they were led over to the lift in the corner by the stairs. Jennifer looked around for Jasmine and Benji, catching sight of them through the glass doors as they walked slowly towards her along the pink-carpeted hallway, staring at everyone and everything they passed. She pushed open one of the doors.

"Come on, you two. We're going up to our rooms." Realizing that the lift was not going to be able to accommodate them all, Sam took hold of Russ's arm and stepped out.

"We'll walk up, Jennifer. It'll do us good." He turned to Jennifer. "Listen, I was thinking on the plane over that maybe we should have a couple of ideas up our sleeves for the meeting tomorrow, so Russ and I are going to put our heads together for the day. But I want you to have the day on your own—take Benji and Jasmine around London or something, and we'll meet down here for a drink at, say, six-thirty, okay?"

"Are you sure you don't need me, Sam?"

He smiled and shook his head. "No. I want you all to enjoy yourselves. If you need anything, though, just give either myself or Russ a call. Room 410 or 416."

"All right. Thanks, Sam." She pushed herself into the lift beside Jasmine.

"Now?" Benji looked up at the bellboy, his finger hovering in front of the fourth-floor button.

"Now," the bellboy replied with a brief nod of his head and Benji punched the button.

Jennifer was allowed only half an hour's respite before Benji began pressing impatiently for her to go out, so, having prised Jasmine from her room, they set off along Piccadilly towards Green Park. Opposite the underground station, they picked up an open-topped tour bus, and despite the blustering coolness of the wind, they succumbed to Benji's insistence that they should ride on the upper deck. Jennifer and Jasmine sat with their coats pulled tight about them, while Benji dived from one side of the sparsely populated bus to the other, as the creamy voice of the tour guide called out each of the sights—Hyde Park Corner, Buckingham Palace, The Mall, Whitehall, The Houses of Parliament—before proceeding along the Victoria Embankment to the Tower. By that point, Jennifer noticed that Jasmine, although pretending bravely to be enjoying herself, looked as if she were in the early stages of hypothermia, so they abandoned the bus and took to the warmer climes of the underground. Taking the Circle Line to Baker Street, they spent the rest of the morning and the early part of the afternoon meandering slowly around Madame Tussaud's, with Benji having his photograph taken with as many of the waxwork celebrities as was possible.

Footsore and weary, they arrived back at the Ritz at two-thirty and, amidst loud protestations from Benji, who was keen to continue with their adventures, they headed off to their respective rooms to recharge their batteries.

"This is going to be boring!" Benji moaned as he threw himself onto the bed.

"You don't have to go to sleep," Jennifer said, taking her wash-bag from the still-unpacked suitcase and making her way through to the bathroom. "Watch TV. But if you don't have some kind of rest, you're just going to flake out tonight."

"No, I won't!" he said, pushing himself off the bed and walking over to the chest of drawers to pick up the remote control. "I'm not tired."

He flicked through the channels, stopping only long enough to give each of the programmes a cursory glance. There was an old black-and-white war film, an Australian soap opera, a cooking demonstration, and something that had just started called "Westminister Today."

"There's nothing on!" he called through to his mother.

"Oh, come on, Benji!" Jennifer shouted back, as she splashed water on her face from the basin. "You've had a pretty good morning. Just make do with what's on."

Benji tutted and threw the remote onto his bed. He pushed his head into the pillow and kicked up his legs, executing a perfect head-stand against the back wall and knocking squint the picture of the galloping racehorse that was hung upon it. A woman's plummy English voice sounded out from the television.

"Good afternoon, and welcome to 'Westminister Today.' We are going to begin our broadcast by going live to the House of Lords where a particularly heated debate on the present government's Companies Bill has been in progress for the past two days. We join it now at the Committee Stage where some one hundred and twenty amendments to the Bill have been put forward for discussion."

"Booriing!" Benji said out loud as he flumped down onto the bed, then kicked his legs up once more against the wall. "Mom?"

"Yes?"

"What's the House of Laawds?" He drawled out the last word.

Jennifer appeared at the door of the bathroom, rubbing at her face with a towel, and looked over at the television.

"I suppose the best way to describe it is that it's like the Senate. You know we have Congress. Well, that's like the House of Commons, and the Senate is like the House of Lords. It's what's called the Upper House of Parliament. We went past there this morning on the bus, remember?"

She smiled at his upside-down face and returned to the bathroom.

"Well, it's pretty boring stuff to put on television. I mean, who's going to watch this stuff?"

Benji watched from his inverted position as the camera zoomed in on a man in a long white wig who was sitting on a huge red sofa.

"We pass onto Amendment Twenty-four. The Lord Inchelvie."

"The Laawd Inchelvie," Benji said, with his mouth drawn down at the sides. "The Laaaawd Inchelvie."

"Your Lordships' Committee might wish to consider the aspect of the Bill that is addressed on page fifty-one, line seven. This sets out proposals for the merger between two companies, where it is presumed that the principal of each company . . ."

Benji fell heavily down onto the bed and stared at the wall, concentrating hard on the voice that was coming from the television.

"There is, however, an aspect that has been overlooked. Even over a short period of time, the management structure of a company can become obscured. And, my lords, if that is the case . . ."

Benji jumped off the bed and ran over to the television. That wasn't Lord Inch—what's-his-name's voice! That was David's! He pressed his face against the screen, trying to make out the figure that was speaking from the long shot being broadcast at that moment.

". . . e.g. discretion may have been given to a certain family and its members to control events, but it may not be clear to the family concerned which board members . . ."

The camera cut to a close-up of the speaker's face. It was! It was David! Benji began jumping around, shaking his hands in the air, his voice muted with excitement.

"MOM!" he blurted out.

Jennifer came running through from the bathroom, a white towelling band pulling her hair back and protecting it from the white cream that covered her face. "What's the matter?" she said in a startled voice.

Benji looked at her, an expression of amazement on his face as he pointed at the television.

"It's David, Mom! Look, it's David! He's on TV! He's in the House of Lords! Look!" He ran over to her, and grabbing her hand, which was slippery with cream, he dragged her in front of the television.

"It's David, isn't it? He's all dressed up, but that's David!"

Jennifer slowly turned from her son and stared at the tall pinstripe-suited figure that stood amongst the red leather seats. Her heart missed a beat as she listened to the familiar voice talking, and Benji watched as her face broke into a huge smile.

"It is," she said quietly, her face registering total dismay. "That's David."

"C'mon, Mom!" Benji said, dragging her towards the door. "C'mon!"

"Where are you going?" she laughed.

"To the House of Laawds! C'mon, we went past there this morning! It's just down the road!"

Jennifer pulled her hand away from Benji's grasp. "Benji," she said, smiling at him and shaking her head. "This must be a recording. David won't be there now!"

"He is!" Benji exclaimed, frustrated. "They said it was live! That means it's coming from there *now!*"

Jennifer turned slowly back to the screen. "It's live?" she said in an astonished voice.

"Yes!! C'mon, Mom, before he finishes! We gotta go and see him!"

Jennifer stood gazing at the screen as the camera zoomed into a tight close-up of David's face. He was sitting now, and she watched as his face broke into a grin over a light-hearted rebuff made by one of the lords on the other side of the house. She knew it so well. She knew that face so well.

"Okay!" She ran through to the bathroom and grabbed a towel, then came back into the bedroom, rubbing the cream from her face. "You go down to reception and get a taxi, darling, and I'll be with you in a minute. I've just got to tell Jasmine and Sam."

Benji rushed from the room, and she heard him running down to the passageway, yelling out "The House of Laawds! The House of Laawds!" over and over again as he went. She picked up the phone and dialled Jasmine's room. A sleepy voice replied.

"Hello, Jasmine here."

Jennifer smiled to herself, wondering if she announced herself that way to everyone.

"Jasmine, Benji and I are going out again."

"Where to?"

"I won't tell you until we get back. But I think it could be a pretty big surprise for you!"

"Oh, okay," Jasmine replied uninterestedly. "I'll just go back to sleep and wait 'till I hear from you then."

"Right." She pressed her finger on the button to disconnect the line and dialled Sam's room number. It was Russ who answered.

"Russ? It's Jennifer."

"Hi! You sound excited. What's going on?"

"It's David, Russ! He's on TV—in the House of Lords. And it's live."

There was a moment's silence at the other end of the line.

"Russ? Are you still there?"

"Yeah, sorry. David's here? In London?"

"Yes!"

"Well, Chrissakes, what did I tell you? Looks like you knocked on the right door! Go for it, Jennifer! Just go for it! Sam and I can handle the meeting. God, what am I saying? Forget us, Jennifer. Just go for it!"

"Will you explain to Sam?"

"Yeah, but he's heard anyway. He's sitting here nodding his head, and if he nods any more, it's going to fall off!"

Jennifer laughed, feeling her eyes prick with tears of elation. "Okay! Okay! I'm going!"

"Good luck, old friend," he said quietly.

"Thanks, Russ."

She put down the receiver and rushed to the door, then turning back to pick up her handbag she took another quick glance at the television. David was standing once more, speaking. She smiled, blew him a kiss, then turned and ran out of the room.

Benji was already sitting in the cab outside the hotel, leaning forward and watching out for his mother coming down the steps. She jumped in and was about to announce their destination when the taxi took off.

"I've told him, Mom! He says he knows where it is!"

"I hope so!" Jennifer laughed. She opened up her bag and took out her make-up, and jammed herself into the corner of the taxi to give some support to her already shaking hand.

By the time they drove down Whitehall, she had finished applying a make-shift covering to her face, while Benji had engaged her in an excited though uncomprehending discussion as to how David Corstorphine had suddenly become Lord Inch—what's-his-name. The taxi drew to a halt outside the Houses of Parliament next to a large statue of a man on a horse, and the driver pulled open the partition window.

"You want to go into the Lords, luv?"

"Yes," Jennifer replied, leaning forward and pulling a ten-pound note out of her purse.

"That's the queue there," he said, pointing to a roped-off section of the pavement. "Not many people. You should get in with the next lot."

"Thanks," Jennifer said, handing him the note. He delved into his pocket for change, but both Jennifer and Benji had jumped out of the taxi.

"Keep the change!" she called back with a smile. "It's worth it!"

"I hope so, luv!" he yelled after her.

As they joined the queue, a man in a uniform came forward and unclipped the white rope and began ushering them into the building.

They entered a huge stone-floored hall and followed the line as it moved sedately along between the stone statues of past politicians. At the bottom of the stairs, the usher turned to them and told them in a lugubrious voice that they would have to wait there in the Central Lobby until such times as the last intake of visitors had left the Public Gallery. Undeterred by this, Benji walked to the front and confronted the man.

"Excuse me, but my mom and I know someone who's in the House of Lords, and we want to see him."

There was a murmur of amusement from the other visitors, as the man bent slowly forward to speak to him.

"I'm afraid that you will have to wait, young man, even though you are acquainted with one of the Peers of the Realm."

Benji turned with a disconsolate look on his face and walked back to his mother, scuffing his feet along the floor as he went. He sauntered over to one of the statues and leaned against the base, watching for any movement coming from the stairs.

Five minutes later, the first of the visitors began to descend, turning eventually into a steady stream of people. Benji sighed impatiently, realizing that it was going to take some time before they would be allowed to go up, and turned to read the inscription on the statue against which he was leaning.

"BENJI?"

The voice echoed around the Central Lobby, and everyone, including the usher, turned to look up at the top of the stairs. Charlie was staring down at him, holding hard to the banister and stopping the flow of people who were coming behind him.

Benji's face lit up as he watched Sophie and Harriet thump against the banister beside him.

"CHARLIE! SOPHIE! HARRIET" Benji yelled out, and ran towards the bottom of the stairs as he watched Sophie and Charlie push their way unceremoniously through the crowds towards him.

When they reached the bottom, they stood three feet apart, looking at each other, incredulous grins spread across their faces.

"What are *you* doing here?" Charlie asked in an amazed voice.

"Mom and I saw your dad on television. We've come to see him!"

"Your mother's here?" Sophie asked, looking around for Jennifer. She saw her, still standing in line, leaning sideways and smiling at her. She took off at a run and threw herself into Jennifer's arms, clasping her hands around her neck.

"What are *you* all doing here?" Benji asked. "I thought you were at school in Scotland!"

"We are, but Granny took us off for two days and brought us down here, 'cos she thought we would like to see Dad talk in the House of Lords."

Benji looked past him to see a tall old lady come down the stairs holding on to Harriet's hand. Charlie ran up the first two steps to meet them.

"Granny, this is Benji, my friend from America. He's here—in London!"

His grandmother smiled at Benji as she approached him, her hand outstretched. "Yes, I can see that, darling. How do you do, Benji? How very nice it is to meet you."

Benji shook her hand and turned to find that his mother and Sophie had come to stand behind him.

"Granny," Sophie said excitedly. "This is Jennifer."

Alicia smiled warmly at Jennifer and stepped forward and kissed her on both cheeks. "My dear, I am so delighted to meet you. I have heard so much about you, both from Sophie and from David." She stood back, shaking her head in astonishment. "I cannot believe you're here! What an extraordinary thing!"

Benji walked up to his mother and tugged at her hand. "Mom, can Charlie and I go and see David now? *He* knows where to go."

Jennifer looked down at him. "In a minute, darling. There are still people coming down the stairs."

Alicia looked around. "Oh, I'll see if we can't pull a few strings."

She walked over to the usher at the head of the queue and talked quietly with him. He nodded and accompanied Alicia back to where they stood.

"This very kind gentleman will take you two up to the Public Gallery. But remember, Charlie, you have to be very quiet."

"All right, Granny!" Charlie exclaimed and both he and Benji began running up the stairs, squeezing past the oncoming traffic, followed as briskly as he was able by the elderly usher.

Being between intakes, the Public Gallery was completely empty, and all was silent except for the single low voice that droned from the chamber below. The usher showed the two boys to the seats at the very front, and stood beside them as Charlie pointed out his father to Benji. He craned forward in his seat, desperately trying to catch David's eye, then turned to Charlie.

"Can't we call him?" he whispered.

"No, it's against the law," Charlie replied sombrely, pressing his mouth against Benji's ear. "Granny says you're not even allowed to wave."

"How can we get his attention then?"

"We can't. We have to wait until he looks up."

Benji gazed down on the house, looking at each of the lords in turn. "He looks as if he's the youngest person there!"

Charlie put his hand to his mouth to stop himself from giggling. "Granny says that some of them have been sitting there so long that they have cobwebs stretching from their heads to the backs of their seats."

Benji too clamped his hand to his mouth, but not before letting out an involuntary snort of laughter. He turned guiltily around to the usher, who put his finger to his lips.

At no time did David make any effort to look up at the gallery. Benji moved his head fractionally from side to side to try to attract his attention, but it was all to no avail. David didn't know they were there. It was all too much. He had to let him know. He stood up.

"DAVID!"

Charlie grabbed at him and dived below the level of the balcony in embarrassment. Every face turned up to the gallery, each issuing loud murmurs of "Order! Order!" The usher gave Benji a hard pat on the back and pointed to the door. But it was all too late. Benji's call had had the desired effect. David started in his seat, and looked up at the gallery in time to see the beaming-faced boy waving at him as he was ushered out. God, it was Benji! What the hell was he . . . ? Charlie's face suddenly appeared from below the balcony, and as he too got up to leave, he gestured with his hand for his father to come out. David shook his head in disbelief, then turned to look around the chamber. All eyes were on him. He handed his papers to the peer directly in front of him, then stood up and walked as fast as he felt was permissible towards the double doors.

Once outside the Debating Chamber, he hurried across the Lords Lobby, pushed hard at the large swinging doors and entered the Central Lobby, arriving just as Benji and Charlie reached the bottom of the stairs.

Benji picked him out immediately from the crowd. "DAVID!" he yelled and ran up to him, throwing his arms around his waist.

David held hard to the boy and bent down and kissed the top of his head. "Benji," he said, laughing, "what *on earth* are you doing here?"

Benji pushed himself away from him, just as Charlie came to join them.

"We saw you on TV. We're staying in the Ritz, and I turned on the TV and saw you. I didn't recognize your name. You changed it!"

"Yes, you're right. I have. Who's 'we,' Benji?"

"Mom, Jasmine and me."

"All of you? You're all here in London?"

"Yup. Jasmine is still in the hotel, but Mom is here somewhere." He turned and looked around the crowded hall.

"There they are!" shouted Charlie, and he and Benji turned and began running over to the entrance door, where Jennifer stood talking to Sophie and her grandmother.

David walked slowly towards them, his eyes fixed firmly on Jennifer. As the boys reached them, she looked around and saw him approach, and her face broke into a wide grin.

He stopped in front of her and thrust his hands into his pockets of his jacket.

"Hi."

Jennifer held her handbag with both hands in front of her, self-consciously swinging it from side to side. "Hi," she replied quietly.

As they stood in silence looking at each other, Alicia put her arm around Sophie's shoulders and, giving her a knowing wink, they followed on after the two boys and Harriet, who had already run out through the doors into the sunlight of the afternoon.

"How are things?" David asked, his face still fixed in the widest of grins.

Jennifer shrugged. "So-so."

"Did, er, everything work out between you and . . . ?"

Jennifer shook her head. "No, it's finished. I did try, David, but he walked out on us in November."

"What a bloody fool," he murmured, staring down at his feet in an attempt to disguise his look of sheer relief. He looked up at her and laughed.

"So . . . how long are you over here for?"

"I don't know."

David acknowledged someone who passed by. "You, er, wouldn't consider coming up to Scotland, would you? I mean, all of you?"

Jennifer contemplated this for a minute, before nodding her head slowly. "You know, I think we might. Nothing else is planned."

They continued looking at each other without either making a move. Jennifer took in a long breath and let it out again. "So, you've changed profession? From a gardener to a lord?"

David nodded and raised his eyebrows.

"Wow!" She gave a little laugh at the incredulity of it all. "That really *is* one for the books!" She pulled a face. "I've never met a lord before. What am I supposed to do? Give a little curtsy?"

David shook his head and moved towards her, putting his arms around her waist and pulling her towards him. "I don't think there's any written law on the subject. So I suppose that we could just make do with a very long and passionate kiss."

And the elderly usher, who had been making his way slowly up the staircase, stopped and cast his eyes around the Central Lobby, wondering why such a profound silence had suddenly descended upon the place.

Starting Over

I wrote this book remembering two of my good friends,
Iain Mallet and Roddy I'Anson.

ACKNOWLEDGMENTS

Thanks to Peter Erskine for supplying me with information about his wonderful new golf course at Kingsbarns; Sam and Jeannie Chesterton for help with all things Spanish; David Greer for his guidance on the oil industry; Winnie Jurk, who rapped my knuckles over my schoolboy German; Aurora Jauncey, who did likewise with my Spanish; Alice Gruzman, who helped refresh my dimming memory of Sydney by running around Vaucluse with a camera; and last but not least, my family, who once more put up with me talking away to myself for the best part of a year.

Chapter 1

A taste of spring. That's exactly how it should be described. Nature pervading the senses with the tangy texture of newly tilled soil, laced with the lightest sprinkling of salt that blew in on the cool breeze from the North Sea. Liz Dewhurst leaned against the rotting strainer-post at the head of the field and closed her eyes, pulling in a deep breath and moving her tongue across her palate to identify more. There *was* something else, but it seemed alien, ill at sorts with this carefully prepared recipe. She opened her eyes and watched the large John Deere tractor sweep past fifty metres below her, the masculinity of its six-cylindered roar giving way to the more genteel sound of the drill-spouts, clicking away like a thousand synchronized knitting needles as each placed its designated quantity of barley seed into the rich dark earth.

Liz smiled to herself and pushed away from the strainer. Diesel fumes. That's what it was. Her moment of sweet communion ended by a technological breakthrough.

"Come on, Leckie!" she called out, shrugging the strap of the basket higher onto her shoulder and scanning the hedgerow for the Jack Russell terrier. He appeared from the undergrowth a hundred yards uphill, like a cork fired from a champagne bottle, and stood looking at her, a small power pack of energy weighing up the odds as to whether obedience should give way to further moments of pure joy.

"Come *on*!"

The tone of voice was enough. Obedience would seem a better option today. Hitting full speed at only two strides into its run, the dog tore down the hill towards its mistress, then veered off and dodged away down the field in front of her.

Liz made for the centre of the field, hoping to coincide her arrival there with the next pass of the John Deere, but as it turned on the end rig, the engine was cut, emptying the air of its noise, leaving only the weaker, yet more melodious sounds of the cab radio to take its place.

Bert was well settled into his lunch by the time she reached the tractor, alternately biting into a white-loaf sandwich and supping away at a plastic cupful of tea. Acknowledging her arrival with a chuck of his head, the old tractorman slid forward in his seat and gave the door a hefty boot open, allowing the fug of sweet pipe tobacco to escape from the cab's airless confines and waft down towards Liz.

"Hullo, Bert."

"Weel?" Bert replied with his customary question to the greeting.

Liz turned and looked down the rail-track straightness of his drilling. "How's it going?"

Bert took a noisy slurp of tea before answering. "Tractor's pullin' braw, but yon machine ahent's a real scunner. Spoots aye seem to be gettin' fell chochit."

Liz smiled up at the old man. Having lived all her thirty-seven years right here on the east coast of Fife, she was proud both of her Scottish roots and lilting voice, but sometimes she found it almost incomprehensible that both she and Bert should come from the same country, so broad was his accent. A native of Aberdeen, he spoke as if every word had been given a good chewing before being sputtered out in a whirring stream. And that lack of comprehension had not all been one-sided. At the *ceilidh* that her father had held to mark Bert's twenty-five years' service on the farm, the tractorman had risen unsteadily to his feet, clutching in his hand a glass of whisky that was as dark as the peat with which it was made, and remarked that "the reason that me and the fermer hev got on sae weel ower the years is that neither of us hev understood a bloody word we've said tae itch ither!"

Liz bent down and picked up a handful of earth, rubbing it gently between fingers and thumb and allowing the crumbled soil to fall back to the ground. "At least the conditions are perfect. I don't think they've been this good in years."

Bert sat back in his tractor seat. "Aye, weel, there's somethin' tae be said fer that at ony rate."

Liz glanced to where the old cab-less Fordson sat idle at the bottom of the field. "You wouldn't happen to know where my father's got to?"

"Aaay. He went off doon the gulley just afore ye arrived." He let out a throaty chuckle. "He'll be sunbathin' on the rocks, nae doot."

Liz laughed at the vision of her father lying prostrate on a rock, his coveralls zipped right up to the neck to keep himself warm. "Aye, nae doot." She gave her head a quick shake of admonishment, realizing that she too was slipping into the vernacular. "Well, I'll away down and see him. I've got his lunch."

She patted the basket with her hand and looked back at the tractorman. But he had already closed the door of the tractor to resume his own.

Liz set off at a brisk pace towards the gulley, hoping to catch her father before he made his way back to the field. As she went, a blinding pinpoint of light from the adjacent field, sun hitting polished metal, caught her eye, and she stopped to see what had caused it. Two distant figures, their fluorescent green coats clearly outlining them against the dark backdrop of the sea, stood on open ground two hundred metres apart. One held a long white pole at the vertical and moved this way and that in response to the hand-waving of the other, who, when not giving directions, was stooped over a surveying theodolite, the source of the reflected light. The sight of this hitherto innocuous task had an immediate effect on Liz, displacing her feeling of complete contentment for the day with a griping sense of foreboding. She watched them for a moment longer, then, with her hand held hard against the basket, she turned and began to run in tottering, uneven steps across the unworked land, as if physical distance might help separate her from the undesirable infringements of the surveyors' actions. Only when she was sure that the undulating contours of the field hid all view of the neighbouring farm from sight did she slow to a walk.

The gulley that led down to the shore was dank and gloomy, the sun's rays being denied access to the dreariness of its inner sanctum by a canopied arch of unkempt hawthorn bushes, their roots exposed like gnarled arthritic limbs after years of undermining by an out-of-control rabbit population. Consequently, the full length of its rutted centre still brimmed with a succession of stagnant brown puddles despite the fact that it had not rained for the best part of a month. Liz kept to the driest part at the edge of the track, her upper body tilted to the side to avoid having her head caught by the tentacled branches of spiky hawthorn, and at the same time keeping an eye on the darting Jack Russell, just in case he decided to up-tail and vanish down one of the all-too-inviting rabbit holes.

With warming relief, she stepped back out into bright sunlight at the bottom of the gulley and climbed up high onto the overhang of craggy volcanic rock to afford her a better view of the shoreline. The wind, now sparkled with moisture from the crashing waves, had become more chilled, and she zipped up her quilted jacket to the neck and pushed away the strand of short blond hair that blew about her face. The dog, who had been vainly sniffing out something of interest in these new maritime surroundings, suddenly let out a short yelp, heralding the discovery of her father's whereabouts, and headed off, his claws scrambling for purchase on the slippery rocks, in the direction of the lone figure that sat looking out to sea fifty yards upwind from where she stood. Liz turned to follow the animal at a more careful pace, her Wellingtons being too loose-fitting to be classed as ideal footwear for the purpose in hand.

Even though he would have certainly been forewarned of his daughter's proximity by the dog's appearance, the farmer continued to look mesmerically out to sea as she approached, the collar of his coveralls turned up as token protection against the wind, his white-browed eyes shielded by the peak of a battered tweed cap. He sat with the wriggling dog in his arms, his hand clamped tight over Leckie's mouth to avoid his over-amorous greeting.

"Hi, Dad," Liz breathed out in a sigh of exhaustion.

At the sound of her voice, the farmer broke from his train of thought and turned to flash her a crooked smile. "Well, lass. How're you doing?" He let go of the dog, allowing it to spill from his arms and run off to explore the peripheries of a nearby rock-pool.

"I thought I'd bring your lunch out to you."

"Aye, well, there was no real need. I'm not that hungry." He gave his head a quick, appreciative nod. "But it's good of you, nonetheless."

Liz sat down beside him on the rock, tucking the bottom of her jacket under the seat of her jeans to avoid its chilling smoothness. She wedged the basket into a crevice, damp with seaweed, behind her, then delved in and took out a Thermos and a plastic container filled with sandwiches. She poured out a cupful of soup for her father and handed it to him.

"Just as well I brought this down. You didn't look as if you were going to bother coming in for lunch."

He took a loud swallow of his soup, but did not follow it up with any verbal response, instead just wrapped his large, calloused hands around the steaming warmth of the cup and cast his eyes far beyond the frothing breakers on the rocks.

Liz reached across and put a hand on his knee. "Are you all right, Dad? You seem to be a bit away with the fairies."

Her father let out a long sigh and turned to her, a wistful smile on his face. "Och, I don't know, lass. Just having a few thoughts."

"What kind of thoughts?"

He took another sip from his cup, then gave a short laugh. "If you really want to know, I'll show you." Handing her the cup, he leaned forward to pick up a pebble before pushing himself to his feet. He stood for a moment, as if readying his tall, angular frame for action, then, with a certain and, to Liz, quite alarming unsteadiness that was probably only to be expected of a man nearing his seventieth year, he jumped his way across the rocks to stand just out of the spattering reaches of the breaking waves.

"See that out there?" he called back to her, his voice barely audible above the noise of the sea. He pointed his finger towards a jagged needle of rock that protruded from the sea seventy metres offshore. Liz nodded in response. He moved back a couple of paces, executed a number of practice throwing actions to loosen off the muscles in his stringy arm, and then, with one ungainly skip forward, he launched the pebble, and almost himself, out into the water. The small stone hit the surface with a feeble plop, not even a quarter of the way to its appointed target. For a moment, he stared at the point of impact, then, letting out a loud exclamation of derision, he made his way back to where Liz was sitting.

She shook her head as he approached. "What was that all about?"

Her father sat down, letting out a heavy blow from the effort, then leaned over and took a sandwich from the box. "I'll tell you." He took a bite and, almost simultaneously, began his explanation. "When I was a wee lad, about ten or eleven years old, my father brought me down here and showed me that rock. He said that the day that I could hit it three times in a row from that point where I just threw that stone would be the time when he'd let me take over the farm. Well, I thought there and then that I'd make him eat his words." He shot a knowing wink at Liz. "Aye but, lass, he was a wise old devil. No matter how much I tried, I fell short of that rock all the way through my teens. Then, once I'd the strength to get the range, it took me another two years to get the control.

And when I eventually did hit it three times, he didn't believe me! So I had to do it all over again, with him standing as witness—and that took another six months!" He laughed. "I was twenty-three by that time!"

Liz smiled at her father. "You'd wonder how he knew that it would take that long. Do you think that *his* father put him through the same test?"

"Oh, aye, he did. And as far as I know, *his* father before that, too!"

Liz was silent for a moment before making the decision to ask the question. "And did you ever do it with Andrew?"

The farmer took another bite of his sandwich and this time said nothing until he had swallowed his mouthful. "Aye, I did—and the lad hit it three times when he was only nineteen." He gave a long sigh and held out his cup to be replenished. "But your brother was never that interested in the farm. And why should he be? I never minded that much. He was always a clever boy. Too bright to spend his days driving tractors about the place. He'd only have got bored. No, he made the right decision, going away to Australia like that. Managing director of a company and all." He drained his cup, and flicking its residue out to be dispersed by the wind, he once more scrutinized the distant rock. "Aye, it's like the family's own stone of destiny, that out there. I suppose it's sort of become like the physical pinnacle of my life, with those pebbles getting closer and closer to it as I grew up, and now, as I get older, getting further and further away. I suppose it won't be long now before I canna even heft them further than the shoreline itself."

Liz took the cup from him and put it back in the basket. "Come on, Dad, you're being a bit pessimistic, aren't you?"

He wiped his hands on the legs of his coveralls. "Aye, well, I've had the mind to be a bit pessimistic over these past few months, as I'm sure you'll understand."

"Yes. I can," Liz replied softly. She screwed the top back on the Thermos and kept hold of it at its tightest position. "You'll be missing Mum a good deal, Dad?"

He pushed back the peak of his tweed cap and scratched at the top of his snow-white tangle of hair before settling it once more on his head. "Of course." He got to his feet and held out a hand to his daughter. "You don't easily forget the scent of a flower just because it's died."

Taking hold of the outstretched hand, Liz felt the power in his grip as he brought her effortlessly to her feet, then, picking up the basket, he set off across the rocks towards the gulley ahead of his daughter.

"Dad?"

"Aye?" He turned back to look at her.

"I haven't ever asked you this before, but—well—you don't blame me, do you? In any way—for Mum, I mean?"

Her father beamed a broad smile at her and shook his head. "No, Lizzie, I don't. And never think it. It was just one of those sad coincidences, her getting ill when you and Gregor parted company. Of course, there was no doubt that we were all affected by it, with our families and the farms being linked so close, but no, lass, I'm pretty sure that it never hastened her end."

Liz leaped the two rocks to where her father stood and put her arms around his chest, pushing her cheek against the exposed front of his woollen jersey and feeling the warmth radiate through from his lean frame.

"I sometimes wonder what it would be like if it never had happened."

"What? You jumping in the back of the Land Rover with young Gregor?"

Liz pushed herself away from him, and looked up at a face that twinkled with amusement. "Dad!"

His grin spilled out into a laugh. "Och, you mean the marriage? Well, I suppose one wouldn't have happened without the other, would it?"

Liz smiled and shook her head. "No, you're right. It wouldn't."

Her father pushed his hands deep into the pockets of his coveralls and gave a brief nod in the direction of the rock, its tip now becoming more pronounced with the ebbing of the tide. "You can't change destiny, lass. You can't get your pebble back once you've thrown it. It's all been. It's in the past. Anyway, you wouldn't have that fine lad of yours if it was different, would you?"

Liz took in a long deep breath and let it out. "I know that." She paused for a moment. "But sometimes I wonder if the future holds anything better." She cast a wary glance at her father. "They've been out on Gregor's farm again—doing more surveying for the golf course."

He nodded. "I know. Gregor phoned me this morning. They want to start here tomorrow."

"What did you say?"

"I told him to hold off until we see what the outcome of the meeting is tonight."

He watched the change of expression on his daughter's face, the usual open, smiling features being drawn down into a hardened glare of determination. "We can't let it happen, Dad. We mustn't let them steamroller us into making a decision."

Putting an arm around his daughter's shoulders, he drew her into his side, and lifting his other hand to her face, he pushed gently at the corners of her mouth with his thumb and forefinger to reinstate the smile. "Listen, Lizzie, we'll see what they have to say, and we'll do what's best." He bent down and planted a kiss on the top of her head. "But I don't want you getting all huffed up and bitter about it all, lass, because that's not you—that's not you at all." He leaned his head forward to make eye contact with his daughter. "D'you hear me?"

Liz looked up into his kind, weather-beaten face and could not help but break into a genuine smile. "I'll try—but it's hard sometimes."

"I know." He grabbed her hand and pulled her up bodily onto the next rock, then turned and gave a shrill whistle for the dog. "Come on, we'd better get going, otherwise Bert will have no worked ground in front of him."

Together they picked their way slowly across the rocks back towards the gulley. Just as they reached the plateau on which Liz had stood to search him out, both caught the distant but constant rumble of thunder crescendoing as it approached them. Instinctively putting their fingers to their ears, they watched as the menacing cross-section of the Phantom jet sleeked towards them, hugging the coastline like a hunting fox, conspiring to keep hidden until the last from its unsuspecting prey. With an ear-shattering roar, it passed overhead, no more than two hundred feet above them, then banked hard to the right and streaked out seaward for the final run-in to its destination at RAF Leuchars.

No more than a minute later, Alex Dewhurst stepped away from the ball, just as he prepared to play his approach to the tenth hole on the New Course at St. Andrews. He took two more practice shots, swinging his number eight iron in slow, rhythmic arcs, desperate to keep his concentration until the Phantom jet, which had set down on the runway at the other side of the estuary, had closed down the reverse thrust on its engines. When the noise had subsided, he re-addressed the ball, flexing his knees to settle his tall frame into the shot, then played through the ball with a swing as smooth as those that he had executed in practice. The ball soared high into the air, starting its flight left of the fluttering flag before catching the stiff sea breeze that blew in across the course. It pitched fifteen metres short of its target, but with no back-spin applied, it ran fast across the hardened fairway onto the razored surface of the green. It caught the borrow and swung in towards the flag, and eventually came to rest no more than three feet from the hole.

Alex kept the final position on his swing until he had seen the ball come to a halt, then let the club rest down on his shoulder. He turned to his opponent, and grinned. "Of course it was meant!"

Tom Harrison's eyes had not left the ball. The captain of the university golf team stood no more than two clubs' distance from Alex, supporting his right elbow with his left hand and biting thoughtfully at a fingernail. He took a deep breath and glanced across at his younger opponent, shaking his head in disbelief.

"That is bloody *ridiculous!* That's about the fourth time today you've laid it dead from that distance!"

Alex stepped forward and scooped up the divot of turf with the blade of his club. "It doesn't always work that way." He replaced the divot and stamped it back into the ground. "But I suppose it does help being brought up on links courses. You just get to know how they work." He speared the club back into his golf bag and swung it up onto his shoulder, then stood watching as Tom walked over to where his ball lay in the short, wispy rough at the edge of the fairway.

No, he thought to himself, it certainly didn't always work that way. Far from it. Despite having a handicap of five, quite often by this stage in a game he would have blown a couple of holes, simply through some niggling apprehension that momentarily bled his concentration. But then it always seemed to be a different matter when he was in a match situation. This was his forte, playing head to head against an opponent, playing to win. And he knew that, in this case, his reward for winning would probably be a place on the team.

Tom played his shot, but badly miscalculated the resistance of the rough, the consequence being that the ball stopped ten yards short of the green. "Damn!" He picked up his bag and walked rapidly forward to catch up with Alex. "So, go on. You were saying that you were at school around here."

"Yes. Madras College. I wouldn't say that I exactly excelled myself there, but that was my fault, not the school's. I spent more time on the golf course than I did in the classroom during my final year, which did play havoc with my grades. But I was the captain of the school golf team, and I took it all quite seriously."

Tom pulled a face at Alex's obvious self-deprecation. "Well, you couldn't have done that badly if you got into the university."

"Only there by the skin of my teeth."

"Aren't we all? So, what are you reading?"

"Languages—German and French."

"Ah, a *leenguist*, huh? And what about digs? I suppose you're in halls, being a fresher."

"No. I still live at home."

"Oh, right! I didn't realize that you lived that close to Saint Andrews."

Arriving at his ball, Tom shrugged the golf bag off his shoulder and pulled out a pitching wedge in one practised move, then, with near nonchalance, stood over the ball and stroked it to within two feet of the hole. He turned to Alex, a hopeful grin on his face. "A gimme?"

Alex nodded. "Okay. A gimme."

Tom crossed over to the ball and pushed it into the hole with the back of his club. "So where exactly are you from?"

Alex took a putter from his bag and walked over to his ball. "Balmuir. You've probably never heard of it. It's just a wee flea-bite of a place seven miles along the coast. My parents both farm out there."

"Oh, I know Balmuir! That's where they're planning to build the new course, isn't it? I read about it in the local paper. 'The best new links course in Britain,' that's how they're describing it already."

From the moment that Alex put the blade of the putter to the ball, he knew that he was not ready for the shot. Thoughts unconnected with the game flashed through his mind, and he suddenly felt apart from the ball, his brain totally out of tune with the movements of his hands. He tried to play for time by taking a couple of practice shots, but was only too aware of a tenseness that grated at the fluidity that been there beforehand. His eyes began to focus on other things—the logo on his ball, lying askew with the angle at which he was preparing to play his shot, a minute blade of grass that seemed to be lying against the grain in the carpet of green. All things that, up until that moment, had remained completely unimportant and unnoticed in the momentum of his game. He took back the club and hesitated. The sin. The cardinal sin. He pushed the ball towards the hole, and knew from the moment that he had hit it that it was to the left and well past.

He watched the ball as it took its designated path, bending his knees forward in the hope that the movement would in some way alter its course to the hole. But psychology gave way to physics, and the ball glided past its target exactly at the point that he had imagined. He stood watching it for a moment, then glanced across at his opponent, cocking his head to the side in an expression of resignation to his own fallibility.

Tom scratched at the side of his face with a finger. "What happened there?"

Alex didn't reply, but walked forward to his ball, hiding his disappointment by scrutinizing the line once more, as if trying to lay blame on something other than his own ineptness at getting it into the hole.

"Is that all right?" he asked quietly. He bent down, his hand hovering above the ball.

"Yes, sure," Tom replied. He exhaled in relief. "Hell, you let me off the hook there, mate. Thought that was definitely me going one down."

Alex scooped up the ball and went to pick up his golf bag, passing Tom without a remark.

Together they walked to the next tee in silence.

Even though it was still his opponent's honour to drive off, Alex watched as Tom dumped his bag on the ground and continued on to the bench that was situated at the side of the tee, nestled under the protection of a rampant gorse-bush. He sat down and folded his arms. "I'm sorry, Alex. I psyched you out just then, didn't I?"

Alex smiled at him and shook his head. "No, it was nothing. Just my concentration went."

"I know. I saw it happen. What was the cause?" He paused for an explanation, but none was forthcoming. He asked again. "Was it something I said?"

Alex shook his head. "It doesn't matter."

"Like hell it doesn't! Listen, forgive me if I come over as being a bit of a know-all, but it's perfectly true that seventy-five percent of this game is played in your head, and to put it bluntly, Alex, if you're going to have any chance of playing for the team, I have to make sure that you don't spook quite as easily as that."

Alex looked back to the tenth hole and watched as a ball came to rest on the edge of the green. "Come on, Tom, we'd better get a move on, or we'll hold up play."

Tom paid no heed to the remark. "Oh, bugger them, let them play through. Come on, tell me. It was something about the new golf course, wasn't it?"

Alex walked slowly over to the bench and thumped himself down beside Tom. "Yes, you're right." He paused. "The plan is to build the golf course on our farms."

Tom nodded slowly. "And you don't want it."

"Do I not! I think it would be a great idea. Can you imagine having a championship course right on your doorstep?"

"So . . . what's the problem?"

Alex shot his opponent a faint smile. "It's a long story—but, in a nutshell, 'family' is the problem."

"Go on."

Alex took off his baseball cap and ran his fingers through his thick brown hair. "Well, if you really want to know—it's a bloody mess, really! My parents split up about six months ago, after eighteen years of marriage, the reason being that my mother found out that my father had been having an affair with this local woman for about two years."

Tom bit at his lip. "Ah, right!" he mumbled quietly.

"And that's only half the complication. Mum and Dad came from neighbouring farms, you see, so their parents thought, well, if the families are to be united in marriage, why not unite the farms as well? So that's exactly what they did. Farming was going really well at that time, and there were these massive grants coming from the European Community, so they were lured into buying tractors and grain-driers and all the latest technology—all against the collateral of the farm, which, as it turned out, was pretty bloody stupid. Anyway, times changed, prices went down, and the business began to suffer. And then, to cap it all, my mother found out about the affair."

Alex stopped talking as the two golfers who had been playing behind them came onto the tee. They exchanged pleasantries about the weather and the condition of the course, and watched as both hit shots that made light of the awesome expanse of gorse-infested rough that separated the tee from the fairway. With a final wave of thanks, the two golfers went on their way.

"So?" Tom asked. "What was the outcome?"

Alex took in a deep breath. "The outcome was that both my parents and the farms split. My father shacked up with his girl-friend at his place, where in fact we'd been living up until that time, and my mother and I moved back to my grandparents' farm. And then, two months ago, just to rub salt into the wound, my grandmother turned up her toes."

Tom blew out a noiseless whistle and leaned forward, resting his elbows on his knees and rubbing his face with his hands. "Bloоody hell!" he exclaimed, almost to himself. He looked at Alex. "As you say, what a mess."

Alex smiled at him. "Exactly. And what's been left is this almighty financial wrangle about who owns what, or, to be more exact, who *doesn't* own what. The bank really has it all. Anyway, going back to the new golf course, my father thought that he had found an answer to all our problems. He'd been approached by this financial consortium that wanted to reinstate an old nine-hole course which had existed on the farm sometime around the First World War. Their plan was to make it into an eighteen-hole championship course—as you say, 'the best new links course in Britain'—which would mean constructing it across the two farms."

Tom nodded his head slowly, beginning to understand the implications. "And your mother's dead against it."

Alex fired his fingers pistol-fashion at his opponent. "Got it in one. And if you think about it, can you blame her? Her husband leaves, and then comes back, all sweetness and light, to ask her if she would mind giving up her family farm so that he can pay off his overdraft and live happily ever after with his girl-friend."

"*Bloоody* hell!" Tom exclaimed again, this time more forcefully.

Both were silent for a moment as each contemplated what had been said.

"Why don't you leave home?" Tom asked eventually.

Alex let out a long breath and shook his head. "I can't. I don't think that would be fair on Mum. Her two men upping sticks and leaving in the space of six months. No, I've got to stay around. It's just that the atmosphere gets so . . . depressingly heavy, and everything is so insular. It's like being caught up in some appalling soap opera. Nothing new—or . . . well—of any consequence is ever talked about in the house. It's all about the wretched farms, and who's saying what behind whose back, and"—he pulled down the corners of his mouth—"'*Whose side are you on, anyway?*' There is just absolutely *no* outside interest taken at all."

Tom got to his feet and stood up on the bench to see how far the two golfers were in front. He jumped off, took a driver out of his bag and teed up his ball. "Well, introduce something." He swung his club back and forth.

Alex looked at him quizzically. "What do you mean?"

Tom turned and leaned on the top of his club. "Well . . . you can't just sit and wait for something to happen, for things to get better, because, you have to admit, it's a pretty hopeless situation. So why don't you try to take the lead? Introduce something new to talk about—I don't know—get a student lodger, or take a girl-friend home or something."

"I don't have one at the minute."

"Well . . ." Tom held out his hands in exasperation. "I really can't tell you, Alex. It's your business, not mine." He stepped forward to his ball and, without any preparation, hit it with enormous power straight down the centre of the fairway. He bent forward to pick up his tee. "But what is my business is the fact that I can't risk having you blow a game when you're on the team."

Alex was silent for a moment as he took in what Tom had just said. "What d'you exactly mean by that?"

The captain of the university golf team smiled at him. "I'm short of a guy on Saturday. Can you play?"

Chapter 2

When Liz and her father arrived for the meeting that evening, the mock-Tudor-beamed lounge bar of the Doocot Arms in Balmuir was already nearing capacity, even though proceedings were not scheduled to begin for another quarter of an hour. Liz took off her coat by the door and cast a concerned eye over the assembled company as they jostled about and craned over each other to study the various plans of the golf course project that were pinned to the display boards beside the bar.

She let out a nervous breath. "I thought that this was to be a closed meeting tonight," she said quietly to her father.

He caught the eye of Andy Brown, the owner of the village store, and nodded him a greeting. "Aye, I was under that impression, too. Looks like they're going all out to drum up local support."

"And I can guess whose idea that was," Liz answered, her voice edged by the thought. She scanned the room for Gregor, but there was as yet no sign of him.

"Mr. Craig! Mrs. Dewhurst!" The voice came from the direction of a disembodied hand held high in the centre of those who perused the plans. For a moment, the volume in the room died as every face turned to look at them. A path was cleared to allow the speaker to make his way forward to where they stood, and as he approached, Liz watched as the company turned to murmur with one another, the subject of their gossiping made all too apparent by smirking smiles and the almost imperceptible jerk of heads in her direction.

That's right, Liz thought to herself. Have a good laugh. Don't worry, I know exactly what you're saying. Look, there goes Liz Dewhurst, the woman who couldn't keep her man. Satisfied him once after a Young Farmers' Dance when they sorely tested out the springs of his father's Land Rover, and then, having paid the consequences, couldn't keep up the momentum. He, on the other hand, with the purring care of that wee blonde-haired bombshell of a divorcée, Mary McLean, couldn't keep it down!

Jonathan Davies approached them, his hand outstretched to her father. "Mr. Craig, how nice to see you." The two men shook hands, and then, to Liz's dismay, he planted a kiss on each of her cheeks. "Well, what a turn-out!" he exclaimed, surveying the crowded room. "I discussed it with Gregor, and we both thought that it was time to let the local residents in on the action."

As I suspected, Liz thought, fixing the man with a false smile of greeting.

Davies put his hands together and gave them a quick, frictioned rub. "So, what can I get you both to drink?"

Liz's father held up his hand. "Thank you, Mr. Davies, I'm not much of a drinking man. If there's a cup of tea going?"

"Right! I'm sure I can arrange that. And Mrs. Dewhurst?"

"Liz—please. I'm not a great one for formalities." Not the true reason, she thought to herself. It's just the name Dewhurst that grates on you.

Davies's face lit up at this welcome overture of friendship. "Of course. Liz. So what can I get you?"

"Just an orange juice, please."

"Right. Well, let's go over to the bar and I'll introduce you to some of the American contingent."

He set off across the room with a springy, purposeful bounce, and Liz and her father fell into step behind him. He was a short man, no taller than her at five feet five, but he was as honed and as well-cut as the tweed suit he was wearing. An ex-naval officer with a bearing that met well with his past occupation, he had made his money with a firm of City stockbrokers before "down-shifting" to Scotland, where he had sought out a collection of other monied parties to start up what had now become an extremely successful venture-capital group. At first, he had concentrated his expertise on identifying small, ailing businesses which he had bought, built up and sold on. Now, with a string of successful transactions to the group's name, he was going for the big one, having gone into partnership with an American-based finance company which specialized in the development of sports complexes.

After putting in his order at the bar, Davies moved over to the group of men that stood in a huddle in the centre of the room, and placed his hand on the bright-yellow-sweatered arm of a large, athletic-looking man to attract his attention. "Michael?"

The man turned, and before Davies had the chance to continue with his introduction, he looked straight at Liz and flashed her a smile that seemed to accentuate both the brilliance of his perfectly set teeth and the nut-brown texture of his sun-tanned face. He was almost too ridiculously good-looking, as if he had just stepped off one of those billboard advertisements for toothpaste that showed a jagged white starburst exploding from the model's teeth and the word PING! in thick black-painted letters inscribed within.

"Michael, can I introduce you to Liz Dewhurst?"

The man reached out and grabbed Liz's hand before she had made any move to offer it and gave it a finger-crunching shake. "Hi, Liz. Michael Dooney. A great pleasure to meet you."

"And," Davies continued, taking a step back to allow clear ground between Dooney and Liz's father, "this is Mr. Craig."

Dooney launched himself forward to Liz's father and repeated his near-crippling action. "Hi, Mr. Craig. Michael Dooney. A real pleasure, sir."

Davies held out his hands in a gesture to signify that all three were included in his address. "We are particularly lucky to have Michael on board for this venture. He has been responsible for designing some of the top golf courses in the United States over the past"—he turned to Dooney for verification—"twenty years, is it, Michael?"

Dooney raised his eyebrows and let out a long puff as he made his own mental calculation. "Nearer twenty-five now, I think, Jonathan."

Davies smiled. "Well, there you are. A veritable wealth of experience." The beckoning of the barman caught his eye. "Right now, I'll go and get your drinks, and maybe, Michael, you could introduce Liz and her father to the rest of your crew."

Dooney flashed Liz his Colgate smile once more. "It'd be my pleasure."

His compatriots were all of a similar size and build to Dooney, although all but one were dressed in more formal attire. Dooney went round the group of four men, introducing them all in turn and giving a short résumé on the involvement of each in the project. Jack Dennis, the accountant; Bill Hennessey, the banker; Shane Reader, the property developer; and Hatton Devlin, the other casual dresser, Dooney's young assistant.

After formalities were completed, Dennis immediately engaged Liz's father in conversation, leaving Liz to the mercy of Dooney's flashing gaze. He moved forward from the other men, in doing so making it obvious to Liz that theirs was to be a one-to-one exchange.

"So, this is all pretty exciting, huh?"

Liz shrugged her shoulders. "Well, it's early days yet, isn't it? I mean, there could be some objections to it." She paused briefly, realizing that her comment might have given away too much of her own feelings towards the project. She smiled up at the course architect and added brightly, "Couldn't there be?"

Dooney chucked his head to the side in appraisal of her question. "Well, from what Jonathan has told me, it looks good at the moment. He's been liaising with the planners, and they seem to be quite pro the idea. It would certainly take the heat out of the golf courses at Saint Andrews, especially seeing that it's going to be a golf *links*, rather than an inland course."

Liz smiled weakly at him. "And that will make the difference?"

"Sure as hell it will! That's why the guys come over here to Scotland—to play the natural courses."

Liz nodded her head. Go on, say it, you stupid woman. Say that you don't want the bloody golf course. Say that you don't want to give up the farm that has been in your family for five generations. Say that your husband has gone off with another woman, and that the last thing you want to do is give the farm over to him, so that he can be happy and—

"I hear your son's quite a golfer."

Liz started at the question, her mind away on another plane. "I'm sorry?"

"Your son. I hear he's a pretty good golfer."

Liz let out a sigh that was entirely unrelated to Dooney's words of praise. "Yes. You're right. He's actually having a trial today for his university team."

Dooney gave her a wink. "Good for him. So I reckon that he'll be over the moon at the thought of a golf course on his doorstep."

Liz opened her mouth to reply, but was cut short by Jonathan Davies's voice rising above the noise in the room.

"I think we should maybe make a start to proceedings, even though Gregor isn't here. He did warn me beforehand that he might be a little late, due to a prior engagement."

To Liz's horror, she was aware of a ripple of amusement running around the room as people took their seats, all due to Davies's unintentional *double entendre*. Her facial expression must have given a concise indication of how she felt, because suddenly her father was at her side, giving her arm a reassuring squeeze.

"Come on, lass," he said quietly. "Let's go and sit down."

He made to move forward, but felt the resistance to his guidance as Liz stayed where she was. He turned to look at her.

"Dad, I don't want to stay here. I think I'll just go home."

The farmer smiled at her and shook his head. "Listen, lassie, don't take any notice of this lot. They're nothing but a bunch of ignoramuses. If you go off now, you'll just be adding fuel to their fire. So what do you say to just sitting down and seeing what these lads have to say?"

Liz bit hard on her bottom lip and nodded slowly, and her father took hold of her arm once more and pushed her quite forcefully up the narrow aisle to the front row.

As they were about to take their seats, the door of the lounge bar crashed open. Both Liz and her father, along with every other person in the room, turned to watch as Gregor blustered into the room, shrugging off his waxed jacket, while at the same time keeping his foot against the sprung door so that Mary McLean could enter unhindered. Again, the slight hum of levity ran around those that were seated.

Liz sat down quickly, keeping her head rigidly to the front. She leaned stiffly over to her father, trying to make it as unobvious as possible to those behind that she was speaking to him.

"What is *she* doing here? This has nothing to with her."

Her father did not reply, but reached for her hand.

Gregor and Mary made their way quickly to the front. "Sorry we're late, Jonathan," he said, leaning across the top table and shaking hands with those who sat behind it. "Hope we haven't held up the proceedings too much."

Davies held up his hands. "Not at all, Gregor. We've just taken our seats, so you've missed nothing so far."

Liz watched out of the side of her eye as Gregor threw his jacket onto a seat on the opposite side of the aisle, then turned to nod her father a silent greeting.

"Right!" Davies called out, giving everyone the benefit of his most welcoming grin. "Firstly, I know that I would go to the ends of the earth for a free drink, but nevertheless may I thank you all for making time in your busy schedules to attend tonight." He paused while the audience gave due appreciation to his humorous entrée. "Now, I know that there has been much discussion in the area about the pros and cons of our project, so I thought that it would be best if everyone had the chance to air his views, and hopefully those present at the top table with me will be able to answer all your questions. It would be my aim tonight to have you all leaving here seeing this not only as an extremely exciting project, but also one which will be of great benefit to the local economy. So, without further ado, and just to whet your appetites, I think it would be best to hand over first to Michael Dooney, who will take you through the exact geographical layout of the course."

From the moment that Dooney stood up, Liz listened only half-heartedly to the whole proceedings, her mind suddenly preoccupied with thoughts of now-distant times when she, Gregor and Alex were a complete and inseparable unit—living together, laughing together, working the farm together. She could picture so clearly those picnics at harvest-time, leaning against bales of sweet-smelling straw and watching proudly as their young son took his first precarious steps, staggering his way from mother to father and back again through the crackling stubble. She remembered watching Gregor at the controls of the giant combine harvester, his shirt-sleeves rolled high to reveal thick brown arms and bulging biceps, and her heart would skip a beat as she considered how the task seemed to accentuate his rugged good looks; and then there were the occasions when he would allow Alex up into the cab and, clamping the young boy between his knees, would let him steer the machine, open-mouthed with delight, across the field. She thought about the hilarious evenings spent right here in the bar after the day's work had been done, then returning home, their minds tingling with the effects of the drink, where their bodies would cast aside the fatigue of their labours, and they would . . .

No. She didn't want to remember that. It was no use remembering that. Those days were all over, finished with, never to happen again. God, had it really been so much her fault? Why had it gone so wrong? Had she really not been a good companion to him, a good lover? She glanced across the aisle to where Mary McLean sat, her head leaned to the side, a look of concentrated interest on her face. Could no one else see how utterly unconvincing that expression was, with her dolly-bird looks and lacquered curls? Liz looked down into her lap and picked at a piece of cotton thread that had come loose at the side of her denim skirt. God, am I that dowdy, that *unsatisfying* that he sees something better, something more pleasing in *that* woman?

It was a question being asked from the back of the room that brought Liz's attention back to the meeting. She looked up at the top table and realized that all the speakers had finished their presentations, and that she had missed everything that had been said. She turned to see who was asking the question, hoping that her action would make it look as if she were genuinely interested in the proceedings. The tweed-enveloped figure of Delia, the wife of Sir Hector Stanfield, owner of Balmuir Estate, stood six rows back, her hands clutched to the metal arch of the chair in front, onto which she leaned her whole formidable frame. This was all much to the agitation of Miss Mouncey, the occupier of the chair, a sparrow-like spinster whose attendance at the meeting heralded the fact that she had, for once, taken a break from her purgatorial pastime of polishing the brasses in the local church.

"You state quite convincingly, Mr. Davies," Delia bellowed out, "that this is going to be good for the area. I would hope very much that this is true, but, to be quite honest, I do have my doubts. In my experience of these new developments, what will take place is that a whole load of people will be shipped out here to work, and we won't benefit at all.

What we'll be left to put up with is a huge increase in the amount of traffic on our roads and hundreds of foreign people making a nuisance of themselves in our village."

Liz could not help but join in with the cacophony of laughter that spread about the room. She watched as Delia took her seat and noticed that, to the woman's credit, a wide smile was spread across her lipsticked mouth. Good for you, Delia, Liz thought to herself, please keep it up. Please keep objecting.

Davies was on his feet and had started his reply before the drone of amusement had died. "Lady Stanfield." Liz studied his face as he waited for silence to be restored, his eyes sparkling with humour as a result of Delia's statement. Goodness, he was good. He had always proved himself to know all that he should about everybody. "Lady Stanfield, the steering committee, to a man, is giving full support to the idea that this project should work for the good of the community, and as such we would hope to offer as many jobs as is thought practicable to those who live in the area. As far as the roads are concerned, we don't envisage that much of an increase in traffic, and for those who do come to use the complex we would hope that, no matter how far they have travelled to reach these shores, they would be more than willing to burgeon local businesses with their custom." He picked up the glass of water from the table and took a drink, giving time for the general undertone of approval to percolate across the room. "Nevertheless, I think that, at this stage," he continued, "we should just take stock of our present position by recapping on what has been said tonight. Outline planning consent has been granted, and as such we have continued apace with the surveying on Winterton Farm." He glanced down to where Liz and her father sat, raising his eyebrows in anticipation of approval. "And we are hoping that, if all goes well, we will be able to move on to Brunthill Farm tomorrow."

Liz turned to her father and gave him an uncertain smile.

"Mr. Davies. Can I ask a question?"

Liz recognized the voice of Danny McKay, another of Balmuir's local farmers, a man renowned as much for his imperiously outspoken views at National Farmers Union meetings as he was for his Bacchanalian visits to the local cattle market.

Davies gave his head a quick nod. "Certainly, Mr. McKay."

"This project is going to be built across Winterton and Brunthill farms, is it not?"

Davies furrowed his brow, wondering if the slight slur in Danny McKay's voice might be the reason for his stating the obvious. "That is correct."

McKay let out a deep, scornful laugh. "Well, taking everything into consideration, it would be in my mind that you would have more chance of flying to the moon than getting the owners of those two farms ever coming to an agreement!"

There was a sudden intake of breath from everyone in the room, followed by total silence only broken by the whispered tones of Danny McKay's wife telling him to sit down.

"Wheest, woman, it has to be said. Mr. Davies, trying to make ends meet in farming is pretty damned hard at the minute, and quite honestly, if I was given the chance of an offer like yours, I'd grab it with both hands. But that's not the case, is it? So, my point is that if one particular party, or parties, has been lucky enough to be given the chance to get out, then they shouldn't be too selfish in making up their minds, so that we can all be in the position to reap some of those benefits that you've spoken about. So, I think I'd be speaking for everyone here in asking for assurance that neither Gregor nor Liz Dewhurst will allow their petty differences to mar the future potential of your scheme."

Liz sat rigid, staring straight ahead at Jonathan Davies, seeing, for once, a flustered expression come over his face. She felt her cheeks flush uncontrollably, and a sudden pounding filled her head. She heard the chair beside her creak and watched as her father rose slowly to his feet. He turned and fixed Danny McKay with a steely glare.

"Mr. McKay, I can tell you that this family has known some suffering over these past few months, yet not for a minute have we allowed this to stand in the way of Mr. Davies and his colleagues in their endeavours to draw up their plans. But nothing is certain just yet, and I can tell you that if a decision is made to end the project at any stage, it will be because of financial considerations made by both Gregor's and my family, and not because of what you term as 'petty differences.' " He looked round to Jonathan Davies. "With apologies to the chair"—he turned back to scowl at the now red-faced farmer—"I take your question, Mr. McKay, as not only being out of order, but also damned right offensive."

An embarrassed silence descended upon the room as both men took their seats again. Liz found herself glancing unwittingly over to where Gregor and Mary McLean sat, and saw her huddling forward in her seat, trying to make herself as invisible as possible.

Davies cleared his throat and rubbed nervously at his forehead. "Well, I think that we have probably discussed enough for this evening. If anybody has any further questions, my colleagues and I are going to be holding back here for a bit, so please feel free to come forward and ask them. So it just leaves me to thank you all for attending."

The meeting broke up with a general movement of chairs and a buzz of hushed conversation. Davies picked up his papers from the desk and pushed them together in his hands, then made his way around the table to the front row where Liz and her father still remained seated.

He leaned forward to Liz. "I'm so terribly sorry about that, Liz," he said quietly. "If I had realized at all that someone would come out with such a crass statement, I would never even have considered an open meeting at this stage."

Liz shook her head. "Don't worry. Something like that would have been said regardless of when you held it. It's the fodder on which our little community thrives at the minute, I'm afraid."

Davies nodded and gladly escaped back to the bonhomie of his American colleagues. Liz let out a long sigh and turned to her father. "Come on then, Dad," she said, taking his arm. "Let's go home. I'll go get the car and meet you at the front door."

The small car-park at the rear of the pub had emptied as fast as the lounge bar after the meeting. Pulling her coat around her to protect her from the chill wind, Liz walked over to the Land Rover and put the key in the door.

"Liz?"

A car door slammed shut behind her, and she turned to watch Gregor walk across the car-park towards her. Breathing out a heavy sigh, she leaned back against the door, casting her eyes anywhere but at her husband.

Gregor stopped a short distance from her and pushed his hands into his pockets. He looked down at the ground and began scraping his shoe at a loose stone in the Tarmac. "I'm sorry about that in there. Your father was right. McKay had no cause to say such a thing. He's just got it in for us—always has."

Liz made no reaction to his remark.

"Have you seen Alex today?"

Liz shook her head.

"Just wondered how he got on at the trial."

Liz shrugged and turned to open the door of the car. "No doubt I'll find out when I get home."

"Liz?" Gregor stepped forward and put his hand on her arm, but immediately withdrew it as he felt her pull away from his contact. "Listen, Liz, we must talk sometime. We have to discuss this whole thing through properly. I had a meeting with the bank today, and they're getting pretty edgy about the overdraft. I don't think it'll be that long before they try to pull the rug out from underneath me—so I would guess that they'd do the same with you. What I mean is that I don't think that we can go on just burying our heads in the sand."

Liz kept her hand on the car door, but turned to look at him, waiting to see if he had anything further to add.

"Liz, come on. Just listen for a minute." He paused and let out a long sigh. "The reason we have to talk is that I'm not so confident that this golf project *is* going to get off the ground. Jonathan said to me today that one of their investors has pulled out, and if his group don't find another investor in the next couple of months, then the Americans are going to cut their losses and move their money over to another project in the States. So, you see, we have to talk. We can't jeopardize this one chance of solving all our money problems. We have to think of our futures, of Alex's future. If we show ourselves to be right behind the scheme, then maybe they will delay making a decision for a little bit longer."

Liz felt a sudden warmth from the realization of hope that built up inside her. Okay, so there had always been uncertainty about whether the project would get off the ground during the earliest of its stages, but over the last month she had been beginning to admit to herself that it was heading towards an inevitability. So to lose a valued investor at this stage would be crucial. This might be the way out. If they couldn't find the money, then her father, Alex and she would be left in peace, and Gregor would be left to sort out his own dirty washing. She folded her arms and stared straight at Gregor.

"Why did you bring her along tonight?"

Gregor bit at his lip. "What?"

"You heard me. Why did you bring her along? It's got nothing to do with her."

"Well, she just wanted to show interest."

Liz let out a short laugh. "I'm sure she did." She turned and opened the car door and got in.

Gregor walked forward and grabbed the door, preventing her from shutting it. "Come on, Liz, you've got to be a wee bit more reasonable than this."

Liz pulled the door shut with unaccountable power. She grabbed hold of the steering wheel with both hands and stared mesmerically at its centre, fighting hard to control her emotions. After a moment she rolled down the window and looked at her husband. "Reasonable?" she said quietly, a laugh of incredulity in her voice. "Why the hell should I be reasonable? When were you ever *reasonable?*"

Starting up the engine, she crunched the Land Rover into reverse gear and lurched back, spinning the steering wheel so that Gregor had to jump aside to avoid coming into contact with the vehicle's already battered wing. As she pulled away, she glanced across at Gregor's pick-up, briefly catching the look of wild astonishment on Mary McLean's face.

She laughed to herself and said out loud, "Oh, dear, oh dear, Barbie gets a fright!"

Chapter 3

The charcoal smell of burnt pastry wafting through the closed door of the kitchen greeted Alex as he entered the house that night, quickly followed by a painful expletive and the clattering bash of hot pie dish being discarded rapidly onto the sideboard.

"Look at that!" He heard edged anger in his mother's voice. "What a damned waste! Where on earth is he?"

Alex stood motionless in the back lobby, physically sensing the air of tension that had become so commonplace in the house over the past six months. He caught hold of Leckie on his fourth attempt to jump up into his arms and stroked the Jack Russell's smooth coat in an effort to keep his welcome silent, at the same time straining to hear his grandfather's quiet but calming response.

"That's as may be," his mother cut in, "but he could have at least called."

Alex took a deep breath to ready himself for the inevitable frosty reception and entered the kitchen, immediately wishing that he hadn't coincided it with giving a visible wince at the acrid fumes that filled the room. His mother stood at the paint-flaked central worktop, its surface cluttered by the opened contents of the day's mail, a large bag of Ewe Milk Replacer and his grandfather's tweed cap, upon which sat a large ginger cat whose tail swished as regularly as a pendulum as it stared fixedly at the pie. His mother looked up, catching his frown of distaste, then continued to busy herself in picking out the least-burnt bits of the steak pie before giving the side of the dish a hard tap with the edge of her spoon. "You may well look like that. It's because you're so late that it's burnt—and don't add to the smell by bringing that dog in here. He's out in the lobby because he's rolled in something."

Alex immediately thrust the small dog out to arm's length, and with an expression on his face that would have well befitted someone who had been asked to dispose of the decomposing body of a rat, he hurriedly projected the dog back out through the door, wiping his hands, on relieved impulse, on the seat of his trousers.

"Alex!"

Letting out a short, manic cry of frustration, he walked over to the kitchen sink and turned on the tap to rinse his hands. The water was scalding. "*Shit!*" He pulled his hands back fast from the steaming torrent, giving them a frantic shake to cool them down. He turned to see his grandfather, who was seated at the table, throw a glance of disapproval in his direction over his half-moon reading spectacles. "Sorry." Alex smiled apologetically. "The water's hot."

"So what happened to you?" his mother asked. "Where have you been?"

"Well, I went to have a drink with Tom in the nineteenth hole and sort of lost track of time."

"You could have called."

He took a dish-towel from the rail in front of the Rayburn and dried his hands. "I know. I would have done. I'm sorry. But I really did lose track of time."

His mother handed him a plate brimming with steak pie, boiled potatoes and broccoli. He stared at it for a moment, considering asking whether she would mind if he put one of the sticks of broccoli back in the bowl, it being his least-favourite vegetable, but thought better of it, thinking that it might not be too diplomatic a move under the circumstances. He walked across to the small table at the window and sat down opposite his grandfather, who was engrossed in the newspaper that was spread out on the yellow oilcloth in front of him.

"And did you drive back?"

"Yes."

"What? After drinking?"

"Yes."

Alex took a mouthful of food and glanced up to his grandfather, who looked at him over his spectacles and gave him a wink. Alex grinned back at him.

"I saw that, you two." She walked across to her father and gave him a slap across his upper arm with her oven glove. "There's no need to encourage him, Dad. He could lose his licence, and then he would be expecting us to drive him in and out of Saint Andrews."

"Coke, Mum. I was only drinking Coke."

"Ah. Right." She stood for a moment realizing her misjudgement of the situation, then covered for her unease by stretching across to remove her father's empty plate, pushed to the farthest side of the table to make way for the newspaper. "Well, that's all right then." She walked back to the kitchen sink and rinsed off the plate before putting it in the dishwasher.

"So," his grandfather started slowly, taking off his spectacles and laying them down on top of his newspaper. He folded his arms on the table and looked across at his grandson. "How did it go then?"

Alex smiled at him. "I never thought anyone would ask," he said, a tone of amusement in his voice.

"Well, I'm asking."

"I got in."

His grandfather brought his hands together in one resonant and triumphant clap. "That's my lad! Well done, you! You played well, then?"

"Well enough. I thought I was going to blow it half-way round, but at that point, Tom Harrison, the team captain, announced that he wanted me to play on Saturday, and after that, I just seemed to pull it all together."

Alex had just taken another mouthful of food when a blue rubber-gloved hand flashed past his eyes and a pair of arms, quite unexpectedly, encircled his shoulders and he felt himself drawn in against the busty softness of his mother's chest. She held him so tightly that there was too much resistance for his jaw to continue chewing, and one of the buttons on her woollen cardigan bit painfully into his ear. But he made no attempt to move away. "I'm sorry, Alex." She kissed him on the forehead. "I had completely forgotten that this was your big day. Well done, darling, I'm really proud of you."

She let go and moved back to the kitchen sink to continue scrubbing at the blackened innards of the pie dish. Alex looked across to where she stood, the harsh glare of the fluorescent light accentuating the paleness of her tired face. Damn this whole situation, he thought to himself. Damn Dad for doing this to her, for behaving like some young stud at *his* age. Because that's all it was with Mary McLean. Just a sexual attraction. He could see that himself. They didn't have anything in common with each other. She never went out on the farm or to the market with him, not as Mum used to do. And when they did speak, there was always an air of falseness in their conversation, as if they were simply a couple who had been thrown together on a blind date. But then he'd made his bed and he was going to have to lie in it.

He pushed the broccoli to the side of his plate and scraped what was left of the steak pie onto his fork. "I also got a job caddying again for the holidays," he said brightly, trying to inject a shot of levity into the gloomy atmosphere.

His mother looked round, pushing back a strand of hair with her forearm to avoid its coming into contact with the greasy froth on her glove.

"Have you? Well done." Alex could hear her making every effort to express enthusiasm.

"Well, I just thought that I'd take the opportunity on the way back from playing, so I looked in at the caddymaster's office. He said there'd be no problem. Just turn up when the semester is over."

The muffled trill of the telephone sounded over the last few words of his sentence. Liz turned from the sink and walked over to the dresser, pulling off her rubber gloves as she went. She stood for a moment looking at the empty base of the portable. "Dad, where's the phone?"

"Ah, yes. Sorry. I used it earlier. I think it's in the hall."

"Well, see if you can remember to put it back in future." She opened the door into the hall and closed it with force behind her.

Taking the opportunity of her absence, Alex got up from the table and took his plate over to the plastic rubbish bin at the side of the Rayburn. He flipped open the lid and slid the watery stalks of broccoli off his plate.

"What's eating Mum?" he asked, reaching back into the bin to cover the evidence with a discarded *Farmer's Weekly*.

"Nothing at all, Alex, is *eating* your mother," his grandfather retorted, a sternness to his voice, "in the same way that nothing is *eating* at that broccoli that *was* on your plate."

Alex pulled a short, embarrassed smirk. "Right. I'm sorry. I didn't mean it to sound like that. It's just that . . ."

Mr. Craig leaned back in his chair. "Aye, I know what you're going to say. But your mother does have reason to be feeling a little upset." He paused and closed his newspaper, and carefully folded it up. "We had the golf course meeting tonight."

Alex poured himself a glass of water and went back to sit opposite his grandfather. "What happened?"

"Just some of the locals behaved a bit unthinkingly towards her. Made her feel a wee bit uneasy. And then she had a few words with your father in the car-park afterwards about the project."

"What was he saying?"

"Och, just that he thought that it was still the only way we could appease the bank and suchlike. He did say that these consortium laddies were having to stall a bit, being in need of another investor." He let out a long sigh and leaned forward to pick up his spectacles, holding them by one leg and twisting them back and forth between thumb and forefinger. "But . . . well, we'll just have to wait and see."

"Do you think it will happen, Granddad? I mean, it's been so on-off over the past year."

"Aye, well, from what I gathered at the meeting tonight, it looks now as if they've got everything in place to get started. I suppose it just depends on whether they get this other investor."

Alex eyed his grandfather. "And what about you, Granddad? Do you want it to go ahead?"

Mr. Craig smiled across at his grandson. "I can't help but admit that I've got awful mixed feelings about it, Alex. The farm's been in the family for five generations, and you know, old habits die hard. But there's no getting away from the fact that we're in a bit of a pickle financial-like." He chuckled. "Maybe in hindsight, we shouldn't have invested so much when we joined up with your father's family after your parents got married, but it seemed the right thing to do at the time." He paused and Alex could hear the glass-paper friction as he rubbed his callused hand across the grey stubble on his chin. "But then all those 'high heid yins' in Brussels changed their tune and told us to start taking land out of production, and that's really when farming changed for me. There was no great pleasure in seeing a good field left to grow weeds, and know that we were taking taxpayers' money for the pleasure of just letting it happen. To me, it sort of undermined the whole integrity and honesty of the business. And now we're being told to diversify *away* from farming, so I suppose we're just heeding their advice." He shook his head. "But I just never thought that it would mean we'd be giving up farming completely. I always had the notion that I'd end my days being a farmer."

Alex stared out the window into the blackness of the night. "Mum really doesn't want the project to go ahead, does she?"

"Not at the minute, no. But I think we can all understand her point of view. She's been hurt quite bad by what's happened—not only with your father, but also losing her mother. And really, since then, she's been running the business side of the farm, so I think she'd be loath to give that up, it taking her mind off everything and all."

Getting up from the table, Alex walked over to the sink and discarded the remaining contents of his glass. He turned and folded his arms. "I just feel that we've all got to keep going, Granddad. Not especially with the farm, but with, well, everything. I mean, I *know* that Dad has behaved like a stupid fool, and I realize that Grandma dying has been hard on both you *and* Mum, but we've got to keep going. To be quite honest, I don't know how much more of this eternal gloom I can put up with."

His grandfather let out a quiet snort and shook his head. "That bad, is it?"

"Yes, actually, it is. You know, Tom asked me today if I'd ever considered moving into digs in Saint Andrews, and for a moment I was really taken by the idea. But I wouldn't do it. At any rate, I couldn't afford it on my grant. But what we need to do is inject a bit of *life* into this household. We can't moulder around in sorrow forever." Alex bit hard on his lip, understanding that he may have gone too far with this last remark. He walked over to his grandfather and put a hand on his shoulder, then pulled out the chair next to him and sat down. "Sorry, Granddad, that didn't come out right. What I was meaning to say was that I just don't like seeing you both so . . . well . . . down all the time."

His grandfather smiled at him. "Listen, lad, I'm not 'down,' as you put it. At my age, you accept the fact that you're getting nearer the time when death plays its part some way or other. Aye, I miss your grandmother, but I'm not 'down.' I've got a great many good memories, you know, and that's what keeps me going."

The door opened and they both turned and watched Liz walk back in. She replaced the portable on its base. "That was your father, Alex. He said well done about getting into the team, and wondered if you would give him a call about shooting pigeon on Saturday. He says they're hitting the oil-seed rape quite badly."

"Did you tell him that I'm playing golf on Saturday?"

"Yes, but he was thinking of doing an evening flight. You'd be through by then, wouldn't you?"

"Probably," Alex replied with little keenness. "I'll give him a call in a minute."

Mr. Craig looked across at his daughter. "Was that all he had to say?"

Liz took the kettle off the side of the Rayburn and filled it with water. "No, he said that Jonathan Davies was concerned that what happened tonight in the pub might colour my judgement on the project, and he asked me to call him."

"And did you?"

"Yes."

"And what did you say?"

Liz spooned coffee into a mug. "That we were still undecided."

He chortled quietly. "Probably not what Gregor had hoped you would say."

"No."

Alex took a deep breath and got up from his chair. "Listen, I don't know what you both feel about this, but, well, I was speaking with Tom about everything on the golf course, and he suggested that we might get someone in—you know, as a paying guest in the house. We've got the spare room empty, and Granddad, you said yourself we were pretty strapped for cash. I just thought that maybe it wasn't such a bad idea. I mean, every little bit helps."

Liz let out a scoffing laugh. "I don't think things are *that* bad, Alex!"

"Maybe not, but at least it would be a bit of money coming in for housekeeping and the like."

Liz took the steaming kettle off the Rayburn and poured water into her coffee. "I think that that would be more trouble than it was worth, would it not?"

"I don't think so, Mum. I mean, a student or someone. They'd probably only sleep here, and I'm going into town every day. I could drive him and get him to pay for some of the petrol, so it would help me." Alex looked from one to the other. "Well, would you consider it?"

His grandfather flicked his head to the side. "Not a bad idea. It may be peanuts, but Alex could be right. Every little bit helps."

Alex looked at his mother. "Well?"

She took a sip of coffee and slowly shook her head. "I don't think we need anyone else in the household at the minute."

Alex lifted his hands in exasperation and slapped them hard on the top of his head. "Oh, for God's sake, Mum, come on! It's exactly what this household needs at the minute! If not for financial reasons, then certainly for emotional ones!" For a moment he stood looking at them both, their faces expressing dismay at his outburst, then, shaking his head at the futility of it all, he turned and picked up the portable. "I'll see you both in the morning." He left the room, closing the door behind him without a backward glance.

Liz made for the door, intending to call him back, but was cut short in her actions by her father.

"Leave him be, Lizzie."

"What did he mean by that?" she asked quietly.

"You've got to understand that he's finding it hard to work out how best to cope with the situation at present. He doesn't like seeing you suffering the way you are at the minute, lass. He's just trying to think of a way to help you out."

Liz moved over to the table and sat down heavily on the chair next to her father. She rested her elbows on the table and rubbed at the tiredness in her eyes. "I know." She paused. "Oh, Dad, I don't know what's wrong with me. My head is so full of *hate* at the minute. It seems to affect everything."

Her father stretched across and gently patted her arm. "Aye, I can tell that. But what Alex was saying to me when you were out of the room is right, you know. We have to keep going. We have to bring life back into this house, otherwise we'll all just sink into a huge bucket of gloom."

Liz looked up and smiled at her father. "It's that bad, is it?"

Her father gave her a wink. "That's exactly what I asked Alex."

Liz raised her eyebrows and blew out a long breath. "So it *is* that bad."

"Aye, I think it must be—for him, at any rate."

Liz nodded. "So we should maybe consider doing what he suggests."

"I don't see why not. As he said, the spare room is free, and he's certainly right in saying that we could do with a bit of extra cash coming in."

Liz put both hands on the table and pushed herself to her feet. "I'll go and have a word with him."

Her father laid his hand on top of hers. "Aye, you do that thing. And remember, lass, you mean more to that boy than anyone else in the world at the minute." He got up from his chair and took his daughter in his arms. "And that goes for me as well, d'ye hear?"

Chapter 4

The pigeon, nothing more than a shadowed outline against the darkening sky, weaved its way across the field towards him before setting its wings to plane down into the small copse at the edge of which Alex had been standing for the past two hours. He kept his head low, shielding his eyes with the peak of his baseball cap, just in case the fast-diminishing light caught in them the merest glint of reflection, enough for the pigeon, through the intricacy of its built-in radar vision, to sense that something was out of sorts with its intended night-time roost. Alex raised the shotgun and took a bead on its head, allowing for its forward motion, putting pressure on the trigger only when the bird had reached the outermost branches of the tree that stood behind him. The gun kicked hard against his shoulder, the air exploding with sound, and as the hollow echo faded away across the open fields, it was replaced by the frantic thrash of wings against branches, as those pigeons which had slipped into the centre of the wood, from directions unguarded by his father or himself, broke cover from the depths of the trees and made their escape.

The Jack Russell, who had been watching the progress of the pigeon as intently as Alex, took off into the wood, yelping excitedly at the prospect of finding another pigeon, fully intending to give it a good mauling before it could be finally wrested from his vice-like jaws.

"Leckie!" Alex yelled after the dog, his voice breaking into a laugh. "Come here, you stupid idiot! I missed it!"

Leckie, however, never deviated from the mission-in-hand, his war-cry diminishing until it was lost to the sound of the freshening wind that had begun to flush out any vestige of warmth that had been hitherto afforded to Alex by the protection of the trees. He pulled up the collar of his jacket and dug his hands deep into the pockets. Leaning back against the tree, he began stamping his feet on the hardened ground in an attempt to rid the tingling ache of cold from his toes.

"I think we've done for the night."

The voice made Alex start, and he turned to watch his father approach through the trees. His shotgun was shouldered with one hand, and in the other he carried a plastic fertilizer bag, the weight of which caused it to knock clumsily against his Wellington as he walked.

Breaking open his gun, Alex took out the unfired cartridges and slipped them back into his belt. "How did you get on?"

"Not too bad. About twenty-three. How about you?"

Alex looked down at the dismal extent of his bag. "I haven't counted yet, but I think only about ten. I'm afraid I was a bit off-target tonight."

His father glanced over to the pile of spent cartridges that lay scattered at the base of the tree. He let out a short laugh. "Aye, I can see that. Well, you start picking those up, and I'll deal with these." He laid down his gun and started to count the pigeon into the bag. "Nine, ten, eleven. One more than you thought." He gave the neck of the bag a twist and slung it over his shoulder, then, putting his thumb and forefinger into the sides of his mouth, he gave out one long, ear-splitting whistle to call back the dog. He bent down to retrieve his gun. "Och well, it's just a drop in the ocean anyway. They'll still be back in force tomorrow, even though they've lost a few comrades tonight." He waited until Alex had finished stuffing the empty cartridges into his pocket, then moved off into the field. "Come on, we'll head for home."

Alex tucked his gun under his arm and stood for a moment watching his father stride away in front of him, his short, muscular frame barely stooping under the weight of the heavy bag he carried over his shoulder. That's a good one, he thought to himself. And whose home would you be talking about?

They made their way in an uneasy silence across the open field, the only sounds being the wind and the brittle crunching of their feet on the frost-spangled leaves of the oil-seed rape. The near-full moon in the cloudless sky lit their way, their shadows cast in front of them in ghostly, yet perfectly focused forms. It wasn't until they had reached the brow of the hill, where the warming rectangles of light spilt out from the windows in the farmhouse to greet them, that his father spoke.

"So the match today was successful, was it?"

"Yes, it was. But only just. We won all the singles, but only managed to scrape a draw on one of the foursomes."

"Who was it you were playing?"

"Aberdeen University."

"Right." His father paused, and Alex sensed that he was uncertain as to how he should continue the conversation. "And then, what about your studies? How are they going?"

"Good enough. I've had a change of tutor for German which I thought might be a bit disruptive, but he's turned out to be a pretty sound guy, *and* he makes himself available for tutorials, which is more than can be said for the last one."

"New, is he?"

"Yes, a Canadian. He's actually a professor, but he doesn't head the department or anything like that. From what I can gather, he's just coming up for retirement and was given a secondment to Saint Andrews from the University of Toronto."

"One of those eccentric old duffers, is he?"

Alex let out a short chuckle. "In ways. He's always pacing around the room as he talks, and he has this pipe in his mouth which he never succeeds in keeping lit. But, funnily enough, I wouldn't say that he really looks *that* old. He sort of reminds me of one of those old Hollywood film actors, but I can't for the life of me think which one."

His father stopped, a querying smile on his face. "Give me a clue, then."

Alex shrugged. "I can't. I just know that I've seen him in one of those old colour films. Maybe one of those 1960s thrillers."

"Alfred Hitchcock?"

"No, that's not him."

His father laughed. "No, you nit, that's the guy who *made* those kind of films about that time."

"Ah. Well, maybe."

"I bet it's Cary Grant."

Alex stopped in his tracks, his mouth open in thought, then he gave a loud click with his fingers. "That's exactly who it is!" he exclaimed. "You've got it! It's Cary Grant."

His father chucked his head to the side and gave his son a companionable bump with his arm. "There you are, then. One thing I know about is my films."

They walked on into the shelter of the red pan-tiled farm buildings and passed round the side of the lambing shed, where his father's small flock of pedigree Suffolks was housed.

Letting the fertilizer bag fall from his shoulder, Gregor flicked on the switch by the door, the action immediately causing a flutter of alarm amongst his ewes as they noisily began to seek out their offspring in the close-stocked quarters. He made his way slowly down the central feed aisle, casting an experienced eye from one side to the other to make sure that nothing was amiss. Alex watched him, leaning his shoulder against the side of the door.

"Dad?"

Gregor reached the other end of the shed and turned. "Aye?"

"Can I ask what you're planning to do?"

His father walked slowly towards him, giving the flock a second appraisal. "I don't really know, Alex. I suppose it has to depend on whether the consortium can get this other investor."

"I didn't actually mean that. What about you and Mum?"

Gregor had reached the half-way support stanchion of the shed. He stopped and looked at his son, but did not answer.

"Are you going to get a divorce?"

His father finished the inspection and came to lean his back against the opposite doorpost. He let out a long sigh. "I don't know, lad. I'm not sure what I should do. I don't know what would be least hurtful to your mother."

Alex shook his head and stared out into the night to avoid looking at his father. "It's not just Mum, you know."

He heard the crumpled rustle of his father's waxed jacket as he moved across the doorway towards him. A strong hand squeezed his shoulder, but he shrugged it off and walked out into the darkness, giving a quick whistle for Leckie, who had been busying himself on a ratting sortie, darting from one building to another.

"Alex!" He could hear anxiety in his father's voice as he walked away from him. "Listen, lad, why don't we go into the house for a cup of coffee and we can have a talk about it?"

"Not tonight, Dad," he shouted back over the sound of the wind. "I've got an early start tomorrow, and anyway"—he stopped and looked back to where his father stood, silhouetted in the doorway by the light that shone out from the lambing shed—"I want to go home."

He turned and made his way towards his car. That should give him a jolt, he thought to himself, that should hurt him. But as he walked he realized from the burning sting of tears in his eyes that the remark had had exactly that effect on himself.

CHAPTER 5

Agnes Winterbotham placed her Nilfisk vacuum cleaner into the cupboard under the stairs, then began her daily struggle of trying to get its unruly tube sufficiently curled so that she could close the door behind it. Giving its escaping spout a final kick with an elastic-slippered foot, she slammed the door and locked it, the action giving her as much satisfaction as if she had just managed to subdue an irascible boa constrictor. Delving into the pocket of her floral housecoat, she pulled out a yellow duster and walked along the swirl-patterned carpet in the narrow hallway, wiping the cloth along the radiator shelf as she went, being careful to avoid knocking off either the cactus plant or the delicate pink figurine of the "Shepherdess with Lamb in Arms." She opened the front door, snibbing it so that it didn't shut behind her, and descended the three steps to the pavement, where she began rubbing hard at the brass plaque which was bolted to the black-glossed iron railings that ran the full length of the little street. When she felt that its gleam was sufficient, she looked to each side of her to make sure that she would not hinder the path of one of the many students who were making their way, in different states of urgency after the weekend, along the street to their lectures. Then, taking two paces back, she first made sure that the name BALLINLUIG GUEST HOUSE stood out well for the benefit of any prospective client, before leaning her head to the side to confirm to herself that the VACANCIES sign in the window of the residents' drawing-room was set in exactly the right place for maximum appeal. Satisfied that all was as it should be, she ascended the steps.

As she reached out to give the brass knob on the front door a quick once-over, it flew open and a young man, dressed in brown terylene trousers and beige wind-cheater, appeared and immediately tripped over the threshold, precipitating both himself and the pile of books that he carried at her feet. She moved to the side and watched as he scrambled together the papers that had flown out of his "Arcadia A-4" file, then, gathering up his books, he got to his feet and gave her a wide, teeth-plated smile, using the corner of the file to push his black bottle-lensed spectacles back onto the bridge of his nose.

He let out a long, embarrassed moan. "Sorry about that, Mrs. Winterbotham," he lisped, his words accompanied by a fine spray of spittle.

Agnes looked kindly at the acne-infested face of the young boy, thinking to herself how unkind nature could be to bestow one person with so many disturbing afflictions. "That's all right, Alasdair. Now, did you remember to call your mother this morning?"

Alasdair let out another indecipherable sound that gave her no real clue as to what the answer might be to her question, then turned and ran off down the street, his scarf flying out behind him like that of a First World War pilot. Agnes watched fondly as he went. What a nice boy, she thought to herself, so little trouble. Just the kind of guest that she liked. She let out a short sigh and glanced up to one of the upstairs windows, the lower half of which was closed down upon two pairs of grey socks that flapped in the morning breeze. Not like others she'd care to mention.

She walked back into the house, dropped the snib, and opened the door into the residents' drawing-room. Adjusting the two lace antimacassars as she made her way around the sofa, she gave each of the three cushions a generous plumping before laying them back in place. Then, running her cloth over the mantelpiece, she lightly dusted the ornaments before taking down the focal point of the display, a fading black-and-white photograph of her deceased husband. She gave the glass that protected the stern, shrouded-eyed face a gentle blow, then wiped the frame and replaced it, adjusting it so that it was exactly positioned where it had been beforehand. Standing back, she smiled at the bleak countenance and said quietly under her breath, "Good morning, Hubert. It's another lovely day. Fresh, but lovely."

A door slammed shut upstairs, so loud that she saw the photograph tremble in the shock wave. With a click of her teeth, she walked over to the mantelpiece, made the minutest adjustment to her husband's image, then hurried over to the door and opened it. She looked up the narrow staircase at the tall man who thumped his way down towards her, struggling to pull on a huge belted mackintosh over his leather arm-patched tweed jacket, while passing a battered leather brief-case from one hand to the other.

"Professor Kempler? Might I have a word?" Agnes held her hands together, squeezing her fingers so tightly that the area around the knuckles went white. She hated confrontation. In the past, she had always left this kind of thing up to Hubert.

"As long as it's quick, Mrs. Winterbotham. I have to give a tutorial in ten minutes."

He always pronounced her name incorrectly. It was pronounced "bottom," not "botham." Hubert would have put him right, probably quietly accentuating his rebuff with some comment about the ignorance of "colonials."

"Professor Kempler, I wondered if you might *try* to make a little less noise. It disturbs the other guests."

The man clamped the brief-case between his legs while he did up the buttons on his raincoat. He glanced up the stairs. "Forgive me for saying this, Mrs. Winterbotham, but as far as I know, you only have myself and that spotty-faced youth as your guests at the minute, and I saw him head off in the most appallingly dishevelled state about five minutes ago."

Agnes felt her face colouring fast. "That is a cruel thing to say, Professor, and neither is it the point. The fact is that I am of a nervous disposition and I don't like noise."

Arthur Kempler did up the buckle of his belt and took the brief-case from between his legs. He stuck his hand in his pocket and pulled out a pipe and a lighter. "I'm sorry, Mrs. Winterbotham. I shall try to make less noise in future." Then, before Agnes could utter another word of reproach, he flicked the lighter and held it to the bowl, emitting from his mouth a puff of smoke that even a myopic Red Indian would have found hard not to see.

Agnes was incensed by his action. "Professor, please do *not* smoke your pipe in my house! I've asked you this before!"

Arthur cast his eyes heavenward, then made an accentuated play of pressing his forefinger into the bowl to extinguish the pipe before returning it to his pocket. "Anything else, Mrs. Winterbotham? I have to go, you know."

Agnes crossed her arms to stop herself from shaking both with anger and nerves. "Yes, as a matter of fact, there is." She bravely took one pace towards him. "I have also specifically asked you not to hang your shirts or your socks on the radiator to dry."

Arthur Kempler held up both hands in desperation. "And I've stopped, Mrs. Winterbotham!"

Agnes continued slowly, trying to control her tone. "Yes, but now you are placing your socks on the window-sill to dry, and, Professor Kempler, it does not look good for prospective—"

Arthur turned full circle this time, his flailing brief-case nearly decapitating the "Shepherdess with Lamb in Arms." "*Christ*, Mrs. Winterbotham, how the *hell else* am I meant to get them dry?"

That was enough for Agnes. She had felt up until now that she could put up with his appalling house manners, simply because in early March room rentals throughout St. Andrews were at a low ebb. But for anyone to take the Lord's name blatantly in vain in front of her! That was unforgivable! What would Hubert have thought at this kind of behaviour going on under *their* roof? There was obviously only one course of action to take.

"Professor Kempler, I am sorry, but you leave me no alternative other than to ask you to leave." There. She had said it, and she was proud that there had not even been the slightest tremor in the tone of her voice.

Arthur stood looking at her for a moment, then swept his hand over his grey-flecked hair, a grimace on his face as he tried to force some kind of reconciliatory meekness into his manner. "Listen, Mrs. Winterbotham—"

Agnes realized immediately that she had the upper hand. "It's 'bottom,' by the way, not 'botham.' "

Arthur nodded. "I'm sorry, Mrs. Winter-*bottom*." Damn it, he didn't mean to smile. Get that smile off your face *now*. "But could we not just try again? I really do promise that I'll make an effort, as I'm sure that you must understand that I don't have much time to look for other accommodation right now, it being in the middle of the semester."

Agnes had caught the smile and gave him one last glare of contempt before turning on her heel and walking along the passage to the kitchen. "I shall give you three days to find other lodgings, Professor Kempler, and I shall *not* be returning your deposit." She opened the door into the kitchen and closed it behind her.

For a moment, Arthur stared at the lilac-blue barrier that lay between them, then blew out one large, loud raspberry. "Damned woman," he said quietly and turned and let himself out of his former residence.

At the first chime of the bell, Alex looked up from his notes and glanced through the dusty panes of the study window at the church clock on the other side of the street. It was midday. He caught the eyes of his three fellow students and raised his eyebrows. From their looks, he could tell that they had gathered as little from the tutorial as he had done, and he was fairly sure that they were all of the same mind in wishing that the professor would come to a halt, so that they could go off to have a well-earned pint in the pub. But he continued to drone on unintelligibly through the twelve chimes, as he had done throughout the whole two-hour tutorial, pacing the floor in front of the huge marble fireplace, every third round holding his lighter to his pipe and letting out one huge cloud of smoke, before taking it from his mouth and allowing it to burn out over the next three rounds.

The professor was definitely having an off-day. Usually his tutorials were fired with debate and humour, and on many occasions he was sympathetic enough to break into English if he felt that the point of discussion was too important to be jeopardized through the students' lack of knowledge of the German language; or, what was more common, if he felt that the punch line of one of his many off-beat jokes might not receive the loudest groans of inappreciation that it deserved. But today had been completely different. Alex sat back in the armchair and picked at the piping on the faded loose cover, allowing his thoughts to meander away from the tutorial, as they had done throughout the session. He thought back to the golf match on Saturday and went over in his mind how much better he could have played the two approach shots to the sixteenth and seventeenth greens, and how they would have secured for him and his partner an outright win, rather than a draw, in their foursomes match. He thought back to his trial match with Tom Harrison, and his golf captain's words of advice. Maybe Tom was right that he should try to get another girl-friend. He hadn't really had a steady one since he had left Madras the year before. Okay, there was that girl he'd met in Freshers' Week, but that had only lasted a couple of weeks. He looked across at the only girl in the room, opposite him on the sofa. She sat, quite obviously doodling on her textbook, her legs curled up under her bottom, her elbow resting on the leather arm as she absently raked her fingers through her straight blonde hair. What about Madeleine, for instance? Yes, what *about* Madeleine? He'd not even considered it before, but why not? She was a really good friend of his, they'd studied a good deal together, and as far as he knew she didn't have a boy-friend. He looked hard at her in appraisal. *And*, what's more, she's pretty. His eyes moved down from her face and took in the curve of her breasts and the protrusion of her nipples against the tightness of her cotton T-shirt, all this being accentuated by the framing folds of her open-zippered waistcoat.

Alex suddenly realized what was happening, and gave his body a shuddering jolt to get himself away from that train of thought. What the hell was he doing? He crossed his legs to relieve the sensual ache that had begun tugging at his lower abdomen. Come on, Professor, finish off this damned tutorial now, before the distractions get worse!

Arthur stopped and looked at his watch. "*Also, was machen wir? Es ist schon viertel nach zwölf! Gut! Machen wir Schluß. Am Freitag sehen wir uns alle wieder hier.*" There was a general creaking of old furniture as the students moved in their seats to gather up their belongings. Madeleine was first to her feet. She threw her books back onto the sofa and pushed her arms high above her head in an effort to stretch out some of the weariness that had assailed her body during the dreary session. "*Und Madeleine,*" the professor continued, "*ich finde es sehr beunruhigend, daß Sie in meiner Arbeitsgruppe keinen BH tragen. Ich bitte Sie, in Zukunft einen anzuhaben.*"

The aftermath of his remark, following the initial shocked moment of silence, could have been much worse, had Madeleine not immediately read the situation as being yet another example of the professor's zany sense of humour, taking it as his preconceived plan to end the otherwise mind-numbing tutorial in a breath-clutching climax. She broke the embarrassed hush in the fusty room with a loud burst of laughter, deciding to give the old boy as good as she had received. "I beg your pardon, Professor!" she exclaimed, a look of surprised horror on her face, her three male colleagues noting, with relief, that there was little change to the colour of her cheeks. "If I choose not to wear a bra, then I won't! Anyway, you're far too old to make a remark like that!" She put together the two ends of her waistcoat zipper, and shut away from sight the subjects of debate.

For a moment, Arthur Kempler stood with one hand holding his elbow, the other covering his mouth. He then closed his eyes and thumped the palm of his hand against his forehead. "Madeleine," he started slowly, "that was an unforgivable remark, and I am totally ashamed of myself for ever having uttered it. You are absolutely right, of course. Not only am I too old, I have no business to make any observation at all on how my students dress. Please accept my most abject apologies. If I can offer any excuse for my unacceptable and unprofessional behaviour, it would be only that I happen to have a few rather distracting thoughts going through my mind at the moment."

Madeleine glanced at her fellow students, then took the opportunity of rubbing salt into her tutor's wounds. "That, Professor, is an understatement."

Arthur held up his hands, as if defending himself from any further verbal onslaught. "I know, I know! It's just that . . . well . . . I have this morning been unceremoniously ejected from my lodgings by a woman who would make Boadicea look like a nurserymaid." He turned to shuffle together the papers on the desk and stuff them into the brief-case. "Consequently, I have been forced to find somewhere else to live in the next . . . three . . . days." Clicking his brief-case shut, he turned and leaned against the desk, glancing around his four students. "So if any of you have a bright idea, I would be most grateful for your assistance."

Madeleine waved her hand in the air. "I don't suppose you'd be interested in a room in our all-girl flat, would you, Professor?" She fluttered in wicked innocence.

Arthur let out a guffaw of a laugh and pushed himself off the desk, walking between his students to the coat-stand by the door. "Madeleine, my dear, with the self-confidence and sense of humour that are obviously in your possession, you will go far in life." He took down his raincoat and began shrugging it on, bowing to Madeleine as he did so. "I thank you for your kind offer, but I must feel obliged to refuse." He did up his buttons. "But if, at any time, you see me emerging from a large cardboard box in a shop doorway on a cold, frosty morning, I would be most grateful if you might ask again." He opened the door of the study and held out his brief-cased hand to usher the group out of the room.

While Arthur locked the door, the students made their way down the stairs, laughing quietly amongst themselves about the tedium of the session and the professor's extraordinary remark, their hushed tones echoing around the chambered confines of the stone stairwell.

When they had reached the next landing, Madeleine glanced up through the iron banister. "Poor old boy!" she said to Alex when she had seen that the professor wasn't following. "It'll be pretty difficult for him to get anywhere at this time of year. He'll probably end up in a doss-house." She laughed. "At least, he's got the coat to go with the image!"

Alex smiled at her observation, then almost immediately stopped dead in his tracks, a frown of contemplation coming over his face. Madeleine had carried on a couple of paces before she realized that her companion was no longer at her side. She turned and gave him an inquiring look. "Alex? What's the matter?"

Alex shook his head. "Oh, nothing much. Probably nothing at all. But listen, you go on to the pub with the others, and I'll meet you there in about ten minutes."

Madeleine seemed still none the wiser for his explanation. "What are you going to do?"

"Nothing. I just want to see Professor Kempler for a minute."

Madeleine shrugged her shoulders and smiled at him. "Okay." She turned and started quickly down the stairs to catch up with the others. "I'll see you in the pub, then."

Leaning his back against the wall, Alex settled down to wait for the professor to appear, and began to work through his mind the practicality of his new train of thought. Was it worth considering? I mean, giving it a bit of lateral thought, would it be such a daft idea? Maybe it wasn't another student that was needed at home. Maybe it would be much better to have someone older, someone with experience in life, who could inject some light-hearted diversity—and even wisdom—into the household. Perhaps it was all too easy, latching on to the first person who just happened to be looking for somewhere to live, but then it just might work. In fact, the more he thought about it, the more *workable* the idea became! The professor was an easygoing guy, he had a good sense of humour—well, a bit odd-ball would be more precise—but he didn't seem to be grumpy or obtrusive or anything like that—and what was more, he *had* to be getting on to be about the same age as Granddad, so they'd probably have quite a bit in common. And it would be much easier for Mum having someone that age, better than having a student whom she might feel she'd have to "mother." Alex pushed himself away from the wall. Well, no harm in putting the idea to him, anyway.

There was still no sign of the professor. Alex turned and made his way back up the stairs again, finding the door of the study open and the professor's keys hanging in the lock. The room appeared to be empty, but the top drawer of the filing cabinet, which was against the wall behind the desk, was open, and files stuck out from it like badly shuffled cards.

"Professor?"

Arthur's tall figure suddenly materialized from below the level of the desk, the look of surprise on his face crumpling into a grimace of pain as his head came into contact with the underside of the cabinet drawer. A sound rang around the room as loud and as lingering as the ringing of a gong. "*Ow! Dammit!*" He closed his eyes tight and rubbed hard at the top of his head. "Alex! What the hell are you doing? Ow, that hurt!"

"Sorry. I didn't know where you were." Alex walked around the side of the desk and looked down at the disordered pile of files and papers scattered over the surface of the floor. Arthur bent down to push them together.

"That bloody woman! Said she wouldn't pay back my deposit. Now I can't find the damned piece of paper I signed."

Picking up the files, he stuck them back, with little regard to indexing, into the cabinet and slammed the door shut. "So! What can I do for you?"

"Well, I wonder if I could have a quick word?"

Arthur's mouth twisted in trepidation at what he thought might well be the reason for his student's returning. "Alex, I hope you're not going to take me to task over what I said to Madeleine. It was a stupid remark, and I really could kick myself for saying it. I hope that you don't think that you need to take it any further."

Alex shook his head. "No, I wasn't going to mention it."

The professor smiled at him. "Good! I'm glad." He sat down on the edge of the desk, crossing his arms. "In that case, please don't think me rude if I say that I hope this won't be too long a discussion, Alex. I really *do* have to find somewhere else to live."

Alex cleared his throat. "Well . . . actually, it was about that."

"Really?" The expression on Arthur's face turned from one of resigned detachment to quizzical interest. "Do you know of somewhere?"

"Well, it depends on whether you want to live in Saint Andrews or not."

Arthur cocked his head to the side. "I teach here, Alex. I can't very well go live on the other side of Scotland."

"I didn't mean that. Would it matter to you if you lived *outside* Saint Andrews?"

Arthur shrugged his shoulders. "At the minute, I'd consider anything. I don't have a car, but as long as there's some kind of regular public transport. . . . What do you have in mind, Alex?"

"Well, it's just that we have a spare room in the house that we were thinking of renting out. I live on a farm with my mother and grandfather about seven miles out of Saint Andrews, and because things aren't going too well with the business, we discussed the idea of letting out a room to help with—you know—housekeeping and that sort of thing."

Arthur nodded slowly, taking in what Alex had been saying. "Can one get into Saint Andrews quite easily from out there? I mean, is there a regular bus service?"

"Yes, from the top of the farm road. But what I was going to suggest is that I drive in to university every day, so I could bring you in. That is, if you could maybe give me a hand with the cost of petrol."

Arthur contemplated this for a moment, then held out his hands as if laying himself open to Alex's tentative offer. "So, where do we take it from here?"

"Well, if you want, you could come out to meet my mother and grandfather, and have a look at the place. I'm afraid I have no idea what the charge would be for the room. You'd have to talk to my mother about that, but I'm sure that it won't be any more than you're paying at the minute in the middle of Saint Andrews."

"Okay then. When would be a good time?"

Alex glanced at his watch. "It couldn't be until a bit later, I'm afraid. I've got two essays to finish off for tomorrow, so I'm going to be spending most of the afternoon in the library. But I reckon I'd be through by, say, half past four. I could take you out after that, if it would be suitable."

Arthur rose to his feet and walked over to the door. "I think—or should I say I hope—that that sounds like a godsend, and because, unlike you, I have little to do this afternoon, I shall rendezvous with *you* at the library at, say, twenty to five."

"Right."

Arthur walked over to the door. "You *will* call your mother about this, won't you, Alex?"

"I could try, but I don't think she'd be in. She spends most of the day out on the farm. But I'm sure it will be all right."

"Okay. Well, I'll see you at twenty to five at the library." They walked out onto the stone landing, and the professor closed the door of the study behind him. "And thank you, Alex. You may have just saved me from a life on the streets of Saint Andrews."

Brian Davidson, Balmuir's master butcher and the man renowned throughout Fife for being the purchaser of the Supreme Champion at the

1989 Smithfield Show, stripped the disposable gloves from his hands and threw them into a waste-bin, then came around the end of the counter to open the door of the shop. "Now, see and enjoy your meal tonight, Liz. You couldn't get better than a roll of Aberdeen Angus beef, no matter what the French may say!"

Liz smiled at the man, the ruddiness of his beaming face quite accentuated by the white coat and mesh trilby he wore on his head. "Thank you, Brian. Let's hope they appreciate the treat."

She left the shop and walked across the narrow main street of the village to where the Land Rover was parked. It had been her intention to leave the package in the vehicle, but seeing Leckie jump across from the back seat and stand with his front feet on the steering wheel, a cock-eared look of eager anticipation as he eyed the bag, she thought better of it and veered past towards the small Spar supermarket.

The bell on the door tinged as she entered, and she scooped up a wire basket from the stack that was pushed in beside the refrigerator unit. She took a pint of milk from the unit as she passed and made her way quickly around the single display section in the centre of the shop to pick up a packet of peas from the deep freeze, her only other requirement for the day. As she turned the corner, her eye was caught by the line of glossy magazines on the shelf. Consequently she did not happen to notice the enormous tweedy posterior that bent forward in front of her, the possessor of which was doing her best to get low enough to retrieve something from the hindmost reaches of the bottom shelf. Liz hit her target at speed, making Delia Stanfield straighten up faster than she might have done in many a year.

Liz clapped her hand over her mouth. "Lady Stanfield! I am sorry! I wasn't looking where I was going!"

Delia took time to turn her formidable bulk around in the confined area, her eyes lighting up when she saw who her assailant was. "Liz, my dear, it's you!" She rolled her eyes and let out a long sigh of regret. "I was so hoping it was going to be some gorgeous young man!"

"Oh dear! What a real disappointment for you!" They both laughed, any potential embarrassment that the incident might have caused tempered by their humour.

Delia linked her arms through the handle of her basket and gave Liz's dress a quick assessment from head to foot. "Well, you certainly are the working girl today, aren't you?"

Liz glanced down at her attire. The legs of her jeans, tucked into her Wellingtons, were smeared with milk from the leaking teat of a feeding bottle, and there was a yellow streak of something much less savoury down the front of her torn jacket where she had had to cradle one of the more sickly lambs. She looked up at Delia, an embarrassed look on her face. "Oh, Lady Stanfield, would you just look at me! I was really hoping that I could make it in and out of Balmuir without anyone seeing me. We're over our heads with work at the minute, what with the sowing *and* the lambing, and I suddenly realized that we didn't have anything for supper. Problem is that Dad and I have all the orphan lambs over with us at Brunthill this year. It just seemed easier with the situation being . . . well . . . what it is."

Delia moved forward and gently put her hand on Liz's arm. "I do understand, my dear." She paused, her glossy lips suddenly pulled tight into a thin line of contempt. "That really was an appalling show at the meeting the other night," she said in a hushed tone. "What a dreadful oaf that man McKay is! I did *so* feel for you. Now, you might well consider it being none of my business, but may I ask how things are at present?"

Liz smiled at the kindness of the woman. "Well, they're not really . . ."

Delia sighed and shook her head. "Aren't men such fools? Only thinking of one thing all the time." She rocked forward in a confiding manner. "Hector had a dalliance once with one of our girl grooms. Didn't last, though. Soon put a stop to it."

Liz found herself having to bite hard on her lip to stop herself from laughing, the image of the upright figure of Sir Hector and a hot-blooded girl groom being too incongruous to imagine. "How did you manage that?" she asked.

Delia shrugged her shoulders. "Found them in a clinch in the discothèque at a Hunt Ball, so got hold of a jug of ice-cold water, walked up to him and poured it over his head. Ha, *that* soon cooled his ardour. Never went astray after *that!*" She put her hand once more on Liz's arm. "Now listen, my dear, I know that the community council are really pushing for this golf thing to go ahead, but *you* must take your time in deciding. If you want any advice, please come to see me. Even though I was lucky enough to curb Hector's rambling instincts, I do understand exactly what you're going through."

Liz smiled a thank-you at the woman. At that moment, the bell on the door sounded, and Delia, having the advantage of height over Liz, craned over the central display to see who had entered. She looked back at Liz, a furtive expression on her face. "Oh, my word, speak of the devil! It's the *other* woman, my dear." She pressed her bulk as far back against the display section as she could to allow Liz to pass. "You go on and I shall waylay her while you get out of the shop."

"That's very kind of you, Lady Stanfield," Liz whispered conspiratorially.

Delia gave her a wink. "Not at all. As I said, I understand the situation." And, as if settling herself to form the last line of defence at the Siege of Mafeking, she turned to block the aisle. Liz quickly retrieved a bag of peas from the deep freeze and made her way to the counter, hearing behind her the sound of Delia's voice reaching decibels never before attained in the shop as she greeted Mary McLean.

CHAPTER 6

Once he had become used to the agricultural state of the interior of Alex's Peugeot van and the heady cocktail of tractor oil and sheep, Arthur had found himself rather enjoying his trip out into the countryside. At the outset of their journey he had thought to break the formality of the student/teacher relationship by engaging Alex in general conversation about his family and his roots in Fife, but noticed that the boy's hesitancy as he drove through St. Andrews and the lack of response to his questioning indicated that he was probably quite new to the art of driving. He decided therefore that it would be less of a distraction to Alex if he just kept quiet, and consequently settled himself back in the torn plastic seat and contented himself in looking out the window.

The little van swept up the hill out of St. Andrews and rounded the corner at the Brownhills junction, leaving the late-afternoon sun to bathe the grey stone houses of the town and the ancient ruins of the cathedral in a strong, shimmering light. The road ran on adjacent to the sea, lying some distance away across undulating fields of newly tilled soil, its burnt-steel surface broken in ribbons of white by the cresting waves as it stretched off to the horizon without hindrance of land or vessel. Single-wired fences atop drystone dikes dipped and rose as they drove by, revealing, at their lowest ebb, fields in which double-tyred tractors toiled with frenetic power to prepare the seed-beds for the summer's harvest. In others, sheep fussed like protective nannies about their unruly young as they bounced on spring-loaded legs around straw-baled shelters tucked well into corners away from the cold cut of the prevailing wind. Occasionally the open view was narrowed as they passed through hamlets of whitewashed cottages, each of different size and shape but granted uniformity by the pan-tiles on their roofs, their terra-cotta surfaces shining to an almost translucent pink in the fiery rays of the dipping sun.

Arthur's relaxed contentment in perusing the scenery was such that, when the incident took place, the most immediate thought that flashed through his mind was that his Maker had predestined the fifteen-minute journey to be a restful and fitting climax to his otherwise disruptive life. They had just driven, at nothing more than a gentle pace, over the crest of a hill on the twisting road when they were suddenly confronted by a speeding car heading straight towards them, its driver having become frustrated at being caught behind a queue of traffic that was fronted by a large, slow-moving tractor. Both Alex and Arthur simultaneously slammed their feet hard down to the floor, and with a degree of luck, rather than of better judgement, the van responded to Alex's guidance by swerving in towards the side of the road and juddering to a stalled halt with one wheel up on the grassy bank. The white-faced driver of the approaching car managed to swerve his way through the narrowest of gaps between the Peugeot and the tractor before being sent scurrying on his way by an ear-splitting blast on the airhorn of the gigantic blue machine.

For a moment, Alex stared straight ahead at the lopsided view of the wall three feet in front of them, then blew out a long puff of relief. "Sorry about that," he said quietly, breaking his seven-mile silence.

"Wasn't your fault," Arthur replied, turning back from viewing the disappearing car through the rear window. "Damned fool's not long from his coffin if he goes on driving like that." He studied Alex's ashen face. "Are you all right?"

Alex nodded. "That's the first near miss I've ever had." His voice shook as he spoke. "Do you think the van's all right?"

"Well, all we can do is reverse and see if a wheel falls off or the engine drops out. But don't worry. You did well to avoid him."

Alex started the engine again and reversed carefully away from the bank. Arthur rolled down the window and craned out to see if he could detect any damage. He brought his head back into the van. "Seems to be all right. Just a few clumps of grass stuck in your fender." He looked across at Alex. "Are you sure you're all right to continue?"

"Yes, I think so. We've only got about another half a mile to go." He engaged first gear and moved away slowly. "That's not the first time that's happened here. Not with me, I mean, but with other drivers. Problem is that the road has Z-bends all the way from Balmuir to here, so it's about the first place you can even try to overtake for about a mile." He gave Arthur a nervous smile. "That's why this stretch is known locally as Smash Alley."

Arthur gave him a reassuring wink. "Well, we live to see another day, thanks to some pretty classy driving."

Alex stuck to a cautiously sedate speed for the remainder of the journey, and Arthur noted the look of quiet relief come over the boy's face when he eventually brought the van down through the gears and indicated left off the main road. They turned in beside a lopsided wooden sign so lacking in paint that it was impossible for Arthur to ascertain the name of the establishment that they were approaching, and headed down a road pitted with pot-holes, the sides of which were spattered with loose Tarmac chips from past attempts at reparation. Alex began threading the van through these obstacles, the now-confident burst of speed at which he was accomplishing the task making it quite obvious to Arthur that he had probably been doing it for a good many years longer than he had been on the open road.

After two hundred yards of fairground driving they pulled into the farm steading, an assortment of buildings which Arthur quickly assessed to have seen better days. The rusted guttering that bounded the loose-slated roofs hung away in places from its mountings under the weight of green tufted weed that grew in its length, and where the unchannelled rain-water had run down the sides of the walls, white mould had clutched hard into gaps left by crumbling mortar. The tongue-and-groove timbers on the weather-bleached doors had swelled outwards, bursting their hold on each other, so that they were now of little use in closing off the darkened interiors of the buildings. And around the extremities of the property, half-hidden amongst tall yellowing clumps of grass, lay a graveyard of disused farm implements.

They continued round to the house, lying on the seaward side of the steading, and the initial sight of it made Arthur's urban-yearning heart drop the final few inches to the level of the metal oilcan that he had been holding upright with his feet for the duration of the journey. The door into the drab, grey-harled extension that jutted out at the back of the otherwise whitish house was an insipid shade of yellow, the lower half of it being almost indiscernible in colour due to the mudded streaks that had been splattered against it both by the elements and passing vehicles. At one side of the well-worn stone steps that led up to the door an old fertilizer bag had toppled over, spewing out its tangled contents of orange baler twine, while at the other side a discarded refrigerator rested hard on its open door, its stained interior filled with a plethora of dark brown medicine bottles.

Alex pulled the car to a halt and turned off the engine. "Here we are, then."

Arthur forced a smile onto his face. Good God, it was worse than Cold Comfort Farm! "It's very nice, Alex."

Alex laughed, noting the distinct lack of enthusiasm in the professor's voice. "No, it's not. It's ropy as hell, if you want the honest truth. Maybe I should explain that this is my grandparents' farm, and I don't think they ever had much inclination to do anything with the place. They just became quite happily used to it being like this."

"But you live here now?"

"Yes." He aimed a finger to a distant group of buildings that was just visible between the end of the house and an open-sided hay barn. "We used to be there until about six months ago, but then . . . well . . . my parents split up, and my mother and I moved back here. Then my grandmother died a couple of months back, so now it's just myself, my mother and my grandfather." Undoing his seat-belt, he made to open the door, then turned back to Arthur, thinking that maybe further reassurance was necessary. "I think my mother has great plans to get the place back in shape again, but time and money are both pretty hard to come by at the minute." He pushed the door open on its creaking hinges and got out, and watched over the roof of the van as Arthur slowly appeared from the passenger's side. "But I think you'll be pleasantly surprised when you get inside. It's very comfortable—and warm!"

Arthur flicked his head to the side. "Well, that's pretty important. My landlady in Saint Andrews had a tight-fisted habit of turning off the heating at six o'clock every night, regardless of how low the outside temperature had dropped."

Alex laughed. "Well, I can promise you that it's like a hothouse in there. Anyway, come on and I'll show you around."

As they made their way across the small courtyard towards the back door, there was a rasping screech as one of the steading doors was slid back on rusting rollers. A tall, thin man with a shock of wild white hair appeared in the doorway, a struggling lamb tucked under each arm.

"Och, it's yourself, Alex," the man said, turning to push the door closed with his elbow. "Wasn't expecting you to be home already. You're not practising your golf tonight?"

"No, not tonight," Alex replied, walking towards him.

Mr. Craig eyed the clumps of grass wedged hard into the bumper of the Peugeot van. "Looks like you've been ploughing a bit, lad."

"I know. I've just had a near miss up on Smash Alley. Someone came at me on the wrong side of the road." He bent down to pull the grass from the bumper. "I don't think there's any damage done, though." He looked up at his grandfather. "Is Mum home, Granddad?"

The farmer gave the steading a quick scan for the Land Rover. "No, I doubt she's back yet. She went into Balmuir for some purchases."

"Right. Well, have you got a moment? I'd like you to meet someone."

He looked over Alex's shoulder to where the tall raincoated figure stood by the back door. "Aye, well, I was just away to feed these wee devils, but I reckon they can hold off for a couple of minutes." Sliding open the door with a shove of his boot, he pushed the lambs back through the gap. "I doubt they'll go far," he said, closing the door on them. Taking an old rag from his pocket, he gave his hands a brisk rub as he walked with Alex across the courtyard.

"Granddad, I'd like you to meet my German tutor, Professor Kempler."

Craig nodded a greeting. "Professor Kempler." He stuck out his hand and Arthur took hold of it, feeling the softness of his own hand grate in the man's calloused grip.

"Very pleased to meet you, Mr. . . . ?"

A flustered look came over Alex's face. "Sorry, I should have said. Mr. Craig."

"Well, it's a pleasure, Mr. Craig."

There was a moment of uneasy silence as the two men smiled pleasantly at each other, both waiting for Alex to begin explaining the reason for the professor's visit. He eventually took the hint. "Granddad, I was having a tutorial with Professor Kempler this morning, and he just happened to mention that he was having to leave his lodgings, so he doesn't have anywhere to stay. I just thought that maybe he could have the spare room—you know, like we discussed."

A look of clarity came over the old man's face. "Ah, I see. Right, well, there's a thing then."

Arthur looked from one to the other, detecting a lack of keenness in the farmer's answer. "Maybe I'm jumping the gun a bit in coming out here today, Mr. Craig. It was just that Alex said that there might be a chance that you had a room to let, and if that is the case, then I could very well be interested in renting it from you."

The farmer scratched at the side of his face with his fingers. "Aye, well, that's what we decided to do." He looked at Alex. "We did have a thought that it might be a student, Professor. I don't know if the room would be quite suitable for someone of your standing."

Arthur laughed. "Mr. Craig, I am sure that what you have to offer would be a veritable palace compared to some of the places that I've ended up in over the years."

The farmer smiled at the man. "In that case, let's away and take a look then, shall we?" Walking over to the door, he levered off his Wellingtons on the doorstep and led the way into the house.

From the moment he entered, Arthur realized that Alex was true to his word. The house was indeed warm, though it was obvious that little had been done in way of decoration for many a year. Moving in single file through the cluttered kitchen and along the narrow passageway to the front hall, Arthur found himself murmuring words of feigned appreciation as he cast an eye over the collection of dull little prints, hung too high on walls lined with a yellowing paper on which it was just possible to make out the dying colours of its flowered pattern. Mr. Craig opened the dark-stained panel doors at either side of the hall, giving Arthur fleeting glances into a stark, formal dining-room and a neatly arranged sitting-room. Both, he determined from their slightly musty smell, had seen little use over the years.

Moving across to the staircase, the farmer bent down to slip home a dislodged stair-rod that held the threadbare beige runner in place. "I'm afraid it all may seem to you a wee bit run down, Professor." He took hold of the carved oak banister rail as if requiring its support, but then began to make his way with surprising agility up the stairs. "My wife and I never had much expertise in this interior-designing lark."

Arthur followed on with Alex hard at his heels. "Well, in that case, you're a man after my own heart, Mr. Craig. All I need of a place is a warm bed and a comfy chair."

"Aye, well, I hope we may be able to accommodate you there."

The stairs led up to a half-way stage, from which a passage ran off to rooms at the back the house, before turning back on themselves to continue up to the spacious front landing. Once there, Mr. Craig walked across the skylighted area and opened a door, standing back to allow Arthur to enter first.

The room was of similar size to the drawing-room below, again with a slightly unused smell and with the same all-enveloping wallpaper, but Arthur judged it to be both clean and comfortable. A double bed, covered with a yellow Candlewick bedspread, was pushed against the wall opposite the window, its oak headboard sporting two frilled reading lamps, while in the highest part of the room a large wardrobe fitted snugly into the wide angle of the ceiling. In one corner to the side of the window an old leather-inlaid desk, probably the most valuable piece of furniture that Arthur had seen so far in the house, doubled as a dressing-table, while in the other a sagging armchair sat at an angle.

Having taken in the contents of the room, Arthur walked into the small recess created by the dormer window and looked out. The sun had by now sunk away, but even in the gloaming of the day he could well see why the house had been situated in such an opportune place. Save for a short foreground of rolling fields darkened by cultivation and a ragged line of windswept hawthorn bushes at the land's farthest extreme, the view was dominated by the North Sea, a colourless canvas that merged with no sign of demarcation into the dulling sky. He pressed his face close to the window. The view remained unchanged either way, except for the cluster of farm buildings that Alex had pointed out to him earlier, lying three fields distant to the north-east.

He turned back from the window to find Alex and his grandfather standing behind him with earnest looks of expectation on their faces.

"Well?" Alex asked. "Do you think it'll do you?"

Arthur nodded. "Looks fine. Perfect, in fact." He looked across to the farmer. "So, have you any idea how much you would be requiring for the room, Mr. Craig?"

The old man scratched at the back of his head. "Ah, well, that's a question now, isn't it? I couldn't rightly say, Professor. I think, on that account, it would probably be best if we waited until my daughter came home, and then you and she can—"

He was cut short by the sound of a door slamming in the hallway. "Dad?" Liz's voice rang up the staircase.

Mr. Craig gave Arthur a wink. "Saved by the bell. There she is now." He walked out of the room. "Aye, we're up here, lass. We're on our way down."

"Dad, is Alex all right? The front of the van looks as if he's hit something."

He raised an eyebrow at his grandson before leading the way down the stairs. "Aye, he's fine. Just had a wee incident on Smash Alley. Not his fault, though."

Liz stood at the bottom of the stairs, still in her Wellingtons, watching as her father and Alex appeared at the half-way stage. "What do you mean, a wee incident? And what *are* you two doing up there, anyway? Has something happ—" She stopped when she saw the stranger appear behind them. "Ah, I'm sorry," she continued quietly, watching as Arthur descended the stairs. "I didn't realize you had somebody with you."

Alex came to stand beside his mother. "Mum, I'd like you to meet Professor Kempler, my German tutor."

"Oh!" Liz uttered in horror. She put her hand to her head and brushed back her hair, an instinctive gesture to try to bring some semblance of decency to her appearance. She watched as the professor approached her, his hand outstretched, a broad smile on his face that creased the lines at the sides of his sparkling brown eyes. "How do you do, Mrs. Dewhurst. It's very good to meet you."

"And you too, Professor." She shook his hand, then held out her palms as she looked down at her filthy attire. "I'm sorry about my clothes. If I'd known you were coming—"

"Oh, please, no!" Arthur interjected. "It is I who should apologize. I have come completely unannounced and certainly should have known better."

Liz smiled at the man. So this was the new German tutor from Canada Alex had told her about. My goodness, he certainly had preserved himself well if he was truly coming up for retirement. And he certainly wasn't her vision of a professor. He was really . . . well . . . almost too . . . dashing! "Well then." She glanced at Alex and her father. "So . . . to what do we owe this pleasure?" The smile suddenly slid from her face, to be replaced by a look of concern. "There's nothing wrong, is there?"

"Of course not!" Alex exclaimed. "What? Did you think I was being chucked out of university or something?"

"Well, I just thought . . ."

"No, it's nothing like that. Professor Kempler has come out here today because he's just had to leave his lodgings in Saint Andrews, and I thought that the spare room would be perfect for him. Anyway, we've just had a look at it, and he thinks it would suit him well."

Liz somehow managed to keep the smile on her face, even though she felt like gasping out in dismay. "Ah!" She nodded slowly, giving herself time to make sure that the smile was well and truly fixed. "Ah! Right!"

Alex studied the inane grin on his mother's face. "Mum?"

"Yes?" The smile still stuck.

"We did agree."

"Yes, we did, didn't we?"

Arthur shifted uneasily from one foot to the other. "Listen, I'm sorry, Mrs. Dewhurst. I can see that I've put you in a difficult situation here. If it is at all inconvenient, I can certainly look elsewhere. I am sure that—"

"No!" Alex interjected sharply. "Come on, Mum! This is what we agreed."

"I know we did, but . . ."

"But what?"

Liz shook her head. "I'm sorry, Professor, it's just that we're so busy at the minute. I don't know if we can . . . well, what I mean is that I didn't realize that Alex would get someone *quite* so soon, and . . . well, to be quite honest, I don't think that we're ready to rent out the room just yet."

Alex threw up his hands in frustration. "Oh, Mum!"

Arthur stepped in to calm the situation. "No, Alex, I can quite see your mother's point of view. But if I might just take a moment to try selling myself to you, I really am very self-contained and I would not make demands on you at all. And I am quite adept at looking after my own room and doing my own washing, and I am also quite prepared to cook my own meals."

"Oh, no, you wouldn't have to do that!" Liz exclaimed. "I mean," she said, softening her tone, "if you were to stay, you wouldn't have to do that."

Alex looked at his mother, realizing the glimmer of hope in her reply. "So?"

"I don't know, Alex. We only discussed this a few days ago, and I didn't think you'd be getting anybody until April or May at the earliest. It's just not a very good time, what with all the farm work, and those men starting to survey the wretched golf course."

"Mum, you heard the professor. He doesn't want anything other than the room—and he's pretty desperate for somewhere to live."

Liz looked across at her father, who had been quietly leaning against the banister, pulling absently at an ear-lobe. He gave her an almost indiscernible nod. She turned back to the professor, a resigned smile on her face. "All right. You can certainly have the room, Professor, but I don't really know what I would charge you."

Arthur pushed his hand into his pocket, taking up a resilient stance. "Well, if you would like to name a price, Mrs. Dewhurst, I'm sure we could come to a satisfactory agreement straightaway."

Liz took a moment to think. Damn it, if he was going to be there, she would have to make it worth her while. "Forty pounds a week, including your food." She watched his face drop, and realized that she had overstepped the mark.

"Forty pounds a week!"

Liz felt her face colouring. "I'm sorry. As I said, I really have no idea about the going rate. What about thirty—"

"Fifty."

Liz looked at him aghast. "What?"

"You're selling yourself short, Mrs. Dewhurst. I am willing to pay fifty pounds a week, including my evening meal. Come on, the view itself is worth thirty pounds a week." He paused. "Wait, on consideration . . ."

Liz looked at him with open eyes, thinking that the deal was now going to fall flat. "What?"

"Fifty-five on the condition that you let me smoke my pipe in my room."

Liz was completely taken aback. "Well."

"Go on, Mum," Alex said, a broad grin on his face. "He never manages to keep the thing lit anyway, so it would be a bargain."

Liz nodded. "All right, Professor." She put forward her hand to conclude the deal, but as Arthur went to take it, she unexpectedly withdrew it. "I would like to make a condition of my own, if I could."

Arthur eyed her. "And what might that be?"

"That you stay and have something to eat with us tonight."

Arthur laughed. "Mrs. Dewhurst—"

"Liz . . . please."

He nodded. "All right . . . Liz, that is not a condition. That is a pleasure!"

"Good. In that case, Professor Kempler, you have yourself a deal."

Chapter 7

Roberta Bayliss pulled the old Holden out of the car-park of the Royal Sydney Golf Club and drove the short distance down Kent Road to the traffic lights at the junction with New South Head Road. At five o'clock on a Friday afternoon, the traffic streamed nose-to-tail out from downtown Sydney, the heat from the cars making the surrounding air shimmer in the still-fierce swelter of the day. She wiped away a bead of perspiration from her forehead and cranked up the air-conditioning to its rasping limit, then sat back to wait for the lights to change, focusing her eyes on the refreshing coolness of the waters of Rose Bay just visible beyond the tennis courts in Lyne Park.

She really did not relish the idea of going to this birthday party. Not that she would ever dream of letting her feelings show in front of her sister Eleanor, for whose sixty-fifth birthday the party had been organized. But it was just that, for her, birthdays were no longer occasions to be celebrated. They only seemed now to serve as unwelcome reminders of years fleeting past, of the ever-shortening climb up the ladder to decrepitude and senility.

But maybe that was a really selfish thought—and even a stupid one, taking into account that here she was, as fit as a fiddle at the age of sixty, playing golf nearly every day. And, what's more, if hereditary factors were to be taken into account, there could be no worry about longevity nor of mental collapse setting in when she had both her parents still alive and kicking.

A short blast on a car-horn sounded behind her, and she glanced up to see that the lights had turned green. Pushing her foot down on the accelerator, she crossed over the thoroughfare and joined the line of traffic heading east along New South Head Road, the speed at which she accomplished the manoeuvre being the fastest that she would drive for the next ten minutes. Finally, having crawled the kilometre's distance, she turned left off the main road by the imposing edifice of Kincoppal School and made her way down Vaucluse Road, its narrow avenue bounded by large rambling houses whose extensive grounds were hidden from view by high stone walls.

At the road's farthest extreme, where it looped round on itself in front of the wooded area of Nielsen Park, Roberta slowly manoeuvred the car through a set of high wrought-iron security gates into a short, brick-paved driveway. Cutting the engine, she took her shoulder-bag from the passenger seat and got out of the car. She stood for a moment making adjustments to her cotton dress, not so much as a preening measure, but more because she felt so unused to wearing one. She found dresses to be such impractical garments, always creasing up or twisting round on her, and anyway, she was always aware that they clung to her body in all the wrong places, revealing herself in her true light as being small and lumpy. Even her friends at the golf club had registered bewildered surprise on witnessing her appearance from the ladies' locker room. How *different* you look, Roberta, they had said. Certainly not how *wonderful* you look! But maybe that was because they had only seen her dressed in trousers or shorts, those being not only her normal uniform for playing golf, but also her everyday wear.

She took a deep breath and began climbing the stone steps that wound their way up through the well-groomed garden in front of the house. She had gone no more than half-way when she heard the front door open and Dana, her niece's help, appeared at the top of the steps. Roberta stopped in her tracks and looked up at the large, smiling woman. "Where's the party then, Dana?"

"Hasn't started yet, Miss Bayliss. The kids all wanted to go to the beach before tea, so they headed down to Nielsen. Becky said you could either stay here and wait, or go down and join them."

"How long have they been down there?"

"No more than half an hour."

"Well, I'll go on down."

"You sure? It's pretty hot out. You're quite welcome to stay."

Roberta smiled. "The walk will do me good. Anyway, I might have a paddle myself." With a wave of her hand, she turned and descended the steps, stopping at the car to take her Titleist sun visor from the golf bag in the boot. With perfunctory care, she pulled it on hard over her cropped grey hair, then walked down the drive and crossed the road into the park.

The tall gum-trees that stood in Nielsen Park gave such cooling shade against the heat of the day that she decided not to make her way to the beach immediately, but instead veered off in a westerly direction towards Shark Point, along one of the many concrete paths that criss-crossed the grassed area of the park. She walked at a fast pace, acknowledging the greetings of those whom she passed, until the trees eventually gave way to the unhindered view of Port Jackson. She stood for a moment watching the yachts out on the wide expanse of sparkling blue water, their multi-coloured sails stretched full in the offshore breeze as they tacked back and forth against the jagged backdrop of the city's skyscrapers. Then, rejoining the path, she headed across the top of the park and walked down onto the beach, where she found its short length lined with a multitude of elderly sun worshippers who appeared to be casting aside any cares about skin cancer in their attempts to soak up the last of the summer's sun. She kicked off her sandals and walked barefoot along the edge of the water, scanning the area for her sister's party.

"Bobby! Over here!"

She turned round to see her sister sitting on the stepped concrete wall at the top of the beach. She gave her a wave and skipped across the hot sand towards her.

Eleanor rose to her feet as she approached. "You got the message then?" she asked, peering at Roberta from under the brim of an enormous straw sun-hat.

"I did." Roberta reached up and gave her sister a kiss on either cheek, their difference in height allowing her to do so without their respective headgear becoming a hindrance. "Happy birthday, darling."

Eleanor laughed as she sat down again on the wall. "I don't know if 'happy' is the word that would best describe it, but at least my well-earned pension matures today!"

Roberta sat down next to her. "Well, I think you look wonderful." She closed an eye to accentuate the scrutiny that she gave to her sister's face. "In fact, I would go so far as to say that you could almost pass yourself off as my younger sister."

Eleanor nodded slowly, her mouth twisting to one side. "I don't know how I'm meant to take that. Do I give you a hug or just tear your hair out?"

Roberta laughed. "Please, not the second! You did *that* often enough when we were kids!"

Eleanor dug her bare toes into the sand and raised her legs so that the two small mounds ran off the sides of her feet. "Only when you deserved it." She paused in a moment of reflection. "Goodness, we fought some, didn't we?"

Roberta nodded. "We sure did." She put her arm around her sister's waist and gave her a squeeze. "It really is great to see you, Ellie. We haven't seen each other for so long. How's life up on the peninsula?"

"Good."

"And Gordon's well?"

"Longing for his retirement in July. He's just had about enough of the journey down to Manly every day. The poor man wanted to come down here today, but he had some meeting which he couldn't put off, so we're going out for a slap-up meal tonight, just the two of us."

"Quite right, too." Roberta cast her eyes along the beach. "So, where's the rest of the party?"

"Becky's on bay-watch duty over there." Eleanor pointed a finger to the far end of the beach where the tall, willowy figure of her daughter, dressed in a white T-shirt and short denim skirt, stood at the edge of the water with her arms folded. "And the racket you hear out in the water sounding like a load of seals being fed at Taronga Zoo is in fact coming from my two grandchildren and their countless friends, who later will be joining me to celebrate my 'coming of age.' " She looked across at Roberta and gave her a wink. "Thanks for coming, Bobby. I was needing a bit of 'mature' support, seeing that big sis Mary found something more important to do with her time. I did have a niggling suspicion that you might have been tempted to have a few extra holes of golf and pretend that you'd forgotten about it."

Roberta smiled and watched as Becky started to move slowly along the beach towards them. "Wouldn't have missed it for the world." The young woman caught sight of her aunt and waved. Roberta raised her hand in reply.

"That's a lie, for a start." Roberta turned to catch a knowing smile on her sister's face.

"Not your cup of tea really, is it? A whole load of screaming kids tearing around at your ankles."

"I don't mind it—once in a while."

Eleanor stood up and looked out across the small bay to where the children were swimming. She called out to her daughter. "Becky, Clem's getting pretty close to the shark-net, isn't he?"

"He's all right, Mum," Becky called back, shielding her eyes against the glare of the sun. "I'm watching him."

Eleanor sat down again. "I hope so," she said quietly. "I don't want my birthday celebrations dampened by one of my grandchildren getting snagged by a shark."

"That's what shark-nets are for, aren't they? Keeping the sharks *out*."

"All right, clever one. I just don't think you can be too careful. Those grandchildren are my pride and joy, you know, but maybe . . ." She stopped.

Roberta looked at her. "Maybe what?"

"Nothing."

"Were you by any chance going to say that maybe I wouldn't understand that, not having grandchildren of my own?"

Eleanor bit at her lip. "Sorry, Bobby. That was a pretty thoughtless thing to say—or *begin* to say."

Roberta shrugged. "Doesn't bother me. I don't really notice it. Those kind of feelings just . . . well . . . have never been awakened in me, so I wouldn't know otherwise." She looked at her sister. "But that doesn't mean I'm not very fond of all Mary's and your countless offspring."

Eleanor nodded. "I know you are, but . . . don't you sometimes think to yourself secretly, deep down inside you, that you've missed out?"

Roberta laughed. "No! Not at all." She paused. "Well, I don't think so. I've never wanted for more than what I have already. I've really been quite content with my life."

"But you could have married, Bobby, couldn't you? I remember there being one or two quite meaningful relationships in your life. What about that Royal Navy guy from England, for instance? He was really keen on you."

Roberta raised her eyebrows. "He was a wimp, Eleanor, and you know it." She eyed her sister. "Anyway, why the sudden interest? You've never asked these kind of questions before."

Eleanor shrugged her shoulders. "I don't know. Maybe today is the first day that I have felt old age creeping up on me. Maybe I just want to settle differences and get to understand everything before . . . well . . . anything happens."

"What an extraordinary thing to say, Ellie. We've no differences to settle." She gave her sister a nudge with her arm. "Come on, nothing's going to happen to you. You're as fit as a racehorse. And as far as getting to understand everything, what *is* there to understand? I never got married. That's it. I'm not the first woman in the world never to have got married."

"I know, Bobby, but I just feel that you've not really done much with your life, other than sticking around at home with Mum and Pop. Here you are, sixty years old, and you're still there, still the tomboy—still the *baby* of the family. Mary and I both made the break when we were just out of our teens. Why did you feel that you couldn't—or even *shouldn't*?"

Roberta frowned in puzzlement at her sister. "I don't know where you're coming from, Eleanor. What are you trying to say? Are you *jealous* or something?"

Eleanor laughed dismissively at the suggestion. "Of course not!" She then glanced across at her sister, realizing that her flat denial to the question had not registered true with either of them. "Oh, I don't know, Bobby. Isn't that just the best? I really don't know." She sighed. "Would you believe it? Sibling rivalry rearing its ugly head at *our* age! I suppose we'd never be talking like this if Mum and Pop were pushing up the daisies. But here we are, two sexagenarians, still enjoying the pleasure of being the 'younger' generation." She was silent for a moment, then reached over and patted Roberta's knee before rising to her feet. "Come on, I think your crabby elder sister has said quite enough on the subject. It must be too much of the sun. Let's walk back to the house together." As Roberta stood up, Eleanor caught her daughter's attention and waved her hands in semaphore style to indicate that they were both leaving the beach.

Kicking the sand off their feet on the concrete stepway that led up from the beach, they slipped on their shoes and began to amble their way slowly along the central path through the park, their arms linked together.

"Tell me about Mum and Pop," Eleanor said. "How are they? I don't think that I've seen them for about two months."

"They're both well enough, I guess." Roberta paused. "No, actually, I have to say that Pop is not his usual sprightly self at the minute. We've only managed to get in three half-rounds of golf over the past week, and those have really knocked him out."

Eleanor chuckled. "Well, he *is* coming up to ninety, Bobby. You've got to realize that twenty-seven holes of golf in a week is something of a marathon for anyone of his age."

Roberta shook her head. "Oh, no, that's not the reason. He's just maybe got a bug or something. He'll soon be right as rain. Anyway, he's got to be, because we're heading off to Augusta for the Masters at the end of the month."

Eleanor stopped walking and looked at her sister. "Bobby, you're asking a lot of him, you know. He *is* old, you've got to understand that . . ."

"No, he's fine. As I said, it's just a bug. It'll soon—"

Eleanor took hold of her arm and held it tight. "Bobby! He's *my* father, too, you know. I happen to be quite concerned about his well-being, because I want to make damned sure that he survives as long as he can."

Roberta pulled away from her sister's grasp and glanced down at her feet, the look on her face immediately stirring an extraordinary realization in Eleanor. Here, standing in front of her, was the little girl she had known so many years before, the same pouting expression on her clear, boyish face, always put on whenever she had been rebuked for some misdemeanour or other. Eleanor understood now that she had not been that far off the mark back there on the beach. Bobby was still the kid of the family. She had never really moved on from her childhood.

She put her arm around her little sister's shoulders and drew her in beside her as they continued walking. "Listen, Bobby, I know you've done more for Mum and Pop over the years than either Mary or I ever could. And we have never doubted the fact that you were Pop's favourite. I think, in a way, that you filled the shoes of the son that he never had, playing golf with him and travelling the world to all those tournaments.

But you're going to have to accept the fact that the time has come for him to start to slow down and take things a little easier. I know it's hard to take this in, but he is an old man now, and the reason why he has probably kept on playing golf is because he doesn't want to let *you* down."

"But if he stops," Roberta replied quietly, "that'll be the end of him. I know it. He's got to keep going, Eleanor."

They walked in silence for a moment before Roberta stopped and let out a heaving breath. "You know what you were saying earlier on about me not getting married?"

Eleanor nodded. "Yes?"

"Well, if you want the honest truth, there was never a time when I felt that I ever wanted to. You see, my perfect role model for a man has always been Pop, and I never really found a man who could quite match up to him. Not that he ever discouraged them or anything like that. In fact, sometimes he was quite blatant in his endeavours to get me married off. The decision was mine, Eleanor. He was, and still is, my greatest friend, and there's been no one in my life like him." She let out a short, unconvincing laugh. "So there you are. After all these years, there's your question answered."

Eleanor smiled at her. "You didn't need to answer it. I knew already." She paused. "Bobby, the reason why I brought this whole thing up is because I'm not just worried about Pop. I worry about you as well, about what will happen to you when he eventually does go. You have to give it thought, my darling, you have to start trying to work out what you're going to do with the rest of your life, because you're too great a person just to curl up into a lonely little ball of sadness and self-pity." She studied the changing expression on her sister's face as emotion began to break through her blind resistance to the reality of the situation. She had made her point. There was no reason to say more. "Look, Bobby," she said, moving across to her sister's side and putting her arm once more around her shoulders, "I think the best idea would be for you and me to strike a deal to keep him with us as long as we can, don't you? My suggestion would be to cut out any idea of travelling to Augusta—or anywhere else, for that matter—and just get him fit for playing his golf. How about that? That should keep you both happy, should it not?"

Roberta nodded in silent agreement.

As they resumed their walk, a profusion of whooping yells grew in volume from behind them on the path, and they were quickly overtaken by a whirlwind of young party guests heading back to the house. Clem slowed down as he passed by. "Hi, Granny! Hi, Great-Aunt Bobby! Come on, get a move on! Dana's got the barbie going *and* I think Mum's been to Doyle's for some oysters for you lot." He turned and sprinted off after his friends.

Eleanor looked at Roberta, a sparkle in her eye. "Do you fancy a race?"

Roberta's crestfallen features slowly broke into a smile. "You've never beaten me before."

Eleanor hitched up her skirt in her hand. "Maybe not, but there's always a first time. Are you ready? One . . . twooo . . . threeee. . . . GO!"

Roberta sprang quickly from her mark, and although she ran at no more than a jog, it was a speed far greater than that mustered by her elder sister, who felt the twinge of arthritis in her left knee as soon as she took her first step. Eleanor continued to walk along the path and watched as her sister ran the whole length of the park, only stopping when she had reached the pavement on Vaucluse Road. Roberta turned to look back at her, and seeing the margin of her win she let out a cheer of victory before crossing the road and making her way up the driveway of the house.

Eleanor let out a quiet laugh. Poor Mum, she thought to herself; how on earth had she ever been able to compete with *that* all her life? Then, as she walked on, the smile at the thought slid from her face and she slowly shook her head. Oh, Bobby, what *is* going to happen to you?

Chapter 8

The old ewe licked hard at the remnants of thin membrane that still covered the body of her first-born lamb as it lay spluttering its way into life beside her head, then let out a long, effort-filled groan as she pushed hard once again to try ridding herself of its more reluctant twin. Gregor Dewhurst disengaged his hand from her backquarters and got to his feet, flexing his fingers in an attempt to ease the numbing pain caused by the contracting of her cervix. He poured a fresh dollop of lubricating fluid into his palm, then knelt down to try again, closing his eyes to concentrate on his sightless task. He carefully pushed in around the lamb's head and felt for its knee joint, hoping to hook in a finger and release a front leg, so that he could align it into a more normal birth position. He sensed the next contraction coming on and grimaced as the ewe's powerful muscle once more clenched his hand in a vice-like grip. The lamb moved only the merest inch forward in the birth canal, but it was enough for him to detect the small triangular opening for which he had been searching. He eased the leg forward until it was free from her cervix, then applied enough downward pressure to bring its shoulder clear. He blew out with effort as he waited for the next contraction, then, feeling her strain once more, he clamped the leg in his little finger and slid the cleft of his fore and middle fingers over the lamb's head and gently prised it free from her womb. Kicking in a clean layer of straw with his foot, he allowed the lamb to flop down onto the ground, and as its small diaphragm began to heave in air, he quickly cleared away the mucus from its mouth with his little finger.

"My word, wee one, that was a tussle and a half, wasn't it?" he said quietly, pulling away the remains of the placenta from its body. He picked it up by its front legs and swung it gently forward to lie at the head of the ewe beside its twin. "There you are, lass, there's another one for you to deal with."

He stood up and watched as the attentive mother began to work on her new lamb, feeling almost as contented as she at the eventual success of the delivery. He took the towel that was hanging over the top rail of the gate and gave his hands a hard rub, then settled back against the gate to make certain that the bonding process had begun.

In all the years that he had worked on lambing, he could not remember one that he hadn't enjoyed. He had never sickened of the job. Even during the one appalling downtime when he had found his flock to be riddled with contagious abortion, the pure surge of joy at finding one alive was indescribable. The creation of life had the ability of touching one's emotions to the core, the power to turn utter adversity and desperation into hope, in the way that a news report might show total jubilation amongst the rescuers of a small child who had been plucked alive from the concrete graveyard of its shattered home, days after the whole area had been devastated by an earthquake. He had never really been a religious man, but there was something so powerful, so tangibly spiritual about the process of birth that, after that particular lambing, he had felt compelled to go to church to give thanks.

And, of course, the feeling wasn't only associated with his lambs. He remembered the day Alex had been born, the whole procedure seeming so uncannily similar that he had felt the strongest compunction to roll up his sleeves and help the midwife with her task. He smiled to himself. Poor old Liz. She could tell what he was thinking by the look on his face. "Don't you *dare* come near me," she had screamed at him. "Don't you think you've damaged me *enough*?"

He raised his arms above his head to stretch out the stiffness in his limbs and the tiredness in his body, which brought on a long and totally unpremeditated yawn. He glanced at his watch. It was six o'clock in the evening. Making a quick mental calculation, he worked out that he had been on the go for eighteen hours without a break. My God, what a difference it was, having to do the job by himself. Before, it had been a time of the year when the whole family had been involved, but now, with his parents living in happy retirement in their little cottage in Balmuir, neither had felt the urge or inclination to come out to give him a hand. But, then again, one of the reasons for that had been Liz. Both his parents had been so thunderstruck by the split-up of his marriage and the barrier it had caused between their two families that hardly a word had passed between them since.

Then of course, there *was* Liz. She had been the master at lambing, having both a patience and stamina that could outlast him at any time, as well as being the possessor of small hands that could extricate the most difficult lambs at birth. Unfortunately, he couldn't say the same thing for Mary. The only time she had ever been into the lambing shed she had almost fainted at the sight of a birth, then had come up with the impractical suggestion that he should give epidurals to all his ewes.

He stared blankly at the new mother and her lambs, his pensive inactivity allowing a comforting surge of fatigue to sweep though his body. He had to admit to himself that he did miss Liz, and not just for the practical reasons. He never meant it to turn out the way it had, but it was just that circumstances had prevailed. He would have dearly loved to have more children, to have experienced once more the exhilaration at the birth of a baby, but it wasn't to be. Three times Liz had miscarried, and thereafter her frustration and disappointment had manifested themselves in complete disinterest and apathy towards sexual relations. It was only a temporary state of affairs as it turned out, no more than three months, but how the hell was he to know that? For a young man in his prime, it was too much to cope with. And then Mary had been there, flirtatious and willing, and she had provided the physical solace for which he so yearned. Yet he had never thought for a moment that it would end in such a calamitous way.

But that showed, on his part, naïveté in its extreme, and he knew now that he had demonstrated a complete lack of understanding towards Liz. She had been deeply hurt by her inability to have more children, and he had only helped to consolidate that pain by having an affair with another woman. It had to have been the final insult, the final kick in the teeth. The outcome was inevitable and the repercussions far-reaching, so much so that the whole situation was now both an emotional and financial mess. He could not bear the bitterness that Liz now felt towards him, nor the resentment Alex showed in his unwillingness to come round to the house. If he could only make Liz understand that the golf project would be a step forward, not only to financial betterment but toward finding some middle ground for an understanding between them. But she wouldn't speak to him. It was well and truly finished.

Nevertheless, he still had Mary, and he had always been both touched and proud at the stalwart resilience she had displayed when faced with the narrow-minded attitudes and behind-the-back remarks of the local people. Yet, as far as being a friend, she had her shortcomings, there being little common ground between them. She was completely ignorant about the ways of farming, and sometimes the artlessness that she displayed in her efforts to appear interested in the golf project annoyed him. That was what he missed most about Liz. Having been married in their teens, they had literally grown up together and had understood everything about each other. But it was totally pointless to make such comparisons now. Liz was gone, Liz was in the past, and it was Mary who was willing to stick by him and share his bed whilst others wouldn't even have him in their house.

The two lambs had struggled to their feet and now stood on splayed legs, pushing their noses into their mother's soft belly in an attempt to find some source of nourishment. Gregor took an aerosol can of antiseptic spray from his pocket and, picking each up in turn, gave their umbilical cords a good covering before latching them on to the ewe's teats. He waited for a further five minutes to make sure that each had enjoyed a healthy intake of colostrum, then, letting himself out of the pen, he walked down the feeding aisle, glancing from side to side to see if any other births were imminent. All seemed quiet, so he left the lambing shed and made his way across the yard to the house.

The airless heat in the kitchen hit him as soon as he entered, making the drowsiness he had felt in the cool of the lambing shed immediately become more like a drug-induced stupor. Pulling out a chair from the kitchen table, he slumped down and leaned his elbows hard on the table's scrubbed surface and began rubbing at his tired eyes. The door opened behind him, but he could hardly find the energy to turn around.

"Gregor!"

He pivoted his face round on his hand to look at Mary. "What's the matter?"

"Look at your boots! They're covered in dung!" She waved her hand in front of her face to waft away the smell to which his own senses seemed to be completely immune, and walked over to the cooker to stir gingerly at the simmering contents of a pan, keeping herself at a safe distance so that she didn't accidentally splash either her pink tight-fitting blouse or her black pencil skirt. As he watched her, Gregor could not help but feel a pang of lust shudder through his body, even in his near-comatose state. It was extraordinary that even in the execution of a task as innocent as stirring a cooking pot, Mary was unable to disguise her natural provocation; the position that she adopted to carry out the task pushing her bottom upwards and outwards so that the fabric of her skirt stretched tight against the curve of her hips, making it ride high up the back of her legs. My word, Mary McLean, he thought to himself, you certainly have quite a body! She looked round at him, catching the look in his eye, and gave him a wink, followed by a remonstrative smile. "I think you should try getting used to taking off your boots by the back door before coming into my kitchen."

Gregor let out a long sigh and bent forward to unlace his boots. *Your* kitchen. Is it really *your* kitchen? Beforehand, he had never really thought of it as being anybody's kitchen.

"Oh, and I nearly forgot," Mary said, pulling off a section of paper towel from its roll and giving her manicured hands a gentle wipe. "Jonathan Davies called you from his car about five minutes ago. He's going to drop in on his way home."

Gregor flicked back his head, a smile of disappointment on his face. "That's a pity." He toed off his boots and carried them over to the door of the back kitchen. He opened it and threw them in. "Did he say what he wanted to talk about?"

Mary shook her head. "Just said that he wanted a word."

"Have I got time for a bath?"

Mary was about to respond when car lights swept across the kitchen window. "There's your answer."

Gregor let out a resigned sigh and returned to the back kitchen to greet Jonathan Davies. Mary watched him as he left, then opened up one of the cupboard doors to use the mirror that hung inside to give herself a quick once-over.

She heard Gregor welcome the man. "Nice to see you, Jonathan, come on in."

Mary scampered back to the cooker and nonchalantly began to stir at the cooking pot. She turned with a beaming smile on her face as the two men entered the room. Jonathan walked up to her, his hand outstretched. "Mary, how nice to see you. Hmm, what a delicious smell! What *are* you cooking?"

Gregor watched with interest as Mary's face coloured as she took his hand, then listened as she began to explain to Davies the contents of her pot, and the many ingredients she had added to embellish their flavour. He had noticed this before, but had never quite been able to pin it down, and it was something he found to be almost unkind or even untrustworthy about Mary's character. She relied on him, she supported him and she was attracted to him, but as soon as another man showed any interest in her or what she was doing, no matter who he was or what age he was, she became singular in her attention to that one. And that was exactly what she was doing right now. It wasn't a mild flirtation, but an all-out offensive to attract the man. As far as Mary was concerned, there were only two people in the room at present—she and Davies. But maybe that was her greatest attraction. Although you never knew quite where you stood with her, while you were the man in her life, you were king.

Davies turned from the cooker, a broad smile on his face. "Sorry to butt in on your supper like this, Gregor."

Gregor shrugged. "No bother. Do you want some? I'm sure there's enough, isn't there, Mary?"

She smiled but did not voice a reply.

"No!" Davies exclaimed, holding up his hands to accentuate his refusal. "I wouldn't dream of it." Walking over to the kitchen table, he sat down on its edge and crossed his arms. "No, the only reason that I wanted to drop by was to tell you that I had a meeting today with an investment company in Edinburgh, and I'm pretty sure that they want to come in on the project."

Gregor gave a double thumbs-up. "Oh, that's great news, Jonathan! So we're still on line, then."

Davies gave a tentative nod. "Of course—from our end, that is." He gave a quick glance towards Mary. "I just wondered if you had had any further feedback from . . . well . . ."

Gregor eyed Mary as she busied herself around the kitchen, quite obviously fully aware of the subject around which they were skirting "No, nothing." He paused for a moment. "I'm afraid that I'm in a bit of a stalemate on that front at the minute. I was just wondering whether it might be a good idea if you made an approach."

Davies slapped his hands down on his thighs. "Did try, old boy. I went round there tonight to spread the good news, but it was only your father-in-"—he checked himself—"her father and your son who were in."

"So where was Liz?" He shot a look in Mary's direction, knowing immediately that he had said it with too much interest. Mary had caught his look, so he made a vain attempt to mollify his inquiry. "I mean, was she out feeding the lambs or something?"

"No. Seemingly she had gone to the theatre in St. Andrews."

Gregor let out an abrupt laugh. "The theatre! I doubt it. That's not her scene at all."

Davies raised his eyebrows. "Well, that's what I was told by Alex. They have one of his tutors from university staying in the farmhouse at present, and she'd apparently gone with him."

For some reason, Gregor felt an unpremeditated rise of envy in his gut. He nodded his head slowly, longing to ask who this man was, but realized that Mary's agitation was becoming all too obvious in the way that she had begun to clatter dishes and cutlery onto the table.

Davies broke the uneasy atmosphere by rising from the table and clapping his hands together. "Well, I must be off." He walked over to Mary and this time bade his farewell by planting a kiss on both her cheeks. "Goodbye, Mary, and thanks for your impromptu cooking lesson. I must get my wife to try that recipe some time."

Gregor followed him through the back kitchen and out into the yard. Davies opened the door of his car, then turned to look at him. "You must see if you can have a word with Liz, Gregor. If this investment company comes good, then we should be ready to start almost immediately, but we really need to have the go-ahead from all parties, otherwise it can never be anything other than a complete non-starter."

Gregor nodded. "Aye, I understand that."

"Okay. Good. Well, give me a call any time."

"Will do, Jonathan. And thanks for dropping in."

Gregor waited until Davies's car had driven around the corner of the steading before walking back into the house. Mary did not look at him when he entered the kitchen, but stood by the cooker ladling out her spicy stew onto two plates. He walked around the table and encircled her waist with his arms. She tried to shrug him away but he held fast. He bent forward and kissed the back of her neck. "Are you hungry?"

"Why?" she asked, a tetchy edge to her voice. "Aren't you?"

He gave her ear a gentle bite. "Not for food, anyway."

CHAPTER 9

A gentle breeze blew in through the window of Liz's bedroom, parting the curtains wide enough to allow a splash of sunlight to flicker momentarily onto her face. She opened her eyes and pushed her toes downwards under the bedclothes in one long, luxurious stretch before turning her head slowly on the pillow to glance at the alarm clock on her bedside table. Her brow furrowed. She quickly raised herself onto an elbow and picked up the clock, giving it closer scrutiny. Oh, for heaven's sake, it was twenty past eight! She picked up the clock and checked the alarm button. It was in the "off" position. Throwing back the bedclothes, she jumped to her feet, discarding the alarm clock onto the bed with little regard to its future functioning. She pulled her night-dress over her head and scrambled around with the clothes on the chair, trying to separate those that she had worn the previous night from her work attire. She pulled on her knickers and hopped around on one foot as she got into her jeans, then walked blindly towards the door, struggling to find the misaligned armholes of her T-shirt and woollen polo-neck. Opening the door, she ran downstairs in her bare feet and raced into the kitchen.

Alex and the professor had just stood up from the breakfast table, their mugs and plates in hand. "Ah, the sleeping beauty doth appear!" Arthur exclaimed, giving a dramatic bow in her direction which made the crockery rattle precariously in his outstretched hand. Fully aware of his past record with breakable objects in the house, Liz moved swiftly forward and relieved him of his load before it too was added to his tally.

"Why didn't you wake me?" she asked, shifting her gaze towards Alex in case it was construed that she was addressing the professor.

Alex opened the door of the dishwasher and slotted in his plate and mug. "I thought that if you were sleeping on, then you were probably needing it."

"But the lambs need to be fed. You know that."

Alex shook his head slowly, as if making out that she was giving him little credit for his own common sense. "Yes, I know that, Mum. That's why I've done them."

"Ah," Liz said quietly. "Right. Well, thanks for that."

Arthur gave her a wink. "Thoughtful boy, eh?"

Liz did not respond to the remark. "And what about Granddad? Have you seen him this morning?"

"He went off at about eight o'clock with the spraying contractor. Said that he was going to do a field walk with the guy, and that he wouldn't be in until about mid-morning. He asked me if I would feed the lambs, because he thought, like me, that you deserved a lie-in."

"There you are, then!" Arthur declared, opening up the cupboard above the sink and taking out a mug. "Everything is organized for you, so if you'd allow me now to do my bit, I'll make you a cup of coffee before your son and I hit the road."

"No, please don't bother. I can do it myself." She moved forward to take the mug from him, but he hugged it to his chest to avoid her outstretched hand.

"No, it would be my pleasure! The kettle's just boiled. White, no sugar, isn't it?"

"Yes. Thank you." She turned to catch Alex beaming a wide smile at her. "What are you looking like that for?"

Alex shrugged his shoulders. "No reason."

"There you are." Arthur handed her the mug of steaming coffee, then turned and headed towards the hall. "Alex, I won't be a moment. I've just got to get my coat."

As the professor's footsteps sounded up the staircase, Alex folded his arms and leaned back against the draining-board. "So, how was it last night?"

Liz took her coffee over to the table and sat down. "Good. It was very funny, actually."

"Not so highbrow as the first play, then?"

Liz laughed. "No, I understood this one." She took a sip of coffee and her face lengthened into an expression of disgust. "Oh, my goodness, that's horrible!" Getting up from her chair, she hastily discarded the contents of her mug down the drain and set about making herself another one before Arthur re-entered the kitchen.

"And he hasn't tried to molest you yet?"

"No, Alex, he has not."

"There you are. I told you that he'd be all right."

Liz smiled at her son. "Alex, I'm sure that molestation is the last thing that a man of his age would be thinking about." She paused. "Anyway, maybe age has nothing to do with it. Maybe I'm now just unmolestable."

Alex flicked his head to the side. "I don't know. I thought you scrubbed up pretty well last night."

"Thanks, Alex."

"Well, come on, it's pretty rare you being seen without a streak of lamb shit somewhere on your clothing."

Letting out a cry of affront, Liz gave her son a sound punch on the arm before making her way back to the table with the new cup of coffee.

"Anyway, I'm not the only one who thought you looked pretty good last night."

Liz raised her eyebrows. "Your grandfather, I suppose. He just says that kind of thing as a matter of course. Trying to boost my flagging morale."

Alex screwed a forefinger into the side of his head. "No, actually, dummy, it was the professor!"

She shrugged her shoulders. "Same thing, isn't it? The kindly compliment of an older man?"

"Oh, come on, Mum! Do yourself a little justice! He may be a bit older than you, but I wouldn't underestimate his judgement. I think he's seen quite a bit of life, you know."

Liz pushed her spoon around in the coffee. "Well, if you say so," she said quietly, taking a sip from her mug. She cleared her throat. "What . . . er . . . exactly did he say?"

"Only that he thought you looked . . ." Alex stopped speaking as he heard the professor's footsteps thump down the stairs. He blustered into the kitchen, his raincoat flapping open behind him.

"Sorry about that, Alex. Suddenly remembered I needed some papers for today. Couldn't find them." He opened his brief-case on the central worktop and untidily stuffed in the ream of papers. "Right!" he said, clicking down the catch and heading for the door. "Come on, then! We're running pretty late!"

As he left the room, Alex let out a short cry of disbelief at the incorrigibility of the man, then walked over to the table and gave his mother a kiss on the cheek. " 'Ravishing' was the word he used." He stepped away from her and watched as her cheeks began to colour and a self-conscious smile stretched across her mouth. "See, I told you that getting someone to live with us would spice up our lives a bit. It's good to see you smile again, Mum."

Liz got to her feet and reached up and ruffled his hair. "You'd better be off, darling. I'll see you this evening."

Picking up a pile of books from the kitchen table, Alex hurried over to the door. "Okay, but it'll be late. I'm playing golf, so don't bother cooking anything for me." He opened the door and immediately bumped into the tall figure of the professor as he came back into the kitchen.

"Sorry, Alex! Forgot to mention something." He turned to Liz. "How about trying an opera now?"

Liz stared at him, aghast. "What?"

"Tomorrow night. The opera in Edinburgh. Suddenly remembered I had tickets."

Liz shook her head. "Oh, Arthur, that's very kind, but I really don't know if I can—"

"It would be a pity not to use them. And I promise you that if you don't enjoy it, we'll get up half-way through and leave."

"No, I honestly think that it would just be wasted on me. I'm sure that you must know someone else who'd be more appreciative—"

"How can you tell?" Alex interjected. "You've never seen an opera."

The professor turned to his student and nodded in agreement. "Thank you, Alex. My sentiments exactly." He looked back at Liz. "Well, will you come?"

Liz pushed her hands into the back pockets of her jeans. "I don't really think I should. I just feel that I've been away quite a bit over the past few weeks, and Dad and I are still extremely busy."

Arthur showed disapproval at her meagre excuse by wrinkling up his nose. "What? Two evenings is termed as 'being away quite a bit'?"

Liz let out a resigned sigh. "Well, I'll have to speak with Dad."

Arthur nodded. "Good. And if you have any problem with him, I shall beat him tonight at cribbage and win the right to take you."

Liz laughed. "You might lose, you know."

"Not even a possibility." He turned and pushed a grinning Alex out the door in front of him. "I taught him to play, remember?"

Liz listened to the sound of the Peugeot van fade off as it turned the corner of the steading, then stood with her arms crossed, taking in the comforting and welcome silence in the house. Alex had been right. Since the professor had moved in, their lives had certainly been "spiced up." No, that was an inadequate phrase. "Disrupted" would probably be more apt. She glanced over to her treasured Rayburn cooker and surveyed what remained of the two identical rubber imprints that had been melted onto the otherwise polished chrome top, a small yet now permanent reminder of the professor's attempt to dry off his hiking boots. That had probably been the worst, but in no way the first indication that he was totally without any idea of house-training. During his first week in residence, he had taken it upon himself to wash a pair of socks in the basin in the upstairs bathroom, even though she had been magnanimous in her offer to add his somewhat threadbare garments to her already burgeoning load. Somehow he had managed to flush them down the lavatory, a misdemeanour that only came to light when the drains began to back up on themselves and the house became permeated with the smell of raw sewage. That, in itself, had almost been enough for her to ask him to pack up his two battered canvas suitcases and leave the house. However, such was the vehemence of opposition to the idea, both from Alex and her father, that she had to recant on her threat, and was left to consider why this man had managed to inveigle his way into their household in such a short space of time. And the more she considered it, the more she began to realize that his attributes far outweighed his shortcomings. The uncertainty of what he was going to do next had created a sense of hilarious urgency amongst her two men, and after her initial negative, and often bad-tempered, reaction to this, she found herself being caught up in the new air of carefree happiness that had descended upon the household. Furthermore, her father had now begun to cast aside his quiet moroseness, his world suddenly stimulated by the intellect and wit of the professor, with whom he had struck up a close relationship. Every evening, they would disappear together into the hitherto unused sitting-room, each carrying a small glass of Jack Daniel's bourbon, and there they would sit, behind closed doors, talking or playing cards until well past midnight. When she eventually took herself off to bed, having enjoyed an hour or two of peaceful solitude in the kitchen, she would hear the laughter from within and smell the rich, heady aroma of the professor's pipe tobacco filter its way into the hall as she passed by.

His presence in the household had also greatly benefitted Alex, in that he was able to receive extra German tuition gratis. It had been the professor's idea that, during their journeys to and from St. Andrews, the Peugeot van should become a far-flung outpost of the German state, and that only the native tongue should be spoken within its mucky confines. Such was the success of the venture that the bounds of the German state were soon increased by the annexation of the farmhouse, but she and her father, mind-boggled by their unintelligible communications in the kitchen, had managed to exercise their full democratic powers of veto, reclaiming the place as sovereign territory.

And what about her? How would she term the effect that the professor had had on *her* life? Negative? No, that was too strong, but certainly he had managed to throw a sizeable spanner into her seething and grinding works. She had in no way been ready for a man to ask her out, in no way *prepared* for a man to ask her out, especially one who had to be near-enough a quarter of a century older than she. But it probably had been that lack of preparation, coupled with the over-enthusiastic, and to what she considered as bordering on downright disloyal, support that the professor had been given by both Alex and her father that had forced her to accept his invitation. Alex had even used the professor's age as a *reason* for her to accept. "Don't worry, Mum," he had said. "You'll be quite safe with him. I mean, just look at his age!" So she had undergone the alien task of "scrubbing herself up," as Alex had so tactfully phrased it, and rummaging through her wardrobe for something half decent to wear. Three times she had opened the door of the bedroom to make her way downstairs, and three times she had closed it to change her appearance. First her dress—Laura Ashley or Debenhams' best? Then her hair—brush it or just scrunch it? Then her shoes—flats or heels? She would have probably been quite happy to stay up there all night had Alex not yelled up the stairs that the professor was getting quite agitated that they might miss the first act. So she had gone, totally mismatched, to make an appearance before her "date," feeling like one of those dressed-up potatoes with the blue hat, red nose and pink mouth stuck into its skin.

And as she walked into the kitchen, Arthur had turned from viewing the kitchen clock and, after taking one long look at her, had let out a loud, extended wolf whistle. Surprisingly, her reaction to that had not been one of anger, but one that precipitated a stream of quite feeble, self-conscious mutterings. "Oh, you're just doing that to be kind, aren't you? I'm afraid that I just have nothing to wear. Everything that I have on is *at least* ten years old. I just hope you don't mind spending the evening with someone who looks like *this*!" And that was when the anger kicked in—not with him, but with herself—for being so wet, for sounding like a simpering, downtrodden wife and making these excuses, for even giving a damn what she was wearing! But Arthur had just shrugged his shoulders and said, "Well, you can think that if you like—but I think you look bloody wonderful, and I'm going to be proud to have you as my companion for the evening—even though you are at least twenty-five years too young for me!"

And that was what had broken the ice. She had thought to herself, Liz, my girl, I think that this man understands how you're feeling. Alex is right. He's no threat to you, so why not just go out and enjoy yourself?

And they had done so—even though she had found the play so highbrow that she had lost track of the plot somewhere in the first act.

But now it was becoming more complicated. She didn't want these evenings to become a feature of her life, nor an intrusion into it. Even though it had only been a case of going to the theatre and coming straight back home again, they had talked in the car and over their interval drinks, and she had fallen victim to his obviously kind but inquisitive nature, telling him about her upbringing, her marriage and the subsequent disaster that had befallen that. And as she had done so, she realized that she wasn't ready for any man to have this depth of understanding of her situation. She was still knotted up inside in the knowledge that his gender was the perpetrator of the brutal hurt she was experiencing, and consequently she wanted to dislike and distrust every man that she met. But, with Arthur, she had found it difficult to keep up this brittle reserve. She had therefore adopted an alternative and finely balanced strategy of trying not to talk directly to him or look at him in the house so as not to raise suspicions in her father or Alex of there having been a fall-out, in the hope that it would discourage Arthur from proffering further invitations. Still, she didn't want to alienate herself from the friendship that he showed, not only to herself but to her father and Alex. And she did like him.

But this *had* to be the last time. They would go to the opera in Edinburgh and she would make a concerted effort not to be drawn into talking either in the car or over their drinks. Thereafter, she would have a quiet word with Alex and her father and ask them to support her in her decision not to go out with him any more. In that way, surely nobody would get hurt.

It wasn't she who made the decision to leave. She was really quite enjoying the whole new experience of opera and the atmosphere engendered by the ornate grandeur of the cavernous auditorium, even though she was completely at sea as to what was happening on the stage. This was demonstrated to her by the fact that, at a point just before the close of the first act, when she thought everything was going just perfectly for everyone concerned, the woman in the seat next to her began to dab at tear-filled eyes with a handkerchief. However, as the curtain fell and even before the house lights had come up, Arthur jumped to his feet and stated in an embarrassingly loud and carrying tone that the heroine had a voice like a bullfrog with laryngitis and that he really didn't want this to be Liz's first taste of opera. So, without even waiting to down their pre-ordered interval drinks, Arthur took her arm and ushered her down the stairs and out into the street.

"Sorry about that. That was a complete waste of time."

"It wasn't at all. I was really quite enjoying it."

Arthur scratched at his head. "Ah. Right. Well, that just shows how selfish a person I am. Would you like to go back in? I suppose I could just about bear another . . ."

Liz shook her head. "No, I'm quite happy not to."

"All right." He stuck his hands into the pockets of his raincoat and blew out a decisive breath. "In that case, I think that the least I could do is to take you somewhere for a bite to eat."

"No, really . . . thanks." She heard her voice sound sharp in response. "I mean, that's a very kind thought, Arthur, but I don't feel that hungry. Anyway, we've got a fairly long journey in front of us."

"Nonsense! An hour would get us home. What's more, I'm feeling pretty hungry. What do you say to just finding a pizza place or something like that?"

Liz let out a short sigh of resignation, realizing that his persistency would far outlast hers. "Okay, then, but as long as we can find somewhere that will serve us quite quickly."

There were two reasons for them not finding anywhere for the next hour. Firstly, the time of night, and secondly, their joint lack of knowledge of Edinburgh. Having walked half the length of Princes Street without finding a suitable establishment that didn't have a queue for tables, they returned to the theatre to pick up Liz's Land Rover. While she collected it, Arthur went into the theatre to ask advice as to where best they should try, but in waiting for him outside, Liz thought to suggest that they should just cut their losses and head for home. The opportunity, however, never arose, as Arthur came bounding down the steps and, with a jubilant cry of success, jumped into the car and directed her towards the west end of town.

The restaurant was only half-full, and Liz could only surmise from the assembly of welcoming waiters in their full-length white aprons, the razor-creased pink table-cloths and velvet-covered gilt chairs that the place was probably far beyond the financial budget of most people. One of the waiters detached himself from the smiling bunch and came forward to take Liz's coat. "Have you a reservation, sir?" he asked Arthur.

"Yes. Kempler."

"Of course, Mr. Kempler," he sang out as if now recognizing Arthur as a regular customer. He quickly relieved Liz of her coat, and its speedy disappearance suddenly made her feel exposed and underdressed in front of the other diners. She pushed down self-consciously at the side seams of her black dress, having experienced great trouble earlier that evening in finding something different to wear and discovering that she was certainly a little plumper since the last time she had worn that particular garment. She turned and gave Arthur a half-smile. "Are you sure this is all right? I mean, it's not exactly a pizza place."

Arthur took off his raincoat and handed it to the waiter, and she immediately took comfort in the fact that her dining companion had obviously made no special effort to dress for the evening other than to add a clean shirt to his customary attire of hairy tweed jacket and stringy knitted tie. "Well, it's Italian, anyway. If you really want pizza, I'm sure that they could rustle one up."

"I didn't mean that. I just thought that . . . well . . . they might take quite a long time to serve us."

He stood aside so that Liz could follow the waiter first to the table. "Just don't worry about it. I'll make sure that we're as quick as possible, but hey, you won't turn into a pumpkin if you're not home by midnight."

The waiter seated them with theatrical flourish, flicking open their napkins with such force that they cracked like whips before setting them with accomplished humility on their laps. He handed them the menus, and Liz swallowed hard in an effort not to gasp in shock at the prices.

Arthur laughed as he studied the menu. "My God, you'd think we'd had enough of the Italian language for one evening, wouldn't you? Still don't understand a word of it."

"I thought you were a linguist."

"If being a linguist constitutes knowing more than one foreign language, then I'm no linguist."

"So why only German?"

Arthur shrugged. "My native tongue, I suppose, in a manner of speaking."

"Oh? Why is that?"

The waiter came back with a wine list and stood by Arthur while he gave his order. Liz sat back in her chair and watched him. Here's your chance, girl, she thought to herself. You ask *him* about his life, you get *him* to talk. In that way, you won't have to talk about yourself. Just don't let him get a word in edgeways.

He glanced over to Liz. "A bottle of white all right for you?"

"Yes, but I'll only have one glass, seeing that I'm driving. Could I have some mineral water as well?"

Arthur slapped the covers of the wine list together and handed it back to the waiter. "A bottle of number twenty-one, please, and a glass of mineral water."

Liz leaned her elbows on the table and looked intently at her dining partner. "Well?"

"Well what?"

"Why is German your native tongue, 'so to speak'? I thought you were Canadian."

"Well, it does happen to be a multinational country. Have you never heard of French-Canadians?"

"Of course! But not German-Canadians."

The waiter came back with a copper tub brimming with ice, from which he took the bottle of wine and poured a little into Arthur's glass. He waved his hand. "Just go ahead. I'm sure it's fine."

"So, are you a native German-Canadian?" Liz asked, persisting with her questioning, enjoying the fact that she, for once, had control of the conversation.

Arthur shook his head. "No. I'm not. I'm Canadian now, but I was born in Germany."

"Really? When did you leave?"

"In 1939."

Liz nodded slowly, understanding the relevance of the date. "Right. Just before the . . ."

"The war. Yes." Arthur took a drink from his glass. "My father was, like me, an academic, a physicist to be precise, and also vice-president of the Technical Institute in Stuttgart. When 'Führerprinzip' was introduced in 1933, all members of staff at the Institute who were of Jewish descent were immediately fired. In other words, all my father's most erudite friends. Mr. Hitler was particularly hostile to any scientific advancement that originated from a Jewish brain, and it has even been mooted that that was why, during the war, Germany lagged behind the rest in the development of the nuclear bomb. Anyway, my father stuck it out for the next six years in the hope that he could help keep up the student numbers, but they declined fast, regardless of his efforts. So you can imagine that when he began to express his sentiments towards all this rather too openly, he was never going to be first in line for a popularity award. Having a wife and three small sons. I being the youngest, he understood only too well the direction in which things were going and he thought that the risk was too great in staying in the country. So, one night, he took what he could carry from the house, bundled us all into his car, and we made our escape. As it turned out, only just in time. My father heard many years later of the fate that befell many of his fellows at the Institute."

"So you went straight to Canada?"

"Yes. In the salubrious elegance of a Dutch tramp steamer."

"How old were you?"

"Two, I think." He smiled at her. "There you are. You can work out my age now."

Liz let it pass without comment. "So what did your father do when he got to Canada?"

"Not a lot to begin with. We were housed in a sort of refugee camp for about four months, and then my father had an opportune meeting with a friend from the university who had emigrated ten years beforehand. It was he who really saved our lives. Within two months, the guy had pulled enough strings to strangle an elephant. We were given Canadian nationality, the man found us a small house in Toronto and a job for my father in a high school there."

"That was a bit of a come-down, wasn't it? I mean, going from a university to a high school?"

"You're right. But beggars couldn't be choosers. He just knuckled down and did his job. But what with the problems in Germany and the fact that he missed his friends and the mental stimulation of working in research, things didn't go well for the old boy. I don't think that I ever remember him being in any mood other than deep depression. He died almost ten years to the day after we arrived in Canada."

Liz bit at her lip. "I'm sorry." It was a falter, but she had to keep pressing on. "And what about you? What did you do?"

"I went to the high school and then on to the University of Toronto." He laughed. "And that's when my story begins to have certain parallels to yours."

Liz's back straightened, relinquishing her relaxed position, and she felt her screen of defence begin to shut down on the conversation. With opportune timing, the waiter came to the table to take their orders.

"Now, what are you having?" Arthur asked.

"I think just cannelloni as a starter, please, and that'll do me."

"What about sharing a green salad with me?"

"All right then."

Arthur looked up at the waiter. "So, that's one cannelloni starter and a lasagna verde, and we'll have a green salad to share."

The waiter wrote quickly on his pad, and with a gracious bow left the table and hurried away to the kitchen. Arthur smiled at Liz. "Go on."

"What?"

"Go on with your questioning. You're doing well."

Liz let out a quiet laugh at the intuition of the man. He knew exactly what she was doing. "I can't remember where we'd got to."

"I said that my life had parallels with yours."

"Ah. Yes. Right, then—in what way?"

"I got a girl pregnant. She was a fellow student—I was nineteen, she was eighteen. It was almost regarded as criminal in those days, so I married her. Actually, it turned out to be a pretty good marriage, even though, to begin with, we lived on air. It lasted twelve years, during which time we both graduated, both got jobs, and we had three children, two girls and a boy. But then I . . . well . . ." He paused, twisting his mouth to the side as if finding it difficult to continue.

"You did what?"

Arthur held out his hands, as if already submitting to her reaction to his confession. "I left them."

Liz's brow furrowed. "For what reason?"

"Because I was selfish, impulsive, bored, wanting to make a success of my life. You think of every bad reason for me to walk out on my family and I can guarantee you that it would have gone through my mind."

Liz said nothing. What could she say? Here they were talking about him, but she could not pass comment without making it seem to be a direct reflection on her own circumstances.

She picked up her wineglass and took a sip, then, catching in his eye an inquiring look to see her reaction, she picked up her mineral water and took a sip from that as well.

"It's pretty shocking, isn't it?" he said eventually.

She nodded. "Yes. It is."

He leaned forward on the table. "I wasn't having an affair at the time, you know. There was no one else—if that makes it any easier for you to understand."

"Not really."

"No. I can quite see that. Anyway, I have started, so I shall keep on going. My wife and I eventually divorced, but I continued to keep them financially, which was pretty hard on the salary that I got. That was probably the main reason why I never married again. Okay, I had some passing affairs, but none that lasted. It was always myself that broke them off. Not because I didn't want them to work. It was just that I never really trusted my instincts ever again."

"But you kept seeing your family?"

"No, I didn't, because there was obviously great animosity between my wife and myself and she didn't want me anywhere near the house, so I just thought it best if I got out of their lives. I took a job in Vancouver and ended up living there for twenty years. However, about five years ago, I had this great impulse to find the children. Don't know what brought it on. Probably approaching my sixtieth year. I found out where each of the girls lived—luckily they were both still in Toronto—and I visited them on the same day, because I didn't want one to put the other one off from meeting me. And there they were, married with children—my grandchildren—and we talked—and we made up—eventually." He paused. "It was the hardest thing I ever had to do in my whole life. For a week, I found myself teetering along a rotting rope bridge over this gaping chasm of rejection, with the haven of acceptance never seeming to get any closer on the other side."

"But you made it."

"Eventually."

"And what about your son?"

"I'm still on the bridge—I think. It could quite possibly be broken."

"How do you know? Did you meet him?"

"Yes, I did—thanks to Angela, my eldest daughter, who filled me in on what he was doing and how to get in touch with him."

"And?"

"He's young—and he's powerful—and he's dead-set against marriage."

"Because?"

"You can probably hazard a guess."

"Yes, I suppose I can. So what does he do?"

"Oil. He's in oil. Everywhere in the world where they speak Spanish, he's in oil."

"Another linguist, then?"

Arthur laughed. "Again, if you consider being fluent in another language qualifying one as a linguist. Doesn't speak a word of German."

"So where is he based?"

"Everywhere. Philippines, South America, Spain, London, Aberdeen . . ."

"Aberdeen?"

"Not very Hispanic, is it? But he does come up here quite a bit. He's in exploration. And that's the real reason that I came over here to Saint Andrews. I had to find a place that I could wait around to meet him, and as you can imagine, I can't afford to do that without working."

"And what happened when you did meet . . . what's your son called?"

"Will. Wilhelm, actually, after my father. Well, just let's say it didn't go off so well as with the girls. Angela had given me his mobile phone number, and through the wonders of modern technology, I eventually managed to track him down in Spain. The great thing about the telephone is that it's pretty difficult to think of an immediate excuse when you're taken unawares, so I managed to arrange a dinner meeting with him for the next time that he was in Aberdeen. It turned out to be pretty disastrous, because despite my consuming more humble pie than was good for my egotistic appetite, he tore strip after strip off my guilt-ridden body. Thank God not physically. You can imagine what he looks like, having worked hands-on in oil exploration. But the one thing he inherited from me was an academic's brain, so he managed to reduce me to pulp within the first hour of our meeting."

"So the rope bridge collapsed."

"I don't know. I'm hoping that it's still hanging by a slender thread."

She looked down at her finished plate, not having realized that she had been served her meal, let alone eaten it. She put her knife and fork together and sat back in her chair.

Arthur looked at her. "Okay. My turn to ask a question. What would you say that you have really missed in your life?"

"In what way?"

"Well, you got married and had Alex when you were pretty young. There must have been times when you were cooped up in the house, bathing him or feeding him, when you said to yourself, 'Gosh, I wish I could be doing *that* right now.' "

Liz considered this for a moment, then shook her head. "No. I can't think of anything. I was quite happy with my lot, and I probably didn't have too high expectations for myself anyway. I suppose I did have some regrets in not going on to college, but that was some time ago." She paused. "What about you? What have you really missed?"

"I didn't think that I had missed anything until I met my children again. That's when I realized that I had really lost out."

"Don't you think that you deserved to lose out?"

"Yes, I did—but you didn't."

Liz did not reply, but instead concentrated on making sure that the smile did not slide from her face.

"So," Arthur continued, leaning forward on the table, "I shall slightly rephrase my original question. Looking at your life as it is now, what do you feel that you have missed out on?"

Liz felt trapped for an instant as she struggled for an answer. Looking at her life as it was now, she could only think of what her wants were at that precise moment, and they were all overloaded with negative intent. She did not want to see the golf course built, she did not want to stop farming, she did not want to see Gregor again. But they were all irrelevant to his question. Then something extraordinary happened in her brain. As she concentrated anew, a chink appeared in the hitherto impenetrable layer of bitter resolve, and through it shone a thin but bright light of happy recall.

"Riding!" she exclaimed, a broad smile suddenly bursting onto her face.

Arthur nodded in appreciation of her answer. "Riding."

"Yes. Dad bought me my first pony when I was eleven, and he used to take me to all the pony-club events in the area. Looking back on it, it was all quite embarrassing, because there were always these smart trailers pulled by Range Rovers, and we used to turn up with a battered old Land Rover and the sheep trailer. Sometimes, if the place where the event was being held was close by, he'd even take the tractor. Anyway, I became quite good at it—I mean, I didn't compete or anything like that, but I used to go out quite a bit with the local hunt and charge all over the county on horseback." She sat back in her chair, a contented smile on her face at the recollection. "Yes, that was fun."

"But you didn't exactly miss out on it, did you?"

She shook her head. "No, you're right. I didn't. But when Alex was born, I had no time to ride any more, and Dad said that it was unfair for my horse to be standing around in a field all day not being ridden, so we sold him." She paused and focused her eyes on the palm of her hand, and began tracing small circles on it with her forefinger. "And along with him went my childhood . . . and I was nowhere near ready to lose either."

"No, I dare say you weren't," Arthur said quietly. He clapped his hands together, as if to dispel the mist of melancholia that was beginning to descend upon the proceedings. "Right! Riding. I'll make a mental note of that one. Anything else?"

Liz sat forward on her chair and rested her elbows on the table. "Erm, let's think now . . . travel! I've always wanted to travel."

"Where in particular? The Far East? Africa? America?"

"Don't mind. Just anywhere out of this country. I was going to go to Austria with some friends just after we finished school, but, well, I became pregnant and my mother wouldn't let me go. I don't know if it was supposed to be for the baby's sake or just my punishment for being such a wild young girl. Anyway, holidays thereafter were few and far between. That's the problem with coming from a farming family. You're either too busy to take holidays, or, when you're not, it's always at a time of year when the weather is telling you that it's the wrong *time* to take a holiday." She laughed. "I remember when Alex was about five, we spent a whole week in a café on the Isle of Mull drinking coffee and watching the rain teem down outside. The kind old lady who owned the café realized we were having quite a time controlling Alex, so she pulled a chair over to the one-armed bandit, stuck him on it, gave him a cupful of tokens and told him to do his best. It could have been the start of a dreadful addiction."

Arthur smiled. "You know, you should do that more often."

Liz giggled. "What? Go to the Isle of Mull?"

"No. Laugh like that. It suits you. Your whole face lights up."

The smile slid from Liz's face.

"Oh, dear, I've embarrassed you."

"No—no, you haven't really," Liz replied quietly. "It's just that I don't, well . . ."

"Don't what?"

Liz looked at him. You can't say it, you know. You can't say that you don't think that he should be saying those kind of things to you, that he's too *old* to be saying those kind of things to you. "It's just that I don't believe in compliments like that anymore."

"Well, you should, because I wouldn't waste my time saying it if I didn't mean it. Anyway, if you weren't embarrassed before, you might well be after I've finished my next statement, so I'd be grateful if you would hear me out, because it might just turn out that it's me that ends up embarrassed." He leaned back in his chair. "Right, are you ready for it?"

Liz laughed weakly, in trepidation of what was to follow. "Go on, then."

"Okay. In two weeks' time, I'm heading off to Spain—to Seville, actually, for Holy Week, or Semana Santa, as they call it. I've yet to witness it myself, but it is supposed to be one of the most phenomenal and spirit-lifting experiences that one can imagine. I thought that it would be an ideal trip for Will and me to do together, hoping that he might be able to coincide it with a business trip, so I went ahead and booked it up about three months ago. When I met him that time in Aberdeen, I was going to put the idea to him, but the whole evening was such a disaster that I just thought that it was the wrong time to ask. So when I returned to Saint Andrews, I sent him the itinerary and the plane ticket and told him to take time to think about it before he made a decision. Unfortunately, I received the ticket back by return post with a letter enclosed saying that he had meant what he said during our dinner together—that he never wanted to see me again. So I have this spare ticket—and I was wondering if you might consider coming with me."

Liz gulped before trying to make a reply. "Arthur, I—"

"I'm not finished yet. I know that I probably should be, but I'm not. Liz, Gregor is a fool. I know that because I did exactly as he did. I left my wife and children—in your case, a child. But you cannot brood on it forever. It would be a waste for someone with your attraction, with your humour, with your beauty, to just slip into a life-style of self-rebuke and misery. I know that I am quite a bit older than you, but I know that I can help—"

"That's just it, Arthur."

"I'm sorry?"

"You're too old for me. You are nearer to my father's age." Liz pushed back her chair and got to her feet. "It just wouldn't seem right."

Arthur looked up at her. "Look, sit down for a minute."

Liz remained standing, casting her eyes around the restaurant so that she didn't have to look at him. She noticed that the occupants of the neighbouring table were staring at them.

"Please?"

With reluctance, Liz resumed her seat.

"Listen, I just want to say that I know how you're feeling. I know that probably the last thing you want to think about at the minute is making any form of commitment with another man—and I find that totally understandable. I didn't actually get my phraseology worked out too well, but what I wanted to say was that it's our difference in age that is the key to the whole thing. I'd be no threat to you, Liz. You wouldn't have to be fighting me off"—he let out a low chortle—"which is more the pity for myself, but I promise you that you would have to make no effort other than to enjoy yourself."

Liz was silent for a moment before letting out a settling breath. "I'm sorry I said that—that thing about your age, Arthur. You're right. I'm probably too defensive for my own good at the minute."

Arthur tilted his head to the side in recognition of her state of mind. "So, what do you say? Will you at least think about it?"

"No, Arthur, I can't. Maybe if you were to ask me the same kind question a year from now, I might give it thought, but there's just too much going on at the minute, too much to sort out—what with the farm, with the golf course, with my family . . . and with Gregor. I would feel as though I'd be running away from my own problems."

"I wouldn't say that. More like you would just be distancing yourself from them. It might give yourself the chance to see them more clearly, to see them more in perspective."

"No, I don't think so." She got to her feet again. "If you don't mind, Arthur, can we just leave it?" She paused. "Listen, I really value your friendship, as does everyone in my family, so please, can we just leave it at that?"

Arthur brought his hands down on the table and pushed himself to his feet. "All right. But I'd have kicked myself for not trying. I'll go ahead and get the bill."

Liz nodded. "Okay. And I'll go and get the car."

She walked towards the door of the restaurant, where their waiter, who had witnessed her first attempt to leave, was already waiting to help her on with her coat. She walked out onto the street and took in a deep inhalation of fresh air. Then, as she turned to make her way to where the car was parked, she glanced at her wrist-watch. It was ten past twelve. She had already turned into a pumpkin.

Chapter 10

Eleanor Bayliss Hamilton took in a deep breath, catching the rich aroma given off by the abundance of flowers that decorated the chapel. Not wishing to witness the final moment, she gripped hard at her husband's hand and looked up high into the airy coolness of the crematorium roof as the priest said the final words, sending the coffin slowly along the soundless conveyor belt before disappearing forever behind the purple velvet curtains. Above the muted organ tones, she heard her elder sister, who sat on her other side, let out a series of short, stuttering sobs as she fought hard to stifle her emotions, and without looking at her, Eleanor felt for her hand and gave it a reassuring squeeze.

Good thoughts and happy memories. It was on these that she had been trying to concentrate throughout the service in an effort to stop herself from crying openly. And it really hadn't been difficult. Her father had had many attributes and few shortcomings. Throughout his life, he had been kind, gentle, supportive to his whole family, and she had had to search hard through her memory bank in order to recall a time when he had ever rebuked them as young children. It had always either been left to their mother, or, if one of their frequent misdemeanours was thought so appalling that his judgement was deemed necessary, he would do little more than chew pensively on the leg of his reading glasses before uttering something quite ineffectual, such as, "Well, I wouldn't bother doing it again, if I was you." Then it would be back to reading the sports section of the newspaper to find out who had won a golf tournament in some far-flung corner of the world.

Yet this disinterest in their discipline was more than matched by the enthusiasm and affection he showed for his daughters, never taking the easier option of treating them as a unit, but always making sure that each received the special encouragement and praise to develop her own individual character and interests. And throughout his ninety years, he had never stopped doing that.

But even as she thought about all the happy times in the past, and recognized the fact that she was truly blessed in having had a loving father for all those years, it was not enough to dispel the emptiness she felt in knowing that he had gone forever. It had all happened so fast, too. The young consultant who had been looking after him in the hospital had said that the heart attack was most likely the follow-on to a mild stroke which had gone undetected. So nobody was to blame—least of all poor Bobby. It had only been three weeks since her own sixty-fifth birthday party, when she had talked so fiercely to her younger sister about her own concerns for her father's well-being. Since then, his health had declined so suddenly that he and Bobby had never set foot together on a golf course again.

The completion of prayers was heralded by a general movement amongst the congregation, accompanied by a short ripple of emotion-clearing coughs. The priest stepped down from the pulpit and moved to the centre of the chapel, directing a kindly and reassuring smile towards the family pew. Opening up his prayer-book, he took out a piece of paper which he settled across its pages. "My friends, I would usually think it appropriate to end a service at this point. However, it was Simon Bayliss's own express wish that we should not bring proceedings to a close on a sad note, but rather on one that celebrated the triumph of his being able to survive for ninety glorious years in God's presence on this planet." A reserved murmur of amusement ran through the congregation. "I would ask you therefore to lift your voices in unison one last time in celebration of his life by singing together 'Jerusalem'—number 578 in your hymnals."

The organ came to life with a loud blast, almost cutting off the last few words of his sentence, and the packed chapel rose to their feet as one. Gordon cupped his hand under his wife's elbow and helped her up, and as she steadied herself, Eleanor leaned forward to glance past him to where Roberta still remained seated beside her mother. Although it may well have been construed otherwise by those who stood in the pews behind, there seemed little sign of mutual support being given, for while her mother bowed her head, Roberta stared hard at the purple velvet curtains, oblivious to all that was happening about her. Her face showed no sign of sadness or loss, but was set in a fixed expression of utter disbelief, her whole comportment making it appear as if she had made up her mind to freeze-frame her life at the point that her father's coffin disappeared from sight. Eleanor looked down at her hymn-book, now feeling the tears begin to prick at her eyes. Oh, Bobby, she thought to herself, I *knew* that this was going to be unbearable for you. I said as much to myself that day in Nielsen Park, but I had no idea that you were going to have to deal with it so soon. And you still have the worst to come.

The family had sat in silence around the dining-room table in her parents' house the night before as the lawyer went through the will, but Eleanor had been unable to hold herself back from letting out a cry of incredulity when he had read through the final paragraph. He could *not* ask that of Bobby. She had immediately launched into a full riposte, pointing out the impracticalities and needlessness of the request, but it was Bobby who had held up her hand to stop her in mid-flow, saying that if it was her father's wish, then she would do it.

But it was to happen so far away. To Eleanor, it was the only unthinking, unreasonable thing that her father had ever asked of any of them.

She pulled Gordon's hand towards her mouth and gave it a kiss, and he turned and gave her a broad smile of love and support. Thank goodness she still had him. She could never imagine what it would be like to lose him.

Chapter 11

The eighth hole on the proposed Balmuir Championship Course was 420 yards in length. It dog-legged at a good drive's distance from the tee around a natural outcrop of scrub-covered granite before sweeping down into the hollow to where the white-staked outline of the green nestled itself against the rocky backdrop of the shoreline. From this high vantage point, Jonathan Davies and Michael Dooney, the course architect, surveyed the topography of the hole, struggling to hold open a copy of the plan in the gusting wind.

The tall American grabbed at the flapping sheet as a particularly strong blast threatened to take it off seaward. "Let's try putting it on the ground. Doesn't matter if it gets dirty."

Stretching it tight between them, they laid it out, placing a large stone at each corner to hold it secure before squatting down on their haunches to inspect it.

"Do you think we're making it tricky enough?" Davies asked, looking up from the plan and squinting in concentration as he tried to imagine the layout of the hole in the open fields.

"Yeah, I think so. Remember from down there, the hole is blind—you can't see it from the tee because of this lump of rock that we're standing on. What's more, it follows a pretty difficult par-five, so it does fit into the general pattern of the course, putting an easier hole after a testing one." He stood up, placing both hands on his hips to stretch out his back. "Anyway, this is only a computer generation of the basic layout of the hole. I can always see how things turn out and bring the rough in from the left a bit or stick a couple of pot bunkers down there by the fence where the dog-leg comes into play."

Davies pushed himself to his feet and carefully dusted from his suit trousers a couple of bright yellow petals that had blown off the flowering gorse. "That'll rather penalize the big hitters, don't you think?"

Dooney flashed his wide, piano-key smile. "It's to be a championship course, you know. The big hitters should know how to avoid them."

Davies nodded. "Okay. If you say so."

Dooney delved into the inside pocket of his wind-cheater and took out a notebook and pen to jot down his observations on the hole, glancing down at the plan and looking out across the hole as he did so. "That fence," he said, pointing out the half-mile line of rickety posts that stretched from the bottom of the field up to the road. "That's the boundary between the two farms, isn't it?"

"Certainly is." Davies let out an exasperated laugh. "Maybe the front line of battle would be a more apt description of it."

Dooney shot him an inquiring glance. "I take it then that you're no further forward with your negotiations."

"No, not yet." The venture capitalist flicked the stones from the plan with the toe of his rubber boot, then bent forward and picked it up and began to fold it carefully along its creases. "I sometimes feel like spouting out the old cliché about 'of all the places in all the world, I had to pick this one.' "

"Yeah, I get your point. But take comfort from the fact that you have chosen the minutest corner of the earth on which I think God had always intended golf to be played."

"Oh, I know that. It's the Garden of Eden, as far as that's concerned. But then God did also create Adam and Eve."

Dooney chuckled. "Of course." He became serious. "So you don't think she'll budge?"

"It doesn't look that way at the moment. I mean, all you have to do is look around. Every field's got some damned crop growing in it. Does it look to you as if it was ever intended that a golf course should be laid out here?"

"Well, I think, on that point, you have to give them their due. If the financial packet had been in place, they might not have felt the need to cover their backs by growing crops this year."

"I'll grant that that may be true of Gregor, but I wouldn't think Liz had any intention other than to see all the crops on Brunthill harvested." Davies took off his narrow tweed cap and swept a hand across his thinning hair. "I don't like being beaten for an answer, Mike, and, to be quite honest, I'm really beginning to despair of this whole project. Here we are, ready to go at a moment's notice, and I still feel as if I'm juggling at least three balls in each hand, trying to get the finance raised and trying to get those two to agree with each other." He paused, letting out a resigned sigh. "A couple more weeks. That's all I can afford to give it, Mike, regardless of the fact that we're going to lose thousands on it. A couple more weeks, and then we head Stateside."

Dooney slapped his notebook closed and slid it back into his inside pocket, the action making it look as if he felt it was worthless to take any more notes. "When do you plan to tell *them* that?"

"Tonight. I have a meeting with Liz and her father in the pub, and I'm just going to take the bull by the horns and invite Gregor to join us."

"The final show-down, then?"

Davies began to pick his way down the narrow path, his wax jacket rasping against the jagging gorse-bushes. "That's it, Mike. The final showdown."

As Dooney began to follow on, the shrill ring of a mobile phone sounded out. He stopped and dug his hand into his pocket. "Mine or yours?"

Davies pulled out his phone. "Mine." He pressed the "speak" button. "Hullo? . . . yes, this is he . . . oh, hullo, Lionel, how are you? . . . good . . . yes, I can speak, but can you hang on a minute? The reception's not very good here." He turned and began to retrace his steps up the slope. As he passed Dooney, he put a hand on the American's arm and gave it a tight squeeze. "Fingers crossed, Mike. This could be it." He continued on to the top of the outcrop and bent down behind a clump of gorse to shelter from the wind . . . "Hullo, Lionel? Yes, that's better, so what's the situation? . . . right . . . okay . . . and you're one-hundred-per-cent sure that's firm . . . right . . . and what about conditions? . . . well, that's great news, Lionel . . . absolutely, it's really lifted my spirits . . . okay then, we'll speak soon."

He pressed the button on his mobile phone and held wide his arms as if in triumphant praise. "You were absolutely right, Mike. God does want a golf course built here after all."

Dooney smiled up at him. "You mean you've got the finance?"

Davies bounded down the slope to where he stood. "Yup. Every last penny—signed, sealed and delivered."

Dooney let out a loud rodeo whoop. "Well done! Now all you have to do is deal with Adam and Eve."

"Well, I have the incentive. It's now just a question of finding a tempting-enough apple for both to bite into." He reached up and placed his arm around the shoulders of the course architect. "But right now, my friend, I would suggest that we might hedge our bets a little and put those diggers on stand-by."

Liz stared out of the kitchen window, aware of the two distant figures moving across the farthest field on the farm, but her mind was too preoccupied for their presence to register any small measure of concern or inquisition. She glanced down at the sheet of letter-head on the kitchen table, then bent forward and picked it up. Once again, she read through its precise wording, her head filled with a mixture of bewilderment and fury as to why news of such overpowering consequences should be imparted in the form of a computerized print-out.

The door of the kitchen opened and her father walked in. She hurriedly folded the letter and moved across to the work island, where she tucked it under the pile of otherwise unopened mail. Taking the cap from his head, Mr. Craig spun it through the air with a deft flick of his wrist. It came to rest only a few inches from where she had secreted the letter. He looked at her concernedly. "You all right, lass? You look a bit washed out."

Liz shook her head. "No, I'm fine. Just seem to have a bit of a headache."

"Take a couple of aspirin, then."

Liz shook her head, but it was more to acknowledge the fact that that seemed to be his answer to all ailments. "It's just come on."

"Right. Well, could you just make a wee note somewhere that we're needing a couple of bags of hen-feed? The last one's just finished."

Liz put both hands on the work surface and gripped hard at its edges, her father's innocent-enough request seeming, at this point, to be as demanding as a child moaning endlessly for sweets in a shop. She felt anger and emotion grip tight at her stomach as the fight and resilience that had been hitherto fired by her break-up with Gregor and her subsequent efforts to keep the family farm intact began to ebb from her body. It would seem now that it had all been for nothing.

"Dad, we cannot afford to buy any more damned hen-feed!" she blurted out through clenched teeth, her eyes brimming with tears of hopelessness and frustration.

The farmer gave her a lengthy stare, his expression registering both concern and a guarded understanding of the reason for her outburst. "What's the matter, lass?" Liz did not reply. "Is it the bank?"

Liz slipped out the letter from the bottom of the pile and handed it to him. "They're going to foreclose on us, Dad," she said quietly, slipping her fingers into the front pockets of her jeans. "So no more hen-feed—no more of anything."

She watched as her father read once through the letter, then, with the slightest nod of acceptance, he folded it up and placed it gently back on the worktop.

Liz stared at the letter, incredulous at his reaction. "Is that it, Dad? Do you not understand that that letter effectively ends a hundred and fifty years of our family having farmed here?"

Mr. Craig walked towards his daughter and encircled her shoulders with his strong lean arms, pulling her tight against him. "Lizzie, I can't allow that thought to pass through my mind, because it would be no use. We have done everything that we possibly could, and I'm that proud of you for giving so much of yourself in trying to keep the place going."

Liz pushed herself away from him. "But you can't accept it that easily, can you? Surely if we asked the bank, they would give us a little time to come up with some alternative?" She turned from him and began to pace back and forth across the kitchen floor, her face a study of concentrated intent, as if she were trying to come up with one last desperate escape plan from a condemned cell. "What about a sale and leaseback? Bob Maclure did that with some pension company about ten years ago, didn't he? That would raise sufficient capital to clear the overdraft."

"Pension companies aren't that interested any more in land, Lizzie. Anyway, by the time we cleared the overdraft, there'd be little left for working capital and we'd just be back to square one in no time at all—this time as tenant farmers."

Liz's eyes widened at another thought. "Well, what about Andrew in Australia? Why don't we ask him to buy the farm? I'm sure that he would help if he knew . . ."

"I've no wish to get Andrew involved in this. He made a decision many years ago that he wanted nothing to do with the farm, and I think it would be unfair to ask him."

"Well then, what about . . . ?"

"Lizzie, stop!" He took hold of her shoulders and guided her towards the kitchen table, then pulled out a chair. "Now would you please, for a moment, just sit down there and be quiet, because I want to say something. All right?"

For a moment, Liz showed every sign of resisting his request, but then, with a sigh of resignation, she slumped down onto the chair. Her father swung one around for himself and sat down, leaning his elbows on the table and rubbing a hand over his gaunt cheeks. "Listen, lassie, we're not the only farming family to have these problems, you know. It's not unique to us, so we don't have to feel guilty or feel that we have failed in any way. There's a good few others like us. I read about them every week in the newspaper or in *The Scottish Farmer*. It's just the way things are in the industry at the minute. But what you have to realize is that many of these families have nothing to fall back on, so they end up just throwing the keys of the farmhouse onto the bank manager's desk and walking off the land." He paused, folding his fingers together and pressing them to his mouth. "I don't want to be forced into doing that, Lizzie, and I'm afraid that we would be if we kept hiding away from the truth any longer. We're lucky enough to have an alternative. It's all there, set in place, even though I know you're not too keen on the idea."

Liz's eyes narrowed. "You're not meaning the golf course?"

"I am."

"But we can't—"

Her father cut short her objection. "Yes, we can—and we're going to!" he exclaimed, a hint of vehemence in his voice. "I'm running out of energy, lass. I'm tired of farming and tired of having to cope with this financial millstone that we have to carry around our necks all the time. But what is of much greater concern to me is that I think it's the only way that we'll have any chance of laying bare those defence barriers that you've been setting up all about yourself." He reached across and touched the side of her hand on the table. "Lizzie, I know what's been driving you for the past six months, and even though I can quite understand it, I don't like it—and neither does Alex. We've all had to suffer great upheaval in our lives recently, but we have to keep trying to make the best of things. You *have* changed, lass, and quite a bit, too. Both Alex and I see it, and I have to say that sometimes it quite frightens us. I've never wanted to tell you this before in such a blatant way, because I know that you've been hurting that badly. But I see no sign of you getting any better, and I think that it's time that you're given a wee push in the right direction."

Liz let out a choking breath and clasped tight the hand that touched hers. "Oh, Dad!" In one movement, she slid off her chair and onto his lap, putting her arms around his shoulders and pressing her face into the nape of his neck, exactly as she had done to seek comfort as a small child. "I'm so sorry, Dad. It's just that I miss everything so much. I want everything to be as it was."

He patted her back gently. "I know you do, lass. I know it too well, and if it were in my power, I'd change it all back for you." He pushed her away so that he could look up into her face. "But things *are* different now and you've got to make a wee bit of an effort—for all our sakes."

Liz nodded slowly and wiped away the tears from her cheeks with the back of her hand. "I know. You're right. I do feel bitter—and angry, not just about Gregor, but Mum as well. I just felt that all our lives had been shattered, and I wanted to hold on to whatever was permanent and safe in our lives."

"I know that—and I don't blame you for trying."

She smiled at him. "So what do you think we should do?"

"Well, firstly, I would suggest that you go to the meeting in the pub tonight and tell Jonathan Davies that we will give his project our full support."

"Don't you want to come?"

"No. I think that I'd better be going into Saint Andrews to see the bank manager, and I'll tell him what we've decided to do. And then I'll just head on over to Cupar to see if I can fix up a date for a farm sale with the auctioneers."

"Already?"

"Yes, already. If we're to stop, then I don't want it dragging on forever."

Liz nodded in agreement. "So that's the first thing. What's second?"

The farmer laughed. "Aye, well, secondly, could you please get off my lap? My old legs are about to collapse."

Chapter 12

The barman of the Doocot Arms sat swinging his legs over the edge of the stainless-steel work surface in the small kitchen that linked the public and lounge bars, throwing back his head in laughter at the joke that the corpulent young chef had just told him. Half-way through the story, he had thought of one himself that would be a perfect follow-on, but just as he launched into telling it, he heard the heavily sprung double doors of the lounge bar bang shut. He held up a finger, listening for a moment, then jumped down off the side. "First customer of the evening, I think."

Four quick steps took him to his position behind the bar and he fixed a smile on his ruddy features as the sprucely dressed man approached him. "Good evening, Mr. Davies. How have things been today?"

Jonathan Davies thumped the thick cardboard file that he had been carrying down onto the polished surface of the bar. "Fraser, I think that I can say in all honesty that things have gone rather well today."

"Glad to hear it. So, what will it be?"

"Just a half-pint of lager, please."

The barman reached up and took down a glass from the rack above the bar. "So what's the latest on the golf course?"

"Things are progressing."

That was as much as he was prepared to say. He had always been careful not to discuss the project too openly in front of the locals, other than with those who were directly involved or when he was keeping to a strict agenda at a public meeting, and he certainly wasn't going to start discussing it with Fraser, the barman. He had learned that lesson the hard way, having once let slip the merest titbit of confidential information to the man, which not only reached the ears of every resident in a five-mile radius within a time span of about four hours, but did so with an appalling degree of distorted embellishment. He had also the strongest suspicion that it had been Fraser's gossiping bar-talk that had provoked the affront that Liz had suffered at the last meeting.

So he simply smiled a thank-you to the grinning barman, picked up the glass of beer and his file, and moved over to one of the tables to await the arrival of the others.

With a synchronous jerk at each trouser leg, he settled himself in his seat and took a sip of beer. Then, flicking the bands off the file, he took out a printed sheet of paper and began to give its contents a final run-through.

Even though it hadn't taken him long to work out what his tempting "apple" was going to be, he still felt a pang of anxiety about the impending meeting. It wasn't so much that he felt that the offer was insufficient, but more that he had begun to have second thoughts about inviting Gregor, thinking, in retrospect, that it may have been more tactful to approach both parties separately. But then, this was crunch time. At this stage, he couldn't afford to appear kind and considerate, even though it went against his better nature. If nothing even remotely began to swing in his favour during this meeting, he would be left with no alternative other than to inform them of his plans to pull out.

But what a bloody waste of time and effort that would be, not least taking into account the resources that his consortium had already ploughed into the project to cover the research and development, the marketing and planning. He had always been able to keep quite upbeat at investors' meetings, because invariably there had been new progress to report, and he had always been able to skirt around any issue that related to the owners of the land. However, if the project were to fall through at this advanced stage, then challenging questions would be asked of him about why he had chosen not to bring these problems to light beforehand, and at that point his integrity and business capability would no doubt become the subject of debate.

He scanned the sheet of paper again. He could offer no more. He simply could not *afford* to offer more. It was crunch time for everyone.

The door opened and closed with a bang, and he looked up to see Liz walking towards him. She was dressed in a short brown corduroy skirt and yellow cotton shirt that she had tucked loosely into a broad silver-buckled belt, and a large leather handbag hung by a long strap from her shoulder. The trailing fringe of her otherwise short blonde hair was swept to the side, held in place above her right ear by a small gold clasp, the full effect being one of wholesome simplicity rather than alluring sophistication. There was no doubt that he found her attractive, but it was more in a protective nature, always being aware that there was an expression of deep hurt and acute vulnerability ever-present in her hazel-brown eyes. She gave him a faint smile of greeting as she approached, and he quickly slipped the sheet of paper back into the file and rose to his feet to greet her. "Liz, how nice to see you." He gave her a kiss on either cheek. "Come and sit down. Is your father on his way?"

Liz slid the handbag from her shoulder and hung it on the back of a chair opposite to the one that he had been occupying. "No, I'm afraid not. He had things to do."

"Oh dear. That's a pity." He made no effort to hide the disappointment in his voice. "Well, what can I get you to drink?"

"Just an orange juice, please."

He walked over to the bar, noticing that Fraser was sidling a glance past him at Liz, a half-laughing sneer of disdain on his face. "One orange juice." He missed out on the "please" on purpose. Leaning both hands on the bar, he watched vacantly as Fraser went about his business. Dammit, this was going to be a disaster. He had been counting on the presence of Liz's father to temper the whole meeting. Now, not only was he going to have to try to sell the addition to his financial package, but he was also going to have to tread as carefully as a bloody marriage counsellor. Hell, why was he worrying about *that?* As soon as her husband walked through that door, Liz was probably going to get up and leave anyway.

The door swung open and Gregor's square, muscled figure appeared. Davies turned, pressing his back against the bar and glancing quickly from one to the other, as if about to witness an almighty shoot-out in a Western saloon. Liz had seen him now—but she made no movement to leave. In fact, she still had that same smile fixed on her face. It was Gregor who looked more ill at ease, taking what seemed like an eternity to walk the short distance from the door to the table, never taking his eyes off Liz, as if he fully expected some show of hostility at his appearance. But nothing happened. Davies turned back to the bar and quickly paid for the orange juice so that he could return to the table to mediate.

"Gregor, thanks for coming," he said, his voice sounding jolly to cover for his uneasiness. "What can I get you to drink?"

"Don't worry. I'll get myself something." He was still looking at Liz as he spoke. He nodded at her. "Liz?"

"Hullo, Gregor." Her voice was calm, almost resigned.

Davies gave an inward sigh of relief. So far, so good. He placed the orange juice in front of Liz and sat down opposite her.

"I didn't know Gregor was coming," she said quietly.

Davies pushed back his chair, then leaned forward, resting his elbows on his knees. He linked his hands and began to turn his thumbs nervously around each other. "I know you didn't. I'm sorry if it upsets you, but I just—"

"It doesn't upset me." Her tone hadn't changed.

Davies nodded and smiled at her. "I'm glad."

Gregor pulled out the chair next to him and sat down, placing his pint of beer on the table. Davies slapped his hand down on top of the file. "Well, I think that we'll just get started, shall we?" He opened up the file and took out the sheet of paper. "Right. I'll start with the good news. I received word today that we have the full complement of money necessary for the project." The news was greeted with silence from both parties. Davies let out a short cough of apprehension before continuing. "Anyway, so we are now in the position to move forward—that is, if we can come to some sort of agreement. Now . . ." he followed on quickly so as to give Liz or Gregor little chance of interrupting, ". . . I have drafted out here a codicil which I would add to the purchase agreement, copies of which you will both have already." He handed each a sheet of paper. "It states that The Balmuir Sports Development Company would be willing to give you full market value of growing crops in all fields which have been designated for development."

"That's my whole farm," Liz murmured, almost inaudibly.

"Yes, I do understand that, Liz."

"Are you talking about market price at time of harvest, or just cost of production?" Gregor asked.

"No, full market price at harvest, taking a mean average of yields in the area. Now I think that this is a fair offer, and one that my consortium should quite rightly put forward, considering that we did not have our financial package in place at the time of sowing." Out the side of his eye, Davies caught Gregor slowly nodding his approval. "So, at this precise time, we are ready to move, and all we need now is your acceptance of the offer."

He sat back and crossed his arms. That was it. He'd said it. Now it was up to them. Either they agreed, or he would have to start telling them of his alternate plan.

Gregor glanced across at Liz, then back to Davies. "Well, you know my answer."

Davies nodded. "Liz?"

Liz picked up her glass of orange juice and drained it, and as she got to her feet and slung her handbag over her shoulder, the two men watched open-mouthed, like children who had had newly opened presents snatched away from them. She saw this and smiled in amusement. "Don't worry. I'm not going to disappoint you both. We'll agree to it."

Davies's mouth fell open even further. "What?"

"Are you sure, Liz?" Gregor asked, a measure of concern in his voice.

"Yes. Both Dad and I are sure."

"My word!" Davies couldn't believe that it had been that simple. "Well!" It was on. The project was going ahead. He slapped his hands down hard on his knees and jumped to his feet. "In that case," he exclaimed, now making no effort to control his excitement, "I think that we should bust open a bottle of champagne right now."

Liz held up her hand to refuse the offer. "Thank you, Jonathan, but it's not really a moment of celebration for my father or me. We heard today that the bank has foreclosed on us and, well, that's the reason why we felt that we had little option other than to accept your offer. But thank you, anyway, and if you will excuse me now, I think that I'd like to go home."

"Of course," Davies replied, recovering his decorum.

Liz smiled at him, then cleared her face of all expression and nodded a farewell to Gregor. She turned and walked out of the lounge bar without looking back.

The two men stood in silence, their eyes fixed on the door of her departure. Gregor turned and picked up his pint glass and quickly drained it. "Give me a moment, Jonathan."

Liz slid into the driving seat of the Land Rover and put the keys into the ignition, then sat back and let out a long sigh. She caught sight of her face in the rear-view mirror and closed her eyes, not wanting to look at the person who had betrayed her ideals, who had given up the fight. It's finished, she thought to herself, you've capitulated—and what on earth are you going to do with yourself now?

She turned the key and the old vehicle spluttered to life. She reversed quickly and spun the wheel, looking to the front in time to see Gregor jumping aside to avoid her. She stopped abruptly. Déjà vu. This had all happened before. She sat watching him for a moment as he made no move to approach her, then slowly she reached forward and turned off the engine.

Gregor walked tentatively over to her door and opened it, and rested his shoulder against the side of the vehicle, his body facing in towards her. "I was just wondering . . ."

She turned to face him. "What?" she asked aggressively.

"If you were all right."

She sniffed out a derisive laugh. "No, not really. Would you be?"

"No. I mean, I'm not—either. I got a letter, too."

She looked straight ahead through the windscreen, fixing her eyes on the lettering of the pub sign. Anything rather than to have to look at him. "From the bank?"

"Aye. They've foreclosed on us too."

Us. That was a good one. She paused before replying. "So that meeting was make or break for you too."

"For all of us, I think." He dug his hands into his pockets and cast a nervous glance about him. "I'm sorry that it had to end this way, Liz."

"What are your sorry about?"

"The farms—that they both went to the wall."

Liz nodded. Ah, that, she thought to herself. For a moment, I thought you were apologizing for something else. "So what are you going to do now?"

Gregor shrugged. "Don't know. I suppose I'll have to start looking for a job in farm management."

"Around here?"

"Not specifically. There's nothing much to keep me around here." He bit at his lip, realizing what he had just said. "Sorry. I didn't mean it that way."

Liz nodded.

"How's Alex?" he asked.

"Fine."

"I'd like to see him sometime, Liz."

"I'll tell him."

"I mean, I really would like to see him."

She understood his meaning. Well, why not? Things were different now, especially if he was going to be moving away. There was no reason to deprive her son of a father, or vice versa. After all, what was it her own father had said about having to start to make the best of things the way they were? She turned to look at Gregor. "I'll ask him if he would come over to see you."

Gregor smiled at her. "Thanks."

There was another uneasy silence. No need for any more, Liz thought to herself. She turned the ignition key.

"I never knew you liked the theatre."

Her hand froze on the key. "What?"

"The theatre." There was a brightness to his voice; she couldn't tell whether it registered inquisition or just interest.

"How did you know about that?"

"Jonathan Davies told me. He came around to your house that night you went out."

"Ah, right. Well, in answer to your question, yes. I do like the theatre—and the opera, for that matter."

"That's good to hear." He let out a long breath. "And this is, erm, Alex's professor that you've been going with."

"Yes, it is."

"Nice man, is he?"

Liz turned to look at Gregor. He stood now with his back to her, his face looking down, and she leaned forward enough to see that it was a six-inch nail that he must have had in one of his pockets that he now turned over and over in his fingers. Why was he asking these questions? He's not—no, surely he's not *jealous*.

"Yes, he's *really* nice." Go on, girl, overplay it. See what happens when you dig in the knife a bit. "He's funny. He's wonderful to talk to. In fact, he's just great company."

Gregor nodded. "I'm glad. I think you, well, deserve it."

Liz turned the ignition key and started the engine. "Yes, Gregor, so do I." She closed the door of the car, and in doing so felt a rush of exhilaration flood through her body for the first time in countless months. She pressed her foot on the accelerator and took off, glancing back in her side mirror at Gregor. What was he doing now? Why was he running after the car?

He pulled open the door, forcing Liz to stop abruptly. As she did so, a small Mini Metro pulled into the pub car-park. "You won't forget to ask Alex, will you?"

Liz did not answer. Her eyes were fixed on Mary McLean as she got slowly out of the car. Gregor turned to follow her line of sight.

"Gregor?" Mary asked. Liz was sure she could detect a tremble in her voice.

"Hi, Mary," he replied quietly.

"What are you doing here?" Yes, there was a definite tremble.

"We had a meeting—with Jonathan Davies, that is."

"Why didn't I come?"

"Well, I . . ."

"I think I'll leave you two to sort this out between yourselves," Liz cut in. She closed the door and drove out to the edge of the car-park, and having checked the road she swept out, catching a glimpse in her rear-view mirror of both Gregor and Mary standing at a distance from each other and staring at her departing vehicle.

Anyone who might have happened to witness her driving through the village and up the hill and around the corner to the farm road might well have thought she was under the influence of drink, because she laughed uncontrollably the whole way at the thought of Mary McLean's simpering hurt. And what made the pleasurable ache in her stomach even more acute was the fact that she *had* been seen. Miss Mouncey, Balmuir's nervous little spinster, had been scuttling along the pavement on her way back from the church, her little basket no doubt containing her tin of Brasso and an abundance of polishing cloths, when Liz had driven past at speed. The sight of her jumping like a frightened mouse and diving into a shop doorway to conceal herself had nearly been enough to cause Liz to steer the Land Rover into a parked car.

She made it to the end of the farm road and stopped, and slowly began to bring herself under control. That had been quite *wonderful*. If she had tried to stage-manage that herself, it could not have turned out more perfect. She imagined what it must have been like for Mary seeing her boy-friend running after his ex-wife's car and yanking open the door.

What on earth could she ever think he was doing, other than proclaiming undying love for his estranged wife? She laughed again at the thought. Perfect retribution without an iota of malice on her part. And what about Gregor? It *had* to have been some kind of jealous pang that had fired those questions. There could be no other explanation.

She suddenly felt a comforting sense of well-being again, of self-control, of self-confidence. She put her foot down on the accelerator, but then immediately took it off as her eyes focused on the farm in front of her, the green fields sweeping down to the shoreline, and a small dark cloud of nostalgia and loss rolled across her bright sun of new-found elation. It was gone. Nothing could save it now—and as Gregor had said, there wasn't much to keep them around now. The glint came back to her eyes. No, there wasn't, was there? And why not? Even Gregor had said that she deserved it.

She slammed shut the kitchen door behind her, catching Leckie as he bounded towards her and jumped into her arms. She made her way through to the hall and opened quite forcefully the door of the sitting-room and walked into a thick cloud of pipe smoke. Her father and the professor sat opposite each other each clutching a fan of cards, two small glasses of Jack Daniel's placed on the carved oak coffee-table between them. Both gave her a look as if they had just been caught red-handed in some illicit speakeasy. Then the farmer saw the expression on his daughter's face and a wide smile spread across his wrinkled cheeks.

Liz let out a long breath. "Arthur?"

The professor pushed himself out of the sagging sofa, his expression of guilt now turning to one of consternation, as if he might be trying to work out what new household misdemeanour he could have committed. "Yes?"

"I was wondering if you had found anyone to go with you to Seville."

Arthur's shoulders dropped quite visibly in relief. He shook his head. "No. Actually, I haven't bothered to try. Why do you ask?"

"May I come with you?"

The two men glanced at each other and Liz detected the merest sense of conspiratorial triumph in their eyes. The professor turned and gave her a gentlemanly bow. "Liz, I would be delighted if you came! And I promise you that I would adhere to all our conditions."

She smiled at him, then looked down at her father, whose face had not yet lost its Cheshire-cat grin. "Hullo, lass," he said.

Chapter 13

The contractors moved in on the last work-day of the second week in April, two days before Palm Sunday. Their heavy machines lumbered down the road to Brunthill, their tyres so wide that, in one pass, they reduced the grass verges to the same level as the road, and when they found that they were unable to make the tight turn around the steading, they took down twenty yards of the roadside fence to gain access to the fields. There was no one at the farm to witness this event, nor to see later, in the bottom field directly below the house, the lush green carpet of malting barley that had shown such promise of yielding a bumper crop being unceremoniously scraped away and thrown into great heaps by the gleaming blades of the bulldozers.

Mr. Craig stayed with Liz and the professor at Edinburgh Airport until he had seen them through to the security section, the latter never giving a backward glance as he disappeared into the screened-off area, his constantly worn raincoat flapping out behind him. Liz, however, turned and gave her father a final wave and he knew from the look on her face that she felt both trepidation and excitement at the thought of her incipient holiday. But she managed a smile and blew him a kiss and then was gone.

He turned and walked slowly back along the wide stone-floored arcade, glancing in at the shops that sold vacuum-packed smoked salmon and ties and pieces of designer luggage, none of them being of any interest to him. He stopped briefly at the newsagent to buy a paper, then descended the stairs and walked out of the terminal building and across the road to the short-term car-park.

The weather in the earlier hours of the morning had promised much, but now the wind had freshened and the sun was allowed only moments to radiate its warmth as high broken clouds slid endlessly across its face in the pale-blue sky. He held hard to the door of the Land Rover as he clambered in, then closed it with a jarring clatter and threw the paper onto the passenger seat. He did not start the vehicle immediately but sat back to watch the endless movement of people around him, every one industrious in his pursuit, whether it was trying to work out how to cram various pieces of luggage into a too-small boot or making a mad dash to catch a soon-departing plane with ticket clamped between teeth so that hands could juggle with brief-case, overnight bag and car keys.

But there was no hurry for him. For the first time in his whole life, there was absolutely no hurry. He had arranged for Bert, the tractorman, to feed the few orphan lambs that were still dependant on the bottle, there being little else left for the old boy to do. That had been a sad moment, bringing to an end his thirty years of loyal stewardship, but he was past retirement age at any rate and it had not been difficult to tell, by the beady glint in Bert's eye, that the news of one month's notice was more than assuaged by the mention of a healthy redundancy payment. However, there was no more tractorwork to be done. The big John Deere and his own trusty Fordson Major, along with all the implements and all the livestock, everything right down to the broken-shafted fencing mallet, would be sold at public auction the week after Liz returned from Spain. He had tried to arrange for it to happen beforehand, but the auctioneers had been unable to come up with an earlier date. So time was his own. There was certainly no need to go back to the farm straightaway.

He parked three-quarters of the way up the Royal Mile and made his way slowly up the cobbled street to Edinburgh Castle. He stood high on the battlements, craning over to look down on Princes Street and its two parallel thoroughfares, George Street and Queen Street, then far out across the intricate layout of the New Town to the river Forth and beyond to Fife. He waited there until he had witnessed the ceremony of the one o'clock gun being fired, and then set off back towards his car, stopping in at an old lead-windowed pub for lunch. He sat in the corner with a half-pint of beer and a plateful of haggis and mashed turnip and read his newspaper, feeling quite out of place in his old market suit amongst the gaudily dressed tourists and the casual refinement of the townsfolk. And it was that sense of not belonging that suddenly made him feel quite lonely, and he thought of Kathleen, his dear, sweet, quiet wife, and wished that she could have been there, to watch and to discuss the people about them, as they had done on countless times before. He folded his paper and got up, leaving his beer and food half-finished, and once outside the pub he felt that he had had enough of the hustle and bustle of the city and decided to start making his way home.

Although the traffic coming out of Edinburgh was light, he took his time in driving back to the farm, criss-crossing Fife on a nostalgic journey along a multitude of B-roads which took him through parts of the county, past farms and properties, that he had not seen for many a year, parts that he had never seen without Kathleen by his side. On numerous occasions, when a memorable view would come into sight, he would pull over into a lay-by and sit for a time just looking—and thinking. Consequently, when he did eventually walk back into the farmhouse kitchen it was evening, the clock on the wall making its last movements towards eight o'clock.

Alex turned as he entered, a cooking pot in his hand. "Hi, Granddad, I was expecting you to be home long before me."

The cap came off the farmer's head and was discarded with customary precision onto the central worktop. "Aye, well, I just thought I'd take my time." He walked past his grandson, glancing in at the contents of the pot. "Baked beans, eh?" He let out a chuckle. "That should get you going."

Alex gave him a sheepish look. "Is that all right? I'm afraid that I'm not much of a cook."

Mr. Craig crossed over to the table and sat down. "Don't worry about me tonight, lad. I had a big lunch. Anyway, I think we might just go down to the pub for something to eat in future, don't you think?"

"Well, it would certainly save you from being poisoned by me." He paused as he stirred the pot. "Only thing is, Granddad, that I did say to Mum that I might head across to see Dad a couple of times."

"Of course you did, Alex. That's a good thing to do."

"So, did they get off all right?"

"Aye."

Alex laughed. "Poor Mum. I reckon that if she had known the state that she was going to get herself into over her passport and trying to find clothes to wear, she might have given the whole thing a second thought."

"Aye, well, I think she did on more than one occasion. But I'm sure that she'll have a rare old time once she's out there."

Alex ladled out his beans onto a plate. "Did you see the state of the road fence on your way in?"

"I did. I suppose that's something that we're just going to have to start putting up with."

Alex carried his supper over to the table and sat down next to his grandfather. "They've started already, you know. Down in the bottom field. It doesn't look that attractive, either."

"No, I don't suppose it does. I think I'll just leave it to the morning before I go to have a look at it myself." He leaned his elbows on the table. "So, what's been happening with you today?"

Alex swallowed a mouthful of beans and bread. "I've been caddying on the Old Course all day."

His grandfather looked surprised. "Have you now? I thought that you weren't going to start that until the summer holidays."

"I wasn't, but I don't have much work on at the minute and I'm in dire need of a few extra pounds in my pocket, so I just went down to the caddymaster's office on spec. He said that there were plenty of golfers needing caddies, and told me to roll up whenever I had time on my hands."

"So it was worth it, was it? Got some big tips?"

"Well, to start with, I thought it was going to be a disaster. I went off with a Japanese foursome at just after ten o'clock, and we took all of five hours to get round. They were in and out of bunkers, taking photographs of each other, and the time that they took to line up putts! You'd think that every one was to win the Open! But, to be quite honest, it wasn't that funny. We were holding up play behind and the course rangers kept giving me and the other three caddies stick for not getting them to move faster. And then, of course, none of the Japanese knew how to speak English—or they pretended not to know—and they never took any notice of our efforts to get them shifting. I mean, even on the eighteenth green, they spent about five minutes bowing to each other and shaking hands after they'd finished."

Mr. Craig shrugged. "Och, well, I suppose one can understand them wanting to savour the moment. It probably was the highlight of their lives, like Muslims visiting Mecca."

"Yes, Granddad, but there is a code of conduct, you know."

He grinned at his grandson's admonishment. "I'm sure there is, lad. So that was it, I take it. You got no more work after that."

"Well, I decided to hang around for a bit, even though the other caddies had decided to finish, and just before a quarter to four the caddymaster called me over and asked if I could do a round with a single person on the Jubilee. So I did—in three hours dead."

"Heavens! You must have been fair hurrying the poor man."

"Well, for a start, it wasn't a man. It was this very small, fairly old Australian lady, and I tell you that I had to stop myself from bursting out in laughter when I first saw her, because she was standing there with this enormous Titleist bag beside her that just about dwarfed her. Anyway, I said to the caddymaster that I would take her out, even though I had a strong suspicion that we would still be playing at midnight."

"And you were proved wrong."

"And how! She turned out to be a terrific golfer! She had this huge swing, which is pretty amazing for someone of her age, and she could hit the ball for miles. She sort of defied all those laws of physics that have anything to do with size and power. She actually ended up going round the Jubilee in only nine over par."

Mr. Craig cocked his head to the side. "Must have been some lady."

"She was. Actually, I didn't know if I was going to like her, to begin with. She didn't speak much other than to ask about club selection and distances. I put it down to her being a little off-hand at first, but as we played, I began to realize that she just seemed . . . well . . . a bit sad, as if she might have been widowed recently. She didn't wear a golfing glove, though, so I could see that there was no wedding ring on her finger. Anyway, I thought I'd make an effort to break the ice a bit, so I told her about how I was at university in the town, and after that she really opened up and showed genuine interest in what I was doing. The long and the short of it was that, because of the way she played and the amount of talking we did, the time went past really quickly, and at the end of the round she handed me a tip that was twice the size of the one I got from my Japanese guy."

"So it was all worth it, then?"

"Yes, it definitely was. In fact, I was just thinking that I might do it again tomorrow and then get back to studying on Monday."

Mr. Craig pushed himself to his feet.

"What are you going to do?" Alex asked.

His grandfather laughed. "What? Now, or for the rest of my life?"

"No, I meant now."

He walked towards the door that led into the hall. "Well, I thought that I might just get myself a wee tipple of Jack Daniel's, and then teach you how to play cribbage." He turned to look at his grandson. "That is, if you've got nothing else to do."

Alex shook his head. "No. You can bring me a 'tipple' too, if you like."

Mr. Craig flicked his head to the side and let out a resigned sigh. "Aye, well, I suppose you're of that age now." He opened the door, and as he entered the hall, Alex heard him laugh. "All these bad habits have been introduced by your professor, you know," he chortled in the distance.

Chapter 14

The moment she slid open the balcony window of her bedroom on the fourth floor of the Hotel Cazaral, the sterile frigidity of the air-conditioned room was invaded by the comforting warmth of Seville's night air. It carried on its breath the aromatic cocktail of watered vegetation mixed with a slight hint of drains and petrol fumes, the latter emanating from the grumble of traffic that moved unceasingly along the wide Avenida de Menéndez y Pelayo below. Liz stepped out onto the balcony and stood for a moment taking in the city's sultry air before moving forward to the iron railings and opening the street map that she had found on the bedside table. Directly in front of her, she could just make out the dimly lit paths of the Murillo Gardens stretching along the backbone of the avenue, the spiky silhouettes of its palm trees only just distinguishable against the dense backdrop of foliage that secreted the Alcázar Palace from view. Beyond that in the distance, scraping at the very roof-top of the city, the cathedral's vast, ornate mass and towering

Moorish spire stood out against the night's horizon, fixed in fiery illumination. She glanced to her left and watched as the traffic merged around the Plaza Don Juan de Austria before breaking free of its constraints down the Avenida del Cid. She stretched her hands along the railings, becoming aware at that point of the unaccustomed smile of contentment that transfixed her face. This was different. This was exciting. Less than one full day away from Scotland, and already distance had begun to create a new perspective in her mind, the whole cultural change and the upsurge in temperature squeezing the rancour from her spirit and overriding the problems and worries that had engulfed her over the past months.

Yet she was fully aware of the fact that the day had not started on such a carefree note. When she had left her father that morning at Edinburgh Airport, she had been a jangle of nerves and of mixed emotions, both at the thought of flying for the first time and by recriminations at leaving him to deal with all the legal papers involving the sale of the farm. Consequently, from the moment that she had turned to give him a final wave and had seen him standing alone and altogether quite vulnerable, she had been totally uncommunicative towards Arthur, the whirlwind of thought that had spun through her brain quite wrongly blaming him for enticing her away from her father and away from home. But, to give him his due, Arthur seemed to have understood this immediately, and his blustering passage through the security channel had been the last solo act that he had carried out. Thereafter, he had been constantly at her side, never making demands on her company or trying to chivvy her along with jolly remarks about adventure and intrigue, but just being there, silently supportive. Then, after white-knuckling the armrests of her seat during take-off, she had sat by the window and watched as the landmarks grew smaller and the fields became nothing more than a quilting of green. It was at that point that she had been suddenly gripped by the exhilaration of it all, the size of the world fast diminishing below her and, along with it, the insignificance and unimportance of her own rankled existence.

The five-hour wait at Gatwick Airport for the Seville flight had been much longer than was normally necessary, but Arthur had admitted that he was always nervous of missing connections and had thus booked it with a safe, though maybe, in retrospect, excessive turn-around interval. Liz had bought a couple of postcards, one of Buckingham Palace and the other of a punk rocker with a bright green Mohican haircut, and had sent them to her father and to Alex, respectively. Then, over a coffee and Danish pastry, Arthur had pulled out a heap of guidebooks on Seville from his brief-case and had proceeded to pick out passages that were relevant to Semana Santa. Glancing at her over his smudged reading spectacles and puffing away on his momentarily lit pipe, he had read them out in a voice that could quite easily have indoctrinated everyone in the restaurant.

It was the thought of the Danish pastry that suddenly made her realize that she was feeling extremely hungry, having had nothing other than that and a few mouthfuls of plasticky airplane food to sustain her during the day. The flight to Seville had been on time, but with the add-on of an hour for time difference, they had not landed until a quarter to ten at night. Consequently, by the time the taxi had dropped them off at their hotel, both she and Arthur had decided that they could wait until the morning before eating. But now, looking out from her balcony at Seville, she found that her appetite and energy had been rekindled.

Going back into the room, she picked up the telephone on the bedside table and dialled Arthur's room number. It rang without reply. Puzzled by this, she opened the door and walked along the corridor to his room. She knocked. Again, there was no reply. She lifted her fist to repeat the action, but at that moment the door sprang open. Arthur stood there in a pair of striped Viyella pyjamas, the top of which was buttoned up to the neck, with a tooth-brush protruding from the side of his mouth.

"Lij! Whashamatter?" he mumbled.

"Nothing. I was actually wondering if *you* were all right. I called you on the telephone, but you didn't answer."

Arthur took the tooth-brush from his mouth. "Sorry, I was in the bathroom. I didn't hear a thing. Why were you calling?"

"No reason in particular. Only I was just going to suggest that . . . well, never mind." She paused and gave his attire a quizzical glance. "Arthur, aren't you feeling quite hot in those pyjamas?"

"No, I'm bloody well not. I'm freezing. I can't find the control switch for the air-conditioning."

"Have you tried ringing reception?"

"Yes, but I couldn't make myself understood to the night porter. He doesn't speak any English."

"Oh. Right. Well, do you want *me* to have a look?"

The expression on Arthur's face registered all too clearly his thought that if he had been unable to get to the root of the problem himself, then there was very little hope of Liz's working it out. Nevertheless, he moved aside to allow her entry before returning to the bathroom to continue brushing his teeth.

Liz stood in the centre of the room and surveyed the walls, but there was nothing obvious, other than the usual light switches. She walked over to the built-in wardrobe. "Have you tried in here?"

Arthur appeared at the door of the bathroom, rubbing his face with a towel. "Sort of."

Liz pulled open the double doors and pushed aside Arthur's clothes, which he had already, quite uncharacteristically, hung up. The control box with the LCD read-out was on the back wall. She pressed the "off" button and immediately the whirring fan slowed down and eventually stopped. She closed the doors. "There you are. You know where it is now. At least for the time being, you won't feel as if you're back in Scotland."

Arthur nodded. "Thanks."

Liz started to make her way back to the door of the room. "Well, sleep well, then. I'll see you in the morning."

"Wait a minute. You never told me what it was that you were wanting."

"Oh, nothing. It wasn't very important."

"Tell me anyway."

She turned and smiled at him. "Well, I was going to suggest that we might go out to get something to eat."

"Oh, I see. But I thought that . . ."

"I know. I did say that I wasn't hungry, but I am now . . . anyway, it doesn't matter."

Arthur held wide his hands and looked down to appraise his own dress. "Well, I suppose I could change, but I don't know if we'd find anywhere at"—he glanced at his wristwatch—"half past eleven."

"Oh? I didn't gather that from your Spanish guidebooks. You read out that they were 'a nation of late eaters,' and on a Friday night, I would have thought that they'd have eaten later than usual." Arthur's reluctance to accept her idea was clearly displayed by the way that he puffed out his cheeks and screwed up his face and scratched at the back of his head. "Anyway," she continued quietly, "please don't think any more about it. I can quite easily wait until the morning."

Arthur's face lightened. "Are you sure? You don't mind?"

"No, of course not."

He moved forward and opened the door for her. "I'm glad. To be quite honest, Liz, I'm feeling really flaked out. Travelling seems to take it out of me nowadays. But just you wait and see," he exclaimed keenly, giving her a light, boys-together punch on the shoulder. "I'll be right as rain in the morning."

Liz smiled at him. "Good night, Arthur."

"Good night."

Liz shut the door of her bedroom behind her and sat down heavily on the edge of her bed. That was that, then. A good idea fallen flat. She could always call room service and order a sandwich, but then she might just get embroiled in an unintelligible conversation with the night porter. Anyway, that really had not been her initial impulse. She wanted to continue the day, to relish this new change in herself. Of course, she could still go out and try to find somewhere for herself, but she had no idea in which direction to go or even how to ask, and Arthur might quite easily be right in saying that it was too late. She picked up the television remote and flicked through the channels, but all the programmes seemed to have a political overtone and all were in Spanish. She turned it off, went over to her suitcase and took out a wedge of shirts and placed them on a shelf in the cupboard. She stopped, her hands still resting on the pile. Come on, she thought to herself, you're behaving like a spoilt schoolgirl. He *is* a bit older than you, although most things about him belie the fact, but you can't expect him to go burning the candle at both ends. And after all, he's been nothing but supportive of you all day, so he's more than entitled to call the tune for a change. In fact, why not try to do something you've been reluctant to do since the first time you met him? Why not just give the man a chance?

CHAPTER 15

Stopping at the bottom of the grassy bank, Mr. Craig leaned both hands on the top of his carved ram's-horn crook and stood for a minute to catch his breath, watching as the Jack Russell flew past him and raced up the slope towards the house. Without hesitating in his stride, Leckie leaped up onto the stone wall that encircled the front garden and turned to watch the farmer, his cocked ears and quivering tail willing the old man to follow at a similar pace.

Mr. Craig laughed and shook his head. "You'll have to hold on a wee bit, Leckie. I canna quite keep up with you."

He set his crook firmly in the ground and began to push himself slowly up the bank, digging the toes of his steel-capped boots into the soft ground to give himself better purchase, but even in doing so, there were a couple of times during the ascent when he had to grab at well-rooted grass tussocks to stop himself from tumbling backwards down the steep incline. When he had made it to the top, his feat was immediately acclaimed by Leckie with a furious round of congratulatory barking before he launched himself off the wall and into his master's arms.

"Canny now, wee lad!" he exclaimed as he fought to steady himself on the narrow plateau. "You'll have me down at the bottom again if you carry on like that." He turned, tucking the wriggling animal under his arm, and leaned against the wall to look back over the route just covered on his early-morning walk. Alex had been right: Even in one day, the contractors had managed to change the whole aspect of the landscape. The cut that they had made through the length of the bottom field stood out in blackened shadow against the verdancy of its surroundings, as brutally administered and as painful to observe as a razor slash on a human face. He let the dog drop gently to the ground and took from the pocket of his overalls the aging Instamatic camera with which he had already begun to record the metamorphosis of his farm. He held it to his eye and lined up the shot, but before he had time to click the shutter, a renegade cloud in the otherwise clear azure sky muscled its way in front of the sun, obliterating the shadow in the excavation and blending it in with the existing contours of the land. Mr. Craig took the camera from his eye and squinted up at the cloud, a wry smile cracking the seriousness of his features. Maybe that's a sign from the Almighty, he thought to himself. Maybe He's saying to me, "Look, don't bother taking a photograph of it looking like that. How about I just move this cloud a wee bit this way? There you are, that's not so bad now, is it?"

He curled the cord around the body of the camera and slid it back into his pocket, and, picking up his crook, he pushed open the gate and walked up the overgrown path to the front door. He turned once more to look out across the fields. The cloud had passed away from the sun and the shadow had reappeared. He reached into his pocket again for the camera, but then stopped and slowly withdrew his hand. No, he thought, it's not worth recording—not in this transitional stage, at any rate. You know yourself that your soul is deep-rooted enough in this piece of land to love it, regardless of its cosmetic appearance, so just be excited about what is to come, and not sad or reproachful about what has been. The vision of what it *was* like is instilled into your very being, so just turn your eyes from it all until such times as you can look down from this vantage point and see the tall fescue grass that will soon cover those stark brown banks waving in the breeze and the morning sun dance those shadows across the undulations of the newly grassed fairways. And be thankful to the Almighty that you'll still be in this house to enjoy it.

He kicked the mud from his boots and opened the front door and made his way as lightly as he could through the hall to the kitchen, knowing that his action of entering by that door while still wearing his working boots had been sacrilege in the eyes of his wife and a ruling still vehemently upheld by his daughter. He took off his cap and flicked it onto the central worktop, then stood surveying the kitchen. In the twenty or so hours of losing its female control, the room was fast coming to resemble a bachelor's residence, the sink brimming with unwashed dishes and the table still strewn with the previous day's newspapers. He took off his coat and hung it on the back of a chair, then set about clearing the surface of the table, folding up the newspapers and placing them on the pile of other reading material on the window-seat. He picked up the used cereal bowl and the half-full bottle of milk, and realized, at that point, that Alex must have already had his breakfast. He added the bowl to the tottering pyramid in the sink, then walked over to the refrigerator, noticing as he passed the worktop the hastily scribbled note half-hidden by his cap. He wiped his hands on the seat of his trousers and picked up the note, holding it at a distance so that he could focus on the writing.

Granddad,

It's 7:30 and I'm heading off. I want to get out early on the course and try to fit in three rounds today—make a bit of serious money. So don't hold back supper for me, because if I'm not too late, I'll probably drop in to see Dad on the way home. Anyway, I've made up a mountain of ham sandwiches, which should keep me going for the day. So I'll see you when I see you.

Alex

"Good on you, lad," the farmer said quietly to himself, balling up the note in his fist. He moved towards the rubbish-bin and then stopped, eyeing the plastic bag that stood on the worktop. He tipped the lid of the bin and discarded the note, then pulled the bag towards him and looked inside. It contained a large bottle of water and Alex's supply of sandwiches.

He shook his head. "Alex, you dunderhead!" He pulled the handles of the bag together and tied them in a knot, then walked over to the back kitchen door and hung it on the latch. The Jack Russell, who had been lying on the window-seat, sprang down and ran towards the door, eagerly anticipating another action-packed walk, but his ears drooped in disappointment when the farmer turned away from it.

" 'Fraid not, Leckie," he said, rolling up the sleeves of his shirt. "And I'm afraid that you're going to have to stay here while I go into Saint Andrews. I'm not sure how long I'm going to be. But first," he gave his hands a decisive rub, "I'd better get this place sorted out." And, moving across to the sink, he began running scalding water onto its overcrowded contents.

Having lost the morning to clearing up the house and to fleeting visits to the supermarket and the bank, Mr. Craig did not arrive at the caddy-master's office until the gold-painted hands on the clock of the Royal & Ancient Golf Club had just clicked into alignment at midday. He took his place at the office window behind the small, immaculately dressed Japanese man in the pork-pie golfing hat who appeared to be having great difficulty with his limited knowledge of the English language in getting himself fixed up with a caddy whose credentials matched his specific requirements. Eventually, after a great deal of slow talking and multitudinous hand signals on the part of the caddymaster, the little man gave him a bow of gratitude and walked away with a smile of bemusement on his face. The farmer walked forward to the window, seeing the caddymaster let out a long sigh of relief. He smiled at the man. "Having a bit of a trauchled day, are you?"

The caddymaster raised his eyebrows. "No more than usual," he replied morosely. "I think sometimes, though, that this job would be more suited to some multilingual high-flyer rather than a mere mortal like myself. Anyway, how can I help you?"

"I was looking for my grandson. He's working for you at the minute. Alex Dewhurst."

"Oh, Alex. Right." He scanned his book. "No, you've missed him. He came in about half an hour ago, but then went straight out again."

Mr. Craig clicked his tongue. "That's a pity." He held up the plastic bag. "He forgot his lunch this morning."

The caddymaster glanced at the bag in his hand. "If you want, you could leave it here for him. Mind you, I don't think that he'd be much further than the third hole, if you want to get it to him quicker. It's getting quite slow out there on the Old Course now."

The farmer nodded. "In that case, I think I'll just take myself a wee walk. It's a good enough day for it."

He thanked the caddymaster and turned to walk down the Tarmacked path that ran adjacent to the first hole. As he did so, the starter's voice sounded out over the loudspeaker. "Next match play off, please." He stopped and looked over to the first tee, where a brightly dressed golfer had already begun to settle himself into his shot. With a fearsome swish of his club, he let fly at the ball, and the farmer squinted his eyes in an effort to follow its path through the air. He lost it for a moment, then saw it land far up the fairway, but over to the right, dangerously close to the nearest point of the Swilken Burn. There was a loud guffaw from the other golfers on the tee as the shot was cheerfully castigated, and Mr. Craig smiled to himself at the good humour of the whole proceedings.

He turned and walked over to the bench that stood in the lea of the caddymaster's office and sat down, deciding that he would stay for a bit to watch the buzz of activity that surrounded this great arena. He was in no hurry, and he was sure that Alex could wait a further half-hour for his lunch.

As the golfers left the tee and began to make their way down the first fairway, he leaned back on the bench and crossed his arms, thinking to himself how easy it was, in living so close to St. Andrews, to take for granted a view that would probably rank as the most famous in the golfing world. Behind the first tee, the imposing building of the Royal & Ancient Golf Club of St. Andrews, with its pale stone walls, roof-top ballustrades and ever-watched-through windows stood proud sentinel over the great links course. At the far side of the broad fairway the deceptively sloping eighteenth green tucked itself hard in against the lattice-fenced bank, defying entry to its inner sanctum like a stag at bay, its front apron guarded by the Valley of Sin, the hidden dip in the ground which captured all those who displayed too much caution in hitting their approach shots to the heart of the green. Beyond that, creating the southerly wall of the rectangular amphitheatre and running almost the entire length of the eighteenth fairway, was the narrow road known as The Links. Its border was lined with an ill assortment of buildings, some whitewashed, others natural stone, some tall and austere, others small and pleasantly faced: shops, private dwellings, hotels and golf clubs clustered together with no regard to size nor shape. Farther out, where the course began to widen without the hindrance of buildings, the Swilken Burn meandered its way across the fairway, its diminutive width spanned in front of the eighteenth tee by the small, stone-arched Swilken Bridge, the definitive foreground for any photograph taken of this great golfing vista. And then, out still farther to the monolithic Old Course Hotel that fringed the seventeenth fairway, its magnificent position on the site of the old railway sheds affording its rooms the prime panorama of the Home of Golf. Aye, he thought to himself, there's many a human being on this planet who would sell his soul to be sitting where I am right at this minute.

He watched the next two foursomes tee off before deciding that it was time that he made a move. Picking up the plastic bag, he pushed himself to his feet and was about to move off down the path when he heard the sound of a woman's voice drifting around the corner from the caddymaster's window.

"Good morning. I was wondering if I could get a caddy to take me out on the New Course." The farmer recognized the rounded tones of an Australian accent.

"I'm afraid that we have no one available, madam," the caddymaster's voice replied. "All the caddies are out on the Old at the minute."

"Oh, *no!*" There was despondency, almost a hint of desperation in her reaction to the news. "What do I do then?"

Mr. Craig looked through the windowed front of the office to see if he could get a glimpse of the woman, but the caddymaster's body obscured his view.

"All I can suggest, madam, would be for you to go down to the starter at the New and he'd be able to fix you up with a trolley."

"But I don't want a trolley. I can't manage one, and anyway, I don't know the course. I really do need a caddy." The caddymaster offered no reply to this, and the farmer heard the woman let out a deep sigh of despair. "Listen, I went out late yesterday afternoon on the Jubilee with a young caddy called Alex Dewhurst. If I waited until later, do you think that he might be available?"

Mr. Craig nodded. He thought that that was who it was. He took a step forward and glanced around the edge of the building. She was dressed in a pale-blue polo shirt and Black Watch tartan trousers, and the arms of a yellow sweat-shirt were draped around her shoulders. The upper part of her face was hidden under a white sun visor, the top of which displayed a head of cropped greying hair. She wasn't as small as he had imagined—maybe about five feet three—but what certainly made her seem more diminutive was the enormous black Titleist golf bag that stood at her side.

The caddymaster let out a laugh. "Ah, young Alex again, is it? He seems to be a popular lad this morning. His grandfather was here earlier on looking for him. I'm afraid Alex is out on the Old at the minute, but if you'd like to come back . . ." The farmer moved behind the woman, into the caddymaster's line of sight. "Oh, look, there's the gentleman behind you." He addressed him. "Did you catch up with Alex, then? This lady was wanting him to caddy for her later on in the afternoon."

The woman turned and tilted back her head so that she could view the farmer from under her visor. He smiled at her. "No, I've yet to go out. I've just been having a seat around the corner."

The woman turned to the caddymaster. "So you've no idea when he'd be available?"

"Sorry, madam. It could be three hours, it could be four. There's no easy way of knowing."

She bit at her bottom lip, then shook her head in resignation. "Well, I suppose it had better wait for another day," she said quietly, almost to herself. She put her arm through the carrying handle of the golf bag and heaved it onto her shoulder and, with her body bent almost at right angles under its weight, she began making her way slowly up the path towards the clubhouse, her white-studded golf shoes clicking on the solid surface as she went.

Mr. Craig nodded a quick farewell to the caddymaster and walked hastily after her. "Excuse me."

She stopped and turned around, letting the bag slip from her shoulder. "Yes?" she said in a clipped voice that made her frustration all too apparent.

"I was just going to say that I'm about to head out across the links to meet Alex." He held up the plastic bag. "The lad forgot his lunch."

"So?"

"Well, I was wondering if you would like me to carry your bag. I'd be quite happy to."

The woman studied him for a moment before a smile came across her face. "That's very kind of you, but don't worry yourself. Anyway, it's a pretty heavy bag."

"Och, I'm sure I've carried heavier bags than this in my time." And before she could open her mouth in objection, he took the bag from her and hoisted it onto his shoulder, his steely frame hardly bending under its weight. "There you are, you see? I may be old-looking, but I've still got a bit of muscle left on me."

The woman let out a quiet laugh. "I didn't say that you were old-looking."

Mr. Craig gave her a wink and patted the side of the bag. "Well, I just thought that you might be thinking that I looked a wee bittie ancient to manage this."

"Not at all. The only reason that I hesitated was that I know that Alex is out on the Old Course, and I want to play the New."

"Aye, but they run parallel on the way out to the turn."

She nodded. "Yes, I'm aware of that."

"Well then, there's a chance that I might catch up with him there, so I'd just nip across to the other course and give him his lunch."

The woman gazed out across the links, contemplating his offer. "Are you sure you wouldn't mind? I mean, do you have the time?"

He let out a laugh. "Right now, I have all the time in the world." He turned and began retracing his steps down the path, and if anyone, at that precise moment, had been looking out of one of the windows of the Royal & Ancient, they might have been quite amused at the sight of the tall, angular figure, formally dressed in a tweed jacket and cap, striding away down the side of the first fairway of the Old Course with the enormous golf bag on his shoulder, while, at his side, the short, stout woman half-walked, half-ran to keep up with his progress.

The New Course starter had been right in saying that play was fairly clear out in front of them because they managed to cover the first three holes in just over half an hour, mainly because the woman never seemed to hit a shot that deviated from a central line down the fairway. Mr. Craig had begun to enjoy his walk, although he was surprised that any effort to make conversation with her was met with monosyllabic answers, and there had been no attempt at any form of introduction. At first, he had put it down to her being a tough little Australian with a somewhat offhand manner, having witnessed at the outset of the round her terse refusal to the kindly invitation proffered by two elderly male golfers for her to join them on the course. But as she played he tempered his judgement, understanding that she was probably more content to be in her own company and to be able to lose herself in concentration on her own game. And then he remembered what Alex had said to him the night before, and he realized just how intuitive the boy had been. There was something sad about this woman, an aloofness, a need to be alone yet finding it hard to deal with her own loneliness. There was no doubt in his mind that those symptoms pointed to some acute loss in her life, for he himself recognized them all too well. But what was her loss? It certainly wasn't a husband. He didn't need to look at her hand to tell that. After forty-five years of married life, he just knew—just felt it in the way that she was, in the way that she acted. Yet it really was not his place to ask questions of her, and at any rate he was quite happy just to be out there on this warm, breezy day, running his errand for Alex and enjoying his impromptu exercise.

They played on to the fourth hole without hold-up, then walked through the narrow gorse-lined path to the fifth tee where, for the first time, they caught sight of the players in front of them, pacing the green 180 yards up the closed-in fairway. As they putted out and replaced the flag, the woman stood with her hands on her hips, contemplating the hole. She turned to look at him, her mouth squinted in pensive uncertainty. "Well, what do you think?"

Mr. Craig stared at her for a moment. "What do *I* think?" He looked up the fairway to the hole. "Well . . ." He placed the golf bag on the ground and walked over to stand beside her. He took his cap from his head and rubbed at the puckered wrinkles on his forehead. "I would say," he continued slowly, "that it would look a good bit shorter—and probably even a good bit narrower than the holes we've played so far." He nodded in finality. That was all he could think of saying about the hole. Nevertheless, he felt quite pleased with himself in being able to formulate what he hoped she would consider a constructive judgement on something about which he knew very little. He replaced his cap and walked back to the edge of the tee and picked up the golf bag. When he turned to look at her, she was standing, still with her hands on her hips, observing him with her mouth hanging slightly open.

"When I asked the question 'What do you think?' I was hoping that you might be able to tell me what club I should use."

He frowned. "Ah. Right." He studied the clubs in the bag for a moment, then pulled out her driver, removing the soft velour cover to expose its gleaming head. He held it handle-out towards her, but she made no move to take it.

"But that's my driver."

"Aye, well, it's the club you've used for your first shots up until now, and I would say that you're doing a pretty good job with it."

The woman came towards him, a light smile stretching the corners of her mouth. "You don't know much about the game of golf, do you?"

He shook his head. "No. Not a thing."

The woman laughed. "I'm sorry. I was under the impression that your grandson must come from a long line of caddies."

He looked at her quizzically. "Now, what would make you think that?"

"Well, you seem to know the layout of the courses well enough—and then, when we started, you said that you'd carried heavier bags than mine in your time."

Mr. Craig's mouth opened in realization. "Ah, well, then it's myself who should be apologizing. I had no wish to mislead you. I do know about the courses because I've walked around them a number of times with Alex. He's a fair golfer himself, you know. And as for the bags, well, I'm afraid that I was referring to fertilizer bags and the like. I've been a farmer all my days, you see."

"A farmer!" the woman exclaimed, her voice breaking into a laugh. "Oh, my word, I had no idea. I am sorry. What a mix-up."

"I should have said something earlier maybe, but I didn't think that there was any need."

"Of course there wasn't! I just naturally thought . . ." She paused for a moment. "I am sorry. You must think me pretty dreadful."

"I wouldn't say that."

"Well, I would. I'm afraid that I've never been too communicative when playing golf at the best of times, especially—" She stopped talking abruptly and dropped her head, clenching her bottom lip between her teeth. Being unable to see her eyes under the sun visor, Mr. Craig could not tell whether the action was to stop herself from saying something that might offend him, or to halt a break-out of emotion. His instinct told him the latter, and he therefore thought to diffuse the moment immediately with a cheerful act of friendliness. He took off his cap and held out his hand to her.

"Well, might I ask for whom do I have the honour of caddying?"

She tilted back her head and smiled at him. He had been right. He could see now that her eyes were glazed with tears. She reached out and took his hand. "Roberta Bayliss."

He felt the strength of her grip in his hand and gave it a solid shake. "I'm very pleased to make your acquaintance, Miss Bayliss."

"Roberta . . . please. And you are?"

"Craig's my name."

"Well, Craig, it's a pleasure to meet you too."

The farmer smiled. No doubt her immediate surmise was that Craig was his first name, thinking that he would be carrying the same surname as Alex. There seemed little point in putting her right. It might just cause another flurry of embarrassment, and he was sure that he could last out the round with the pretence. Besides, he had never been too enamoured with the Christian name that his parents had bestowed upon him. He glanced back up the fairway to the hole. "Well now, Roberta Bayliss, let's get back to our game of golf. What do you reckon we should be using here?"

Roberta smiled at his inclusive remark. "I think, Craig, that *we* should be using a four-iron."

And so they continued the round of golf, conversation between them thereafter coming a little easier when her concentration on playing would allow. Nevertheless, the farmer was always aware of the marked reservedness in her nature, almost an unwillingness to offer any information about herself, and the questions she asked of him appeared quite forced, as if stemming from an obligation to be polite, rather than a need or desire to form any degree of friendship. However, in giving his answers as they walked, he had ample opportunity to study her features without giving rise to any affront on her part. She wasn't beautiful or pretty in the classic sense—she was too small and too solidly built for that—but there was a naturalness about her, a youthfulness that made it difficult for him to judge her age. Fifties? Yes, he thought probably, mid-fifties. Her face was untouched by make-up, yet it was remarkably smooth and unlined despite the fact that he could tell from the healthy glow of her skin that she was not one to spend many hours indoors, away from the heat of the Australian sun. When asking a question, she would tilt back her head to look up at him and he could make out below her visor a pair of striking blue eyes which he knew at one time must have sparkled with laughter and wicked humour, but now seemed filmed by dullness, like a metal that had lost its lustre.

Once free of the dense gorse-bushes that chevroned away from the eighth tee, the fairway of the long par-5 widened out to touch with the farthest reaches of the Old Course, at that point affording a close view of the players on the four "loop" holes. Having waited until Roberta Bayliss had played her second shot, Mr. Craig walked over to the fringe of rough grass that separated the two courses and, shielding his eyes against the glare of the sun, scanned the area for Alex. There was no sign of him. He glanced at his watch and made a quick mental calculation, working out that there was no way that he could have gone farther than this. He turned and made his way up the fairway to where Roberta was already standing by her ball, working out her next shot. She turned as he approached. "Did you see him?"

He shrugged the bag off his shoulder. "No! I doubt he's yet to reach here."

Roberta was silent for a moment, her eyes drifting off to the left of the line that she would be taking for the next shot. She raised her arm and pointed. "Would you think that's the furthest outward point on the Old Course over there?"

He followed her line of sight. "Aye, it would be."

She let out a sigh that seemed to quiver with trepidation. "Well, in that case, I am going to want to excuse myself there for a bit, so I'm quite happy for you to wait until Alex arrives."

"Will you not mind the gentlemen behind coming through?"

"No. I'm in no hurry."

In playing out the hole, Mr. Craig witnessed for the first time Roberta missing a shot, her third scuttling no more than twenty yards along the ground, and once she had made it to the green, she walked over to her ball and picked it up without bothering to putt it into the hole. She came over to him and put the ball back in the bag, then unzipped one of the larger pockets and took out what appeared to be a large, silver-topped Thermos flask.

She looked up at him, cradling the flask in both hands. "Where will you wait for Alex?"

"I'll have a wee seat over there," he replied, pointing to the bench that was positioned high at the back of the eighth tee on the Old Course.

"All right. Well, I'll just come to get you when I'm through."

She turned and walked up onto the dunes and he stood watching her progress until she disappeared from sight. He hefted the golf bag onto his shoulder and set off across the rough grass to the eighth tee on the Old.

The timing of their meeting could not have been better planned, because as he made it over to the bench he could see Alex approach the seventh green, skirting around the large bunker that stretched across its front. His grandson stopped and pulled a club from the bag and handed it to the golfer, and in casting a glance towards the hole, he caught sight of his grandfather. After a brief moment of uncertainty, he raised his hand in greeting, then, having watched the golfer play his ball to the green, he exchanged club for putter and walked across to where his grandfather was now seated on the bench.

"Hi, Granddad! What are you doing out here?"

Mr. Craig held up the plastic bag. "You left this on the kitchen table."

"Oh, thanks, you're a star!" he exclaimed, taking the bag from him. "I hadn't realized that I'd left it all at home until I parked the car in Saint Andrews." He frowned in puzzlement when he caught sight of the golf bag that leaned against the bench. "What are you doing with those?"

His grandfather chuckled. "You'd wonder, wouldn't you?"

Alex dropped the golf bag that he was carrying to the ground and went over to take a closer look at the clubs. "I know them. They belong to that Australian woman I caddied for yesterday afternoon."

"Aye, they do. I saw her at the caddymaster's office and recognized her from your description. She wasn't able to get a caddy for the New Course, so I thought to kill two birds with one stone and volunteered my services."

"Good for you. I hope she's paying you well."

Mr. Craig squinted the side of his mouth in dubious consideration of his grandson's remark. "Well, if reward is based on knowledge of the game, I think I'd probably end up having to pay her!"

Alex laughed and turned to survey the area around them. "Where is she, then?"

He pointed a thumb over his shoulder. "Up behind there on the dunes. She wanted to excuse herself."

"Ah, right. So she's playing by herself again."

"Aye, she is."

"Not much fun for her, is it?"

"No, I wouldn't think it. I would guess that she's quite a lonesome person."

The large group with whom Alex had been caddying—four Americans with their respective camera-laden wives and three other caddies—had finished on the seventh green and were making their way across to the tee. Alex stooped to pick up the golf bag. "Well, I suppose I'd better go and make myself useful."

"Aye, you do that, lad, and I'll see you later on this evening."

Alex nodded. "All right, and thanks, Granddad, for bringing out my lunch."

Mr. Craig winked at his grandson. "No bother."

He watched the four Americans drive off, each of their shots making the green and being met with loud whoops of congratulations from the four wives, and as they set off down the short fairway, Alex turned and gave his grandfather a brief wave. He reciprocated, then settled back to wait for Roberta Bayliss.

There was still no sign of her by the time the second group of golfers following Alex's game had played from the tee, and at that point he began to feel a small measure of concern about her well-being. He glanced at his watch and worked out that he had been there for nearly forty minutes. Surely whatever she had to do wouldn't take her that long? He got to his feet and picked up the golf bag, and walked back onto the New Course and across to the edge of the last green that she had played. He laid down the bag in the short rough at the back of the green, then began to climb up onto the dunes, pushing aside the spiky reeds to clear a path for himself. Every ten steps or so, he stopped and called out her name—he thought, in this case, that it would be more fitting to address her as Miss Bayliss—but there was never any reply.

At the top of a large dune, he stood scouring the long ridge for any sign of her, his eyes sweeping round to take in the wide Eden Estuary, stretching across to the RAF air base at Leuchars on the other side. The tide was on the turn, the currents sweeping away at an alarming rate around the Out Head and into St. Andrews Bay. He felt a knot of apprehension grip at his stomach as his mind raced back over his own assessment of her apparently sad demeanour.

"Oh, my word, lass!" he said out loud. "I hope you haven't gone and done something foolish."

He took a step nearer to the edge of the high bank and once more scanned the ridge. Something caught his eye fifty yards over to his left, a splash of bright yellow against the pastel background of the dunes. It was the woman's sweat-shirt, laid out on top of the reeds as if to dry. He made his way towards it, moving as quickly as he could over the rough ground. And then he saw her, sitting on the pebbled beach below him, her back against the stone breakwater, staring blankly out across the estuary. He walked to within twenty yards of where she sat, then stopped, concerned that she might be still occupied in doing something to which he should not be witness.

"Miss Bayliss?" he called out quietly, so as not to startle her. "Are you all right?"

She did not seem to hear him. He stood for a moment before making the decision to move closer. He moved down to the bottom of the bank and crunched noisily across the pebbles, hoping that the sound of his footsteps would warn her of his presence. He walked up and stopped directly in front of her. She had taken the sun visor from her head, and her cropped grey hair was ridged at both sides from where the band had held it tightly in place. She sat motionless, resting her chin on her knees, her hands clasped around her legs. The Thermos flask was wedged between her feet.

"Miss Bayliss, I don't mean to disturb you, but I was just getting a wee bit concerned. Are you all right?"

Still she neither answered nor made eye contact with him, and the farmer, taking this as a clear indication that he was intruding on her privacy, turned to leave. "Well, I'll just away back and wait for you by the green."

"Craig?" She spoke quietly, a choking falter in her voice.

He turned. "Aye?"

"Please don't go." She placed her hand on the ground beside her. "I wouldn't mind having some company."

Mr. Craig eyed the place that she had indicated, thinking to himself that it offered a mite less comfortable seat for his bony posterior than it did for her own. "All right, then." He took off his jacket, and folding it up to afford himself some degree of padding, he walked across and placed it next to her, then slowly lowered himself to the ground, glancing across at her as he did so. He could tell from the puffed ruddiness of her cheeks that she had been crying. "So what's been happening to you, lass?"

She turned and smiled at him, then let out a short laugh that immediately subsided into a tremble of emotion. "Lass. If only. I'm nearly sixty-one, you know!"

Plucking out a white-bleached twig that lay caught between two large pebbles, the farmer drew up his long legs and rested his elbows on his knees, and began twiddling it between the thumb and forefinger of both hands. "Well, you'd hardly think that."

Without looking at him, she reached across and brushed her balled fist across his shirt-sleeve. "Thanks for that."

They sat together in silence, looking out across the estuary, a stretched arm's distance apart, but their adopted positions mirroring each other, the only sound being the swish of the light wind in the reeds above them and the rippling sweep of the waters being carried away on the tide. It was he who eventually spoke. "So, Roberta Bayliss, what are you doing here so far from home?"

Roberta glanced down at the large Thermos flask that she held between her feet. She reached forward and picked it up. "Do you really want to know?"

"Aye, if you want me to."

She undid the top of the flask and handed it to him. He looked inside. There was no trace of liquid, but a light covering of grey dust clung to its cream-coloured plastic interior. He looked at her inquiringly.

She reached over and took back the Thermos, and having replaced the lid, she gripped the bottom of the flask in the palm of her hand and held it out in front of her, her elbow supported on her knee. "That was my father. He is now no more. That's it." She carefully placed the flask back between her feet. "I brought him all the way from Sydney," she continued, casting her eyes about her, "and now he's where he wanted to be, blowing about in the wind on the furthest point of the Old Course at Saint Andrews."

Mr. Craig nodded slowly, everything now becoming clear in his mind, all the thoughts and theories that he had had about her suddenly beginning to fall into place. He wondered if he should say something, some standard form of condolence, but then felt that it might sound too glib or even too familiar. Better to remain silent and allow her to do the talking.

"He loved this place, you know. Of all the courses in the world that he had played, this was the one he loved the best. And probably the proudest moment of his life was when he was made a member of the R and A. It didn't happen until he was sixty, but by golly, from then on, he was over here whenever he could find reason, that usually being either the Spring or the Autumn Meeting. It was really the only time during the year that I didn't travel with him. He always said that it wouldn't be much fun for me, because when he wasn't playing golf, he'd spend his time sitting in the Big Room in the clubhouse, and as you probably know, women don't go in there." She shook her head and let out a heavy sigh. "Pretty ironic, isn't it? This is the only time I've ever got to come here with him."

"And I would think," the farmer said slowly, "that it must have been an awful hard thing to do."

Roberta smiled wistfully at him. "Too right, it was. I had absolutely no idea that this was what he had planned until the lawyer read out the will to us all. My two sisters were really opposed to the idea. They said that it was too much to ask of me, having to come all the way over here and then having to play a round of golf during which I was to scatter his ashes." She paused. "But I knew I had to do it. It was my duty. You see, he wasn't only my father, Craig, he was my best friend as well."

"Could you not have got someone to come with you?"

"No, not really. My two sisters are married and have their own families to worry about, and Mum's too old to take on such a huge trip. Anyway, Dad and I were always together on the golf course, so it just seemed right that we were together here."

Mr. Craig flicked the twig into the air and watched the freshening wind take it off. "So you'll now be having to make the long journey home?"

"Not until Tuesday week. I managed to get a cheap air ticket, but it meant staying quite a bit longer than I had intended. So I'll just be killing time until then. I might play a few holes of golf, if I feel like it."

"Are you staying in the town?"

"Yes, in some guest-house. It's run by a pretty pernickity widow called Mrs. Winterbotham."

Mr. Craig laughed. "Och, her! I know of her!"

"Do you?"

"Well, not personal-like. But I have a good friend who's had the displeasure of receiving the rough side of her tongue."

There now being a coolness to the wind, Roberta got to her feet and pulled down her sweat-shirt from the bank. She put it around her shoulders before resuming her seat. "Tell me about your family, Craig," she said quietly.

He pushed out his legs and turned to lean his weight on his elbow. "Well, to begin with, I have a son who lives in your country."

"Really? Whereabouts?"

"Oh, a good way from you. Over on the west coast, in Perth. He's been out there for twenty-three years now. Married an Australian girl and they've got two kids, both at university."

"Do you see them at all?"

"Just once in the last five years. Andrew has his own engineering business, so he's kept pretty busy. But then I have a daughter back here."

"Alex's mother?"

"Aye, that's right. She and Alex live with me, seeing how's her marriage broke up last year."

"And your wife?"

"I'm afraid that she passed away last year as well."

Roberta turned to look at him. "I'm sorry. What a horrible year you must have had."

"Aye, well, things got kind of bad, but we're beginning to pick up the pieces and get on with our lives."

Roberta gazed once more out across the estuary. "Right now, I can't ever imagine myself being able to pick up the pieces."

"Aye, you'll be thinking that at the minute, but you will do eventually. I felt the same way for a good few months after my wife died, but then different things began happening about us, and they all helped to bring a new focus into my life. It's a bit like driving for hours on a main road, and then turning off onto one that runs parallel and finding the scenery completely different, even though you're still heading more or less in the same direction. But you do need guidance to pick the right turning—if you like, someone who can do the map-reading for you. It won't happen any other way."

There was a moment's silence before Roberta spoke. "That's all very well, Craig, but in my life, my father was both the driver and map-reader, and I'm afraid that there's no one waiting in the wings to take over from him."

Mr. Craig pushed himself to his feet and stooped down to pick up his jacket. "Well, I wouldn't be so sure about that. When you get back home, you try putting out your indicator for a time, just to show that you're ready to make the change, and I think that you might be surprised at who's waiting in the shadows to take over." He held out his hand. "But right now, we'd better be making a move before someone gets the idea that you've given up on golf and decides to walk away with your clubs."

Roberta reached down to retrieve the flask and her sun visor, then took his hand and found herself pulled effortlessly to her feet. She smiled up at him without relinquishing her grip on his hand. "Thanks, Craig, for your time. I have to say that I'm glad that I met you today."

The farmer found himself quite nonplussed both by this physical contact and by the degree of affection in her voice, so he broke the moment by giving her hand a firm shake, as if being introduced to her for the first time. "And that goes for myself as well, Roberta Bayliss."

He stood aside to allow her to walk in front of him along the beach, and as she passed him by, she stopped. "Craig, would you mind if we didn't play on the way in? I don't really feel like it any more."

He nodded briefly. "Aye, that's fine by me. That'll give me time to hear more about yourself."

They took the most direct route back to the town, following the track that cut through the gorse-bushes between the two courses. Occasionally they stopped, either for him to drop the golf bag to the ground and to rest his shoulder for a while, or to allow players to drive off from a tee without distraction. Roberta talked animatedly as they went, recounting stories of her life in Sydney and of the travels that she and her father had experienced in visiting golf championships throughout the world, her only regret being that she had never once attended a British Open with him. They walked in at an easy pace, so much so that when they eventually passed by the caddymaster's office, the clock on the R&A clubhouse was fast approaching five o'clock.

The guest-house where Roberta was staying was a good distance from the course, so Mr. Craig was insistent that he should give her a lift, saving her from carrying the golf clubs any farther. They collected the old Land Rover from the car-park that lay adjacent to the Golf Museum, and then cut up through the town to her destination. Roberta pointed out the house as they approached, and he pulled the vehicle over to the side of the road beside the black wrought-iron railings. They both got out and he opened up the back door of the vehicle and took out her golf clubs.

"I can manage from here, Craig," Roberta said, offering out her arm for the clubs.

"I wouldn't hear of such a thing," he retorted, slinging the bag up onto his shoulder. "A few more yards won't hurt me."

Roberta smiled at him. "Thank you." She turned and walked up the steps to the front door and rang the doorbell. It was a full minute before the door was opened by a thin, austere-looking woman wearing a pink nylon housecoat and a pair of turquoise fluffy-toed slippers, her pale, powdered face set as expressionless as a death-mask. She stood in the doorway, as square as her meagre frame would allow, making no effort to move to the side.

"Have you not got your key with you?" the woman asked, glowering at Roberta through narrowed eyes. Mr. Craig was amazed that she could utter a word with her mouth set in such an admonishing manner. He felt a smile come to his face. If there was ever a hen's arse of a mouth, that woman was the proud possessor of it.

"No, I'm sorry, Mrs. Winterbotham," Roberta replied, sounding like a schoolgirl who had just been reprimanded by her teacher. "I'm afraid that I left it in my room."

The woman folded her arms and stood aside. "Well then, it's lucky for you that I was in the house."

As Roberta made to enter the house, the woman glanced down at her feet and immediately stepped in front of her to deny her access once more. "Those wouldn't be golfing shoes you have on, by any chance?"

Roberta looked down at her shoes. "Yes, they are."

The woman let out a petulant groan. "Well then, if you had taken time to read the pamphlet in your room, you would have noticed that I have banned golfing shoes from being worn in my house. They do untold damage to my carpets. So please kindly take them off here on the doorstep."

Roberta turned away from the woman and raised her eyebrows at Mr. Craig, then sat down on the top step and began to unlace her shoes. He gave the golf bag a quick shrug-up onto his shoulder, then strode up the steps and, pushing past the woman, entered the house. "Where can I put this?" he asked abruptly, a tremor of anger in his voice.

The woman made a show of rubbing at her elbow where the end of golf bag had lightly brushed against her. "What do you . . . ?"

The farmer pointed to his feet. "Listen, you crabbit besom, these are not golf shoes, so where do you want me to put this?"

There was a snort of laughter from Roberta as she bent over to pull off one of her shoes. The woman heard it and shot a lasered stare at the back of her head. She turned to Mr. Craig and gave him the benefit of the same look. "How dare you call me—"

"Och, woman, if you've got nothing nice to say, then don't bother saying anything at all." He leaned the golf bag against the radiator shelf in the hallway, pushing aside a small figurine of a "Shepherdess with Lamb in Arms" to make room for the club-heads. As he walked out of the door, the woman turned away, muttering to herself, and picked up the golf bag and started to struggle with it up the steep staircase.

Roberta pushed herself to her feet, golf shoes in hand, the expression on her face registering both mirth and nervous apprehension. "Golly, Craig, I hope she doesn't throw me out after you saying that to her."

He shook his head. "No, she wouldn't dare. She's the kind who's all a-bluster until she gets challenged. Anyway, it just doesn't seem right that people come here to Saint Andrews to have a good time and then get confronted with someone like that."

Roberta sighed. "I know, but at least the place is cheap and she does keep it spotlessly clean." She passed her golf shoes over to her left hand and held out the other. "Craig, I won't hold you up. I can't tell you how much I have appreciated your company today. You've really helped me through something that I've been dreading for ages."

Mr. Craig took her hand and shook it. "Aye, well, people meet sometimes when they shouldn't and sometimes when they should, and I think that we've probably both been on a lucky streak today."

"So do I." She walked up the steps and into the house, then turned, her hand on the door. "And please give my kindest regards to Alex, and say how much I enjoyed meeting him."

"I will do." He watched as Roberta gave him a final wave and closed the door.

He made his way down the steps and around the back of the Land Rover, waiting there until a car had passed by on the narrow street. He opened the driver's door and clambered in, and sat with his hands resting on the wheel. Up until the moment that they had arrived at the house, he had felt only deep sorrow for Roberta Bayliss, having made the long, lonely journey from Australia to scatter her father's ashes. But now guilt seemed to play its part in the equation, and he felt a responsibility in allowing her to be abandoned for over a week in that unfriendly household with that dragon of a woman who just happened also to be his fellow countryman. He thought back over what he had said to Roberta out on the golf course, and wondered if he had been stupidly insensitive in saying that someone might step out of the shadows when she got home. Having heard her story, he realized now that there had been no one else in her life besides her father. She would be returning to nothing, except a deep void that would never be filled.

He started up the Land Rover and put out his indicator to turn onto the street, and the very action in doing it and the clicking sound that emanated from somewhere behind the stark display panel made him stop the vehicle abruptly. He sat for a moment staring straight in front of him, then slapped his hand hard against the centre of the steering wheel. Dammit, he thought to himself, you're a stupid man. You couldn't see the wood for the trees, could you? You were so busy expounding your naïve philosophies on life, all about finding a map-reader and putting out an indicator, that you couldn't tell that her indicator was already out. If there was ever a time that Roberta Bayliss needed help, it was right now, and she was a hell of a lot more likely to benefit from it in this country than when she returned to her empty, pointless life in Australia. You've got the time, man, and so does she.

He sat for a further five minutes, his mind churning with thought, then he got out of the Land Rover and made his way up the steps to the house and rang the doorbell. The woman took less time to answer it, but her reception was decidedly more frosty.

"What do you want?" she asked curtly.

"I'd like to see Miss Bayliss, please."

Without uttering a word, the woman closed the door on him. He waited for a full minute, and had just about come to the conclusion that she had ignored his request, when the front door opened and Roberta appeared. Her face lit up when she saw him. "Hullo, Craig. Did you leave something in the golf bag?"

He shook his head. "No, nothing like that." He took off his cap and scratched at the back of his head. "I was just wondering if you'd ever heard of Carnoustie?"

Roberta looked at him quizzically. "Of course I have."

"What about Gleneagles?"

"Yes."

"Troon?"

Roberta laughed. "Of course."

"Well, I was sitting in the car just then, and I thought to myself that I didn't have much to do over the next week, and I wondered if you would like to go and play them. I mean, I would just drive you and carry your clubs. I couldn't play or anything like that."

The sparkle that he sensed had been lost from Roberta's eyes suddenly returned. "Are you being serious, Craig?"

He nodded. "Never more so. I am in need of a bit of a distraction myself at the minute, and I just thought that it might be nice to see those places."

"Well, in that case," Roberta replied, her voice now alive with excitement, "I would love to do that."

"Good. I'm glad. There is another thing, though. I reckon that we'll have to be starting off quite early each morning, so I think it would be best if you saved me the trip into Saint Andrews by coming to stay with Alex and me out at the farm."

Roberta shook her head. "Oh no, Craig, I couldn't—"

"Aye, you could. It's part of the package. You can't have the one without the other."

Roberta bit at her lip. "But what would I say to Mrs. Winterbotham?"

"Let's deal with one thing at a time. Do you want to take up the offer?"

She nodded eagerly. "Yes, I'd love to."

"Right." He walked up the steps and into the house. "Well then, in that case, you just leave Mrs. Winterbotham to me."

Chapter 16

Mary McLean leaned forward over the dressing-table and studied her face carefully in the mirror, rolling her lips together to make sure that her lipstick was applied evenly. Satisfied that there were no obvious smudges, she distanced herself slightly from the mirror and gave herself a final viewing, at the same time placing everything back in her make-up bag and fastening the zip. She glanced at her watch. It was ten past seven. If she didn't get a move on, she was going to be late. She lobbed the little bag into the hold-all on the floor and, jumping to her feet, scooped it up without bothering to close it. She walked quickly towards the bedroom door, stopping for a moment in front of the full-length mirror on the wardrobe to get the overall effect. She was pleased with what she saw. Her blonde hair was held back off her face by a pair of Calvin Klein sunglasses that perched on the top of her head, and her well-proportioned figure was perfectly complemented by the new Nike track suit, its pale yellow looking demure yet sporty against the tan she had acquired courtesy of the sun-bed at the games club. Okay so she might not be as good as the rest of her playing partners at badminton, but she certainly could knock spots off them when it came to appearance.

She hurried down the stairs and made her way along the corridor to the kitchen, starting in surprise at the sound of a dish crashing to the ground in the larder as she passed by. A loud expletive followed. She stopped and looked in to see Gregor standing with his check-shirted back to her, one hand on his hip, the other rubbing at the back of his head, as he perused the splintered ashet on the ground, framing the remains of the roast lamb as if it were some obscure piece of modern art, while a mud-slide of gravy oozed slowly across the stone floor.

"Gregor? What on earth are you doing?"

He swung around to face her. "I'm looking for the beer. What have you done with it?" His voice was edged with nervous irritation.

"I've put it in the fridge, where I always put it."

"I didn't see it."

Mary let out a sigh and walked across to the fridge, putting down her hold-all on the table as she passed by. She opened the door and removed a large tub of margarine and a carton of orange juice, revealing the cans of lager, still attached by their plastic ring holder, at the back of the rack. She stood aside and, with a sweep of her hand, invited Gregor to take a look for himself. "There you are. Six cans of beer."

He thrust his hands into the pockets of his jeans and shook his head. "Well, I didn't see them," he mumbled.

Mary smiled and walked towards him and gave him a kiss on the cheek. "Don't get into such a state, Gregor. It'll be fine. He's your son, after all. Just be natural with him."

Gregor flicked back his head. "I thought I was the last time, but it just ended up with him walking away from me."

Picking up her badminton racket from the sideboard, Mary put it in the hold-all and did up the zip. "Well, the difference is that this time he called *you,* so he obviously wants to see you, and what's more, he hasn't got his mother around to poison his mind against you." She paused, leaning her hands on the top of the hold-all as she looked at him. "Listen, I have to get going, otherwise I'll be late."

"When will you be back?"

She picked up the bag and moved over to the kitchen door. "Not sure. I might stay and have something to eat afterwards." She opened the door and turned back to look at him. "Anyway, it's better I'm out of the way. It'll be easier for you to talk things through without me being here."

Gregor nodded. "Aye, I think you're probably right." He walked over to her and planted a kiss on her cheek. "Thanks, love."

Mary gave him a smile. "And while you're waiting for him, you can clear up the larder."

He laughed. "Thanks, love."

For once in his life, Gregor was pleased that there was a mountain of paperwork to be cleared in his office. He worked his way methodically through the outstanding bills of the farm, paying off those which had final reminders, then moved on to updating his stock records on the sheep, making sure that all was in order for the farm sale that was scheduled in two weeks' time. Glancing at the clock on the wall at a quarter to nine, he closed his battered notebook and turned off the computer and sat back in his chair, wondering if Alex had had second thoughts about coming to see him. He picked up the copy of *The Scottish Farmer* from the desk and began to leaf through it, and a feeling of dark despondency came over him at the thought that the information which was contained within its pages, and which had hitherto been integral to his life, was now irrelevant and unimportant. New sheep vaccines, new machinery developments, market reports on livestock and cereal prices—they would be of no use to him in the future. He flicked through to the end page and scanned the employment section. There were a number of jobs for casual tractor drivers, a few for hill shepherds, and one for a sales representative with a mineral-supplement company. But there wasn't one for a managerial position. He discarded the magazine onto the desk, and linking his powerful, calloused hands behind his head, he breathed out a long sigh of discontentment. What the hell was he going to do now? Two years off his fortieth birthday and he was out of a job. No, not just out of a job—out of a way of life. He knew nothing other than how to farm. He stared through the window as the setting sun gathered in its crimson rays, draining colour from the sky through the corrugations in the high, static cloud formation. Well, be thankful for small mercies, he thought to himself, at least for once the weather's on your side. You'd feel a lot worse if your depression were matched by the elements.

He heard the car change down a gear as it came around the corner of the steading, and the engine screamed mercilessly for a second before it came to a skidding halt on the loose chips in the courtyard. He got up quickly from his chair and walked through to the kitchen just as the back door slammed shut. Alex appeared, his face aglow both from his day on the golf course and the adrenaline rush of a hurried journey.

"Sorry I'm late," he said, standing on the threshold of the kitchen door as if waiting to be invited into the house.

"You're not at all," Gregor replied. "I mean, you didn't have to rush back for me. I was just going to expect you whenever."

Alex nodded. "Right." He cast an eye around the kitchen. "Is Mary in?"

Gregor let out a grunt of a laugh. "No, you'll be all right. She's gone out to play badminton."

"Oh, I didn't mean it in that way! I was just, well, asking."

Gregor moved over to the refrigerator and opened the door. "Do you want a beer?"

"Yeah. That would be great."

He took out two cans and lobbed one over to his son. The ring-pulls came off simultaneously. "So, how did you get on today?"

Alex took a drink from the can and wiped the back of his hand across his mouth. "Good. I managed to fit in three rounds, which all goes to help the bank balance a bit."

"That's pretty fast going. What time did you finish?"

"Well, it was getting pretty dark. I'd say just before eight o'clock." He paused. "But then I bumped into a friend from university, and she insisted that we go to have a drink."

Gregor raised his eyebrows and a teasing smile tilted the side of his mouth. "She sounds keen."

Alex dismissed the remark with a shrug of his shoulders. "Not really. She's just a friend in the same German tutorial group as me."

"So she's from Saint Andrews, then?"

"No. Down south. I think she lives somewhere near Swindon."

The smile remained on Gregor's face. "And she sort of stayed up here for the Easter break so that she could see you."

Alex blew out derisively. "No, she did not. She wanted to do some extra study before next term, so she got a part-time job waitressing in a restaurant in town." He looked hard at his father. "Look, it's no big deal. She's just a friend. Anyway, I think it's pretty dumb for anyone to get caught up in any kind of 'heavy commitment' at this time."

Gregor nodded slowly, realizing that his attempt at generating some sort of easy banter between them was beginning to falter, and the guilt that he still felt over his break-up with Liz hit at a paranoic nerve, and he wondered if Alex's last remark was not aimed directly at their own failed relationship. It was he now who was more eager to end that particular conversation. "You're quite right," he said quietly, "I think that's a wise thought." He moved towards the door that led out onto the paved terrace. "How about we sit outside for a bit? I think it's warm enough."

The breeze had died down with the ebbing of the tide, and an airy coolness had settled over the barley field in front of the house, extracting from the green tillers of the growing crop a sharp pungency that struck at the senses more effectively than a powerful decongestant. Feeling goose bumps rise on his forearms, Alex placed his beer can on the small cast-iron table and took his jersey from around his waist and pulled it over his head. They dragged out metal chairs and sat down, Gregor tilting his onto its back legs and putting his feet up onto the low stone wall that surrounded the terrace.

"So how are you and your grandfather getting on without Mum being around?"

"All right. Neither of us are that brilliant at cooking, though, so we might quite easily starve by the time that she gets back."

Gregor took a sip of his beer. "Have you heard anything from her?"

"Not yet. Mind you, she wouldn't have arrived in Seville until late last night, and then I was out of the house first thing this morning."

"Of course."

"Granddad might have by now, though."

Gregor nodded but didn't reply.

"He was out on the New Course today."

Gregor turned to look at his son, a frown on his face. "Who?"

"Granddad. He was out caddying."

Gregor laughed. "Never."

"Yup. I'd left my sandwiches at home this morning, so he brought them out to me, and on the way he just happened to bump into this Australian lady whose bag I'd carried yesterday and whom I had told him about last night. Anyway, he recognized her from my description, and seeing that she couldn't get a caddy, he thought that he'd just kill two birds with one stone and help her out."

Gregor cocked his head to the side. "Well, good for him. Obviously there's still life in the old dog."

Alex silently acknowlegded his father's witticism with a smile and looked about him. On the small patch of lawn on the other side of the wall the old swing stood in retirement, its four tubular legs surrounded by tall clumps of dead grass, while, on its swinging chains, rust had taken hold where the black paint had peeled away. Beyond that, over by the vegetable patch, he noticed that a section of wood on the rectangular box that his father had embedded into the ground to serve as a sandpit had succumbed to wet-rot, and lay, white with fungus, where it had broken off. All monuments to a past childhood. His childhood. He felt a surge of nostalgia weigh heavy in the pit of his stomach. This place had been his home, and now it had been made alien to him. He turned back to look at his father, who had his chair tilted even farther back and was gazing straight up into the clear, but as yet starless, sky.

"How's Grandpa and Grandma?"

His father contemplated the question for a moment, then kicked his feet off the wall and sat forward in his chair, placing his can of beer on the table. "They're well enough, I think."

Alex watched him. "Meaning?"

"Meaning I haven't seen much of them recently. I'm not exactly the most popular person in their world at the minute."

"Because of having to sell the farm?"

Gregor looked at him and smiled. "No, Alex. They can understand the reasoning behind that. It's over you and your mother."

Alex nodded. "Right."

His father let out a deep sigh. "You know, Alex, no matter what age you are, it's a pretty hard thing to take when you can't speak to your parents—especially your father. Dad was always a much better farmer than me, so I miss him a lot, for his advice and support, especially at the minute."

Well done, you, Alex thought to himself, that's quite a clever angle. He drained his can of beer. "Maybe then you should take time to go to see him too," he said quietly. "Just have a conversation with him, like we're doing now."

Gregor scrutinized his son's face, hoping that he was on the verge of a breakthrough. "And you think it would help, Alex?"

"Yes, I think so, once everyone has accepted the fact that the situation isn't going to change."

"And have you?"

Alex pushed himself to his feet. "To be quite honest, not really. But life's too short, isn't it?" He picked up his empty can and made his way over to the door. "Do you want another?"

Gregor sprang to his feet. "Look, you sit down. I'll get them."

"No, don't bother. I can do it."

They came together in the doorway, Gregor's powerful shoulder accidentally knocking the taller yet slighter frame of his son against the doorpost. Both stood back, two feet apart, to let the other enter into the kitchen first.

"I'm sorry," Gregor murmured.

Alex shook his head. "No bother. It didn't hurt."

"No, Alex. I mean I'm really sorry—for everything. I'm sorry that both you and your mother ever got caught up in my life, and that you've both been so badly hurt by it." He rubbed hard at the back of his head. "Shit! Listen, Alex, I'm not a great man with words and I don't even know if I'm putting this across the right way, but—"

"Look, Dad," Alex cut in. "Let *me* put it across for you. If I hadn't got caught up with your life, I wouldn't be here. It's as simple as that. You're my father. You could be dead, or you could have run off with Mary to the other side of the world. But you're still here—and we're still talking, and I would guess that you're probably still quite concerned about Mum and me. Okay, so you're right in saying that you've hurt us both really badly, but you're not, as you think, the most loathsome bastard that this world has ever produced, so please don't give yourself the pleasure of being that hard on yourself."

Alex's voice had risen in volume so much throughout his statement that his last syllable echoed around the farm buildings. The two looked hard at each other and Alex watched as his father drew in his breath. He had seen him do this before, when he was about to lose his temper. But this time he just snorted out a laugh.

"Yes," he said, nodding his head slowly. "That was probably what I was going to say."

Alex spun the empty can into the air and caught it. "But if it makes you feel any better, I still think you're a bit of a bastard."

Gregor smiled and reached out and gripped his son's forearm and guided him towards the door. "Well, I think on that point, we might have come to some sort of an agreement."

The car swept around the corner of the steading and came to a halt facing them, catching them both in the blinding glare of its headlights.

Gregor put up a hand to shield his eyes. "Now who the hell could that be?"

The engine was cut and the lights went out, and before they could accustom their eyes once more to the falling darkness they heard the door being opened and slammed shut and the sound of footsteps approaching them.

"Good evening, Gregor."

He recognized immediately the clipped English tones of Jonathan Davies.

"Jonathan! This is a surprise. I didn't expect you."

By the time Gregor had finished his half-hearted welcome Davies had sprung up onto the terrace wall and had come down into the weak pool of light that shone from the lamp above the kitchen door. He was dressed casually in a maroon cashmere jersey and yellow corduroy trousers, sporting at his neck a neat blue cravat instead of his customary tie. In his hand he carried a large plastic bag, the contents of which had clinked noisily as he had executed his hurdle. "Oh dear!" he said, grimacing as he looked from Gregor to Alex. "I hope I haven't come at a bad time."

Gregor shook his head. "No, not at all. You know Alex, don't you?"

Davies smiled at Alex and shot out a hand. "Indeed I do. How are you, Alex?"

Alex clasped his hand. "Well, thank you, Mr. Davies."

"Jonathan—please."

Gregor turned to go into the kitchen. "We're just about to have a beer, Jonathan. Will you join us?"

Davies held up the plastic bag. "Well, I was wondering if I could interest *you* in the contents of my bag. We haven't really celebrated the start of work on the golf course yet, and seeing my wife has gone down south to visit her mother, I thought that tonight might be quite opportune."

Gregor laughed. "And what, may I ask, do you have in your bag?"

Davies put it down on the table and delved in his hand to produce a magnum of Taittinger champagne, two packets of Kettle potato chips and a box of Havana cigars. He stood back so that both Gregor and Alex could feast their eyes on his booty. "So what do you think?"

Gregor scratched slowly at the side of his face, making it look as if the decision were a hard one. He looked over to his son. "Difficult to judge, isn't it? Beer or champagne."

Alex gave his head a quick shake. "No competition," he said, making his way quickly into the kitchen. "I'll get the glasses!"

Mr. Craig picked up his mug from the kitchen table, then reached across for the one that sat in front of Roberta, his action being prompted by his house guest stretching her arms above her head and letting out a loud yawn.

"I'm sorry, Craig," she said, pushing herself to her feet. "That was pretty rude. I think that I must still be suffering a bit from jet lag."

"Och, it's hardly surprising that you're tired," he replied, walking over to the sink and washing out the mugs under the tap. "You've had a pretty exhausting day, what with one thing and another." He glanced at the kitchen clock and his mouth opened in horror when he saw that it was a quarter past eleven. "Heavens, what am I thinking about, keeping you up to this time? I had no idea that it was that late. You should have said something before now."

Roberta took a dish-towel from the rail in front of the Rayburn, and picking up one of the mugs from the draining-board, she began to dry it. "Not at all. I wouldn't have wanted to turn in any earlier. I haven't had the opportunity to talk so much for goodness knows how long."

"Well, I hope I didn't bore you," he said, taking the mug from her and hanging it on a hook on the dresser. "My life has been fairly humdrum in comparison to yours."

"I wouldn't say that for a minute! I found it all fascinating, especially those new plans for the golf course. I can't wait to have a look at it in the morning."

"Well, you'll be able to get a good view of it from your bedroom window. Not that there's much to see at the minute, what with them just getting started." He took the other mug from Roberta and hung it up. "Now, I would suggest that we just play it by ear tomorrow. If you're still feeling a wee bit tired, we can give the golf a miss and you can just have a lazy day here."

"No way!" Roberta exclaimed. "I'll be fine! I wouldn't give up the chance of playing Carnoustie for all the tea in China."

He smiled at her. "Good. In that case, I'll knock on your door at, say, eight o'clock, and we'll have a bite to eat for breakfast and then leave here around nine. How would that be?"

"Perfect," Roberta replied, trying to stifle another yawn. "By Jiminy, I really have got the gapes."

"Well, get yourself away to bed then. You know where everything is?"

Roberta nodded. "Yes, thanks."

"Right. In that case, I'll just get the dog put out for a minute before I turn in myself." He opened the door that led into the hall and stood aside for Roberta, but they were both beaten to it by the Jack Russell, who muscled his way between their legs and stood panting in eagerness at the front door.

"Goodness, I wish I had that much energy," Roberta sighed, walking to the bottom of the stairs and beginning to climb them quite laboriously.

Mr. Craig laughed. "I think it might be spurred on by the fact that he knows he's taking a loan of me. He knows full well that he's not allowed to put so much as a paw into this part of the house when my daughter's here." He turned the heavy key in the lock. "Go on then, you wee devil, I'll let you get out here this time." Giving the door a sharp tug, he immediately jammed its underside on the doormat, but it left a wide-enough gap for the dog to squeeze through and disappear outside, barking frantically. Mr. Craig bent down and pulled away the mat, then opened the door fully and looked outside. He stood there for a moment, gazing out at the night, then turned and took a pace back to the bottom of the stairs. "Are you away to bed yet?" he called out.

Roberta appeared at the bathroom door, tooth-brush in hand. "No. Why? What's the matter?"

"Nothing. I just think it's worth you coming down to have a wee look out here."

She came down the stairs and they walked out into the garden and stood side by side on the small stretch of lawn. The moon was full and perfectly formed, hanging in the star-lit sky like an anchored balloon above the distant sea, its light so intense that it was possible to make out the movement of water in its reflection. The fields below the house were bathed in an ecliptic glow that picked out every contour of the land as far as the eye could see, and the air was so still that all that could be heard was the muted sound of the waves tumbling idly against the rocks on the shoreline and the eerie hoot of an owl which, although perched somewhere in the trees away down by the gully, sounded as clear as if it had been sitting on the garden wall.

"Craig, this is *so* beautiful," Roberta whispered, as if she felt that her voice might introduce an alien sound to the tranquillity of Nature's night.

"Aye, it is." He paused for a moment to allow the owl to hoot unchallenged. "It always is."

"And look at the lie of the land. It really will make the most wonderful golf course."

"Do you think that?"

"Oh, without a doubt! It's a natural." She cupped her hands around her eyes to shield off the glare of the moon. "I hope the guy who's designing the course knows what he's doing."

"Aye, well, he seems to. He's an American lad. Done quite a number all over the world."

"Yes, but even I can see that this is going to be a completely different challenge. This'll be a links course, not a manufactured one. It'll have to be treated with such delicacy."

Mr. Craig turned to look at her, a grin on his face. "You give me the impression that you're a bit of an expert yourself."

Roberta shook her head. "Not me. Dad. It was always his dream to design a golf course. He read every book possible on the subject. His idea was always that one shouldn't *build* a course, one should sculpt it. He said that, wherever possible, it should blend in with the physical layout of the land, and that could be simply matching the existing undulations or even creating lines that mirror the hills on the horizon." She let out a deep sigh as she once more swept her eyes across the glowing landscape. "My word, he would have fallen in love with this place."

The farmer cocked his head to the side. "Well, he'd be a man after my own heart then." He saw Roberta give an abrupt shiver and she folded her bare arms across her chest to ward off the cold. "Come on," he said, moving back up the garden path, "let's get inside. It's getting quite fresh out here."

On reaching the front door of the house, he turned to see that Roberta had yet to move, her eyes now transfixed on something in the direction of the neighbouring farm. She raised her arm and pointed a finger. "There's no road over there, is there?"

"No. Just a track that links this farm with the next."

A puzzled frown wrinkled her brow. "Well, there seem to be headlights coming this way."

The farmer could now hear the sound of a diesel engine blowing out noisily through a cracked exhaust pipe. He took a few steps down the path and looked out in the same direction as Roberta. "Well, I never. That's Gregor's fork-lift."

They watched the lights slowly approach, and as the vehicle got nearer they were able to make out, above the grumble of the engine, the sound of voices singing in what seemed like a tuneless descant. The fork-lift momentarily dipped into a hollow, then reappeared, and at that point the farmer realized that they had not been listening to the rendition of one song, but two, both being belted forth at full volume, as if those who were performing them were trying to compete for air-time.

Roberta let out a laugh. "It sounds to me as if a party's just been had. Who is it?"

The farmer smiled and shook his head. "I'm not sure at the minute, but when you get to hear 'Flower of Scotland' and 'Swing Low, Sweet Chariot' being sung together like that, it usually means that there's a Scotsman and an Englishman having a wee bit of a musical difference."

They moved forward and leaned on the garden wall and watched as the fork-lift pulled to a halt at the bottom of the bank. The two singing figures were sitting in the bottom of the grain-bucket, only their heads visible above its steel rim, on to which both clung hard, having been transported the half-mile along the bumpy track high up in the air. The driver slowly lowered the bucket to within three feet of the ground, then tipped it forward, and the musical duet immediately slid up-scale into a cry of protest as the two figures were unceremoniously dumped out. The engine was cut and the driver clambered with what seemed like infinite care from the cab, only to have his true colours shown when his wavering foot completely missed the final step and he swore out loud as the serrated metal rasped against his shin.

Roberta let out a short laugh but immediately stifled it with her hand when she saw the farmer hold a finger to his lips. He cleared his throat. "And *what* do we have going on here?" he called out, his voice sounding as stern as that of a disgruntled schoolmaster. The two figures scrambled unsteadily to their feet and, now joined in line by the limping driver, all three stood peering up at Mr. Craig and Roberta. One of them detached himself from the group, took a couple of steps back and ran at the bank, only managing to make it to the top on his third attempt.

Alex swayed slightly as he stood in front of them, an inane beam on his ruddy features. "Hullo, Granddad."

The farmer acknowledged the greeting with a brief nod of his head. "Alex. You know Miss Bayliss, of course."

Alex grinned at Roberta. "Hullo, Miss Bayliss. What're you doing here?"

"You'll get an explanation of that later," the farmer cut in, "once I've heard yours."

Gregor now made an appearance at the top of the bank, still rubbing at his aching shin, and Alex cast him a glance as if requiring immediate moral support. Gregor noted the farmer's look of disapproval and made an effort to appear as compos mentis as he possibly could. "Well?" That was all he could manage in greeting.

"Gregor. This is Miss Bayliss. Miss Bayliss, this is Alex's father."

Gregor came forward, wiping his hands on the seat of his trousers. He shook Roberta's hand. "Pleased to meet you, Miss Bayliss."

The third figure appeared now at the top of the bank, blowing forcefully with the effort of the climb. Jonathan Davies took a silk handkerchief from the pocket of his soil-streaked corduroy trousers and wiped his brow, then came forward and tripped over a clump of grass, only managing to break his fall by splaying his hands out on the wall.

"And here we have Mr. Davies!" exclaimed Mr. Craig, turning to Roberta to hide the fact that he was now finding it quite hard to control his own laughter. "Miss Bayliss, this is the gentleman to whom we have entrusted the task of turning this farm into a championship golf course."

Davies looked up at him, a pained expression of embarrassment on his face. "Good evening, sir," he said quietly, keeping one hand on the wall to steady himself and putting out the other to the farmer. It was shaken with force. "Mr. Davies, may I introduce you to Miss Bayliss—from Australia."

"How do you do?" he said weakly, shaking Roberta's hand.

Mr. Craig clapped his hands and rubbed them together. "Right! Now that we have the introductions out of the way, let's hear what you've all been up to."

There was a general casting of looks between the three before Gregor took the lead. "We've just been over at Winterton having a wee celebration . . ."

"Oh, a *wee* celebration, was it?" the farmer remarked, rubbing interestedly at his chin.

Gregor cleared his throat before continuing. "Well, Alex and I were just having a beer together when Jonathan here arrived with some champagne . . ."

"Ah, champagne. That's nice, though."

Davies pushed himself away from the wall and looked as if he were about to fall over. "Would you mind awfully if I sat down?"

"Not at all, Mr. Davies. You go right ahead."

Davies walked as if on rubber legs over to the top of the bank and slumped down on the damp grass, his legs dangling over the edge.

"So, have you been enjoying anything other than champagne then?"

Gregor looked across at Alex. "Well . . ."

"Havana cigars," Alex interjected, the smile that remained transfixed on his face making him seem utterly pleased with himself.

"Ah, then. Champagne and Havana cigars." Mr. Craig shook his head. "Well, lad," he said, looking at Alex, "I would say that you're in for a real humdinger of a hangover in the morning."

The statement seemed to be sufficient to wipe the smile from Alex's face. He dug his hands into his pockets and looked down at his feet, and began scuffing at a loose stone with the point of his shoe.

Gregor rubbed a hand across his mouth. "Listen, I'm sorry about this. It was my fault. I shouldn't have maybe let him drink so much."

"Ah, well," Mr. Craig started slowly, "maybe you shouldn't have. Keep in mind, Gregor, that I have a responsibility for him too, while his mother's away." He let out a long sigh. "On the other hand, a wee tick of grease is sometimes needed if one wants to get rusty machinery to turn easy again." He smiled at them both. "I'm glad that you two are on course again."

Gregor nodded. "I didn't let him drive."

"I can see that." The farmer flicked his head in the direction of the fork-lift. "Mind you, it's a toss-up as to which would have been the safer mode of transport."

Gregor scratched at the back of his head. "Yes, well, I think that Alex and I could have walked, but we were a bit concerned about Jonathan over the . . ." He had turned to look to where Davies had been sitting, but stopped abruptly when he realized that the bank was now unoccupied. He walked quickly to the edge and looked over. "Oh, for goodness' sake!" He disappeared down the bank. Mr. Craig pulled open the garden gate, and both he and Roberta hurried over to stand next to Alex. They watched as Gregor examined the body that lay curled up in a foetal position at the bottom of the bank.

"How is he?" Mr. Craig inquired, a note of concern in his voice.

Alex looked up and let out a short laugh. "Sleeping like a baby."

There were sighs of relief at the top of the bank. The farmer turned to his grandson. "You'd better get down there and give your father a hand to bring the man inside. I don't think he'd survive a homeward journey in that grain bucket." Alex's fixed grin returned and he slid down the bank to help his father.

Mr. Craig put his hand on Roberta's arm and guided her back through the gate. She stopped and turned to him. "You're a pretty understanding man, aren't you?"

He shrugged. "Och well, there's no harm done. I'm quite sure that it won't become a habit. I remember when I was a wee bit younger than Alex, I had a few too many pints of beer at the Harvest Home and was sick as a dog all night. The headache that I had the next morning was a great help in teaching me to act in moderation from then on." He paused for a moment. "I hope you're not feeling too off-put by all that's gone on tonight. I can vouch that it's not a regular occurrence."

Roberta smiled at him. "You know, Craig, I don't think I've had so much entertainment for, well . . . ever!"

"Good," he said, as they walked together up the garden path. "I'm glad that you see it that way." He opened the front door and ushered Roberta into the house.

Chapter 17

The *paso* (large platform), that bore El Señor de la Presentación, a massive eight-figure display portraying the presentation of Jesus to the people by Pontius Pilate, swayed its way up the narrow street. Its forward motion seemed imperceptible as the *costaleros*, who remained hidden from view beneath the embroidered side canopies, shuffled forward with the immense weight of the float upon their cushioned shoulders. Myriad candles bordered its ornate plinth, sending up a plume of smoke into the cool night air that drifted unbroken past open windows and crowded balconies, their railings draped with fringed rugs or interwoven with an abundance of flowers that would eventually be dispersed by the unfelt breeze swirling softly about the roof-tops. In front of the procession, ordered lines of *nazarenos*, members of the fraternity to whom the *paso* belonged, cleared a way through the thronging crowd, their identity concealed beneath full-length white robes and tall purple conical hoods. And behind the float came the masses, an ever-changing multitude who joined the procession from side streets or doorways or bars as others left for rest or much-needed refreshment.

Liz concentrated hard as she followed on amidst the crowd, her own movement being regulated by the uneven pressure on her upper body exerted by those behind and in front of her. Despite the freshness of the night, she felt hot and sticky from the heat generated by so many people in such close proximity to one another, and her eyes smarted from the constant waft of cigarette smoke that hung like a rain-cloud about their heads. Desperate to keep her balance in the jostling crowd, she fought an unseen battle for space on the ground, endlessly stepping on toes and smiling apologetically at those who she thought might be their owners. On many an occasion over the past three days, her own feet had fallen victim to this painful, yet unavoidable, abuse, and she had resorted to buying a pair of heavy leather boots, both to protect her feet and to help them cope with the many miles that both she and the professor had walked through the streets of Seville.

But sore feet was a pittance of a price to pay for the pleasure of actually being there, being part of this incredible happening. She had never been particularly religious in her life, but she now found herself captivated by the contrasting atmospheres of reverence and celebration engendered by the colourful parades, the *pasos* depicting the Passion of Christ that she had followed or watched pass by during the course of Semana Santa now giving a tangible meaning to a story that she had known since she was a little girl. She felt closer to it all than she had ever done before, and sometimes wondered how little difference there must have been in her watching events unfold before her eyes here and actually having been in Jerusalem all those years ago, and following Him through the streets and on to Golgotha, and watching Him being nailed to the Cross.

She looked around to see if she could discover the whereabouts of the professor, eventually catching sight of his tall figure ten yards behind her. He had taken off his jacket, revealing a pair of bright-yellow braces which, worn over a dark blue shirt, contrasted quite irreverently with the funereal dress of those about him. He was attempting to stand still in the jostling crowd so that he could read about some point of interest in his guidebook, whilst emitting from his pipe a cloud of smoke that was adding quite effectively to the general tobacco smog. He looked up, catching her eye, and gave her a fixed grin which seemed to register more desperation than contentment, then began to push his way through the crowd towards her. As she watched him approach, Liz found herself once more reflecting on how selfish she had been towards him when they had first arrived, because, as it had turned out, he could not have been a more perfect companion and guide, having demonstrated from the outset both an unrelenting energy that belied his age and a ceaseless enthusiasm during all their sightseeing quests. Together they had marvelled at the Moorish splendour of the Reales Alcázares, become hopelessly lost in the maze of streets that made up the Barrio Santa Cruz, and imagined the fiery atmosphere in the Plaza de Toros de la Maestranza. They had stood at the top of the towering Giralda, high above the cathedral, looking out over the roofs of the city, and away to the north, beyond the many bridges that spanned the waters of the Guadalquivir River, to where the foothills of the Sierra Morena pimpled the horizon. They had taken a horse-drawn carriage along the tranquil avenues of the Parque María Luisa and had had their photograph taken by their sombre coachman on the semicircular esplanade in front of the Plaza de España. And then they had stood patiently outside basilicas to witness the first sighting of one of the flower-bedecked *pasos*, the images greeted with whoops of joy and cries of admiration, before following on in the procession, walking for hours through the narrow labyrinthine streets of the city. And never had there been a moment when she had needed to ask a question on who, why, or wherefore, because the professor was always there with his guidebook, keeping up a constant yet engrossing commentary, tinged with his own dry humour, on whatever they were seeing.

He squeezed his way between the short, stout Spanish couple that stood directly behind her in their Sunday-best attire, and blew out with exertion when he arrived at her side. "My God, I'm hot!" he exclaimed, taking a red-spotted handkerchief from his trouser pocket and wiping the glistening beads of sweat from his forehead. "Listen, there's a street just coming up on the left. What do you say if we just dive down there and go find somewhere quiet to get a drink and some tapas?"

Liz stretched up on her toes and peered over the heads of the crowd to where the platform was being carried, seventy yards ahead of them. "What about waiting until it gets to the end of this street?"

He followed her line of sight. "That's another four hundred yards! It could take at least another hour to get there." He made to wipe at his forehead again with the handkerchief, but in doing so in such a confined space his elbow caught the side of the mantilla-covered head of the small Spanish señora whom he had just passed. He gave it such a healthy blow that her finely arranged bouffant hair-do slipped to the side, making the black lace shawl that covered it now resemble more a badly erected tepee.

"I'm sorry!" he said, instinctively grabbing hold of the woman's arm to steady her. "I mean, er, *lo siento*." The woman pulled her arm from his grip and gave him a look that could kill. He turned to Liz and pulled a grimace that barely disguised the fact that he was about to burst out laughing. "My word, what a way I have with women!"

Liz closed her eyes tight with embarrassment. "I think you're right, Arthur. Time to beat a hasty retreat." She began pushing her way diagonally through the crowd, making for the refuge of the little street that the professor had pointed out.

They had just extricated themselves from the worst of the throng when the sound of a deep baritone voice rang out across the street in a long, warbling wail. Liz walked to the edge of the pavement and looked up to the balcony where the singer stood, directly above the *paso*, his arms outstretched in mournful supplication.

"Oh, for goodness' sakes!" the professor groaned. "Not another bloody *saeta*."

"Come on, Arthur," Liz said reproachfully, giving him a bump with her elbow, "they're wonderful. I think they're really moving."

"Which is more than the crowd will do for the next fifteen minutes."

Liz gave him a bewildered look. "What's the matter? You're not being your usual bright self."

He let out a long sigh. "I know. I suppose it's just the heat—and all these people. I'm just beginning to feel a bit tired and crabby."

"Come on, then," Liz replied, taking him by the arm. "Let's go. I think we've probably done enough for tonight."

"Listen, I don't want to be a killjoy," he said, pulling away from her grasp to allow clear passage for a woman and her two small daughters to hurry up the street to join the parade. "We could have a quick drink and then catch up with it all later."

Liz glanced at her wrist-watch. "No, it's a quarter to twelve. I'm quite happy to call it a day, if you are."

Arthur nodded. "Glad you said that. My legs are beginning to feel decidedly wobbly. I don't think I've quite recovered yet from our climb to the top of the Giralda."

"Right. Well, let's get back to the hotel then—if we can find our way."

"Just leave that to me!" he exclaimed, his good humour seemingly restored by the prospect of returning to the hotel. He stopped to peruse the street map in the back pages of his guidebook. "Now, if we go down here, turn left, then right, then left . . . then right again, we can cut through the Barrio de Santa Cruz and out by the Jardines de Murillo." He smiled at Liz. "How does that sound to you?"

Liz shrugged. "I'm afraid you can't ask me, Arthur. I still don't have a clue about this place. If it wasn't for you and your map, I'd probably be lost here forever."

He slapped shut the guidebook and took hold of her arm. "In that case, stick close to me and I will guide you through the wilderness." He moved her off down the street at a jaunty pace, his head held high in a display of exaggerated smugness. "Oh, how wonderful it makes me feel to be considered so important!"

They lost their way after the third turning, having come to a small junction from which five narrow streets led off, and subsequently choosing one that took them in the opposite direction to their planned route. A quarter of an hour later, they regained their bearings outside the Iglesia de Santa Cruz, by which time their camaraderie was under severe duress, the professor now furious at the fallibility of his own map-reading skills and becoming quite desperate to get back to the hotel.

"Thank God for that! Come on, this way!" he called out, waving his guidebook like a flag. He had begun to walk at such a frenetic pace that Liz had to break into a jog to keep up with him. She stopped for a moment to catch her breath, but seeing him disappear around the corner of the church and frightened that she might lose him, she set off after him.

The cry was loud enough to bring the crowd's babbling noise to a momentary silence, then people started moving quickly down the street from where it had sounded out. Liz found herself caught up in the hurrying masses, and as one man ran past her he slipped and grabbed at her arm to steady himself. "*¡Cuidado, señora!*" he laughed. "*Hay mucha cera aquí.*"

Liz smiled at him, not understanding a word that he had said, but thinking it better to make some sort of reaction to his joking comment. She stepped off the pavement and her foot immediately slid out in front of her, and she too found herself having to grab at a passer-by to maintain her balance. She looked down at the cobbled surface of the street and noticed that its length seemed to be glistening in the lights that shone out from the shops. She scuffed her shoe against a cobble and noticed a whitish residue build up in front of her toe. Bending down, she brushed a finger against it, then smeared it with her thumb, realizing immediately that it was wax, deposited there by the hundreds of candles that had been carried up and down the street.

"Don't try to get me up, you fool!" Liz heard Arthur's voice cry out from the centre of the crowd that had gathered farther down the street. "Can't you see the bloody thing's broken!"

"Oh, no!" Liz muttered to herself in horror. She made her way as fast as she dared to the back of the crowd and began pushing her way to the front. "Arthur?"

"Liz! Where the hell are you?"

The crowd moved aside to allow her through, and she found Arthur leaning heavily on one elbow in the middle of the street. His feet were splayed out in front of him, his face ashen-white, and his lips were drawn back to reveal teeth clenched in pain. Liz looked down the length of his body and immediately saw the impossible angle at which his left foot stuck out from his leg. She dropped to her knees beside him. "Arthur, what have you done?"

"What the hell do you think I've done? Some stupid bastard has sprayed the street with bloody candle-wax! My sodding foot's broken!" He let out a loud moan. "Oh, God, it hurts!"

Liz got to her feet and looked desperately around at the crowd, who just stood eyeing Arthur as if he were some kind of unclean being. "Can someone not call an ambulance?" The onlookers turned to each other and shrugged their shoulders. Liz tried again. "Ambulance!" She held out her hands, trying to think of some word that might resemble the Spanish equivalent. "*Ambulante?*"

A tall young man, impeccably dressed in a light blue linen suit, pushed his way through to the front and, delving into the inside pocket of his jacket, produced a mobile phone. "*Ambulancia, señora. El quiere una ambulancia.*"

"Yes!" Liz nodded frantically, "Yes, please—and quickly!" She knelt down beside Arthur again and took hold of his hand. She felt his grip tighten like a vice around her own, and she knew then that he was in desperate pain.

"I'm sorry, Liz. What a stupid, bloody thing to do! This was *not* what was planned."

"Don't worry. Please don't worry. The important thing is to get you to a hospital as quickly as possible."

"I know, I know, but what are you going to do now? How are you . . . ?"

"Just don't worry about me, Arthur. I'll be fine." She felt a hand on her shoulder and turned to look up into the face of the young man.

"The ambulance comes now, señora. She comes now."

Liz smiled at him. "Thank you so much."

"*De nada.*" He turned and began to push his way through the crowd.

Liz pulled her hand free from Arthur's grasp and stood up. "Excuse me!"

The man turned. "Señora?"

"Do you speak English quite well?"

He smiled. "No." He held a thumb and forefinger millimetres apart. "Only a very little."

"Well, that's enough." She gave him her most pleading look. "Do you think you could just stay with us until the ambulance arrives—please? Neither of us understands a word of Spanish, and I have no idea what to say when it comes."

The young man held out his hands in apology and cast a glance towards the bar at the side of the street. Liz followed his gaze to where a girl sat at a table, her dress expressing sophistication, but her features little humour. She watched the commotion with only a modicum of interest and raked back her long dark hair with fingers that also held a newly lit cigarette. "I am sorry, but I cannot. It is—how do you say?—my first time?"

Liz let out a long sigh. "I think you probably mean your first date."

The man laughed, understanding the subtlety of her point. "Yes, you are right. My first date. Now you understand how bad is my English."

Liz nodded. "Well, thank you for your help, anyway." She turned around to find that the majority of the crowd had dispersed, and an old woman in a black dress had come out of one of the adjacent houses and had kindly put a blanket around Arthur's shoulders and one across his legs. She now stood beside him jabbering her heart-felt condolences in

Spanish. Liz walked over quickly to his side and knelt down. "Why the hell do all the Spaniards smoke so much?"

Arthur managed a querying look through his pained expression. "What?"

Liz shook her head. "Nothing. Just give me your hand."

The ambulance took fifteen minutes to reach them, but once the two paramedics had given Arthur a pain-killing injection and had carefully placed him onto the stretcher and loaded him into the back of the vehicle, it took only a further seven to get to the hospital. Liz sat beside him on the way, holding hard on to his hand as the ambulance sped through the crowded streets, its siren wailing like a banshee. Her concern now was not only for him, but also because even she could tell that the direction in which they were travelling was taking her farther away from the hotel.

Swinging off the road into a narrow service lane, the ambulance came to an abrupt halt under the brick-pillared entrance of the hospital. Quickly opening up the back doors, the two paramedics wheeled Arthur out, and having been given no indication as to what she should do, Liz followed on as they pushed the trolley through the frosted-glass swing-doors, above which was written the word URGENCIAS in dark red letters. There was a turmoil of activity inside, the long hallway crammed with doctors in green fatigues trying to organize and administer to the hordes of patients in need of attention. Young children with pallid faces sat quietly in oversized wheelchairs, whilst mothers monopolized the showing of grief, stroking fiercely at their child's head and dabbing theatrically at their own tear-filled eyes with the edge of a handkerchief. An old woman, dressed in a black shapeless dress, moaned in pain as she was helped slowly to her feet. She clutched fiercely at her rosary beads and struggled to cross herself as her arms were clamped in support by medical staff who, emitting quiet words of sympathy, began to move her off at a snail's pace along the corridor. There were others who appeared to be there for no reason apart from the show, leaning unconcernedly against walls with their hands in their pockets, and murmuring to each other every time another trolley was wheeled in through the entrance doors.

Liz was threading her way through the melée in pursuit of Arthur when one of the paramedics turned around and noticed that she was following. He waved a finger at her.

"*¡No aquí, señora!*"

"Could I perhaps come with you?" Liz asked.

He came back towards her, and taking her by the arm, guided her back to the double doors. He opened one and pointed at the words NO PASAR that were written across the frosted glass. Liz held out her hands, signifying to the man that she didn't know what she was meant to do. He pointed at a plate-glass window behind which was the reception desk, and beyond that, a stark waiting room with lines of green chairs anchored together on long metal tubes. He walked out of the door and pointed to one that was adjacent. *"La entrada está allí."*

Folding Arthur's jacket over her arm, she went into the waiting room as directed and sat down, and watched through the plate-glass window as the paramedics wheeled Arthur away down the corridor.

The two women who sat behind the reception desk eyed her momentarily, then spoke furtively with each other before one came through from the office and approached her with a clipboard. She gave it to Liz, along with a pen, and made a writing motion with her hand to indicate that she wanted the admittance form that was clipped to it filled in, then left her and returned quickly to the office. Liz cast an eye over the form. It was all in Spanish. She could make out a few of the headings, and began filling in the professor's name and a sparse address—Hotel Cazaral, Seville—being unable to remember the name of the street on which it was situated. But that was as much as she could do. She got up and walked over to the office window and handed across the clipboard. "I'm sorry, but I can't understand the rest." The woman looked at the form and smiled at her. "*¡No se preocupe! Es suficiente.*"

For one and a half hours Liz sat in the waiting room, watching people come and go. Complete families, all with worried faces, entered the reception area, where they would fret over the condition of one of their own with the two receptionists. Then, having received much mollification and reassurance, they would come to sit on the seats next to Liz and continue their overwrought banter. On many an occasion, Liz found it difficult to work out exactly which of their group was requiring the urgent hospital treatment, so melancholy was their joint demeanour.

She was watching an old man, dressed in a pair of worn corduroy trousers and drooping cardigan, a black Basque beret set rakishly forward on his bristling grey head, as he shuffled slowly along the corridor with the support of a heavy cane walking-stick, when a young doctor with black-rimmed glasses came into the waiting room and approached her, the white coat that he wore over his green fatigues flapping open as he walked. He held in his hand the clipboard that she had given back to the receptionist.

He smiled at her. "*¿Señora, no habla español?*"

Liz shook her head.

He sat down beside her and took a pen from the cluster that was clipped to the top pocket of his coat. "My English is no good, but we try, yes?"

Liz sighed with relief on hearing words that she could understand. "How is he?"

The doctor scratched at the back of his head with the pen. "He is all right, but it is not a good break. We have to give him . . ." He paused as he searched for the word. ". . . *sedativos?*"

"Sedatives."

"Yes, we have to give him sedatives to pull the foot straight."

"Can I see him?"

"Not yet, señora. First, I must ask you some questions." He studied the form on the clipboard. "Now, has he . . . *alergias?*"

"Allergies?

"Yes."

Liz shook her head. "I don't know. Can't you ask him these questions?"

"No, señora. He sleeps."

"Well, I'm afraid that I don't know these kind of things about him. He's just an acquaintance, a friend."

The doctor nodded slowly in realization. "Ah! So the señor is not your husband, then?"

Liz let out a short laugh. "No, he's not! He's just my tenant."

"Tenant?" the doctor asked, looking perplexed by the word.

"He lives with me."

"Ah, he *lives* with you, then."

"No! I mean, not like that!"

The doctor shook his head in confusion. "Señora, I am sorry if I do not understand, but I must have a *firma* . . . to give permission to do the operation." He held out the clipboard and pen. "Can you please do this?"

Liz took them from him and sat for a moment with the pen poised above the consent form. She *supposed* he was all right. After all, he had managed to storm his way through life this far, smoking his wretched pipe and drinking quantities of bourbon. And anyway, there was no doubt that he needed to undergo the operation. She signed the form and handed it back to the doctor.

"Thank you, señora." He got to his feet.

"Do you think that I should wait to see him?"

The doctor glanced across at the clock on the office wall. "I think not. We will operate now, but then he will not be awake until much later. I think you will be better to go back to where you stay and return in the morning."

"All right." She stood up and slung her handbag onto her shoulder. "Could you then tell me the name of this hospital?"

"La Macarena."

"What? As in the Virgin?"

The doctor smiled. "*Exactamente*. As in the Virgin." He turned to leave.

"Just one more thing," Liz called after him.

"Yes?"

"Have you any idea how I get back to the Hotel Cazaral?"

The doctor thought for a moment. "I'm not very sure of this hotel, señora. I am from Córdoba." He held up his hand. "But please wait. I shall ask." He walked over to the office window and handed back the clipboard, and engaged one of the women in a few seconds' animated conversation, during which there was much hand-waving and reaffirmation of directions. He came back over to her. "Right, señora. It is quite good. I take you to the door." He walked beside her to the entrance. "Ah, yes, I forget to ask! Can you bring some clothes and tooth-brush for the señor in the morning?"

"All right. And by the way, he's a professor." She thought it best to tell him this, in the hope that it might save Arthur from getting needlessly rankled in his efforts to explain.

"Ah, he is a teacher."

"No, he is a professor. It's his title." The young doctor looked none the wiser. "In a university."

"Ah!" he declared, appearing now to understand what she was saying. "A *catedrático*. A very clever man, then?"

Liz sighed, realizing that her attempts to explain were bearing little trace of enlightenment. "Yes, I suppose so. A very clever man who can't walk down a street without falling over."

"I'm sorry?"

Liz shook her head. "Never mind."

They walked out through the door, and Liz immediately felt a considerable decline in the temperature since she had entered the place. Taking her jersey from around her waist, she pulled it over her head as she walked with the doctor across the service lane and out onto the pavement.

"Now, señora, you go up to that street there," he said, indicating the fast-moving carriageway to her left, "then go to the right for two hundred metres, and then to the left, and when you are there, you do not leave this road. It is very big all the way to the Avenida de Menéndez y Pelayo, and your hotel is there."

"Right. And how far is it?"

"I believe about three kilometres."

"Three kilometres! I didn't think it was that far! I'd be better getting a taxi."

The doctor let out a sigh. "You want to take a taxi now?"

"No, don't worry," she replied, realizing from his tone that she was fast becoming a nuisance to him. "I'll just walk. And thank you for all your help."

The doctor gave her a smile, then made his way quickly back to the entrance, dodging around a newly arrived ambulance as he crossed the service lane. Liz watched him until he had disappeared through the double doors, then turned and set off on her way back to the hotel.

The walk across the city was, as the doctor had suggested, quite straightforward, and there was never a moment when she felt uncomfortable in being out alone at that time of night because the streets were as busy as they had been during the day. On countless occasions, she had to step off the pavement, finding her path blocked by swarms of children who played like puppies around the street-side tables at which their parents sat. She would return a smile if she caught the eye of a doting mother, but that was as far as she could go in communicating with anyone, and it was this inability and the fact that she now had no one with whom to interact that made her start reflecting on her own isolation and loneliness. Other than Arthur, she knew absolutely no one in this vast, humming city. Thinking about it, she knew no one in this *country*! She couldn't talk to anyone, she had no idea of how to get around the place by herself, and she now realized how much she had come to rely on Arthur for the companionship and security that he offered. She felt an aching knot tighten in her stomach as the alien sensation of homesickness engulfed her, and all she wanted to do now was to return to Scotland, to see her father and Alex, and to talk with them. Yes, that was it! Just to talk to someone without having to help others search for words, or for herself to try to understand this wretched language.

By the time that the vertical blue-lit sign on the side of the Hotel Cazaral came into view, she was almost running, desperate to get back to the haven of known territory. She pushed through one of the heavy glass doors and entered the foyer, and even though the pale-green marbled décor was as warmly welcoming as an unfilled swimming pool, she breathed out a sigh of relief at the familiar sight of the two sludge-brown armchairs, incongruously positioned to draw attention to the hotel's ornate wall-hanging and the model of the Spanish galleon in full sail that stood below it on the corner of the carved pine chest.

A man was standing at the reception desk, his luggage clustered around his feet, as he talked animatedly in Spanish with the young girl who manned the desk, and whom Liz had not seen before. Her fingers danced in stuttered bursts over the keyboard of her computer, and a look of puzzled anxiety creased her forehead. The man reached across the desk and swung the screen around so that he could look at it himself, and the girl took a pace back and nervously twiddled her pen in her fingers as she watched for his reaction to what he was viewing. He slowly shook his head and spun the screen back to face her, and came out with a short expletive that, judging from the look on the receptionist's face, Liz understood to be a particularly potent swear-word. The girl took a deep breath and spoke to him in a thin, wavering voice but he cut in, his raised tone resounding around the marble walls of the foyer. He held up his hands as if admitting defeat and gave each of his suitcases a hefty dunt with his foot, making them slide across the highly polished floor towards one of the armchairs. He turned and followed their path and slumped down into the chair.

Liz walked forward to the desk, hoping to take advantage of the momentary lull in their heated debate. She was feeling tired and low-spirited and she didn't want to have to witness any more of this haranguing match. "Excuse me," she said, giving the girl a wide smile to assure her that she was going to be friendly.

The girl continued to punch the keyboard, but lifted one hand to stop Liz from speaking further. "*Un momento, señora. Tengo que asistir a este caballero primero.*"

Liz turned and looked across the foyer to where the man was sitting, resting an elbow on the arm of the chair and rubbing at his eyes with his fingers. He was probably in his mid-thirties, broadly built, and was dressed in a light fawn corduroy jacket, white open-necked shirt and jeans, and although he was tanned, he certainly did not have the colouring of a Spaniard. A tangled mass of sandy-blond hair curled over his collar, and the cuffs of his jacket were drawn back enough to reveal a profusion of freckles covering his wrists and hands. He sat with his legs crossed, showing off a pair of high Spanish riding boots with crossed ankle-straps under his jeans. He dropped his hand to the arm of the chair and looked straight at Liz, fixing her with a pair of startlingly blue eyes. He pulled down the corners of his mouth and held out the palms of his hands, as if to signify that matters were out of his control.

"*¿Señor?*" the girl called out to him.

The man made no move to leave the chair. "*¿Sí?*"

"*Lo siento, pero yo tendré que llamar el gerente.*"

"*Si cree que es necesario, pero primero quisiera una copa.*"

"*Desde luego. ¿Qué quiere usted?*"

"*Whisky, un whisky doble, y una botella de agua con gas.*"

The girl smiled at him, relieved that he seemed to be becoming better-humoured. She made to move from behind the desk, then, as an afterthought, turned back and looked towards Liz. "*¿Señora?*"

"Thank you . . . yes. Could I have the key to room four hundred and ten, please?" She blurted it out quickly, longing just to get to her room and go to bed.

The girl looked perplexed, not having picked up what she had said. "*¿Llave?*"

Liz let out a long sigh and shook her head. "I don't know!" She pointed towards the rack of keys that hung behind the girl. "Key—for room four hundred ten."

"The Spanish for key is *llave*." The voice, slanted in an American accent, came from behind her.

She turned and looked at the man. "I'm sorry?"

"The girl asked you already if you wanted your key."

Liz bit at her lip. "I didn't know that. I can't speak any Spanish."

The man shrugged. "Well, you shouldn't expect everyone here to speak English, then."

"I don't," she replied, giving him a look of bewilderment at his rudeness before turning back to the girl.

"Well, then, ask for it in Spanish. The word is *llave*."

Liz felt her cheeks flush with anger, not only because of his attitude, but because, for some stupid reason, she realized that her eyes had begun to well up with tears. Dammit, she thought to herself, what the hell are you doing? You've gone through worse emotional moments than this over the past few months. You can cope with this. She brushed fiercely at a cheek to wipe away an escaping tear. On the other hand, why on earth *should* she have to cope with this? She was tired and alone and all she really wanted to do was to go to bed now, and having longed to hear just one English word spoken to her for the past three hours, when it did eventually materialize, it was just . . . so unfriendly.

"Go on, try it. The word is *llave*."

Liz spun round and glared at the man. "Why don't you just shut up?" The quiver in her voice made the rebuke totally unconvincing.

She noticed the expression of self-amusement drain from the man's face the moment that he caught both her intonation and her look. She turned back to the receptionist, willing her to find the key so that she could get away, but the girl just cast bemused glances from one to the other, her hand poised over the rack of keys, in the hope that someone would give her verification as to which she should hand over.

The man appeared at Liz's side. "*La llave para la habitación cuatrocientos y diez.*" The girl quickly took the key from the rack and gave it to Liz.

"Thank you." She turned and lowered her head as she passed him, but he took her by the arm to stop her.

"Listen, I'm sorry. I didn't mean to be rude."

"Well, you were," Liz replied curtly, focusing on the hand that clenched her arm. She glanced up at his face, narrowing her eyes, and realized that his tan was mostly made up of an abundance of freckles. "In fact, I think you still *are* extremely rude."

He let go of her arm immediately and held out his hands. "Look, I've just apologized. What more do you want?"

Liz gave him what she hoped was her most sardonic smile. "Nothing at all." She broadened the smile momentarily, then made her way towards the lift.

"Okay, I really, really am sorry." The man continued to walk by her side. "I was just being bloody-minded. I don't want you to go off thinking I'm a first-rate bastard, because I'm not. The fact is that I was meant to be here five hours ago, but my plane from Madrid was late, and I've just got here, and, well, I don't really want to be here, but now that I am, they don't have a damned room for me, and . . . I'm sorry, but I just suppose that I took it out on you."

Liz stopped abruptly and turned to look at him. "And I also have had a horrible night. My friend has broken his ankle, he is now in hospital on the other side of this . . . city, and I . . . just want to go to bed." In saying this, her emotions seemed now to get the better of her, and for the first time she was conscious of tears running unguarded down her cheeks. She made her way quickly up the stairs and around the corner to the lift and pushed hard at the button. The man came after her.

"How about joining me for a whisky or something?"

Liz shook her head.

"What about a coffee?" he said quietly, his voice almost pleading.

As the lift arrived, Liz suddenly remembered the doctor's request. She turned to the man. "No . . . thank you, but if you want to be helpful, you could maybe ask at reception for the key to my friend's room. I have to take some of his clothes to the hospital tomorrow."

"Of course. What's his room number?"

"Four hundred eighteen." She shook her head. "No, it's not." What *was* the number? She hadn't been to his room or had reason to contact him there since the first night. "Maybe it's four hundred twenty."

The man smiled at her. "Look, there's no problem." He began to make his way back to the reception desk. "Just give me his name."

"Professor Kempler."

He stopped dead in his tracks and slowly turned to look at her, the friendly smile visibly sliding into a questioning frown. "Professor Arthur Kempler?"

Liz took in a breath of surprise. "Yes, that's right," she replied, her voice suddenly bright in the comforting realization that Arthur might be a common link between them. "Do you know of him?"

"Arthur Kempler is your friend?"

"Yes," she replied, her moment of elation turning to one of puzzlement as she viewed the stony expression on his face. "Why do you ask that?"

The man shook his head slowly. "My God!"

"I'm sorry?"

The man walked two paces to the wall and leaned his back against it, folding his arms across his chest. "The man is incorrigible! He's completely *insatiable*!"

Liz walked over and stood in front of him. "Listen, I'm sorry, but I don't know what you're talking about. How do you know Professor Kempler?"

He let out a mocking laugh. "So you're the new woman in his life, are you?"

"I beg your pardon? No, I am not the . . . look, I don't need to explain myself to you! Who are you anyway?"

"Who am *I*?" The man shook his head again. "Well, madam, I just happen to be his son."

The word hit Liz as if a church bell had been sounded too close to her ear. It rebounded from one side of her head to the other, the resonance of his tone thrashing around in her brain as if desperate to escape from its confines. She just stood staring at him with her mouth open. "You're . . ." She gulped to try to bring some moisture into her mouth. "You're Will?"

A cynical smile spread across the man's face. He looked down at the ground. "Of course. You would know all about me, wouldn't you?"

"Well, yes, I do, but only because Arthur told me that you weren't going to be coming out here with him. I wouldn't be here otherwise."

"That'd be right," he murmured.

"Yes, as a matter of fact, it is!" Liz exclaimed. "It's absolutely right! You told Arthur that you didn't want to come. In fact, I think that your exact words were that you never wanted to see him again."

This obviously struck a delicate chord. He paused before replying. "Well, that's between him and me, isn't it? That's for a father and son to sort out."

"Of course it is. I have never wanted to get involved in Arthur's affairs."

"Oh, Arthur's affairs!" He let out a scoffing laugh. "That's an extremely apt choice of words. Well, I can tell you that there have been plenty of them."

Liz swallowed hard, realizing that she had said completely the wrong thing. She felt her face colour with embarrassment at the line of conversation and she didn't want to be drawn into it any further. "I wouldn't know about that," she said quietly. "That's none of my concern."

"Oh, isn't it?" he replied, looking hard at her, his blue eyes afire with contempt. "Maybe you just wouldn't *want* to know."

This final innuendo hit hard at Liz. She let out a short cry and shook her head in disbelief. "You think I'm having an affair with your *father*?"

The man shrugged. "And why should I not think that?"

"Well, for a start, he's about twenty-five years older than me!"

"Age difference has never bothered him before."

"*Him?* We're not talking about him! We're talking about *me*! It would bother me. I don't need to go chasing after older men. I have a husband . . . or *had* a husband." She shook her head. Her argument was becoming confused. "Anyway, why am I saying all this? I don't have to prove anything to you." She paused for a moment, wondering if it wouldn't be better just to leave things right there, but then decided to set the record straight once and for all. "Listen, I'll explain the situation to you, so please get this into your extremely suspicious mind. Your father is my son's German tutor at Saint Andrews University, and as he had nowhere to live, my son persuaded me to allow him to come to lodge with us on our farm. He has become a good friend of *my* father, and also to us as well. Now, our farm has just gone bankrupt and we're having to sell it, and that is after five generations of our family having farmed it. As you can imagine, that is quite a devastating blow for us all. What's more, my husband has just walked out on me. So to get a little distance between myself and the place, I accepted your father's *extremely* kind offer to accompany him out here—and to be quite honest, the longer I spend here, the more I wish that I had never, *ever* set foot in this wretched city." She looked away from the man, her eye caught by the appearance of the young receptionist. She glanced from one to the other, a look of fear on her face as she held up her hands in an attempt to quieten their incomprehensible and hostile exchange. "I'm sorry," she said quietly to the girl. She took in a deep breath and looked back at him. "Now, if you'll excuse me, I am very tired and I'm going to bed." She put her hand on the lift door and pulled it open.

"What about the old man's clothes?" the man asked, his voice subdued.

She glared contemptuously at him. "I shall get the *llave* tomorrow morning and collect them then." She entered the lift and pressed the button for the fourth floor.

He quickly came to stand in front of her. "And what about him?"

"I don't know," Liz answered as the inner door closed in front of him. "Isn't that for you to decide?"

Letting herself into her room, Liz walked straight over to the bed and sat down heavily upon it. She put the palms of her hands against her brow and rubbed it hard in an attempt to relieve the throbbing in her head. "Oh, my goodness, what *is* going on?" she said out loud, then fell back on the bed and closed her eyes, and in feeling its longed-for comfort beneath her, the last vestiges of resistance to sleep quickly drained from her body.

Chapter 18

Jonathan Davies rounded off the address on the envelope with a precise underline, gave the ink a quick blow, then replaced the top on his fountain pen and picked up the folded letter from the desk and tucked it inside. He bent over the flap to seal it, but then paused, having second thoughts as to whether its contents had said enough. He took out the letter and reread it.

He hadn't had to write many letters of apology before. He had always prided himself on his own decorum, his naval training having instilled in him a discipline of courtesy and gentlemanly behaviour. He therefore understood how appallingly he had let himself down at the farmhouse the other evening, not only embarrassing himself but also the farmer and his lady guest. And what was more, his inability to hold his drink had resulted in his forcing his presence on the household for the whole night. And dammit, he had come to respect that family so much, in the way that they had been able to handle the countless adversities that had been heaped upon them. Yet throughout his association with them, they had always remained friendly and accommodating toward him at a time when they could quite easily have regarded him as the enemy.

The contents of the letter, he decided, could never humble himself as much as he would like, but it would just have to do. He replaced it in the envelope and sealed it, then, getting up from his chair, he made his way over to the door of his office. The telephone on the desk rang. He tucked the letter into the inside pocket of his jacket and retraced his steps and picked up the receiver.

"Jonathan Davies . . . yes, hullo, Lionel . . ." As he listened to the words spoken to him he felt the colour drain from his face and the sting of adrenalin ran up his nerve ends to explode in his brain. ". . . You can't be serious! . . . but you *assured* me that they were going to back the project! Had they not signed the agreement? . . . Yes, but the work's well under way, Lionel! The earth-movers are working right at this minute! . . . Well, it's all very well for *you* to suggest that we stop them, but don't you understand what this means? . . . No, it is *not* a temporary hitch. We now do *not* have the complete package in place at the time of commencement, and that was the condition upon which the American consortium insisted. Did they give any reason for pulling out? . . . Oh, come on, Lionel, that is a technicality! I think they're acting in a totally unprofessional manner. They shouldn't be in the business of lending money if that's their policy. . . . I dare say you won't be recommending them again, Lionel, but that's no help to us. Do you realize that this will probably spell the end of this project? . . . I'm afraid that's no help. I could never continue on such a speculative basis. . . . Yes, I know I have little choice. You don't have to point that out. . . . All right, one week, that's all I can afford to give you, and in the meantime, I'm going to have to suspend all work. . . . Right, well, you do that and just keep in touch."

He replaced the receiver with force, then slammed his fist down on the desk. He slumped back into the chair and covered his face with his hands. This just could not be happening, he thought to himself, this is a complete nightmare. What the hell was he going to do now?

He had been raising capital for this project for the past four years, so there was really no hope of raising a sixth of the full amount within the space of a week, *and* he had an interim progress meeting with the principal backers in ten days' time.

Maybe he shouldn't bother waiting the week. Maybe it would be better just to pull the plug on the whole project right now. It seemed to have been dogged with bad luck from the moment of its inception, and he really could not afford to take on any more of the capital burden himself. He had already funded the research and development by taking out a double mortgage on his house, and his own assets within the venture-capital group were also tied up as collateral. So there was nothing left on which to fall back. He couldn't afford to go on and he couldn't afford to stop.

He reached across the desk to pick up the telephone to call the contractor, and as he did so the envelope in his inside pocket crinkled gently. He took it out and leaned back in his chair and studied the address. *What* was he going to say to them? How on earth could he break the news? All he had really succeeded in doing was leading them down the garden path with his grandiose ideas. Okay, so Gregor's farm was still intact, but how could Liz and her father ever begin to market their farm in its present condition? And there was simply nothing left with which to help them reinstate it.

He picked up the receiver and dialled a number. "Willie? Good morning, it's Jonathan. Listen, what are the boys doing at the minute? . . . Well, you'll have to stop them. . . . I know, Willie, but there's been quite a major hiccup, so just get them to stop for now. Is Michael Dooney on site? . . . Right, well, could you ask him to wait there until I come over? . . . probably in about an hour. I have to go to Winterton first to see Gregor, and then Mr. Craig at Brunthill, but after that I'll just walk down to see you both . . . all right. Thank you, Willie."

The farmyard at Brunthill was still wet following the cloudburst that had occurred during the previous night, and a deep, muddy puddle stretched the length of the flight of steps that led up to the back door. Jonathan Davies skipped over it, took a deep breath, then climbed the steps and gave two sharp knocks on the door. He heard first the muffled bark of a dog from the depths of the house, then someone allowed it through to the back kitchen, where it stood yelping and scratching on the other side of the door. It opened and the small dog, taking little notice of his presence, ran past him down the steps, hurdled the puddle at pace and disappeared off into the steading.

"Mr. Davies!" The farmer stood in the doorway, his quite conservative attire of tweed jacket, cavalry-twill trousers, checked Viyella shirt and knitted tie being incongruously offset by a pair of white trainers and a dark green baseball cap with GLENEAGLES emblazoned above its peak in gold lettering.

"I'm sorry, Mr. Craig. Is this a bad time? Are you just going out?"

"Shortly, but not quite yet. Come on in." He stood aside to allow Jonathan to walk in front of him to the kitchen. "Now, you remember Miss Bayliss, don't you?"

The diminutive woman had just entered the room by the door leading from the hall. She was carrying a small suitcase. "Of course," said Davies, his hand outstretched as he approached her. She put down the suitcase next to the set of golf clubs that leaned against the kitchen sideboard, then turned to greet him.

"Hullo, Mr. Davies. How nice to see you again."

He cast an eye over the luggage. "I'm sorry, I should have rung first. I see that you *are* both going out."

"No, not at all," replied the farmer. "I'm a long way from being ready to leave yet. Would you like a cup of coffee?"

"No, please don't bother yourself."

"It's no bother. We're about to have one." Mr. Craig tipped back the lid of the Rayburn and placed the kettle on the hot plate.

Davies slid his hands into the pockets of his suit jacket. "Right, well, that's very kind," he said quietly, feeling quite ill at ease. "So . . . where are you off to today?"

Leaning back against the Rayburn, Mr. Craig crossed his arms and smiled broadly at Roberta Bayliss. "Well, we're heading westward, Mr. Davies. We've played Carnoustie, Gleneagles and Rosemount, so we've decided to ring the changes and go off for a couple of days to play some of the courses on the other side of the country."

Davies tried to show interest in what was being said to him, but his mind was more occupied in working out how best he could break the news. He flashed the farmer an apprehensive smile. "Well, what a good idea!"

Mr. Craig walked across to the sideboard and took down three mugs from their hooks. On his way back to the Rayburn, he was intercepted by Roberta. "Listen, I'll make the coffee," she said, taking the mugs from him, "and then you and Mr. Davies can have a talk."

"Well, that's very good of you, Roberta!" He turned and placed his hands on the central worktop. "So, Mr. Davies, I might well be wrong, but I'd say that you're looking a wee bit worried about something."

Davies let out a short laugh. "You could say that, sir."

Mr. Craig nodded. "Then we'd better hear it, hadn't we?"

Davies cleared his throat. "Well, for a start, I had written you a letter this morning concerning my behaviour the other night."

The farmer frowned in puzzlement, yet it did little to disguise the smile of amusement that wrinkled the sides of his mouth. "The other night? I don't recall there being much amiss with your behaviour the other night."

Davies shifted edgily on his feet. "That's kind of you, to see it that way. However, I believe there was, and I hope very much that both you and Miss Bayliss will forgive me for appearing at your house in such a state, and also for my unscheduled overnight stay."

Mr. Craig shook his head. "In my mind, there's nothing to forgive, Mr. Davies. It was a pleasure to have you stay under my roof." Pushing himself away from the worktop, he walked over to the fridge and opened it and took a bottle of milk from the door-shelf. "So you can now stop looking so worried about life and just enjoy your cup of coffee."

"I would very much like to, Mr. Craig, but I'm afraid that I have some other quite distressing news."

The farmer turned and slowly began to unscrew the top, his eyes fixed on Jonathan Davies. "And what might that be?"

Davies took a deep breath. "I'm afraid that one of the backers has pulled out."

His hand did not make even the minutest waver as he poured milk into the three mugs. "And what exactly does that mean, Mr. Davies?"

"It means a suspension of work. An indefinite suspension of work."

Mr. Craig came over and handed him the mug of coffee. "And have you broken this news to Gregor yet?" he asked.

Davies nodded. "Not yet. I've just been over to Winterton, but he wasn't there."

The farmer carried his mug over to the window and stood with his back to Davies, staring out across the fields. "So you would be reckoning," he said slowly, "that this golf course won't get built."

"I don't know, Mr. Craig. I spoke this morning with our business consultancy in London, and they're going to see if they can raise the shortfall in the City over the next week."

"And do you hold out much hope for that?"

Davies paused before replying. "I have to say that I'm afraid I don't."

Roberta Bayliss had been standing by the Rayburn, listening intently to the conversation but feeling uneasy about her presence while such dire news was being imparted. "Excuse me," she said quietly, "I realize that it is probably not my place to speak, but I just wondered if you were a golfer yourself, Mr. Davies."

Davies smiled at her. "I'm afraid I'm not, Miss Bayliss."

"Well then, as a keen golfer myself, I hope you don't mind my saying that it would be a crying shame if that golf course wasn't built. It is probably one of the most beautiful sites I have ever seen, and I can tell you, Mr. Davies, I've seen some of the world's best."

"I am fully aware of this, Miss Bayliss. Michael Dooney, the course architect, agrees with you wholeheartedly on that point. But we have strict conditions in place, one of them being that if we don't have the full financial package at the due date of commencement, then our major backers in America wish to pull out and redirect their money into a new golf course over there."

Roberta nodded, understanding his problem. "They're frightened of speculative ventures, right?"

"Exactly."

"And you've already started."

"Yes." Davies looked towards the lean figure of the farmer, silhouetted against the window. "I'm so sorry about this, Mr. Craig. I don't know what else to say."

The farmer turned and let out a long sigh. "No, I appreciate that, Mr. Davies, and I appreciate you coming to tell me. I can see that it must be very hard for you too. You've put a good deal of your own money into this project as well, haven't you?"

"Yes, I have." He drained his mug and place it on the sideboard. "I know that Liz is in Spain at the minute, Mr. Craig, but I hope very much that when you speak to her, you'll pass on my heartfelt apologies to her."

"Well, I won't be telling anyone just yet, Mr. Davies, and I would hope that you might take my advice in doing exactly the same. Not even Gregor." He turned to Davies. "Let's just give it the week. Something might turn up, and then hopefully we can just forget that this conversation ever took place."

Davies shook his head. "I'll have to tell the contractor, Mr. Craig, and Michael Dooney."

"If you haven't told them yet, I wouldn't bother doing so. If you have to hold off construction for a wee while, I'm sure that you can think of an adequate excuse. Remember that this farm has served my family for five generations, Mr. Davies. A week in the life of this place is very short, and it could quite easily result in its future being made secure. I would like to think that we owe it that at least."

Davies contemplated this for a moment. "All right, I'll try to come up with something."

"I'd be most grateful if you could do that," Mr. Craig replied, making his way towards the door that led into the hall, "because if I don't get myself ready for this trip, we'll never get off." He put out his hand to Davies as he passed him. "Goodbye, Mr. Davies. We'll just keep our fingers crossed." He looked quickly in the direction of his house guest. "Maybe you could show Mr. Davies to the door, Roberta."

Roberta smiled at the two men. "I'd be glad to."

He hadn't been away from the house for so long that he could not remember even if he still owned a suitcase. He went through every cupboard on the upper floor of the house, eventually tracking down a dusty object with a handle in the roof-space above the back bathroom. He carried it carefully to his bedroom, opened the window and gave it a few solid whacks against the side of the house, then, laying it on his bed, he stood back to appraise it, hands on hips. It wasn't the most salubrious piece of luggage he had ever seen, definitely not as smart as Roberta's, but it had two good catches, even though they were slightly rusted, and what's more, it wasn't filled with junk. He threw back the lid, then opened his cupboard door and scratched at the back of his head as he considered which of his meagre supply of clothes would be most suited for the trip.

Half an hour later, he came down the stairs with the burden of a severely overfilled suitcase to hand, the cover of a *Farmer's Weekly* flapping out of one of its bulging sides. Ripping it off, he crumpled it up and put it into his jacket pocket, then quickly made his way through to the kitchen. As he entered, he heard Roberta saying words of farewell to someone at the back door. She closed it and came back into the room.

"Sorry I was so long," he said, dropping the suitcase by Roberta's luggage and trying to position himself in such a way that she didn't see it.

"I'm a wee bit out of practice in knowing what to take on a trip like this."

Roberta smiled at him. "That's all right."

He looked towards the back door. "Who was that you were talking to?"

"Oh, only Jonathan Davies."

"What? He's only just gone?"

"Yes, well, we got talking about Australia. He'd been to Sydney once when he was in the navy."

"Had he now?" He took hold of the strap of Roberta's golf bag and swung it onto his shoulder, then picked up a suitcase in each hand. "Right, are you ready to go?"

Roberta made no move towards the back door. "Listen, are you quite happy to go—under the circumstances, I mean?"

Mr. Craig nodded. "Aye, perfectly. We can gain nothing at all by worrying about it at present, so I suggest that we follow the party line and have no mention of it for the next week. So let's away and enjoy ourselves."

"All right. Did you leave the note for Alex?"

"It's on the table."

"Okay then!" She walked through to the back kitchen and opened the door, standing aside to let him out with his load. "He's pretty old-fashioned, isn't he?"

"Who?"

Roberta dropped the snib on the door and pulled it shut behind her. "Jonathan Davies."

He heaved the luggage into the back of the Land Rover. "In what way?"

"Calling you Mr. Craig."

He slammed the door of the vehicle shut and rattled the handle to make sure that it was closed properly. He then leaned his elbow against it and took off his baseball cap and smoothed back his hair. "Well, maybe I should confess something to you."

Roberta gave him a quizzical look. "What?"

"Craig is my surname."

Roberta looked aghast. "You're joking!"

"Not at all."

"Do you mean to say that I've been calling you by your surname all this time?"

"Aye, you have."

"But that's . . . that's dreadful! I mean, why didn't you tell me earlier?"

"Well, just because you started calling me that and I thought it would be an embarrassment to us both if I was to enlighten you, and, well, as it happens, I'm not awful partial to my Christian name in any case."

"And what might that be?"

He laughed. "I'd just rather you called me Craig."

"Come on, tell me your Christian name."

A pink flush rose to his cheeks and he crossed his arms, then unfolded them and scratched at the back of his head. He took a pace towards Roberta and whispered something in her ear, then stood back to watch for her reaction. The expression on her face, however, registered surprise rather than the hilarity that he had anticipated.

"I don't see anything wrong with that name," she said.

The farmer smiled. "Well, it's never been one that I've ever got used to. It was always considered a bit out of the ordinary around here. When I was at the school, it left me open to all sorts of nicknames. "

Roberta nodded. "I've got a pretty silly nickname too back home."

"Have you now?" he sang out, his eyebrows raised in interest. "And what might that be?"

"Bobby. Stupid, isn't it? It's a boy's name."

"Aye, but it's a good name. I had a sheep-dog once called Bobby."

Roberta let out a cry of astonishment. "A sheep-dog!"

"Aye, and an awful loyal one at that." He put his fingers to his mouth and let out a shrill whistle to call in the Jack Russell.

Roberta laughed. "Well, I think that it would be best if we gave that name a miss, just in case you get tempted to start whistling me up!"

Mr. Craig opened up the passenger door of the Land Rover for her. "Aye, well, there might be a good chance of that happening. And I think we'll just stick to Craig as well, shall we?"

Roberta climbed into the vehicle. "Are you sure you don't mind?"

The farmer waited for the dog to scuttle in beside Roberta's feet before slamming the door closed. "Nothing would make me happier."

CHAPTER 19

Liz entered the dining-room of the Hotel Cazaral at exactly eight o'clock the following morning and was surprised to find that, even at that relatively early hour, it was almost full to capacity. As she was shown to a table in the corner of the room she cast an eye around those who were having breakfast and sighed inwardly with relief when she realized that he was not there. She had no idea—nor did she care—whether he had managed to get himself a room in the hotel, but she was taking no chances, her plan being to get away from the place before he put in an appearance. Consequently, as she sat down at the table, she immediately ordered coffee and toast before the waiter had the chance to leave her.

Realizing that she was now going to have to cope with being alone for the duration of her stay, she had been up early that morning to give herself time to go through her Spanish phrase-book, writing down on a piece of hotel letter-heading some sentences that she felt might be of some use to her. She was studying these, head resting in her hands, when a shadow fell across the paper and she looked up with a smile of anticipated gratitude on her face, expecting it to be a waiter asking her if she wanted anything more. But there *he* stood before her, a hold-all in his hand and a watchful look of uncertainty upon his face.

He faced the palm of his free hand towards her and held up two fingers. "Can we declare a truce?" His voice hit a momentary silence in the dining-room, and Liz looked around, noticing that a large family seated three tables away from her own had overheard the remark and were now watching them with intent, having obviously understood his remark. She really did not want him anywhere near her, but on the other hand she didn't want to cause a scene. She gave a brief nod.

"Can I join you?" he asked, pointing to the empty chair at the table.

"If you must, but I'm not going to be here for much longer. I have to summon up my courage to go and ask for a *llave*."

The man twisted up his face, as if he had just received a hard slap on the cheek. "Ouch! I reckon I deserved that." He pulled the chair out and sat down, placing the hold-all beside him. "Actually, as it happens, you don't have to ask for that any more."

"Why not?"

He pointed to the hold-all. "I've been to his room and got everything for you." He paused, scrutinizing her reaction to this. "I hope you don't mind?"

Liz shrugged. "Why should I mind? You're his son and I'm just a friend."

He leaned forward across the table. "Listen," he whispered furtively, "can we just get rid of this hostility bit? I really am trying my best to make amends."

Liz drained her cup of coffee and sat back in her chair, staring at him for a moment. "Could you answer me just one question?"

"Sure."

"What are you doing here?"

He considered this for a moment. "I don't really know."

"That's no answer."

"Maybe, but it's the truth. I was in Madrid on business and I had a couple of days clear, and I knew that my father was in Seville for Semana Santa, so I thought I'd just make a trip down here."

"Because you wanted to see him again."

"Well," he replied, making a gesture of indecision with his head, "let's just say that I was going to leave my options open."

"That's a bit of a change of heart, isn't it? Arthur said that you had returned your plane ticket and that you had said that you didn't want to see him again."

"Yeah, I did say that," he drawled, "but in retrospect I think that it was a pretty childish thing to say."

"But how did you know that he was here in this hotel? You returned everything to him."

"No, not everything. He'd sent me an itinerary along with the plane ticket, and for some reason I held on to that."

A waiter appeared at their table and Arthur's son ordered coffee and toast for himself. He asked Liz if she wanted anything else, but she declined the offer.

"Anyway," he continued, "even after I'd finished my business in Madrid, I was still of two minds as to what I should do. So I just sat in the coffee shop at the airport staring out the window at the planes taking off, trying to work out whether I really wanted to see him again or just forget the whole idea and take a flight back to London. And then I decided that it was pretty dumb going through life not knowing one's father when there was an opportunity of getting to know him, even though he had done irreparable damage to the lives of everyone in my family." He paused for a moment and glanced at Liz. "Maybe you don't know the whole story."

Liz nodded. "Yes, I do. He told me, and I have to say that he did make himself out to be the villain of the piece."

He blew out derisively. "Well, if he told the story straight, he wouldn't have been able to make himself turn out anyway else."

The waiter made his way over to their table, a tray held aloft on his upturned hand. He placed a laden toast-rack on the table and poured out a cup of coffee for the man. "*¿Algo más, señor?*"

He held up a hand. "*No. Nada más.*" He took a sip of coffee, then rested his elbows on the table, linking his hands together. "So, after much deliberation, I booked a flight to Seville. The only trouble was that it was five hours' late, and I arrived tired and angry, mostly because I'd had time to churn things over in my mind and, as a result, had begun to doubt my initial judgement. You know, all those things about a leopard not being able to change its spots." He sat back heavily in his chair and pushed his hands into the pockets of his jacket. "And that was why I jumped to the wrong conclusion with you last night—and if it helps any, I am still *very* sorry for what I said."

Liz bit at her lip, not knowing what to say, his explanation having been so succinct that she now understood totally his reaction to their meeting. She cleared her throat. "So where did you stay last night?"

"Here." He let out a quiet laugh. "Actually, I nicked the old man's room."

"They allowed you to do that?"

"Once they'd studied my passport and seen the names were the same." He leaned forward, his hand outstretched. "Talking of which, I'm Will Kempler."

Liz looked at the hand for a moment, then reached out and took hold of it. His grasp was firm, the palm of his hand surprisingly rough. "And I'm Liz Dewhurst."

He let out a sigh of relief. "Well, Liz Dewhurst, I have to tell you right now that I have been up half the night, cursing my own stupidity and ignorance, and wondering if I would ever get the chance to find out your name."

At that point, they both became aware of someone standing at their table and looked up to see the father of the family which had shown such interest in their initial interchange. He grinned inanely at them, an expression that was mirrored on the faces of the other members of his family, who had all been making moves to leave, but now stood in the centre of the dining-room, gawking in their direction. He craned forward over their table as if he were about to take them into his confidence, and clasped his hands tightly between his knees. "I do hope you don't mind my coming over," he said quietly in a twanging English accent, "but my wife and I couldn't help but notice that you were having a bit of a hard time, and we just wanted to say how delighted we both are that you seem to have made amends, because Seville is just too beautiful a place at the minute to have one's differences." He stood upright and held out his hands. "Now you don't have to say anything, but my wife and I *and* my whole family would just like to let you know that our prayers go with you." He turned to his family, raising his eyebrows to signify a successful mission and bathing them with a smile of self-benevolence before he moved over to where they stood. Then, straddling an arm around the shoulders of both his buck-toothed wife and a stringy teen-age daughter, he led his flock out of the dining-room.

Will screwed his head round to watch them for a moment, then turned back to face Liz. She continued to track them, her mouth open in amazement, as they descended the stairs and walked through the small seating area before disappearing around the corner to the hotel entrance.

Will chuckled. "Wow! That was a bit deep, wasn't it?"

Liz snorted out a laugh. "Deeply embarrassing, more like."

"Oh, well," he said, throwing up his hands dismissively. "Each to his own." He took a drink of coffee and leaned forward on the table. "So, Liz, what are we going to do with Arthur?"

The smile left her face on hearing the word "we." She had never thought for a moment that she would be having to consider the "we" situation. "Well, erm, I . . . I don't really know. I mean, well, what are your plans?"

Will shook his head quite forcefully. "I don't really know either."

There was a moment's uneasy silence. "Maybe," Liz said eventually, "it's for you to decide. You are his son, after all."

Will let out a grunt. "Yes, I was afraid you'd say that."

"What did you expect me to say?"

"No, no, I mean I agree with you entirely. It's just . . . quite difficult."

There was another silence. They both opened their mouths to speak at the same time.

"Sorry."

Liz shook her head. "No, you go on."

"Well, I was going to suggest that we should both go to see him, and then . . . take it from there."

"Don't you have to go back to work?"

"Yes, I do—eventually, but under the circumstances, maybe I shouldn't." He scratched at the back of his head. "Listen, I'm sorry, I'm not being very decisive about this, but the ridiculous thing is that you, as a friend, know him much better than I do, as a son!" He continued his display of uncertainty by pulling hard on his ear-lobe, then suddenly brought his forefingers down hard on the table and beat out a quick drum-roll. "Come on, we'd better try to be methodical about this. When is your return flight booked for?"

"Next Tuesday."

"Right. Well, I would reckon that he'd probably be able to fly home by then, so maybe the best idea would be for me just to stick around and fly back with you. After all, I think it's going to be pretty important that you have someone around who can speak Spanish."

"That's exactly the point that I was going to make. Only my feeling is that now you *are* here, it might be better all round if I just flew home straightaway."

Will shook his head. "That is not a good idea."

"Why not?"

"Because I am fairly sure that Arthur will have booked early to get a discount rate, and if that's the case, your ticket will be non-transferable. If you do change flights, you'll have to pay a hefty surcharge."

Liz felt her heart sink at this news. She had been hoping that this would be considered the optimum idea, not through any disloyalty to Arthur on her part, but because she realized that if she did stay, there would be little alternative other than to spend time with this man whom she really didn't know and of whom she was still quite uncertain.

"And also what has to be taken into consideration," Will continued, "is that you are my father's friend. I think that if you did take an earlier flight home, it may be construed that I'd forced you to do that, and I can tell you that my father and I certainly won't be needing to look for reasons to fall out." He let out a short laugh. "And that's the other reason I don't want you to go. Both my father and I may well need the services of a friendly ombudsman."

Liz looked long at her hands clasped tight together on her lap. There was little alternative. She was going to have to make the best of the changed circumstances, regardless of what they might throw up. She let out a long sigh. "All right." She discarded her napkin onto the table. "Well, maybe we should go to see him."

"Okay!" Will exclaimed, pushing back his chair and getting up. "But before we go, do you have your plane ticket?"

"No, Arthur does. They could be in his room, though."

"I wouldn't know where to look. Can you remember what airline you travelled with?"

"GB Airways."

Will nodded. "Well, my reckoning is that they probably have only one flight a day. I'll have to warn them that they have a passenger with a broken leg, so they can arrange for him to have a row of seats to himself."

Liz took in a long breath. "Goodness, I never thought of that. Do you think that'll be possible right after Semana Santa?"

"No idea." He gave her a wink. "But I can be very persuasive." He picked up the hold-all. "So I'll meet you down in reception in a quarter of an hour."

"All right."

Liz got to her feet and began to follow him out. He had only taken a few paces when he stopped and turned, and she could not avoid bumping into him. He smiled at her. "I really am sorry about last night."

She nodded slowly. "Well, let's hope that we don't have to mention it again."

Arthur was feeling disgruntled. Things were beginning to annoy him intensely, especially the man in the bed next to him. Having regained consciousness after his general anaesthetic, he had been wheeled into his room at four o'clock in the morning, and had hoped that his drowsy state would allow him to continue sleeping. However, it was not to be, because the man, who appeared to have no visible sign of injury or illness, took one look at Arthur's heavily plastered leg and immediately took it upon himself to demonstrate to his new companion that he was the one in much greater need of medical care and attention. Arthur had therefore spent the remaining hours of the night listening to his neighbour turning constantly in his bed, each move being accompanied by a long moan or a loud groan. The noise, what's more, was further exacerbated by the vociferous, though no doubt comforting, tones of his middle-aged and quite unattractive daughter, who was having to stand night-time vigil over him, snatching at rare moments of rest in the discomfort of what looked like an un-upholstered dentist's chair.

Besides all this, he had begun to feel quite alone—and quite bored, and even though he was being fed a regular supply of pain-killers his leg still ached, and he was becoming increasingly conscious of an itch that had developed under his plaster-cast, somewhere just up from his fourth toe. He also missed his pipe sorely. He knew that it was sitting in his bedside cabinet, but he could neither reach it nor was he allowed to smoke it. The nurse who had assisted in the operation to set his leg had made this abundantly clear to him when she had wrestled it from his clutches in the operating theatre, giving him express instructions by way of sign language not even to think of putting a match to it in the hospital.

Nevertheless, of all his concerns, his greatest was for Liz. He hadn't realized that she wasn't with him until he had woken up just before they took him down to the operating theatre. He had become quite agitated about her whereabouts, but the young doctor, who bore a somewhat disconcerting resemblance to Buddy Holly, had explained to him in pretty poor English that he had suggested that she should return to the hotel. When he had then let slip that he had given her directions to walk, Arthur had blown up, asking why the hell he hadn't thought of getting her a taxi, because she was incapable of finding her way to the bloody cathedral in Seville, let alone her hotel. This had obviously been the wrong simile to make with the young man, because at that point he had walked away from Arthur without response, only returning to administer an injection with about as much delicacy as a bayonet thrust.

He now lay prostrate on the bed, staring at the blank white walls of the room. There was no chance that he could go back to sleep, the man next to him now snoring away quite contentedly. He pushed himself up awkwardly to a sitting position and turned around as far as he could to try to rearrange his pillows, but in doing so he caught the blanked-off needle that stuck out of the vein in his forearm. "Damnation!" he cried out in pain. "What the hell is this thing doing in my arm anyway?" The man's daughter looked across at him, a pleading look on her face as she held a finger to her lips. She pointed to her slumbering father. "Oh, that's a good one!" he mumbled to himself. "It's a damned pity you can't make *him* shut up for a minute."

At that point a well-built nurse, dressed in a white uniform that strained across her ample frontage, came bustling into the room and unclipped the chart from the bottom of his bed.

"Excuse me," he asked, his voice edged with irritation. "Could you tell me why is it so necessary for me to have this thing in my arm?"

The nurse did not reply, but simply smiled at him, replaced the clipboard and left the room.

"Oh, for heaven's sakes!" he exclaimed in a loud voice. "Why can't anyone speak English around here?"

"Well, if there's anyone in this hospital who does, they'll no doubt have heard you by now."

He turned to see Liz smiling at him in the doorway. "Liz! Am I glad to see you! I was wondering whether you'd ever made it back to the hotel or not."

"Arthur, don't you think you should talk a bit quieter?" she said, glancing at the sleeping man as she walked around the bottom of his bed. "You'll wake him up." She cast a sympathetic smile at the woman who sat beside him, clutching his hand.

"Good riddance, too. He's kept *me* awake ever since I got in here."

"Arthur!"

"Don't worry! Neither he nor his daughter can understand a bloody word I'm saying."

"Maybe not, but I'm sure that she can understand from your tone that you're not being over-friendly." Liz eyed the plastered leg, supported by a cantilevered bracket above the bed. "So how is it this morning?"

"Bloody sore."

"I'm sure it is. Are they giving you pain-killers?"

"Yes, but I don't think they're strong enough."

"What? Not up to Jack Daniel's, then?"

Arthur grunted a laugh. "Certainly not!" He leaned forward towards Liz, a furtive look in his eye. "Talking of which, you don't think you could . . ."

"Not on your life, Arthur! Just wait until you come out!"

"I thought you might say that," he groaned, slumping back against his pillows. "So that's it—the holiday period's over, is it? You now change back into being the Scottish schoolmistress."

Liz reached a hand slowly forward towards the needle that protruded from Arthur's arm. "Do you want me to give that a not-so-gentle turn in your arm?"

"Don't you touch that!" he cried out, covering the needle with his hand.

"Well then, don't be so grumpy, and don't go taking your misfortunes out on me. Anyway, there's someone here to see you that might cheer you up a bit."

"Who?"

"I'm not telling you. It's a surprise."

"Male or female?"

"Male."

Arthur raised his eyebrows. "Hell's teeth, I break my leg, end up in hospital, and you go off picking up stray men all over the place."

"My word, you *are* feeling sorry for yourself, aren't you? As a matter of fact, I did not pick him up. He was at the hotel when I arrived back there last night."

"Good-looking, is he?"

Liz laughed. "Arthur, he is devastating! But I have worked out that it's probably in his genes."

"That's all I need," he droned. "Some dark-eyed Spaniard coming to ogle over my . . ." He turned around when he became aware of the figure that stood in the doorway, clutching a hold-all in both hands, and the gloom lifted like a veil from his eyes when he saw who it was. "My word! Will! What on earth are you doing here?"

Will entered the room and came to stand at the bottom of Arthur's bed. "How are you feeling?" he asked, putting down the hold-all beside the bed. When he straightened up, Liz could tell that the smile on his face was forced.

Arthur pushed himself up in the bed. "Fine! Fine! Never better." He looked at his son, shaking his head in disbelief. "Well, this is wonderful! I wasn't sure whether . . ." He trailed off and reached for the glass of water on the bedside cabinet and took a drink.

Will frowned. "You weren't sure whether what?"

Arthur fixed a broad grin on his face. "I wasn't sure whether it was you at first in the doorway. But how marvellous that you've come."

"Well, it was an on-the-spur decision," Will replied with little animation in his voice. He looked down at Arthur's leg. "So how is it? Nothing too trivial, I hope."

Liz saw immediately from Arthur's open-mouthed expression that the remark was hurtful. "Will," she said guardedly.

Will let out a quiet laugh. "It's all right. It was meant as a joke." He placed both hands on the rail at the bottom of the bed. "So, what's to be done with you?"

Arthur shook his head. "Not a lot, I wouldn't think. I have no idea how long I'm going to be here."

"Three days at the most," Will replied, pushing himself away from the bed. He leaned back against the wall and folded his arms across his chest.

Arthur's eyes widened at the news. "How did you find that out?"

"I've just been to see your doctor. He wants you out of here as soon as possible. He says that you're too much of a liability."

"I am not! I've been a model patient so far."

"Oh, yeah? And model patients try to light up their pipes in the operating theatre, do they?"

Arthur bit at his lip to suppress a grin. "Well, I was slightly disoriented."

"I'm sure you were."

"Listen," Liz interjected, trying to balk any chance of a confrontation between the two men. "Now that we know that Arthur will be out of hospital by the weekend at least, maybe we should think about what we're going to do."

Will screwed up the side of his mouth as he considered the scant alternatives to hand. "Well, we can't do much other than get him back to the hotel, and kill time there until we fly home on Tuesday."

Arthur shot a querying look from one to the other. "We?"

Will unfolded his arms and dug his hands into the pockets of his jeans. "Yes, well, I didn't think that it would be fair for Liz to struggle back with you by herself, so . . . I've rung the office and told them that I'm going to take a week off."

"Right," Arthur said quietly. "Well, that's very kind of you, Will."

"Don't mention it. I couldn't very well abandon a sinking ship, now could I?"

There was a definite note of provocation in his final delivery. However, the need for an answer was avoided by the appearance of the busty nurse, who sailed into the room and cleared a space around Arthur's bed without issuing any form of command, relying solely on her considerable size. She stuck a thermometer under Arthur's tongue, unhooked the notes from the bottom of his bed, squeezed the big toe of his plastered leg until she saw him wince, wrote something down, withdrew the thermometer and wrote down the reading, then replaced the clipboard and walked out of the room, saying something in passing to the sleeping man's daughter, who sniggered and turned to look at Arthur, making no attempt to hide the smile of amusement on her face.

"I bet that nurse said something about me," he said out of the corner of his mouth, his eyes narrowed in suspicion at the woman.

Will laughed. "Yes, she did, actually."

Arthur glanced up at his son. "Dammit, of course! I was forgetting you speak this language! What did she say?"

"You wouldn't want to know."

"I certainly would."

"All right. She said that she was sorry that this woman here had to suffer being in a room with two grumpy old men."

"She never did!"

"God's truth."

Arthur humphed. "What nerve! I'm at least ten years younger than him."

"I think that we should get back to talking about the plan of action," Liz cut in, not wishing to give Will the chance to needle his father, even though it was being done ostensibly with humorous intent. "Are you happy with what's been suggested, Arthur?"

He turned to gaze out the window as he contemplated Liz's question. "No, not really."

"What do you mean, not really!" Will exclaimed, frustrated at his father's apparent belligerence. "There's no altern—"

"I know! I know!" Arthur broke in, holding up his hands defensively. "Please just let me explain before you bite my head off!" He paused, watching Will closely. "All I was just wondering," he continued in a slow, reasoning voice, "was whether we couldn't get away from Seville for a bit. If I go back to the hotel on Friday, I doubt I'm going to get much rest at all, what with Semana Santa coming to its climax. And there's surely going to be a great many more people around over the weekend."

"Maybe we should consider first what Liz wants to do. She might still want to see it all."

The two men looked in her direction, awaiting her reply. She shook her head. "What I want to do is the least of our considerations. Arthur has to be the priority now."

Arthur smiled at her. "I'm sorry about all this, Liz. It's really mucked everything up, but you do still have until Friday. If you do want to go and join in with the parades, I'm sure Will would accompany you." He glanced at his son. "Wouldn't you, Will?"

"Of course."

Arthur brought his hands down on the bed, as if he had successfully put an auction lot under the hammer. "Good! That's decided then."

"But have you any idea where we would go?" Liz asked, "or, more to the point, *how* we would go? You're not going to be fit for travel, are you?"

"I don't see why not. I'd have to get back to the hotel somehow, so I'm sure an extra few hours in a car wouldn't harm me."

"But we don't have a car."

"I'm sure we could hire one, couldn't we, Will?"

Will nodded. "I would think so. It would have to be a pretty big one to allow you to get stretched out in it."

"Great! In that case, fix it up, could you? I'll pay for it and claim it back on my travel insurance."

Liz laughed. "But we still don't have a clue where we would go!"

"No, we don't, do we?" Arthur scratched pensively at the day's growth of stubble on his chin. "You know Spain, Will. Do you have any ideas?"

"None at all, I'm afraid. I don't really know around here too well.

Madrid's been my stamping ground." He pushed himself away from the wall. "But I'm sure that the hotel would be able to recommend someplace. Liz and I could go back there now and make some inquiries."

A dark expression of gloom came over Arthur's face at this suggestion. "You don't both need to go, do you?"

"What?" asked Will. "You want Liz to stay here to hold your hand?"

"I don't mind staying," Liz said quickly.

"Look." Will bent down and picked up the hold-all and placed it on the bottom of the bed. He undid the zip and took out two paperback books and threw them into Arthur's lap. "Those should keep you entertained."

Arthur held one of the books at arm's length as he viewed the title. "My goodness! Mickey Spillane! I haven't read one of these for ages."

Will shrugged his shoulders. "Well, I don't remember much about you, but I do recall there always being a pile of those books by your bed."

Arthur looked up at his son, wide-eyed in wonderment. "You remember that?" He laughed. "Not the most auspicious memory for a son to have of his renegade father, but nevertheless, I am deeply touched that you can recollect anything of me at all. Thank you." He reached across to the bedside cabinet for his reading spectacles and put them on, then opened the book and began reading immediately.

"So do you want me to stay?" Liz asked him.

Arthur glanced at her over the top of his spectacles. "What?"

"I asked if you wanted me to stay."

"No! No!" Arthur replied, finding it difficult to drag his eyes away from the book. "It'd be much better if you went with Will. He'll probably need a hand choosing a place to stay."

Liz laughed. "So we have your permission to leave you."

Arthur had gone back to reading the book. He looked up. "Of course, of course!" he said, waving his hand in dismissal. "You head off."

Will gestured to hurry her away before Arthur changed his mind. She gave a friendly smile to the daughter of Arthur's room-mate in passing as she and Will walked quickly to the door.

"You will come back, I trust?" They both turned simultaneously to look at Arthur. His eyes still hadn't left the book. "These won't keep me amused forever, you know."

Liz caught Will raising his eyes heavenward. "No, Arthur, we'll be back later."

"And when would that be?" he asked, this time looking up at them.

Liz opened her mouth to reply, but Will pre-empted her. "When we have everything sorted out, all right? Probably this evening."

Arthur nodded. "Good. I'll see you then."

Will pressed the button on the lift and stood back to watch the lights above the door flash out the changing floor levels. "So what do you feel like doing today?"

"Not a great deal, to be perfectly honest," Liz replied, leaning her shoulder against the wall of the corridor. "I'm feeling quite washed out after all the goings-on over the past twelve hours. If you wouldn't mind, I think that I might just go to bed and try to catch up on some sleep."

The lift doors opened and they both entered. He pressed the button for the ground floor. "Well, that suits me fine. I've got a bit of work to do anyway, *and* I'll have to try to find somewhere that we can all stay." The lift clunked to a halt and the doors opened. They made their way along the corridor towards the main entrance. "I would suggest that we maybe meet up later this evening and go get something to eat."

"What about seeing Arthur?" Liz asked, stopping momentarily to allow the automatic doors to open up in front of her.

"We don't have to make it that late. Anyway, I'll take on visiting duties. I'm going to have to spend the night with him, at any rate."

"Is that necessary?"

"So the doctor told me. Seemingly, it's the way the system works over here. They look after him during the day, but at night, it's over to the family."

They had reached the pavement beside the bustling Ronda de

Capuchinos, and Will walked over to the edge of the thoroughfare and looked both ways for a taxi. Liz went to stand beside him. "I could do that, if you like."

Will shook his head. "No, I think you deserve to take it easy tonight." He turned and gave her a wide grin. "Besides, it'll give us an opportunity to do a bit of father-son bonding, and no doubt we'll get on a hell of a lot better if he's asleep for most of the time!" He let out a shrill whistle and waved his hand at a taxi that was approaching them on their side of the road. They watched as it veered across from the central lane in a heart-stopping manoeuvre before coming to a standstill beside them. He spoke briefly to the driver and opened the door for Liz, and they had hardly the time to settle themselves in their seats before the man took off again, pulling out into the street without a backward glance, his actions resulting in a sickening squeal of brakes behind them and the furious pumping of at least three car-horns.

Will was silent for a moment, then blew out a sigh of relief. "Okay, so if we're lucky to make it back to the hotel in one piece, what time do you want to meet up this evening?"

Liz did not reply immediately, but stared out of the window at the passing traffic. She turned to look at him, a half-smile on her face. "Listen, please don't feel that you have to take me out, just because of the way things are at the minute. I can understand that it must be quite awkward for you . . . as it is for me." She paused for a moment, but continued when she saw that he was about to speak. "You see, I'm not very good company right now, as you can probably guess from what I told you last night. I was all right with Arthur, because he knew . . ."

"I'm looking forward to taking you out."

Liz cast him a querying look. "Why?"

"Because I need to talk, and I think that you probably need to talk as well."

She shook her head. "I have nothing that's worth saying any more. I mean, not just to you . . . to anyone. To go over the same old ground again would just be self-indulgence."

"Great! So let's be self-indulgent! Maybe it's fate. Maybe we've been thrown together in this far outpost to be self-indulgent together."

Liz laughed. "I think that you could be manipulating the path of destiny just to suit yourself."

"I know! It's fun, isn't it? So, I shall ask you again. What time tonight?"

"I don't know," she replied quietly.

"What? I don't know, you don't want to come; or I don't know, you don't know what time to make it?"

Liz smiled at him. "The second, I suppose."

He nodded at her, a triumphant grin on his face. "Good! In that case, we'll meet at seven o'clock in the bar."

"I don't have much to wear; I mean, for going out."

He cast an eye over her from head to foot. "I'm sure you'll look just fine."

At a quarter to seven that evening she was looking anything but just fine, due to the fact that she had slept as if comatose throughout the day and had forgotten to set her alarm clock. It was only Alex's telephone call at half past six that had woken her, and when, during the course of their conversation, he had announced in quite a matter-of-fact way that he was alone in the house because his grandfather had gone off to the west coast with an Australian woman to play golf, she had questioned him for much longer than time allowed. She now ran around the bedroom in her bra and knickers, her mind buzzing with mixed emotions about the inexplicable antics of her father, while at the same time wondering why it was that every time she had to go out in the evening she went through this palaver of trying to decide what she should wear. She pulled her meagre supply of dresses from the wardrobe one by one and held each up in turn in front of the full-length mirror on the wall before discarding them onto the bed, at the same time rubbing hard at her wet hair with a towel. They all seemed so unsophisticated, so . . . country-bumpkin-like. When the wardrobe was completely devoid of articles of clothing she went through the process in reverse, eventually settling for a pale-blue short-sleeved summer frock, more out of desperation than choice. She pulled it on over her head and contorted her arms around the back to pull up the zip, then gave the wrinkles a forceful brush-out with her hands. She found a lamb's-wool cardigan that was as good a match as she could muster, then made her way quickly through to the bathroom to put on her make-up.

Having made a hurried job on her mascara and eye-liner, she screwed out her lipstick and puckered up her lips, but then stopped with it held inches from her mouth and stared at her reflection in the mirror. Her pursed mouth matched perfectly the look of contempt in her eyes. What on earth did he think he was doing? His wife, her mother, had only died less than a year ago, and surely theirs was now a happy and complete-enough household without some other woman being introduced into it. Heavens, she'd only been away for five days and he was already galli-vanting around with some person that she'd never met! She stopped her thoughts there, suddenly realizing how much she was distorting the truth, beginning to understand that she herself was the source of her anger and frustration. She slowly let her hands fall to the edge of the basin and lowered her eyes to avoid looking at her own reflection. Why are you reading into this something that you know full well isn't there? Just think on what Alex took time to explain, you stupid, embittered woman. Your father was doing this out of the kindness of his heart, to help someone who was in need of friendship, of company, of solace. You're resentful of his selfless nature, jealous of his ability to carry on with life, while you cannot cope with what you have lost. She looked back up at the mirror and saw the freshly applied eye make-up run in blackened streaks down her cheeks. She coughed out a sob, and then felt other sobs take hold, juddering her body and gripping her stomach as fiercely as birth-pains. She bent down and laid her face on her hands. Oh, Dad, I'm so sorry. I'm so sorry. I didn't mean to think that of you. My mind is just so twisted, so resentful. She bent up her head so that she was looking at her poor, pathetic reflection in the mirror. Oh, Gregor, why did you do this to me? Why—did—you—do—this—to—me?

The telephone rang insistently in the bedroom. She listened, but made no move to answer it. It kept ringing. She pulled a long strip of lavatory paper from the roll and wiped her eyes, then blew her nose as she walked through to the bedroom. She picked up the receiver. "Hullo?" she asked, her voice croaky.

"Hi. It's me. Will."

"Oh, hullo," she replied, trying to lighten her tone to sound as if she were pleased to hear from him. It came out thin and wavery.

"It's ten past seven. Just wondered how you were getting on."

She took in a deep breath to try to steady her voice. "Will, would you mind if we didn't go out tonight?"

There was a silence at the other end of the line. "Are you all right?"

She cupped her hand over the receiver and cleared her throat. She brought it back to her mouth. "Yes, I'm fine. I'm just not feeling very well."

There was another silence. "Okay," he said quietly. "There's always another night."

She replaced the receiver and sat down on the bed and covered her face with her hands. Well done, she thought to herself, there's one more missed opportunity. No doubt you'll be making those kind of feeble, stupid excuses for the rest of your sad, lonely life. She gave her nose a hard blow on the piece of lavatory paper and got up and walked slowly back to the bathroom, taking off her cardigan as she went. She chucked it over the towel-rail and turned on the hot-water tap in the basin, and cupping her hands under the steaming flow, she threw water onto her face, caring little for the fact that it was almost too hot to bear. She took a towel and rubbed hard at her face, looking in the mirror to see if she had managed to remove every stain of make-up from her cheeks. She had been successful on that account, but what proved indelible were the puffed eyes and red nose. She shook her head. How attractive. How wonderfully, bloody attractive.

There were two sharp knocks on the door of her room. She stood with the towel pressed against her mouth and listened. Whoever it was would go away again if she didn't answer. She walked quietly through to the bedroom and stared at the door. There were two further knocks. "*¿Señora?*" The voice seemed extraordinarily high-pitched, but she was sure it was male. She took two steps towards the door.

"Yes?"

"*Servicio de habitaciones, señora.*"

Liz threw the towel onto the bed. "All right. If you could just give me a minute, please." She gave each eye a rub with the back of her hand, pulled in a long sniff and walked over to the door and opened it.

Will stood with the side of his head in his hand, his elbow resting on the door-frame. "Hi. I thought you might not answer the door if you knew it was me."

Liz looked at him. His hair, still wet from his shower, was swept back sleek across his head, and she noticed that the collar of his corduroy jacket was damp where the mass of sandy blond curls touched it. He was dressed no differently from when she had seen him last, but his shirt and jeans were freshly laundered. She lowered her head, so that he couldn't see her face and so that she didn't have to look into his piercing blue eyes. "Will, I really meant what I said. I'm not feeling very well."

"Right. So that's why you've got yourself all dressed up, is it?"

"I am not dressed up. This . . . thing is as old as the hills."

"It doesn't matter how old it is. It's how you look in it, and I think you look pretty good."

She heard a rustle as he moved his position, and felt his hand cup under her chin. He lifted her face to look at him. "What's happened, Liz?" he asked quietly.

The kindness in his voice was too much for her to stand. She felt the misery well up inside her again, and her face crumpled. "I just feel so . . ." She could say no more, the convulsive sobs returning.

He put an arm around her shoulders and pulled her close into his body. "Hey, hey, hey," he said soothingly. "Come on, things can't be that bad."

"Can't they?" she sobbed. "How would *you* know?"

"Okay, okay, so maybe I don't know." He took her arms and put them around his body. "But how about a hug between friends to get things on the right road?" He held her tight to him. "There, that's better, isn't it?"

The feel of his body was too familiar. The taut muscles in his back, the squareness of his frame, the power of the arms that enfolded her. Only the height and the smell, some expensive aftershave that Gregor would never dare or afford to wear, were different. She pushed herself away from him and stood back, knowing that the look she gave him was filled with contempt. He read it well, and took in a deep breath, placing his hands on the small of his back. "I'm sorry," he said quietly. "I didn't mean to—"

She held up her hand to stop him. "No. It's not for you to apologize. Only maybe now you realize what kind of wilting flower you're dealing with."

"I don't think you're a wilting flower. You may be a deeply hurt person, but you're no wilting flower. But, on the other hand, maybe you understand now how I feel about my father—someone whom you love deeply, whom you trust, who one day just . . . gets up and walks out of your life." He stuck his hands in the pockets of his jeans. "I know what you're talking about, Liz. I've been there. The circumstances may be different, but it never stops hurting."

Liz turned to look at him. "But you're all right. You're not like me."

"Really? I have a job that takes me all over the world. Why? Because I don't want to settle down. Why don't I want to settle down? Because I don't want to meet a girl and marry her. Why don't I want to marry? Gadzooks! The problem has just been solved." He paused for a moment and cast his eyes around the room. "You can never get away from it all, you know, but you sure as hell have to make the best of what you've got." He walked across to her and took hold of both her hands. "Tell me, what was your husband called?"

She looked up at him. "Why do you want to know?"

"I just want to know his name."

"Gregor."

"Well, in that case, *fuck* you, Gregor, and *fuck* you, Dad." He looked at her, a broad smile on his face. "You should try saying that—not about my dad, that's my prerogative, but you can say that about your husband."

Liz shook her head. "No, I couldn't. I've never said that about him."

"But I sure as hell know that you felt like saying that about him."

Liz lowered her head to hide the smile that had unwittingly come across her face. Once again, he cupped his hand under her chin and pulled it up so that she was looking directly into his eyes. "Go on, say it."

She paused, finding it difficult to stop the smile creasing her face. "Fuck you, Gregor," she said quietly.

"No, no." He considered her delivery like a stage director might rehearse one of his star actors. "Not enough feeling. Try it again."

Liz didn't know if she was laughing or crying. "FUCK YOU, GREGOR!"

"Good for you," he said quietly. He put his arms around her shoulders and once more pulled her close to his chest. She pushed her face against the lapel of his jacket, feeling the tears run down her cheeks, yet knowing there was a broad smile on her face. It slipped slowly away when her eyes focused on the open door of her bedroom. She pushed herself away from Will and made a gesture with her eyes for him to look behind him. Will turned and together they stared out into the corridor. There stood the family—the father, the buck-toothed wife, the stringy teen-age daughter, and all the rest of them. Will turned to Liz and bit on his lip to stop himself from laughing. He looked back at the family and gave them a wave with his hand. "Hi, there," he called out in a cheery voice.

The father did not reply, but gave them both an icy stare before walking away, his body bowed in dejection. Only the wife flashed them an uneasy smile before they all scurried off after their leader.

"Oh dear," Will said slowly. "I think that we two lost souls are just about to become the 'intrigue' of the hotel."

Liz blurted out a laugh. "It's your fault if we are."

Will shrugged his shoulders. "Yeah, I suppose it is." He let out a deep sigh. "But that's what happens when I get hungry. I get all sort of tensed up and say outrageous things." He smiled warmly at her. "So, how about joining me for something to eat, so nothing more outrageous can be said?"

Liz hesitated for a moment. Go on, she thought to herself, get on with life. Don't be such a miserable idiot. She nodded. "Well, you'll have to give me time to put on some make-up."

"Don't you know," Will said, leaning back against the wall and folding his arms and crossing one leather riding boot over the other, "that time means very little in Spain?"

From the outside, there was no way of knowing that it was a restaurant, save for the small glass cabinet that housed the menu, handwritten in Spanish on pink paper, which was attached to the wall at a height that deemed it only readable by someone over six feet tall. Will opened the heavy, riveted wooden door and ushered Liz into a small high stoned-walled courtyard, the length of which was lined with round white-clothed tables, each lit by a single candle held within a bulbous and ornately engraved glass hurricane lantern. A wooden pergola stretched the full length of the terrace, laden with an unruly twist of vines that drooped so low in places that the black-waistcoated waiters had to dodge their heads to the side as they hurried between the kitchens and the farthest tables, where the majority of those already dining were seated. At the other end of the courtyard open French windows led inside to a small room that only had space for four tables, all occupied.

Will glanced in at the crowded area. "Are you going to be all right eating outside? It's not that warm, is it?"

Liz looked around the restaurant. "This is wonderful. I would hate to eat inside. There's so much . . . atmosphere out here."

A grinning waiter approached them, deftly flicking his white dishcloth over his shoulder as he walked. "*Buenas noches, señores.*"

"*Buenos noches. He reservado una mesa.*"

"Vale. ¿Su nombre, señor?"

"Kempler."

"Por supuesto. Sigame, por favor."

He led them to a table half-way along the terrace, an agreeable distance from the main cluster of diners. He pulled out a chair for Liz.

"¿Es un poco frío esta noche, verdad?" Will remarked.

The waiter laughed. *"Sí, señor, pero no aquí. Tenemos braseros."* He bent down and lifted up the white table-cloth and the thick woollen blanket that lay beneath it. A wooden deck, matching the size of the table-top, was attached to the legs of the table just above ground level, and a hole had been cut into its centre to accommodate a large cast-iron pan that brimmed with glowing embers. *"¡Hay mucho calor aquí, señor!"*

Will smiled at him. *"Muchas gracias."* He pulled out his chair and sat down opposite Liz.

"That's a bit dangerous, isn't it?" Liz remarked furtively, once the waiter had left them.

"Not if you work it right. Pick up the blanket, stick it over your knees and put your feet up on the platform."

Will watched Liz as she did as he had suggested, and saw the comforting smile come over her face as she began to feel the heat from the brazier. "That is remarkable!"

"Well, in rural areas of Spain, it's still the main heating system for many of the houses. That's why so many Spaniards suffer during the winter from frost-bitten faces and chilblained knees."

"They don't really, do they?"

Will laughed. "No, I doubt it. I think it's what one might call an old wives' tale." He caught the waiter's eye and beckoned him over to the table. "Now, what would you like to drink?"

"I think, er, just a glass of white wine, please."

"Well, let's go mad and have a bottle." He glanced up at the waiter, who had come to stand beside their table. *"Una botella de vino blanco de la casa."*

"Sí, señor." The waiter turned to go, but spun round when Will called him back.

"Y queremos comer pronto."

"Vale. Les voy a traer la carta." He turned, ducking his head instinctively to avoid the trailing vine, and headed off quickly towards the interior restaurant.

Will pulled his chair forward and leaned his elbows on the table. "So where have you been eating with my father while you've been out here?"

"Nowhere like this. We usually just grab something in a tapas bar, and then head off again to join in with the processions."

Will nodded and let out a sigh. "I'm sorry about all this happening. It's rather ruined your reason for being out here. If you want, we could always go out after dinner and see what's happening."

"No, thank you!" Liz replied, holding up her hands in refusal of his offer. "I can tell you, it's quite a relief not having to walk the soles off my shoes for one night."

The waiter brought over the menus and the bottle of wine and poured a splash into Will's glass, who waved his hand for the wine to be poured without being tasted. Then, picking up his glass, he held it forward to the centre of the table. "So, what shall we drink to?"

Liz waited for her wine to be poured, then picked up her glass and gave his question a moment's thought. "Arthur's speedy recovery?"

"Good one." He reached over and clinked Liz's glass. "Arthur's speedy recovery . . . and starting over."

She gave him an inquiring look. "What do you mean?"

"Well, I think it's probably time that we all stopped living in the past, and tried to make the best of what life will deal out for us in the future, don't you?"

She slowly lowered her glass to the table and averted her eyes from his. "That's a difficult one."

"I know it is, but we all have to start somewhere, don't we?"

She looked up. His glass was still raised. She smiled at him and held up her glass. "I suppose so." They brought their glasses together once more.

"So, Liz Dewhurst, what about telling me your life story?"

Liz shook her head. "There's not much to say, other than what I told you in my garbled version last night. I'd much rather hear about you. Arthur told me that you were in oil."

"For my sins, yes."

"Why do you say that?"

Will shrugged. "Well, things change. What I do now is a world apart from when I first joined the industry."

Liz settled her arms on the table and watched him intently. "In what way?"

"It's not very interesting, you know."

"And neither is my story."

Will laughed. "All right, if you insist. Where do you want me to start?"

"At the beginning?"

"Okay. Well, I was brought up in a suburb of Toronto with my mother and two elder sisters—and no father, of course."

"Was your mother blonde?" Liz cut in.

"No." He smiled and ran his fingers through his hair. "Ah, you're wondering about my colouring, aren't you? I don't know where that came from. Somewhere in the hidden depths of my family background, no doubt. When I was young, I remember my father saying that it was the milkman, and being pretty naïve at that tender age, I always thought that the milkman had changed the colour of my hair by pouring milk all over my head when I was a baby. It wasn't until I was quite a bit older that I realized what he really meant. Anyway, to continue, I went through high school there, and at the age of eighteen—I was just about to go to a local college when the last of my sisters got married—it was then that I decided to leave home."

"Why then?"

"Well, I didn't want to be the only one left at home, and it seemed a better time than any. My mother had just met up with this man who made her as happy as she had been since my father left her. He then became a sort of fixture in the house, and seeing that I didn't get on too well with him, and the feeling was obviously reciprocated, I thought it best if I wasn't around to rock the boat."

"So what did you do?"

"I managed to wangle myself an American work permit and headed up to Alaska, where I got a greenhorn job as a right-of-way inspector and surveyor on the oil pipeline that linked Prudhoe Bay on the Arctic Ocean with the terminal at Valdez. I was up there, freezing my butt off for nine months, before a whole squad of us were moved down to Argentina to work on a new oil development project that was starting up there."

"That sounds a little more exciting."

"It was, and also pretty educational. That's where I learned to speak Spanish. Anyway, after six months there, I was assigned to the drilling division of the company as a surveyor. We worked way down in the south of the country in the Comodoro Rivadavia area on wild-cat exploration, which means that we carried out high-risk investigation of prospective development sites. We became quite a tight-knit team, all hands-on, and because of the nature of our work we were treated with a healthy respect by the other rednecks who worked the routine development wells and work-over rigs. When we went on leave to Rio or Buenos Aires, we'd walk into a casino and the regulars would stand aside and allow us unhindered passage to the bar. No one messed with us. Mind you, it was probably because we all stank after a month of wild-cat drilling."

Liz laughed. "So, what happened then?"

"Well, a number of things. The oil prices crashed a couple of years beforehand, the economy was up the creek and corruption was rife. So my company decided to stop all further exploration in Argentina, and we were packed off to new pastures."

"Did oil production stop completely there?"

"No way. It's still going strong. There was a wave of privatization in Argentina a few years ago, and quite a number of Spanish companies returned there in force. That's why I come out to Spain so much now. Most of our Argentinian operation is handled from Madrid."

"So where did you go then?"

"The North Sea for eight years. Based in Aberdeen." He juddered his shoulders. "God, that was cold work! And then we went over to the Philippines."

"Now, *that* must have been considered a cushy number!"

"You'd think so, wouldn't you? As it happened, it was, and still is, a difficult *and* delicate assignment. When we first arrived out there, offshore oil exploration was in its relative infancy, but nevertheless, by this time 'the environment' had become a buzzword, and we found ourselves having to carry out lengthy negotiations at every level—provincial, regional, national, governmental—before we were able to do so much as lift a finger."

"Why there so much?"

"Because the Philippines happen to have one of the most pristine physical environments on earth. Each of the seven thousand islands is surrounded by coral reefs and phenomenal marine life."

Liz gave him a knowing look. "And you would rather have just gone in and drilled."

"No, actually, I have to say that that is the fallacy! Contrary to what everybody thinks, oil companies are pretty careful when it comes to protecting marine environment. In fact, I sympathized so much with the conservational aspect of it all that I always found myself saying the right thing in front of the governmental officials, and they got to like me—and trust me. And all this came to the attention, or maybe was *drawn* to the attention, of the big brass in the Madrid head office, and before I could say 'oil boom,' I was made Chief Negotiator on Environmental Issues for the company."

"And that's what you are now."

"In a way." He grimaced. "Only now I have a grander title. Health, Safety and Environment Manager of Kalmex Oil Exploration, Inc."

"Wow!" Liz looked suitably impressed. "But you said earlier on that things had changed. In what way?"

Will shrugged. "Because I don't drill any more. I am a negotiator, an ambassador, a corporate diplomat, and I'm pretty good at all of it, if you can excuse me for blowing my own trumpet. But I'm a harder and more knowledgeable man than I was back then. I have to be. And sometimes I don't like myself for it. I'd rather be back working with the team."

"Are they still together?"

"A few of the diehards are. I caught up with them the other day in Aberdeen, and having a couple of days to kill, I went out with them to one of the rigs. It was pure nostalgia. For the first time in goodness knows how long, I got my hands dirty again." He stretched the upturned palms of his hands over the table for Liz to view them. At the base of each finger and across the lower joints was a multitude of broken blisters. "And sore."

Liz laughed. "Yes, I can see those are worker's hands."

She found herself totally unprepared for his next move. He reached across and took hold of the hand with which she had been supporting her face, turning it so that the palm faced upwards. He brushed a finger across its surface. "And so is that."

The physical, almost intimate contact hit her like an electric shock. Abruptly, she pulled her hand away from his grasp and sat back in her chair to distance herself from him. "Yes, well, needs must," she said curtly, glancing around the restaurant, anywhere to avoid coming into eye contact with him.

Her moment of embarrassment was broken by the waiter, who came to stand by their table, a smile on his face and a pen poised expectantly over his pad. Will picked up the menu.

"Right. So what do you feel like having?"

Liz shook her head. "I'm not sure."

Will glanced quickly at the fare. "Okay. In that case, do you like pork?"

"Yes."

"Good. Well, that's a safe bet around here." He looked up at the waiter. "*Dos solomillos.*"

"*Vale, señor. ¿Con patatas y verduras?*"

"*Sí.*"

"*Gracias, señor.*" He whisked the menu from Will's clutches and headed off towards the kitchen.

Will leaned forward on the table and watched Liz closely. He had noticed in the instance before she had averted her eyes from his that they had registered a completely different reaction to the one he had witnessed in her hotel bedroom. There was no contempt this time, only a profound fear. "I'm sorry. That was an insensitive thing to do. I think it's probably because I've been in male company too long. I don't get much chance to understand the finer points of life."

Liz shook her head in dismissal of his apology. "Have you never had a girl-friend?"

He gave the question thought before replying. "No. Not really. I've had the occasional fling in different parts of the world, but that's all they were. I'm just too busy to get caught up in any long-term commitment, and because I'm never in one place for more than a couple of days, I don't think that it would be fair."

Liz let out a sigh. "Well, it's a good excuse, anyway."

Will laughed. "Yes, it is, isn't it?" The smile slid slowly from his face, to be replaced by a frown of serious contemplation. "I've seen it happen all too often before, the offspring from a split marriage ending up in a mirror situation. Working in the oil industry turned out to be the best way to avoid it all."

"And you have no regrets?"

"Not really. Well, maybe a bit, but I think that's just me getting a bit more sentimental with age. Anyhow, I've been on my own for so long now that I reckon I'm far too self-centred and set in my ways to impose myself on anyone."

"So what's all this about 'starting over' again, then?"

He grimaced. "Ah. Well, I was really meaning with my father. I don't think that I'll be introducing any other discipline into my life."

The waiter glided across the paved courtyard towards them and slid the brimming plates onto their place-mats with practised aplomb. "*¡Qué aproveche, señores!*" He gave a short bow, then turned and left.

"Goodness! I don't think I've eaten as much as this since I've been here," Liz exclaimed, studying the mountain of food on her plate.

"Well then, I would suggest that it's time you started filling yourself up a bit. The best way to curb emotion is to fill your stomach, and what better way to do it than with a good chunk of Iberian pig." He took a mouthful of food. "By the way"—he stopped talking until he had swallowed—"I found a place for us all to stay."

"Did you? Through the hotel?"

"No. I thought it best not to get them involved. I borrowed a map, though, then picked an area and found it on the Internet."

"How did you do that?"

"I have a laptop with me all the time. It's invaluable for keeping in touch."

Liz sliced through the tender meat as easily as a hot knife went through butter. "I'm a complete dunce when it comes to the Internet. Alex, my son, tried to teach me once, but I found it all far too confusing. I've only just learned to master doing the farm accounts on the computer. So, go on, where is this place?"

Will put his hand in his inside pocket and produced a piece of hotel letter-heading. Liz saw that there were a few handwritten notes scribbled upon it. "Well, it's a small private hotel in the Sierra de Cañareas," he read out, talking as he was eating, "about one hour and a half north of here. It's set in one hundred acres of chestnut and cork trees, and every room commands a wonderful view, which, on a clear day, can mean seeing right across to the next province."

Liz laughed. "How far is that? About two hundred metres?"

"Probably! Anyway, what sold me on the place is that it's run by an English couple, so you won't have to scramble for your phrase-book every minute of the day, and my father won't need to lose his rag at not being able to understand what's being said to him."

She raised her eyebrows. "Yes, well, that'll be a good thing. Did you tell them about him?"

"What? Losing his rag all the time?"

"No!" She smiled at his joke. "About his leg."

"Yes. They said that that was fine. The whole house is built on one floor and they have one bedroom which is set up for wheelchair access. So, the long and the short of it is that I've booked ourselves in there from Saturday until Monday. We have to get Arthur back to hospital on Monday afternoon so that the doctor can make sure that he's all right to fly on Tuesday. Seemingly there can be the risk of deep-vein thrombosis if one flies too soon after sustaining an injury like that. So we'll just drive down here on Monday morning and get him checked."

"And you've managed to get a car as well?"

"Yes, all fixed. I called around the hire companies and explained our problem, and eventually tracked down a vehicle called a Seat Alhambra. The guy said that it had seven seats, and if there were only going to be the three of us, he could take out the middle row, so that the old boy could stretch his leg out in the back."

"Well, that all sounds perfect."

There was a lull in their conversation while they ate, only broken by the occasional utterance of appreciation about the food. As soon as Liz had laid her knife and fork together, the waiter appeared at their table and whisked away the empty plates. "*¿Algo más, señores?*"

"Do you want anything else?" Will asked.

She shook her head. "No, thanks, I'm fit to burst. That was delicious, though. Thank you."

Will looked up at the waiter and smiled at him. "*No, nada más. Solamente la cuenta.*"

"*Por supuesto, señor.*"

As the waiter left them, Will studied Liz intently. "So, you mentioned your son Alex earlier on. I'd like to hear about him—and everything else, for that matter."

Liz placed her napkin on the table. "No, not tonight. I'm not feeling like telling that story tonight. Maybe another time . . . maybe." She glanced at her watch. "Anyway, if you don't go to see Arthur soon, he might 'lose his rag,' as you put it."

Will nodded and pushed himself to his feet. "Okay, but I will hear it, even if I have to negotiate it out of you, and as you know, I'm pretty good at that."

Liz got to her feet. "We'll see." She began to walk towards the wooden door in the wall, but then turned and looked up at him as he followed. "Thank you, Will, for tonight."

"Not at all. It was a pleasure having dinner with you."

"I didn't mean that so much as, well, just acting as a friend."

He gave her a wink. "I wasn't acting."

Chapter 20

The cold west wind blew in hard from the Atlantic, whipping up the dark waters of the sea loch into angry waves that beat heavily against the boulders on the shoreline, throwing a frothy spray across the wide green verge to leave large rippling puddles on the uneven Tarmacked surface of the road. Mr. Craig pulled hard at the door of the red telephone-box in an attempt to shut out the rain hurled in stormy gusts against the window-panes. However, sometime in its more recent history, either a heavy-handed person or a previous storm had wrenched the door from its top hinge, making it impossible to shut. He bent forward in the confined space and screwed up his eyes to focus on the zip fastening of his waterproof jacket, and, once connected correctly, he pulled it up to his neck. Delving into the pocket of his trousers, he took out a handful of change and placed it on top of the telephone. Once again he strained his eyes to read through the operating instructions, just to refresh his memory on its use. He picked up the receiver, dropped a pound coin into the slot and dialled the number.

It rang four times before being answered quite unexpectedly. "Hullo?"

"Alex, is that you?"

"Hi, Granddad, how are you? How's the caddying going?"

The old man chuckled. "Och, I'd say that I still have a lot to learn. Why are you not away out today? I was getting myself all ready to speak to that wretched answerphone."

"Well, I did go out early this morning, but the weather turned bad and I got soaked, so I just came home and had a bath. How about you? Is it the same where you are?"

"Aye, it's dreadful." Mr. Craig replied, rubbing the sleeve of his jacket against one of the panes of glass and staring out at the elements. A small lobster boat was bobbing its way courageously down the loch towards the Ballachulish Bridge, its square, concrete structure nothing more than a vague outline in the rain-heavy mist. "So we decided that it was best to give the golf a miss today as well."

"But it's been all right up until now?"

The farmer stuck a finger in his free ear. "You'll have to speak up a bit, Alex. It's awful difficult to hear you with this wind."

"I said it's been all right up until now?" Alex yelled down the line.

"Aye, couldn't have been better. We managed to play around Prestwick on Tuesday afternoon, then Turnberry on Wednesday and Troon yesterday."

"That's pretty good going! And you had no trouble getting on any of the courses?"

"Och, we had a wee bit of a wait each day, but we were always lucky enough to join up with another game, which made it all the more enjoyable for us both."

"And have you been staying in first-class hotels?"

Mr. Craig chortled. "No, nothing like that, son. We just made do with a couple of small B and Bs, which I would say were probably just as comfortable."

"And did Leckie get to go in as well?"

"No, he did not. He was quite happy making a bed for himself on my jacket in the Land Rover."

"Just as well. So, is this you on your way home now?"

"Not quite yet. Miss Bayliss bought herself a wee book on the golf courses of Scotland, and she's taken quite a shine to the idea of playing Dornoch and Tain, so we're on our way up north."

"Heavens, Granddad! You'll be away for ages! When does Miss Bayliss have to fly home?"

"Not until Tuesday, but she's awful keen to be back in Saint Andrews by Sunday evening for some reason or other, so we'll be returning then, come what may."

"Right." There was a pause, during which Alex obviously took a mouthful of food, because when he spoke again, Mr. Craig could hear that his grandson's words were muffled. "So, whereabouts are you right at this minute?"

"Just before the Ballachulish Bridge, if you know where that is."

"I've heard of it. Never been there, though."

"Well, we've just had a pretty miserable journey up from Crianlarich and through Glencoe, and the weather's that bad that I think we'll just get to Fort William, and stop off early for the night."

Alex grunted a reply which the farmer knew from past experience meant that his grandson was either being distracted by the television or simply wanted to end the telephone call. He had more questions to ask, so he persisted with the conversation.

"And have you heard from your mother at all?"

"Yeah," Alex replied, his voice sounding quite bland. "I called her a couple of nights ago. Oh, wait!" A tinge of humorous excitement lifted his tone. "You'll never guess what's happened."

"Tell me."

"The professor's broken his ankle."

"Ach, never!"

"Yup, he has, and quite badly, too."

"How did he do that?"

"Slipped on some candle-wax in the street."

The farmer clicked his tongue. "Och, that's awful bad luck." He paused for a moment, giving quick thought to this new development. "Maybe I shouldn't go north then. They'll no doubt be coming straight back."

"No, they're not. The professor's son said he'd fly back with them—"

"The professor's son!" the farmer broke in. "So he *did* get out there."

"Seemingly. Mum said that he turned up at the hotel just after it happened, so he's going to arrange for them all to fly back on Tuesday."

"Well, then, it sounds as though they have everything under control. So you don't think there's a need for us to change any of our arrangements?"

"No, not at all. And by the way, talking of your arrangements, she didn't half fire questions at me about you and Miss Bayliss."

Mr. Craig laughed. "Aye, I can well imagine that she did. I hope you gave a true account of what's been taking place now, Alex."

"Of course I did. She got into a bit of a tizz about the whole thing, so I had to!"

"Good for you, lad. Now one more thing before you go . . ." The telephone started to signal the need for more money. "Hang on . . ." He put in another pound coin. "Alex? Are you still there?"

"Yes."

"Listen, lad, the main reason for my calling is just to explain something to you. You may have noticed that work has stopped on the golf course. Now, I'm pretty sure that it's only a temporary measure, so when you next speak to your mother, I don't want you to bother even mentioning it, all right?"

There was a silence at the other end of the line. "I don't know what you mean."

"Well, I'll explain it all when I get home, but in the meantime, if you could just keep it quiet from your—"

"But, Granddad," Alex interjected, "work hasn't stopped."

"I think you'll find that it has, Alex," Mr. Craig replied quietly, taking his grandson's remark as a pleading objection to the idea.

"But it hasn't. I know that for a fact. Dad and I were down there yesterday afternoon with Michael Dooney and Jonathan Davies. Michael even asked me for my thoughts on his easing out the dog-leg on the fifth hole. That doesn't sound as if work's been stopped, does it?"

Mr. Craig breathed out a long sigh of relief, feeling a huge burden of worry lift from his mind. "Well, I'm awful glad to hear that, Alex. Things must have been sorted out much quicker than we had all anticipated."

"That's good, then," Alex replied, his tone dropping once more, denoting a further waning of interest in their conversation. "Is there anything else, Granddad?"

"No, I don't think so." He paused. "So, what's on television?"

Alex laughed. "Football. Scotland's playing Sweden in a World Cup qualifier."

"Ah, well, lad, I won't hinder you. I'll call you from Dornoch."

"All right, Granddad."

Mr. Craig replaced the receiver, scooped up the remainder of his change and pulled up the collar of his jacket in readiness to meet the storm. He opened the door carefully, wary that one good blast could well separate it altogether from the telephone-box, and hurried across to the lay-by where he had parked the Land Rover. He had left the engine running in an attempt to keep Roberta warm, but in doing so, the windows were misted with condensation on the inside, there only being one pin-point of clarity where, in searching for its master, the Jack Russell had been pressing his nose against the glass. Mr. Craig opened the door and clambered in as quickly as he could, the small dog jumping across onto Roberta's lap to make way for him, and then leaping back onto his as soon as he was settled in his seat.

"All well?" Roberta beamed at him. She was dressed as if setting off on an Arctic expedition, and the knitted hat that had been just one of her many purchases in the factory shop on the edge of Loch Lomond was pulled down over her ears so that her small bright eyes were just visible beneath its woolly brim.

"Aye, all well. He hasn't burnt the house down yet." He took hold of Leckie and returned him to Roberta's knee. "I'll tell you the best news, though," he said, turning to her with a broad smile on his face. "Work's still going ahead on the golf course."

"Oh, that's wonderful!" she exclaimed, giving her hands a single triumphant clap, the sound being deadened by her gloves. "You're right, that is the best news. I couldn't think of anything worse than knowing it would never be completed."

"And those are exactly my own sentiments." He put the vehicle into gear and slowly moved out of the lay-by and onto the road. "Right then, let's go! Fort William next stop!"

They spoke little during the remainder of their journey, Roberta knowing that her travelling companion was finding it difficult enough to concentrate on driving in the appalling conditions without her adding to his problems by asking questions on points of interest. So she contented herself in gazing out at the mist-shrouded countryside, directing any comment that she had to make on its stark and untamed beauty to the dog. She didn't mind the silence. It gave her time for her own thoughts, to consider the extraordinary change of circumstances that had come about in her life over the past week. When she had first arrived, she had felt that there was little left to be happy about, yet now she was aware of the smile of contentment that seemed to be fixed permanently upon her face. And it was all due to this extraordinary man, someone whom, in her closeted existence back in Australia, she would have more than likely passed in the street without giving him a second thought. His wisdom, though simply portrayed, was deep and understanding, and his attitude towards life and death, through his own experience, had helped to pierce the dark and hopeless despondency she had felt since the loss of her father. It was a friendship, an easy companionship that she could never have imagined existing again in her life. And that's all it would, or could, ever be. They were too old, too different and their geographical distances too great for either even to consider a permanence between them.

Roberta turned in her seat to track the progress of a small ferry that pushed its way across the choppy waters of Loch Linnhe. She let out a long sigh, realizing immediately that it was one that tingled with excitement, not regret. For she knew now that the special bond that had formed between them would never be broken, even though they were to live the rest of their lives on the opposite sides of the world to each other.

The rain became marginally lighter as they drove along the side of the loch and into Fort William. Though the wind remained strong, clouds still clung low to the surrounding hills, shrouding the upper reaches of Ben Nevis and diminishing its usual towering presence over the town. As they made their way along the main thoroughfare, Roberta looked out at the drab line of shops that bordered both sides of the street. Grim-faced pedestrians hurried along the pavements, clutching at coat-necks with hands that were white with cold or struggling with umbrellas to keep them from turning outside in. Mr. Craig slowly edged the Land Rover past a vociferous contretemps between a meek-looking traffic warden and an irate young businessman who had displayed a bullish disregard of parking laws by leaving his large four-wheel-drive vehicle on a double yellow line outside the bank. A major traffic snarl-up had ensued, which impatient motorists were beginning to celebrate by leaning hard on their horns or rolling down their windows and shouting out in biased support of the young man. At the far end of the street, Mr. Craig pulled into a large car-park which was empty save for three identical tour coaches, recently arrived from Glasgow. They were in the process of disgorging their passengers, a profusion of white-haired ladies in thin summer mackintoshes who sought shelter from the cut of the wind by huddling together at the front of the coaches while struggling to secure the ties of plastic fold-away rain-hats under their chins. There was, however, obviously a strict timetable for the day's outing, because, besides the weather, they were having to cope with the impatient and quite hostile attentions of one of the bus-drivers, a sour-faced man with an incipient moustache and a white-shirted beer belly that bulged well beyond the fastening capabilities of his maroon blazer. Waving his arms in the air as though herding unwilling sheep into a dip-tank, he edged them away from their refuge towards an aging clapboard café where a sign with fading illustrations of multicoloured ice lollies was all that enticed them into its gloomy interior.

Roberta looked around at her companion, who sat chewing at the side of his mouth as he stared out the window.

"Makes me feel cold just looking at that sign over there," Roberta said quietly.

Mr. Craig nodded slowly. "Aye, I was thinking that myself." He leaned back in his seat and thumped the palm of his hand down on the steering wheel. "Not really what we're used to, is it?"

Roberta laughed. "No, it isn't. I'm afraid that I have to say that I find it all quite depressing. Those poor old dears over there really make me feel my age. I mean, some of them couldn't be that much older than me." She paused as she watched one of the ladies attempt to return to the bus to collect something that she had obviously forgotten, only to have her arm taken by the driver and forcibly marched back to the café. "You don't think that *we* look like that, do you?"

"No. But if we stay here any longer, we could be running the risk that others might think that of us."

"So what should we do?"

Mr. Craig looked at his watch. "Well, it's only two o'clock now, so I suggest that we just keep going. We should be able to make Dornoch in two to three hours."

"But what about you? Will you be all right to drive all that way?"

He craned his neck forward to look up at the sky. "Och, it's not so bad now. I've an inkling that it might start clearing as we head up the road." He took a last glance around him before crunching the Land Rover into gear. "Anyway, I think it would be a better option, don't you?"

He had been right about the weather. By the time they had driven the length of Loch Ness, the wind had abated to such an extent that its waters now mirrored the reflection of the surrounding hills in glassy calmness. Sunlight, as weak as a luminous watch that had been starved of light, broke through the dwindling clouds and bathed the countryside in a shadowless glow. And when, in the late afternoon, they passed by the war memorial and drove down the gentle slope into the main street of Dornoch, the sky above the dark slate roofs and smoking chimney-stacks was a cloudless blue, and the sun, now recharged but defeated by the passing of the day, thrust forward a last defiant burst of light that cast out before them the lengthy shadow of the Land Rover, a harbinger of their arrival.

The small, stone-built villa stood back from the main street in its own carefully tended garden. Protruding over its boundary wall was a dark green sign with gold italic lettering that announced it as "Craig-na-Fhalde, a bed-and-breakfast establishment that has been Highly Recommended by the Scottish Tourist Board for the past four years." Below the main sign, hung on brass cup-hooks for easy detachment, was a smaller one on which was written in similar script: "Vacancies." Mr. Craig turned into the short gravelled drive and pulled to a halt as close to the crocus-filled flower border as he could, allowing room in case another car had to park alongside the Land Rover.

He turned off the engine and leaned forward to survey every aspect of the property through the windscreen. "Now, would this seem all right to you?"

Roberta, however, had already opened the door and was clambering out of the vehicle. "It looks absolutely perfect. Come on."

He got out and shrugged off his jacket, placing it on the driver's seat as a bed for the dog, then walked around the back and took out their two cases. Together, they made their way the short distance to the arched front porch, where they found that the door had already been opened to them by an elderly couple.

"Hullo and welcome!" they said in unison, both sporting enthusiastic grins. The woman took over. "We heard you arriving." She rubbed her hands briskly together. "Oh, my word, the chill's fairly come down, now that the sun is away. Come on, let's get you inside."

They were shown into a narrow hallway, cluttered with unmatching, though neatly arranged, pieces of furniture. A staircase, lined with small water-colours depicting Scottish landscapes, rose steeply to the upper floor. There was a comforting warmth about the house, and the smell of pine logs burning in an open fire seemed to complement the welcome that they had been given by their hosts.

"Now, first things first," the woman said in an airily organized voice as she closed the front door behind her. She turned to the small half-moon table that sat next to a burgeoning coat-stand and opened up a leather-bound visitors' book. "Would you mind just signing your names here before I show you to your room?"

"It would be two rooms that we require," Mr. Craig stated quickly. It was not the first time that he had had to say this, but he still felt his face colour, more for the embarrassment that it might cause Roberta rather than for himself.

"Of course it would be," the woman replied without altering her tone. "My apologies." She handed a pen to Roberta. "Now, might I ask if you've eaten tonight?"

He shook his head. "No, not yet."

"Oh, now that's a pity, because we usually do offer our guests an evening meal, but I'm afraid that both my husband and I are going out to a *ceilidh* tonight. However, there are some good places to eat in Dornoch, and we'd be more than happy to point you in the right direction before we go."

Roberta stopped writing in the book and looked up at the woman. "Can I ask what a *ceilidh* is?"

It was the first time that Roberta had spoken, and the woman reacted to her Australian accent with a kindly eagerness. "A *ceilidh*! Well, it's just a party where we have a bite to eat and sometimes a wee bit to drink, and dance a few Scottish reels."

"That sounds really good fun!" Roberta replied, smiling at the woman before she continued to write.

Mr. Craig had caught the twinkle in Roberta's eye, and a frown of consideration came over his face. "Now, would this ceilidh be a private function?"

"Oh, not at all!" the woman replied. "It's just being held at a local hotel as a fund-raiser for our local branch of the Women's Rural Institute, so everyone who turns up is more than welcome." She glanced at her husband, wondering whether she had been correct in her reading of the farmer's question. "Of course," she continued in a tentative voice, "if you would like to come, we'd both be more than delighted to take you with us."

The farmer glanced at Roberta. "What would you feel about that?"

"Well, it sounds a wonderful idea. Only problem being that I haven't got a thing with me that I could wear to a party."

"Oh, it's not that smart at all!" the woman declared. "Just a simple dress would do."

Roberta bit at her lip. "That's what I mean. I don't have a dress." She looked apologetically at the farmer. "I didn't even bring one with me from Australia. I didn't think I'd be needing one."

"Och, it couldn't matter less," he said, smiling reassuringly at her. He took the pen from her and began to write his name in the book.

Roberta noticed that the woman cast a brief look at her from head to foot, as if sizing her up. However, it was more than apparent that anything her hostess had to offer would be too slim-fitting for her own plump figure.

"I suppose it would be too late to buy something, wouldn't it?" Roberta asked.

"Well, I didn't want to have suggested it myself, but"—the woman held her finger pensively to the edge of her mouth—"let's just see what we can do, shall we?" She took the telephone receiver off its wall mounting and dialled a number. "Hullo, Jean? . . . It's Isla here. . . . Aye, we're fair looking forward to it. Now, Jean, I know that you'll have closed up for the night, but we have some visitors here, and they were considering coming to the ceilidh, but unfortunately the lady doesn't have a dress. Would it be an awful imposition if I brought her along, just to see if you had anything that might be suitable? . . . Are you sure, Jean? . . . Well, that's very kind of you, dear. . . . Yes, very good. . . . Right, in ten minutes. . . . Thank you, Jean . . . goodbye." She replaced the receiver and turned to Roberta with a grin of success. "Well, that's settled then."

"That's so kind of you," Roberta said, taking hold of the woman's arm and giving it an affectionate squeeze. "It's Isla, is it?"

"Yes." She turned to her husband. "And this is Gordon."

"Well, it's really good to meet you both. I'm Roberta, and"—she glanced at the farmer, a broad grin on her face—"this is Craig."

There was a general shaking of hands before Isla held up a finger to command attention. "Now, I don't think we should keep Jean waiting at the shop, so I suggest that Gordon quickly shows you to your rooms, and then Roberta and I can nip down the road to see if we can find her something to wear. How would that suit you?"

"That would be perfect," Roberta replied. "Can I ask at what time we would need to be ready?"

"We should be trying to get there for seven-thirty," Gordon answered, "if we want to get a good place to sit." He glanced at his watch. "That would mean leaving here in about two hours."

"More than enough time," Roberta exclaimed, grabbing hold of her suitcase and readying herself to follow Gordon up the stairs.

"Please, Roberta!" Isla gasped. "Gordon can quite easily manage that!"

"She won't let you, you know," the farmer said with a wry smile on his face. "I can carry her golf clubs, but not her suitcase."

A polite tingle of humour buzzed about them before Gordon, taking note of the farmer's comment, began to climb the stairs empty-handed. "So you're here for the golf, then?"

"Yes, we are," Roberta replied as she followed on behind.

"And have you played Dornoch before?"

"No, never. This is the first time."

"Well, if you like, I'd be more than happy to join you on the course tomorrow and show you the way round."

"Are you sure?"

"Of course. It would be my pleasure."

"In that case, thank you, Gordon. We'd love that." Roberta turned to look at Mr. Craig, who was two steps below her on the stairs. "A party *and* a golf game organized," she said quietly. "Who says we're getting old?"

He flicked his head to the side. "Not me, lass."

Even though he had had the heater on in the Land Rover, Mr. Craig had begun to feel a painful stiffness in his back and shoulders due to the persistent dampness of the day and his many hours of being at the wheel. Consequently, once he had seen Roberta off on her shopping trip with Isla, and having fed the dog and taken it for a short walk, he returned to the house and ran himself a hot bath, knowing that he had enough time to have a long, self-indulgent soak.

And so he lay there, with the water lapping under his chin, feeling his eyes grow heavy as the ache in his body succumbed to the comforting heat.

"Hullo, Nathaniel."

The voice came to his ear as quiet as a whisper, yet its pitch was as clear and as recognizable as the call of a songbird on a frosty morning. He turned and looked across to where she sat on the lid of the small white chest by the window, her back upright, her legs together and her thin hands resting upon her knees. She was wearing her floral apron over the faded green woollen dress, her white hair neatly permed, and her pink spectacles, still with the piece of Sellotape binding on one of the legs, perched on the edge of her pretty, fine nose. A wistful smile touched at the corners of her mouth, and she watched him with tenderness in the eyes.

"Hullo, my darling," he replied in as quiet a tone as her own. "How are you?"

"All is well with me. All is well."

"I miss you so much."

"I know you do, and I miss you."

"I talk to you all the time."

"And I hear you."

"You're always with me."

"And you with me."

"I'll never forget you. You know that, don't you? Whatever happens, I'll never forget you."

"I know you won't. You're a good, gentle man, Nathaniel Craig. That's all I wanted to say. You're the best man I ever knew."

He woke with a start, feeling immediately his skin prick with goose bumps in the cooling water. He turned to look at the small white chest in the window, but there was no one there. Only his neatly folded towel, which he was sure that he had thrown down on the bathroom floor, occupied the space.

An hour later he descended the stairs, running a finger around the collar of his shirt in an attempt to relieve its tightness. He stopped in front of the mirror in the hallway and gave himself a last once-over. Even though he had had the tweed suit since his twenties, it still fitted him well enough, but the lapels were slightly frayed at the edges and the years had knocked most of the coarseness from the material. He was just smoothing down his unruly white hair with the palm of his hand when the door adjacent to the mirror opened and Gordon appeared, resplendent in a kilt and tweed jacket, his green-stockinged legs criss-crossed with the long tasselled laces of a pair of dancing pumps.

"Craig! I thought I heard someone coming down the stairs." He stood to the side of the door and held out a hand to invite the farmer into the room. "Come away in and we'll have a wee dram before we go. There's no telling how long the ladies are going to be."

They entered the small sitting-room, where the farmer felt the heat of the roaring fire hit him immediately.

"Now, take a seat over there," Gordon said in his melodious Highland voice, pointing to the deep armchair that was drawn up to the fire. He walked over to a tall cabinet that stood against the back wall and opened its doors with a flourish, then gave his hands a single clap and rubbed them together as if meaning business. "Right. What will it be?" He surveyed the abundance of bottles on the shelves. "I have our local tipple Glenmorangie, or there's Glendurnich, which is a Speyside, or maybe it's an Islay you prefer, in which case it would be Laphroaig."

"You'll think me an awful heathen, Gordon," Mr. Craig said as he sank back into the armchair, "but I'm not really much of a drinker."

"Are you not? Oh dear. So I won't be able to tempt you with anything?"

Mr. Craig detected from the despondent tone in Gordon's voice that it could quite easily be taken as an affront if he didn't accept something. Pushing himself to his feet, he made his way over to the cabinet. "Well, let's see now," he said, studiously appraising his host's supply. "Would that be a bottle of Jack Daniel's you have at the back there?"

Gordon raised himself onto the toes of his dancing shoes and peered into the cabinet. "My word!" he sang out, reaching for the black bottle. "I'd clean forgotten that that bottle was there. I think that it was given to me by an American couple who came to stay with us last year." He held the bottle out at arm's length to read the label. "Jack Daniel's. Well, I never! That's exactly what it is." He twisted off the top. "You'll have one of these, then."

The farmer judged this to be more command than question. "Just a wee one by itself would do me fine."

The measure poured was much greater than he could cope with, so he was quite relieved when Isla eventually entered the room to interrupt their fireside chat. "We'd best be going, Gordon, otherwise we'll be late," she said, pulling on a fleece-collared coat over her party dress.

Gordon drained his glass. "Is Roberta ready yet?" he asked.

"She's on her way."

Mr. Craig followed them out into the hall. "And did you have some success at the shop?" he asked.

A door slammed shut upstairs and Roberta appeared, making her way quickly down the stairs. Isla smiled up at her. "You two can judge that for yourselves."

The long-sleeved dress was ochre-yellow and spotted all over with a blue design that resembled sea-gulls in flight. It was meant to be worn closed at the neck, but Roberta had chosen to leave the top two buttons undone, folding back the flaps into narrow lapels. A dark blue belt gathered the dress at her ample waist, and on her feet she wore a new pair of shoes, their uncreased leather the same colour as the belt. The farmer watched her closely as she descended the stairs. It was no remarkable transformation. She hadn't suddenly become a beauty. If anything, the dress was slightly unflattering to her fuller figure, but the expression on her face made up for any minor faults, being filled with girlish enthusiasm and excitement at the prospect of the party.

"You look fine, Roberta," Mr. Craig said as she came to stand in front of him in the hall.

Roberta looked down at the dress. "I don't feel it. Not that there's anything wrong with the dress, only I just look a frump in it." She let out a long sigh of resignation. "I'm afraid that I've never seen eye to eye with dresses."

"Absolute rubbish," Isla clucked admonishingly. "It suits you perfectly."

"Aye, it does," the farmer agreed. "You look very . . . elegant." He wasn't quite sure if that was the word for which he was searching, but Roberta seemed pleased enough with the compliment.

"You two men look very handsome as well," she said, looking both him and Gordon up and down. She focused on Gordon's neatly laced pumps, then turned her eyes to view the farmer's well-polished but heavy black boots. "Are you sure you're going to be able to dance in those, Craig?"

"Of course. Like you, I didn't bring anything else other than these, but that doesn't mean I can't skip about a bit."

"Come on then," Isla said, opening the front door. "Let's away and see you prove that."

The hotel function suite, which stuck out from the back of the main building, was one of those suspect structures that looked as if economy rather than longevity had been the more important consideration at the time of construction, and the musky whiff of damp in the long, low-ceilinged room confirmed this to Mr. Craig on entering. Nevertheless, it was pleasantly warm due to the abundance of electric heaters that were strategically set about the place and the throng of people, already laughing and drinking, that filled it. Gordon led them to the bar, exchanging greetings with those who stood aside to allow his party through.

"Right! What's it to be?" he asked.

"No, no! I'll not hear of it," Mr. Craig retorted, delving into the inside pocket of his suit jacket for his wallet.

Gordon held up a hand. "Plenty time for you to buy a round, Craig. Now, Roberta, what would you like?"

If anything, the smile of excitement on Roberta's face had grown even wider since entering the room. "Oh, I don't know." She turned to her hostess. "What are you going to have, Isla?"

"I think just a small glass of wine."

"Okay. I'll have one too."

"Two glasses of wine coming up!" Gordon exclaimed, holding up a ten-pound note between his fingers to attract the barman's attention. He turned and gave the farmer a wink. "And I know what you like, Craig, don't I?"

"Not for me, thank you, Gordon. One is quite enough for me for one night. An orange juice will do me just fine."

"All right. Now, you lot clear away and get a table, while I order these up."

By the time that the two-man band had readied their instruments—an accordion and fiddle—their little party had finished their meal of meat-loaf and stovies, something at which Roberta had initially cast a sceptical eye before being informed that it was nothing more exotic than potatoes and gravy mixed together. Then, with a long and somewhat squeaky chord, the band brought silence across the room.

"Ladies and gentlemen," the fiddler announced into the microphone, then turned briefly to play with the knobs on the amplifier to get rid of the ear-splitting feedback. "Ladies and gentlemen, please take your partners for a Gay Gordons."

Gordon and Isla joined others in jumping to their feet. They took their place on the small parqueted dance floor beneath the multicoloured glare of the revolving disco globe. With hands and feet poised in the correct position, they readied themselves.

"Right!" Mr. Craig declared, slapping his hands on both knees and getting to his feet. He held out a hand to Roberta. "Come on, let's see what we can do."

"No, not just yet, Craig," Roberta said, shaking her head and holding her hands firmly together on her lap.

"There's nothing to it," he replied in quite a forceful tone. "All you have to do is watch the couple in front and allow me to guide you through it."

"Is it not really difficult?"

"No more so than swinging a golf club. Come on!" He pulled Roberta to her feet and all but dragged her onto the dance floor. "Now, put your right hand up to your shoulder—that's it—and take my other hand with your left in front. Well done. Now, we're set to go."

"Do I walk or skip?"

"No, no, just walk through it for now. We'll leave the pas-de-bas to the experts."

The band played another resounding introductory chord and then they were away. At the first turn, Roberta was so tense that she resisted her partner's guidance to turn and they bumped head-on into the couple who had been in front of them and who were now coming back towards them. However, there was no anger or animosity at the clash, just a hoot of laughter from the couple.

"Just relax!" the farmer shouted to her above the volume of the jigging music. "I'll take you through it."

After that, they were away, Roberta closely watching the movements of the other dancers and responding to Craig's verbal commands and to the guidance of his hands. "This way! Good! Now turn! That's it! And now birl!" And he would spin her around, holding her right hand aloft, forcing her to go faster and faster. By the time they were into the second rendering of the dance, she had it perfectly and his commands stopped, and she now began to take note of his neat little steps as he rocked gently from side to side up and down the floor. She became aware of the coarseness of his calloused hands rubbing like sandpaper against hers as he spun her around, and then, when she came out of it, giddy enough to fall over, he would pull her to him and they would circle in a fast polka step, he keeping her inches away from the couple in front. And then it dawned on her that this was the first physical contact that she had had with this man, the first physical contact she had had with *any* man since . . . well . . . since she could remember.

The band brought the dance to a close with a final chord and everyone clapped, the couples on either side of them giving special praise to Roberta for picking up the routine so quickly. She beamed at them, her face flushed with both the effort and the elation of having mastered the dance. She turned to Mr. Craig, who stood looking down at her, a gentle, proud smile on his face. On impulse, she reached up and put her hands on his shoulders, and pulling his head down towards her, she planted a kiss on his cheek.

"Thank you, Craig, that was wonderful fun!"

The farmer's face coloured as he put his hand up and rubbed at the place where she had kissed him. "Oh, well, we've only just started, Roberta," he said, giving his head a questioning flick to the side, though there was a teasing glint in his eyes, "which leads me to wonder what my reward might be once you've mastered the more difficult reels."

Which, during the course of the evening, she did. They always started at the bottom of the dance set to give her an opportunity to watch how it was done, but by the time it came to their turn, she had studied the others with such intent that she went through the complicated movements without hardly putting a foot wrong. There were only a couple of occasions when Mr. Craig had to give her a gentle push to guide her in the right direction. She had even been able to work out the basic rudiments of the pas-de-bas, practising the steps below the table during dances that he had deemed, quite disparagingly, as being "nothing more than just a stupid kerfuffle" and "not worth getting up for." By the end of the evening, the intricacies of the Duke of Perth, the interweaving complications of the Eightsome Reel and the arm-wrenching frenzy of Strip the Willow were now emblazoned upon her mind. As they made their way home in Gordon's car, she sat silently in the back while the others chatted away, her feet aching gloriously and her head pulsating with the lingering sound of the music to which she happily kept dancing away in her mind's eye.

"Who's for a nightcap, then?" Gordon asked as they entered the house and he helped his wife out of her coat.

"Not for myself, thanks, Gordon," Mr. Craig replied, stifling a long yawn with his hand. "It's been a pretty long day, so I think I'll just go and let my dog out of the car for a minute and then head up to bed."

Isla turned sharply from hanging up her coat. "Oh, my word, I never realized you had a dog with you! Do you want to bring it in for the night? Gordon and I wouldn't mind if you did."

He shook his head. "No, no. Leckie's happier sleeping in the car. He kind of treats it as his own territory."

Isla smiled at him. "Well, if you're quite sure."

He turned the wooden knob of the front door and was about to open it when it occurred to him that his hosts might well have retired by the time he returned. He stopped and looked back at them. "I would just like to thank you both for taking Roberta and me with you tonight."

"Me, too," Roberta followed on immediately. "Without any doubt, I think that it has to be the highlight of our little trip." She beamed at the farmer. "Don't you, Craig?"

He nodded in agreement.

"Don't even mention it," Gordon replied. "It was a pleasure to have your company."

"And I second that entirely," Isla said, taking hold of her husband's arm. "Now, just before we go our separate ways, maybe we should have a quick discussion about breakfast. When do you think you'll be wanting to play golf?"

Roberta held out the palms of her hands. "Well, if Gordon would really be kind enough to join us on the course, then we'll go along with whatever he thinks."

"It would probably be best in the morning if the weather's good," Gordon replied, "so maybe a nine-o'clock breakfast? Would that suit?"

Roberta glanced at the farmer. "Is that all right for you, Craig?"

"I'll fit in with whatever's going on."

"Right!" said Isla. "Nine o'clock it is! And we'll see you both in the morning."

Leckie shot out of the Land Rover as soon as the door had been opened for him, and immediately sniffing out the back wheel, he lifted his leg for such a lengthy period of time that Mr. Craig thought that he might keel over as relief set in. Eventually he finished and then set about accomplishing his next priority of greeting his master.

"That was awful unfair, wasn't it, wee laddie? I shouldn't have left you for so long." He picked up the dog by the scruff of the neck and tucked him under his arm, and then allowed him to lick enthusiastically at the side of his face.

"Is he all right?"

He turned to see Roberta standing on the front porch. Her arms were folded across her chest and she rubbed at the sleeves of her new dress to ward out the chill of the night.

"Aye, he's fine. Just a bit desperate to relieve himself."

Roberta walked over to stand beside him and looked up at the clear, starlit sky. "What beautiful nights you have over here," she said quietly.

He followed her gaze. "Well, *you've* certainly been blessed with them over the past week. It's not always like this." He looked down at her and noticed that she was shivering. "Come on." He opened the door of the Land Rover to let the dog jump back in. "Let's get back inside before you catch your death."

Roberta shook her head. "Don't worry about me. I'm fine." She paused until he had locked up the vehicle. "Craig, thank you for tonight."

"You've got nothing to thank me for."

"Yes, I do. I've got everything to thank you for." She paused for a moment, then let out a little laugh. "Do you know that when I came over here from Australia, I was as naïve and as vulnerable as a little child? You see, I'd been protected all my life, and there was never the need to grow up because I always had my father with me. I lived in a time warp. But since being here in Scotland, with you, the extraordinary thing is that I don't feel vulnerable any more. In fact, I feel more confident, more alive than I have ever done before. I really think that now I'll be able to cope with whatever crosses my path in the future, Craig, and it is entirely your doing that I feel this way. I know that our ages probably aren't that different, but I was always aware that maybe, inwardly, I was just treating you like another father-figure, relying on you for your capability, and your calmness, and your kindness. But I know now that that is not the case, because everything you have said to me, everything that you have discussed with me has given me strength. And I cannot thank you enough for that."

The farmer said nothing for a moment, then folded his arms across his chest and gave her a wink. "Well, the same goes for me, lass. I never thought that I'd ever jig again."

Roberta let out a quiet laugh, then, walking over to him, she once more pulled his head down towards her, this time giving him a kiss on both cheeks. She stood back and looked up at him. "You're a good, gentle man, Nathaniel Craig. In fact, besides my father, I think you're probably the best man I've ever known."

And as she turned and walked back towards the house, the farmer simply stood and watched her go, aware of the comforting sense of inner peace that gently swept its way through his being, because he knew, from that moment on, that everything would be all right for both of them.

Chapter 21

"Will you two speak up?" Arthur shouted from his semi-supine position in the back of the Seat Alhambra. "It's pretty lonely being back here, and I can't hear a word that you're saying to each other."

Will glanced at him in the rear-view mirror. "We're not saying anything of great interest, you know," he called back over his shoulder. "We're just looking at the map and trying to work out where the hell we're going."

Arthur was silent for a moment. "Well then, maybe you can put on some music."

"No, we cannot. We need to be able to hear each other."

Arthur let out a long sigh of discontent. "I don't see why you had to get such a stupid vehicle. In a normal-sized car, I'd have been able to hear you as well."

Will turned around and glared at his father. "Come on, if we had a normal-sized car we wouldn't have been able to get you in. Now just let us get on with finding out the right route, or I'll turn round and take you back to the hospital."

"Will, watch out!" Liz yelled.

He turned back in time to see that he was heading straight towards an articulated lorry coming from the opposite direction. He veered back onto his own side of the road, causing the wheelchair that was folded up in front of Arthur to shoot violently across the floor and thump hard against the rear passenger door, missing his outstretched plastered leg by a matter of inches. The lorry flashed past, its airhorn blaring.

"Steady on! Remember you've got an invalid in the back here. . . ." His voice trailed off when he saw Will look back from the driver's seat, his face ashen with shock and anger. He watched as his son took in a long breath through clenched teeth, ready to let fly at him, but Liz premeditated the outburst by putting her hand on Will's arm and saying something that was once more indiscernible. She turned, a smile on her face. "Listen, Arthur, we *will* speak to you once we know which way we're meant to be going. It's just a bit difficult at the minute."

Realizing that Liz had probably saved him from a forceful reprimand, Arthur thought it best to heed her plea and keep a low profile for a while. He turned in his seat and looked out of the window at the wide rolling plains that spread away to the cloudless horizon, their sparse-looking crops beginning to yellow prematurely from lack of rain, and even to his unagricultural eye, he was amazed at how much farther on they were in comparison to the crops that he passed by on his way back and forth between St. Andrews and Balmuir. Few buildings graced the countryside save for the occasional large white-walled farming complex seemingly stuck out in the middle of nowhere, with no visible sign of a road or track connecting it with the main highway. And that, too, was of little interest, a ribbon of black that dipped and swayed and turned on its way north through the empty landscape, its sides falling away into deep ditches that were filled with detritus jettisoned by passing vehicles and the occasional half-decomposed body of a dead animal.

He put his pipe in his mouth but thought better of lighting it. Maybe he had been acting a bit like a bear with a sore head. He had already complained of the speed at which Will had driven through Seville, but everyone agreed that Arthur had had good reason for that. Being taken from the restful security of the hospital and catapulted into the fast-moving mayhem of the city streets had felt as if he had hitched a ride with Michael Schumacher. Nevertheless, he just felt so damned useless, and his leg still ached. He had made light of it that morning, being terrified that they would keep him in hospital over the weekend and that he would have to suffer the consequences of yet more sleepless nights in the company of that wretched man and his daughter. But there again, he hadn't been alone, had he? He had been quite amazed and touched by the fact that Will, of his own volition, had spent every night with him, sitting up in that appallingly uncomfortable chair, even though, after the first two nights, the doctor had told him that there was little reason for him to do so.

They drove at pace behind a Lisbon-bound fish lorry through a small town, its low, whitewashed houses clustered tight to the sides of the road, as if it were their lifeline to civilization. A frail metal barrier protected their front doors from the speeding through-traffic, and the narrow pavement that ran between them relinquished most of its precious space to a line of sickly looking orange trees battered by the blast of passing vehicles and poisoned by the inescapable breath of carbon-monoxide fumes.

He was confused about his feelings towards his son. He hadn't really expected him to come out to join him in Seville, yet of course he was delighted that he was now with them. He and Liz would have found their situation almost impossible without him. He was also gladdened by the way in which both he and Will seemed to be getting on, and he hoped beyond hope that the time that they had spent together in hospital might finally have put to rest the ghosts of their past. That was, of course, barring that little episode a few miles back, for which he knew that his own irascibility was to blame. But maybe even that was part of his confusion. He knew that he should be intelligent and mature enough not to bother about it, but he could not help feeling a deep pang of jealousy in the way that Will was spending, or, more aptly, was *able* to spend, so much time with Liz. Up until the time he had broken his ankle, it had been *he* and Liz who had been the inseparable unit, but now it was Will and Liz. He felt himself excluded from the party, and no more so than now. Sitting right at the back of this wretched vehicle, he was having to watch them chit-chat away to each other without being able to hear a damned word that was being said.

He took the pipe from his mouth, unable to extract much joy from its smokeless bowl, and discarded it with little care onto the seat beside him. He sighed. It wasn't that, though, was it. This situation was always meant to have happened. As he said, he hadn't expected Will to join them, but that was what he had hoped would be the case. The whole idea had been complete pie-in-the-sky when he had discussed it with Liz's father over one of their nightly games of cribbage. But they had both thought that if his plan was to work out, then it would benefit Liz in forming a new friendship, or even relationship, with someone of her own age outside her own claustrophobic environment. And he had based the whole crazy concept on the fact that Will hadn't returned the itinerary.

Then, in its extraordinary way, fate had played its part, and here they were all together. Not as had been planned, but they were together. And now, in retrospect, he realized that it had been a stupid, irresponsible idea, brought about by two conniving old men who thought that they had the right to interfere in the emotional lives of their children. He laughed derisively to himself. Yes, *old* boy, that's what you are now, and that, in truth, is what is hurting you. You've been able to swan your way through life without care, without baggage, without any tangible measure of your age, and now you have been hoisted by your own petard. Liz is not *your* age, she's your son's, a mature woman with a son of her own. How could you think that she might ever have become interested in you?

He came away from his thoughts on hearing Liz utter the words "All the way to Cañareas," and he watched as she folded up the road-map and tossed it onto the front sill of the dashboard. She turned round in her seat and smiled at him. "That's it. I think we know which way we're going. How are you doing back there?"

"All right," Arthur mumbled.

"How's the leg bearing up?"

"It aches quite a bit."

She smiled warmly at him. "I'm sure it does. The movement of the car won't help either. Do you want to stop for a bit?"

Arthur shook his head.

"Right. Well, we're on the Lisbon road now, so we reckon that it won't be much more than three-quarters of an hour from here." She paused, briefly looking out through the windscreen at the road ahead. She turned back. "Would you like me to get you a pain-killer?"

"No, it's all right. I'll wait until I get there."

Liz nodded. "Okay." She had now turned her whole body in the seat and was leaning her arms on the back head-rest, looking at him. Arthur's attention, however, was drawn to her tucked-in knees, which brushed against Will's forearm as he drove. Neither seemed embarrassed by the contact, and neither made a move to shift position. "So what do you want to talk about?" she asked, a teasing laugh quavering her voice.

In that instance, Arthur felt his irritation subside. She was at ease, she was happy, she was completely different from the woman he had known back in Scotland. He may have been the one who had had the truth thrust upon him, but he knew now that the plan had worked. He blew her a long kiss. "Nothing. I'm fine. I was just being a grumpy old bastard back there. You look ahead. It's not good for you to turn around in a car like that. There'll be plenty of time to talk once we're there."

"Are you sure?"

"Of course. Anyway, we don't want to miss any of this, do we?" He held out his arms in a magnanimous gesture as if to embrace the new countryside through which they were driving. And it certainly had changed. Now in the foothills of the sierra, the empty plains had given way to smaller fields that were enclosed by heavy-staked fences or stone walls. Gnarled acorn oaks grew in abundance, amongst which lean

Retinto cattle grazed at the lush covering of grass interlaced with an abundant mosaic of wild flowers, while black Iberian pigs rooted around under the trees to escape the unseasonal warmth of the midday sun. Beyond, where the land had begun to rise up to dark-wooded hills, gleaming white pueblos touched colour to their sombre appearance, with houses, like timid children, hugging close to the tall central figure of Mother Church.

The traffic had eased considerably since leaving the main highway north, and Will was now able to drive at a much greater pace. Nevertheless, they were still overtaken, even on blind corners, by a variety of fast cars with Seville number plates, their occupants also escaping the city's Semana Santa crowds for the weekend. Although Arthur found their driving skills quite alarming, his concern was much greater for those elderly members of the local population who had chosen to take their morning stroll along the sliver of asphalt at the edge of the road, and even more so for the two old men with flat caps on their heads who sat, hands resting on walking-sticks, on the crash barrier at a near right-angled corner, idly watching the traffic go by.

"What's that?" Liz exclaimed at a volume that he was able to pick up. She was pointing towards the outline of a huge fighting bull that stood, his head turned towards them as if his attention had been caught by their arrival, on a low hill a mile or so in front of them.

"That's the Osborne bull," stated Will.

"The what?" Arthur called out from the back of the car.

"The Osborne bull," Will yelled. "It's an advertisement for one of the Jerez sherries. You'll see them all over the southern provinces of Spain. I reckon that that one's probably the most northerly that you'll find, seeing that we're just about to leave Seville province and enter Huelva."

As they drove past the figure, Arthur was amazed at the enormity of it, and he thought about passing comment on certain oversized parts of its anatomy, but then felt that it was maybe not one to make with female company present. So he just said it to himself and laughed quietly at his own joke.

They came across Cañareas quite unexpectedly, rounding a corner at which there appeared to be little sign of urban civilization to reveal the town, bathed in sunlight, sitting contentedly below the new ring road in a deep basin in the hills. It was dominated by a large church and the ancient ruins of a Moorish castle that stood high on the outcrop of rock towering above it. As they approached the first entrance to the town, Will slowed the car down, noticing that there was a large queue of traffic, fronted by a packed bus, waiting in the central slip lane to cross the road.

He turned in his seat. "I was going to drive through town so that we could have a look at the place, but I think we'll give it a miss. The Saturday market will be on, and then there'll be the parades later, so it'll be teeming with people. What do you think?"

Arthur nodded. "I'd rather just get to the place that we're staying. I'm beginning to get cross-eyed, if you get my meaning."

Will put his foot down on the accelerator and shot past the line of traffic. "Okay. I don't think it's that far now." He took a piece of paper from his shirt pocket, and unfolding it with the help of his teeth, he laid it across the steering wheel. "I'd say no more than a couple of miles."

At the highest point of the ring road, Will turned right onto a wide dirt track that led away from the town, and immediately the full beauty of the mountainous countryside was laid open to them. Steep-faced hills that merged into one another were wooded with wide-leaved chestnut and dark-blooded cork trees, sweeping down to green fertile valleys pock-marked with small white dwellings. In the distance, beyond the lake that nudged its way into view between the hills, the land was in stark contrast to this, soaring to an even higher skyline that appeared as barren and colourless as a desert. They passed by a succession of old men trudging their way back towards the town, some carrying gardening implements and sacks across their shoulders, while others slowly ambled along with their hands clasped behind their backs, every one of them turning to face away from the road to avoid the choking dust that was being whipped up by the tyres of the vehicle. Then, rounding a gentle bend, Will had to brake sharply to avoid ploughing into a muleteer who led his two sad-eyed charges along the centre of the road, their backs burdened by hessian panniers brimming with firewood. In his own good time, the old boy guided the mules to one side of the road, then lifted a hand either in acknowledgement or apology and shot them a roguish grin which spread like a crease across parchment on his weather-beaten face, revealing two widely spaced and perfectly useless teeth.

There was no sign to herald the fact that they had arrived at their destination save for a pair of fading green iron gates hung from rough-built stone pillars, which were prevented from swinging closed by two rocks that had at one time been part of the now crumbling drystone wall that surrounded the property. Will drove slowly through the gates, then stopped with his wheels straddling the wide cattle-grid and once more checked his directions. No one spoke. No one dared to make a remark about what might be at the end of the track. He studied the piece of paper for a moment, then balled it up in his fist and threw it into the well at Liz's feet. He clutched the steering wheel and let out a deep sigh. "Well, let's see what we've let ourselves in for, shall we?" he said quietly.

The track broke free from the shade of the chestnut trees and swung around the side of the hill, dipping, then rising again into a wide turning circle. Will pulled the car to a halt and turned off the engine. "Thank goodness for that!" he exclaimed, letting out a long sigh of relief and running the fingers of both hands through his hair. "For a moment back there, I thought we were going to end up staying in a mountain shack."

The whitewashed house was cut into the side of the hill, so that where they had parked was at the level of the long, pan-tiled roof, faded pink by the sun. It had been built in an L-shape, but was squared off by a large courtyard enclosed by a high wall, in the centre of which was a heavy studded oak door set into a pan-tiled overhang. In one corner a small pavilion had been integrated into the surrounding wall, and a covered terrace ran around the inner part of the building, giving shade to the main entrance door and to the French windows that opened out onto the courtyard.

"This is fantastic, Will!" Liz breathed out quietly. She opened the door of the car and got out and walked over to the edge of the car-park. She turned, her mouth open in wonderment. "Come and have a look at this!"

Will got out and stood for a moment with his hands in the small of his back, stretching it out, before walking over to stand beside her.

"Look down there."

Thirty feet below the house, following the ever-decreasing contours of the land, wide stone steps flanked by ornate urns brimming with crimson geraniums led to a paved terrace where light shimmered on the dark blue waters of a large square swimming pool. Below that, further steps led to another terrace, this one half-moon, that fronted an ancient *casita,* its uneven walls covered with a wild bougainvillaea that crept around the windows and tumbled over the sagging lintel of the entrance door.

"Well done you, Will. This is a wonderful find!"

Will shrugged his shoulders. "That's the power of the Internet for you."

"Excuse me!" The voice was muffled behind the closed windows of the car. They turned to see Arthur slowly waving to them, as if accentuating the fact that he was trying to attract their attention. "I'm still here, you know, and if you don't get me out quite soon, something quite untoward might happen."

Letting out a gasp, Liz ran back to the car and opened up the door. "I'm sorry, Arthur." She clambered in beside him and sat down heavily on the seat next to him.

"Watch my pipe!"

"Sorry." She bent forward and removed the pipe from under her bottom and handed it to him. "Isn't this just the most wonderful place?"

Arthur nodded and awkwardly began to push himself forward in his seat. "I'm sure it is, but at this precise minute, my greatest priority is *not* looking at the view."

"Ah, yes. I was forgetting about that. Right, well, let's get you out of here."

It took all of five minutes to extricate Arthur from the car, and once they had managed to get him esconced in the wheelchair, he announced that he couldn't wait and that he wanted to get out again immediately to relieve himself. Liz was quite happy to leave this particular duty to his son and walked around to the other side of the car to wait for them.

The sound of a stone rolling down the car-park banking caught her attention, and she turned to find a tall, lean man with tufts of grey hair sticking out from underneath his camouflage jungle hat standing ten feet away from her, his long, sun-tanned face drawn into a knowing smile as he caught sight of Will and Arthur. He was dressed in a pair of blue coveralls that hung from his body like a clown suit, and he carried in his rubber-gauntleted hands a dismantled set of draining-rods. Liz opened her mouth to speak, but he held up a rubber finger close to his lips to stop her.

"Right now," Will's voice sounded out, "just hop back a bit. I've got the wheelchair, so put your hands on the sides and support yourself. Now, just ease yourself down." There was a thump and a groan of relief from Arthur. "Well done, you've made it."

The man dropped the draining-rods to the ground and approached Liz, pulling off his gloves as he walked. "Well, that was one of the more bizarre arrivals that I've witnessed," he said in a brusque English voice. He held out his hand. "Johnnie Harker. Welcome to Finca de Rodrigo."

Liz took his hand and shook it. "How do you do. I'm Liz Dewhurst."

"Nice to meet you, Liz."

She looked round as the wheelchair brigade approached them. "Will, Arthur, this is Mr. Harker."

"Johnnie, please." He shook their hands, then stuck his fists on his hips. "Well, you poor old devil," he said, looking down at Arthur. "What a bugger of a thing to happen! Knackered the old holiday a bit, hasn't it?"

Arthur let out a sigh and nodded. "I would say so."

"Well, never mind, once you've stayed here, you'll wonder why you ever bothered going to Semana Santa. All those damned crowds, and Seville can get so wretchedly hot, even at this time of the year." He looked about him. "Not here, though. Always a cool breeze, even in the middle of summer." He let out a contented breath, then lobbed his gloves over to where he had set down the draining-rods. "Right, Liz, if you can manage to guide Arthur down the slope over there to the courtyard, I'll give Will—it is Will, isn't it? Spoke to you on the phone. Good. I'll give you a hand with the luggage, then show you the lay of the land in the house."

Liz gave the wheelchair a push towards the slope, but Arthur held up his hand to stop her. "You weren't once in the army, by any chance?" he asked.

The man looked surprised. "Yes, I was. Now how on earth could you tell that?"

Arthur gave him a wry smile. "Oh, I just had an inkling. Guards, was it?"

"Good God, no, old boy! Couldn't give a toss for all that square-bashing. No, I was a Gurkha. That's why I'm so at home in the hills. Trained a hell of a lot in the Himalayas." He followed Will over to the back of the car. "I'll tell you all about it over dinner, if you're interested."

"I bet you will," Arthur murmured under his breath and he gave the wheels a hefty push to help Liz get started.

Liz leaned forward as she steered him down the slope and whispered in his ear, "When it comes to gruffness, Arthur, I think you may well have met your match."

He glanced round. "Come on! I'm never *that* bad—am I?"

Johnnie Harker led his guests across the courtyard to the front door, which was set into the right-angle corner of the house. They entered into a high pine-beamed hallway, unfurnished except for a round mahogany table that stood in the centre of the rustic-tiled floor, its surface covered with objects as if laid out for a memory game: two videos, one shopping basket, a pair of gardening gloves, countless envelopes (both open and unopened), a man's wallet, a set of car keys and two tin cigar cases, all set around a blue Spode china pot which held a flourishing aspidistra. To one side of the hall a carved wooden railing guarded a flight of steps which surprisingly descended to a lower level, while at the front a full-paned window lay open, revealing beyond an iron grille and over the tops of the chestnut trees a stunning view across the lake and away to the distant hills.

"Right," Johnnie said, "easy layout. From here, all bedrooms are to the right through that arch, and living-room, dining-room and kitchen to the left. No need to go downstairs. That's where Annabelle and I hang out, so you can scoot around up here, Arthur, without a care in the world. Right, follow me!"

He strode off along a wide passage that ran the full length of the rear section of the building, its roof so high that it was like walking down the aisle of a cathedral. Rounded arches split the area into three equal sections, each supporting an inverted arch that concealed the only source of artificial light in the passage, while above, sunlight flooded in through three small oblong windows, projecting their focused shapes onto the walls opposite. Below them, the height of the area was cleverly foreshortened by the hanging of sombre but richly coloured Turkish rugs, except at the far end of the passage, where there was a towering life-sized portrait of a nude woman who clutched in both hands a straw hat, strategically placed to cover her tummy button—and nothing else. Having entered the bedroom opposite, Johnnie turned to give more instructions, but caught Arthur eyeing the painting with interest.

"Good, eh? My fortieth birthday present from Annabelle. Damned nearly twenty-one years ago now."

"It's wonderful," Arthur replied, being glad of the chance to view it more closely. "Good-looking woman, too."

"Yes. Mind you, she was thirty when it was done, but, by God, she's still kept her figure."

Arthur spun round to look at him, his mouth dropped open. "You don't mean that that's . . ." He trailed off, realizing that he had probably just put his foot in it.

"What? Annabelle? Yes, of course it is." He laughed. "You don't think that she'd allow me to hang pictures of other nude women around the place, do you?" He turned to assess the room, leaving Arthur speechless. "Right, Arthur, this is your room. Bathroom over there, with lots of handles with which you can heave yourself about. Easy bed to get into. Bell on the wall in case you fall out of bed, or"—he looked out of the door at the portrait of his wife—"you suddenly decide that you want to sleep with the door open." He laughed again. "So, all right for you?"

"Yes, it's perfect, thank you," Arthur replied, wishing that he wasn't so disadvantaged by his wheelchair.

"Good. Now, Will, you're in the next bedroom and Liz next door to that."

He marched briskly out of the room, and before Will and Liz had a chance to follow him his voice once again sounded forth. "Annabelle, darling! Come and meet our guests."

Arthur suddenly seemed to become quite eager to reach the door, pushing himself away from Liz's clutches, and making his way adeptly across the room. Annabelle, however, entered before he had completed his manoeuvre, resulting in his catching his fingers in the spokes of the chair as he brought it to a halt inches from her legs. There was no blasphemous cry of agony, no pained expression on his face as he looked up at the tall, slender woman. He found it quite difficult not to glance past her and make comparisons as to how she looked both clothed and unclothed. There was, however, no doubting the fact that Johnnie had been right. She appeared exactly as she did in the portrait, her figure still perfect under the blue-striped butcher's apron, her face smooth and unwrinkled, the only difference being that her long dark hair had now turned a lustrous grey and was gathered up in a loose bun at the back of her head.

Johnnie introduced them in turn, and Arthur was gladdened by the fact that he didn't demean him by making any further comment about his indisposition. Annabelle beamed a smile at them. "Forgive me for not shaking hands," she said, holding up her own to show that they were covered with flour. "You caught me in the throes of getting the evening meal ready, but I thought I must come through and say hello. Anyway, it's wonderful to meet you all. Did you have a good journey up from Seville?"

"Went without a hitch," Will replied. "We did wonder, though, if we had the right turning at the top of the road. I didn't quite know what we were going to find at the end of the track."

"That's Johnnie's idea," she said, making a face that registered both long-sufferance and humour. "He thinks that it puts off unwelcome visitors."

"And so it does," he retorted. "Right now, what time is it?" He pulled up the oversized sleeve of his coveralls to glance at his wrist-watch. "Hell's teeth, it's five past two. I've taken four hours to clear that bloody drain."

"Did you manage to do it?" Annabelle asked, giving him a look of surprised admiration.

"Course I did. Mind you, it's amazing what you find in drains—"

"All right, darling," she interrupted him. "I don't think that we want to hear the grim details." She turned to her guests. "Now, you haven't had lunch yet, have you? No, good, because I've made a huge pot of soup which Johnnie and I will never finish in a month of Sundays, so why don't you all get settled into your rooms and we'll eat in about fifteen minutes."

"Which gives us all quite enough time to have a small refreshment first, don't you think?" Johnnie continued. He took hold of the handles of Arthur's wheelchair and manoeuvred him through the door. "Come on, Arthur, we'll see if we can't get a quick one in before the others join us."

They had lunch outside on the large vine-draped veranda that fronted the drawing-room, a leisurely, drawn-out meal that lasted for much longer than it took them to finish off the soup and the slab of locally produced goat's cheese that Annabelle had bought in the market that morning. Arthur was quite content in being placed next to her at the table and, with an enraptured expression on his face, proceeded to engage her in a one-to-one conversation, leaving Liz and Will to be entertained by Johnnie. At first, Liz felt the men's company quite overpowering, finding herself completely out of her depth while the two spoke at length about the oil industry, Johnnie being well-informed on the subject as a result of a year's tour of duty in Oman during his army career. However, just when she felt that she was going to pass the whole meal without opening her mouth, Johnnie abruptly terminated his conversation with Will and, physically turning away from him, directed his attention totally to her.

"Now what about you, Liz? What do you do to keep the wolf from the door?"

Liz took in a deep breath. "Well, nothing really, other than being a mother to my son."

"I wouldn't say that's nothing! Damned difficult job. What age is he?"

"Eighteen. He's in his first year at Saint Andrews University."

"Good for him. We've got two boys as well, both at different stages at Durham University. We get e-mails occasionally from them, and I sometimes wonder from their content whether they're doing any work at all."

Liz laughed. "I'm sure they are. I think that they just find playtime more fun to talk about than work."

Johnnie raised his eyebrows in consideration of her wise remark. "Maybe. Let's hope you're right."

"I don't think Liz is doing herself justice either," Will cut in, smiling across the table at her. "She's lived on a farm all her life, so she's probably worked harder than we ever have."

"On a farm?" Johnnie exclaimed, his eyes sparkling with interest. "But that's wonderful! You don't happen to know anything about sheep, do you?"

"Well, yes, I do. Quite a bit, actually."

"My word, you're a godsend! Listen, I've just become the proud possessor of ten sheep and a motley-looking ram, and I know damn-all about them."

And he proceeded to launch into a barrage of questions about sheep husbandry: how long he should run the ram with the ewes, how often he should worm them and what would be the correct time to clip them.

When he realized that every one of his questions was being answered with authority, he called along the table to Annabelle, telling her to stop talking to Arthur and to listen, because they were lucky to have in their midst a real expert on sheep.

Once he felt that his knowledge was replete, which coincided with a point when the two bottles of red wine lay empty in front of them and coffee-cups sat drained of their contents, Johnnie linked his hands behind his head and leaned back in his chair. "Well, Annabelle," he said, grinning at his wife at the far end of the table, "all I can say is thank God this lot are here!" He turned to Liz and gave her a wink. "Believe it or not, we get quite starved of intelligent people out here." He threw himself forward and slammed his hands down on the table. "Talking of which," he muttered conspiratorially, "I think it only fair that you should be warned about our other guests tonight."

"Johnnie!" Annabelle gasped, a look of consternation on her face. She glanced furtively through the wide French windows into the house as if to make sure that no one had walked into the drawing-room unnoticed. "You're a dreadful man, you know! You're breaking the cardinal rule"—she leaned forward and put her hand on Arthur's arm—"which is one should never be rude about one's guests—especially in front of other guests." She glared back at her husband. "You've obviously had far too much to drink."

"Oh, probably," he laughed, "but sometimes it's such fun to speak one's mind."

"Well, you mustn't." She gave him a crooked smile. "Now to absolve yourself of this quite appalling misdemeanour, I would like to know what little job you have lined up for yourself this afternoon now that the drains are cleared, because . . ." She drew out the word as if she knew already that what she was about to suggest was going to be met with disapproval.

"No!" he interjected. "I'm not paying bills today. I'll do them tomorrow. I've got to mend that fence up in the olive grove, otherwise the sheep will end up getting splatted all over the road."

"All right, but you *must* do them tomorrow, otherwise everyone in the town will start denouncing us." She turned to her guests. "Now, what do you all feel like doing for the rest of the afternoon? We don't have dinner until nine o'clock at the earliest, so you've got plenty of time for whatever you want."

It was Will who spoke first. "Would you mind if I hooked into a telephone line for a couple of minutes? I'm technically still at work, I'm afraid, and I never got the chance this morning to pick up my e-mail."

"No problem, old boy!" Johnnie said. "Just head down the flight of stairs in the hall and turn left. That's my study. A bit of a mess, I'm afraid, but clear a space for yourself and get plugged in."

"Thank you. I don't reckon I'll be that long. I thought then that I might try to clear my head of your wonderful wine and walk into Cañareas." He looked across the table at Liz. "How about it? Do you want to come?"

Liz nodded. "Yes, I'd like to . . . that is, if you don't mind, Arthur."

He shot her a grateful smile along the table. "No, you go ahead. I'll just take myself quietly off to my bedroom and read a book."

"I'm hoping that you'll do no such thing!" Annabelle retorted. "There's nothing I like better than being entertained in my own kitchen by an intelligent and quite charming gentleman."

Liz noticed colour rising to Arthur's cheeks for what she judged to be the first time since he had suffered his accident. "In that case," he replied, bowing his head slightly toward his hostess, "I would be delighted to engage you in conversation for what's left of the afternoon."

By the time Liz had given Annabelle a hand to clear the table Will had finished his work and, at Annabelle's insistence, they were sent packing from the house, leaving her in the company of Arthur, who seemed perfectly content in cutting up carrots on a chopping board that she had placed across the arms of his wheelchair. It took them no more than twenty minutes to walk into town, beating the same track they had seen taken by the old man when they arrived. Crossing over the main road, they made their way down a narrow cobbled street where housewives wearing bright aprons that contrasted with their black dresses gabbled loudly to each other as they swept clean the pavement outside the doorways of their small houses, the multitude of pot plants that hung from the balconies splashing a profusion of colour onto their white frontages.

The street wound round past an open-fronted greengrocer's shop where both customers and staff seemed more concerned with chatting rather than carrying out any form of transaction, and then swung left into the large paved *plaza major* that lay half in shadow and half in bright sunlight. It was thronged with people who milled about the parallel lines of orange trees or bunched together on the wooden benches that were set against the iron railings surrounding the area. A little girl, dressed in her best party outfit, used those who stood about like traffic cones, weaving in and out of them on her small plastic tricycle. In the far corner of the square a noisy game of football was in progress, being watched by a gathering of teen-age girls with sun-glasses perched, as if part of a uniform, on the tops of their heads. They clustered about the dome-topped confectionery kiosk and screamed in delighted horror if the ball was kicked anywhere near them. Beyond the railings, the road that encircled the square was crammed with parked vehicles or encroached upon by tables and chairs that spilt over from the pavements outside restaurants, making it an almost impossible task for those who tried to manoeuvre their cars around the heavily congested area and up the quieter side-streets that led away from it.

Deciding also that the *plaza* was too overpopulated, Will and Liz wove their way across the square and took a street that rose sharply up towards the church that overlooked the town. Half-way up the hill, the street opened out into another square, smaller and less crowded, where they stopped for a moment to catch their breath.

"How about a cup of coffee?" Will asked, pointing to a small restaurant whose few tables and chairs lay out in a sun-trap in the corner of the square.

"I think that's a very good idea," she replied, squinting her eyes against the sun to look up at the church that still lay a good six hundred yards up the steep road. "I don't think that I could make it up there today."

As soon as they had occupied two of the plastic chairs, a waiter appeared through the bead-curtained entrance of the restaurant at a speed that would have suggested that he had been physically ejected from the place. "*¡Buenas tardes, señores!*" he sang out, giving the surface of the table a quick wipe with his dishcloth. "*¿Qué quieren ustedes tomar?*"

"What would you like?"

"Just a cup of white coffee, please."

"*Un café con leche y un café solo.*"

"*Desde luego, señor. ¿Y algo a comer?*"

"Do you want anything to eat?"

"No, thanks!" Liz replied, blowing out a breath at the thought. "I'm still wondering whether I'll have enough room for the meal tonight!"

Will laughed. "*No, nada más. Los cafés solamente.*"

"*Gracias, señores.*" He skipped off towards the door, calling out their orders as he pushed his way through the curtain.

Liz leaned back in her chair and, tilting up her head, closed her eyes to the warming rays of the late-afternoon sun. "This is real bliss," she said in a slow, languid voice.

Will watched her. "Not like Scotland, then?"

"No. Definitely not like Scotland."

"So what's been happening up there?"

"A bit of sun, a bit of rain, but we never get heat. Not at this time of year, anyway. In fact, come to think of it, we hardly ever get it at all nowadays."

"I wasn't really talking about the weather," Will said quietly.

Liz opened her eyes and looked at him. "What do you mean?"

Will rested his elbows on the table. "Well, what's been happening to you? You gave me a garbled account that first time we met in the hotel, and then, in the restaurant, you didn't want to talk about it. So how about now? I'd quite like to hear a fuller version."

Liz shook her head. "You wouldn't find it that interesting."

"Honestly, I'd like to know."

The waiter appeared from the doorway and placed their cups in front of them on the table. Will ripped open the small packet of sugar and poured it into his coffee. "Well?"

Liz let out a sigh. "All right, but if I see your eyes drooping for even a second, then I promise you I'll stop and I won't say a word more about it."

"Okay. It's a deal."

During the next two hours, however, his attention never faltered for a moment as she went through every detail of what had happened to her over the past year. She even surprised herself at the apparent ease with which she was able to divulge information hitherto too sensitive to relate. She told him about Gregor's long-standing relationship with Mary McLean and how she had been left with no alternative other than to move herself and Alex back to her parents' house. She found herself choking back tears when she told him about the death of her mother, and then the subsequent demise of their farm. She continued talking once they had left the restaurant and made their way back through the town, avoiding the square where even more people seemed to be gathering early for the town's *Soledad* parade that night. By the time they arrived back at the gates of the *finca*, she had told him about her vehement opposition to the construction of the golf course and how it had nearly led to her being ostracized by the local community, and then how Alex had brought Arthur home to live with them and how he had managed to breathe new life into their otherwise sad, introverted life.

"And that's about it," she said, as they cut up over the hill to approach the house from above. Will made no reply but continued to walk, his head bowed low as he kicked out at a stone, sending it spinning up the small track. "You see what I mean now. It doesn't make very good listening. It's all pretty self-pitying stuff."

He closed the gap between them and, looping an arm around her shoulders, he gave her a tight squeeze. "I don't think that at all. As a matter of fact, I was just thinking about what a jerk I was to blow off at you like that on that first night we met." He stopped, pulling her to a halt beside him. He put both arms around her neck and held her tight in a powerful bear-hug. "Jeez, you *have* had one hell of a year, haven't you? I'm not surprised you don't trust anyone anymore—well, anyone of the male gender, that is."

Without having to push him away, Liz disentangled herself from his clutches. "I know," she said, continuing to walk. "I try not to make it show, but obviously it does." She let out a short laugh. "The funny thing is that Arthur has helped me quite a bit, in his own rather peculiar way. I think I've grown to trust him."

"And what about Gregor?"

She turned and raised her eyebrows at him. "That's a pretty silly question. Of course I don't trust him."

"I wasn't actually getting at that. I mean, what are your feelings towards him?"

"I hate him," she responded immediately. She stopped and pushed her hands into the pockets of her jeans. "I think." She smiled at him. "Come on, let's get back to the house before you draw anything else out of me that I might regret saying later."

He reached out and clutched her arm. "Hold on a minute."

She looked at him quizzically. "What?"

He let go and stood back from her, crossing his arms as he looked at her. "Well, I'm now going to say something which I might regret saying later, but before you go back to that house, Liz, I think that you should know a few home truths about yourself. In my eyes, I think you're pretty fantastic, and I don't mean, you know, just the normal things like your looks. You are an extremely engaging person. Your whole aura captivates me. Now, to break that down into easily digested segments, I find you intelligent, fun to be with and wildly practical, and I can quite honestly say that if I had run across you before in my life, then my high-handed opinion on marital involvement would probably have been blown out the window"—he clicked his fingers—"just like that." He paused, noticing that her cheeks were beginning to flush with embarrassment. "And that's the main reason that I had to get that story out of you, because had I not known that you had been so badly hurt, there is no doubt in my mind that at some time over the next few days, I would not have been able to stop myself from making an almighty, no-holds-barred pass at you." He moved over to the old drystone wall and leaned against it. "Now, what I would like to know is how that makes you feel? Are you saying to yourself, 'Oh, he's just saying that to be kind,' or are you saying, 'This man must have gone stark-raving mad!' or maybe it's, 'Hell, this man's just trying to get me into bed for his own gratification.' Or, as I hope it will be, you are saying, 'Wow, I think he means it.'" He paused again and swept a hand through his hair. "Okay, that's it. I've said it all. The ball's in your court now."

It may have been, but Liz found herself unable to formulate any answer at all. She had no inclination to speak. No one had ever said anything like that to her before. Not even Gregor. There had never been any call for it. He hadn't had to court her in that way, because . . . well . . . because of Alex. They had just fallen into a relationship. Maybe that had been their trouble all along. Maybe they had both bypassed the first stages of love. She looked over to Will and saw herself impaled by his eyes. She had to avoid them. She lowered her head and copied his action of flicking at a loose stone with her shoe. What had he said all that for? Was he just being kind? No, he'd plugged that bolt-hole. In fact, he'd been clever enough to plug *every* bolt-hole. He had pre-empted everything that she might have thought about what he had said. Surely he couldn't mean it? Surely it's not *me* that he's talking about? She looked back up at him. He was pretending to appear unconcerned about her lack of response, averting his eyes from her and whistling nonchalantly. Suddenly, he fixed her once more with his eyes. "Well, what's your answer?"

She smiled at him, and Will realized immediately that he had made a breakthrough. Her whole being seemed to shed the brittle edginess that had been so apparent before, and the expression on her face encapsulated a new-found contentment. "I'm afraid that I don't know what to say."

Will punched his fist into the palm of the other hand. "Great! That's all I wanted to hear. You are quite simply one of the best, Liz, and never, ever think otherwise of yourself." He pushed himself away from the wall, then immediately held up a finger. "Just one more thing that you should know before we forget that this conversation ever took place, and that is that you can trust me, too, Liz. I promise that I would never do anything to hurt you."

"BUGGER THIS SODDING MACHINE!" The voice rang out from behind the small shed that lay fifty yards above them on the track, its echo ricocheting off the hills on the far side of the valley. They looked at each other for a moment before both burst out laughing.

"I think that sounds as if Johnnie is having a little bit of trouble with something, don't you?" Will said, an analytical expression on his face. "Maybe we should go to see if we can lend a hand."

As he set off up the path, Liz stayed where she was, watching his robust figure stride away from her. "Will?"

He turned back. "Yes?"

"Thanks—and I'm sorry."

Will shrugged his shoulders. "Don't be." He held out his hand to her. "Come on, let's go see what's troubling Colonel Gusto."

They found Johnnie crouched at the side of an old Fordson tractor, his head resting against its bonnet, as he struggled to turn an unseen nut somewhere in the innermost bowels of its engine. As they silently approached him, he stood back from the machine and threw the spanner to the ground in defeat. "*Ballocks!*"

"Having a spot of bother?" Will asked, his question laced with humour.

Johnnie started suddenly at the sound of his voice and spun around. "Oh, it's you lot." He looked back at the tractor and put his hands on his hips. "Bloody thing's stopped dead on me. I was just on the way back from mending the fence, and then, fart! it just gave up the ghost." He bent down to pick up the spanner, then turned to Will. "You must have had some experience of diesel engines in your time. Any idea what could be the trouble?"

Will scratched at the side of his face. "Sounds like fuel starvation to me."

"That's what I thought, but I've been pushing away at that little lever on the fuel pump to no avail at all."

"Have you bled the injectors?"

"As best as I could. The wretched thing is so old that one of them is seized right up."

"That could be the problem then. Maybe you would be best to get someone out to free it?"

Johnnie flicked back his head. "Easier said than done out here, old boy. It'd cost me a fortune that I don't have."

"Could you try turning the engine over for a moment?" Liz asked.

The two men slowly turned to look at her.

"What?" Johnnie asked, his tone almost registering annoyance.

"Just press the starter lever for a moment."

Johnnie shot Will a glance, then moved forward to the tractor and executed Liz's request. The engine turned slowly, its battery nearly dead from Johnnie's insistent cranking.

"White exhaust," Liz said quietly. "I think you might have got water in your fuel system."

"How the hell could that have happened?"

Liz shrugged. "I don't know. Do you fill it up from a tank or with jerrycans?"

"Usually jerrycans."

"Then that's probably what caused your problem."

Johnnie let out a long sigh, as if uneasy at having his lack of mechanical skills exposed by a woman. "So is there anything we can do about it?"

"Well, we can start by taking off the fuel filter."

"Right!" said Will, rubbing his hands together and moving forward to the tractor. "I'll be your apprentice. How do we do that?"

Liz began rummaging through the tin box in which Johnnie kept his ill assortment of tools and came up with an adjustable Stillson spanner.

She unscrewed it to its fullest aperture and handed it to him. "That should do it. Now, take it off as gently as possible so you don't damage it."

Will placed it against the filter and began to adjust it to fit.

"Erm," Liz said softly, "that's actually the oil filter, Will. The one for the fuel is next to the injection pump."

Johnnie let out a raucous laugh. "Bloody hell! We men are really being taught a lesson here, aren't we?"

Having been guided to the right place, Will gave the spanner a slow twist and the fuel filter came free. He screwed it off with his hand and handed it to Liz. "Right, over to you, boss."

Liz stood back from the two men and poured its contents onto the ground, then, raising it over her shoulder, she brought it down in a whipping movement to remove all residue from it. "Have you got any clean diesel, Johnnie?"

"Coming right up!" He rushed off into the shed and returned with a plastic fuel can. "This should do you."

Liz filled up the fuel filter from the can and went through the motion of emptying it again. Then, filling it up once more, she walked over to the tractor and screwed it back onto its seating. "Okay," she said, wiping her hands on the seat of her jeans. "You can tighten it up again."

Will leaped forward to carry out his task. "Now what?" he said, standing back from the machine.

"We bleed it," Liz replied. "Here, give me the spanner."

The two men craned over to watch as she first turned the bleed screw on the bottom of the lift pump, then the one on the side of the injection pump. Once she had diesel seeping from the small aperture, she told Johnnie to crank the engine once more. "Right, that's enough," she said, tightening up the screw. "Now, we've got to check if there's fuel going through to the injectors." She eased off those that she was able, and breathed out an inaudible sigh of relief when she saw diesel running down the side of the engine block. Tightening up the holding nuts, she stood back and lobbed the spanner into the tin box.

"Is that it?" Johnnie asked.

Liz nodded. "I hope so. Does the tractor have a heating coil?"

"Yes."

"Well, you don't have much power left in your battery, so just give it ten seconds before you fire the engine."

There was silence as Johnnie held down the button beneath the steering wheel, and Liz found herself crossing her fingers behind her back. "Right, try it now."

He pressed the starter lever and the engine turned over slowly, but failed to fire. "Stop!" Liz called out. "It's nearly there."

"How can you tell?"

"You're getting black exhaust now. Just put the heater switch on again."

They waited a further ten seconds. "Right, try again," Liz said quietly, "but this time, push your throttle fully open."

Johnnie pressed the starter lever once more, and on the third wheezing crank, just when the battery gave every sign that it was going to die for good, the tractor spluttered into life, sending up a cloud of acrid black smoke into the air.

"You bloody marvel, Liz!" Johnnie exclaimed. "You are nothing but a bloody marvel."

She moved forward and shut down the throttle, the tractor ceasing its metal-shaking scream and settling into a steady idle. "I'd leave it running for an hour, just so that the battery can get charged up again."

She turned to find the two men standing side by side with blatant admiration written all over their faces. Will shook his head. "Now where on earth did you learn to do that?"

Liz laughed. "It's not as good as it looks, you know. My father has one of these at home—forty years old and still his pride and joy. I've just grown up with it. It's almost part of the family, so I know all its idiosyncrasies. Now, if it had been a John Deere or a Massey Ferguson, I'm afraid that I wouldn't have had a clue."

"Well, I certainly couldn't have done it," Johnnie said, bending down to gather his tools together. He closed the lid of his box and stood up, a thoughtful frown puckering his forehead. "In fact, you couldn't teach Annabelle how to do it, could you?"

Liz laughed. "I don't think so."

"No, maybe not such a good idea. Better that everyone sticks to their domain, what!" He took the tool-box over to the shed and threw it carelessly inside, then, closing the door, he snapped shut the padlock. "Right, let's get back to the house and tell the world about your expertise."

As it happened, Liz's "expertise" in tractor maintenance turned out to be a perfect ice-breaker at the pre-dinner drinks, as the couple from the Isle of Wight, who obviously had become quite intimidated by Johnnie's brusque manner during their stay at Finca de Rodrigo, now appeared dumb-struck by the arrival of new guests in their midst. Even after having been introduced, they sat together on the sofa at the side of the roaring log fire, clutching their glasses of Oloroso sherry and smiling nervously at each other as Johnnie recounted to all Liz's tremendous feat, his tone becoming more vociferous and more animated as he went on.

It was Liz who managed to draw them into the conversation, at a time when she felt that Johnnie had slightly overplayed the subject and was beginning to sound quite chauvinistic in his appraisal of how unexpected it was to find a woman who could do such a job. "I don't think that's right at all," she said quite sharply. "In certain cases, women can be much more practically minded than men." She turned to the woman on the sofa. "What do you think, Valerie?"

The woman shot an apprehensive glance at her husband before replying. "Oh, well . . ." she stuttered. Then she gave a definite nod with her head, as if taking courage from Liz's remark. "Yes, you *are* right. Just before we came out here, my dishwasher went wrong and I fixed it myself."

"Yes, she did," her husband agreed, smiling proudly at his wife. "And it was quite complicated, too."

"Jolly good for you!" Johnnie exclaimed. "Every time I try to do something with one of those infernal machines, I usually end up having to call out an engineer, and then find out that I've succeeded in making the problem a hundred times worse than it was originally."

Thereafter, during dinner, conversation flowed between them, so much so that when Annabelle drew their attention to the fact that it was almost one o'clock in the morning, they were still seated around the dining-room table. "Now just leave everything as it is," she said, getting up from her seat. "Johnnie and I will clear up in the morning."

There was a moment of polite dissent before everyone dispersed to their bedrooms. Liz helped Arthur negotiate his wheelchair past the few obstacles in the corridor, then, leaving him in Will's hands to help him get ready for bed, she made her way back to her own room, only to stop short at the door when she heard the clatter of plates being cleared from the dining-room table. She walked back to find Annabelle there by herself, carrying a heaped tray through to the kitchen, the pale-blue dress that she was wearing now protected by her butcher's apron.

"I thought you said you were going to leave this until the morning."

Annabelle stopped abruptly in the doorway of the kitchen and turned around. "Liz!" She grimaced, as if being caught carrying out an illegal act. "You weren't meant to hear me. Johnnie must have left the hall door open when he went out. You wouldn't be kind enough to shut it for me, would you?" She continued on her way to the kitchen and Liz went over to shut the door.

"You caught me out," Annabelle laughed, on re-entering the room.

"In what way?"

"I always say that I'm going to leave the clearing up until the morning, because it gives the guests no option other than to go to bed. Then, when I think the coast is clear, I slip back in here and do it myself. So much easier, because I know exactly what has to be done."

"Would you prefer if I went, then?"

"No! Not at all." She went around the table, picking up wineglasses between her fingers. "It's just that I don't ever get much time to myself, so I try to grab every opportunity."

Liz picked up the salad bowl from the centre of the table. "It must be a real strain having people in your house all the time."

"It is, but it's what we do to make ends meet. We've learned over the years how to work around our guests, so that lessens the load a bit."

Liz took the bowl through to the kitchen and placed it on the draining-board. "How long have you been doing this?"

"Almost ten years now. When Johnnie came out of the army, he had a series of what he termed 'dead-end jobs,' working for a time in financial management, and then, when he became sick of that, working as a glorified travelling salesman for a timber company. And then, one miserably wet day, he stormed into the house and blurted out that he had had enough of England, its weather *and* the government, and he wanted to live abroad. And I, for once in my life, agreed with him. So we sold our ugly old house in Wiltshire for an exorbitant sum of money and we were able to buy this little patch of heaven and build the house with the proceeds. And then, one day, when the builders and the painters and the removal men had all left, we sat down on our newly arranged furniture and looked at each other and said, 'Right. So what do we do now?' That's when panic set in. We had nothing left, nothing to live off. Then, almost the next day, a friend of mine who worked for a fashion magazine in London telephoned and said that she wanted to use Cañareas as a location and could I provide board and lodgings for six models, a photographer and his assistant and an art director? Since then, we haven't looked back." She turned the dial on the dishwasher and pressed the button. "So whenever I have a particularly tiresome set of guests, or I get sick of cooking and the clearing up after people and washing interminable amounts of sheets and towels, I just think back and realize just how lucky we have been."

Liz sat down on the edge of the kitchen table. "I still admire you for doing it. I only have one house guest at home—Arthur, as it happens—and although he's pretty unobtrusive, I really find it difficult having someone other than my own family around the place all the time. You can never, well, relax."

"No, you're right. You can't," Annabelle replied. She took two large wineglasses from the wooden washing-rack above the sink and split the contents of a two-thirds-empty bottle of red wine between them. She handed one to Liz. "Can I ask you something, Liz, without, I hope, sounding rude?"

Liz gave her a questioning look. "Yes, of course."

"It's just that I'm quite intrigued with your situation, and I was wondering—what it is, really."

"In what way?"

"Well, with your menfolk. I can't quite work it out."

Liz took in a breath. "Well, there's nothing really to work out. I'd like to say that I'm young, free and single, but I'm definitely not young, and at the minute I'm not single, because I'm separated from my husband, which I suppose cancels out the 'free' bit. So maybe the best definition would be old, tied up but alone."

"But . . . what about Will?"

"Will? He's just Arthur's son. I came out here with Arthur for Semana Santa and he turned up a couple of days ago, just after Arthur broke his ankle."

"So you're . . . you're not with Arthur either."

"Goodness, no! I'm not with anyone—not in that way, at any rate."

Annabelle shook her head. "I'm sorry, I shouldn't have asked. It's just that I was rather confused about how you three all fitted in with each other."

"And are you any more the wiser now?"

She laughed. "No, not really." She took a drink from her glass. "But if you hadn't made it clear otherwise, I would have suspected that you and Will were an item."

"Will and I? Heavens, no!" She hesitated for a moment. "What made you think that?"

Annabelle shrugged. "I don't know." A smile spread slowly across her face. "Probably just the way he never took his eyes off you the whole way through dinner."

"Ah," Liz replied quietly. She bit at her lip. "Actually, we were talking about things this afternoon, and he did say something along the lines of what you've just mentioned, but I don't feel ready to start another relationship just yet, Annabelle. The last one hurt me deeply and put me very much on self-defence."

Annabelle drained her glass. "Can I ask when this happened?"

"Last year. He went off with another woman."

"Last year! Well, in that case!" She went into the larder and came out with another uncorked bottle of wine. She refreshed both their glasses. "Look, maybe I shouldn't say this, but sometimes a relationship with no ties, with no commitments can be the best therapy for a wounded heart. There can be nothing better than to feel wanted, to be made to feel attractive again. Not that *you* need to be made to feel attractive. Will wasn't the only one making eyes at you across the dining-room table. I don't think that I've seen my husband in such good form for quite a long time. So, my suggestion would be that while you're out here in Spain, far removed from your problems back home, you should just tuck them away to the back of your mind and let things happen. And if the opportunity arises for you to have a wonderful, rip-roaring affair with a man whom I certainly wouldn't throw out of bed on a cold night, then I would grab it with both hands." She put her hand across her mouth and let out a short, high-pitched giggle, realizing what she had just said. "Figuratively speaking, of course."

Liz laughed. "Of course!" She watched her feet as she swung them back and forth under the table. "Have you . . . well . . . ever done anything like that before?"

There was a moment's hesitation before Annabelle replied. "Yes, as a matter of fact, I have." She pulled a face. "My word, the secrets are coming out tonight, aren't they?" Placing the bottle of wine and her glass on the table, she pulled out a chair and sat down. "When Johnnie left the army and couldn't get a job, he seemed to change beyond recognition and he began to take all his problems out on me. We stopped speaking to each other, we never made love, so, as you can imagine, our relationship was heading straight for the rocks. So I upped sticks and headed off to France for a couple of weeks with a friend, just to get some clear thinking time, and while I was there, I met this man and we had a wonderful time together, and I felt loved again—and wanted again. Then, when I returned to England full of trepidation at what the future might hold, Johnnie had found himself a job and everything just went back to normal again. Only this time it was better, because he, too, had had time to think and he understood that the gulf that had appeared in our relationship was entirely down to him. I never told him about my . . . little affair, not because I wanted to continue to deceive him. I just knew that we would be together from then on and it would have done no earthly good if I had confessed all. But I do know that it works."

Liz let out a sigh. "Yes, I can see that it probably would do. It's just that I don't know if I'm quite ready for it. I'm also probably not quite so . . . well . . . liberated as you."

Annabelle laughed. "Heavens, how wonderful! You make me sound like a loose woman." She reached over and placed her hand on Liz's arm. "Listen, Liz, I promise you that I'm not trying to force your hand on this. I just thought it might help to hear another woman's point of view."

"Oh, it does, and I appreciate you talking to me about it. I just wonder if it wouldn't make things . . . quite complicated."

"In what way?"

"Well, I suppose really that my loyalties should still lie with Arthur."

"Oh, don't bother about Arthur! He's perfectly happy, and he's in no fit state to go spying on your every move. Anyway, you just leave Arthur to me. I think that we've developed quite an understanding ourselves." She placed her hands on the table and pushed herself to her feet. "Now, if I don't get to bed quite soon, Johnnie will be through here to find out what's happened to me. So I would suggest that you go off to your room and have yourself some sweet dreams." She walked across to the sink and rinsed out her glass under the tap. "Even after ten years of being here, I still feel that this place has an air of unreality about it. It's like Never

Never Land. What happens really doesn't exist, so you should just take advantage of it."

She switched off the lights in the kitchen and together they walked through the sitting-room and out into the hall.

"Good night, Annabelle," Liz whispered. "Thank you for your words of wisdom."

Annabelle moved towards her and gave her a kiss on the cheek. "Good night, Liz." She turned and began to descend the stairs. "And by the way," she called out softly without looking back, "Happy Easter!"

Chapter 22

The armchair and low coffee-table were not permanent fixtures in the kitchen, nor were they ever likely to become so in the future. Their present positioning successfully blocked up the already restricted floor space and hindered anyone trying to make their way around the central worktop. But then again, Alex wasn't using the room as a place to throw together culinary delights for himself. He had converted it into his living-room, a supremely comfortable area where he had managed to cut legwork to the minimum. He could walk into the house, open the fridge door, take out a beer, make himself his customary life-supporting snack of cheese and Tak's curry-pickle sandwiches, get everything to the coffee-table, flump down into the chair and press the television remote without having to move more than seven paces. It had taken him a good half-hour of back-breaking labour to manouevre the two bits of furniture along the narrow corridor and squeeze them through the doorway into the kitchen. However, it had been worth it for the few hours of relaxation that he was able to enjoy every evening after returning footsore from his daily tramp around the golf courses in St. Andrews.

The only problem was that the amount of exercise that he was taking, coupled with the heat being thrown out from the Rayburn cooker, provided for a soporific cocktail which had prevented him on more than one occasion from ever reaching his bed. Such was his state of being that night, having sat down to watch the late film and fallen asleep before the titles had even finished, that he would no doubt have been heading for yet another stiff-limbed morning had he not been abruptly awakened by the shrill ring of the telephone. He jumped awake, his flailing hand knocking over the half-full can of beer that had been resting on the arm of the chair.

"*Shit!*" He struggled forward in the sagging armchair, picking up the receiver with one hand while trying to retrieve the can with the other before it had a chance to spill every last drop of its contents on the tiled floor. "Could you hang on a moment?" he called into the receiver. He got up and threw the phone on the chair, then stood still for a moment with the can in his hands, blinking his eyes to try to clear the disorientation from his head. He placed the can on the worktop, spun off an overindulgence of paper towels and wiped the floor. Lobbing the sodden mass into the sink, he picked up the receiver and sat down heavily once more in the chair.

"Hullo?"

"What on earth were *you* doing?"

"Oh, hi, Dad. Sorry, I was asleep when you rang and I've gone and knocked over a can of beer." He let out a long yawn and scratched fiercely at his head. "What time is it anyway?"

"Quarter to twelve."

"Hell, you're calling a bit late, aren't you?"

"I know I am, but I've been trying to get hold of you all evening."

"Ah, right. Well, I'm not long back from Saint Andrews. I met up with a couple of friends after I'd finished work."

"You weren't drinking, were you?"

"No, Dad, I was not. I'm not a complete idiot."

"All right, I believe you. Is your grandfather not back yet?"

"No. They've headed up to Dornoch, but he said that they'd be back tomorrow evening."

"My word, I'd no idea that he was planning to be away for so long. If I'd known, I would have suggested that you come to stay here."

"No, I'm fine where I am. Anyway, I have to man the telephone in case Mum calls."

"Have you heard from her at all?"

"Yes, most days. She rang early this morning to say that they were just about to leave Seville and head up into the hills somewhere." He stretched out his legs and rested them on the coffee-table. "So, what have you been doing today?"

"Och, just driving about the countryside looking for jobs. I went over to an estate near Comrie this morning for an interview."

"And?"

"And nothing. It was advertised as a farm manager's job, but I reckon that I'd have been nothing more than a glorified shepherd, working a handful of Blackface ewes on three thousand acres of hill. The house was in the middle of nowhere as well, so I don't think I came over as being that keen."

"It would be a long way from here too, wouldn't it?"

"Aye, you're right. Those were exactly my sentiments. Anyway, on the way home, I came up with a new idea and went straight round to see Jonathan Davies about it."

"That being?"

"Well, it was just that I was considering everything, you know, having this house here and my roots being here and you being just across the field, and I thought to myself that I didn't really want to move away. At any rate, I certainly didn't want to end up being stuck on top of a mountain in some dreich farmhouse. So it occurred to me that maybe there was something that I could do around here once the golf course had been constructed."

"Don't tell me! You're planning to become Balmuir's first golf professional."

Gregor laughed. "That'd be right. I'd swing a golf club like a fencing mallet! No, lad, I'll leave that job to you."

"So what's the idea then?"

"Well, I'm thinking of going back to college."

"*What?* Where? I mean, to study what?"

"Greenkeeping."

"Greenkeeping?"

"Yes. Why not? I remembered that they ran courses at the agricultural college in Cupar, so I thought that I'd go and sound out Jonathan about it. He was all for it. He also reckoned that I would probably be able to get a fair-sized grant, you know, for retraining."

"I wouldn't think it would be that well paid, Dad."

"Hell, Alex, I'm not a big spender. I don't need huge amounts of money. Anyway, I don't think I've done anything other than *lose* money for the last five years, so getting a cheque of *any* size in my hand would be a step in the right direction."

"Yeah, I take your point."

"And once Jonathan's deal goes through and I've paid off the bank, I'll at least have a house with no mortgage, and the golf course is right here on the doorstep. What pleases me most, though, about the whole idea is that in a roundabout way I'd still be working my own land . . ." He paused. "So what do you think?"

"Yeah, go for it. It's a great idea. What does Mary say about it?"

"She doesn't know yet. She's away for the weekend, playing in some two-day badminton jamboree over near Edinburgh. That's actually the reason why I was calling. Seeing you and I are by ourselves, I was wondering if you'd like to go to the kirk with me tomorrow, you know, for the Easter service."

Alex sucked in a breath. "Dad, I can't. I'm afraid that I've arranged to play golf."

"Have you? Och well, never mind. It was just a thought."

Alex could hear the disappointment in his father's voice. "Listen, we could meet up after I've played and have something to eat."

"No, I'll tell you what. I won't bother going to the kirk. I'll just come with you and carry your clubs. How about that?"

Alex clenched his teeth at the suggestion. "Er, well the thing is, Dad, that I already have a caddy—of sorts."

"Ah. Right." Alex heard him chuckling. "It wouldn't be the girl in your German tutorial, would it?"

"It might be."

"Good for you. Well, then."

"And her name is Madeleine, before you start trying to wheedle that out of me as well."

"Madeleine. I like that. That's a nice name." His father let out a deep sigh. "Oh, well, have yourself a good time."

There was silence at the end of the line. Alex shook his head in defeat. "All right, Dad, if you want, you can come too."

"Wonderful! That's great, Alex, and I promise you that I won't go putting my foot in it."

"You'd better not."

"You can count on me, lad. So what time?"

"I'll pick you up at eleven."

"Eleven it is. I'll be ready. And, Alex . . ."

"Yes?"

"Happy Easter."

"And the same to you, Dad."

CHAPTER 23

Having lived all her days on a farm, Liz had evolved over the years into being both a light sleeper and an early riser. Yet, that next morning, she was completely unaware of the person who entered her bedroom and walked purposefully across to the window. It was only when the heavy wooden shutters were banged open that she woke abruptly and found herself blinking hard at the bright sunlight that flooded into the room. She pulled the top sheet over her face to protect her eyes.

"Come on, madam." It was Will's voice. "Time to get yourself into gear. We've got things to do."

She was about to throw back the sheet, but then realized, in her drowsy state, that she probably looked as if she had been dragged through a hedge backwards, so she kept herself hidden underneath. "What time is it?" she mumbled, her breath lifting the sheet from her mouth.

"Ten o'clock."

"What!" She sat bolt upright. "It can't be!" She glanced over at her clock. "Oh, God, it is," she moaned, rubbing at her eyes with the palms of her hand. "Someone should have woken me earlier. Have you all been waiting for me?"

"No, not really." She watched him as he made his way back towards the door. "Everyone seems to have been a bit late this morning. But there's something planned at ten-thirty, so you'd better get your skates on."

"What kind of thing?"

"That's for you to find out."

"Oh, Will, that's no help at all! Come on, I'm in a panic. What do I wear?"

"Exactly what you wore yesterday. Just a pair of jeans and a T-shirt. Maybe bring a jersey with you."

Liz brought her knees up to her chin and gently rested her forehead on them. She let out a groan. "I think that I've got a bit of a hangover."

Will laughed. "You're not the only one. Everyone's pretty fragile this morning." He opened the door. "Never mind, what's planned will soon blow away the cobwebs."

"Have I got time for a shower?"

"Sure. Do you want some breakfast?"

Liz ran her tongue around the inside of her mouth to try to judge if she could stomach any food. Things didn't taste too good. "Thanks, but no thanks. Could I just have a cup of coffee?"

"It'll be ready in the kitchen when you come through." He walked out of the room, closing the door behind him.

Liz threw back the sheet and swung her legs over the edge of the bed. Building herself up for the effort, she got to her feet and stood for a moment, her eyes clenched shut as she gave the throbbing in her head time to abate. She then moved across to the small bathroom and turned on the shower.

When she arrived in the kitchen twenty minutes later, she was relieved to see that there was no great flurry of activity. Annabelle, Arthur and

Will were sitting silently around the kitchen table, clutching steaming mugs of coffee in their hands.

"Good morning, Liz," Annabelle said as she entered. "How are you feeling this morning, or am I right in thinking that's rather a silly question?"

Liz let out a weak laugh. "Yes, I'm afraid that I think it is."

"I know. We're all feeling a bit like that." She got to her feet and walked over to the sideboard and poured Liz a mug of coffee from the percolator. "I don't know what kind of wine we were drinking last night. I'm pretty sure that we didn't overindulge that much. I must tell Johnnie to avoid it like the plague in future."

Liz pulled out a chair and sat down next to Arthur, who was wordlessly slumped in his wheelchair, focusing his eyes on a pepper-pot in the middle of the table. Annabelle placed the mug of coffee and a couple of aspirin in front of her. "Thanks." She popped the pills into her mouth, then picked up her mug and raised it to eye-level. "Well, Happy Easter, everybody."

There was a forced murmur of amusement from all at the thought that anything could be considered happy right then. The silence was resumed, only broken by the sound of heavy footsteps coming up the outside steps and onto the kitchen balcony. Johnnie entered through the open door.

"Morning, everyone." His voice reached parts of their heads which would have been better left untouched. "What a great day!"

Annabelle sighed as she noticed everyone wincing at his voice. "Johnnie never suffers," she said through clenched teeth. "The man has the constitution of an ox."

He poured himself a mug of coffee. "You're all a bit pianissimo this morning, aren't you?"

"Yes, we all are," Annabelle replied tetchily. "What on earth did you give us to drink last night?"

"I'm not sure. I think it was something that Fidel in the supermarket recommended."

Annabelle raised her eyebrows. "Do you owe him money?"

"Probably. Why?"

Annabelle shrugged. "Maybe this is his way of giving us a gentle reminder of the fact."

"Come on. It wasn't that bad."

"Johnnie, it was appalling, and if you have any left, I would suggest that you take it straight back to him."

"Oh, all right then. If you insist." As he sat down next to Will, he brought his hand hard down on his shoulder. "Are you quite happy with everything—for your day, I mean?"

"Yes, I think so."

"No questions on your route or anything?"

"No. I think you explained it all pretty well."

"Good. Well, whenever you're both ready," he said, looking at Liz, "you should head off."

"What?" Annabelle asked, her voice lifting with excitement. "They haven't arrived yet, have they?"

"Yup." He nodded his head towards the open door. "They're waiting patiently at the bottom of the steps as we speak."

Annabelle jumped to her feet and walked quickly out onto the balcony and looked over the wall. "Oh, Johnnie, they're beautiful!"

"Yes, they are rather elegant, aren't they?"

Liz looked across at Will, a frown of concern on her face. "What are we going to be doing?" She looked around the table and suddenly became aware of the fact that all three men seemed to be grinning at her.

"You should maybe ask my father," Will replied. "It's all his idea."

She shot him a querying glance. "Arthur?"

"Well." He broke his focus on the pepper-pot, cleared his throat, then lifted his hands as if trying to work out how to start his explanation. "It was just that I remembered a conversation that we had some time ago, about things that we missed doing, or things that we felt that we'd missed out on. Anyway, during those long nights that Will and I spent together in hospital, we had time to talk and I found out that he enjoyed doing exactly the same thing as you. So I thought that it might be an idea to try to organize something for you both."

Liz stared at him, trying to remember what it was that she had said. Then a smile slowly crept across her face. "It's not . . ." She stopped, thinking that she could well be on the wrong track.

"It's not what?" Arthur asked.

"Horse riding?"

Arthur flicked his head to the side. "Could be."

"Oh, do stop teasing the poor girl," Annabelle called out from the balcony. "Of course it's riding. Come over here, Liz, and have a look at these two beauties."

Liz sat open-mouthed, glancing from one man to another, then, pushing back her chair, she walked quickly across the kitchen and out onto the balcony to stand beside Annabelle. She looked over the wall and could not help but let out a gasp of wonderment at the sight below her. Two pure-bred Andalusian stallions stood side by side, tethered to the grille of the downstairs window, so similar in appearance that one could have been the reflection of the other. Their black coats gleamed like polished metal in the morning sun and their long, groomed manes fell seductively down the sides of their arched necks. She could hear the tinkle of metal as they champed impatiently on their bits, and from time to time they turned to face each other, flaring their nostrils and tossing their heads as if readying themselves for a confrontation. Across their powerful backs were slung large Spanish saddles, their dark brown leather tooled with swirling patterns and inset with polished buttons, and over their high-backed seats were thrown thick woollen blankets with coloured stripes so vibrant and set so close together that they were dazzling to the eye.

Liz made her way quickly down the steps, then slowed her pace as she approached them, talking quietly as she went, wary in case she frightened them. She smoothed her hand across the neck of the horse closest to her, feeling its powerful muscles tighten at her touch, then, ducking under the tethering rope, she stood between them.

"Hullo, boys," she said, almost in a whisper. She let them nose her hands, feeling the softness of their muzzles and the gentle warmth of their breath against her skin. Their eyes shone through their trailing forelocks like polished coals as they scrutinized her, vigilantly at first, and then, as they became used to the sound of her voice and the manipulation of her hands, they relaxed their heads and fluttered their long-lashed eyelids open and closed, as if being hypnotized by her actions.

"What do you think of them?"

Liz turned to see that Will had come to stand beside the horse to her left. He reached up and stroked one of its ears.

"They're beautiful. I don't think I've ever seen anything like it before. They just seem so . . . noble. Do you know what they're called?"

"No idea. I suppose we could find out." He looked up at the balcony. "Johnnie!" he called out, the sound of his voice making the horses flick back their heads momentarily in alarm.

Johnnie's head appeared over the wall. "Yes?"

"Liz wants to know if the horses have names."

"Hmm." Johnnie looked thoughtful. "Eduardo's on the left, Carlos on the right."

Liz craned her head back to look up at him, catching the twinkle of humour in his reply. "Are you being serious?"

"Er, not really. I actually forgot to ask that question, but I'm sure they wouldn't mind being called those names for just one day."

Liz looked back at the horses. "No, I'm sure they wouldn't. Hullo, Eduardo. Hullo, Carlos."

Will turned and made his way back up the steps. "Come on, we'd better start making tracks. Have you got everything you need?"

"Where are we going?" Liz asked as she followed him.

"Around and about. Johnnie has shown me a route on the map which should take us off for most of the day."

When they re-entered the kitchen, Arthur had not moved from his position at the table, but noticing the look of almost child-like excitement on Liz's face, he settled back, leaning his elbows on the arms of the wheelchair and touching his forefingers against the grin of self-satisfaction that stretched across his mouth. She walked straight over to him and placed her arms around his neck and gave him a kiss on both cheeks. "Arthur, you shouldn't have done this."

"I don't see why on earth not? As I said before, it's never too late to start doing all these things over again."

"I know you did." Her eyes scanned the plastered leg that stuck out on its metal support on the wheelchair. "But I just feel bad that you can't join us."

"Dammit, I've never been up on a horse in my life. In fact, to be quite honest, I hate the wretched animals. If Will wasn't here, I wouldn't have dreamt of organizing this whole day. You'd only have tried to force me into coming with you."

Liz smiled at him. "Are you sure you're going to be all right here by yourself?"

"He's not going to be by himself, Liz." It was Annabelle who spoke. Liz turned and watched her do up the buckle of a bulging rucksack that was resting on the table. She handed it to Will, then glanced at Liz and gave an almost imperceptible wink. "Arthur and I are going to spend a very happy and fulfilling day together, so don't you even think about him."

Her words jerked at Liz's memory, and she remembered their conversation of the night before. She felt her cheeks begin to flush. "Right!" she exclaimed, rather too heartily in an attempt to cover for the fluster in her mind. "Well, that's fine then." She turned to see Will shrug the rucksack onto his shoulders and walk out of the door. "In that case"—she pointed after him—"I'd better be off."

Arthur gave her a double thumbs-up. "Have a good time."

"Yes." She shot him a glance, then looked back at Annabelle. "Yes, of course."

As she made her way over to the door, Annabelle came round the side of the kitchen table, took her arm and guided her out onto the balcony. "How's the head feeling?" she asked as they walked down the steps together.

"Subsiding, gradually."

"Glad to hear it." She paused. "Listen, Liz, I don't want you to go worrying yourself about what we talked about last night. I think, in retrospect, that it was quite presumptuous of me to give you advice of that nature. Probably the wine. It does have the tendency to make me talk too much."

Liz stopped. "No. Believe me, it was wonderful to talk to you. I don't ever get the opportunity to have a . . . female chat like that. I always seem to be surrounded by men."

Annabelle laughed. "Wow! *I* should be so lucky!"

"No, what I mean is, my father and my son—and Arthur—and now Will." She laughed. "In fact, I think the last time I had a discussion like that was probably in the school playground!" She paused, brushing a wisp of hair off her face and tucking it in behind her ear. "To be quite honest, it's given me a buzz, and it's made me feel . . . well . . . like a woman again for the first time in I don't know how long." Her gaze flickered momentarily over the top of the whitewashed wall to where Will was tightening the girths on the saddles of the two horses. "I can't say if anything . . . *romantic* will ever develop between Will and myself, but I am going to take your advice and just have a good time."

Annabelle put her arm around Liz and gave her a squeeze. "You do exactly that, and just see what happens. Nothing need be forced upon you." She gave Liz a gentle push. "Now, you get going and we'll see you both this evening."

Liz made her way quickly down the steps to where Will was now standing with the two horses. He handed her the reins of the one Johnnie had christened Carlos. Whispering reassuringly to the horse, she expertly swung herself up into the saddle without needing to make use of the offered leg-up from Will. As soon as the horse felt her weight on his back, he took a number of high-stepped paces sideways, eager to be off. She kicked her feet into the stirrups and pulled gently on his mouth, bringing him to a standstill.

Will put a hand on the toe of her boot. "I just judged the stirrups. What are they like?"

Liz stood up in the saddle. "Fine."

"Right." He gathered in his reins and effortlessly mounted his horse. "Okay, let's get going."

They set off up the track at a bouncing walk, the two stallions impatient for the chance to rid themselves of pent-up energy. Liz glanced over her shoulder to where Annabelle still stood half-way up the steps. She gave her a quick wave, and Annabelle responded by bringing her hand to her mouth and blowing a kiss.

Before the coming of the motor car and asphalt roads, the remote pueblos that were scattered throughout the hills and valleys of the Sierra de Cañareas were linked by a network of ancient thoroughfares known as *caminos réales*, stone-cobbled tracks bounded by drystone walls, wide enough only to allow unhindered passage for a donkey with its panniered load. In most parts, the cobbles were now hidden below a thin covering of turf, emblazoned with the purple and pink of wild flowers, and the walls had fallen victim to age, crumbling away into adjoining fields. However, the paths were still kept clear of encroaching vegetation by those who came out from the town and used them for access to their small vegetable *huertas*, and by the local parks department, which managed them for the good of the multitude of hikers that visited the area each year.

It was these tracks that Will and Liz followed, one behind the other, the paths being too narrow for them to ride abreast. They wound their way through the countryside in the cooling shade of chestnut trees and cork oaks that leaned out from the side banking, their branches hanging above them like the misshapen arms of some grotesque monster waiting for the right moment to pounce upon them. They passed by small, hidden-away pockets of fertile ground where ordered rows of onions and potatoes and carrots grew, not tended that day as their elderly caretakers would have been at home recovering from the night-long festivities that brought Semana Santa to its climax. Then, as the land began to rise, they left behind them the more ordered low ground and rode up into dense scrubland where the spindly trunks of self-seeded pines grew too close together to afford any view. The horses' hooves struck hard at the ground as they climbed, their powerful shoulders brushing aside the tall brittle cistus plants that grew in across the now no longer tended path. At the top of the gradient, they broke out into open ground and rode side by side along the wide fire-break. They followed the line of the ridge, looking out across the wooded hills that stretched like a ruffled green blanket away to the distant horizon, the unseasonal warmth of the day finally draining their contours of all colour and merging them without a line of demarcation into the pale-blue sky.

The fire-break dipped and rose for more than five miles, and where it eventually petered out they caught sight of a cluster of white houses in the valley. Carefully picking their way down the steep descent towards the village, they entered at its highest point and rode down through a narrow maze of streets hemmed in by houses on whose flat-topped roofs lines of washing swung lazily in the midday breeze. There seemed to be little sign of life anywhere, though voices, intermingled with the clamant strains of television, could be heard through open doorways. They were guided by the church spire, eventually finding their way to the village plaza by way of a lane no wider than the *caminos* that they had been following that morning.

The Café El Borriquero could quite easily have passed as a private house had it not been for the large sign advertising Cruzcampo beer above its open door. They dismounted outside, and while Will disappeared into the pitch-black interior of the establishment, Liz led the two horses to the circular drinking trough that acted as a centre-piece for the paved seating area of the plaza. By the time they had quenched their thirst and Liz had secured them to the hitching rings that were set into the concrete beam above the permanently running water spouts, Will had returned with two glasses of beer, frosted with cold. He set them down at the side of a wooden bench, shaded from the sun by a tall palm tree, and let the rucksack slip from his shoulders.

"It's all very quiet," Liz said as she approached the bench. "Where is everybody?"

Will cast an eye around the empty square as he undid the buckles of the rucksack. "More than likely catching up on their sleep after last night's festivities. We've actually been damned lucky to find that bar open. Easter Day has always been very much a family day in Spain, so I doubt we'll be seeing much action around."

So they sat together in solitude on the bench, drinking their beer and eating the sandwiches that Annabelle had made up for them, and talking away to each other about their own experiences of riding. There happened to be no real common ground in that, Liz having done most of hers in small pony club events that were organized down to the last detail by a brigade of forceful women. Will, on the other hand, had learned it on a much grander and more liberated scale, working when he was in his mid-teens on a cattle ranch in Manitoba, spending twelve hours a day during his three-month school holiday in the saddle. However, for once Liz did not feel herself immediately belittled or self-conscious about her own lesser achievements, because there had been a time—before she had become pregnant, before she had married Gregor—when she had been just like any other normal teen-age girl, eating, sleeping and talking horses. And now, after so many years, she had returned to that. She felt exhilarated, happy and carefree in the company of this man who talked with as much enthusiasm about it all as she did. What's more, she felt safe with him. Will knew her whole story and had said himself that he would make no move on her. So there was no need, no pressure to take their relationship any further. This was as good a therapy for her, and much less complicated, than what had been suggested by Annabelle.

They would probably have sat there for much longer had not the sun moved around from behind the tree, and they were dazzled into realizing that time was marching on. They left by the bottom end of the village and followed alongside a river-bed that trickled down the hillside. Its bouldered starkness was brightened by the crimson flowers of oleander bushes that grew on its banks, relying on lengthy tap-roots to eke out moisture from the parched ground. As they descended the hill, the land became more arid and colourless, and they had to snake their way through huge rocks that lay bare and smooth in their path. They passed by the ruins of a small *casita*, its walls constructed with stones similar to those that were strewn about the place, and Liz wondered to herself how it was possible that anyone could have picked out a living on such an infertile landscape.

They followed the meandering course of the river for an hour, and just when they had begun to express doubts as to whether it was leading anywhere, it suddenly rounded a sharp bend and the land opened out, and the river disgorged its meagre flow into the vast lake that had been visible from Finca de Rodrigo.

It had been Will's intention to explore the environs of the lake for a time, but because of their prolonged lunch he realized that they were running well behind schedule. So, having given the horses five minutes to graze on the lush green grass that bordered the lake, he decided that it would be best for them to take the shortest route back home, and they set off up the winding road that linked the lake with the town of Cañareas. They rode as fast as they felt the tiring horses could manage, the sun's heat now intensified by its absorption into the asphalt surface of the road.

By the time they turned into the gates of the *finca*, the sun was touching the tops of the hills, casting deep shadows through the chestnut trees that fell away below the road. As they climbed the final slope to the house they spotted Annabelle sitting at the bottom of the steps that led up to the kitchen, talking animatedly with a man whom they concluded to be the owner of the horses. She got up as they approached and came forward to meet them.

"My word, you look a healthier person than the one that left this morning!" she said, putting up her hand to stroke the nose of Liz's horse. "Your face is veritably sun-kissed! How did you get on?"

"It was wonderful!" Liz replied. "The countryside around here is so . . . different." She slid out of the saddle, fully intending to continue her eulogy to the day, but was silenced by the sudden sharp pain at the base of her spine. "Ooh!" She took a couple of stiff paces forward. "Goodness, I'm not used to that!"

Annabelle laughed. "Well, nothing that a good soak in a hot bath won't sort out. How did you manage with the horse?" She glanced round at the owner, who had stepped forward to take hold of Will's reins while he dismounted. "I think Andreas here was a bit surprised to see you back in one piece. He said that there was no way that a woman could keep this big boy under control."

"She rode him as if she had been on him every day of her life," Will interjected before Liz had a chance to answer. He pointed at her. "*She* is a true horsewoman. I've seen seasoned wranglers not being able to handle a horse like that."

Annabelle pulled a face at Liz. "Well! That's praise indeed." She turned and said something in Spanish to the owner. He looked at Liz, a broad grin on his face, and taking off his battered straw hat, said something in a high-pitched chatter before giving her a flourishing bow. Will let out a loud laugh and slapped the man on the back.

"What did he say?" Liz asked.

"He apologized for doubting your ability," Annabelle replied with a chuckle, "and that he was sure that his horse enjoyed having someone as beautiful as you astride his back all day."

Liz frowned dubiously. "How am I meant to take that comment?"

"I'm not quite sure myself," Annabelle replied, her mouth drawn tight. "But I think you'd better make yourself scarce before he starts making advances."

Liz walked over to the man and held out her hand. "*Muchas gracias, señor.*"

He clenched her hand, then brought it up to his stubbly mouth and gave it a kiss. "*De nada, señora, de nada. Es un placer.*"

At Annabelle's suggestion, dinner that night was earlier, seeing that the couple from the Isle of Wight had rung to say that they were going to be spending the night in Seville. Moreover, Johnnie had managed to push Arthur's energy resources to the limit by wheeling him into town and spending the best part of the afternoon drinking copious amounts of Spanish brandy in his local bar before both made their somewhat wobbly way home again.

They ate out on the wide balcony at the front of the house, Johnnie deeming the evening warm enough to do so, and conversation during the meal was occasional but relaxed, all of them feeling pleasantly exhausted after their respective exertions of the day. Liz hardly spoke but sat with a smile on her face, listening with only half an ear to what was being said and allowing herself the luxury of reliving every minute of her day. She couldn't remember the last time she had been able to do exactly that. Over the last eighteen years, she always had to think of other people. Her father, her mother, Alex, Gregor. She began to repeat his name over and over again in her mind, waiting for the clenching knot to tighten in her stomach, for the bitterness to well up from her innermost being. But nothing happened. Only good thoughts came to her, and memories of the past that had hitherto been too powerful and too disturbing to recollect flashed harmlessly before her eyes. And it was at that point that she knew that she had unconsciously turned a corner, and that she was at peace with the past and content with whatever the future might hold for her. She looked around the table, watching individually each of the four people who sat with her, and she realized her deep fondness for them all. After all the shunning and ostracizing that she had suffered over the past year, she was now in the company of friends, *her* friends, and she knew that they took her at face value and liked her for what she was.

"Did you see that?"

"What?" Annabelle asked, following Johnnie's line of gaze up into the sky.

"I've just seen the most incredible shooting star." He thrust forward an arm and traced its path. "It went from there right over to there, bright as anything."

Annabelle got up from her chair and went over to the metal balustrade that surrounded the veranda and placed her hands upon it. She looked up into the sky. "Goodness, I hadn't realized how clear it was." She turned back, a sparkle of excitement in her eyes. "You know, this is a perfect night for star-gazing. Who wants to go down to the swimming pool?"

"Swimming pool?" Arthur exclaimed. "Not on your bloody life. It's far too cold."

Annabelle laughed. "Not to swim, Arthur. To star-gaze. It's the perfect place. We turn off all the lights, and you can just lie down on a sun-lounger and look up into the sky. It's quite fantastic. You don't know just how insignificant you are in this world until you've done it."

Arthur humphed. "I don't want to know how insignificant I am. I have enough trouble convincing myself that I'm some kind of worthwhile entity at the best of times."

His gloomy statement was met with long groans of sympathy from the assembled company, Annabelle emphasizing hers by walking over to him and patting the top of his head as she might have done to a sad dog.

"Annabelle?"

"Yes, Johnnie, my darling."

Johnnie gritted his teeth. "I was hoping that we might take advantage of the fact that we'd eaten earlier tonight."

Annabelle clasped a hand to her chest and stared at him in surprise. "Johnnie! What a strange thing to say in front of our guests."

"No, no, not that! I was wondering if you wouldn't give me a hand to finish off paying the rest of the bills."

Annabelle looked visibly deflated. "Oh, what a disappointment." She let out a long sigh. "All right, I suppose I could." She began to clear the table. "*Bang* goes the star-gazing idea, though."

"Well, I'm up for it," Will declared, jumping up from his chair. "What about you, Liz? Do you feel like giving it a go?"

Liz got to her feet. "Okay, but only on the condition that we give Annabelle a hand to clear up first."

"Don't you even think about it!" Annabelle exclaimed. "You're all paying for the privilege of *not* doing that kind of thing." She put down her load of plates on the dining-room table and walked quickly out into the hall, returning a few seconds later with two heavy woollen blankets. "Here, take these with you. It's surprising how much colder it is down there by the pool, even though it's only a few feet lower than the house."

"Are you sure we can't give you a hand?" Liz asked tentatively.

"Certainly not. I'll cut your fingers off with a carving knife if you so much as touch a plate. Now get going, both of you." She shooed them away with her hands. "I'll turn on the pool lights long enough for you to get down there so that you don't fall down the steps."

They hurried their way through the kitchen and out onto the balcony, then ran down the two flights of steps to the swimming pool, laughing like kids as they tried to get themselves organized before Annabelle switched off the lights. They pulled two sun-beds together and had just wrapped themselves in the blankets when Annabelle's voice sounded out from the house.

"Are you ready?"

"Not quite!" Will called out.

"Too late!" came the response and the lights went out.

"Dammit!" Will laughed. "She could have waited! I can't see a thing!" He groped around for the sun-bed. "Where are you?"

"Here."

"Where's here?"

He felt a hand touch his arm.

"Right. You take the farthest away sun-bed," he said.

"But I can't see anything either," Liz replied.

"Well, don't go falling into the wretched pool!"

Liz giggled. "No, hang on, I've got it now." She shuffled over to her sun-bed and lay down, and heard the one next to her creak slightly as it took Will's weight. He breathed out heavily. "Right then, what can you see?"

"Nothing yet. I think we'll need to get our eyes accustomed to it all."

They lay in silence for a minute, staring up into the sky.

"Wow!" Will said, almost in a whisper. "Would you look at that! Have you got it too?"

"Yes."

"That . . . is . . . incredible!" He disentangled an arm from his blanket and pointed up into the sky. "Look, there's Orion's Belt."

"Where?"

"There. Can you see it?"

"No, not yet."

He freed his left arm and put it behind her shoulders. "Right, come right across and have a look."

She moved her body over to his and laid her head on his chest and squinted up his outstretched arm, using it like the sight of a rifle. "Yes, I've got it now." She made to move back onto her sun-bed.

"Just stay where you are. It'll make it much easier." He moved his hand across the sky. "There's the Plough. Have you got that one?"

"Yes." She felt his chest rise and fall under her head and the soft blowing of his breath on her hair. She let out an involuntary shiver.

"Are you cold?" he asked.

"Yes, I am. Freezing," she replied, thinking it best to cover up the real reason.

"Well, move for a minute and we'll get rearranged." He pulled away their two blankets and put them together. "Right, come in close." He threw the blankets over both of them and lay back. "Okay, tuck your side in and resume position number one."

Liz laid her head back on his chest and felt the warmth of his body next to hers, now conscious of the fact that the whole length of their legs were touching and her hip dug into the hard muscles at the side of his stomach. She didn't know what to do with her hands, so she folded her arms.

"Is that better?"

"Yes, much."

"Okay, so no talking until we pick out another."

They lay together in silence, staring up into the sky. "Can I say something?" Liz asked.

"Not unless it's the name of a star."

"Well, it's about them. Annabelle was right. It really does make one feel so small and insignificant. I think it has to be one of the most powerful and most beautiful sights that I have ever seen."

"I was just thinking that myself," Will replied quietly.

There was something about the sound of his voice that puzzled her. She turned her head and looked up at his face. He was not gazing up into the sky, but looking directly at her. She felt his hand touch the top of her head, and he twisted a finger around a strand of her hair.

"Will." She felt a constriction in her throat. "I . . ."

"I know. Don't worry. Nothing will happen."

She did not turn her face again, neither did she stop him from playing with her hair. For the first time she was conscious of his smell, a mixture of the same musky aftershave that he had been wearing when he had first held her in the hotel in Seville, and the heady pungency of male body. It had been so long since she had lain this close to a man, so long since she had felt the touch of a man. Annabelle was right—she was always right. It was what she needed to be made to feel whole again. And she knew that it was Will—funny, kind, understanding Will—who was the man who could do it for her. She brought up her hand discreetly under the blanket and undid the buttons of her shirt.

Will raised his hand and pointed up into the sky. "I'm pretty sure that's the Pole Star," he said quietly.

She reached up and took hold of his hand and slowly pulled it down under the blanket, then, slipping it under her bra, she guided him to her nipple. She felt his body tauten beside her.

"Liz, you don't—"

She put a finger up to his lips. "I know I don't."

He was silent, and she could feel his heart thumping like a sledgehammer beneath her head. Then his fingers began to move slowly on her nipple, and it responded immediately to his touch. He moved his position, and she felt the arm below her back lever her sideways onto his sun-bed and then he was above her, obscuring the stars in the night sky from sight. He remained motionless for a moment, staring down at her face.

"You are truly beautiful, Liz."

Then he lowered his head, and she felt his lips brush hers. He pulled away again, but she reached up and put her arms around his neck and brought him back to her, and when their open mouths met and their legs entwined, Liz began to feel the long-missed energy of a man flood through her being.

Chapter 24

Despite the fact that it was five o'clock in the afternoon after a bright but cold Easter Day, a long line of holiday traffic slowly snaked its way along the approach to St. Andrews, stringing back as far as the outer point of the Strathtyrum Golf Course. As the Land Rover approached the rear of the line, Mr. Craig blew out resignedly and dropped into a lower gear, jerking out the clutch sufficiently to make the Jack Russell, who had been quivering with excitement on Roberta's knee, scrabble for a foothold. She caught hold of the dog before he was pitched forward into the footwell and looked across at her travelling companion.

"You must be feeling tired."

He cocked his head to the side. "Aye, a wee bit, but it's been an easy-enough journey."

"How long has it taken us?"

He glanced at his wrist-watch. "Four and a half hours."

Roberta let out a sigh and looked forward at the line of traffic. "And now we're stuck in this. So near, yet so far."

"Och, it won't take that long to clear. I reckon that most of this lot will be heading off in the direction of the beach. Once we're through the town, it'll be plain sailing."

Roberta bit at her lip. "Craig, would you mind awfully if we stopped for a minute?"

"What? Right now?"

"No, I mean when we get into town."

"Surely. Where would it be that you're wanting to stop?"

Roberta pushed the dog onto the centre seat and rummaged in the pocket of her jacket. She took out a piece of paper and unfolded it. "It's a place called the Scores Hotel."

"Well, that'll be easy enough. It's just on the way in." The queue of traffic had begun to speed up and he once more engaged a higher gear. He glanced across at Roberta, wondering why it was that she needed to stop in that particular hotel, and noticed that she suddenly seemed quite agitated. "Everything's all right with you, is it?"

"Yes, fine," she replied airily. "I just have to make a telephone call."

The farmer chortled. "Another one, eh? Well, well!"

Roberta reached over and gave his arm a gentle punch. "What's that supposed to mean?"

"Oh, nothing." He shot her a teasing smile. "I was just thinking that for someone who wasn't that well acquainted over here, you've been making an awful lot of phone calls over the past few days."

Roberta picked up Leckie and replaced him on her knee. "Oh, I know a few people," she declared in a self-satisfied tone. "The important ones, at any rate."

Three-quarters of an hour later, they turned off the main road and made their way down the bumpy farm-track towards the steading. Mr. Craig looked out across the land that had become, over the many years he had been there, the greatest part of his life, knowing every inch of it as well as he knew the back of his hand. But, for once, it was not happiness that he felt at being home. Having physically distanced himself from the place for the best part of a week, he had been able to put to the back of his mind all the problems and sorrow that had been manifest there over the past year. And now the sight of the two bottom fields, their gently undulating topography now changed beyond all recognition, exacerbated his down-heartedness.

"You're not too glad to be home, are you?" Roberta said quietly.

He turned to face her. "What was that, lass?"

"I've been watching you. You've got sadness written all over your face."

He gave her a forced smile. "Aye, well. It's difficult to imagine what it's going to be like never seeing crops growing and sheep grazing in these fields again." He steered the Land Rover around the corner of the steading and pulled to a halt in the courtyard. "I really never thought that I'd see the day." He opened the door, allowing the dog to jump out immediately and disappear into the steading, eager to make up for lost time in the hunt for rats. Mr. Craig clambered out slowly, then, placing his hands in the small of his back, he gave it a long stretch before moving around to the rear door to start unloading.

"Hang on a minute!" He felt Roberta take hold of his hand in a powerful grasp, and he nearly lost his balance as she pulled him towards the corner of the house.

He laughed. "Now where are you taking me?"

"Just come with me," she replied without turning back. She made her way purposefully around the side of the house and into the small front garden, then marched him over to the garden wall and stood beside him, looking out across the fields below the house. From that vantage point, it was even more obvious how much work had been completed in the time they had been away, and he felt his heart give an extra twist at the sight.

"Do you remember when you brought me out here that night when the moon was so brilliant that we could see every inch of this land?" she asked.

"Aye, of course."

"Well, what made that so special for me was that I could physically feel your love for this place, in the way that you spoke about it, in the way you seemed so completely in tune with it all. One thing you did that night that I remember so clearly was that you were explaining something to me and you suddenly broke off mid-sentence just to let an owl, away in those trees down there, hoot away uninterrupted. Bet you can't remember that, can you?"

He shook his head.

"Well, there you are then. You do it subconsciously. This farm *is* you, Craig, this land is you, no matter what it looks like. And even if it doesn't belong to you, you belong to it, as do the trees and the birds and everything else that grows and lives here." She leaned her hands on the top of the wall. "Don't get despondent by all this. I've seen golf courses under construction before, and they all go through this stage of growth where nothing seems to fit, and then suddenly everything becomes clear, and the ugly duckling turns into the most beautiful swan. You *will* be proud of it, Craig, I know you will, and you will love this land again as much as you ever did before."

They stood in silence for a moment, then Mr. Craig moved towards her and put an arm across her shoulders. "Thank you, Roberta," he said, smiling down at her. "I was needing to hear that."

"I know you were." She took hold of his hand. "Come on, let's go and get those things out of the car."

He was just pulling the last of the luggage out of the back of the Land Rover when he heard the car changing down a gear as it came around the side of the steading. He stood waiting for it to appear at the corner, clutching Roberta's golf bag in his hand. It was Jonathan Davies. As he pulled to a halt beside him, Roberta came down the back door steps. Davies threw open the driver's door and got out.

"Good to see you back!" he exclaimed heartily, approaching them both and shaking their hands. "How was the golf?"

"Couldn't have been better!" Roberta replied. "Every course as beautiful as the one before." She bent forward to peer through the windscreen of Davies's car. "Did you meet up with him?"

Davies glanced at his car. "Yes. He's feeling the cold a bit, I think."

Roberta hurried over to the passenger door of the car and opened it, then, leaning in, she helped an elderly man with thinning grey hair to his feet. He clutched a brief-case to his portly frame, while at the same time attempting to pull the flaps of his raincoat around him. "Hullo, Maurice." She put her hands up onto his shoulders and gave him a smacking kiss on each cheek. "You really are a star to do this."

"I've never travelled so far in all my life, Bobby." He spoke in a soft Australian accent. "And I don't think I've ever been so *cold* in all my life, neither."

She took him by the arm. "Come on, then. Let's get you inside." She guided him across to where the farmer was standing, a look of curiosity on his face. "Craig, I'd like you to meet Maurice Roache."

The farmer put forward his hand. "Pleased to make your acquaintance, Mr. Roache."

The man shook his hand. "And yours too, Mr. Craig."

The farmer's intrigue was further heightened. How could this man have told, from the way in which Roberta had introduced him, that that was his surname?

"Can we go inside, Craig, before Maurice gets frost-bite?"

"Of course." He walked over and placed the golf bag with the rest of the luggage beside the steps, then opened the back door and stood aside for the party to enter into the house. "I'm afraid that you might find the place in a bit of a mess. My grandson has been here by himself for a week."

"I don't mind what it looks like," Maurice Roache replied. "As long as it's warm."

"Well, I think you'll be all right on that account."

Mr. Craig was pleasantly surprised to find that the kitchen was in an orderly state, although mobility around the room was somewhat hampered by the presence of an armchair and a coffee-table, both of which he recognized as belonging in the front sitting-room. "Please have a seat at the table, gentlemen," he said, taking the kettle from the side of the Rayburn and filling it with water from the tap. "Would anyone care for a cup of tea?"

Roberta walked over and took the kettle from his grasp. "You go and sit down, Craig. I can do that."

"No, no, I can . . ."

"Please, Craig. I would *like* you to go and sit down."

The farmer pulled a face at her. "All right, I can take a telling."

As he pulled out a chair and sat down, he noticed that Maurice Roache had opened up his brief-case on the table and was busying himself laying out papers in front of him. He turned and looked questioningly at Roberta, who leaned against the Rayburn, her hands spread along the chrome towel-rail.

"Craig, Maurice here is my family lawyer, and it is to him, and to Jonathan, that I've been making all these telephone calls over the past few days. At my request, Maurice has flown over here from Sydney, and hopefully those papers that he has in front of him will explain why he has made such a long journey at such short notice. Maurice, I think that this might be a good time for you to take over."

"Certainly, Bobby." Placing a pair of gold half-moon reading spectacles onto the tip of his nose, he picked up the bundle of papers and knocked them together on the table. He grinned at the farmer. "Mr. Craig, would I be right in thinking that you are unaware of what Bobby is intending?"

He looked up at Roberta, who beamed a smile at him. He shook his head. "No idea at all."

"In that case," the lawyer continued, "it would probably be best if we started at the beginning." He took up the top sheet of paper. "Right, then. Roberta Josephine Bayliss, who happens to be here in our presence, is the third daughter of one Simon Anthony Bayliss, residing at—"

"Maurice?" Roberta cut in.

"Yes?"

"As Dad would say, could you cut the waffle and get on with it?"

The lawyer let out a resigned sigh and shook his head. "Oh dear, like father, like daughter." There was a chuckle of amusement from the others. "All right, then, if that's the way you want it, Bobby." He laid down his paper and took off his spectacles and, linking his hands together, he rested them on the table. "Mr. Craig, Bobby's father, Simon Bayliss, was an entrepreneur of some note in Australia. He began as a young man in engineering, starting up his own company which he successfully adapted to producing munitions during the Japanese conflict. Thereafter, he began to diversify, investing mostly in small businesses that he felt had a chance of growing. I had the honour, Mr. Craig, of being Mr. Bayliss's lawyer for over fifty years, and I can quite truthfully say that I know of only two of those businesses that eventually failed. So, as you can imagine, he accumulated quite a fortune, in fact enough for him to retire at the age of fifty-two and concentrate on his one complete and utter passion—golf. It was one that was also shared by his youngest daughter, Roberta. They went everywhere together, all over the world, not only to play golf but to watch it as well."

He coughed into his fist to clear his throat.

"When Simon Bayliss sadly passed away in March at the grand old age of ninety, he divided his estate among his three daughters, but—and it's a big but—the lion's share of his wealth was to go to his youngest daughter, with two major conditions attached. Firstly, that Bobby accompany his ashes over here to Scotland and to see to it personally that they were scattered on the furthest outreach of the Old Course at Saint Andrews. Secondly, that for the remainder of her mother's life, Bobby should stay to look after her in the family house. Both conditions were subsequently agreed to by Bobby." He replaced his spectacles and shuffled through his papers, eventually extricating one from the middle of the pile. "Now, this is where I have to rely on the written word, I'm afraid." He held the paper up at an angle so that the light above the table played upon it. "It is Bobby's intention to set up a fitting tribute to her father, one of which she feels he would not only totally approve, but also one of which he would be overwhelmingly proud. She has therefore asked me to draw up papers to inaugurate a trust, which will have as its sole purpose the investment of monies into the development of new golf courses around the world. Bobby has also intimated that she wants the course here at Balmuir to be the first beneficiary, and I have here an agreement made up between the trust and Mr. Davies's venture capital group which I very much hope we'll be able to sign this evening." He took off his spectacles and sat back in his chair. "So that's it really"—he shot Roberta a wry smile—"without any legal speak whatsoever."

The two men looked expectantly at Mr. Craig, but he sat in silence, staring blankly at the lawyer, his elbow resting on the side of the table and his hand spread across his mouth, as if preventing himself from saying anything. Jonathan Davies shifted uneasily in his seat, realizing that the farmer's eyes were neither focused nor blinking. Both he and Maurice Roache turned simultaneously toward Roberta. She did not catch their look. She bit apprehensively at a finger-nail as she watched Craig, the glow of excitement that had been on her face now replaced by a frown of concern. Then she moved tentatively forward and placed her hand gently on his shoulder.

"Craig?" Roberta said almost in a whisper. "What do you think?"

He started at the sound of her voice, as if being woken from a dream. He let out a deep breath, then, placing both hands on the table, he slowly pushed himself to his feet. "Would you please all excuse me for a minute?" he said, his voice croaky. He squeezed his way between the armchair and the central work station, moving now like a very old man, and without casting a glance in Roberta's direction he shuffled his way over to the door that led into the hallway of the house. They followed him intently with their eyes as he left the room and then heard the door of the front sitting-room opening and closing behind him.

No one spoke in the kitchen, the only sound being Maurice Roache putting together his papers and placing them back in the open brief-case. He closed the lid and softly clicked the fasteners shut.

"Maybe I should go and have a word with him," Jonathan Davies volunteered quietly.

Roberta shook her head. "No. I think it's up to me to do the explaining."

"Should we make ourselves scarce?" he asked.

Roberta did not reply to his question, but simply held up her hand before she left the room.

She stood outside the door of the sitting room, her hand on the brass knob, ready to open it. She hesitated, then raised her hand and knocked quietly on the door. There was no response. "Craig?" she called out quietly. Still no response. She turned the knob and opened the door and put her head around the side. There were no lights on in the room, but it wasn't entirely dark, only cold and unwelcoming. He sat in his armchair, his hands resting on its arms, staring straight ahead at the space where the one from the kitchen should have been. "Craig? Can I come in?" He glanced at her for only a second, then looked away again. She walked around the side of the sofa and stood in front of him. "Craig, are you all right?" She knelt down on the floor at his feet and placed a hand on top of his. "I wish you'd say something to me."

He looked at her, and she could plainly see the distress in his eyes.

"Craig, what is it?"

He slowly shook his head. "Why have you done this?" he asked quietly.

"Why? Because . . . I wanted to, for my father."

"But you knew the whole story, didn't you? I remembered. You were here when Jonathan Davies came round that time just before we left for the west coast. You knew that if he didn't find someone else to invest in this project, then it would never happen. So when did you speak to him?"

Roberta ran a fingertip up and down the back of his hand. "When you were packing."

The farmer nodded. "Ah, yes. So it wasn't all about his naval times in Sydney, was it?"

"Well, we did talk about that . . . but not all of the time, I admit."

"Then he would have told you about our insolvency problem, and how if this project didn't happen, then we would have nothing left."

Roberta hesitated before replying. "Yes, he did."

He lifted his free hand and dislodged the tear that hovered on his bottom eyelid. "Lass, I really can't allow you to do this. I can't let you save my family like this."

Roberta pushed herself between his knees and grasped both his hands. "Craig, listen, how else would I spend the money? I'm a spinster with an elderly mother. How else?" She paused. "You know when I said back there in the car that I knew some pretty important people over here? Well, no one is as important to me as you are. You, quite simply, have single-handedly turned my life around. I thought that coming over here was going to be the end of everything . . . but it hasn't turned out that way. You have renewed me, Craig, my time with you has given me a new life, and I can't even begin to repay you for that." She bent forward and laid her cheek on his knee. "I can't bear to think that I'm going to have to leave you in a couple of days. I want to stay. But I can't. I have a duty to go back and look after my mother. Dad knew that I would anyway. He just wrote it up in his will so that he could leave me his money and to make it easier for my sisters to stomach the fact." She looked up at him. "But, don't you see, I can now use the money to my own advantage. If I invest in this golf course, I don't have to be away from you forever. I have a cast-iron excuse for coming back again and again." She laid her head back on his knee. "I can use it to buy some happiness."

She felt the rough surface of his hand touch her neck. "You're a great wee lass, you know."

She looked up, resting her chin on his knee, and caught the look of fondness in his eyes.

"I really have grown so fond of you, Craig."

He bent forward and took her face in both hands and planted a kiss on her forehead. "Well, lass, I can tell you truly that it has come to work both ways." He gave each of her cheeks a gentle pat. "So maybe we should get ourselves back into that kitchen and sign those papers before your lawyer runs off home again."

The tall blonde girl bounced her way across the brightly lit restaurant and placed the bill on the checkered table-cloth in front of Gregor and Alex. "There you are, gentlemen." She leaned over towards Alex. "I've managed to wangle a staff discount for you."

He shot a look at his father, then grinned up at Madeleine. "Thanks for that."

"It comes with my compliments." She straightened up. "So when will I see you again?"

Alex scratched at the back of his neck. "I don't know. What are you doing tomorrow?"

"Nothing much. What are *you* doing?"

"Caddying probably in the morning, but if you want, we could meet up for lunch."

"Okay, give me a call on my mobile." She turned to see that a group of people had entered the restaurant. "I'd better go. Duty calls." She bent forward and gave Alex a kiss on his cheek, then turned to Gregor and held out her hand, a broad smile creating small dimples in her rosy cheeks. "Really nice to meet you, Mr. Dewhurst. That was great fun today."

He took her hand and shook it. "I enjoyed it too, Madeleine. And, as I said before, it's Gregor . . . please."

"Oops, sorry," she chuckled, putting her hand over her mouth. "I promise I'll remember next time." She gave Alex a quick wave and went over to welcome the newcomers.

Gregor reached across the table for the bill.

"I'll do that, Dad," Alex said, shifting his bottom on the chair so that he could take his wallet from the back pocket of his trousers.

"No, you won't. It's my shout. It's the least I can do after butting in on your day off."

"You didn't butt in at all. It was great fun. Madeleine thought that you were pretty chilled out."

"Do I take that as a compliment?"

"Of course you do. It means that you're a pretty sound guy."

Gregor gave his son an uncertain look. "I'll take your word for it." He picked up his glass of beer and drained it, and on hearing Madeleine let out her distinctive laugh, he looked over to where she was taking the order from the group of people. "She's a nice girl."

"Yes, she is. She's a good friend."

"Is that all?"

Alex leaned towards him, his eyes widened emphatically. "Yes, Dad, only that."

"Right."

"Anyway, I wouldn't tell you otherwise."

Gregor laughed. "I know you wouldn't." He brought his hands down hard on the table. "Right, shall we make a move?"

Alex pushed back his chair. "Ready when you are."

The cold night air immediately hit Gregor when he stepped outside. He fastened the zip of his jacket up to the neck and thrust his hands into the pockets and stood stamping his feet, waiting for Alex to come out. He turned and saw him through the fogged-up window saying a final good night to Madeleine. A young couple veered off the pavement to enter the restaurant and he stepped aside out of their way. As they opened the door, Alex came out.

"Hell, it's a bit cold, isn't it?" he said, rubbing at the sleeves of his jersey.

"Bloody freezing." He gave his son a powerful thump that was designed to throw him off balance, then turned and began to sprint away up the street. "Come on," he called out, "I'll race you back to the car."

Alex laughed as he watched his father's compact figure race around the corner and out of sight, but he didn't bother following at his pace. Even with his extra height and longer legs, he knew that he still hadn't the speed to keep up with him. He decided therefore to take his time, and allow his father yet again the pleasure of being the victor, even though he knew that he would be teased unmercifully about his lack of stamina and pace all the way home.

But it was good to have been out with him again. He *was* a pretty chilled-out guy, even though he was his old man. And come on, he wasn't even that old. Hell, there were guys still playing professional football who were older than him. Even Madeleine said he was pretty fanciable.

He turned the corner into Market Street and saw his father in the distance, sitting on the bonnet of the Peugeot van with his arms crossed, his legs swinging nonchalantly over the side. He could imagine the smug grin that he would have on his face, so he decided not to give him the satisfaction of thinking that this was a famous victory. He slowed his pace, taking time to look into the windows of the shops and restaurants that he passed, stopping every now and then to make it seem as if he were genuinely interested in what they had on display. He was now in voice range, and he could hear the gibes that were being called out to him.

"Come on, you bloody tortoise!"

This he heard when he was only twenty yards away from the van, and he knew that if he looked towards him, his father would see the broad grin on his face. He turned away and studied intently the whirled-glass windows of a small Italian restaurant. He couldn't really see anything inside, the glass distorting any chance of clear vision, but it gave him time to bite at the sides of his mouth so that he could regain his composure and produce once more a perfect poker face. Then, as he walked slowly on, he suddenly found himself looking through a pane of clear glass that must have been put in as a temporary replacement. He could now see everything that was happening in the restaurant. It was one of those places that had booths, shaped rather like the old cattle stalls in the Winterton steading, where people could sit at their tables in privacy.

He wiped at the pane with the sleeve of his jersey, as if trying to wipe away the reality of what he saw. But there was no doubting his initial appraisal of the situation. It was the hair he had recognized first, the short, bobbing blonde hair. At first he thought it could have been an innocent-enough liaison, but then it was the position of her hands that told him the whole story, clasped together with those of the man who sat opposite her. They leaned towards each other, their faces inches apart, then he watched as they both rose from their seats and kissed across the table before sitting down again, laughing at their actions.

"All right, come on, you've made your point."

He turned to see his father walking towards him. He gave a reactive glance towards the window, then made off quickly towards the car. "Let's go, Dad."

Even in the dim glow of the street-lights, Gregor noticed that his son's face had drained of colour as he walked past him. "What's up with you?"

Alex turned and walked back to him and grabbed his arm. "Nothing. Come on, Dad, we're going home."

Gregor stood where he was. There were ten yards separating them. "What did you see in there, Alex?"

"Nothing, Dad. Please just come home."

Gregor watched him for a moment, then turned and walked back to where Alex had been standing.

"*Please*, Dad, just come away from there."

Alex could make no further move. He had done all that he could to prevent his father from seeing. He watched as Gregor stood in front of the clear pane and peered into the restaurant, his hands thrust into the pockets of his jacket. He took a step nearer, then, looking for a moment longer, he lowered his head as if he didn't want to see any more of what was going on. He turned and began walking back along the street, and as he passed by his son, he glanced at him and Alex could see the deep hurt in his eyes. "Thanks, Alex," he said quietly, his voice quavering. "Thanks for trying, lad."

Alex stood watching him as he walked slowly back towards the van, his shoulders down, his head bowed, the body language of a broken man. He set off after him, and on reaching the car he unlocked the driver's door, then looked across at his father. "Maybe it's just a good friend."

Gregor blew out derisively. "Aye, a *bloody* good friend." He shook his head slowly. "She said that she wasn't going to be back until tomorrow." He brought his fist down hard on the roof of the van. It resounded like a gong, and Alex stared at the large dent that the punch had made. "What a *bitch!* What a conniving, good-for-nothing *bitch*!" He slumped forward, his forehead resting on his forearms. "What a mess I've made of my life, Alex, what a sodding mess!"

Alex opened the door and reached across to unlock the other, then he walked around and put a hand on his father's shoulder and opened it for him. "Come on, Dad, I'll take you home."

They drove in silence out of St. Andrews and climbed the hill, leaving behind them the ghostly amber glow of the floodlights that played upon the ruined walls of the town's ancient cathedral. Alex pushed the van fast, out of anger at the hurt that Mary McLean had caused his father and eagerness to get him back home as quickly as possible. He flashed through villages and swung the little van at pace through the bends, and for once, as he approached the stretch known as Smash Alley, he threw caution to the wind. There were, after all, hardly any cars on the road. He drove so fast over the first blind summit that the van lifted off the road and his head touched the plastic covering of the roof. He glanced to his left and could see the outside light of the farmhouse at Winterton shining out across the fields. He turned to his father. "We're nearly home now, Dad."

His father lifted his head, but he did not look towards Winterton. His eyes were suddenly wide open, transfixed on the road in front of him. "Watch out, Alex!!"

Alex turned back to see the two sets of headlights, side by side, coming straight at them over the next summit of the road. There was no way that he could possibly avoid them. "*Shit!*" he yelled out at the top of his voice, and slammed on the brakes, pulling the steering wheel hard over to the left. The van hit the verge at pace, and as it rose in the air, there was a resounding bang as the bonnet caught the top of the drystone wall, and then there was a moment of terrifying limbo when he realized that he was probably in the last seconds of his life, and he gulped a breath as he watched the light of Winterton farmhouse floating away at the top edge of the windscreen. The van hit solid ground with a bone-jarring thud, but then it seemed to bounce off again, and the world spun around in the beam of the headlights before it thumped down for a second time. The lights went out, and there was the deafening noise of tearing metal and shattering glass as the panels crumpled around them and the windows disintegrated with the force of the impact.

In the sudden, unworldy silence that followed, Alex still held tight to the steering wheel, and it was only when he felt the cold night air on his face that he realized that he was still conscious. He tried to orientate himself, but his senses were then invaded by the excruciating pain in his neck. He attempted to move his head, but it was bent sideways, stuck hard against a solid object. He became aware of the seat-belt cutting into his shoulder, yet he didn't seem to be in contact with his seat. He tried moving his legs, but his right foot was numb and there seemed to be something heavy weighing it down.

"Dad!" He reached out and felt the sleeve of his father's jacket and gave it a shake. Something felt sticky on his hand, but he couldn't manouevre it around to see what it was. "Dad! Are you all right?" He reached out again. "Dad!"

He could now hear his father breathing heavily. "Hang on, Alex," he said weakly. "Hang on, lad, we're upside down. I'll try and get my seat-belt off."

"Dad, I'm stuck. I think I'm jammed against the roof and my foot won't move."

"All right, lad, just hang on. I'll get you out."

"Jesus, I think there's smoke, Dad. Something's burning."

"Hang on, Alex," his father shouted back.

He caught the desperation in his father's voice, and it was then that he knew that there was no way that they could help each other. He started to cry now, understanding the hopelessness of their situation.

He could hear his father thumping his shoulder against the caved-in door, then he let out a growl that crescendoed into an ear-splitting yell as he threw the whole force of his powerful body against it. There was a loud creak as it gave way a fraction, then he felt his father manoeuvring around and suddenly the back of his head came into sight below him.

"Just keep calm, Alex, we'll get out." He kicked out backwards like a mule, kicking and kicking at the door, each one making its mangled hinges screech in protest. He could hear his father's breathing getting faster and faster with the effort.

"Right, Alex, I think I've got it." He began to edge his way backwards.

"Don't leave me, Dad."

"I won't leave you, son. Just hang on."

He heard the sound of voices outside. A man's voice wailed, "Jesus, I'm sorry, I'm so sorr——"

"Fuck off!" He heard his father yell. "Just go and get an ambulance and the fire brigade."

"Dad! Quick! Look down at my feet!" Alex coughed out, as a flicker of yellow flame appeared in the footwell, glowing through the acrid smoke in the car.

He felt his father crawling back in again, and this time he saw his face looking up at him. In his hand, he clutched a penknife, its open blade glinting yellow in the light of the flame. "Just hang on, lad, I'll get you out."

"My feet, Dad, look at my feet!"

Alex watched as his father reached up into the footwell and beat at the flickering flames with his bare hands. They seemed to die away, and then he felt his father's hand slide up the upper part of his leg.

"Right, I've got it now, Alex. I've got what's trapping you." He felt his father's body shudder with exertion as he pulled at something in the footwell. "Try moving, Alex."

"*I can't.*"

"Right, I'll try again."

"Dad, look above you! They've started again!"

He watched once more as his father hit out at the flames with his hands. Again, he managed to dampen them. "Right," his father breathed heavily, "let's try again." This time, he let out a scream of effort as he pulled hard at the metal above Alex's leg. "Okay!" he yelled out through gritted teeth. "Try now, boy."

Alex used his hands to give extra leverage to his legs and then suddenly the one that had been trapped came free. "Yes, that's it, Dad. I'm out."

He saw the knife blade come up and slide under his seat-belt. His father pulled hard on its handle, and the seat-belt gave way, pitching Alex forward on top of Gregor's body.

"Right, crawl, Alex; crawl for your bloody life!"

Mr. Craig flicked on the switch at the back door of the house and light flooded into the courtyard. He opened the door and stood aside to allow Roberta and the two men to file out before him. They descended the steps and walked over to the car.

"We'll pick you up at ten o'clock on Tuesday then, Maurice," Roberta said, as she opened the passenger door for the lawyer.

"I'll be ready, my dear." He slowly clambered into the car. "It'll be good to have some company on the way home."

"That goes for me too." She leaned inside and gave him a kiss on his cheek. "And again, Maurice, thank you so much for coming over. I really do appreciate it."

He smiled at her. "I think you've got your father's business acumen, Bobby. I'm pretty sure that this one'll go as well as anything that *he* invested in."

"You're right. I know it's going to be a winner." She closed the door and gave him a wave as she came around the side of the car.

Jonathan Davies held out his hand to her. "Thank you, Roberta, for everything. It's wonderful to know that we can just get on with things now."

Roberta ignored the hand and reached up and gave him a kiss on either cheek. "I have to thank you as well, Jonathan, for giving me the opportunity of a lifetime." She turned and took hold of Craig's hand. "You just keep me informed of everything that's going on."

Jonathan patted the top pocket of his blazer. "I have your fax number right here. I'll give you weekly bulletins, I promise you." He put forward his hand to the farmer. "I think Liz will be well pleased, Mr. Craig."

He shook his hand. "Aye, I have no doubt that she will be, Mr. Davies."

Davies opened the driver's door. "Have a good trip home, Roberta." He hopped in and fired up the engine, then, reversing quickly, he took off around the corner at speed.

They stood for a moment until they heard the car accelerate up the farm road, then he gave Roberta's hand a gentle squeeze. "Right, what say you to a wee glass of something to celebrate?"

She smiled up at him. "I think that's probably the best idea you've had all day, Craig."

They walked back over to the house and climbed the steps. Mr. Craig turned off the courtyard light and was about to close the door behind them when he stopped, looking up into the night sky. He went back out and stood on the steps.

"Craig?" Roberta asked with concern as she came back out of the kitchen to join him. "What are you looking at?"

He pointed above the roof of the steading where a red glow lit up the night sky, interspersed with the flicker of blue light. In the distance, coming from the direction of St. Andrews, was the wail of a siren.

"What's happened?"

"Looks like there's been an almighty car smash up on the main road. There's one on fire at any rate." He turned back into the house. "I'm afraid that it won't be the last on that stretch, either."

Roberta still stood out on the steps. "Do you think we can do anything to help?"

"No, I don't think so. The emergency services are there. We'd just be a hindrance." He held the door. "Come on, lass, get yourself inside. I don't want you catching a cold before you go home."

Annabelle crossed over the cobbled courtyard to the flower-bed that ran alongside one of the high enclosing walls, and began plucking off the deadheads of the rambling rose that grew abundantly across it. She had been meaning to do this for the past week, but she had never seemed to find the time. She heard the large oak door swing open and turned as Johnnie walked into the courtyard.

"So what have you got planned for this morning?" she asked, throwing a handful of dead petals into a cardboard box that, conveniently, happened to be there.

Johnnie sat on the low stone wall that surrounded the small fountain in the centre of the courtyard. "Nothing much. I thought that I might go into town and return that wine to Fidel."

Annabelle smiled wistfully at him. "Now, that's a very good idea."

"Yes, maybe it is." He let out a deep sigh. "You know, my love, I don't often say this, but I think I'm going to miss our guests."

Annabelle walked over and sat down beside him. "I know. It's not often one gets on the same wavelength, is it?"

Johnnie shook his head.

She slapped him on the knee. "Never mind, we've got a free night. No one to think about but ourselves." She gave him a nudge with her arm. "What fun we could have, eh?"

He laughed and put his arm around her and gave her a kiss on the cheek. "You know, I just might hold you to that."

The telephone sounded out through the open door of the kitchen. Annabelle smiled at her husband. "That, though, could quite easily spell the end of our plans." She got up. "I'll answer it."

She hurried into the kitchen and took the receiver off the hook on the wall. "*Digame*, Finca de Rodrigo . . . Yes? . . . Oh, hullo . . . No, I'm sorry, Mr. Craig, you've just missed them. They left about five minutes ago. . . . No, I've no idea where they'll be staying. Will has a mobile phone, though . . . Oh, I'm afraid that I don't have it either. Is everything all right? . . . I see. . . . Well, I'm sorry I couldn't have been more help . . . goodbye, Mr. Craig."

She hung up the receiver, but kept her hand upon it and stared pensively out of the kitchen window.

"Well, was it another booking?"

She turned to find Johnnie leaning against the doorpost. "No. It wasn't. It was Liz's father," she answered quietly.

Johnnie noticed the look of concern on her face. "Has something happened?"

Annabelle shook her head. "I don't know. But there was definitely something about his voice."

Johnnie approached her and put his arm around her shoulders. "And there's something about my voice too," he said in his most seductive tones.

She smiled at him, then pushed him away and walked over to the kitchen sink. "I know there is, Johnnie. It's normally far too loud."

CHAPTER 25

Mr. Craig followed the lumbering figure of Maurice Roache across the crowded concourse at Edinburgh Airport, struggling with the unruly luggage trolley on which he pushed Roberta's two suitcases and golf clubs. There was nowhere near the same number of people waiting to check in as when he had seen Liz and the professor off to Seville, so they were able to zig-zag their way straight through the cordoned aisle to the desk. He positioned the trolley next to that of the old lawyer and turned to scan the area for Roberta. He caught sight of her through a blur of hurrying travellers, standing outside a newsagent and leafing through a book. She looked up, and seeing that they were waiting at the desk, she hurried over, rummaging in her handbag for her tickets.

"Sorry!" she said, placing her tickets on the desk. "I just wanted to get something to read before I left."

Having booked them in, the cheery-faced girl handed back their tickets, informing them that their luggage would go all the way through to Sydney, so there was no need to worry about it at Heathrow. They thanked her and wheeled their empty trolleys away to the stacking area.

"Right!" Maurice said, shifting his brief-case from one hand to the other. "I've got a couple of telephone calls to make, so I'm going to head straight through security now." He held out a hand to the farmer. "It was a pleasure to make your acquaintance, Mr. Craig. I'm only sorry that what should have been a happy occasion was overshadowed in such a way."

"I know, Mr. Roache, but nevertheless it was good to meet you too." He shook his hand. "I hope that our paths might cross again sometime."

The lawyer let out a short laugh. "I doubt very much that that'll happen, unless you come over to Australia. I think it would be wise for me to leave any foreign travel in the future to a younger colleague."

"Aye, I can understand that. But I trust that you'll still be looking after Roberta's affairs."

"Oh, I don't think I'll be wanting to pass up on those for a good bit yet." He smiled down at her. "I'll see you upstairs, Roberta."

"All right, Maurice. I won't be long."

"No hurry," he said, making his way across to the escalator and lobbing a wave over his shoulder. "You take as long as you like."

Craig and Roberta stood watching until he was out of sight, then once more she delved into her handbag. "Look what I've bought!" she said, an excited glint in her eye. She took out a small book with a tartan cover and handed it to him. He held it out at arm's length and read the title. *An Idiot's Guide to Scottish Reels*. He smiled and flicked through the pages, then handed it back to her.

"It should have been the expert's guide that you got."

"Oh, that's rubbish!" she exclaimed. "I couldn't have done any of those dances without you. But you wait until the next time. I promise you that you won't have to give me a word of guidance."

"I'll look forward to the pleasure of seeing that." He gave her back the book, then immediately brought his hand up to his mouth in an attempt to stifle a long yawn. Roberta noticed it.

"Craig, there was really no need for you to bring us over. We could have just as easily got a taxi."

"No, no, I'm absolutely fine. Just feeling a wee bit tired."

"Not surprising. You've hardly had any sleep over the past two nights."

"Neither have you."

"I know, but I can catch up on the plane."

The farmer reached out and took hold of her hand and gave it a pat. "I've got to thank you for your support, Roberta. I don't think that I could have managed without you."

She smiled at him. "Oh, Craig, I was just so glad that I was around and that I could be of some use."

"Well, you certainly were that, lass."

"Are you sure you're going to be all right telling Liz about it?"

"I think so. I've just got to make sure that I get my wording right so that she doesn't start jumping to the wrong conclusions."

Roberta let out a sigh. "It was just such a pity that you missed them in Spain."

"Aye, it was. Mind you, I don't think she would have been able to get back here any quicker, so I suppose it's saved her a day's fretting over the whole thing."

"When does their flight arrive?"

"In about three hours."

"That'll be a bore for you having to wait around."

"Not at all. I'll just pass the time in the Land Rover." He smiled at her. "I'll be needing to keep Leckie company now. He'll be missing that comfy knee to sit on."

Roberta moved towards him and put her arms around his lean chest. "I'm going to miss him and I'm going to miss you, Nathaniel Craig. I can't even begin to tell you how much I'm going to miss you."

He placed an arm around her shoulders and drew her plump little body close to him. "Aye, and I'm going to miss you too, Roberta Bayliss. You just come back whenever you can, and the three of us will head off again, and we'll golf by day and jig by night."

Roberta looked up into his face, tears bubbling in her eyes. "I'll hold you to that, my dear man. I really will."

He gently pushed her away and cast a glance towards the escalator. "You'd better be off, Roberta. You don't want to miss your plane."

She wiped at her cheeks with the back of her hand. "Will you come up with me?"

"No, lass, if you wouldn't mind, I think I'll just head back to the Land Rover now. I'm not awful good at saying goodbye to my womenfolk."

A broad grin stretched across Roberta's face. "Am I one of your womenfolk, Craig?"

"Aye, you are. And a very special one at that."

She reached up and pulled his head down towards her and gave him a kiss on either cheek. "Goodbye, my dear. I shall write to you every week."

"You do that."

"And I shall expect you to write back."

The farmer chuckled. "Och, you'd have a hard time trying to read *my* writing."

"I don't care." She took hold of his hand. "Now, don't you go caddying for any more strange ladies on the golf course, do you hear?"

The farmer shook his head. "No, I won't do that. I'll tell everyone that I'm booked."

She smiled. "You do that, Craig. You tell them that you're well and truly booked." She reached up and gave him a final kiss, then slowly letting go of his hand, she turned and hurried across the concourse floor and, without looking back, made her way up the escalator with the agility of a girl.

The Jack Russell caught sight of him as he approached his Land Rover, and began to tear back and forth across the front seats in excitement. He opened the door carefully, putting in a hand to prevent the dog from jumping out. He slid in behind the steering wheel, hardly being able to settle himself before Leckie bounced onto his lap.

"Well, my lad, it's just you and me again," he said, rubbing at the dog's head. He watched as a plane rose up above the terminal building, its engines roaring as it powered its way into the sky. He shook his head. "Who would have thought that that would have happened to us, Leckie?" he murmured. "Who would ever have thought it?"

The arrivals hall was already thronged with passengers from the flight by the time that they appeared. It was Arthur he saw first, being pushed in a wheelchair by a sandy-haired young man who wore a fawn corduroy jacket over his square-set frame. Arthur's son, he concluded. It was only then that he realized that the woman who bounced along beside them, chatting away to them both with such spirited animation, was his daughter. He could hardly believe the transformation. Her hair was much blonder than when she had left, and the features of her sun-tanned face were lit up with a happiness that he had not seen for many a month. She bent forward to hear something that Arthur was saying to her, then, throwing back her head with laughter, she cast a sweeping look around the hall. She caught sight of him and ran over to meet him.

"Hullo, Dad!" she exclaimed, reaching up and giving him a kiss on either cheek. "How are you?"

The farmer smiled down at her. "I'm well, lass, I'm well. My word, you look terrific."

"I feel terrific, Dad. We've just had a truly wonderful time." She took hold of his hand and began to drag him over to where Arthur and the young man now stood beside the luggage carousel.

"Dad, this is Will, Arthur's son."

"Pleased to meet you, Will," he said, extending his hand.

Will shook it. "And good meeting you too, Mr. Craig. Liz has told me a great deal about you."

The farmer directed his attention to Arthur, placing a hand on his shoulder and giving it a squeeze. "So what's my friend, the professor, been doing to himself?"

Arthur did not turn to look at him, but blew out a disgruntled puff.

"Why is it that because I'm in a wheelchair, everybody has to ask about my welfare through a third party?"

"I *was* actually speaking to you, you crabbit old devil!"

Arthur looked up and laughed. He nodded at Mr. Craig. "I can't tell you how good it is to be back. I've missed our time together."

Craig glanced at the professor's leg. "Aye, well, it looks as if we might be spending a good sight more of it over the cribbage board than we've done in the past."

Liz touched her father's sleeve. "Dad, I thought that you might have come over with Alex," she said breezily. "Is he working today?"

Mr. Craig had not been prepared for this. He had been hoping to get her by herself before he told her. He took off his cap and scratched at the back of his head. "No, he's not, lass."

Liz's smile fell. She could tell instantly from the look on her father's face and by his actions that something was wrong. "Dad, what's happened?" she asked, her mouth open.

"Well, before I go any further, I have to say that Alex is all right."

"What's happened?"

"He's had a bit of an accident."

"What kind of accident?" There was desperation in her voice.

"A car accident." He noticed now that both Arthur and Will had turned to look to him, expressions of apprehension on their faces.

Liz clapped her hand over her mouth. "Oh, my God! But he's all right, Dad?"

"Aye, he is. He's got a badly bruised leg and his neck's in a brace, but he'll mend."

Her hand moved to her forehead. "Oh, thank goodness! Thank goodness!" She let out a shuddering sigh of relief. "So where did it happen?"

"Up on Smash Alley."

"Oh, no—not there! Was it his fault?"

"No, it definitely wasn't. The young man who caused the crash has been charged with dangerous driving."

"And there was no one else involved?"

Mr. Craig swallowed hard. "Aye, there was."

"Who?"

He hesitated for a fraction of a second before answering. "Gregor was in the car."

"Gregor? Gregor was *with* him?" She paused, and the farmer noticed the colour drain from her lips as she pulled them tight against her teeth. "Who was driving, Dad?"

"Alex."

Her shoulders heaved and she crossed her arms, turning away from her father. "Well, thank heavens for that. If it had been Gregor, I would never—"

"Gregor saved his life, lass."

She slowly turned around to look at him once more. "What?" she asked quietly.

"Well, I had been planning not to tell you the whole story, but I don't see how I'm going to avoid it now. It was a pretty horrific accident, Liz. Alex was trapped upside down in the car and it caught fire. Gregor crawled back in and managed to release him."

Liz just stared at him, and he could see the look of hostility in her eyes drain away into one of deep concern. "And . . . Gregor?" she asked, as if not wishing to know the answer.

"It's all right, lass. He managed to get out . . . just, but he got himself quite badly burnt in the process. Alex told me later that he had actually used his bare hands to douse the flames." He paused for a moment. "It was an awful brave thing that he did, Liz."

Liz nodded slowly. "Yes, it must have been." She gave her head a quick shudder as if to break herself away from the nightmare of the spectacle. "Are they both in hospital?"

"No, back at Winterton. Alex was released yesterday morning, and then Gregor discharged himself last night. He said that he'd got things to do and that he'd rather be at home with his son."

A questioning frown wrinkled her forehead. "Yesterday morning? But when did this happen, Dad?"

"Sunday evening."

"Sunday evening? But why on earth didn't you get in contact with us?"

"Because I wasn't informed about it until much later on that night, and I headed straight over to the hospital in Dundee. I never got home then until the next morning, and when I tried to phone you, the woman said that you'd just left."

Liz turned to see Will pulling their suitcases off the carousel. He caught her eye and they stared at each other for a moment before she turned back to look at her father. "I've got to go straight to Winterton, Dad."

He nodded. "Aye, I thought you might want to do that. That's why I'm going to suggest that the professor and Will take a taxi back to Brunthill. It'll be a more comfortable journey for the professor at any rate."

They drove to the Forth Bridge without speaking, Mr. Craig not wishing to disturb his daughter in her thoughts. He knew that as soon as he had told her about what Gregor had done, it would raise in her mind a turmoil of conflicting emotions. It was better that she had time to think about this and work out how she was going to react when she saw both him and Alex. He glanced across to where she sat, absently stroking the dog on her knee and staring out of the window at the ribbed surface of the cold grey water far below them.

"I've met someone, Dad," she said quietly without turning to look at him.

He smiled to himself, but did not reply immediately. Then he pushed himself back in his seat, straightening his arms on the steering wheel. "Aye, I thought you had." He cast his eyes sideways without moving his head and saw that she was looking at him, a smile on her face. "Is it Will?" he asked.

"Yes."

"I'm glad." He glanced in the rear-view mirror at the lorry that drove feet away from his back bumper and reacted by pressing his foot down further on the accelerator. "I met someone too."

"I know. Alex told me."

"Ah, did he?"

"What's her name?"

"Roberta Bayliss."

Liz waited for him to expand on the subject, but he said no more. "And where is she now?"

"On her way back to Australia."

"Right. And . . . how do you feel about that?"

He looked at her and gave her a wink. "I feel very happy about everything. Very happy indeed."

Liz smiled at him. "You must tell me about her sometime."

"I will, lassie. Don't you worry. I will."

An hour later, Mr. Craig pulled the Land Rover to a halt outside the Winterton farmhouse and switched off the engine. He turned to his daughter and saw that she was looking past him, staring apprehensively at the door into the house. "Are you sure you'll be all right?"

Liz nodded. "Yes." She paused. "It's just that this is the first time that I've been back."

"Aye, I was thinking that. Listen, I can easily wait if you want."

"No, I don't want you to do that. I'll just walk back across the fields." She opened the door and got out. "I'll see you later."

The farmer watched as she made her way across the courtyard to the house. She stopped for a moment before entering, and he wondered to himself whether she wasn't considering knocking, but then she opened the door and went inside.

Liz was overcome by a disturbing melancholy from the moment that she walked into the house. She hadn't really expected that so little would have changed. The Wellington boots were still scattered about the floor of the back kitchen, despite the row of squint, but well-spaced shelves that she herself had erected specifically to house them. The long, windowless corridor still glowed with the orange paint that she had splashed on the walls one afternoon on realizing that Gregor's oily handprints were the first form of decoration one came across when entering the house. She let out a long sigh in anticipation of her feeling when she entered the kitchen.

She walked along the corridor and opened the door quietly, hearing immediately the sound of the television drifting over from the sitting area. She glanced around the kitchen, noticing once more that everything was much the same, then caught sight of the back of Alex's head over the top of the armchair in front of the television.

"Alex?" she called out softly.

She saw him straighten in his seat, but he didn't turn around. "Is that you, Mum?" He pushed himself slowly to his feet and it was then that she noticed the white surgical collar around his neck. He reached onto the table for something, then turned slowly towards her and moved around the side of the armchair, supporting himself on a stick. He smiled at her. "Hi, Mum. You look good. Did you have a good time?"

Hearing those words suddenly hit home. She might never have had a son to say those kind of words to her again. "Oh, Alex, my darling boy." She burst into tears and ran towards him and threw her arms around his neck.

She immediately felt his body go rigid against her. He let out a cry of pain. "Ow, Mum! That's agony!"

"Oh, sorry!" She let go and stood away from him, gulping out a tearful laugh. She shook her head. "I can't believe this happened, Alex."

"I know," he replied quietly. He shifted himself sideways to a kitchen chair and sat down again. "I was bloody nearly dead, Mum."

Liz's body shook as she fought to control her emotions. "I know you were. Granddad told me."

"If it hadn't been for Dad," he paused, biting at his lip, "I would have—"

"You don't have to say it. I know it all."

There was a loud crash from somewhere within the main part of the house, followed by the sound of a heavy object falling down the stairs. Liz started. "What was that?"

Alex looked towards the door. "A suitcase, or should I say the third suitcase."

Liz shot her son a quizzical look. "What's he doing?"

"Well, he's not able to carry anything heavy because of his hands, so he's just manouevring them to the top of the stairs and giving them a kick."

"But where is he going?"

"He's going nowhere, Mum. It's Mary McLean who's leaving."

Liz stared at her son. "What's happened, Alex?"

"What do you think? She's been playing around, hasn't she." He pushed out his long legs and folded his arms across his chest. "I feel sorry for him, Mum, I really do, even though he's been caught out at his own game."

They looked at each other in silence, then Liz pointed at the door. "I think that I should go and see him."

Alex nodded. "Yes, I think you should."

She moved towards the door.

"Mum?"

She turned back. "Yes?"

"He saved my life."

She nodded and walked out into the corridor.

The first of the suitcases that had descended the stairs had left a deep white scar where it had slid across the polished teak floor in the hall. She edged past the other two that had stacked up behind it and looked up the stairwell. She could hear him moving about in the bedroom.

"Gregor?"

The footsteps above her stopped, and then she heard him moving over towards the door. His head appeared over the banister, and she caught sight of his bandaged hands resting on them. He looked at her, upside down, but said nothing.

"Can I come up?" she asked.

He drew back out of sight. "If you want," he eventually replied.

She walked up the stairs and edged into the bedroom, not so much in trepidation of seeing Gregor, but of going into the room where they had once slept, where they had once made love. She glanced around, taking in the open wardrobe and the pulled-out drawers of the large pine chest. All the same furniture, just in different positions. Articles of clothing were strewn across the floor and over the lilac satin sheets of the unmade bed. It looked like a whore's boudoir. How fitting *that* was. At least he had had the decency to get another bed.

He was stuffing a pair of Mary McLean's pale pink trousers into a suitcase that she recognized as having been her own at one time, using his foot to compress its contents. He turned to look at her. "Well, what do you think of this?"

Liz shook her head. "I don't think anything of it. I'm . . . just sorry that it's happened."

Gregor threw back his head in derision, then slammed shut the lid with his hands. He stood up, clutching them under his armpits and grimacing with pain, then brought his foot down so forcefully on its cardboard top that it ripped. "Why the hell should *you* be sorry that this has happened?"

Liz bit at her lip. "Gregor, I didn't come to talk about that, and I certainly didn't come to gloat. I had no idea that this had happened until Alex told me downstairs."

Gregor looked at her, and a smile broke across his stern features. He shook his head slowly. "You look good, Liz. In fact, you look terrific."

Liz swallowed hard. She couldn't remember the last time he had said that to her. In fact, she couldn't remember if he'd *ever* said that to her. "Gregor, I just came to say thank you for what you did for Alex."

He snatched one of Mary's brassieres off the bed and began to ravel it up in his bandaged hands. He noticed that Liz was looking at it, and suddenly realizing what it was, he held it out at arm's length and let it drop back on the bed. "He's my son as well as yours, you know, Liz. I would do anything for that boy."

Liz nodded. "I know you would." She paused. "You shouldn't be doing all this, you know. Your hands."

He looked at his bandaged hands and gave a quick shrug of his shoulders. "You're not going to offer to help, are you?"

She smiled and shook her head. "No, I certainly am not."

He let his hands drop to his side and let out a heaving sigh. "Lizzie, Lizzie, what a bloody stupid idiot I am. None of this would have happened if I'd just used my damned sense."

Liz didn't reply, but watched him as he walked over to the window. He stared out across the fields. "I never actually fell in love with her, you know, Lizzie. Not like I did with you." He turned to look at her. "I just have to tell you this." He turned away again. "I just happened to get caught up in a situation that I was too bloody weak to handle. I'm afraid that my brain got firmly wedged between my legs. I never considered you, and I never considered Alex, and I'm truly sorry for that. I really am *sorry*." He paused, bowing his head. "I'm not just saying this because she's gone, or because I want you to feel pity for me. It's just . . . well . . . the truth."

Liz stood immobile watching him, then she let out a long, calming breath. "Fuck you, Gregor," she said, almost incoherently.

He turned to look at her, his forehead creased into a frown. "What was that you said?"

She shrugged her shoulders, almost to signify that she hadn't realized what she had said herself. "I said, 'fuck you, Gregor.' "

His face broke into a smile, then he let out a laugh. "That's what I thought you said." He shook his head disbelievingly. "I've never heard you say that before in your life!"

"Well, there you go. You obviously don't know everything about me, do you?"

Gregor shook his head. "No, obviously not." He sat down heavily on the bed and looked around the room. "I'm not going to start on about turning back the clock, Liz. That would just be selfish and futile. I know the damage that I have done and know that it's beyond repair. But what I would like more than anything else is to get the chance to win your friendship back. I have missed that so much. Over the past year, I have felt my soul being physically ripped from my body, hearing the hostility in your voice whenever we talk." He paused and looked down at the bandaged hands resting on his knees. "And I can't go on like that." He slowly rose to his feet and walked back to the window. "And even if you feel that you can't do it for my sake, please try to do it for Alex's."

There was a silence, only broken by the distant sound of the television permeating through the house from the kitchen.

"Gregor," Liz said quietly.

"Yes?"

"I've met someone." Her eyes never left him as she said it. She wished that she could see his face. He stood motionless for a moment, then slowly nodded his head.

"In Spain?"

"Yes. He's over at Brunthill right at this minute."

He turned to look at her, a smile on his face. "Good. I'm glad for you. In fact, I'm really, really pleased for you, Liz, because you deserve every moment of happiness that you can get for yourself from now on." She could hear his voice beginning to break with emotion. "You just go right out there and nail him." He clenched his fist to emphasize the point, forgetting about his bandaged hand. He quickly managed to turn the grimace of pain back to a smile. "Because if he makes you look as beautiful as you do now, then he's the man for you."

Liz's face crumpled and she felt the emotional convulsions well up from deep within her. "Gregor, why are you such a bastard?" she blurted out. She turned and ran out of the bedroom. "Why are you such a mean *bastard?*"

She ran down the stairs and along the corridor, narrowly avoiding running into Alex as he hobbled out of the kitchen to come see what was happening.

"Mum?"

She heard him call out but didn't slow her pace, and, opening the back door, she threw herself outside and slammed it shut behind her. Everything suddenly was quiet. She stood in the courtyard, gulping in the cold air with sobbing breaths, then she covered her face with her hands. "Oh, God, what am I meant to do now?" She took off into the dark, following the track that was known so well to her that she had no need for a guiding light. If only, she thought to herself as she went, I could have made my way through life this easily.

Chapter 26

Nathaniel Craig placed the two logs on the sitting-room fire and stood over it until flames began to lick up around them. He walked back to his armchair and sat down with a thump. He picked up the glass of Jack Daniel's and raised it in the air.

"Well, here's to your speedy recovery, Arthur, and good health thereon."

Arthur sat in the armchair opposite, his plastered foot resting on the low coffee-table in front of him. He raised his glass. "And here's to you, Nathaniel." He took a sip, then studied its contents. "Mind you, I don't think we'll be able to drink each other's health for much longer if we carry on like this."

"In what way?"

"Nathaniel, I haven't had a Jack Daniel's at eleven-thirty in the morning since the time in my life when I found myself in imminent danger of sliding towards alcoholism."

The farmer laughed. "Well, I was just thinking that a wee celebration was in order, seeing that everybody is back home in one piece." He eyed Arthur's leg. "Or nearly." He placed his glass on the table beside him. "I didn't realize that breaking your leg was an integral part of your plan."

"My plan! It wasn't just *my* plan. I seem to remember you having quite a hand in it, too."

Nathaniel twisted up his mouth. "Aye, you're right." He let out a reprehensive sigh. "I have to say, though, that after you'd gone, I had second thoughts about it all. I wondered if we weren't playing with fire."

"I know," Arthur replied quietly. "I had the same notion."

"Mind you, I never quite shared your confidence in thinking that Will would join you."

"Well, if you want to know the honest truth, I wasn't that confident about it all, either. Okay, I had a hunch when he didn't return the itinerary with the tickets, but it was a long shot." He leaned across to retrieve his glass and rested it on his lap. "And then when he did turn up, I have to admit to you, Nathaniel, that I suffered a fairly prolonged moment of confusion during which I wished to hell that he *had* never appeared."

Nathaniel noticed a heaviness come over Arthur's eyes. He nodded slowly, understanding the look. "Do I take it that passion flickered in your own bosom for a time?"

"Yes. It did." He blew out a long breath. "And that was when I realized that I was just being a stupid old goat—old being the operative word."

"Och, you shouldn't be so hard on yourself. You've got a good few years in you yet."

"Yes, lonely years."

Nathaniel laughed. "That's a load of poppycock, Arthur! I can tell you that life has a funny way of throwing up the least expected things."

"You sound pretty convinced of that," Arthur replied morosely.

"I am, Arthur, I am totally convinced of that." He picked up his glass and took a drink. "So, you think that there's quite a spark between Liz and Will?"

Arthur laughed. "A spark! I'm surprised that they didn't blow up the plane on the way over."

"What do you think will happen now, then?"

"I can't be certain on that account. Depends on what Will's going to do." He wedged his glass between his legs and delved into his inside pocket and took out his wallet. "But, I tell you what. I am willing to bet you this crisp new Scottish ten-pound note that when they return to the house from their walk, they will have something to tell us."

For a moment, Nathaniel eyed the note that he held up in his fingers. "I'm not so sure."

"Can I ask why?"

"Because she's back home, Arthur. She'll have a great deal more to consider here than she would have in Spain, especially in the light of that accident. You saw yourself how upset she was when she returned from Winterton last night."

"But that's hardly surprising. She'd nearly lost her son."

"And her husband."

"Yeah, maybe so, but not much of a husband, regardless of his heroics." He rustled the note between his fingers. "So, what do you say?"

The farmer smiled at him and pushed himself out of the chair. "You're a terrible influence on me, Arthur Kempler, trying to make me gamble for money under my own roof."

"Are you on, then?"

Nathaniel took the bottle of Jack Daniel's from the mantelpiece and replenished Arthur's glass. "I would be an ungracious host if I refused, now wouldn't I?"

Liz stood on the outcrop of rock, her hair blowing around her face in the stiff breeze, watching the sea-gulls out on the water dip and rise with the movement of the waves. A spatter of surf hit her cheek, and she put up a hand to brush it away, the action being sufficient to break her from her thoughts. She turned and looked twenty yards along the shoreline to where Will was using a long strand of seaweed to play a ferocious tug-of-war with Leckie. He looked in her direction and gave her a wave, and she set off across the rocks to join them.

"What do you think of it, then?" she asked as she approached him.

Will cast his eyes out to sea. "It's great. Mind you, I've spent so much time on oil rigs that I've seen enough water to last me a lifetime."

"Yes, but this is different."

"Oh, really? Why?"

"Because it's mine."

Will laughed. "Oh, I'm sorry. I was under the impression that the oceans moved around, you know, with the gravity pull of the earth."

Liz gave him a hard punch on the arm. "Well, it's mine while it's here."

"Sort of a surf-loan arrangement, is it?"

She made to hit him again, but he grabbed her in his arms. She didn't resist, but pressed her head against the now familiar feel of his corduroy jacket. He rocked her back and forth as they stood there in silence.

"It's different, isn't it?" he said.

She didn't move. "What is?"

"Seeing someone on your own patch. You suddenly see them as alien."

Liz smiled to herself. "You're not alien, Will."

"Maybe not, but you're the one that belongs here, not me."

She looked up at him, a frown of concern on her face. "What is that supposed to mean?"

He laughed and shook his head. "No, sorry, that didn't come out right. All I meant was that I'm not enthusing about this place as much as you are."

She laid her head back on his jacket. "That's all right, then." She felt the comforting warmth of his body against her. "Will?"

"Yes."

"What do you want to do?"

"I don't know. What do *you* want to do?"

"I asked you first."

"Hmm, yes, you did, didn't you?" He paused. "Well, I've got to go back to the Philippines."

He felt her weight slump against him. "I know you do."

"And I would like you to come with me."

She smiled up into his face. "You could have said that in one sentence."

"Yeah, I realize that. I just didn't want to push it." He paused. "What do you think?"

"I don't know. I just don't know." She let out a sigh. "It's a pity that things just couldn't have stayed the same as they were in Spain."

"What's changed?"

She gently pushed herself away from him. "Being back. That's what's changed. Having considerations other than myself."

"I can understand that. But remember that I do come back here every two months, so you can always return with me then to see your father and Alex."

"Yes, I know."

"And anyway, I'll be wanting to see more of my own father."

She smiled at him. "Of course you will." She turned and looked along the rocky coastline. "I don't know if I can leave just now, though. So much has happened."

She heard him sucking in his teeth in consideration of what she had just said. "Do you want to flip a coin?"

She laughed. "No, I do not."

"Well, how do you want to decide the issue?"

"I'm not sure." She was about to turn back to look at him when her eyes came to rest on the thin jagged rock that protruded from the waves fifty yards out to sea. A smile slowly crept across her face. "Yes, I do," she said, almost to herself. She looked at Will. "What are you like at throwing stones?"

"Throwing them at what?"

She pointed a finger. "Can you hit that rock?"

Will narrowed his eyes against the glare as he scrutinized the target. "I reckon I could. Why do you want me to do that?"

"Because that's my father's stone of destiny. He told me that his father wouldn't allow him to take over the farm until he could hit it. It took him years."

Will laughed. "And you're now willing to rest your own destiny on the throw of a pebble, is that it?"

Liz shrugged. "It's no worse than tossing a coin."

Will bent down and picked up a pebble. "All right, then, you're on." He eyed the rock. "How many attempts are you going to allow me?"

"Three or four," she smiled at him, "or maybe seven or eight."

"Okay. Here goes!"

He took off his jacket and handed it to her, then gave the ground on which he was standing a quick check to make sure that it was even enough. He weighed the pebble in his hand for a moment, then ran forward and launched it off. They stood watching as it arced through the air and landed, sending up a small plume of water six feet to the left of the rock.

Liz flicked back her head in scorn. "You missed."

"Not by much," Will laughed, bending down for another pebble. "That was just a range finder. You watch this one." He moved ten feet farther back. "Are you ready?"

Liz kept her eyes on the rock. "Go on then."

The pebble came over far quicker than she had anticipated. She watched again as it spun through the air and even at its highest trajectory she realized that this time he was right on target. As the pebble began to descend, she suddenly became aware of the metallic taste of panic rising in her mouth. Oh, no, she thought, why did I agree to this? This is not right. This shouldn't be decided like this. I'm not ready to leave Alex or my father, and I'm certainly not ready to leave here.

The pebble hit with such force that it splintered off a shard of rock. It tottered on its axis for a moment, as if it, too, were vacillating over whether to stay or leave, then it slowly keeled over into the sea.

Liz stood staring at the place where it had disappeared beneath the waves. "Well done," she said, her attempt at a light-hearted tone doing little to disguise the hollowness of her congratulations. "You've done it."

A pebble landed beside her right foot and she looked down at it, wondering where it had come from.

"That wasn't me," Will said quietly.

Liz turned to look at him.

"What?"

He pointed a thumb over his shoulder, and Liz slowly followed its direction. On a rock twenty yards behind them stood Gregor, an unravelled bandage fluttering out of his trouser pocket in the breeze. He clutched at the wrist of his throwing hand with the other, still bandaged, and just stared at her.

She glanced at Will, meeting in his eyes the same steely glare as Gregor's. She moved across to him and placed a hand on his arm. "Just wait, Will. I'll be back in a moment."

As she walked over to the rock on which Gregor stood she noticed that his eyes followed her every inch of the way. She stopped below him. "What are you doing here, Gregor?"

He raised his face and looked out to sea. "Just watching you throw stones at the Craig Rock."

She was silent for a moment. "How do you know that's called the Craig Rock? I didn't even know that myself."

"It's what my father calls it."

"But how would your father know?"

"Because he used to come down here most days after school with your father to practise hitting it. In the end, they were both equally good." He looked down at her. "It was my father who gave me a bit of coaching."

"Why would you need coaching?"

"Because being able to hit it twice in a row was a condition laid down by your father before he allowed me to marry you."

"Why would he do that?"

"Well, his actual words were that he was passing on to me something that was as precious to him as his own farm."

Liz swallowed and lowered her head. "He never told me all this."

"No, he wouldn't. I think it's sort of a male thing."

Still carrying Will's jacket over her arm, she picked at a small white thread that protruded from under its collar. "And would it have made any difference if you had missed? I did have something in my belly at the time which I would have thought made the outcome of your little test somewhat immaterial."

"But I didn't miss, did I? I hit with the second and the third pebble." He stared at the rock once more. "I've never hit it with the first pebble before now, but by God, this time I was willing for it to hit with every part of my being."

She looked up at him. "How did you know we were here, Gregor?"

"I saw you walking across the fields together."

"But why did you follow us?"

"I'll tell you why, Liz Craig." He squatted down on his haunches, still clutching at his hand. "Because, before I never get the opportunity of saying this to you ever again, I just wanted you to know something that, for so many years, I realize now that I have just taken for granted." He hesitated, and she knew only too well from the look on his face that he was scrambling for the right words in his mind. "What I want to say is that I have always loved you, Liz, and I always will love you. I think you're beautiful, I think you're funny, and you have always been and always will be my best friend. And every day from this moment on, I am going to say those words, even if you're not with me. Because now, with Mary gone, I'm free to say them and, for about the first time in about two years, they have made me feel contented about myself." He paused and took the bandage from his pocket and began to wrap it around his hand. "I'm not trying to have my cake and eat it too, Liz. I know that I'm not in a position to fight for you any more. That's all passed. But I just had to tell you all that *once* to your face."

Liz turned away from him and looked towards Will, using the moment to wipe away a tear that had come to trickle down her cheek. Will noticed the action and lowered his head.

"You screwed up, Gregor Dewhurst," she said without looking back at him. "I hope you realize just how much you screwed up."

"I know I did, and I've got to live with the consequence of that for the rest of my life."

"And so do I."

"Yes, I know," he replied quietly. She heard him rise to his feet behind her. "But I did hit that rock, Lizzie, and I can keep on hitting it time and time again."

Liz stood where she was for a moment, then slowly set off back across the rocks towards Will. As he watched her approach, the smile that he gave her slowly slid from his face.

"Uh-oh," he said quietly. "This doesn't look good."

She ran her hand over the rough texture of his corduroy jacket before holding it out to him. "Will . . ."

"Liz," he cut in, taking the jacket from her. "I can't even begin to negotiate on this one, even though I would love to try. It would be no use for me to influence you one way or the other. You have to be absolutely sure in what you choose to do. You're back in the groove now, everything should be right for you, and you will have to decide for yourself what is best for you."

"I know, and I am so glad that you said that, otherwise it would have made this even more difficult for me." She paused for a moment to collect her thoughts. "Will, I belong here. I can't leave. My soul is part of this place, and I know now that I cannot physically take myself away from it. No matter how fond I am of you, I would be miserable in the Philippines, and I could never allow myself to burden you with that."

Will glanced towards Gregor. "Will you go back to him?"

"I can't tell you that at this minute, because you are far too prominent in my heart and in my mind. But he's not the only consideration, Will. I have to think of Alex, and if there's any way of giving him back his parents, then I'll push the boat out for it. If I were to go away now, it would be exactly the same as what Arthur did to you. You do understand that, don't you?"

Will nodded. "You mustn't let him hurt you again, Liz."

"He won't. I know now that he won't." She moved towards him and took hold of his hand and looked up into his pale-blue eyes. "What worries me more is the hurt that I'm doing to you."

He threw his head to the side as if he had just received a heavy punch to the chin. "Ouch!"

"I'm sorry, Will. I really am sorry. I didn't use you, I promise you."

Will let out a silent laugh. "I know you didn't, Liz." He blew out a long breath and looked out towards the rock. "Well, at least I lost in battle fair. It's just a pity that he arrived before I had a few more practice throws."

Liz moved forward and reached up and gave him a kiss on the cheek. "Thanks, Will." She kissed his other cheek. "Thank you so much for everything."

He put his hand out and cupped it under her chin, tilting her face up towards him. "And thank you, Liz. I think we both taught each other how to love again, didn't we?"

She took hold of the hand and kissed its rough palm. "Yes, we did. We certainly did."

The two men looked up from their game of cribbage as the door of the sitting-room opened, and both watched intently as Liz and Will walked in. Arthur caught the smile on his son's face and glanced quickly across to Nathaniel Craig, giving him an almost imperceptible wink.

The farmer, however, was less convinced of its meaning. It was not a smile of great joy and happiness, but more one of gentle kindliness and acceptance. And while Liz came to stand with her hands resting on the back of the sofa, Will remained distanced from her beside the door.

"Dad," Liz began quietly. She stood up and stuck her hands into the pockets of her jeans. "I have something to tell you."

Arthur shot Nathaniel Craig a furtive smile over the fan of cards that he held in his hands.

"I've just had a long talk with Gregor."

The fan of cards dropped like a stone onto Arthur's lap and he glanced from Will to Liz with an expression on his face that resembled that of a confused goldfish.

Will cleared his throat. "I think while you're explaining it all, Liz, I might just go up and start packing."

Nathaniel Craig saw both deep fondness and regret in his daughter's smile when she turned to acknowledge him. Once Will had left the room she took in a deep breath and proceeded to tell Arthur and her father of the decision that she had made, and how close she had come to choosing the alternative that had been offered.

"And now, if you will excuse me," she said when her explanation was complete, "I'm going to go upstairs to talk to Will while he's packing. So please feel free to continue your game."

The two men sat in silence after the door had closed behind her. They even avoided looking at each other. Then Nathaniel Craig laid down his cards on the arm of his chair and rose slowly to his feet. He picked up the ten-pound note on the table and, taking a step towards Arthur, tucked it away into the breast pocket of the professor's tweed jacket. "What did I tell you?" he chuckled quietly, giving his good friend a pat on the shoulder. "Life does have a funny way of throwing up the least-expected things."